SUNSHIELD

ALSO BY EMILY B. MARTIN

Creatures of Light series

Woodwalker
Ashes to Fire
Creatures of Light

SUNSHIELD

A NOVEL

EMILY B. MARTIN

HARPER Voyager
An Imprint of HarperCollinsPublishers

SUNSHIELD. Copyright © 2020 by Emily B. Martin. All rights reserved. Printed in the United States of America. No part of this book may be used or reproduced in any manner whatsoever without written permission except in the case of brief quotations embodied in critical articles and reviews. For information, address HarperCollins Publishers, 195 Broadway, New York, NY 10007.

HarperCollins books may be purchased for educational, business, or sales promotional use. For information, please email the Special Markets Department at SPsales@harpercollins.com.

Harper Voyager and design are trademarks of HarperCollins Publishers LLC.

FIRST EDITION

Designed by Paula Russell Szafranski

Maps and boot illustration by Emily B. Martin

Library of Congress Cataloging-in-Publication Data has been applied for.

ISBN 978-0-06-288856-3

20 21 22 23 24   LSC   10 9 8 7 6 5 4 3 2 1

To Mom and Dad

THE
OCEAN
WEST

the Outer Islands

Cape Coraxia

N

W   E

S

MOQUOIA

the
rinno Desert
ALCORO

CYPRIEN

LUMEN LAKE

THE
SILVERWOOD
MOUNTAINS

WINDER

PAROA

THE
EASTERN
WORLD

LARK

The stagecoach is visible only by the cloud of dust it kicks up along the track. It's moving at a fast clip, probably hoping to get to Snaketown before sundown.

Pickle shades his eyes next to me. "Bad position, Lark. Maybe we try tomorrow morning?"

"No. If they reach Snaketown, the ridgeline will block out the sun until nearly noon tomorrow. We'll miss the opportunity entirely. One coach, alone—it's too good to pass up." I tilt my hat brim to block the sinking sun. The greasy eyeblack on my cheeks helps deflect some of the residual glare. "I can get them turned around. No problem. You focus on jamming the wheel."

"There are guards," he says.

"I'll take the guards," Rose says on my other side. She shifts in her saddle, tightening the straps of her false leg. Sedge is checking his own gear, making sure his crossbow quarrels are in easy reach. Saiph keeps nervously threading the end of his brush whip through his fingers—it's only his third raid, and he's eager to do it right.

Pickle sighs and adjusts his grip on his long metal staff. "*I wanted to have a nice relaxing soak today, but no . . .*"

"Get ready." I look down at the ground, where my mutt, Rat, is crouched. He nearly blends into the dusty desert rocks— it's the coyote in him. His silly, too-big ears are perked up as he watches the approaching stage.

"Ready, Rat?" I say to him.

He rises from his haunches. I loosen my sword in its scabbard and adjust the straps of my buckler on my left forearm.

"On," I say.

Rat obediently jumps forward through the sagebrush and lopes down the hillside. He angles to intercept the team of horses, snarling as he reaches them. They don't panic, but the pace of the stage slows as they assess the danger.

"All right," I say. "On."

I urge my horse from the shadow of the boulders. The others do the same. We canter down the hillside in a V—Rose and Sedge swing for the front of the stage, and Saiph and Pickle veer for the back. There's a shout from the driver as we're sighted. His whipcrack splices the air.

I dig my heels against Jema's flanks, and she tosses her mane. A crossbow quarrel whizzes over her flank—she snorts. I kiss the air to encourage her and run her directly into the path of the oncoming stage. Rat is nipping at the hooves of the horses, who shy sideways. The rear guard is scrambling for a perch on the far side of the coach, trying to keep Pickle in his sights. The fore guard jams another quarrel in her crossbow. She cranks the lever, her jaw set and her eyes on me. She'll have a straight shot this time.

I wheel Jema around and sling my buckler over my fist. The late sun shoots straight across the sagebrush flats and ricochets off the mirrored curve of the little shield. I wash the light across the guard's face—she throws her arm up to block the glare. With only half a second to aim, I slap my crossbow over the top of my buckler and fire—I tag her calf. I swear under my breath—I'd been aiming for the empty space beside her, but a nonlethal hit is better than landing a killing strike without meaning to. At least it will keep her busy. The guard slumps; her crossbow clatters to the bottom of the driver's box. Her quarrels spill, flying into the air one at a time like little birds taking flight. While I wheel Jema around to canter ahead of the team, Rose takes aim at the rear guard—she releases just before he can pull his crank. It's a beautiful shot, flying so close to his ear I could swear it nicked him. She's always been able to tread that line between a shot to kill and a shot to startle, and unlike mine, it works. The guard curses and dives for cover behind the roof bench.

Saiph's alongside the team of horses now, flicking his brush whip to encourage them to veer to the right. Rat snarls at their hooves. But the driver is holding the reins steady. He switches them to his whip hand, groping with the other for the guard's fallen crossbow. He'll have a time trying to fire while keeping a firm hold on the team, but I'm not going to give him the chance. I twist in my saddle to wash the glare from my buckler over his eyes, and when he squints, I fire. *Shwizz.* The quarrel thumps into the wood just over his whip shoulder. He shouts and drops the reins. The stage rattles as two of its wheels catch in the rutted ditch.

"Come on, Pickle," I mutter, falling back to help Saiph steer the team.

Pickle bursts along the far side of the stage. He hefts the dented-metal staff and flings it at the front wheel. I hold my breath. He doesn't always make a clean hit—the staff is more likely to bounce off the axle or shoot under the carriage. But today it lands true, driving right between the spokes. The wheel catches for half a heartbeat, and then, with an ugly splintering crack, it shatters. The stage tips wildly; the team shies to the side. Rat narrowly avoids a hoof across his spine. Pickle spurs his horse clear just in time as well.

The stage rattles. It lurches. It bounds uncontrollably off a rock. And with a resounding crash, it smashes onto its side.

I let out my breath, easing Jema to a halt. Dust rises in a cloud. The horse team dances in their harnesses, kicking their heels and snorting, tangling their lines. The two wheels facing the sky spin crazily, *tika-tika-tika-tika*, like a rattler's tail.

I hook my crossbow onto my saddle and unsheathe my sword. The rear guard is motionless on the ground, but the driver and the fore guard are groaning and trying to rise. Sedge jumps from his horse and hurries to hold the guard down, putting a big knee on her back and jerking the quarrel out of her calf. Ignoring her swearing, he pulls out a length of bandage and sets to work binding the wound.

I slide off Jema's back, surveying the damage. Honestly, we *do* try not to make this big a mess. It's a measure of self-preservation. It would be easy to kill every driver and guard team that comes through, or run off with the horse teams and leave the travelers to die. But I expect the sheriff in Snaketown and the higher-ups in the more habitable parts of Alcoro would take a stronger initiative to root me out if I left a trail of bodies in my wake.

There's only one kind of traveler I make an effort to kill, and that's the slavers.

This coach doesn't belong to a slaver, though, and I'm hoping the fact that we've wrecked it isn't going to come back to bite us. We've never tipped a stage. A busted wheel and a jammed axle are our usual outcomes, if luck is with us. Today, not so much. But we can't change the past, although it looks like the driver still thinks he can change the future. He's sprawled halfway out of the box, trying to wiggle a carving knife from his boot. I lay the edge of my sword gently across his neck.

My red bandanna puffs over my lips as I speak. "How about you take a little rest?"

He drops his knife. I kick it away and move aside as Rose reins her horse to a halt in my place. She trains her crossbow down on him. He flops his head back against the rocky sand with an angry sigh.

A groan comes from inside the stage. I go to the skyward-facing passenger door and haul it open. Slouched against the far side is just about the palest person I've ever laid eyes on—I've seen the moon reach darker shades. He's old, too—his blond hair and reddish beard are shot through with silver, and he's alone. This will be an easy job. He squints up at me, bleeding from a cut near his right ear.

I angle my sword down into the coach. He doesn't move or even look at the point.

"You're the Sunshield Bandit," he says.

I tilt my sword so the light glances off the blade. He blinks against the glare but doesn't throw up his hands.

"If you know who I am, you know what I'm after," I say.

"I do. And I'm grateful for it. I believe what you do is quite commendable."

I narrow my eyes over my handkerchief. "I'm about to rob you blind, old man."

"Oh, go ahead," he says with a sigh, leaning his head back against the cracked glass on the far window. "I've hardly got much of value, unless you enjoy historical accounts of Moquoian permaculture. The money's in the leather valise. There should be an extra pair of boots in the trunk—nice ones, too, with silver buckles. Otherwise it's mostly traveling garb and books."

"Pickle, open the trunks in the back," I call. He's already performing this task, but the man's indifference irks me. I crouch at the door opening and jump down into the carriage interior. It's an awkward fit with the stage on its side. I sheathe my sword and draw the big hunting knife from my belt.

"Hold still," I say—unnecessarily. The man's eyes are still closed; he may as well be about to doze off. I take his bearded chin and tilt his head back and forth—no earrings in his ears. No chains or baubles around his neck. No rings on his fingers or pins on his lapels. The edge of a tattoo peeks out from his rolled-up sleeve—the prow of a sailing ship, it looks like. The ink is faded but still crisp, unlike most of mine. I grit my teeth—I have a low regard for ships.

"I've got a good case of matches in the pocket of my cloak," he suggests, waving to the garment now crumpled on the bench. "Cypri-made. Might be useful for you."

My irritation spikes, and I swipe up the cloak and toss the whole thing out the stage door. "Take off your boots."

They're old boots, with no buckles or adornments, covered

in telltale dried mud that means he must have come from Moquoia. But I don't care—I just want to rattle him at this point.
Slowly he kicks off each one. I stoop to pick them up and throw
them outside as well.

His eyes are still closed. I hiss and lean forward, letting the
edge of my knife touch his neck. "You seem very easy about
life and death. If you travelers are this unconcerned, perhaps I
should make an example out of you. How would you like to be
tied to a horse and dragged the rest of the way to Snaketown?"

"I would not like that at all," the man says, opening his
eyes. They're blue—an uncommon color. He's got freckles, too,
mixed in among the age spots. "But there are folk in Alcoro who
would notice my absence if I don't show up in a week's time
for the start of the semester, and the provost will be *extremely*
displeased with anyone who holds up classes." His gaze gets
a bit sharper. "And anyway, that's not your particular style—
torturing captives. If it was, I imagine the Alcorans and the Moquoians would have put more effort into rooting you out."

"Cases emptied, Lark," Saiph calls from the back.

"Lark," the old man says, as if testing the word.

I swear behind my handkerchief. Saiph is wiry and fast, but
he's a clodhead, a reason I haven't let him come on raids until the
last few months.

"Turn out your pockets," I say. "Now."

He does, but he continues to talk. "What you do is exceptional, Lark." His voice is suddenly less light—more grave. "The
human trafficking in the desert has become an international crisis. Your commitment to confronting and freeing slave runners'
wagons is desperately needed. But it must be hard to live the
way you do. How many freed captives live in your camp? How

many children you haven't managed to reunite with their families? How many hungry mouths?"

"Shut up." I pluck the lone coin he's fished from his pocket out of his palm. Still holding the knife against his throat, I sweep my other hand under the cushions on the coach seats. But they're tacked down to the wood—no space to hide valuables.

"Do you know about Queen Mona of Lumen Lake?" he asks with a touch of urgency in his voice. "Do you know about the Cypri ambassador? Have you heard about what happened to one of their children?"

"Ready the horses, Pickle," I call outside.

"There are extremely influential people who are *very* interested in what you do," he continues a little faster. "Life could be different for you and your fellows. I encourage you to consider . . ."

I hear a shrill whistle from Rose. The luggage is loaded onto the horses. I put one hand on the frame of the stage.

"Lark," says the old man.

I whirl around and drive the butt of my knife against his cheek. His head slams back against the wooden siding.

"I told you to shut up," I say down at him. He groans again. I put both hands on the carriage door and hoist myself out of the stage. The others are already mounted, their horses burdened with goods. Rose still has her crossbow trained on the driver. The fore guard is struggling to sit up, examining her bandaged calf. The rear guard is moaning about a broken arm.

I swing onto Jema's back.

"Come on, Rat," I call.

He leaps from his crouch by the agitated horse team and together we wheel for the hillside. The sun is halfway below the horizon, its curve red and shimmering in the dust. I glance back over my shoulder before we reach the safety of the towering rocks. The old man is standing up in the stage, holding on to the frame for support. I can see the moment his face turns from the driver and guard up to us. I swear again and face forward, kicking Jema.

"Saiph," I call angrily over the hoofbeats.

He groans. "I know, I know. I'm sorry."

"You call me Lark outside of camp again, and I'm stretching your hide on the tanning frame."

"Spare him the lecture, Lark." Pickle's voice is triumphant. "Hey, I made a pretty sharp throw, didn't I?" He edges his horse in front of mine and spurs it to kick up dust. "First one to camp gets the old fella's boots!"

I spit out Pickle's dust and urge Jema after him.

TAMSIN

I open my eyes on yet another morning.

Still not dead.

I suppose that's good.

Before I move, I take stock of my body. Over the past few days I've learned that moving too suddenly can send me into a whirl of pain and nausea. So I lie still on my mat, the dirt floor cool under my palms, staring at the tiny window near the ceiling that has become the most interesting feature in my life.

I am pleasantly surprised to find the pain less intense today than yesterday. My head hurts the most, of course. My mouth is still tender and swollen. I resist the urge to probe my lips and instead touch my scalp. I can feel the crusted parts where the cuts from the razor are scabbing over. My hair prickles my fingers, the barest fuzz covering my head. For my own sanity, I've been focusing most on that sensation—the lightness of my head with all my hair gone, the automatic gesture to tuck loose strands behind my ear before remembering there are none. It helps to focus on this—the most trivial and reversible facet of my present state.

There's a scrape at the foot of the door, and in slides the morning's meal. The slot was hastily hacked away after I arrived here—this room clearly wasn't intended to hold prisoners—and some of the corn mush in the bowl is knocked onto the floor.

"Careful not to choke today," comes a serious voice through the little barred window set into the door—another addition, along with the removal of the interior door handle. "Poia has the keys, and she's down at the well, so I can't come in to save your life."

I don't respond. I lie still, looking up at the window on the far wall. How ironic, the thought of either of them running in to save my life, when for three weeks their sole intent seems to be keeping me as close to death as possible without actually kicking me off the edge.

I'm in a strange limbo right now. My life's worth lies somewhere between half a bowl of corn mush and an entire country.

"We'll have another letter written later," Beskin continues. Unlike Poia, she has both her eyes, and they're wide-set and buggy. "Try not to shake so much when you sign your name—it needs to be legible. This is our last sheet of parchment, at least until one of us can go into town."

My fingers pluck the packed dirt floor like the strings of my dulcimer, not a shake in them. It doesn't even occur to her that ruining their last sheet of parchment would be entirely in my favor now that I know they're running low.

I shake my head. Will someone remind me again how a handful of crones this stupid could be orchestrating such a nuanced political coup?

I need that parchment, though. I need them to send it, whatever hash-up of a ransom note is inside.

"I'll be back later to empty your bucket." Of my two improvised captors, Beskin is the one with the closest approximation of a conscience, even if half the time it's accidental. She's tidy and orderly more than anything, and while Poia might be content to let me rot in my own filth, Beskin probably couldn't stand the smell. "Try not to spill the corn mush today."

Oh, Beskin, you're hilarious, and you don't even mean to be.

I remain in my silent, supine position until I hear her footsteps fade away. Only then do I carefully roll onto my side and push myself into a sitting position. The pain in my head spikes, and I let it hang for a moment—it feels like a rock on my neck, solid. Once the throbbing has subsided, I scoot to the bowl. Inwardly I curse my captors. The corn mush is undoubtedly salted—I haven't been able to tell if it's extra spite or if they're too thick to consider the sting of salt in a wound.

But I'm hungry.

Silently, slowly, I raise my fist to the door and hook my pinkie finger at the empty barred window, the rude gesture learned from the streets of Tolukum and subsequently unlearned in more genteel company. It feels good to flaunt it now after so long kept primly discreet. I hold it there as I scoop a spoonful of mush and eat.

VERAN

Dear Veran,

I'm writing to tell you that our stage was waylaid outside Snaketown by bandits on the first of July. Don't panic. We all made it through just fine, though I lost a few pairs of shoes. I am back in Callais now in time for classes—I will merely be showing up to my first one in slippers. Don't tell Gemma.

Here's the real bit of news—it was the Sunshield Bandit and several associates who stopped us. I'd suggest you not share this in conversation. I know there are those in both Moquoia and Alcoro who would very much like to get their hands on her—perhaps folk who aren't far away from the top rungs of society, even among the allies you all will be trying to make. The trafficking business is driven by wealth and power, and despite the fact that the Sunshield Bandit did indeed rob me of everything of *monetary value, I'd rather she be allowed to continue her work.*

I did find out one significant thing—her name. It's Lark. If she has a surname, I didn't hear it. Again, don't share this information. But you know how dear the case of missing captives is to us. If the Sunshield Bandit has a camp full of recovered slaves, there is a possibility that Moira Alastaire is among them, or that she knows where she might be. It's a long shot—Moira would be an adult now, if she's still alive. But all the same, it's as much of a lead as we've had for the past fifteen years.

I am not sharing the news with Mona yet, and I'd encourage you not to share it with Rou or Eloise, either. I've written them a separate letter without this little detail. I don't want to give them false hope when it could all turn out to be nothing, and I don't want to crack open that vault of old grief with so many other pressing matters at hand. But I am telling you. Keep your ear to the ground. Maybe amid all the other talk you'll hear something.

We're thinking of you here. Take care of yourself. Write to your parents. I already have four letters on my desk from your mother demanding news of our trip.

Wishing you well,
Colm

I lower the letter and lean against the rain-streaked glass, gazing absently over the waving treetops. Professor Colm waylaid by bandits . . . I'd been gnawing on this possibility from the moment we parted ways in Pasul. The Ferinno Desert has become an insanely dangerous place to travel, and I worried about him making the return trip without the caravan we journeyed with back in June. He had assured me the smaller numbers meant they'd travel through the worst country at greater speed.

Liar.

A sharp rap comes from my parlor door, and without waiting for an answer, it's thrown open. I stuff the letter in my jacket pocket.

"Veran!" Eloise calls. "Are you decent? Even if you're not, you'd better come on—we're late!"

I stand from the window. "That's an interesting suggestion—which do you think would be worse, appearing in court wearing the wrong color, or appearing in court naked?"

"I'm willing to bet color. You are wearing turquoise, aren't you?" She steps around the door and sighs in relief at my silk jacket and trousers. The Moquoians observe twelve months like we do back east, but more important than the season is the corresponding *si*—twelve distinct colors, not seven. With the first day of August, we've transitioned from green to turquoise, and heavens forbid one appear in the wrong colors on the first day of the *si*. Eloise is in a long gown the color of a Paroan lagoon. Her dark brown corkscrew curls are piled on top of her head and secured with strings of opals.

She spreads her arms. "What are you doing? We should be downstairs by now—Papa's already there."

"I was . . ." I recall Colm's words not to share the news about the attack with Eloise or her father. I gesture to the wooden box on the coffee table, the linen inside askew. "I was just working up the fortitude to put on the shoes."

She *tsks* in annoyance. "I'm sorry, Veran—I know they hurt your feet, but we really don't have time."

Hurt your feet is an understatement. I've worn my fair share of foreign wardrobes, but not once have I ever had to trade out my soft-soled leather boots. Even at the University of Alcoro, Silvern students are allowed to wear our native boots, as long as there aren't bells on the fringe. But here in Moquoia, men wear breathlessly tight silk breeches, fastened with large, jeweled buttons up the calves. It was a shock, that first day we arrived in court, when I realized my boots wouldn't fit over the embellishments. In their place, the stiff, hobnailed slippers don't so much blister my feet as eat them away one layer of skin at a time. Almost four weeks into our diplomatic trip, and I'm still no better at walking in them than day one.

Eloise removes the shoes from their wrappings and holds them out. "Come on—once we get downstairs, you can sit, but we need to go."

Biting back my dread, I set the shoes down and slide my battered feet into them. Pain spikes in the blisters along the pads of my toes. Eloise picks up the jeweled wooden walking cane fashionable with young Moquoian men and hands it to me. Shifting my weight to my heels, I plant the cane on the floor and rise. Eloise nods in satisfaction and turns for the door. I wobble gracelessly after her and out into the hall.

The first impact of my heels on the hardwood floor sounds like a clap of thunder. I hurry after her, my collar hot, almost reluctant to use the cane and add a third *clack* to the cacophony. I think of my mama's forest scouts—in order to earn the rank of Woodwalker, they have to be able to tread past a series of blindfolded sentries so quietly as to escape detection, all while carrying a forty-pound pack. I, at the moment, sound like a drunken elk on cobblestones.

We pass into the atrium at the end of the hall. Like the other windows in the palace, the ceiling is constructed from absolutely massive panels of glass—Moquoia's primary industry and probably the single greatest feat of manufacturing of our age. I still haven't gotten over my awe at the soaring panes, the biggest three times my height and half that across. Water runs down them in rivers, muddling the view of the stormy sky and tangled forests rolling away from the palace.

"I wonder if we're ever going to get a tour of the grounds beyond the palace," I say, straining to see past the streaming rain. I want so desperately to get out into those forests, to see more of the giant maples shaggy with moss and the bracken ferns dense enough to swallow a coach. I want to travel south along the coastline and see the fabled redwoods, trees that I've heard surpass even the grandmother chestnuts back home in height and girth. We only caught distant glimpses of the groves as we traveled to Tolukum, and since we arrived, we haven't left the palace once.

"Probably not with that fever on the rise," Eloise says. "Everyone's been so anxious about venturing outside for too long."

I frown, remembering all the dire warnings about rainshed fever we received when we first arrived. *Keep all windows closed*, they told us. *Sleep in long sleeves. If you must go out, wear lemon balm or cedar oil.* The illness is apparently carried by mosquitoes, which thrive in the humid forests, and as such—even on rare days when there's a break in the rain—the palace has remained sealed tight as a bubble. It makes me feel like a goldfish turning circles in a bowl.

"I still don't understand why the fever is so bad here in Tolukum, when we barely heard about it in the towns we passed through on the way here," I say. "The environment along the coach road was no different from here, but we saw plenty of open windows and folk moving about."

"Well, it's a curiosity we probably won't have time to investigate," Eloise says, picking up her hem in anticipation of the approaching staircase. "We're not here to sightsee in the countryside. If we *are* able to secure any kind of outing, it should be to the sand quarries and glass forges—they're the main thing this alliance is hinging on. In fact, I hear Minister Kobok is back from his tour of the glassmaking factories. We should try to schedule an appointment. Can you take the stairs?"

My collar heats more. "Yes."

She starts down the sweeping staircase, her shoes barely clipping against each step. I clamp my hand on the railing and follow, my own heels cracking like a smith's hammer.

"At least we get a taste of the forests inside," she says, gesturing into the open space on either side of the staircase, where we're almost instantly surrounded by living branches. *Trees planted inside*—another astounding facet of Tolukum Palace. Their crowns reach up toward the glass ceiling; their roots are buried five floors below, flanked by tiled pathways, carved fountains, and vibrant flower beds.

"These forests aren't real," I say, the pain in my feet making me irritable. "They're just a show—all make-believe. The trees may be alive, but I haven't seen a single brown leaf or bent twig in four weeks. No worms in the soil, no pollinators on the flowers. They must have an army of servants just to groom everything to perfection."

"Veran . . ."

"Have you noticed—they don't even take the folk names,

like we do. We've always called them *Tree-folk*, because of the redwoods, and the northern rainforests, but they consider that archaic, like they don't even care about the forests at all—"

Eloise stops on the landing so suddenly I run into her. I splay my cane out to keep from falling. She turns to me, her usually cheerful face arranged into displeasure. She purses her lips—she looks startlingly like her mother when she does that.

"Oh," I say, realizing what I'd just said.

"Veran . . ." she says again.

"I'm sorry," I say quickly, embarrassed. "That was rude of me."

"Yes. It's just . . . I know Moquoia is different from the Silverwood—in a lot of ways—but you can't let it affect your respect for the people in court." She looks out at the cedar trees, their needles immobile in the enclosed air. "Do you remember what Uncle Colm always said at the beginning of each semester?"

Do I. His was my very first class at the university, and those introductory words became the undercurrent for my studies from there on out. I can hear him now, plain as that day.

"*Ethnocentric bias*," he said.

The scent of evergreen and the drumming of rain on glass give way to memories of cool adobe and dry, sunny skies.

"*Ethnocentric bias*. Cultural supremacy," Colm said, standing in front of a massive map, his gray university bolero piped with the same blue as the illustration of Lumen Lake. "Everyone has a lens through which they view the world, and the inherent urge to classify everything within your lens as *right* and everything else as *wrong* is the most basic and fundamental error you can make. The notion of cultural supremacy ruins the scholar's ability to adapt to new ideas, to work collaboratively, and to create peaceful relationships. Never allow yourself to devolve into a dichotomy of right and wrong, of normal and not normal. This is the most important thing you can learn from me."

None of his students would dare challenge the validity of that statement. We'd heard the stories, we'd read the history accounts. He was *in* many of the history accounts, along with his wife, Gemma, the provost of the university and Last Queen of Alcoro. To a group of starry-eyed freshies, they were living legends. To me, the awe always went a step further. A mention of Colm's name is usually never far away from his sister Mona's, queen of Lumen Lake, or Rou's, her husband and international ambassador . . . or my own parents', king and queen of the Silverwood Mountains.

The familiar weight of all their names, titles, accolades, and accomplishments settles over me like a blanket, stifling my breath.

So much is riding on us not screwing up. On *me* not screwing up.

"Sorry," I say again. "I wasn't thinking. I'll be more respectful."

"I know the Moquoians manage their forests differently than your folk do," she says. "And don't get me started on their trade records—my mother would have a fit. But it's not necessarily wrong, Veran—just different."

"Ethnocentric bias."

"Right." She nods down the next staircase, and we keep going. *Clip clop, clip clop.*

Four flights later, we reach the main landing and the roots of the cedars. The shade would be nearly impenetrable if not for the galaxy of lanterns hanging along the path. Glowing sconces illuminate ornate wooden planters—until yesterday they had been filled with thick green ferns and hostas. This morning they're overflowing with cascades of teal-tinted orchids. The palace must have been an absolute anthill last night—all the green draperies swapped out for turquoise ones, the gardens replanted, the colored lanterns replaced. Despite this, I can't help but notice that we've hardly seen any servants beyond the ones who bring us our meals. It's another strange anomaly I can't quite wrap my head around.

Ethnocentric bias, Colm whispers.

Standing in the light of the closest constellation of lanterns, studying a creased sheet of parchment, is Eloise's father, Ambassador Rou Alastaire. At the first clap of my hobnails on the hardwood floor, he looks up.

"By the Light, it's about time—I thought I'd have to come hunt you down." He kisses Eloise's forehead. "You look perfect, lolly, and you're not half bad yourself, Veran. We'll have to commission a portrait before we leave, or your ma will never believe it."

I gesture to his wardrobe, a Cypri-style vest and loose trousers. "How come *you're* not in Moquoian dress?"

He pats the wide sash around his waist, the same teal as his ascot. "I'm the old, out-of-touch ambassador, so I get to pass off my outlandish—but ultimately harmless—cultural practices as charming eccentricity. But you two are the young, trendy liaisons who are up on all the latest court fashions."

"You just don't like wearing the pants," I accuse.

"I *hate* wearing the pants," he agrees. "And nobody wants to see me in them, anyway. Maybe twenty years ago, when I was a handsome stripling like you, but not now."

Eloise groans and passes a hand over her eyes. "By the Light, Papa."

He grins and offers her his arm. "Now come on—they'll be starting soon, and I need to brush up on my terminology before I cause another international incident." Rou has a passing grasp on the Moquoian language, but his accent is absolutely terrible, and he has difficulty with a few important inflections. Eloise is better, but not fluent—which is why I'm here. Rou nods at me. "Say the name of the month for me again?"

"*Mokonnsi*," I say as we start down the path. "Keep the *k* in the back of your throat, otherwise it means *garbage*."

"Right. And the color is turquoise, not green like last month, and the meaning is—serenity."

"That's *Bakksi*, Papa—October," Eloise says. "*Mokonnsi* celebrates friendship."

"Correct," he says, ducking under a lantern hanging too low in the path. "I was testing you."

Eloise sighs and catches me chuckling. "Of course you were. Do you need to test me on what this morning's ceremony is all about?"

"I'm offended, lolly," he says with exaggerated affront. "Of all people to know about court jesters, none should be more well versed than your father. Ambassador was always my second career choice."

"I hope you haven't referred to the *ashoki* as court jesters," Eloise says. "They're more like storytellers."

"The closest translation is actually *truth teller*," I say. "Sort of a cross between a jester and a bard. From what I've read, they're the only ones who can publicly poke fun at politics, the monarchy, the court—they're sort of a catharsis for everybody."

"And today Prince Iano names a new one," Rou says, grinning at our hurried efforts to correct him. "I know. This is an important day—we might be the first Easterners to witness the start of an *ashoki*'s career. By my understanding, an effective *ashoki* can alter the entire political climate of the court. We should hope whoever is appointed is in favor of our work in the Ferinno. Speaking of." Rou gestures to the folded parchment in his free hand. "We got a letter from your uncle Colm this morning. He was attacked by bandits outside Snaketown."

Eloise gasps, whipping her head to her father. "Is he all right?"

"It sounds like he was just robbed, and not hurt," I say absent-mindedly, distracted by a tiled pool filled with wending fish—dyed a startling shade of teal. They *dye their fish*.

"How do you know?" Rou asks in surprise. "That is—you're right, but how did you know?"

I jerk my gaze away from the pool. Well, that was hardly discreet. Both he and Eloise are looking at me, confused. "Uh . . . he . . . he sent me a letter, too. Just to say . . . that I should write to my parents." I shrug. "You know, updating me on what's happening at home."

"What's happening at home?" Eloise asks.

"Nothing." I instantly flush at the stupid comment, realizing I should have made up something harmless. "But uh . . . about Colm."

Eloise fortunately shifts her focus back to her father. "Yes, about Uncle Colm. Is he really all right?"

"The two guards came away with some injuries, but either Colm came away unhurt or he's purposefully not telling us." We round a bend in the path, and golden lamplight shines in slices through the dark cedar trunks. The buzz of voices filters toward us. "I'm wondering if I can get in touch with the coach driver—I'd be *highly* interested to know who waylaid them."

I glance at him, Colm's tidbit about the Sunshield Bandit rushing back to me. "Why's that?"

"Because right now the Ferinno is one big boiling pot of trouble—if we're going to lay a real road through it, it'd be nice to know which bandits claim which territory," Rou says. "That section along the South Burr is going to be a crucial stage to keep passable. There's no other water for fifty miles."

I relax a little. He's obviously not thinking about his oldest daughter's abduction a decade and a half ago, or the possibility that she may be in some outlaw's camp in the middle of the desert.

So, of course, *my* thoughts slide to Moira Alastaire—which is strange, because I don't remember anything about her. I've seen a portrait of her exactly once, when I crept along at Mama's side in Queen Mona's chambers while visiting Lumen Lake. The picture was tucked inside the rolltop of the queen's writing desk, and I spotted the two identical brown freckled faces and cascading curls gazing out from their childhood portrait. I haven't thought of that picture in years. As we enter the glow from the hall up ahead, I glance surreptitiously at Eloise.

I guess Moira would look the same now, if she's still alive. I frown at the somber thought, but I can't see how she's not dead.

That said, neither Eloise nor Rou have any cause to connect the attack on Colm's stage to the Sunshield Bandit or long-lost Moira. I try to follow Rou's previous comment back into safer territory.

"We should get good insight to bandit activity near the border if we can get conversation moving in court," I suggest.

"On that note." Rou turns to Eloise. "Have you had any better luck with Prince Iano? I meant to check with you yesterday, but I've been wrapped up with Queen Isme."

"Well—some," she says. "He's still being . . . difficult to interact with."

I can hear the reluctance in her voice—Eloise isn't one to speak badly of others. I admire her for that, but I can't deny that she's dramatically downplaying the ill temper of the Moquoian prince. My work has mostly been at Rou's side, since Eloise's grasp on the language is better than his, and from what I've witnessed of their stilted interactions, I don't envy her in the slightest.

"He just . . ." She pauses, then begins again, pursing her lips and pondering her words. "He seems . . . well, sad, to be honest. He keeps to his rooms so much, he talks to almost no one in court, and he certainly never smiles. And I know it's not a language barrier—he's more fluent in Eastern than I am in Moquoian, but having a conversation with him is like . . ."

Talking to a brick wall, I finish silently for her.

"Well, it's challenging," she says.

"Did you get this impression of him when you exchanged letters last year?" Rou asks.

"Not at all. Did you, Veran?"

She's being kind, asking for my opinion. She's the one who drafted all the letters to Iano—I merely proofread them for grammar. I shake my head. "He seemed perfectly friendly in his letters, and ready to negotiate."

"That's right," Eloise agrees. "He had all kinds of ideas on partnering with the university, funding the Ferinno Road, transitioning industrial labor away from bond labor, all that. But since we've gotten here, any time I bring up policy, he almost pretends not to hear me."

"Hm." Rou frowns in thought. "I wish I could say I'm surprised, but herein lies our biggest challenge with this Moquoian effort. All the courts back east are familiar to us—we share a language, and borders, and cultural groundwork. But the sea and desert routes have distanced us from Moquoia for centuries. These are new steps we're taking, and it's likely there are norms in place we don't understand yet. If I had my way, we'd have a year just to familiarize ourselves with the Moquoian people before broaching policy at all. But the trafficking uptick in the Ferinno has accelerated everything, and instead of a year, we have eight weeks—and we've already used up four of them."

A golden gleam breaks through the dark cedar trunks and turquoise lanterns. Up ahead, the Hall of the *Ashoki* is brimming with light and noise, threaded with the spicy scent of hot cream tea. Rou eyes the approaching doors, and he slows down, patting Eloise's hand.

"Tell you what, Lady Princess," he says. "What if Veran joins you this morning, instead of coming with me? It might come across as more casual—a pair of friends instead of a lone diplomat."

A spark of unease flares in my stomach. "I'm not trained in policy, though." Not to mention that alongside people like Eloise and my oldest sister, Viyamae, both heirs to their respective thrones, I'm generally as helpful as a toddler playing make-believe. Eloise may only be two years older than me, but I've always felt she's on a rung I'll never quite reach.

"Let's leave policy alone for the morning—though you're better than you think you are, V." Rou bumps my elbow reassuringly and then gestures at the turquoise banners hanging from the trees. "It's the first day of the new *si*—a day for celebration. Perhaps we haven't been striking the right chords. Just be friendly, and maybe the prince will warm to negotiations. You can even try the junior delegate route, if you think it might work—maybe Iano will open up if he thinks he's mentoring somebody."

Eloise doesn't look convinced, casting a doubtful glance at her father. "Can you manage with Queen Isme without Veran translating for you?"

He closes his eyes, pained. "Once again, lolly, I am *offended—*"

"Two days ago you told her Moquoia is like a verdant tumor," she interrupts with reproach. "Whatever *that* was supposed to mean!"

I snort and then stifle it. Rou *had* said that, with a completely straight face, and I had to keep from laughing while I offered the similar-sounding *paradise* to the scandalized courtiers.

"Ah, but there are so many *worse* mistakes I could have made," Rou says, half wincing, half grinning. "And I still maintain that there is absolutely *no difference* between those two words." He waves at us both as we jump to insist on the subtle inflection. "I'll manage for the morning. Her courtiers think my slipups are amusing, and I plan to mostly listen to the gossip about the new *ashoki*, anyway. What do you say, Veran? Join Eloise for a little while, see if you can warm Iano up?" He gives a quick nod to Eloise. "Not that I think you haven't done a supreme job already . . ."

"No, I'd be glad for your company, Veran," she says. "If I'm honest, talking to Prince Iano has been the most vexing thing I've ever attempted. Perhaps he'll be more interested in you than in me. Just as long as you don't start an international incident, Papa."

Rou grimaces. "I've done that before, and it's exhausting. My revolutionary days are over—that's your responsibility now."

He gives a bark of laughter at the absurdity of his comment given his present company—the exemplary diplomat and the tagalong interpreter—and shepherds us toward the gleaming doors.

LARK

"There you go, Whit." I tighten the last strap on the little girl's feet. The traveling boots I took off the bearded man in the stage are miles too big for her, but she's outgrown her last pair of shoes and has been padding around with her toes sticking out. I've used leather thongs from an old bridle to cinch them to her feet. Not pretty, but it works.

She mumbles a thank you, the *th* sound distorted by her cleft lip, and shuffles away, leaving tracks in the dirt. I sit back on my heels and take off my broad-brimmed leather hat. The creases are lined with dust, and I beat it against my calf a few times. Nearby, Rat lifts his head at the noise, his bat ears perked up.

"Dust, dust, dust," I say to him. "Sometimes I wonder if we're all really purple or green underneath, but we've all turned the color of dust."

He yawns and shakes his head, flapping his ears. A dirty cloud drifts from his fur.

Saiph emerges from the bushes, his dark hair plastered to his forehead, toweling himself off with a piece of sacking. "Seep's free, Lark."

"About time." I get up and head through the scrub oak. Rat follows at my heels.

The seep sits against the wall of the canyon, deeper than a puddle but not enough to be a real pool. It's born from our water pocket, the natural well in the rocks above that provides all our daily water. The pocket was how Rose and I first found our way into Three Lines Canyon, following the old three-lined petroglyph carved down near the mouth that proclaimed a source of water. The top of the pocket sits high up the canyon wall, and it takes a burning climb to get up to it, but in my four years holing up here, it's never run dry. The water is cool and sweet, and as it trickles down the rock face, it leaves slick black streaks that attract clouds of yellow butterflies and dozens of sandy lizards that snap up flies.

The seep is low today, barely covering the pebbly bottom. It's why we've designated this a washing day—if things dry up any more, all our water will have to be drawn and hauled down from the pocket, and after cooking and drinking there'll be almost none to spare. Lila's turn comes after mine today, and she's pushy on washing days—there's no time to waste. I start stripping off my clothes. Off comes my vest and dust-colored shirt. I kick off my boots—the only part of my wardrobe that's really worth anything, as I lifted them off a well-dressed stage traveler a few months ago. After pulling off my trousers and holey stockings, I finally unhook my breast band and drape everything over a juniper bush.

The breeze is shearing up the canyon like it sometimes does, so I prop up the windbreak—a stiff old bison hide on a wooden frame—and settle down on the rocks lining the seep. I wiggle my feet through the grit and pebbles, letting them grind away the dirt creased between my toes. I bend forward, stretching out my neck, and untie the strip that holds my dreadlocks out of my face. My hair has been locked for as long as I can remember. I have vague memories of tangled curls, but whether my hair locked itself naturally or someone got it started back in Tellman's Ditch, I was too young to remember. I have no desire to change it—I like how easy it is to keep up. No endless brushing, like Lila, to keep the knots and burrs out. No need to wrap it every night, like Rose, to keep it from drying out in the merciless desert heat.

I pinch a few of the locks in my fingers—I'm well past due for a wash, but our soap in camp is running low, and I'm almost entirely out of oil. It's a shame—I found the bottle of high-end scalp oil by chance in a peddler's trunk Pickle lifted in Bitter Springs. It's *perfumed*, light and sweet—certainly the nicest-smelling thing I own, and I've been savoring it drop by drop for almost six months. Now it's nearly gone, and I don't have enough coin to justify buying another bottle, even the cheap stuff I can sometimes find in town. Sighing, I run my fingers through my hair, feeling the grit and grime along my scalp. No, I'll have to wash today, oil or no, and bear the frizzing and dryness that will come along with it.

I cup handfuls of water and splash my arms and neck, leaving little tracks of slightly cleaner skin. I wipe at the dirt covering the tattoo on the inside of my right forearm, glad to see the ink isn't bleeding. This tattoo—my longsword—and the other on my left forearm—my buckler—are two of my oldest. The point of the sword drives into the scarred concentric circle on my wrist, the brand all nonbonded laborers got in Tellman's Ditch. I frown at the back of my hand, where the sun—my most recent tattoo—looks a little blurry near the ends of the rays. Ah, well. Rose told me the ink might not be as strong as it should be for that one.

The two words circling my wrists are clear, though. *Strength* on my right, my sword arm, and *Perseverance* on my left. I had to ask Saiph how to spell that word, and he stood over Rose's shoulder as she worked, scratching out the letters in the dirt one by one so she got it right.

I twist to check the vaguely larkish bird on my right shoulder, and then lean back to check the coyote on my rib cage, its head thrown back in song like Rat sometimes does when he gets a wild hair about him. In this position, I see the six spots making an off-center circle around my navel. I rub at them. Sometimes what I think are marks are just flecks of stubborn dirt, but these have always been here. I think perhaps next I'll have Rose connect them in a star. I saw the Alcoran flag once hanging on the wall of an outpost—a shiny white jewel surrounded by six-pointed stars. The idea of tattooing one of their national symbols onto my skin makes me smirk. It gives me the same satisfaction as naming my horse Jema after hearing about some famous old queen. Or young queen, or not-a-queen-anymore—I don't know what the politics are. I just liked the idea of adding a fancy, stolen name to a fancy, stolen horse.

I splash my face and then crane my head to look at my last, and oldest tattoo. A river, starting at the top of my left shoulder and streaming down the outside of my arm. This is the only one Rose didn't start, though she's added to it over the years, making a sleeve. I got it started when I still worked in the rustlers' camp. The big, dirty cowhand had just finished cutting a curvy lady into the big, dirty bicep of the cook when I sat down in front of him.

He had eyed me, scrawny and scratchy as a scrub oak, as I rolled up my dusty sleeve.

"What'cho want, Nit?" he had asked with some amusement.

"Water," I said. "A whole bunch of water, like the South Burr." That was the most water I'd ever seen in my life, a sluggish, dirt-colored channel, thick with the smell of cows.

He'd laughed. "S'gonna hurt some."

"I'll tell you if it hurts," I said.

I watch a trickle run down the path of the river on my arm now. I've since seen bigger stretches of water—the river the South and North Burr run into, for one, and a reservoir a half mile wide. But it's never enough. I have distant memories of the sea, which leads me to believe I started off somewhere in Paroa, or perhaps Cyprien, but these memories are laced with the taste of salt and a thirsty breeze, and they don't entice me to seek out the coast. Fresh water, the most precious of all resources in the Ferinno, is what I constantly crave.

Thinking about the sea and tattoos and dirt and grime spurs a now-familiar memory that's been dogging me for weeks—the voice of that bearded man with the ship tattoo in the stage outside Snaketown. His words have been nettling my thoughts since we wrecked his coach, usually at times like this, when I pause for breath between all the work around camp.

There are extremely influential people who are very interested in what you do. Life could be different for you and your fellows.

I close my eyes. Of course things could be different. But

it's easy for rich folk like that man to assume such a feat would be simple, because it all comes back to the system they've built, where they sit at the top and pretend not to notice what it is they're sitting on. *Who* they're sitting on. Rose, and Sedge, and Lila, and Saiph, and Andras, and little Whit—and all the uncounted scores of others who get eaten up by the bond labor system.

And we're the lucky ones—the ones who got away. Rose had the shortest stint in the quarries of all of us—after her parents died, she entered herself into a three-year bond at the quarries down in Redalo, and when that was up she joined the cattle-rustling operation that found me. But Lila, the oldest among us, was trafficked her whole life, with no inkling of where she comes from beyond the evidence of her pale skin and dirty blond hair, which tells us she must be at least part Lumeni, a story she feeds with tales of shiny pearls and waterfalls she claims to half remember. But she's not a full-blood—none of us are, except Rose and Andras, with their umber skin and curly black hair from the deep south of Cyprien.

Unlike Rose, though, Andras was stolen, and unlike Lila, he remembers his home and his parents. He's my most recent rescue, and I'm working on finding a way to get him back into Cyprien without running up against the trafficking trade again. It's tougher than the others I've managed to send back to their families in Moquoia and Alcoro—Cyprien is on the other side of Alcoro and is apparently half made of water, if tall tales can be believed, but I've never been anywhere near it and don't have the first notion of how to get there.

Saiph is the only other one who recalls anything of his parents. His father was a drunk, he says, a failed trader from

Moquoia who headed east into Alcoro to try his hand at cattle ranching. His mother worked for the Alcoran turquoise mines before they were all shut down with the opening of the fancy university. She gave him life and his Alcoran name, but she couldn't give him much else, and after she died, his father handed him off to the first band of slavers for a sack full of drinking money. He, like me, didn't have a bond and would have spent the rest of his life a slave if Rose and I hadn't pulled him out of the wagon.

The rest of us are merely castoffs, with no history and no family. I scooped Pickle and little Whit up from the wagon train after bandits sold them to the slavers. Before them came Lila and Sedge, our big, sandy-haired probably Alcoran who still has the iron ring around his neck we found him with. On nights when there's nothing else to do, we often take turns with our worn-out file, working on eventually cutting through the metal. We've got one full cut made, but it's going to take two to get it off.

And then there are all the others who aren't with us anymore—the ones I've managed to return back to their families. Bitty and Arana and Voss and half a dozen others, mostly little kids stolen from the desert towns and ranches. One or two had been sold by their families, and the best I could do for them was take them to a lodger in Teso's Ford, where they had the chance of finding work. But doing that costs money—Teso's Ford is a long way off, and the lodger won't take anybody for free—and I can't do it with the younger kids like Whit and Saiph. They're stuck out here in this burned-out canyon until Rose and I can figure something out.

Rose has been with me longest—she and Cook found me half dead in the desert after I escaped the wagon. She's the closest thing I can imagine to family. My skin is tawny brown to her deep umber, but it's clear I'm part Cypri, like her. That's my mother's side in me—that I know from my hazy handful of bleak memories. Not that I remember *her*, per se, but I remember my father. Or at least, I remember his Alcoran name.

But I don't like remembering. It's a useless, painful pastime, and anyway, we have plenty of real-life problems to fret over instead. I flex my hands and splash water over my face again, trying to banish that sour feeling in my stomach. Droplets trickle over my lips, salty with my dried sweat.

In truth, we're all a mess.

Rose's false leg doesn't fit her. Sedge fashioned it after seeing someone wearing one in Snaketown, but all the parts are random scraps—old leather saddle straps and a woolen shirt and buckles from who knows where. She walks with the stump end dragging in the dirt. Sedge is determined to make her a better one, but despite his capability with turning odds and ends into other odds and ends, a false leg is more complex than a slingshot. He tries, bless him, because he loves Rose with all his heart. I think if he could cut off his own leg and give it to her, he might just do it.

I might, too, for that matter.

She's hardly the only one with something wrong—Pickle gets sores all over his lips that nothing seems to cure, adding to the old scars left over from a bout of childhood smallpox. Andras is always getting eye infections, pink and weeping. Lila doesn't talk about it much, but I know she worries about her periods—they're irregular and painful, sometimes just a few droplets, sometimes an intense flow that sees her puking for the better part of a week.

Whit worries me the most—her cleft lip affects her speech

to the point that she often prefers to stay silent, but it's not her only issue. Lately she seems to be disappearing bit by bit, her eyes sinking deeper into her paling skin. I wonder sometimes if she's sick with some invisible disease. She needs to be seen by a healer, but the closest one is in Snaketown, a three-hour ride away—and besides, we don't have the money to pay for that kind of medicine or surgery.

Sedge is probably the healthiest, or maybe Saiph—and I'm just waiting for the day one of them cracks their head open during a raid. Saiph, being the most educated among us, often has to serve as healer, despite him being younger than most of us and knowing practically nothing besides how to stanch blood flow.

And me. I suppose I'm healthy, too, unless you count a body that creaks and groans from constant abuse, a quarry cough that flares up now and then, and a gnawing anxiety that the bottom is about to drop out of everything. That someone will finally give in to one of the million things ready to kill us. That the posses from town will finally decide we're a scab that needs to be picked and root out our camp hidden up in Three Lines Canyon. That Whit and Andras and Saiph and all the rest will go back in the wagons, their lives bought and sold and dragged to whatever labor industry needs an extra pair of hands.

That, ultimately, the same thing will happen to me.

I sink my hands under the shallow water and leave them there, letting the weight of my hair stretch out the rod of tension in my neck. This is why I hate slowing down—when I'm busy stocking camp and caring for my campmates, I don't have time to dwell on all the trouble lurking just outside our fire ring. But thanks to that jumped-up bearded stage traveler, all the little anxieties keep finding their way into the rare quiet moments.

Life could be different.

I frown, balling my fists under the water. I would *love* for things to be different. Pickle could get the right medicine for his skin. Whit could get real food and real care. Andras could go back to his family in Cyprien. Rose could get a false leg that fits, not one that blisters her thigh or slides off when she rides. Sedge could get a paying job, Lila could creep back to Lumen Lake to figure out if that's really where she comes from. Saiph could go to school.

But rich folk like the man in the stage—folk who have never been on the slimy fringes of society—don't understand the risk those things cost. If I walk into the nearest town with sickly little Whit, or chapped Pickle, or wayward Andras, what happens next? There's no scenario I can think of—no plausible scenario, anyway—where someone doesn't end up on the side of the road, or in prison, or back in the slavers' wagons.

There's a clatter of rocks from beyond the windbreak.

"Lark, are you done?"

Lila. I flip my locks back behind my head and look over the hide. She's standing expectantly by the tiny creek that flows away from the seep, already unbraiding her dark blond hair.

"No," I reply.

She huffs. "It'll be dark soon."

"So?"

"So it'll get *cold*, and don't tell me to get the fire pit going, because then there'll be smoke, and the whole reason for wash day is to *not* smell like smoke for a few hours."

I sigh, splashing a last few handfuls of water under my arms and behind my neck. I could point out that the smoke keeps the flies from biting, but the truth is, I *don't* want her starting the fire—over the years, we've picked Three Lines so clean of easy firewood that we have to ration it for the cookfire. Lighting a fire just for bathing would be a stupid waste of fuel.

"Fine," I call. "The seep is yours." I try to keep the irritation out of my voice—Lila can be annoying, but if she's vain about her appearance now, it's only because she finally has the freedom to be that way. I slick some of the water from my skin and stand from the rocks. The breeze up the canyon slices over the water left on my skin.

Lila already has half her clothes off and is standing expectantly at the edge of the seep. I pick my way out of the water, and she instantly takes my place. I collect my clothes from the juniper bush and make my way down the little creek, shivering in the breeze. She was right—the sun is edging toward the canyon rim, and the air is cooling quickly. I push through the willow shrubs along the creek until I get to a good flat rock that's still in full sun, and I settle down onto it, my feet in the creek. I'm not quite ready to leave the water, as little as there may be.

Rat snoots around in the water, pawing at the rocks and then sneezing when he splashes his nose. In the distance, a pack of coyotes takes up an early-evening chorus, a rattling of yips and long, high howls. Rat lifts his head, looking up at the canyon wall.

"You're a mutt like the rest of us," I say, rubbing a shred of sacking over my skin. "Don't belong here, don't belong there. Who was the coyote? Your ma or your pa? Or do you know at all?"

He looks back at me, one ear still cocked backward at the carefree singing of his half siblings. His name is like most of ours, too—made up. When I found him as a pup, he had mange

so fierce he looked like a drowned rat, his tail bald as a whip.
Now his coat is thick and coarse and studded with burrs.

I reach out and scratch his ears, his fur sticking to my wet
skin. He half closes his eyes lazily.

"You've got it the best of us, though," I say. "At least you
can survive on mice and carrion."

He licks a patch of sweat I missed on my arm. The cool air
sweeps across my bare back, stealing away the last of the water
from the seep.

Through the bushes comes Rose's telltale step-drag. I
straighten as she approaches, her own sack towel draped over
her shoulder.

"Is the seep free?"

"Lila beat you to it."

She swears mildly, setting her sack down. "So it'll be a while."

"Probably." I dig among my clothes for my precious sliver
of soap as she eases herself down on a rock by the creek. As I
pour a few handfuls of water over my head, she unfastens the
straps on her false leg, sighing as she slides the cuff off her knee.

"Are the new buckles helping?" I ask, rubbing the scrap of
soap into the barest lather.

"No. They're stronger, but now they blister." She hisses as
she rolls back her pant leg, revealing a neat line of welts along
her knee. "Don't tell Sedge."

I massage the soap into my scalp. "Maybe you need something quilted to line the cuff, like one of those fancy saddle
blankets. They sell them in Snaketown."

"And what will we buy one with? Our good looks?"

"We've got the coins from that old man's purse. There are a
couple of silver keys, at least."

She snorts, dabbing a few of her blisters with creek water. "I'm not wasting a key on a blanket, not when we're running out of cornmeal and you're handling your soap like it's a biscuit hot off the griddle."

"If it keeps the stupid thing from hurting, Rose . . ."

"No. I'll get a blanket somewhere else. Use the money on Whit, or Andras." She pauses for a moment, examining the ragged scar above her knee, the only other remnant of the goring from the out-of-control bull, crazed by branding, that claimed her calf. "Speaking of which, have you . . . noticed anything about Andras?"

I let out a sigh. I'd been wondering if *I* was going to have to bring up the subject with *her*. "I noticed he missed the grab on a bucket handle last week. It was sitting there plain as day."

She nods. "This morning he poured a stream of coffee straight past the cup and onto the ground."

I dip my head forward and pour another few handfuls of water over it, watching it wash the precious suds downstream. I stay that way, leaning over my knees, my locks hanging down around my face. They form a curtain—I can almost imagine the whole world consists just of this little patch of running water between my feet, clear and cold.

"He needs medicine," Rose continues. "Something for his eyes, before it's too late."

"He needs to get back to Cyprien," I say. "Back to his family."

"And how is that supposed to happen? He can't make that trip. He'd be snapped up by the slavers again, or robbed . . . blind." The last word trips out almost by accident.

"I'll take him."

"And how will *you* make the trip? I know you can survive

on sand fleas and good luck, but he's just a little kid, and that kind of travel costs money—for food, at the very least, if not lodging and supplies. Our couple of keys would barely get you to Teso's Ford."

I take one of my locks and roll it between my palm. The damp hair curls up by my scalp. "I'm working on it. If we save some of the coin we have now, all we need is another good hit or two on the stages."

She goes quiet for a moment. "So that's our long-term plan, is it? Just keep turning over stages?"

"What other option is there, Rose?"

"One of us could get a job."

I twist another lock and then start on the next. "Yeah, taking up space in the town prison. Who's going to hire us?"

"I believe the Alcoran Senate has expressed interest more than once."

"I'm not turning myself in to them."

"I didn't say you had to. I could."

I twist my next lock with vigor. "So they can give you a badge and push you back out in the desert to take all the same risks as before, only for *their* benefit?"

"At least there'd be money," she shoots back. "There'd be food, and blankets, and medicine. Whit and Andras could be taken care of."

"In an overcrowded public orphanage, if they're lucky—more likely prison, just like Voss. The same goes for the rest of us."

"It's worth a shot."

"It's just a different form of slavery!" I yank my next lock a bit too vigorously. "They'll own you again, only with papers this time."

"What do you suggest?" she asks sharply. "Holing away out here in Three Lines for all eternity, while we all drop off like flies? The little ones can't survive like this forever, Lark. We're playing a dangerous enough game as it is. When you and I found this place four years ago, neither of us thought it was a permanent home, just a place to hide from the rustlers."

"And then we found the water pocket and turned over our first coach," I remind her. "And we realized it's as good a home as we're ever going to get. I'm not taking the others in to town. I'm not putting them at the mercy of a bunch of lawkeepers who wouldn't care one scratch if we all went back into the wagons." I roll another lock. "I'm not letting us all get scattered—you really want them to take little Whit or Andras away?"

"Are you scared about what will happen to them without you, or are you scared about what will happen to *you* without *them*?"

"I'm not *scared*." I spit the words out and they hang between us. My scalp stings where I overtwisted my hair.

I'm not scared.

I'm terrified.

For all of us.

Rose sighs. She heaves herself off the rock and gives a little hop on her good leg so she can settle down behind me. She threads her fingers through my locks and rolls one in her palms, twisting more gently than me.

"I know you're not scared," she says. "The Sunshield Bandit isn't scared of anything. But you *are* worried. You'd be stupid not to be. I'm just trying to consider all our options. We owe it to the little ones."

I blow out my breath. "I know. And I'm going to make it

better for them, starting with Andras. I'll figure out a way to get him back to Cyprien. But don't run off and turn yourself in to the Alcorans yet. Give me some time. I'll figure it out."

She snorts softly. "I'm sure you will."

"I'm serious."

"I am, too. Your life is one long *I'll figure it out*. And you usually do." She smooths a few of my locks down my back. "Just . . . remember that all that figuring doesn't have to happen by yourself."

I sigh and close my eyes. She's probably right, but I can't help but want to keep us all tucked up in the relatively safe haven of Three Lines Canyon.

The fewer of us actively battling against the Ferinno, the fewer it can claim.

TAMSIN

Still not dead.

And able to chew again, hurrah!

I've tried to request a notebook and writing utensil from Poia and Beskin, but they've refused.

"We're out of parchment," Beskin says pragmatically.

"But you wouldn't get any anyway," snaps Poia.

"No, you wouldn't, but especially because we're out of parchment," Beskin adds.

Poia's uncovered eye twitches in vexation, rumpling the pox scars that dot her skin. I hold back a broken laugh from where I'm sitting slouched in the corner (I'm choosing to view this as a silver lining of endless prison: the freedom to slouch). Honestly, these two could perform a marvelous comedy routine—oblivious, orderly Beskin, grinding unconsciously on Poia's singular remaining nerve. Apparently Poia was an armed guard for the Moquoian stage line, possibly with a few black marks in her ledger. I'm sure the only thing that keeps her from wringing Beskin's neck is the necessity to leave one person here in the compound while the other resupplies. Oh, it's fun to watch her boil, though.

To think I get all this entertainment for free.

I would very much like a notebook, however. I'm never without one—I had no less than four in my satchel when the coach was attacked, but I suppose they're all ash now. Months of work gone, verses and notes and turns of phrase. Destroyed. Plus my sheet music, with the nearly complete chord progression I've been wrestling with since *Akasansi*.

What does it matter, I suppose—it's not like I'll be plucking any dulcimer strings for rapt ears anytime soon. Or ever again, likely. My fingers press imaginary frets into the packed dirt floor, wilting petals sinking toward a still-frosted earth.

That's not a bad fragment, actually. I wish I could write it down.

Great Light, I am beyond bored.

That's okay, though. Being actively, aggressively bored distracts me from everything else. It distracts me from the fact that I've lost weight. Not much—I still have an appreciable swell to my hips and stomach, but weeks of bad food have left my skin loose and wrinkled, not smooth and taut as before. That's another thing that's worrying me. My skin, once a mellow golden brown, has turned dingy and dry, thanks in part to the stale, thirsty air and the lack of accessible daylight. The tiny window near the ceiling is about a hand square, but the bright patch of light it casts never hits the ground—it just travels across the opposite wall like a lighthouse beacon. Wherever I am, my room must face north.

My hair is the tiniest bit longer now, mossy and tufted. The razor cuts have all healed over. I ignore the pang of indignity in my stomach and instead imagine what I'd look like with all my favorite ornaments stuck on my shorn head—the jeweled combs, carved pins, and glittering baubles all sticking out of my black hair. Back before leaving Tolukum Palace, I had sat for a preliminary sketch for the portrait artists, strategizing different hairstyles and accessories. We'd decided on a string of amber marigolds connected with cascades of superfine gold chain. With my long hair piled high on my head, I thought they looked like sunlight glancing off dew. Now I expect it would look like I got my head stuck in a cobweb. I smile at the thought.

That hurts. It turns into a grimace instead.

Lest I be accused of laziness, I have already worked my little cell over multiple times a day. But there are only three things of interest I've found besides my own body, my own waste, and, twice a day, food. One is the bucket that holds my waste. I've gotten to know it well, but I doubt it will serve me beyond its implied function. It's a wooden bucket with two metal rings holding the thing together, and it's too short to give me any leverage up to the little window. Even if it wasn't, I couldn't turn it over without spilling the contents, and my conditions are already bad enough.

The second feature is my bed, which consists of a woven reed mat and a woolen blanket. The reed mat is scratchy and only marginally better than sleeping directly on the dirt floor—I know, I tested it. The woolen blanket is too short—my feet stick out the far end. Me, short and stubby, and they couldn't get a blanket long enough to cover my whole body? I imagine it must have been a conscious effort on their part.

The third feature is the window, which I suspect is actually a vent for this repurposed storage room. There's nothing to grab to haul my face up to the hole. Even if there was, I doubt I'd be strong enough in my current state. The most I can do is stick my hand up into the little square of sunlight as it moves across the far wall. I can see no trees or foliage through the window, no matter where I stand. This tells me for certain I'm not in Moquoia any longer, along with the dry air and adobe walls. I'm in the Ferinno Desert for sure, probably in the no-man's-land east of Pasul.

It has not slipped my notice that this tiny patch of sky provides the only spot of color in my cell. My wardrobe is colorless as well as shapeless, as are my mat and blanket. The waste bucket is only a darker shade of nothing than the packed dirt floor. Even my sickly skin is slowly turning the same faded, dirty dun of the adobe walls. Sometimes I wonder if my eyes are still their same dark brown, or if they've drained of color, too, leaving me washed out in a washed-out world. No *Kualni An-Orra* here, no Prayer of the Colors or rush to catch a glimpse of the sky—even if there was enough moisture to generate a rainbow, it would have to appear in just the right place for me to see it through my tiny window.

But even if it's not *Kualni An-Orra,* there is one thing that happens here, wherever I am—one wild, beautiful thing. It terrified me the first time, entrenched in pain and panic and wondering what scaffold of sanity had finally given way. But now that I've convinced myself I'm not hallucinating, it's become the highlight of every passing day.

Bats.

Thousands of them, millions. Every night, as dusk turns blush to blues outside my window, they stream into the air, a living storm cloud. I don't know where they come from—caves, I assume, though I can't recall any caves in my little knowledge of the Ferinno. But it must be a huge space. They wheel past my window in rivers so thick the sky turns black, chattering and squeaking. After those first surreal days, when the pain in my head became more bearable, I stood under the window, watching, listening, smelling—by the colors, they stink of guano and ammonia. But so do I in my fashion, so we're siblings in that way. Now they've become a fixture for me, a timepiece. It's bat-time. Their return is more dispersed and happens after I've drifted into sleep, so it's their first mass flight that has become the most treasured tangible thing in my life. My lifeline.

With a tremendous amount of luck, they may just be my salvation, too.

So this is my life at present—four walls, a floor, a ceiling, a few muted objects, and the window to the world. Bats and air. When my head is clear, I sit and watch the colors turn in my little squint of sky. Pale pinks and yellows in the morning fade into a crystalline blue, to orange, to indigo, to bat-black, to night-black, and then back around again. Pretty soon I'll be able to come up with brand-new names for each minute color change. I'll be able to tell every breath and whisper of a different hue. I'll be more intimate with every spot on the spectrum than any *ashoki* ever was.

Either that, or I'll die of boredom.

If my escape plan doesn't work out, I imagine that's the more likely outcome.

VERAN

The Hall of the *Ashoki* shimmers with every imaginable shade of turquoise, starting with pale robin's-egg blue and going straight through to an iridescent green so dark it's nearly black. I pause on the threshold with Eloise, taking in the sight of the room. Peppered throughout the excited crowd are larger-than-life statues on marble pedestals, their white stone garments frozen in flowing movement. Each one holds some type of instrument—a finger drum here, a harp there. The *ashoki*—the legendary wordsmiths that shape this country's politics. Fragments of poetry and lyrics are carved into their pedestals—memories of their most beloved verses.

"Oh look," Rou says cheerfully behind us. "Young'uns in their natural habitat." He points to the long banquet table laden with an array of finger foods, where several older children of Moquoian ministers and a few young politicians are socializing—including Prince Iano. He shoos us in that direction. "Go on, make friends."

I lean toward Eloise as he takes off toward Queen Isme. "He knows we're adults, and not six, right?"

"I think he stopped making any distinction after about age ten. Don't tell me your parents aren't the same."

"With five of us? They tend to group us into the older three and younger two. It lets them hover for other reasons."

She gives a smile of commiseration. "Well, there's certainly plenty to hover over between the two of us, isn't there?"

I grimace. Eloise is the single direct heir to the throne of Lumen Lake, and her parents—Rou in particular—have always been protective of her. Being the fourth out of five children, I don't have that excuse, but that doesn't mean my childhood wasn't as closely watched as hers.

Perhaps more.

We weave among the silk jackets, long skirts, and glittering hair jewels, catching snatches of conversation, all of it focused on speculation for the upcoming announcement.

"—heard that Oiko fellow can play sixteen different instruments, that's got to count for something—"

"—amazed the queen is letting her son make the appointment, even with her upcoming abdication; it's highly irregular—"

"—but the politics are the most important thing, of course. That Kimela, now, I'm told she's a real champion of industry. If the prince hopes to preserve the traditional values of this country, he'd be wise to appoint her—"

I glance at this last voice—it belongs to Hetor Kobok in-Garnet, the minister of industry just returned from factory audits. It's taken me a while to remember the color titles of various nobility in court, but Kobok's isn't difficult—he wears his traditional color bracelet over the sleeve of his turquoise jacket, the gold links studded with fat garnets that flash in the light. Even without this indicator of status, it's not hard to tell that he's an influential member of court—transfixed nobles stand around him in a half circle, hanging on his words.

"I didn't think to do any inquiring about the candidates for *ashoki*, did you?" Eloise asks as we squeeze past the group of ministers. "I've been too wrapped up trying to make progress with the Ferinno Road."

"I wouldn't exactly call it thorough, but I've picked up a little from listening to the queen's attendants," I say. "Of all our options, it sounds like Oiko—that one who can play a million instruments—is best for our interests. I heard one of the ladies on the Citizen Welfare Committee saying he's in favor of phasing out the use of bond labor. I think the one we least want is Kimela—she sounds vocal about maintaining things as they are, including limiting Moquoia's relations with its neighbors. I expect we'll have a much harder time gaining any ground if she's appointed."

"Well, let's hope Iano still upholds the same convictions he did in his letters," Eloise says, eyeing the prince as we draw near the flock of young courtiers. "Even if he's given us no indication of such since we've gotten here."

We reach the skirts and jacket tails of several diplomats, and they make way excitedly for us, greeting Eloise warmly. She responds with seemingly effortless cordiality and introduces me to the handful of courtiers I haven't met. All of them are positively brimming with excitement over the upcoming announcement. In fact, the only person not visibly enjoying themselves is Iano.

True to the first day of the *si,* the prince is decked in deep turquoise silk, his sleeves and collar piped with gold. Beads of jade and tourmaline flash from his embroidery and the lobes of his ears, and the gems down the legs of his trousers are each as big as the seal my father wears on his thumb. Gold winks from the jeweled pin holding his long black hair in a half tail, and it shines on the hilt of the ceremonial rapier on his belt. The only thing outside his *Mokonnsi* color scheme is his *si* bracelet, by comparison a much plainer band of stamped bronze, set with a cluster of lapis and worn with age. On our first day in court, I was surprised to see such a shabby token of his titular colors when so many other courtiers' *si-oque* drip with gems, like Kobok's, until I found out that it's an heirloom piece several hundred years old, the colors replaced for every heir.

"Good morning and a bright *Mokonnsi* to you, Prince Iano," Eloise says, careful to get the customary greeting right. "How exciting to be here for this day."

Iano adjusts his grip on a glass cup of cream tea, his lips set in a frown. "Mm, I'll bet it is."

I can safely say that that's *not* the proper response to the greeting on the first day of a new *si*, but Eloise doesn't let him deter her. She fixes him with a warm smile, believable enough to look genuine to the untrained eye, and gestures to me. "You have already met our translator, Veran Greenbrier—as you can see, he is joining me for the announcement of the new *ashoki* this morning."

I bow slightly, the shift in weight making my blisters sting. I rack my brain for the right thing to say. "We are very much looking forward to it."

His eyes narrow just slightly, but a bubbly girl at his elbow is the first to reply. "We've tried *everything* to get him to tell us his choice, even a *hint*, but he hasn't budged. What a surprise it's going to be!"

"For most," Iano says flatly, looking away toward the stage at the end of the hall.

I throw a quick glance at Eloise, but she's still not deterred by the prince's dour behavior. She gives the barest flick of her eyes in my direction, as if in warning, and then says, "I thought it would be beneficial to Veran if you were to share some of your process for choosing the *ashoki*. It must be such a . . ." She pauses, her brow furrowing. After a moment, she glances at me, lapsing into Eastern. "I can't remember the word for 'significant'—it's not *bengka*, is it? That's 'loud' . . ."

I'm about to offer the translation, when Iano replies in accented Eastern—I've forgotten he's nearly fluent. Both of us have forgotten, apparently. "The word is *aquagii*, and yes, it is *quite* a significant decision."

I almost jump in surprise, but Eloise doesn't flinch. "Yes, of course," she says coolly, still smiling. "Perhaps you could tell Veran about the audition process."

"And why, I wonder, is the Eastern delegation suddenly so interested in the choosing of the *ashoki*?" Iano looks from Eloise to me, his lips set in a thin line.

I'm not sure how to respond. The other courtiers shift with a false front of cheerfulness—none of them can speak Eastern, but it must be obvious we've irritated the prince.

"We . . . have just heard of their importance in court," I stammer. "I read all about them at home."

His eyes narrow, and he looks away, back to the empty stage at the front of the hall. His free hand fingers the gold fringe hanging from his rapier hilt.

After the silence stretches out too long, the bubbly courtier from before jumps to strike up conversation again. She reaches for my lapel.

"Oh, how lovely!" she exclaims. "And look how it matches the new *si*!"

I look down to where her fingers are brushing the silver fili-gree firefly pinned to my jacket. The Lumeni pearl in its abdo-men does have a turquoise color to it, to mimic the blue ghost fireflies that swarm around the palace in the summer. It was a gift from Mama on the steps of the Alcoran Senate building as we were about to depart in June.

"To remember your roots," she'd said, stabbing the pin through my tunic like she had a grudge against the fabric.

"I'm not going to forget, Mama," I'd said, holding still lest I be stabbed, too.

"I hope not, because Colm will have to answer to me if you do." She'd capped the pin and started absently neatening my tu-nic laces. "You listen to Rou. And do your best to help Eloise."

"I will."

"Remember to drink more water than you think. Stick to the shade—and don't be afraid to ask the others to take a rest. They'll listen—"

My face had flushed. "I know, Mama."

"I know you know. Just . . ." She'd taken a breath, her hands pressing my shoulders, grounding me. "Earth and sky, just *be careful*, Veran. Listen to your body."

I tear my attention back to the group of courtiers around me, trying to keep my collar from growing hot like it did that day in Alcoro. The bubbly girl—I need to ask Eloise her name—just said something that I didn't catch.

"Sorry?" I say.

"I said, your pin—it's the *ernduk*, the light beetle that is holy to your people, yes?"

"Uh, yes. It's firefly season back home."

This is hilarious for some strange reason, sending everyone—except Iano and Eloise—into fits of delighted laughter. At least I think it's delighted. My collar heats despite my best efforts.

"I wonder if it will glow at the *Bakkonso* Ball next week," says another. "Wouldn't that be charming!"

"You *are* coming to *Bakkonso*, aren't you?" the first asks.

Eloise gives our confirmation that we are, in fact, coming to the fabled ball, though neither of us are sure we understand it. The name translates to "indigo lamp," and the information we've cobbled together involves a mineral powder that glows bright white under a particular kind of blue-shielded lantern. I haven't quite figured out what one does with the powder, or how it figures in with the dancing, but the younger echelon of the court has been chatting about it nonstop for several days.

"And do you have an *ernduk* pin as well?" our friend asks Eloise.

"We are not from the same country," Eloise begins, but neither of us have the chance to elaborate on the differentiation between Lumen Lake and the Silverwood Mountains before a series of chimes sound from the end of the hall. A few excited murmurs go up, and folk press toward the soaring curtains hanging over the stage, the fabric changed from green to turquoise overnight. The courtiers around us start to jostle and whisper.

"Excuse me," Iano says, setting his tea down—he must be about to make his announcement. But instead of moving directly for the stage, he takes a short, sharp step toward us. I step quickly to one side, but I run into Eloise. My wooden heel wobbles and my ankle turns awkwardly. I feel a blister burst.

I bite back a grimace as Iano leans in close, so quickly it must only look like a nod of his head to an outside observer.

"I have people watching you," he murmurs in Eastern through gritted teeth. Then he straightens, turns, and strides effortlessly through the turquoise crowds. They part like ocean currents around him.

"What?" I say aloud.

"What?" Eloise echoes. "What did he say?"

I straighten off her shoulder, watching him walk toward the stage, the golden pin in his black hair glinting.

"I'm . . . not sure," I say. I try to process his words again—had he gotten his translation wrong? Why would he say something so ominous out of the blue? Was it directed to both of us . . . or just to me?

People watching *me*?

I shift on my sore feet and wince at the torn blister on the pad of my foot. I lean too heavily on my walking cane, my stomach turning at both the pain and the uncomfortable end to our interaction with Iano. "Eloise, I'm going to sit down for a second."

She turns to me, her face instantly changing from puzzled to concerned. "Why? Are you all right?" She hurries to thread her arm under mine, getting her weight under my shoulder, but I wave her away.

"Not like that. It's these damned shoes—they're eating my feet."

She glances down, still holding me under my shoulder, fully

prepared for me to buckle on the spot. "Oh. Well, can you make it closer to the front? I want to be with Papa when Iano makes the announcement."

I get an image of me studiously observing my weeping blisters in the midst of the elegant Moquoian court. "No, let me just . . . I'm going to sit back there, just for a moment. I'll come find you."

She looks doubtful, but the crowd is pressing eagerly toward the stage, jostling for the best vantage points. I slide out of her grip, smiling as robustly as I can to convince her I'm not about to collapse. After another moment of scrutiny, she turns and hurries to join the tide of courtiers. I draw in a breath and walk as normally as I can in the other direction, toward the back of the hall. I pass a giant statue of a woman with ribbons flying from her hair and holding a tambourine, and then I spy a small bench next to a black-clothed block. The block is an odd shape and height, too tall to be a table, but it doesn't concern me now—it's the bench I'm after. I teeter toward it and collapse, discarding my cane on the floor.

I wriggle my cursed shoe off my foot and sigh in relief as it pops off. The blister stings in the open air, and carefully I set it down on the cool hardwood floor. I'm going to need to start wrapping my feet in bandages to stave off infection.

It's going to be a long walk back up six flights of stairs.

Queen Isme is making her way onto the stage, gems glittering in her hair like raindrops. I lean down to slide my other shoe off, just for good measure, when I catch sight of the object underneath the black shroud beside my bench—it's not a table as I first assumed, but solid white stone, like the statues in the hall. I reach forward and twitch the shroud back a few inches, revealing the same tiled pattern along the bases of the *ashoki* statues. It's another pedestal . . . but with nobody on top.

I'm about to lift the cloth higher, to see if there's a name, when the barest breath of air moves against my neck.

I have people watching you.

Instinctively, I drop the cloth and whip my head around. Crouched in the shadow of the shrouded pedestal is a person, dressed in black and holding so still that I'd looked right past her. She's holding a dustpan and brush frozen in midair, as if she'd halted as soon as I sat down.

"I'm so sorry, lord," she whispers. "I didn't think anyone would require this space. Forgive my presence."

"Not at all," I say, trying to shake off my nerves. "I simply needed a place to sit down out of the way."

She ducks her head, showing a few streaks of gray in her brown bun. "I will return at a later time."

"No, by all means, don't let me interrupt you. I'll be gone in a moment. It's just my silly foot."

Her gaze drops to my feet and the line of angry red sores along the knuckles of my toes.

"If it would be convenient for you, lord, I have some lengths of clean linen that could serve you for bandages," she says.

"Oh . . . well, yes, actually, I would very much appreciate it."

With movements small and subtle, as if used to remaining unnoticed, she sets down her brush and pan. Out of the shadow of the pedestal, I can see her more clearly—a kind-faced woman perhaps three decades my senior wearing the all-black attire of the palace servants. She comes around the bench and kneels down in front of me, drawing a few cloths from her apron pocket. I reach to take them from her, but she either doesn't see my hand or ignores it. She starts to wrap my right foot in linen.

"Thank you," I say, embarrassed.

"I will have the valets request a more proper fit for you," she says, looping the cloth around my foot. "You will need sturdy shoes to dance at the *Bakkonso* Ball next week."

"I'm afraid it's my feet, not the shoes," I say with false cheer. "Where I come from, we only wear soft soles. I have no skill with wooden heels."

She finishes wrapping my foot. Peeking from one of her long sleeves is a *si-oque*—rather than the flashy metal brace-lets of most of the court, hers is brown hemp corded through a string of colored glass beads, each a different color. It's the first time I've seen a commoner's *si* bracelet.

"Why are there so many colors on your *si-oque*?" I ask without thinking.

She pauses and glances up at me, and then down at her bracelet. Hurriedly she tucks it back under the hem of her black sleeve. "I have no children to pass them on to."

"Pass them on?" I strain my thoughts back for recollection on this practice—some countries back east pass on hereditary names, like Lumen Lake and Cyprien, but I thought the Mo-quoians were like my folk, taking their epithets independently.

She looks up at me again. Her lined brown eyes are crinkled with suppressed—perhaps sly—amusement. It's not an unkind expression, but I realize I've betrayed my foreignness, if my accent and appearance hadn't already done the trick.

"You are one of the Eastern ambassadors?" she asks.

I nod in concession. "Yes—I'm the translator for Ambassador Rou and Princess Eloise. My name is Veran. What's your name?"

"It's Fala, lord." Swiftly, she hooks the hem of her sleeve back again to show me her *si-oque*. With a better look, I see eight small irregular beads, each flawed with bubbles and scratches. The dye in one didn't mix all the way, creating a green streak through the clear glass. One is little more than a chip, and so worn I can't tell the color.

"Common folk have no title," Fala explains. "The ability to take a *si* is either inherited, or granted by the king or queen. We are generally given a color by our family based on anything—the *si* we were born, an ancestor's wishes, a favorite color." She touches a faded violet bead at the end of the bracelet. "I was a sweet child, and so my mother gave me *quahansi*, the color of kindness. But it's not a title, and it has none of the weight of an official *si*. Merely a childhood token." She runs her finger across the beads to the far end, to the scuffed, colorless chip. "They're passed on to be worn by children, but as I said . . ." She gives the tiniest of shrugs and pulls her sleeve back down.

"You don't have any other family?" I ask.

"None," she replies, going back to the bandages. "My work has always come first, I'm afraid."

"What do you do here?"

"I am the head of palace staff," she says. "Interiors, grounds, gardens, kitchens, and utilities. This room is normally cleaned at night, but I am short-staffed at the moment—" She cuts herself off, as if realizing she's about to reveal some kind of defect to me.

"Because of the fever?" I ask.

She draws in a breath. "It is of no importance."

But she's the first person I've been able to talk to about what goes on behind the veneer of the court, and I don't want her to close down. "I find the work you do fascinating—it must be quite an operation to keep this palace as orderly as it is. I've never been in a place so well-kept."

"You're very kind," she murmurs. She makes a small, sympathetic noise at the state of my left foot, arranging and rearranging the linen.

I look up toward the stage. I wasn't paying attention to Queen Isme's words, but now she's gesturing to Iano to join her. I should hurry and try to find Eloise and Rou before the announcement is made, but there's no way I can re-join the throng unobtrusively now. Besides, I want to keep talking to Fala. Perhaps she'll be more forthcoming than the politicians in court.

"May I ask you a question, Fala?"

"I am at your service, lord."

"Princess Eloise and I corresponded with Prince Iano over the past year, and in his letters he seemed pleased that we were coming, and happy to discuss his agenda with us. But since we arrived, he has barely wanted to speak to us at all. Do you have any idea why that is?"

Her face is bent toward my foot, so I can't see her expression, but her shoulders take on a hint of tension. "I am sure I don't know, lord."

"Nothing at all? Did something happen recently? His father passed away last year, didn't he?"

"A year and a half ago, rest him."

I thought as much—we offered him condolences in some of our earliest letters, and even then he seemed ready to discuss policy. "What could it be?" I ask. "Is he ill? Are we appearing too agga . . . acca . . . *aggressive*?"

She shakes her head despite my fumble. "While I can only

make guesses, lord, I expect the transitioning of the *ashoki* has been very trying for him."

"Oh, is that all?" I ask, before realizing it came out wrong. "That is, I know it is an important office, but what makes the transition so difficult? What happened to the last one? Did they . . ."

I rack my brain for the word *retire*, but before I can recall the translation, Fala sighs. "Yes, may she rest in the Colors."

My brain stumbles over the implication. "Oh, she—she died?"

"Yes, indeed." She gestures around us at the darkened hall. "There's always a difficult mourning period after an *ashoki* dies. Your arrival has come at a bleak time for us."

"I had no idea," I say, filing the information away. Rou and Eloise need to hear this—nobody in court has seemed particularly bleak except Iano. All the talk has been about the selection of the new *ashoki*, not the fate of the old one, so none of us had stopped to wonder if something might be amiss. I gesture to the empty pedestal. "Is that where her statue will go?"

"Yes," she says. "It should have been here by now, but there's been some delay with the order. A disagreement, I believe, on the text to be placed on the stone. She had highly . . . irregular views, many would say."

"Did she? How so?"

But she bows her head farther, busying herself with the linen. "It's not my place to gossip. Speculating about the past hardly has its place today. The beginning of an *ashoki*'s career is a momentous occasion for all Moquoians."

"Will it affect your workforce?" I ask, leaning forward slightly. "If someone with more traditional politics is appointed—

someone who wants to preserve bond labor—will it affect your staff?"

She takes a breath, and I realize she's been unwrapping and rewrapping the arch of my foot, as if she can't get it right. She shakes her head. "It is not for me to comment on, lord."

"I understand, and I don't want you to get in trouble, but, Mistress Fala—Ambassador Rou and the princess . . . we are trying to work with Prince Iano to phase out indentured service and bond labor. Would you consider speaking with us— speaking with my ambassador—to give us better insight on how it might affect—"

A sudden hush falls so quickly and absolutely over the gathered crowd that I bite off my next words. I look over Fala's head to the stage, where Prince Iano is standing rigidly in the harsh limelight. The crowd seems to lean forward as one. Along the left side, I spy Eloise's cascading curls as she tilts her head closer to her father's. Fala's fingers slow on the linen. I find myself wrapped up in the tension of the moment, straining not to miss Iano's words.

I shouldn't have worried. His voice is clear and firm, and sharp as the decorative rapier at his side.

"Your one hundred and twenty-ninth *ashoki*," he says, "appointed on this the first day of *Mokonnsi* by Prince Iano Okinot in-Azure, is Kimela Novarni in-Chartreuse."

A rumble breaks through the crowd like a wave, voices gasping and exclaiming and murmuring all together. Through the commotion, Eloise and Rou look at each other. My eyebrows shoot skyward. Kimela? From the wings comes a stately woman in turquoise silk so vivid it's nearly green, clutching a golden harp. She offers a deep curtsy first to Queen Isme, then to Prince Iano, and then to the court, buoyed by applause.

Queen Isme gestures delightedly at the crowd, calling over the din, "Kimela will make her debut as your *ashoki* on the day of my son's coronation, in one month's time. May her words speak truth to his reign!"

I don't understand. Everything I've heard about Kimela suggests she's one of the old guard, wedded to the antiquated ways of the country, where labor is based on slavery and industry on resource depletion. I look to Iano—he's standing to the side, so stiff I expect one knock would keel him over. What happened to all the things he wrote out in our letters? All the timelines for transitioning the workforce, all the steps to leasing the sand quarries from Alcoro, all the budgeting for building the Ferinno Road? Up until now I was willing to believe Rou, Eloise, and I were just hitting the wrong notes, that we'd eventually arrive at the same page as he. But this—this is massive. A lifetime appointment for the most significant political post in the country, and it goes against everything we agreed to?

Who is this Iano?

Fala's hands are still. I glance down to see her staring into the middle distance, her face unreadable. She must sense my gaze, though, because hurriedly she finishes wrapping the linen up my ankle—with far less fuss than a moment ago—and ties it off.

"Mistress Fala," I say. "What does this mean for you?"

She rises from her knees and begins to stand. I offer her my hand, but she doesn't take it.

"I am grateful for the wisdom of our prince," she says simply.

"But . . . for it to be Kimela, from all I've heard . . ." I trail off at the way her face closes warily. "I understand if you don't feel comfortable talking to me, here and now, but if Princess Eloise were to ask, if Ambassador Rou were to ask, in all confidentiality, only to make more informed decisions . . ."

"Prince Veran Greenbrier," she says, and I stop in surprise. I never told her my epithet or my official title, but in the next moment I realize that as head of staff, she likely knows much more. I was silly to think I was introducing myself to her for the first time. She probably knows all about my soft-soled boots, the books on my bedside table, how I take my tea.

She probably knows everything.

She takes a breath and lowers her eyes to her folded hands. "Please, Prince Veran, what is done is done. *Ashoki* is a lifetime position, one that cannot be taken away. And if you do not wish to jeopardize your stay here, I implore you not to fret about the intricacies of this court. It will endure."

I lean forward, trying to see her face more fully. "What do you mean by that, Fala? What's going on?"

But she only shakes her head and steps away, circling back around the bench to retrieve her dustpan and brush. I rotate on the bench to follow her path.

She offers me a deep bow. "It was an honor to meet you, Prince Veran. And I am glad you are here to witness such a historic occasion. If you want to know Moquoia—truly know it, at our heart—there's no truer place than in the words of the *ashoki*."

Before I can respond, she straightens and hurries into the shadows at the back of the hall. She presses a wall panel to reveal a hidden service door and disappears through it.

Slowly, bracing my bandaged feet against the floor, I turn to the pedestal. All the other statues have words carved at their bases, but Fala said there had been a disagreement about the text for the past *ashoki*. I pinch the edge of the black cloth and lift it—sure enough, the marble is smooth and unmarked.

I drop the cloth and look back over the glimmering hall. The court is breaking up, some pressing toward the stage, some cloistering together to discuss the announcement among themselves. Minister Kobok is shaking hands in a circle of his peers, looking smug. Eloise is in deep discussion with Rou, her brow creased. She lifts her head and finds me across the room, and I can read the same anxiety on her face that's now gnawing at me.

Our work just got much, much harder.

LARK

The thunderhead builds behind me, sending its snarls and rumbles out over the sagebrush flats and broken rock arches. I breathe deeply from Jema's back, relishing the cool blue feel of the air. I need rain. The desert always needs rain, but these past few days, in particular, I especially need the rain. I need it to rinse the mats from Rat's fur and replenish the water pocket in Three Lines. I need it to flush out creatures from their dens, to draw them down to my deadfall traps. I need it to bring a bloom to the yellow lilies and yampa so I can dig up their bulby roots without crawling around the rocks trying to guess if a certain weed is poisonous or not.

But I need the rain for myself, too.

The anticipation of a good thing is always better than actually having the good thing, because good things never last. Soft blankets get gritty and threadbare. Fresh cornbread goes hard and stale if it's not eaten quick enough. And the rain-washed desert dries up all too fast, the sudden blossoms and rushing gullies giving way back to tough plant flesh and cracked earth.

No, give me the expectation of a thunderstorm over its aftermath any day. At least when it ends, it ends in the actual event, rather than the memory of the event.

I whistle to Rat, who has paused to sniff out some creature denning under a dead sagebrush. His head pops up, his big ears pivoted forward.

"Come on, dummy," I call. "Let's get into town before we start getting ground strikes."

He lopes over the rocky ground, and I nudge Jema down to the dirt track leading into Snaketown. It's a three-hour ride from camp, but I took the long way along the river to take advantage of the cattails, and it's already late afternoon. I've developed a healthy appreciation for cattails—Rose and I learned to collect the roots, shoots, and seed heads back with the rustlers. Cook used to send us into the streams to gather the heads for boiling and the roots for mashing into starch to bake into biscuits. It was one of the few chores I enjoyed, relishing the freedom to splash along the muddy banks and sit in the water to wash off the roots.

Unfortunately, we're too late in the season for the heads to be green, and the shoots are now too tough to be tasty. But I gathered a pouch full of the fine yellow pollen that grows on the spikes of the plant—we'll be able to mix it with the sack of cornmeal I plan to buy in Snaketown to make it stretch further.

The first raindrops begin to fall as the ramshackle town comes into view over the rise. Snaketown is a dusty little outpost, hardly more than a single street and a collection of scattered homesteads. It was a miners' town back in the day, but when the mines closed it came to rely on a handful of ranchers and those desperate enough to take the stage farther into the desert. The splintery wooden buildings creak in the wind gusting from the thunderhead. I urge Jema toward Patzo's general store, the shabby red paint darkened by streaks of rain.

Patzo knows I'm the Sunshield Bandit—it's hard to keep your identity a secret when you match all the descriptions frightened travelers bring in from the road—but he had a nephew abducted by slavers a few years ago, and he's always turned a blind eye to me coming in for supplies as long as I have coin to pay for it. Besides that, I'm good for business—the travelers I rob inevitably have to replace their wares from Patzo's store, and I spend all the money I win back in town anyway. I'd like to think I keep Snaketown on the map.

Still, it's always smart to maintain a low profile. I toss a glance at the sheriff's office down the street. She always mysteriously has piles of paperwork that keep her inside when I come into town, but there's no need to push my luck.

My poking through the cattails earlier today means I'll be spending the night, but I don't mind—sometimes Patzo will let me split wood for a hot meal and a bed in the storage room. *Mm*—just think about it, a full belly and a roof echoing with the drumming of rain . . . it's almost too delicious to dwell on.

Yes, give me the anticipation of something good any day.

By the time I rein Jema to a halt in front of the general store, my clothes are drenched. I swing from the saddle and rope Jema's lead to the hitching post. Shaking the rain from my hat, I tell Rat to stay under the porch he's ducked beneath, and I head into the store.

Patzo's helping someone at the counter, a burly lady in a

dark cloak, with a strip of blue fabric wound around her head as an eyepatch. Her hands wave agitatedly as she talks, but in the few moments they're still, I can make out the discolored pox scars stippling her skin, like Pickle's. She's arguing about the mail in Eastern blurred with a heavy Moquoian accent, trying to make Patzo promise the stage will reach Tolukum on an exact day. He's doing an admirable job in keeping his manners—if it were me, I'd just laugh in her face. You want something delivered on a specific day, you're better off making the trip yourself rather than relying on the overland stage.

I head to the medicine cabinet to start strategizing my purchases. The stock boy is unloading crates of castor oil—he looks me up and down with wide eyes. I gift him an eagle-eyed glare, and he scampers clear into the back room.

I peruse the bottles of various tinctures and cure-alls, mentally calculating what I can afford along with the dry goods I need. I may not be able to spell reliably, and my reading is slow, but years of stretching coppers has made me decent at mathematics. Good enough, anyway, to know there's no way I can afford Golden Butter Skin Balm for Pickle or Doc Yaxa's Miracle Tonic for little Whit. I consider filching a bottle of castor oil to replace my bottle of dwindling scalp oil, but I decide against it. I like Patzo, and I have no desire to cheat him. I remove a cheap bottle of coneflower tonic and some blister cream for Rose.

The stocky lady stomps out, clutching her parcels and a package of parchment. As Patzo rummages under the counter, I cross the store and set down my bottles.

"Afternoon, Patzo."

He drops whatever he's digging for and straightens as if struck by lightning.

"Lark," he says hoarsely.

"I need ten pounds of cornmeal, and a few measures of beans and some lard. Plus a length of canvas, if you've got any—and I wouldn't say no to filling your woodshed for a bed in the storeroom."

His copious black mustache quivers, and he cuts his gaze sideways, falling on a wall scattered with bold adverts for life-changing products and curling political announcements from the capital.

And my face.

I blink several times, at first doubting my own eyes. The nose is too slender, but that's inconsequential among everything else—the thick eyeblack, the wide-brimmed hat, the frayed bandanna, the long locked hair.

WANTED ALIVE: "LARK," THE SUNSHIELD BANDIT
SKIN: BROWN
EYES: BROWN
HAIR: DARK BROWN
NOTABLE FEATURES: TATTOOS ON HAND
AND WRISTS
MULTIPLE PIERCINGS IN BOTH EARS
WEAPONS: SWORD, BUCKLER, CROSSBOW,
HUNTING KNIFE
PRESUMED LOCATION: INDETERMINATE,
BETWEEN SNAKETOWN AND PASUL, EAST OF
WATER SCRAPE
REWARD FOR LIVE CAPTURE: 150 CE SILVERS
NO REWARD GIVEN UPON DEATH

"They brought them in a few days ago, a whole passel of 'em," he says. "Soldiers from Callais, they posted them all over town. Gave the sheriff a big old fright. Said if word came back that you'd been through town without being locked up, she'd answer to the Senate. Then she came and hollered at me, made me swear to hand you over next time you came in . . ."

Heat flushes through me, driven by my spiking heartbeat. Through the dingy store window, I see the stock boy racing through the rain, angling toward the sheriff's office. He must have lit out the back door, through the storeroom I'd been hoping to sleep in tonight. I look slowly back to Patzo.

"Patzo." I try to keep my voice calm. "Listen, I've never once done you a bad turn. I've paid you for every speck of corn I've ever bought, haven't I? I keep an eye out for your nephew, don't I?"

"I know it, Lark, I do, but I can't go against the law . . ."

"Hold on." I spread my hands on the counter. "Do me a favor—just get me the bag of cornmeal. That's all—just the cornmeal, and then I'll leave." I dig a haphazard handful of coins out of the purse and push them across the counter. "Please."

Thunder cracks the air; lightning splits the room into light and shadow. It seems to startle him into a decision. He leaps for the crossbow under the counter and scrambles to pull the lever.

I toss up my hands. "Patzo!"

"If the sheriff sees you strolling out of here with goods, it'll be me in the stocks, not you—you get out of here, and don't come back round again. I'll turn you in next time—I mean it!"

Through the rain pouring off the porch roof, I see the door to the sheriff's office open. Swearing, I scoop my handful of coins back into the purse—several of them ping off the floor, little lost promises rolling away under the shelves. Despite the point of the quarrel trained in my direction, I swipe the two bottles of medicine, too—turns out I should have gone for the fancy stuff after all. Without waiting any longer, I bolt from the store.

The rain is falling in sheets now, whipping the sign hanging over the door. Jema is tossing her head, her coat and saddle drenched. I loosen her lead from the post and vault onto her back. A shout rings out—I look over my shoulder to see the sheriff splashing up the road, jamming a quarrel into a crossbow. I wheel Jema around and spur her in the opposite direction. Rat races along at her side. The sheriff shouts again, but it's lost to the next peal of thunder. A quarrel whizzes past my shoulder. I swear, put my head down, and focus on trying to see through the driving rain.

We gallop out of town, mud spraying from Jema's hooves. It coats my back and hair; I pull my bandanna over my mouth to keep it from spattering my lips. We streak back up the rise, the rock arches and sagebrush flats blurred by rain. I give Jema her head, letting her race down the washed-out track, praying to whatever entity that watches over this strip of nowhere that she doesn't set her footing wrong.

A bolt of lightning strikes the ground in the distance. I bite down a sense of panic—out in the middle of this wide-open land, I'm the tallest thing there is. I should pull over and take cover down in the ditch—but what if the sheriff comes after me? Will she give chase in this weather? Or will she count on the elements taking care of me before I'm a mile out of town? Tomorrow morning she'll be able to trot out here and retrieve my body, charred black as a burnt biscuit.

At the next ground strike, perhaps a mile in front of us, I throw caution to the wind and guide Jema off the main track. She veers into the sage. Rat runs along behind, winding in and out of the brush. His ears are flat against his head, tail slightly tucked. I try to whistle some encouragement to him, but it's lost to the next crack of thunder.

The world goes white. The bolt hits so close I can feel it buzz through my body. Jema pulls up short, whinnying. Without waiting to be thrown from the saddle, I swing to the ground and gather up her reins. Dipping my hat against the driving rain, I run, dragging Jema blindly behind me.

There's a jut of rock a stone's throw away. It's hardly taller than me—crap for cover, but at least we won't be the tallest targets. I haul Jema into the lee of the rock and turn her head out of the wind. Rat slinks around her hooves, his thick, coarse fur shedding water. I want to collapse against the rock, but I know better—sitting flat against a tower of rock is a sure way to take a bolt of lightning up through the buttocks. Working Jema's girth strap with slick fingers, I heave the saddle off her back, toss it down on the ground, and crouch on top of it, trying to avoid any contact with the earth. I'll squash the already beat-up leather, but it's a far cry better than being struck by lightning.

Squatting in the driving rain, I bow my head forward into my hands. Water streams from the brim of my hat. My face on the poster swims in my vision again. They found me. After years of vague descriptions and halfhearted bounties, they found my face and my name. A hundred fifty keys! Fire and rock, I could buy a year of room and board for every person in camp with that money. I was in Snaketown last month without any whisper of a bounty . . . I stocked Patzo's woodshed and passed the night stretched on the milling sacks, stomach full of fried grouse and baked beans and sweet cornbread made without a single grain of sand gritting it up. What changed? What went wrong? How have they finally found me?

That man.

The one in the stage, the rich one with the books and the boots. The one whose purse I hoped to trade for supplies we desperately need in camp. The one who heard Saiph—*stupid blockheaded leatherbrained Saiph*—carelessly drop my real name. That old man took the information back to wherever he came from.

Callais. The capital. The Senate. He name-dropped the provost of the university. I'd thought he was just searching for something to scare me off. But he certainly had the look of an academic type, and the Senate is never far away from a mention of the university. *Dammit.* I grip my head in my hands. The man took my name and description back to the Alcoran Senate. Are they fronting the money for my capture out of the government treasury?

Because it *is* a capture, not just a bounty. It's not the ambivalent *dead or alive* so many other bandits get branded with. They want me brought in breathing. But that's far from reassuring—I can't imagine they have anything pleasant waiting for me in Callais. Is this about hunting slavers for them? Is it to serve punishment for robbing that old man and a dozen-odd others? Is it about making a statement? Are they hoping to do something gruesome to my body—hang me from a wall somewhere as a warning to any other bandit foolish enough to threaten a spotty old professor?

Jema stomps her hooves, sending Rat scooting to my side. He leans against my calf, and I absent-mindedly scratch his ears.

Great Light, without Snaketown, our closest bit of civilization is Pasul—almost a day's ride in the other direction. It's a Moquoian town on the very edge of the border, where the sagebrush flats start to rise and buckle to create the little range of mountains that traps all the water on the far side. I'll have to take Saiph with me. He, at least, can pass for Moquoian, and his language is better than mine—mine is out of practice since my days in the sand quarries of Tellman's Ditch. We'll have to change currency, too—I'm sure there's a bank there, but the idea of spending unnecessary time showing my face around town makes me nervous. And that's assuming this bounty hasn't traveled that far—I've broken open enough Moquoian slave wagons to make them happy to turn me over to Alcoran authorities. If they aren't looking for me yet, they probably will be soon. I swear and rub my eyes—and then I swear again as I get Rat's wet fur stuck in my eyeballs.

Lightning flashes again, followed by thunder a second or two later. The storm is blowing south—they never last long out here, but damn if they don't throw everything they have at you in the meantime. I look up dejectedly, soaked through and starting to shiver. I wish I hadn't spent all that time collecting cattail pollen—it'll be soggy and useless by now. As it is, I won't be able to get all the way back to camp tonight, especially since I'll have to pick through the flats away from the main road. Come to think of it, I should probably get on the far side of the caprocks, to hide from view in case the sheriff decides I'm worth chasing before the sun goes down. I didn't bring any gear with me—no blanket or tinderbox. I'd planned at least on stretching out in the town stables, if not in Patzo's storeroom. I barely even have any food beyond wet cattail pollen.

It's going to be a long, cold, wet night.

The rain is slackening. I tilt my hat back and look up at the sky, letting the droplets sting my face. Water. Precious water. It's all or nothing out here—raging thunderstorms, sleet, hail, flash floods . . . or nothing. That, it seems, is the model for Three Lines, too. Feast or famine. All or nothing.

It's not nothing, though. Not yet. I lick the raindrops off my lips. Storms pass. Ours will, too. We can ride it out—find cover and dodge the lightning strikes.

I just have to figure out how.

TAMSIN

It's raining. It began a little while ago, and it's lasted longer than any of the other fizzly showers in the last few weeks. Wafts of cool, moist air have been curling from my window, bringing the scent of wet earth with them. I won't pretend I can imagine myself back in Moquoia, not even when I close my eyes, but it's a comfort to hear that steady patter, broken by rumbles of robust thunder. It's like my heart has been parched along with my skin and sanity, and the sound of rushing water cools me like a river stone in a gully.

I stand under the window, letting wind-caught droplets spritz my cheeks. The other nice thing is that the rain drowns out Beskin's muttering. Poia left yesterday morning to resupply, and Beskin is tiresome when she's alone. She seems to adore reorganizing the kitchen, and the resulting clatter and banging of crockery and pots sets my teeth on edge.

Now that I'm awake more, I've been spending the past few days puzzling over who Beskin and Poia are working for. I can't see either one of them as the mastermind behind my capture. Disregarding their questionable grasps on strategy, they can't just be mailing their blackmail letters straight to Tolukum—the couriers would be able to track them right back here. They must have a middleman, and the attack on my coach needed several other accomplices. There must be someone in Tolukum, perhaps someone right in court, who is quietly pulling all the strings. For hours and hours I've pored over all the people I knew, as well as the ones I didn't, who might like to see me locked mutely in a storeroom in the wilderness.

The growing length of the list is . . . dispiriting.

My head still hurts from the attack, and nursing so many unanswered questions is making me agitated. Beskin's compulsive nattering doesn't help. Truly, I can see why Poia spends an hour getting to and from the well every day. I wonder if she'll take her time coming back from town, too, or if her need to keep me secure will outweigh her hatred of her coconspirator.

I also wonder if there's any higher chance of them lending me writing material once they have parchment again. It's not as if I can send letters to anyone, so I don't see why they should care, unless keeping me idle is just another form of torment. Pointless torment—I'm hardly a threat now. But I never appreciated just how much I process the world by writing it down. I know *why* I'm that way, of course. My parents were scribes.

It's a little outside the norm for an *ashoki*. Most of us are born into political spheres, surrounded by diplomats, advisers, and courtiers—building up our nuanced understanding of the court and how to shake it without toppling it completely. Some other *ashoki* come straight from an entertainment background, having popped out of the womb clutching a harp or finger drum.

Such tellers are quick-witted enough to pick up the culture of the court by observation.

I come from neither of these backgrounds. My parents shared a large, airy office with the other scribes in Tolukum's main library, copying pages of text to send to the book binders. I started coming with them while I was still in the nursing sling on Mami's chest. They were fast writers—Papi could turn out a hundred pages a day. I loved Mami's handwriting best, though—broad and even, every curve perfectly proportioned. In my young opinion, the rich scholars who received books written in her hand were the luckiest of all the scribes' clients.

It was no surprise to anyone when I learned my letters very early on and took to thumbing through books in my parents' queues to pass the time while they worked. Sometimes I helped the other scribes in small ways—fetching parchment or ink or quills, turning up the lanterns on the days it got dark early, or rushing bundles of finished pages to the binders' offices downstairs.

But the lifestyle of a scribe, while earning a comfortable wage, takes its toll on the body. A full third of the workers in the office walked with a cane, even some of the young ones—a product of spending days hunched over the angled drafting tables. Many were forced to retire when their eyesight weakened, or when it became agony to hold a quill in their ruined fingers.

It was Papi who started to show signs of wear first, and it was his eyesight that went. I remember him squinting at pages, his nose barely an inch away, to be sure he got the transcription correct. I festooned his desk with lanterns to keep the lighting bright, and I made sure his ink was always good and dark. But nothing I did seemed to make a difference. Until one day.

"Tamsin, come here."

I put down the quills I was trimming and trotted over.

"This sentence—I can't make heads or tails of it."

To be fair, the previous scribe's handwriting was uneven and lightly drawn. "It says, *Allow the host or hostess to sample first, unless they direct otherwise.*"

Papi grunted and began to copy it down, his eyes screwed up. "Thank you. This text is impossible."

I noticed he'd made very little progress for the morning—he hadn't even completed the first chapter yet. I scooted onto the stool next to his desk. "Want me to read the next line?"

"Do you have something else you're supposed to be doing?"

"Not really."

He sighed and rubbed his eyes. "Sure. Read me a few paragraphs. Give my eyes a break."

I read a few paragraphs. And then a few more. I read to the end of the chapter. It was an etiquette manual for hosting a formal dinner party, and in that short time, I learned two brand-new words, *desultory* and *ideological*. Papi's pace picked up, his quill moving with more assurance now that his gaze didn't have to jump back and forth. When I finished the chapter, he asked if I wanted to stop.

I didn't. I'd just learned how one should gracefully handle a clash of opposing political views. This was getting interesting.

We continued. For the rest of the day, I read the text aloud to him, stopping only to get a giant glass of chilled tea. I sipped it between sentences, allowing his quill to catch up.

So began my role as an orator, narrating the texts so Papi could copy them down. When we finished the etiquette manual, we moved on to a book of stormwater management, and then a history of glassmaking, and then a guide to falconry.

I learned about stage theatrics from a drama technicians' guide. I learned the fundamentals of the dulcimer after dictating an entire manual on their manufacture and technique. I picked up the beginnings of Eastern after painstakingly reading a translation guide, spelling out each foreign word, their consonants clipped and impatient and practically spit from the tongue. I learned the cadence of songwriting and poetry recitation from a six-volume set of classic ballads and epics.

One of the last things I helped Papi with, before he retired to nurture what was left of his eyesight, was ten copies of the intricate court fashions for the upcoming social year. I read it aloud from cover to cover ten times, but rather than getting bored, I found it *fascinating*. Not necessarily the frittering over embroidery and lace, but the way it was all *saturated* with politics. The precise cut of silk for the *Bakkonso* Ball could convey the wearer's status, intentions, and political leanings. Matching patterns with others in court could instigate alliances; hair accessories made by a certain jeweler could signify not just that you *had* wealth, but how you came by it, what you used it for, and how you were willing to invest it. And the colors—every minute tint and shade had a different ramification depending on the event.

By my tenth recitation of the *Social Calendar Exemplar*, it was like a worm had wriggled into my brain. Or a seed had sprouted, if you like—that's a bit less disgusting of an example. Either way, the intricacies of the text buried deep in my psyche, and I found myself drawn to the idea of the Moquoian court— not for its politics, not for its society, but for the fusion of those two things. How they influenced and fed off each other, how they manifested and grew and shaped the daily life of an ordinary citizen like myself.

I wanted more.

When I was thirteen, Papi died after a bout with pneumonia. It wrecked me—for two months I couldn't even look at a book, much less read one. But Mami had trouble keeping our income afloat—her hands were becoming gnarled with scriveners' arthritis, and she could only work a few hours a day—so I was forced out of my stupor of grief by necessity. I picked up the extra hours Mami couldn't handle, coming straight to the library after school to work until suppertime. It was during this period that I delved into the details of Moquoian history, our trade alliances, our relationship to the islands and the countries to the east. I won't pretend I retained every scrap of information I read, but it's hard to copy a text word for word, sometimes multiple times, and not absorb much of it—especially when the subject fascinates you.

The ultimate result is well known in the palace—everybody loves a good *ashoki's journey* tale, and for several months after my appointment, the court was awash in embellished stories of my audition and selection. I even heard one rendition where my apparently mystical skills on the dulcimer had compelled a kindhearted quarry overseer to shorten my bond, on one condition—that I travel to Tolukum to play for the king. In that tale, the overseer supposedly gifted me a coin, which I carried with me, step by step, to purchase an audition for a royal audience, and the rest is history. Oh, what a noble, wise man that fictional overseer was, to spot the country's *ashoki* when she was but a lowly bond slave.

Never mind that the truth is far less glamorous, and far more insidious.

That's how truth generally works.

But only one person knows the full truth—the real truth—and I've been aggressively trying not to think about him at all, because it fills my sore head with a different kind of ache. As depressing as it is, dwelling on the people in court who might like to see me maimed and imprisoned is a more pleasant use of my time. My *endless, empty, wordless* time.

The storm outside has made its way directly overhead, the thunder booming out the same second the lightning hits, making the walls shake. I stand under the tiny window and stare up into the square slice of storming sky. My waste bucket is partially full, so I can't turn it over to stand on it. With a kind of stumbling impulse, I back up as far as the room allows, setting my palms on the far wall.

And then I push off and lunge forward, taking four giant steps before hurling myself upward toward the vent. One hand finds the lip of the hole, but it's wet now, and there's not a shred of strength in my arms. I slide down the solid adobe wall, landing in a crumpled heap on the floor.

I scraped my wrist, right where I used to wear my *si-oque* with the amber cabochons, which they took off me after the attack four weeks ago. Dazed, slightly intrigued by the absolute lack of substance in my muscles, I roll painfully onto my back and suck the raw spot. Flecks of rain continue to spatter my face, speckled bits of a world that has continued on without me.

I wonder if the bats will fly tonight. They must, I suppose, if they want to eat, heedless to the raucous thunder, cruel in their freedom and fitness for their purpose.

I, on the other hand, fall asleep.

VERAN

It's the day before the *Bakkonso* Ball, famous for its indigo lamps and glowing powder. The custom before this event, as I tried to explain to Ambassador Rou as he was arguing with his valet over wardrobe options, is to promenade around the glassed patios and strategize one's color scheme for the next day. He's paired me up with Eloise again, perhaps to continue our attempt to appear youthful and friendly rather than anxiously politic, which has been our primary state since Iano's announcement a few days ago. But Eloise, it seems, has more ambitious plans today. I follow her as she weaves among the buzzing nobility, listening to the negotiations—some to match their partners and allies, some to stand out in the crowd, many designed to communicate political leanings and business intentions, and at least one calculated to humble a former lover.

It's still pouring down rain, the thick greenish glass smeared with water. While Eloise stops to retrieve a cup of chilled *tul* from a black-clad servant, I tilt my head against the window, looking down the dizzying height to the treetops waving below, the leaves showing their pale underbellies in the wind. I press my fingertips to the glass—it's double-paned, muffling the sound of the storm. Not for the first time, my chest twinges with longing for a feel of moving air or trickling water, fever-bearing mosquitoes or no. I get a vision of spending our remaining four weeks slowly wilting under glass.

Ethnocentric bias, Colm whispers in my head.

Out of the corner of my eye, I see something move. I angle my head and nearly gasp out loud—there's a person just off to the side of the bank of windows, climbing nimbly downward. His clothes and hair whip in the wind, along with a jumble of objects around his waist. I squint through the pouring rain, recognizing a flat handheld mop flapping loosely from his belt—a glass cleaner. He's climbing down a metal ladder driven into the narrow space between the massive windowpanes. By the Light, there must be hundreds of them built into the side of the palace, highways for the battalion of servants who must clamber over them night and day. I crane my head to follow his progress—in no time at all he's descended the vertical length of the patio and is lost to my sight.

"Right," Eloise says, returning to my side with her cup of *tul*. I reel back from the window, a little dizzy from the thought of all those workers climbing those tiny ladders in the driving wind and rain. I brace myself on my walking cane. Eloise sips her *tul*, her face businesslike. "Here's the plan. I've been digging around, and it sounds like the two allies we need to make are the chairwoman of the Citizen Welfare Committee, and the minister of industry."

"Minister Kobok?" I ask. "I thought he leaned the other way from the chairwoman."

"Very much so—preserve the traditional labor model, and all that. A lot like the *ashoki*, Kimela." She scans the crowd, her gaze lingering on Minister Kobok. "But from what I've read, if we can appear to ally with both, it may communicate that the East is not out to destroy Moquoian industry, only to stop the practice of abducting Alcoran citizens for bond labor."

"And close down the sand quarries they operate illegally on Alcoran land," I point out.

"Well, yes, and that, but baby steps, you know?" She nods across the room, where the chairwoman is chatting with a few other courtiers. "So I'll go talk to the chairwoman. You go talk to Kobok."

"Alone?" I ask. "Shouldn't we . . . I mean, don't you need me to translate?" I know it's a hopeful statement—in truth, I need her much more than she needs me.

"From what I've heard, the chairwoman is friendly—friendlier than Kobok, anyway. I think she'll be patient with my grasp on the language. He probably won't be. That's why you need to talk to him—he'll have a harder time brushing you off. Show our interest in his work. Try to figure out what colors he's wearing to *Bakkonso*, and then see if you can secure the promise of an audience—a hard date and time would be best." She squares her shoulders. "Okay?"

"Um . . ."

"I'll meet you back here afterward to discuss our options." With that, she takes off across the long patio, her lavender skirts billowing behind her. She chose her colors today specifically to convey friendliness and approachability.

Friendliness. I can be friendly, can't I? I look down at my tunic—one of my typical shades of green, which is closer to the Moquoian *si* for optimism . . . unless it's dark enough to be regret.

Maybe I should have given the color more thought.

I can't change it now, though. I swallow and turn for Minister Kobok. He's mingling not far from the group clustered around Queen Isme. Ambassador Rou is among them, his ear cocked to keep track of the rapid Moquoian. He sees me across the crowd and gives me a wink. I give what I hope is a normal-looking grin in response, trying to keep from conveying my nerves.

I focus back on Kobok and the knot of courtiers around him, pushing forward until I'm standing beside them. I hover awkwardly, waiting for him to finish his conversation, drawing the curious gazes of several of his companions. When he's unable to ignore me any longer, Kobok turns to me, eyebrows knitted. His ensemble for today is a subtle gray-blue—water under a steely sky. Solemnity? Serenity? I can't recall what his precise shade means, so I focus on other clues in his appearance, though it doesn't tell me much. Rather than a fashionable bun or braid like many of the younger Moquoians, his long salt-and-pepper hair is swept back loose to brush his shoulders. His only adornments are two small gold bands securing his hair away from his graying temples, and an opal ring so large it spans his entire knuckle. His elaborate *si-oque* rests over his cuff, studded with garnets.

"Yes?" he asks brusquely.

I straighten, trying to channel Eloise. "Good afternoon, Minister. We haven't had the chance to officially meet—I'm Prince Veran Greenbrier, of the Eastern delegation."

"Oh, yes—the translator. I've seen you bobbing around the

ambassadors' elbows," he says. I can't tell if it's meant unkindly or not—his tone is certainly sharp, but perhaps it's just his usual manner. It doesn't escape my notice, though, that he identified me as an accessory to the ambassadors, not an ambassador myself. I squirm under the eyes of the other courtiers. Dammit, why did Eloise think this was a good idea?

"Yes. I am . . . pleased to meet you," I offer.

His gaze drops to my empty hand—my other is occupied with my cane—and then he snaps his fingers at someone over my shoulder.

"*Tul*, maid, if you please."

"Oh," I say quickly. "No, it's all right . . ."

But a servant slips into our midst before I can finish. I start to wave her away, when I recognize her—it's the head of staff from the Hall of the *Ashoki*. "Oh, hello, Fala."

Her gaze flicks up to my face and then back down, but she doesn't answer, merely offering her tray of *tul* to me.

"No, thank you—really," I begin, but Kobok lifts a glass from the tray and thrusts it toward me.

"I trust you are enjoying the hospitality of our court?" he asks pointedly. I swallow—the question feels almost like a threat. My fingers close unsteadily on the glass.

"Yes, sir, very much so."

He swats the air dismissively, and Fala obediently curtsies and melts away. I'd prefer to scurry after her, but I force myself to stand my ground, trying to shake off his scrutiny—I can't waste this opportunity. *Show our interest in his work.* "I understand that you have been on a tour of the glass facilities. How does the industry fare?"

"Halfway to cannibalizing itself," he says with disapproval.

"Everyone from the foremen to the quarriers shouting for union-izing and wage hikes, pretending those things can be conjured from thin air." He's still examining me, clearly not to be deterred. "You don't look Alcoran."

"No, sir. I'm of the Wood-folk in the Silverwood Mountains."

He leans back, his brow furrowing, and too late I realize what I called my folk. I keep forgetting that the Moquoians consider the traditional folk names outdated. A few of the other courtiers shift and mutter, and I flush. "Oh . . . forgive me. At home it's considered acceptable to refer to each country by their folk name."

The minister's nostrils flare. "So I expect we are referred to as the *Tree-folk*?"

I think of the mighty redwoods and lush maple forests and silently suggest it's an admirable association. *Ethnocentric bias.* "It is sometimes used, but . . ."

"Without a thought to oversimplification. There are trees in the Silverwood, are there not?"

"Yes, sir . . ."

"And hills in Lumen Lake, but they are called *Lake-folk*. Rivers in Winder, but they are called *Hill-folk*. Coastline in Cyprien, but they're called *River-folk*. Shall I continue?"

I swallow again. "I apologize, sir, I didn't mean to offend—"

"Do you see how the antiquated characterization of each country serves to diminish it?"

Great Light, he's making me feel like a backward rube. I try to straighten, my knuckles white on the glass in my hand. "Yes, of course you're correct. Forgive the slip of my tongue. It's my hope that with a strengthened partnership between

Moquoia and the East, this old-fashioned verbiage will fall out of favor."

It seems to satisfy him. He nods shortly and gives a little "hm." Several courtiers copy his movement. I allow myself the briefest of congratulations for dodging that particular strike. He takes a sip from his glass and studies the firefly pin on my lapel. "Will you pronounce your surname again, please?"

"Greenbrier," I say, trying to organize my thoughts in Moquoian. "But it's not exactly . . ."

"I don't recall that name in Silvern records."

"No," I say. "It's not a surname. We take . . . we have . . ." I can't remember the Moquoian word for *epithet*. "A name you choose for yourself. Not family names."

"A *si*," says one of the courtiers, using the name of the color titles Moquoian nobility take. It's not the word I would have chosen, but the others nod in sudden understanding.

"What color does it represent?" Kobok asks, his gaze flicking over my forest green tunic. "Is it a form of *Iksi*? I have been told you overwear that color."

It's hardly my fault that nearly all my tunics are the color of my parents' banner. The momentary relief at my tiny victory dissolves away. "Greenbrier . . . it does have *iksi* in its name, but it's actually a vine. A little thorny vine."

"What concepts does it represent?" asks the first courtier.

"It . . . doesn't, really, it's not the same—"

"Why did you choose it?" asks another.

"Because . . . I just . . . liked it," I lie—even if I wasn't floundering with the language, I can hardly air my quiet, childish secrets to this group of foreign politicians. I cast frantically for another topic, trying to remember what Eloise wanted me to achieve here. "Minister, Ambassador Alastaire and Princess Eloise were hoping we might coordinate our colors with you for tomorrow's *Bakkonso* Ball."

Kobok lifts an eyebrow, and I run back through my statement, hoping I got all my wording correct. Silence stretches out, first thoughtful before quickly becoming awkward. I shift on my blistered feet.

Finally he turns his attention back to the group of courtiers. "Ladies, gentlemen, if you don't mind, I would like a private word with our guest."

The cluster obediently breaks up. Some take up positions only a few feet away, probably hoping to eavesdrop.

Whether he's expecting this, or whether he's simply an expert at scare tactics, Kobok steps closer to me. I lean back, gripping my cane.

"I do not mean to be rude," I say. "I am still learning the language."

He doesn't respond to this. His ample mustache curls as his lips purse. "Ambassador Greenbrier, if you please, enlighten me. I heard of your proposed presence in our court at the beginning of the year, and since then I have wondered—what is the real reason you are here?"

I blink again. "I'm sorry?"

"It is all very benign on paper," he continues. "New economic opportunities and safer trade routes and such, but this is only with our neighbor Alcoro. You are not Alcoran. Your master is not Alcoran, and neither is the princess. In fact, if my facts are correct, Alcoro is the historic enemy to all three countries you represent. What has suddenly created a bond so strong that you can speak for their government?"

"Alcoro and the Silverwood have been allies for almost two decades," I say, taken aback. "As have the other Eastern countries. We represent the allied East."

"Mm," he says again, his eyes narrowing. "Are you quite sure there isn't a more intimate reason?"

I'm so mixed up that I wonder if I heard him correctly. I repeat his word back to him. "Intimate?"

"Yes, intimate."

"I'm not sure I understand."

"No, I don't think you do." He takes another step forward—a tiny one, but it makes me shift backward all the same. "Do you know when I took this office?"

"No," I say.

"Fifteen years ago," he says. "Do you know what happened in the sixth month I held the office? I received a letter. From Lumen Lake. For over a month it had traveled around the cape and up the coast—this was before the desert routes were even remotely passable. Queen Mona Alastaire risked a ship full of soldiers—Lumeni, Cypri, and Paroan—to bring me this letter."

Ah, I'm starting to understand, and I'm entirely at a loss for what to say back. Of all the topics I'd anticipated discussing today, Mona and Rou's long-lost daughter was hardly among them. I cast a panicked glance at the crowd—Eloise is clear on the other side of the patio, and Rou is engaged with Queen Isme.

"It was quite strongly worded, written once in both Common Eastern and a rustic attempt at Moquoian," the minister continues. "Suggesting that if I had any information on a recent shipload of captives bound for my glass forges, I should surrender everything I knew. Particularly information regarding a little girl, five years old, named Moira Alastaire."

He exaggerates the Lumeni pronunciation, putting a too-heavy twist on the *oi* in Moira's name. I look again toward Eloise. It's not hard to imagine how Queen Mona would have detailed her missing daughter in her letter, an unmistakable blend of the queen's fair complexion and freckles and Rou's warm brown skin and fine smoke-gray curls. Eloise laughs at something the chairwoman says, her nose and eyes crinkling. I think again of that portrait in Queen Mona's desk, two sets of sparkly brown eyes and cascades of tawny hair.

Her sister must have been so scared.

"In that same letter," Minister Kobok continues, and I wrench my focus back to him, "I received the distinct suggestion that the very foundation of the Moquoian workforce would soon be under scrutiny of the East, and that we should be prepared to acquiesce to a long list of foreign demands or risk the allied enmity of the Eastern World." He snorts derisively. "Enmity! From a collection of countries strung together in a haphazard alliance, whom we can barely make contact with twice a year! The sheer arrogance, the utter compunction of such a threat, to undermine our very economy and infrastructure. But I soon found that Queen Mona's threats were only that—threats, and empty ones. She could do nothing from a little dock in her faraway lake but shake her fist in Moquoia's direction—a grieved mother, an embarrassed monarch. I penned a brief response, which I am not sure ever reached her, and did not give a second thought to that letter. Until I heard that none other than her husband, younger daughter, and now, apparently, the fourth child of the Silverwood monarchy, were coming for a friendly visit."

I'm staggered. I bristle at the way he's talking about Queen

Mona, by all rights one of the most powerful and legendary monarchs in Eastern history, and that's even when standing alongside my own parents and Gemma Maczatl, the Last Queen of Alcoro. To write off Mona's correspondence—a well-placed one, if we're being honest, because where else do seabound captives go but around Cape Coraxia—to dismiss it as a meaningless product of grief and *political embarrassment* rankles me. It would rankle Mama even more—she poured her own blood and sweat into searching for Moira Alastaire, and I suspect her response to the minister would rely mainly on her closed fist.

But the ugly truth is that if we're going to get anywhere with Moquoian infrastructure, we need to be in this reprehensible man's good graces.

If such a thing is possible.

"We're not here on any personal errand of Queen Mona's," I say, with what I consider to be an admirable amount of diplomatic restraint. "The abduction of Moira Alastaire happened when I myself was a child, and it would be odd timing to suddenly bring it all back up now for no reason—at least, none that's apparent to me." I eye him, hoping I've at least irked him in as polite a way as possible. "As I said before, we represent the allied East and the University of Alcoro. Ambassador Rou was sent because he was one of the founders of the Eastern Alliance and has served as a liaison in all the courts of the East. Princess Eloise was sent because she is the next queen of Lumen Lake. I was sent based on my language study to open dialogue for a potential partnership. If such a thing is achieved, perhaps the next ambassadors will be more to your liking."

His mouth twists under his mustache. He straightens.

"I must decline your request to ally with my colors tomorrow evening," he says. "It would not sit well with many of my donors to see me mirroring *si* with our Eastern delegation, particularly not when there are so many questions about the murder of our previous *ashoki*. Oh yes," he says to my sudden look of consternation. "I know the rumors, and a fair amount besides. You do our court a disservice by carrying on as if everything has been done by the book. Should you be interested in my advice, here it is: you gain nothing from hounding the prince. Rather than treating your stay like a farcical diplomatic summit, consider it rather a show of Moquoian hospitality—one you've worn rather thin so far."

I'm gaping at him—I can't help it. I can't think of a single thing to say. Kobok doesn't wait for me to come to my senses. He gives a clipped bow and then turns back for the nearest group of courtiers, all standing in conspicuous silence just a few arm's lengths away.

My head reels with his tirade of accusations. A search for Moira Alastaire? The death of the previous *ashoki*? *Murder*? I look desperately for Eloise, but she's nowhere in sight. As I make a second sweep of the room, I spy Mistress Fala standing near a cluster of couches. Anxiously, I set my unwanted cup of *tul* down on a side table and make a beeline for her.

"Good afternoon, lord," she says, lowering her eyes. "How are your feet?"

Awful. "Fine, thank you. May I ask you an important question?"

Her gaze flickers to the tray. "I suppose it is not to ask for *tul*?"

"No, and I understand it may be delicate, but I desperately need an answer. Fala—how did the previous *ashoki* die?"

She stiffens. "That is . . . not strictly public knowledge, lord."

"So I'm aware. But I think it may be impacting our work here, and I expect you know the truth. You must hear all the rumors, all the secrets. Please, if I can't find out the answer, I worry we will only continue to make things worse and worse here, without knowing how or why." I gesture in the direction of Prince Iano, his cheerful lemon jacket contrasting with his wan face and shadowed eyes. "I worry we will only bring Iano more stress, more grief."

She takes a little sip of air, glancing toward the prince, and then she deliberately sets about pouring me a glass of *tul*.

I wave at her. "I don't need a glass . . ."

"Yes, lord, you do," she murmurs. "You are already attracting too much attention speaking with me—the ministers are watching you. It will look highly irregular. Understand that it is not my place to know what happened to the last *ashoki*."

I blink in confusion at her last statement, until I realize that she's pouring the glass of *tul* exceptionally slowly. Buying me the briefest moment of decorum. I nod vigorously and then, remembering Iano's threat of having me watched, turn it into a curt movement, one a nobleman might be expected to give to someone inferior.

"I won't tell a soul who told me," I say quietly.

She takes another breath, her eyes on her work, and in the time it takes her to top off the glass and set the pitcher down, she says all in a rush, "The previous *ashoki* was killed in an ambush by the Sunshield Bandit, as her coach was nearing Vittenta for the night at the start of *Iksi*."

I lean back from her in surprise. "The Sunshield Bandit? What on earth does that have to do with us?"

"Here is your *tul*, lord," she whispers. "Now please, go back among the court, before you cause a scene. I implore you not to talk similarly to any of the other staff. It will only damage your image."

Dumbly I take the cup. As soon as I have, she turns and hurries away, head down. I clutch the cup without moving, staring unseeing at the shimmery mosaic wall over the couches.

The Sunshield Bandit. My mind races back to the letter Colm wrote me, the tidbit he told me but not Rou or Eloise, about who robbed his stagecoach, and what he found out about her.

Lark.

Just in case.

But . . . I still don't understand why such a thing would solicit such hostility from Iano. The Sunshield Bandit operates in the Ferinno, it's true, but surely he can't think we're involved just by that alone? If she really did attack and murder the previous *ashoki*, it would be the first such attack I've heard of—I thought the only people she killed were slavers.

Still, Eloise needs to know, and she can decide if her father needs to know, too. I set the second cup of *tul* down, hoping it will be the last such offer. I'm about to turn back to the humming crowd—my debacle with Kobok now an afterthought—when a beam of sunlight manages to break through the rolling clouds outside. It's brief, but significant—the glass patio brightens, dazzling the wet glass. The mosaic tiles over the couches flare, throwing off little pearly glints. A murmur swells through the court at the sunburst. Many people press toward the windows, craning to see if there's any chance of *Kualni An-Orra*—a rainbow, the manifestation of the Light here in Moquoia, accompanied by the twelve-verse Prayer of the Colors. It's the rainy season, though, and the weather hasn't broken enough in four weeks to produce a rainbow. I start to turn toward the bank of windows, but a flash at the corner of my eye makes me stop.

As everyone presses toward the glass, I turn slowly back to the shining tile mosaic. The sun transforms what had been a pattern of tiles into a gleaming mass, a blinding mirror that stings my eyes. In another breath, the light is swallowed up again, and the room plunges back into ambient light. A few people murmur in disappointment. The mosaic resumes its pattern of geometric flowers, dull and dreary after the flash.

Hurriedly I search for Fala in the crowd, wanting to clarify something she said. But she's gone, invisible among the other black-clad servants.

I don't have any idea why it should matter, but it stands out, odd and irregular, as unexpected as the sunburst.

Fala said the *ashoki*'s coach was attacked as it was nearing Vittenta . . . *for the night.*

By a bandit who uses the sun as a weapon.

LARK

I pick through the scrub, leading Jema behind me. My body aches and groans from spending the night on the ground, bunched up tight to keep warm in the chilly darkness.

I'm famished—I haven't eaten since I left camp yesterday, and I'm still two hours away from Three Lines. I spied dust along the road this morning, coming from Snaketown, so I expect the sheriff is out trying to pick up my trail. I hope she doesn't have dogs, but just in case I've been turning up and down every draw and drainage I come across, trying to muddle our trail. I've swung so far south of the road I'm nearly to the tower mesas that rise like giants from the horizon. What should have been a three-hour ride from Snaketown has turned into a six-hour slog cross-country, but I'd rather the authorities think I'm fleeing south than along the river. Three Lines is well hidden, but the fewer folk poking around north of the road, the better.

Problem is, I'm well outside my usual stomping ground—if we're drawing lines in the sand, this is technically Dirtwater

Dob's territory. He's more of a poacher than a bandit, skirting around hunting restrictions for bison and pronghorn, which are less plentiful down here than up on the prairie, but we've crossed paths more than once. Back before I was able to send Bitty and Arana back to family in Callais, we had a full-out brawl with Dob's posse over access to the stage road. We drove him off, though Bitty came away with a broken hand, and since then Dob has mostly stayed to his side of the mesas. Still, I'm keeping a sharp eye out. I'd prefer to avoid any run-ins. I'm tired and beat-up, and I don't have Bitty's tree-size biceps or Arana's twin knives or Rose's crossbow to back me up.

Rat sauntered off a little while ago in the direction of a willow seep, probably sniffing out ground squirrels. Jema's hooves are making a fair amount of noise over the stony ground, and I'm distracted with wondering if I can risk turning north again—when I round a cluster of boulders to find I've walked right into an armed robbery in progress.

Sun be damned, it *is* Dirtwater Dob, as if conjured from my thoughts, though he seems to be down a couple of allies—there are only two beefy bandits backing him up, with a third rolling around on the ground with her hands to her bloody face. In their midst is a stout woman with a strip of blue fabric tied over one eye—it's the Moquoian woman from Patzo's general store, the pox-marked one arguing about the mail. She's facing the three bandits with a confident grip on a broadsword, but she's also favoring an ankle and backed into a tangle of juniper. A horse's panniers are scattered across the ground, parcels and parchment strewn on the rocks. The horse is nowhere in sight.

Everyone stops midmotion to stare at my sudden appearance, save the bandit on the ground, still clutching her face.

"The Sunshield Bandit," Dob says in surprise, his grungy eyebrows flying skyward.

The victim doesn't lose her head and uses my momentary distraction to plunge for Dob. He recovers a second too late, parrying slowly with his dinged-up mattock and earning a glancing blow to his forearm. The other two waffle between jumping in to assist and wondering what I'm planning.

Joke's on them—I have no plan. But I have to say, I don't particularly like the odds here. I could side with Dob in the hopes of splitting the victim's panniers, but it's more likely he'd remember the brawl over the stage road and turn on me as soon as he finishes his target. Besides, I'm not big on killing innocent travelers. I'll take all their stuff, sure, but I try not to take happenstance lives or strand anybody where they're going to die of thirst.

Yeah, yeah, the old man's stage. He was just outside Snaketown, though, and clearly he got back all right, didn't he?

My face on the wanted poster flares up again, and without waiting any longer I slide my longsword out from under my saddle. I could run, I guess, but if Dob kills this traveler, in the same terrain I fled after Snaketown, in all likelihood the crime will be pinned on me, and then they might strike out the *Alive* part on my bounty. I spur Jema forward.

"Hey, Dirtwater! Don't you have bison to poach somewhere?"

One of Dob's cronies has joined in the struggle with the traveler, but the third wheels back to me as I bear down on them. He's got a nasty-looking scythe in one hand, and he whirls it toward Jema's shoulder, but I sling my buckler forward. A splash of afternoon sun washes over his eyes, and he flicks his head. It's enough—I kick out with the toe of my boot and connect with his jaw. A tooth flies like a junebug. He spins a full circle and drops.

I make sure Jema steps on him as he screams and curses on the ground, and then I'm on the second bandit. He's got a length of chain—did these guys just raid a logging camp for their weapons? He's on my sword side, and I angle my blade, preparing to deflect a swing of the heavy metal links—but he whirls them instead at Jema's nose. She tosses her head and sidesteps, treading again on the scythe bandit but throwing me off-balance. I grab a tighter hold on my reins and arc my sword just in time to parry a jab from a hunting knife. He's quick, going for Jema's flank, and I put all my strength into an awkward strike with my hilt. It cracks against his skull, and he drops both chain and knife, clutching his forehead.

"Hold! Hold—Mosset, hold." Dirtwater Dob tosses up his hands, mattock hanging pick-side down from his wrist. His gaze flicks over his groaning companions and then up to me. "You're a ways off the road, Sunshine."

"And you're getting a little bold, Dirtwater." I adjust my buckler to make the most use of the glare. "Are the bison too smart for you? You've had to stoop to jumping single travelers?"

"At least I haven't blundered into tripling the price on my head." He palms the slice on his forearm. "Heard you held up one of the university deans and got your face on a bunch of posters along the road. Is that why you're sneaking around down here? Sheriff on your tail?"

I don't know what a dean is, but it's my luck that the old man was somebody important.

"There's been a price on my head for three years, and they haven't flushed me out yet," I say. On my right, the bandit called Mosset adjusts his grip on his chain, the links clinking. I lay the edge of my sword along his neck. He freezes, scowling. There's a welt on his forehead the size of an egg.

Dob huffs. "All a matter of time, Sunshine, and then you won't be lording over the road any longer. Come on, Mosset, Berta . . . Goon, quit rolling around under the horse."

"She knocked out one'a my teef!" whimpers Goon.

"You got a bunch left. Come on." Dob flicks his head at the one-eyed traveler. "Lucky day for you."

The traveler doesn't reply, just glowers at the posse as they collectively stagger to their feet and file away through the sage.

I grind my teeth, watching them go. I watch until I'm sure they're really retreating and not just bluffing, and then I turn back to the traveler. She's warily collecting the goods from her panniers, though one fist is still closed on her broadsword. She eyes me as I slide from Jema's saddle.

"What're you traveling around here for?" I ask.

She doesn't answer, reaching for a bag of cornmeal that's threatening to split along the seam.

"Want help?" I ask. "I wouldn't mind helping you pack up in exchange for a meal." *Plus I just saved your ass*, I decide not to add.

She grunts, though I can't be sure if it's in agreement or not. I kneel and reach for a bundle of blank parchment that's spilled across the ground, many of the sheets peppered with somebody's blood—probably Goon's. Before my fingers close, though, she whacks my hand with the flat of her blade.

I jerk my hand away. "Hey!"

"*Niq-otilai.*"

Moquoian—right. I'd forgotten. My Moquoian is rusty—I haven't had to use it since the mines.

"Again?" I ask, the foreign word awkward on my tongue. "Slow?"

"I said, *go away*," she repeats.

I scowl, but I'm not fluent enough to snap back or suggest she offer a thank-you instead. From a little ways off, I hear Rat's coyote yip-yip—perhaps at a wandering, riderless horse.

"You ride a horse, yes?" I ask flatly in my uneven Moquoian, eyeing a packet of thick jerky. "If I am go to get your horse, you can share a food?"

She huffs. "No. Go away."

"I can rob you." The threat sounds pitiful in my broken speech. She scoffs. I'd scoff, too.

"I fight better than that group of nobodies. Go away."

"Fine." I'm too tired and hungry for a devoted swordfight anyway. I put my hands on my knees, preparing to stand, when she moves suddenly—her hand lashes out to grab my sleeve. She pushes it back to reveal my longsword tattoo—and the old, scarred circular brand. Her face goes as dark as yesterday's thunderstorm.

She drops my sleeve like it's poison, steps back, and slings her sword toward my face. I'm still in a half crouch, and if she hadn't had the decency to give an angry yell, she probably would have landed her blade right between my eyes. But her roar startles me, and I haul my buckler impulsively to block my face, bracing against the impact.

"Hey!" I shout, scrambling to find my feet. "What's wrong with—"

She swings around again, and this time, I pull my sword out in time to lock her hilt in mine, hoping to wrench it out of her grasp. But just as I clamp my hand over her wrist, I'm hit with an intense, unmistakable smell, rippling off her clothes. The stink of guano.

Without warning, a memory floods my unguarded mind.

Clouds of little black bodies streaming out from cracks in the rocks, cheeping, swooping, their calls not quite drowning out gasps of pain, the ragged grind of a bow saw. The reek of ammonia mixed with the thick scent of blood and sweat and liquor.

I suck in a breath at the rush of vivid sights and sounds that awful smell has conjured. I drop her wrist and leap back, our swords disentangling with a metallic whine.

"Utzibor?" I say without thinking.

She grits her teeth and readies her sword again, but I don't wait to parry her strike. I wedge my foot in Jema's stirrup and slap her rump before I've thrown my other leg over. She starts forward, her hoofbeats clamoring with the string of Moquoian curses the traveler is shouting. I glance back over my shoulder— the woman is yelling with her fist in the air.

I don't even care why—perhaps she recognized my tattoos and realized who I am, but all I can focus on is the ugly memories dredged up by that smell. My stomach boils with a misplaced sense of dread. I whip back around and urge Jema faster. We break from the scrub and out into the sage flats.

Sure enough, Rat is hopping around the girth of a dun-colored mule, its reins dangling freely. For a brief second I consider scaring the mule farther away, or even taking it with me, to keep the woman off my tail, but I'm overridden by the desperate desire to get far away from that stench and the sick memories it's brought with it. I whistle to Rat and kick Jema into a canter, veering north for the distant road.

Utzibor. Nothing good happens at Utzibor, nothing, nothing, *nothing*.

I just want to be back home.

VERAN

I clatter down the hallway, unsteady but rushed—my shave and hairstyling took longer than I anticipated, and I'm running late. The *Bakkonso* Ball starts in just under fifteen minutes. I'm a little surprised Eloise didn't come find me—it probably means she's sitting expectantly in her parlor, ready to give me an earful.

I rap on her door and stand back. But there's no call from inside or quick rattle of the doorknob. I wait, shifting on my blisters.

I knock again. "Eloise?"

There's a tread of approaching feet, and the door swings open to reveal Rou, holding a mug. His collar's undone, and his face is stoic.

"Oh good, you're here," he says. He hands me the mug. "Hang on to that while I hunt down a fresh pot."

"What?" I ask as he sweeps past me. "Is Eloise ready? We should be heading to the ballroom."

"She can't go," he says. "She's not feeling well."

His grave tone makes my stomach plunge, but then Eloise calls from the other room. "I'm *fine*, Papa, don't get everyone worked up! Veran, come here!"

Rou hurries away down the hall, and I turn for the bedroom. Eloise is propped up in bed, her hair wrapped in her silk bonnet. A small caravan of mugs waits on the bedside table.

"What's wrong?" I ask, adding the mug Rou gave me to its fellows.

"It's nothing. Just sniffles from all the damp." She waves at the window, streaked as always with rain. "And you know how Papa is. He thinks every hiccup is consumption. I'm fine."

My thoughts fly to the reports of rainshed fever, despite her windows being sealed shut. "Are you sure?"

She nods and sips from one of her mugs. "I'm more irritated than anything—I wanted to go to the ball."

"I'll be sure to tell you all about it."

She shakes her head. "I don't really care about the dancing. But I wanted to start trying to clear things up with Iano, now that we know some of what's bothering him."

I'd filled Eloise in on the attack on the previous *ashoki* and Iano's apparent persisting shock. I'd left out my confusion about the involvement of the Sunshield Bandit, as well as the extent of my failure with Minister Kobok, only telling her that he'd declined to share his colors with us and leaving out the part where he suspected we were only here to frame him for having a hand in her sister's abduction fifteen years ago.

Eloise sips from her mug. "It's no matter, I suppose—Papa's not going to let me out of bed as long as I'm sniffly. You'll just have to do it instead. Try to get him alone, if it's possible. Tell him that we're sorry for his grief, but that we had nothing to do with the attack—and then make it clear that if we can go through with some of our original agreements, we can bring the desert bandits to justice. Emphasize that especially—building the Ferinno Road could stamp out not just slavery, but banditry, too."

"I'll do my best," I say hesitantly. Already my stomach is turning anxiously at the thought of attempting such a verbal dance on my own, particularly after my debacle with Kobok.

"I know you will. Come right up after the dance—I want all the details." She coughs, delicately at first, but then it deepens. She turns her head away—I grab for her teetering mug as her chest spasms.

"Ugh." She takes a deep breath, pressing her palm to her chest.

"Are you sure you're going to be all right?" I ask.

"I'll be fine with some rest. Too much running around."

"Have you considered . . ." I begin hesitantly. "It's just . . . that fever, you know."

"I'm not feverish," she says with finality. "And I've kept my windows shut, just like they told us to. I'm just run-down. I'll be fine in a few days."

She takes her mug back and savors a sip. "Why don't you go on—you're going to be late enough as it is. Papa should be along shortly if I can convince him I'll survive the hour."

The door to the hall swings open, followed by Rou's voice. "Eloise?"

"Still alive, Papa," She rolls her eyes at me, but I can't help noticing the rattle in her breath. I bite back a comment, though, and get up as Rou comes in with a fresh pitcher of steaming water to add to the flock of undrunk tisanes on the bedside table. I slip out as quietly as my shoes allow as he swoops down to check her forehead and throat and pupils, plying her with endless questions.

I hurry through the atrium and down the staircase, clutching the rail all the while, my thoughts back up with Eloise. I hope she's right, that whatever she has is just a passing illness. Surely if she had been exposed to the mosquito-borne fever, others in the palace would have been, too, and then the place would be in a panic.

Right?

I'm so distracted I barely notice where I'm going, and as I pass through the doors to the social wing, I'm startled to be plunged into darkness. I pause as my eyes adjust—it's dim, but not completely dark, and it's certainly not silent. An accented beat punctuates a rousing bass line of strings, threaded with the murmur of moving crowds. Lining the hall are burly lanterns, their flames burning behind thick indigo shades. A flash on my chest catches my eye, and I look down—the pearl in my firefly pin's abdomen is gleaming bright white under the strange lamps.

A figure approaches me, and I jump—the servants are even more invisible in the dim light. To my surprise, it's Fala.

"Oh, hello," I say.

She bows. "Good evening, lord. May I take your cane?"

I hand it over, hoping I can keep my balance without it.

"Where is the princess?" she asks.

"Not feeling well," I say. "She sends her regrets."

"What a shame." She hands me a little drawstring bag, bulging but weightless. "Your powdered *adoh*," she explains. "Watch the caller for cues to throw it—and try to avoid getting it in your eyes."

"Thank you," I say, relieved. "Is that what I do with it? Throw it?"

"Only on the cues. You'll hear them. I'm sure you will do marvelously, lord."

I'm decidedly less sure, but another group is entering behind me, and Fala turns to approach them with her basket of *adoh*. I grip the drawstring bag and hurry toward the ballroom.

It's a sight unlike anything I've seen before. In a perverted way, the closest comparison I can make is my folk's firefly revelry. But unlike the fireflies, there's nothing gentle or quiet about the scene in the ballroom. The darkness is punctuated by streaks of bold blue-white, glittering underfoot, peppering clothes, dusting hair. Folk grin, their eyes and teeth dark against their luminescent skin. I spot Iano circling with several others near the center of the room. A caller up near the orchestra lets out a shout, releasing a pinch of dust from her bag. In response, with a great deal of whooping, a hundred other hands arc through the air, streaming with glowing *adoh*. It settles in a haze over the dancers.

"Blessed Light," I mutter aloud, utterly at a loss. How I'll describe this to Eloise, to *Mama*, earth and sky . . .

I inch along the periphery of the room until I spy what must be the royal balcony. The queen is there with her entourage. I spy Kimela, the newly appointed *ashoki*, as well as Minister Kobok. I swallow, and my gaze goes to Iano's embroidered capelet draped over an empty chair near the rail—perhaps he'll return when he's not dancing. I'll wait there, station myself by his seat so as not to waste any time.

That's what I tell myself, anyway. I'm being proactive, not spooked by the alien frenzy of *Bakkonso*.

I edge through the crowd, my ears full of the driving drumbeat and hollers from the dance floor any time the powder is tossed into the air. I climb the steps to the balcony, relieved to find the noise and fever diminished.

Two guards block the entrance at the top.

"Good evening," I say. "I'm, um, trying to get in, please."

They stare, silent.

"I'm Veran," I say. "Greenbrier. I'm with the ambassador? He's—not here yet."

Nothing.

Heat rises under my collar—what if I can't get into the balcony at all? What if I waste all my time waffling in front of the guards? What would Eloise do if she were here? What would she say to prove her credentials?

"Ah, Prince Veran Greenbrier."

I look past the guards to see Queen Isme standing past them with a glass of *tul* in her fingers. She brushes the shoulders of her guards with a feathered fan.

"It's all right, let him through."

Wordlessly they part, and I sidle between them. Trying not to pant or shake, I bow to the queen.

"Thank you, Lady Queen."

"Of course. It wouldn't do to miss your first *Bakkonso* because of a few stubborn guards." She smiles warmly, gesturing me to the cluster of seats she had been occupying. "Where are the ambassador and the princess?"

"I regret Princess Eloise is unable to attend tonight," I say, trying to salvage my manners. "She is feeling unwell at the moment. Ambassador Rou should arrive shortly."

"I am sorry to hear that. I hope she recovers soon." She speaks slowly and clearly to me, probably used to Rou's occasionally mangled Moquoian. Smiling, she gestures to an empty seat on her opposite side beside Kimela. Minister Kobok is one chair over, regarding me over a cup of *tul* clutched loosely in his hand. Turns out he's wearing pale greens today—almost exactly the same shade as Kimela, which makes sense, given her color title *Chartreuse*. If I'd thought harder about it, I might have guessed, but I was too preoccupied with the news about the Sunshield Bandit. He eyes my eggplant-colored jacket coolly—the color Eloise hoped would match the chairwoman, though I haven't seen for myself.

Queen Isme, also in light greens, waves to a chair. "Please sit. I believe you have yet to formally meet our new *ashoki*."

Growing ever more anxious—a cozy chat with the queen and her most influential associates was not at all what I'd anticipated—I sink into the proffered chair, remembering to bow halfway through to Kimela, producing an awkward tilted crouch. "I'm honored to meet one of the fabled *ashoki* at last."

Her smile grows. I wonder if she's making mental notes for her debut performance in a few weeks. "The pleasure is mine, Prince Veran of the Silverwood Mountains. I regret that I have not seen your home country myself—I have only made it as far west as the border of the Ferinno, and I found it much too dry and brown for my liking. But your country is more akin to our own, is that right?"

"Yes." I glance at the dance floor—another cloud of glittering *adoh* has gone up. Partners spin in the falling cloud, catching the powder on skirts and jacket tails with the loudest cheer yet. "We have chestnuts the span of a six-horse coach, and poplars as tall as the palace, but nothing comes close to your southern redwoods."

"I hear your silver mines have great potential," Kobok says.

It seems an odd thing to say—our silver mines have been in production for centuries. I think I'd move that past *potential*. Before I can think up the right answer, Kobok clarifies his point for me.

"My sources tell me there's a fleet of restrictions in place designed to limit production, instated by an old political faction. Why artificially force a low yield? Does it cause civil unrest?"

By the Light, he means Mama and the Woodwalkers. *Artificially force a low yield . . .* responses race through my head, each one of them in rapid Eastern. *Unrestricted mining destroys the slopes and waterways, you twit, it kills hamlets and resources, it affects timber and roads . . . and how could our mines have lasted this long if we were in a race to deplete them? How exactly do you run your mining operations, Kobok?*

"Ethnocentric! Bias!" Colm yells in my head, though I can't be sure if he's yelling at me or Kobok.

"Oh, Minister, you bore our guest with industry," the queen says merrily while I gape like a beached fish. She waves an airy hand at the surging dance floor, her wrist jeweled with white beads that glow like teeth under the indigo lamps. "Tell us about your dancing, Prince Veran—how does ours compare?"

"Marvelous," I manage automatically, unable to think of a real response. Earth and sky, I wish Eloise was here. Down below, with a final tremendous chord, the dance finishes. A haze of powder settles over the crowd as they applaud the musicians, and then there's a milling of bodies as the dancers leave the floor. I spy Iano weaving toward the staircase to the balcony.

"And the rain?" Kimela asks with a touch of amusement, waving to the distant glass overhead, black as night. "Do you have our rain?"

I try to pull myself together. "We certainly have a lot—but not as much as you. And no domes of glass, either—we instead have the fortitude to bear the elements."

Her smile goes from amused to stoic, and oh damn, I realize I've gotten my translation muddled. I meant to imply that her folk had the technological advantage over mine, but somehow it morphed into a jab. My cheeks go hot.

"I . . . er, that's not what I . . ."

The queen makes a flat little hum and sips her *tul*. "Such an amusing group, our Eastern ambassadors. So witty."

"Very witty," echoes Kimela, scrutinizing me. Kobok doesn't say anything. The *ashoki*'s lips are pressed permanently into that inscrutable smile, and too late I recall that our delegation might be mistakenly tangled up in the death of her predecessor. And I've just made a joke at her country's expense.

The dancers are reassembling into two wide circles, fluid with the ripple of skirts. It looks like a ladies' dance—all the men are lining the walls, taking drinks from near-invisible servants. Where is Iano? I glance back toward the guards, trying not to appear as if I'm planning an escape. The *ashoki* leans forward toward me, her silk rustling. A smudge of *adoh* gleams on her cheek. "Be careful how much you compare the customs of your culture to ours. It doesn't do to compare the virtues of a tree to a seed."

"Yes—no, I . . ." Suddenly I'm flushed with that familiar

stuffy heat. An immediate sweat breaks out around my collar and under my arms. The slips and glares of blue white stand out bold as midday sun, fuzzing my vision. The panic of that old feeling momentarily untethers me completely, and I lurch to my feet, shoving my chair back a few inches. The queen and the others all give little starts of surprise.

At that moment, Iano materializes on the balcony, and my knees nearly give out in relief. He doesn't seem to see me, though—distracted and glowing faintly, he drifts to his empty chair. A small battalion of servants approach him as he sits—a server with a plate of sweets, another with a chilled glass of *tul*, one with a towel, one with a letter on a silver tray.

The music begins, and a great hurrah goes up with arcs of *adoh*. I jerk my gaze back to Kimela, who's still looking at me despite the spectacle below.

I bow, making the burning blood slosh around my head. "Forgive me—I would like to talk to Prince Iano about the dancing. I'm very pleased to make your acquaintance, *Ashoki* Kimela. I look forward to your first performance."

"Yes, be sure you're there," she says.

I don't know what to say to that, and my brain is fizzling anyway, so I simply turn and hurry for the other side of the balcony.

To my surprise, Iano has risen from his seat just seconds after sitting down. He's rigid, gripping the rail of the balcony with one hand and staring at the commotion below. The air is bright with powder, lighting the ladies' hair and bare arms.

I try surreptitiously to loosen my hot collar as I sidle alongside Iano. His valets have dressed him for the occasion down to the smallest details—his normally gold hairpin has been swapped out for one of bone and pearl, to shine in the indigo lamps, and twin studs gleam similarly in his earlobes. His jacket is dark, the better to show off the intricate white embroidery. If it weren't for the powder glowing faintly on his skin, he could pass for a miniature galaxy.

He doesn't look at me. His normally distant eyes are wide and bright, his gaze fixed on some unmoving point in the whirling circles of dancers.

"Good evening," I croak. "What, um, what an exciting event this is."

He doesn't answer, only jams his fist in his jacket pocket. Across the hall, the caller raises her voice, and with a twirl of skirts, the circles change direction. Laughs and cheers ring out. Iano remains silent, still fixed on the floor below.

I cough, only partially fake. Earth and sky, I need a glass of water. "Princess Eloise gives her regrets—she's not feeling well and is unable to attend today."

No response. Light be damned, does *anything* make an impact with him?

I press on regardless. "I do have something I'd hoped to speak with you about. Princess Eloise and Ambassador Rou are growing concerned at our lack of progress. They had hoped by now we may have at least sketched out the terms of a partnership, if not started planning the funding of the Ferinno Road. They're concerned we're running out of time before we return to the Alcoran summit in *Tukurmsi*."

There's a change in the music, the tempo quickening. The ladies change direction again in a cloud of glitter. My flush now washes from my collar down through the rest of my body, my fingers and toes warm and buzzing. I swallow and look hurriedly back to Iano. He hasn't moved, hasn't spoken, and suddenly I'm angry as well as panicked.

"Iano, listen—we've heard about what happened to the former *ashoki*," I say. His posture goes, if possible, more rigid than before. "And I understand it's a significant transition for the court, and that the decision has been difficult. Eloise and I both wish to communicate our condolences. But if you suspect that we had some knowledge of the attack beforehand, or were somehow involved, we weren't. We had no knowledge of it until this week. So I hope . . . I hope that is not what is stalling our discussions." I continue despite his persisting silence. "Because the fact remains that your country and ours spent a great deal of time and money to organize this visit. We traveled for weeks to get here. We prepared for years. Perhaps our plans were ambitious, but when you and Eloise and I corresponded, you made it sound like Moquoia was ready, that with your throning we would begin a new alliance—"

He turns to me so suddenly I'm thrown off-balance. I grab the rail to keep from stumbling. His glassy, inscrutable face has suddenly become a torment of creases and furrows.

"You don't know *anything*," he snarls.

And then he bursts into tears.

With a whirl of glowing silk, he turns and bolts across the balcony, his hands clapped over his face. He rushes past his mother and courtiers without slowing a single step and plows through the two guards at the head of the stairs. Every single head turns to follow his flight.

And then they pivot toward me.

The ambient chatter goes deadly silent, leaving only the pulsing music and cheers below. Where there was a hot flush before, now there's only frozen shock. I clutch the rail, staring at the empty doorway as thirty-some-odd of the most influential people in this whole strange, terrifying country lock onto me like sights on a crossbow. Minister Kobok gives a quizzical glare. Next to the queen, Kimela tilts her head, as if observing an unrecognizable animal.

I swallow, and with a huge amount of effort, I put my head down and shuffle across the balcony toward the guarded stairs. I place one foot in front of the other, still gripping the bag of *adoh*.

I stumble past the guards and down the darkened stairs. At the bottom, I almost run into Rou, his pale silk ascot glowing in the weird light. He's looking in the direction Iano must have fled, and he turns just as I reach him.

"Veran—was that the prince? What's going on?"

"I need—I need to get out . . ." I push past him, jostling my bag of *adoh* and sending a luminous cloud into the air. Coughing on the powder, I skirt the edge of the ballroom, squinting against the hazy glare dusting every surface. Dropping my bag in a potted plant, I push into the outer hall, the whirling music chasing me out. I pick up speed until I'm practically running, my soles clopping dangerously against the floor. I worry that Fala will stop me, fretting kindly, but she's not there anymore, and I race out of the hall without stopping to retrieve my cane. *Adoh* dusts off me like ash, rendered into unremarkable white powder out of the light of the blue lamps.

I turn corners, not caring or paying attention to where I'm going, until I'm confronted with a ubiquitous glass wall, its sides smeared with rain. I don't slow down; in fact, I speed up until I practically collide with it. I press my hands and face against the glass, my breath fogging the surface.

Trapped, closed in, boxed up in a dome of pretend air. I gasp against the glass. Is the rain even real? Are there real, moving trees out there, waving in a wind? I can't breathe, can't see straight. I stagger along the wall, one hand on the cold panes, scrabbling at every seam and bracing. I come to a garden bed at the edge of the path and clamber through it, stomping through trimmed moss and everlasting blooms, my heels sinking into the dirt. I push aside the pruned fronds of a date palm and am confronted by a small door, a service entrance for gardeners, so they might do their secret cultivating out of sight of the rest of the palace, lofting the grand illusion that these plants trim and water themselves, that the dead blooms vanish in the night, that worms and bugs simply don't exist. I throw myself at the door; it gives easily to my dramatic heave, and I pass through two panels of double-thick glass to stagger drunkenly into the shocking rain.

It is, indeed, real, pouring from the sky in sheets, spattering against the cold gray paving stones. I'm instantly soaked, my hair falling from its curls to plaster against my forehead. My jacket gains ten pounds in water, and my shoes flood, making the hobnails slick as ice. With a fierce vehemence, I kick them off, setting my bruised feet on the cold stone in shocking relief.

This courtyard is little more than a platform, surrounded by a low wall. The stinging rain feels delicious against my sensation-starved skin, but I want more. I want wind and soil. To the left is a ladder, extending both up and down—the scaffolds I'd seen the glass cleaner climbing yesterday. Attempting a ladder in my current state is a terrible idea, particularly a narrow metal one clinging vertically to the side of a glass building, at an unknown height, in the rain.

I am *just* in the mood.

Leaving my shoes, I swing onto the rungs, the metal bit-ing my fingers. They're cut with hatching to provide purchase when wet, and, trusting in that alone, I begin to clamber down them. It was a good idea to take off my shoes—my knees are wobbly, and my panic hasn't fully subsided. Chances are good I'd have slipped straight off if I was still wearing those wooden soles.

Fortunately, the ballrooms are on the lower floors of the palace. I reach another platform, and then the greenish glass walls disappear, replaced by the palace's immense stone founda-tion, buttressed by dark soil. I hit the landing at the bottom and immediately step off the pavers into the rich, wet earth.

My breath escapes my chest like a plunging bellows, and I curl my numb toes into the dirt. The ground is covered with thick ferns, except in the two feet or so along the palace founda-tion, providing a well-maintained service path. I give a passing thought to mosquitoes, but the next moment I realize they won't fly in the pouring rain—they'll stay under the thick tree canopy and the overhangs of the palace windows. Keeping one hand on the stones, I follow the service path, heading around the curve of the wall until I reach a place where the ground slopes away, affording a rain-muddled view of the forests beyond.

I succumb to the weakness in my knees and drop to the ground, tucking my feet under me. I've ruined this outfit, but at the moment, I can't make myself worry about it. I set my head on my knees, drawing in great gulps of chilly, living air, the wind shivering over my wet skin.

By the Light, what a mess I am. What a joke—a throwaway prince stuffed into foreign clothes, playacting at diplomacy. I should never have agreed to a political discussion without Eloise. I'm not even sure I should be here at all. Surely someone else has the same grasp on Moquoian that I have. Surely Prince Iano's handle on Common Eastern could have sufficed otherwise.

Lightning flashes, and I curl my arms over my head, blocking out the jarring light. A juvenile wave of homesickness compounds my lightheadedness. *I wish you were here, Mama. Papa. Viyamae.* Mama would make no pretense at tiptoeing around the etiquette and polite society. She'd stand in the middle of the crowd in her tunic and Woodwalker boots and cut straight to the chase—*What exactly is going on here?* Papa would have the patience of the mountains themselves, and my oldest sister, Viyamae, would know precisely the right words to gain results. Earth and sky, even my other siblings would produce better results than me. Vyncet would puzzle things out in his methodical way, Susimae would charm everyone with her sweetness, Idamae would just fight anyone who looked at her crossways. Any one of them could do a better job than me.

I shouldn't have come.

I wiggle my feet deeper into the rich muddy soil, staining the embroidered hems of my trousers, taking morose pleasure in mirroring my own wallow in self-pity. The air is heavy with the smell of rot and ripe earth, but after weeks in the sanitized forests of the palace, I inhale it like a tonic. The ache for the firefly slopes of Lampyrinae lodges deep in my gut.

Slowly, the panic and dizziness brought on by the harsh light in the ballroom lessens, leaving my head aching. I massage my temples—I'm going to have a lot to atone for when I go back inside. I let my hands fall to the ground and then pause when I feel something besides mud. I look down.

Under my fingers, curled on its side, is a small, bright yellow bird—a goldfinch. The black and white bars on its wing are so crisp I'm surprised I didn't see it when I threw myself into this spot. I pull my fingers away. Its head is bent at an odd angle, its legs curled like twigs in a frost. Dead.

My gaze is inexplicably drawn past it, along the palace foundation, to another tiny mass on the ground. This one is easy to miss—a dun-colored sparrow—but it, too, is on its side, its head twisted backward.

Setting my palms against the soaring stone foundation, I get stiffly to my feet. The mud squishes through my toes as I pick my way along the curved wall. Beyond the sparrow is another, and then a bluebird, and then several warblers nearly right on top of each other. When I get to another goldfinch, I stop, staring at its bent head. Goldfinch is a popular epithet in the Silverwood, it's bright *per-chick-o-ree* the song of summer.

I look down the row of dead songbirds I just walked past, and then farther down the curve of the foundation, where I can see more—a flash of red here, a huddle of brown there. Each of them curled in the mud, their heads bent on broken necks.

I look up.

The rain stings my face as I stare at the massive expanse of glass soaring into the sky, the greatest feat of modern engineering, the pinnacle of progress.

The birds *hit the glass.*

My embarrassment in the ballroom is overwhelmed suddenly by the sinister reality of this palace, this marvel of shine and gloss and see-through walls. Why had the thought of birds striking the glass never occurred to me? At home we string mirrored pendants from the main windows, and during migration season any windows higher than the tree line have to be slatted. But this place, this city of glass . . . by the Light, how many birds must die in a day? A hundred? A thousand?

A flare of anger bursts to life inside me, my fists balling at my sides. I'm nearly ready to turn and race up the ladders and staircases to Eloise's room, full of fury, but in the next moment, I wilt again. Eloise can't be bothered by this, and neither can Rou. While they'd surely care about the deaths of scores of birds a day, they simply can't afford to waste effort on it— particularly not now when all our attempts seem to be taking us backward.

I should have told Eloise the whole truth about my failure with Kobok—between that disaster and today's, there's no chance she'll send me off on my own again. Hopefully she'll be well enough in another day or so to salvage some of the wreckage I've caused. I'll go up to her room now and confess. It's going to hurt, detailing my dismal attempts at diplomacy to her, but at least she'll be able to make informed decisions from here on out. Birds or no birds.

A gust of wind picks up, sluicing along the palace wall. I shiver violently, my earlier cloak of frustration and self-pity gone. Now I'm just cold and wet, my feet numb and my head muddled. Dejected, I trudge back along the line of dead songbirds to the service ladder. In a fog, I clamber back up and pass back into the palace, leaving a small stream of water over the tiled floors and carpeted staircases.

Bakkonso isn't over yet, so the halls are quiet, save for a few soft footsteps here and there as servants slip into service doors or alcoves as I pass by. It makes me uneasy, this rigid protocol between the court and the staff, but I've already made enough blunders. I put my soaking head down and don't try to make any eye contact.

The climb up to the guest wing leaves me winded, and the atrium flickers with the continued lightning outside. With one hand on my forehead, I reach Eloise's door and knock. There's no answer, but I expect it's because she's still in bed. I crack the door open.

"Eloise?" I call.

The parlor is dim and silent. She must have fallen asleep. I'll talk to her tomorrow, then.

There's a whine by my ear—I jump as a mosquito sails out of the darkness, on its way into the hall. I smush it against the door frame, crushing it. I wipe my hand on my soaked jacket and then ease the door shut. Turning, I tread toward my room, congratulating myself for keeping my shoes quiet.

No, I'm an idiot. I left my shoes outside the vexing service door. I've been so quiet because I'm barefoot. Lightning splashes against the hallway windows. I clamp my hand over my eyes, leaving just a sliver to see through, as much a motion of dismay as discomfort.

Feeling exceptionally stupid, as well as tired, sore, and cold, I reach my door and turn the knob, desperate for the oblivion of sleep.

TAMSIN

I found a thumbtack!

It's actually always been with me. I've just been too dense to appreciate it for what it was. Believe it or not, it was driven through the metal band of my waste bucket. There are four of them, two on each band, to hold them in place. One was loose. After a bit of finagling and a broken fingernail, I worked it out of the wood (my bucket was empty at this point). Now I hold it in my hand, a prize, barely the length of my thumbnail.

Hello, little friend!

Poia came back a while ago, and she was extra surly, barking at Beskin about the smoke in the rafters and the scorpion in the rice jar and the pointless reorganization of the coffee cupboard. From the snippets I could hear, I gather she had some kind of run-in with bandits on the trip, though she clearly came out on top—just after she returned, she had unlocked my door and kicked it open, brandishing an inkwell and sheet of parchment.

"Time for you to sign your name," she'd said.

"Is this *blood* on these sheets?" came Beskin's voice from around the corner.

"Not my blood," Poia shot back, shoving the materials into my hands. "Anyway, it may work in our favor—who's to say it's not hers?"

As I juggled the writing materials she had thrust at me, my gaze had fallen to her feet, planted impatiently before me. One of her trouser legs was rolled up to show a dusty bandage wrapped around her ankle. But it wasn't the injury that had drawn my attention—it was the edge of a tattoo peeking above the cloth. Two small curved lines, arcing toward each other like parentheses.

My eyes narrowed.

She'd snapped impatiently. "Come on, your name, and make it legible this time."

I did what she demanded, puckering my lips as I focused on forming the letters. Afterward she whisked the parchment away, grumbling about having to head right back out into the cursed wilderness to deliver the thing on schedule. Her slam of the door toppled my empty bucket, which led me to set it upright and discover the loose edge of the thumbtack poking out of the metal band.

Sitting in my palm, it feels like a weapon.

I think back to the tattoo peeking above the bandage on Poia's ankle. It's a mark I haven't seen since arriving at court—not something a high-ranking noble would flaunt to their colleagues. But I'm not surprised to find it on Poia's skin, and I wouldn't be surprised to find that some of the people on my list of enemies may bear the same ink. I close my fingers on the thumbtack.

What to do with this new information? I wonder.

What to do with my friend, as well?

The bats are flying outside, making the air thick with their chatter and distinct odor. They billow against the deep turquoise sky, a true *mokonnsi*. Between this and my new prize, my spirits are lighter than they've been in weeks. The pain in my body is distant and familiar. Best of all, I have the capability to do something.

To leave a trace.

Carefully, I pinch the thumbtack and press it into the adobe wall. But as I attempt to drag it in a line, the adobe only crumbles. Hm. No good.

I scoot to the cell door. It's made of wood. I press the point into the grain and drag it. It makes a minuscule scratch. Carefully, I smile. It hurts less now.

The bats wheel outside. I drag the point over the line again.

LARK

Thwack.

The blunt ax head buries in the thick round of pine. I jerk it out and swing it high again, the muscles bunching in my back. Sweat pours between my shoulder blades, and I can feel the sun crisping my skin bared in the absence of my shirt and vest. But I don't care. I can't split wood in my vest, and to be honest I can't afford the possibility of busting the seams in my shirt sleeves—that's what happened to my only spare—so I split wood in my breast band, and I brown darker than the wet riverbank in the meantime.

I bring the ax down again. Despite tireless sharpening, the head has almost entirely lost its edge. It bites into the wood only a fraction of an inch. I work it back out, feeling the handle wiggle loosely in the metal fitting. It doesn't help that the wood slice I'm working on is two feet around. Our firewood is dwindling in camp, and we're down to these stupidly thick lengths of pine. Crappy wood, and impossible to split. I'd use a wedge and a sledgehammer, but surprise—we don't have any.

I hear Rose's step. Rat lifts his head and thumps his brushy tail.

"You're muttering to yourself," she says.

"I am not." I wiggle the head out of the wood again—damn, this handle is getting loose.

"Something about a sledgehammer."

"Oh. That was out loud?"

She bends her knee—she's not wearing her false leg today, relying on a crutch to hop around. Her trouser leg is tied below her stump. She lowers herself to the ground near the last few lengths of pine and takes out her pocketknife. She picks up a splinter of wood and starts shaving bits off to wrap into kindling bundles.

We're quiet for a moment, the silence broken only by the dull thud of the ax and the scratching of her knife. It was a blow to the others in camp when I returned two days ago with the news from Snaketown. I kept quiet about the scuffle with Dirtwater Dob and that gut-awful smell of guano coming off the traveler. I gave the blister cream to Rose and the tonic to Whit and Andras, but dinner that night was corn cakes hard with grit, and broth boiled from the last of a grouse carcass Sedge had trapped. Since then I sent Saiph and Pickle to the river to gather more cattail pollen and roots, and we've doubled down on laying game traps. We've been lucky—one of Sedge's snares caught a jackrabbit, and I got a fat gopher in one of my pits. We set to smoking the meat yesterday—but that burned through the last of our wood. Which is why I'm here, fighting with a massive block of pine.

"We need to take the horses down to the river and drag up one of those cottonwood falls," Rose says, tying kindling into a bundle. "Then we can split it here in camp."

"I know, but there hasn't been time. I need Saiph and Pickle for it, and they're watching the road today."

"Sedge could probably help."

"I guess." Sedge is big and muscular, but his longest stint in captivity was splitting wood for the glass forges in Moquoia, and he killed his back as a result. He can't lift an ax above his head. But he could probably help hitch up a fallen tree.

Silence falls between us again. My breast band is drenched in sweat; I pause to wipe my face with my bandanna, avoiding her gaze. I've been avoiding it since I came back, trying not to swirl up that sickly dread from a few days ago.

"Are we going to talk about what to do about Snaketown?" Rose asks.

I tie my bandanna back around my forehead and lift the ax again. "What's there to talk about? I can't go back. We'll have to go to Pasul."

"Pasul's a long way."

"A day's ride isn't too bad." I try to keep the unease out of my voice at the thought of leaving the others in camp for three, maybe four days.

"You don't look Moquoian."

"Well, I don't look Alcoran, either."

"You can pass for it, though—a Cypri-Alcoran mix. And folks were used to seeing you in Snaketown. But you'll stand out a lot more in Moquoia."

"Well—so I'll stand out. I'll take Saiph with me. He can do most of the running around. We don't really have another choice."

"*I* could go to Snaketown," she says.

I swing the ax up again. "Nope."

"Why not?"

The ax falls. "You think *I* stick out, Rose? How many one-legged Cypri girls go riding into Snaketown?"

"Oh, I'm a girl now? I thought we agreed I'm at least two years older than you. If I'm a girl, you're a tot, and a whiny one at that." She bends her right leg and rests her arm on her knee. "You're not the sole protector of Three Lines, Lark. You're not our canyon queen."

"Well, someone has to be."

"No, someone doesn't. You're just one of us. I appreciate you taking charge, I do, and the little ones look up to you. But you can't pull all the weight by yourself. You have to let some of us do it, too."

I lean on the ax for a moment, looking at her. "Look, I know you think otherwise, but I'm not just being stubborn. What's it going to look like if I get chased out of Snaketown, and then a few days later a raggedy stranger comes riding in to get the same supplies? Patzo's not an idiot. He'll know you're coming in my place. Then they'll have a poster up with *your* face on it, if they don't just toss you in jail right away."

"It's a chance we may have to take, Lark."

"*No*, it's not. And I won't send Saiph or Pickle in for the same reason. Lila can't defend herself. Sedge can't go in because of the slave ring around his neck. Snaketown is out for us, Rose. It's Pasul, or nothing—and that's assuming they don't have bounty sheets posted there, too."

"Then I'll go to Pasul."

"What is wrong with you? No, you won't!"

"What's wrong with *you*?" she shoots back. "You act like I

haven't helped you turn over a dozen stages and twice as many wagons. Is this some kind of fake survivor's guilt? Are you still carrying around my calf like it's a penance?"

My next swing has a flush of anger behind it—the head bites deep into the wood. I go to wrench it free—and the handle pops clean out, leaving the head stuck fast. I swear in frustration and hurl the ax handle. It spins end over end and disappears into a thicket of scrub oak.

Rose snorts derisively. "I was going to say at least the handle didn't break, but . . ."

I sit down hard in the dirt, rubbing the back of my hand across my forehead and leaving it there. The smell of bats ghosts in my nose again. "Why did you have to bring that up?"

"I'm not the one obsessed with the memory."

No, because it hadn't been her fault, and she'd been either liquored up or unconscious for most of it. I remember every second—the full momentum of the bull, the sight of its horn puncturing clean through Rose's calf. Rose sailing through the air, Rose coughing through the whiskey they dosed her up with to start the surgery right there in the branding ring. The bow saw, the *sound* of the bow saw, how its teeth sank into her skin and below, grinding *back*, *forth*, *back*, *forth*. The cowhand's set jaw, his dirty fingers around the handle, his sharp curse.

"Damnation, Nit, shut up and hold her still. If you'd held the be-damned gate like I said, this wouldn't have happened."

I rub my eyes. "It was my fault. I was supposed to be keeping the gate closed."

"Girl, that bull was well over a thousand pounds of muscle and madness. If it wanted to bust through the holding pen, your skinny little ass wasn't going to stop it." She flicks a splinter of wood at me. "Besides, it gave us the chance to get away from the rustlers, didn't it? They underestimated me, and you. Aren't you glad about that?"

"*No.* You *don't have a leg.*"

"Dammit, I don't have a calf, and *so what*? You act like a person needs to be whole to be considered a person at all. That crap's tiring, Lark. I don't move as fast anymore, but I ride just as well, and I'm a damn sight better shot than you. Quit treating me like a cripple on bedrest. Grow up. Worry about your own issues before you worry about mine."

I hear a deep sigh from Rat—he does that when tensions are running high. Rose glares at me with one eyebrow raised. I give my own sigh.

"I don't want anything to happen to you," I say, unable to add *you're the only family I've got.*

"That's something none of us can promise," she says, resuming her work at splintering the pine fragment. "Least of all you. Listen. Let me and Saiph go into Pasul. We'll set out tomorrow. While we're gone, you take Pickle and Sedge down to the river and haul up a cottonwood. Let Andras help. Build up a wall of firewood eight feet high. Then when we come back, we'll have ourselves a feast of beef and potatoes and real honest-to-goodness griddle biscuits. All right?"

I blow out the rest of my breath. "All right. Get some lard, too."

She nods. "And beans."

"Blankets."

"Soap," she says. "The kind with flower petals in it."

"Perfumed scalp oil." As long as we're getting fanciful.

"Plus twelve head of cattle."

"And a marble fountain of crystal-clear water."

"Bandages," she adds. "We do actually need more. I'm bleeding right now, and Lila's been cramping—she'll probably have one of her blow-outs this time around. Sorry—the fountain reminded me."

I grunt and wipe my forehead with my bandanna. "Then get some of that Missus tea." I think of the ax head buried in the wood. "And a new ax."

"Absolutely not." She points into the bushes. "You go get that handle from the scrub, and if you get scratched up, it's your own fault."

"You provoked me."

"You provoked yourself, my love." She ties a last bundle of kindling. "Take it to Sedge. He's been dying for something to keep his hands busy. I don't want him adding wheels to my leg or anything."

I sigh and get to my feet. She reaches out to let me help her up.

"Rose, I'm sorry," I say as she tucks her crutch back under her arm. "I don't mean to act like you can't take care of yourself. I don't know what I'd do without you."

"Probably rage-fling everything in camp into the scrub." She pushes me toward the bushes.

Before I can work up the fortitude to plunge into the scratchy mess of branches, running footsteps thump toward us. Saiph rounds the big boulder at the edge of the splitting ring, his angular black eyes lit with tense excitement.

"What's the matter?" I ask. "Stage?" I'm not going after any stagecoach right now.

"No," he says, his face fierce. "Wagon."

VERAN

I wake up on the floor.

Dammit.

I pushed myself too hard last night. I should have known better.

A knock is coming from my parlor door—the sound must have jarred me awake. I flail in a web of sheets, my limbs hollow and watery. My elbow throbs, which means it probably took the brunt of the fall. I clamber to my feet, woozy, and stumble out into the parlor. I turn the wrong way at first, toward my glassed porch, before windmilling in a full circle and staggering to the door to the hall.

On my threshold stands a black-liveried palace servant, holding a box in his hands.

He says something, jumbled words that make no sense. His statement ends with a lift in his voice, as if he's asked me a question.

"What?" I slur.

He blinks at me.

"What?" he echoes.

Oh—*oh*, right, the language. Moquoian. He's speaking Moquoian, I think I answered in Eastern. I shake my head as if to rattle my brain into place. My whole body hurts.

"Sorry," I say in Moquoian. "I, uh, did not sleep well. What did you say?"

"Have you lost a pair of shoes?"

A pair of shoes? "I don't think so."

"I've been told these are your shoes, sir," he says, lifting the lid.

I stare, befuddled, at the shoes in his hands, gripping the doorframe to counteract my dizziness. The purple silk has been cleaned and dried, and they're tucked neatly in place with a swath of linen.

"Mistress Fala said one of the groundskeepers found them outside the mezzanine garden entrance," he explains, slowly, as if I'm a toddler—with good reason; I'm feeling about as coherent as one. "She inquired with the cordwainers, who matched them to your wardrobe. Or were they in error?"

"Uh, no—no." The patchwork memories of the previous night blink back to me like a guttering lantern. "No, they're mine. Yes, the garden entrance. I left them there. By accident."

I take the shoes from him and tuck them under my arm. With the memories comes the mortification of my slipups on the royal balcony, along with the conviction to tell all the details to Eloise and start trying to fix a few things. Following that comes the unexpected image of a dead songbird lying broken in the mud.

I rub my eyes. "If you please," I say to the servant. "Do you know if the ambassador and princess are awake?"

"I expect so, sir—it's past breakfast. Shall I inquire with them for you?"

"No, thank you—I'll go myself." I turn over my palm, which he stares at. Too late I remember that my folk's automatic gesture of thanks isn't universal. Hurriedly I tuck my hand back under my arm. "Thank you for returning my shoes."

I wait until he bows and heads away, and then I duck back inside my parlor. I set the shoes with the mud-stained outfit from the previous night and head to the trunk in my bedroom. I'm too achy from the night to attempt another Moquoian jacket and jeweled trousers—if Rou can be charmingly outlandish, so can I. I pull out the topmost pair of tunic and trousers, along with a leather belt and my softest, most comfortable pair of boots, the ones with the chevron fringe. I fumble to pull everything on.

I'm just tugging my second boot over my toes, mentally rehearsing what I'm going to say to Eloise in a few minutes, when I'm startled out of my thoughts by a clanging bell. I pause, straining to hear.

"Kualni An-Orra! Kualni An-Orra! To the northwest rails—Kualni An-Orra!"

Colors in the sky.

A rainbow.

I wrench my boot onto my foot and stagger upright. The clanging continues as I run back to the parlor door and out into the hallway, soon accompanied by other cries in the corridor. Maids are dropping laundry baskets in corners, and other guests of the Moquoian palace are darting from rooms, pulling on jackets and shoes. I catch a whiff of lemon balm as one lady smears insect repellent over her face. I shuffle down the hallway a few steps, one hand on the wall.

I'm halfway across the atrium when I realize I should have knocked on Eloise's door—at least to see if she's well enough to come outside. But I don't want to miss the start of my first *Kualni An-Orra* prayer or run the risk of the rainbow fizzling out before I can get to a northwestern patio. Perhaps I'll meet her outside and then, once the event is over, we'll sit down and talk.

The main doors out to the atrium porches are thrown open at last, with mosquito netting just barely forming a barrier to the open air. Folk slip through the netting, heedless of the damp wind gusting into the palace. The breeze rustles the tops of the indoor cedars, shaking needles from their usually stagnant branches and filling the air with a sharp evergreen scent. I grip the rail around the waving crowns, following the colorful silks of the last few Moquoian guests, one of whom has suds streaming from her wet hair.

I'm slow, and a little nauseated—the night was harder on me than I thought—and by the time I get around the circle of the atrium, everyone in the wing has already poured out. I can see them through the windows, rushing around the wraparound porch to the right, seeking those northwestern viewpoints. The rain has stopped, lighting up the glass with patchy sunlight, and through the panes I think I can see it—a smear of colors growing bolder as the clouds shift, forming a definite arc.

I don't know what makes me do it—everything worth seeing is happening outside, on the terrace, in the sky; I've been looking forward to a *Kualni An-Orra* since we arrived, and I've been dying to get out in the free air, last night's ill-planned excursion notwithstanding. But for whatever reason, despite the rushing breeze and billowing clouds, just before I release my grip on the rail, I look down, into the cedar trees. Normally, six stories up, the crowns block the view of the gardens below. But now, with the boughs bending in the wind, I catch a glimpse of the distant pathway, where I see a flash of gold-piped capelet flickering through the branches.

I turn fully to the rail, leaning over to be sure my dozy brain isn't playing tricks on me. No, there's his golden hairpin. While every other soul in the palace is rushing outside, Iano is stealing off the path through the cedar gardens. And not simply skulking or moping, either—he's moving with purpose among the boles, pushing aside ferns and flowers with a destination in mind.

I waver, looking again out the open doors. But it doesn't take me long to make a decision—his snap and flight last night repeat in my head, coupled with the painful memory of all the eyes turned my way.

He's up to something, and I'm just off-kilter enough to decide it's my business.

Besides that, today I'm wearing my boots, not tippy hard-soled slippers, and that makes me feel invincible.

Emboldened, I reverse my direction and head back for the staircase, slipping down the first few steps with blissful silence. Up above me, a single bell chimes, and a swarm of voices rises en masse in the first line of the twelve-verse prayer, starting with *tekonnsi* scarlet and the call for energy. The voices grow distant as I reach the third-floor landing and peer into the trees again. I can just see a flash of gold through the trunks, but Iano's moving away fast. I don't want to lose him—I'm moving faster than

I ever could in the Moquoian shoes, but by the time I reach the gardens below, he may have vanished in the greenery.

So, on impulse, probably channeling more of my mother than may be wise at the moment, I throw my leg over the rail, reach for the nearest stout limb, and swing into the branches.

I'm showered with fragrant needles, and my palms are instantly tacky with sap, but it feels strangely glorious to shimmy and twist down through the branches. I'll be the first to admit I've lived a sheltered life, but I've seen Mama scramble up an endless number of trees, bear bag in hand, and I've practiced on my own during the chancy stolen moments alone in the forest. I'd get an earful if Mama knew, or a full-blown panic attack if Papa found out, but I've learned to be fast and quiet enough not to raise suspicion. Besides, these trunks are strong, trained by centuries of pruning to grow in attractive arches thick enough to hold glassed lamps and pendants. I slither easily from branch to branch, angling down toward the ground in the same direction Iano disappeared.

A small side path winds through the trees a few yards to my right, one of many little pleasure jaunts in the grove. But Iano is cutting a line to my left, leaving a swath of squashed fern heads and heeled footprints in his wake. I stop just short of dropping to the ground and instead crab through the understory, occasionally jumping to my next perch when the branches become too slim. None of the sunlight and breeze from the open doors penetrates this far in—it's still and quiet as a first snow. I pause against a trunk, and then I hear it—a low murmur, and a hush of whispers. I peer around the trunk—Iano's turquoise capelet flashes through the branches about a stone's throw in front of me. I can't make out any words from here, but blessedly there's a hefty split trunk perfect for hiding just one branch over. I splay my feet on the branch, just like on the scout walkwires at home—another thing I'm not supposed to do—and pad silently down the limb to the crook of the tree. I flush with pride at that successful traverse as I wiggle into the space between the split trunks—my brother, Vynce, still has trouble with his traverses, and he's damn close to earning his Woodwalker boots and cord.

I force my thoughts away from my own silly victories and peer through the open space between the trunks. Iano is a little to my right, half hidden behind another tree, but I have a clear shot at the person he's talking to—it's Mistress Fala. She's more distraught than I've seen her any other time, her hands clasped before her, and her motherly face creased in desperation. Stifling my breath, I lean forward as much as I dare.

". . . I don't know who it was, my prince, I swear I don't . . ."

"Light be damned, maid, how can you *not know*?" The anger in Iano's voice startles me—he sounds even fiercer than last night. One fist is balled by his side, trembling. The other hand rests on the ceremonial rapier always attached to his waist. A flicker of unease needles my brain—I've never stopped to wonder if he's actually proficient with the elegant weapon. Surely he wouldn't use it against an unarmed, distressed subject.

Would he?

"He wore a hood and cape," Fala answers tremulously. "And a cloth over his face, and he had a *bintu* knife in his belt, and he was so big . . . he made me kneel and keep my eyes on the ground while he gave me the message."

Iano gives an exasperated growl. "And? What did he have to say this time?"

Fala's voice drops quieter, her hands clutched in front of her lips. I strain forward even more, one scant grip on a scrubby branch the only thing keeping me from pitching headfirst out of the tree.

"Speak louder, dammit! *What did he say?*"

"He said . . . he said the eyes in the court are many, and that you . . . you must make a better effort at appearing n-natural. H-he said if you cannot keep up appearances, then . . . oh, please my prince—"

"Then *what*?" There's panic alongside the anger in Iano's voice now, thrumming through the air. The cord on his rapier swings.

"Then you may start to receive—items. He said . . ." Fala's voice is shaking so badly, I can barely translate her words. "He said she . . . she has enough f-fingers and toes to send a daily reminder until your c-coronation."

Iano's breathing is so loud I can hear it above Fala's voice, until she breaks down, her palms pressed over her face to muffle her crying. My stomach squeezes at her distress, but Iano makes no move to console her. He's quiet for several long breaths, and when he speaks again, his voice is low and dangerous.

"And you have *no inkling* who this man is?"

Fala shakes her head, lifting her splotchy face from her hands. "He's only found me twice, each time when I was alone and in the dark—first cleaning the lamps in the portrait hall, and second when I was washing the breakfast room windows. The other times he's left the letters—he puts them in with my other correspondences in the mail room . . ."

"Have you spoken with your mail workers?"

"They've never seen him. The letters are simply in the collection box when they come in the morning." She fishes a handkerchief out of her pocket and blows her nose. "I am so sorry, my prince—I wish by the Light he had not sought me out, I wish by the Light he was not tormenting you with her safety, but what can I do—what can I do?" Her final words are akin to a wail.

Iano's breath streams out his nose. "Next time, come to me straightaway—I don't care what time of the night it is. If he approaches you again, you come wake me immediately."

"He says if I do so he'll—"

"I don't give a damn what he says he'll do. This is more important. *She's* more important. And if you'll just keep your head next time, we may be able to stop him tormenting the three of us altogether. Do I make myself clear?"

"Yes, my prince, yes."

He flaps a hand at her. "Go. Report to me *immediately* with any scrap of information."

She bows herself in a half circle around him, her hands clasped before her again. "Yes, sir, I promise."

I lean back quickly in the tree as she turns and hurries away, frantically wiping her tears. She stumbles through the ferns, her sniffling fading away.

Iano, meanwhile, stands stone-still under the trees, still gripping his rapier. In the new silence, I drag my tunic collar over my mouth to try to stifle my breathing. He stays there, rigid, for countless minutes, until I have dents in my palms from the cracks in the bark.

Somewhere in the faint distance, a bell rings out again, and then another, and another, their constant ringing becoming a full-on peal. The *Kualni An-Orra* is over. The rainbow has been swallowed up by the clouds again.

Iano makes a sudden movement, unsheathing his rapier and

slicing it expertly through the ferns, leaving a perfectly flat gap in the brush.

"*Kuas!*" he shouts.

I don't know that word, but something tells me it's probably not in my *Standard Primer of Moquoian Vocabulary*. He turns toward my tree for the first time, scrubbing his palm over his face. I hold my breath as he sheaths his rapier, but he pays no attention to my tree as he winds back among the trunks. He trudges slowly through the ferns, his shoulders slumped in defeat. I hold still until I can no longer hear his footfalls, and then I relax against the crook of the cedar, letting my breath out in one long stream.

Well.

Someone is blackmailing the prince.

A *he*.

About a *she*.

Well, well, well.

TAMSIN

I have one whole letter carved in the door.
H

LARK

I crouch on the rocks, peering over the twisted trunk of a fallen ponderosa pine. Below us, the thin ribbon of the South Burr slices through the flats. A meager road follows the near bank of the river, barely more than two parallel ruts offering a break in the scrub. We're four miles off the split with the stage road, which angles toward the North Burr on its way to Pasul. This one continues along the South Burr for another mile. A cart towing a large wooden wagon bumps slowly along the track, its wheels and gears groaning against the rough terrain. The wagon is pulled by oxen, not horses—that's what allows these travelers to take this remote road, rather than the main stage routes. And they know they're in dangerous territory—three armed guards face each direction, quarrels loaded into crossbows. The driver snaps a whip, urging the team to move through this treacherous bottleneck faster.

It's a good position. The sagebrush flats are wide but rocky, and the wagon won't be able to veer off the main track without breaking apart or falling in the river. We'll move faster than the oxen team, even at their full speed. We outnumber the armed guards. And to top it off, they're heading west—directly into the vicious late-afternoon sun shooting straight across the flats.

I crawl back up to the stand of living ponderosas, where the others are waiting.

"All right," I say. "We'll do this the usual way. Saiph and Pickle, you draw fire in front and give Rose and Sedge a shot at the guards. I'll work on the driver. If they try to outrun us, Pickle, you go for the cart wheel, not the wagon. Don't get your head bashed in."

"Wouldn't think of it!" He's eager, his horse sidestepping and snorting underneath him, feeling his energy.

"All right." I put my toe in the stirrup and sling my leg over Jema's back. I check my sword, buckler, and crossbow and then look down at Rat. "Ready, Rat?"

He rises off the ground.

"Don't you get your head bashed in, either," I say to him. "Oxen are stupid, but they don't shy like horses. Stay clear of those hooves."

He puts one ear back and gives a short, perfunctory yawn of tension.

"On," I say.

With a swish of his brushy tail, Rat slinks through the ponderosas and begins to lope down the hillside. Saiph and Pickle urge their horses after him. Rose checks the release on her crossbow—sometimes it sticks—and nods to me. I move forward after the others.

We weave down the rocky slope, angling toward the oncoming wagon. I can see the moment we're spotted—the three armed guards wheel from their watchful but casual positions to full alert, scrambling to make sure their quarrels and knives are easily accessible. Rose and Sedge split off to take a line behind the wagon. Pickle is out in front, swerving smartly around the rocks, muddling the aim of the guards. By the time we're within range, we've hit the track, and the sun is at our backs.

Rat snarls, and one of the oxen bellows in response. A quarrel whizzes somewhere close by, and I hear Pickle cheerfully chide the guard's poor aim. He wheels his horse in the opposite direction, and I see three quarrel points shift to follow his path. One fires and misses. Before the other two can release, Sedge materializes alongside the driver's box on the far side. I don't see everything that happens next—there are a few shouts, and then one of the guards topples from his perch. The wagon makes several sickening jolts as two sets of wheels bounce over the body. We canter on—I look over my shoulder to see the huddled form lying motionless on the side of the track, swept by a cloud of dust.

But if I thought that meant we were down a guard, I was wrong—the driver slaps the reins against the galloping oxen's rumps and pulls her own crossbow out from under her seat. Setting the reins under her boot heel, she stands up in the driver's box. One of Rose's quarrels flies past her ear. The driver swings her sights to me and fires—I veer Jema out of the way just in time. A near miss—but it's made me give up my position ahead of the wagon. I slap Jema's haunches and urge her back up the track, hoping to regain my ground before one of the guards trains their sights on me again.

Rose aims and fires—she catches a guard in the shoulder, and I hear him swearing colorfully as I catch back up to the wagon. My gaze sweeps over the door—sometimes the wagons are canvas, able to be ripped into, the victims inside hauled to freedom before running the wagon into the rocks. But this one is solid wood bolted shut with a heavy lock, not an easy thing to undo at a gallop over rough terrain. No, we're going to have to bring the thing to a halt, a gentle one, too, if we don't want to hurt those trapped inside.

There's a shout of dismay, and I look back to see Saiph falling behind. His mule, Weed, is stumbling over his foreleg. He must have taken a bad step. I turn forward again—I can't worry about Saiph at the moment. Truth is, all the better if he's out of harm's way.

The driver wheels her crossbow around to me again, thinking she has the edge with the sun now in my eyes, but I'm ready for her—I tilt my buckler straight toward her face. She squints, but she's smart enough to duck behind the driver's box just as I pull the trigger on my crossbow. My quarrel skips off the top where her head had been.

"Lark—to your left!"

I twist in the saddle just as a crossbow releases. I swipe my buckler up impulsively, and the quarrel glances off. But Jema weaves away from the groaning wagon, and as I scramble to keep her line, my own crossbow slips from my fumbling fingers. It smashes on the rocks below.

"Dammit!" I spur Jema to get her ahead of the creaking wood and metal coupling. "Pickle!" I call. "Jam the wheel!"

He swerves along my other side. Another quarrel whistles between us. "The driver's hot!"

"I don't care—get this thing stopped!" I lean low over Jema's neck, pulling my sword from its sheath. A whip cracks. Jema snorts nervously.

Pickle shouts to his horse, Scrub, and spurs him around the back side of the wagon. The remaining uninjured guard tracks him, his fingers tensing on his lever. I grab for my crossbow before remembering it's in pieces behind us. I glance for one of the others—all I see is Rose. She aims and pulls her crank.

It sticks.

The curse forms on her lips as she rejams her quarrel, but in that split second the guard fires. There's a shrill whinny from Scrub and as the wagon lumbers on, I see the horse on the ground, flailing in the dust. But no Pickle.

"Pickle! Damnation—Rose! Sedge!" We've got to get some order back on this thing.

There's a shout, and suddenly the top of the wagon sports not two figures, but three. Pickle dives into the guard box, swinging his metal staff.

"Pickle!" I shout in frustration. The driver snaps her whip. She's trying to outrun us.

And the way things are going, she's likely to succeed.

Gritting my teeth, I spur Jema forward again. If I can get near the oxen with my sword, I may be able to cut through some of the harnesses, or wound one of them. Anything to slow this thing down. Rose is coming up along the carriage, still fighting with her crossbow. Sedge is trying to draw fire from the guards, but he can't get a clear aim with Pickle in the tussle. I can't see Rat, and we've left Saiph far behind.

I hug the cart as closely as I can to avoid the driver's crossbow. But as I clear the box, I find that her focus isn't on me. She's standing up again, the reins back under her boot. She cocks her whip arm back and flings it along the top of the wagon. I can't see where it lands—I only hear the snap splice the air, a startled shout, and then two bodies topple off the swaying top. The swerve of the wagon sends them into the rocks along the ruts, where, unable to roll, they simply smash in a heap.

My guts freeze.

A metal staff bounces off the roof. It catches Sedge's horse, Pokey, flat across chest—the horse shies and bolts into the scrub. Rose swerves around the loose staff, twisting in her saddle to confirm her fears. Seeing Pickle on the ground, she turns back around and, with a yell, forgets fixing her crossbow and spurs Blackeye faster. The final guard stands up unsteadily on the wagon roof, wrestling with the crank on his crossbow.

"Rose!" I call. "Stop the wagon!"

Her thoughts are the same as mine. She disappears around the far side of the wagon. Gritting my teeth, I turn back for the driver's box.

Now. This driver.

Jema is wary and tiring, but I bring her flush with the racing cart again. The box is on my left. It'll make for an inelegant thrust, but all I want is to make contact—to wound enough that she'll give up the race. I slide my buckler up to my forearm and switch my sword into my left hand. I slap Jema's rump and clear the driver's box, arcing my sword toward the driver's calves.

She sees me at the last second and gives an ungainly hop to avoid my blade, dragging the reins with her. The panicky oxen low and weave toward the rocky bank. The wheels leave the ruts of the road and instantly tear apart on the rocks. If we were going more slowly, the whole thing might skid to a stop. But the cart and wagon are racing almost out of control now, and instead of slowing down, the whole cart jumps skyward. The wagon follows it with freak suddenness, and there's a breathless moment where every remaining wheel is off the ground.

The whole thing lands in the ditch with a smash, followed by a shriek of pain.

Everything in my body seems to lurch upward into my throat. *Rose.* There's an astounding moment of silence that follows, as if everything is drawing breath. Then the sounds begin. A wounded bellow from one of the oxen. The grind of a spinning axle. The tinkling of shattered glass. A moan from near the wagon.

A moan from inside the wagon.

I pull Jema up short and swing from her back. I run on watery legs for the locked door, but another sharp moan from Rose makes me veer for the other side of the destroyed wagon. *Please no. Please no.* I don't know what I'm praying to or for—just *no, no, no.*

I round the corner.

It's not as bad as I feared.

It's worse.

One of the oxen is on its chest, its foreleg bent clean in half. The other is tugging agitatedly at its yoke, lowing and tossing its horns. Rat is crouched in front of them, one paw tucked gingerly under his chest. What remains of the final guard is dashed on the rocks a full fifteen feet from the side of the road. There's no sign of the driver.

In the ditch is Rose, flat on her back. Her false leg has been twisted under her, caught in the movement of the wagon as it reeled out of control. The foot end is splintered. The strap end, where it attaches just below her knee, has taken her knee with it. A white knob of bone protrudes from her skin. My stomach sours, and I wrench my gaze away, dropping down to her side. She's breathing feebly, staring straight up at the sky, not seeming to see me. Her fingers are hooked into the dirt on either side of her, trembling.

"Rose," I whisper, brushing her forehead. Her skin is slick with sweat. "Oh Light . . . Rose."

She licks her lips, tear tracks staining her cheeks. "Is it bad?" She's whispering, too.

What do I say? I dare a glance at her leg again. *Why isn't there more blood?* You'd think there'd be more blood. No, there's only her knee rent to one side, as if someone twisted the top off a jam jar.

"It's," I begin. "It's . . ."

"Rose!" Sedge has caught back up, clutching the loose reins of Rose's horse, Blackeye, as well. He wheels Pokey to a halt and vaults from his back before the dust has settled. "Rose!"

He sweeps down beside me, clasping her face. She closes her eyes and brushes his arm with one set of shaking fingers.

There's a click of a heavy lock, and the groan of hinges.

"Dammit!" I push myself off my knees. *The driver.* I should have gone for the wagon first, should have checked to see if she'd been killed in the impact . . .

I skid back around the ruined wagon, gripping my sword with white knuckles. *Calm down. Keep control.* I round the door of the wagon, buckler up, just as the driver crawls inside.

After the harsh brightness of the desert sky, I have trouble making out the shapes inside. There seem to be three—the driver and two others. I'm not sure what the driver is doing, but I'm not going to wait to find out. I reach in to grab a handful of the closest captive's tunic and haul the person out into the sunlight.

I only have the barest moment to register a tiny girl, copper-skinned and dark-haired, before the driver spins around in the hold of the wagon.

"You hold it right there," she demands.

I push the captive behind me, placing myself between her and the gaping wagon door. The driver is kneeling on the straw-strewn floor, her chest heaving in and out. Crouching in front of her is the second captive, a man a few years older than myself. He's pinched and drawn, his skin a pallid gray, his hair colorless and wispy. With his arms shackled in front of him, I can see the line of mine tattoos running up his forearm. He's likely been a slave all his life.

The driver holds his head back and presses a knife to his throat. She's got a gash on her forehead that's bleeding heavily into her eye—I'm surprised she hasn't passed out yet. She wobbles slightly, unsteady, but her mouth and eyes are hard with anger.

I adjust my grip on my sword. "Let him go," I say. "And I'll let you walk away." I'm hoping she won't see through the promise—I plan to take her oxen with me, and if dehydration doesn't get her, blood loss will. She's already weaving, her right eye gummed shut.

She hisses through her teeth. "How does the loss of life feel to you, little girl? Does it make you feel powerful? Does it make you feel good, to murder three hired guards with nothing against you—who were only hoping to go back to their families in Vittenta?"

"They knew what their cargo was," I say. "They're no less innocent than you."

"But more so than you. You have more lives lost to your

ledger than me. You already have four today—maybe five." She jerks her head toward the back of the wagon, where I'm trying to ignore the sounds of Rose's labored gasps. *Four lives.* That's the three guards . . . plus Pickle.

My stomach heaves, and I take a step closer, sword up. "Let him go."

"No, darling. You've ruined me in a matter of minutes—destroyed my property and my investments. You'll forgive me if I deny you the satisfaction."

She jerks her wrist just as I lunge into the dark. My sword-point finds the soft spot beneath her ribs, and I drive it upward, forcing a bubbled gasp from her lips. It's not the only one. As she wilts forward, her blood washing my sleeve, the victim curls up beside her, a deep gash sliced from ear to ear. Thanks to the angle of the wagon, they both sink forward onto me, the weight of their fading bodies throwing me against the straw-strewn floor. I heave against them—someone's blood dribbles across my throat, sliding up along my jaw. Sick, flushed with rage, I grasp the edges of the wagon door and haul myself out from under them, landing hard on the rocks. The man falls halfway out, his head dangling down, a steady stream of blood trickling over the parched earth.

I breathe heavily for a moment, suddenly aware that the first captive is standing just over my shoulder. I look up into two massive green eyes framed by thick lashes. Dressed in a tunic cut from a rough cornmeal sack, she's staring, stricken, and shaking all over.

I try to unstick my tongue from the roof of my mouth, to tell her that she's safe, that she'll be all right, but I can't seem to force the words out. The beat of uneven hooves approaches, and

I lift my head to see an ashen Saiph pull up short with Pickle slumped in his arms.

"Lark!" His voice is broken. My stomach drops at the unnatural angle of Pickle's head. I roll onto my knees as Saiph slides from the limping mule's back, his breath coming in throaty gasps. He hauls his friend off the horse in a heap, dropping to the ground with him in his arms. He bends over Pickle, crying into his shirt. Pickle doesn't move, his arm bowing awkwardly out of Saiph's embrace.

I crouch on the ground and grip my head in my hands, shaking. Oh Light, this is the worst failure yet. In all my years chasing slavers' wagons, it's never gone this badly.

It's never gone so wrong.

The little girl begins to cry.

I'm too numb to join her.

VERAN

"She grows more ruthless by the week!"

Minister Kobok slams down a stack of parchment. "On this particular wagon, not only were the driver and guards slain, but the passenger was, as well. All items of value were stripped from the coach, including one of the oxen. Everything else they set on fire, burned to a crisp."

I glance at Rou beside me, who's listening with a concentrated frown. When we heard about this emergency meeting following the reports of the Sunshield Bandit's latest attack in the Ferinno, we were cautiously optimistic—making the desert safer is, after all, one of our major goals. But I expect Rou, like me, is irked by the fact that it was an attack on a slaver, not a passenger coach, that's caused this uproar.

"Bandits have been a thorn in our side as long as we have peacefully quarried the desert border," the minister continues. "And for years, the council has ignored my regular pleas to authorize organized force against them. The reason given has always been that the bandits—the Sunshield Bandit in particular—seem only to kill either themselves or wandering criminals. But I hope it is now clear that this is no longer the case. These are vagabonds, lawless and ready to murder anyone for material gain. How soon before they waylay a full stagecoach? How soon before they start raids on the quarry outposts?" He slaps his palm over his parchment. "I put forth to you now—if you are still in favor of inaction, you are more concerned about public image than the safety of our citizens and the economic future of our country."

Around the room, folk shift in their chairs, murmuring. I look to Prince Iano, sitting next to his mother and staring at the table. This is the first I've seen him since eavesdropping from the trees a few days before. I can't tell if he's taken the grisly threats to act natural to heart—his stoic gaze could just as easily be attributed to the news of this latest wagon attack.

Rou is silent, his knuckles over his lips. He's got circles under his eyes—product of checking in on Eloise through the night. She's still not feeling well, her rattly cough lingering in her chest. When I sought her out yesterday afternoon to parce out everything I've learned, Rou practically fenced me away with the fire poker, arguing that she was finally getting some sleep in between coughing fits and I could turn myself right around.

Now he lifts his knuckles from his lips to mutter to me. "Catch me up—the Sunshield Bandit attacked a Moquoian wagon, and he's wanting to go after her?"

"Banditry in general, it sounds like," I murmur back.

He frowns, but before he can say anything, the queen clears her throat. "What do you suggest, Minister?"

Kobok flips the top page of his stack with vehemence. "Set

a bounty in all the border towns. Station a small garrison in Pasul."

"No," Iano says suddenly, and all the attention in the room rivets on him. He sits up, a new ferocity on his face. "No bounty or garrison is going to do the work for us. We need soldiers out in the desert itself. It's time to start organizing searches. Hunts. It's time to start flushing them out of their hideaways."

Several eyebrows raise, including the queen's and Kobok's.

"Your support is encouraging, my prince," the minister says. "Perhaps if we begin small, with an armed presence in Vittenta and Pasul, we can start to gather intelligence on the whereabouts—"

"No, I want a sweep," Iano says. "And I want it now. Before *Mokonnsi* ends. This lawlessness has gone on far too long."

Kobok takes a little breath. "I doubt I need to point out that the Ferinno is a huge place, my prince. The type of active presence you're suggesting would take weeks just to organize— posses would have to be formed, with a budget, and a strategy. We cannot simply scatter soldiers across the desert . . ."

"Then get on it," Iano says. He turns to a startled woman with a badge pinned to her lapel. "Map a course for ten groups of fifteen soldiers each, with suggestions for provisions and base camps—"

"Wait just a minute," Rou says suddenly.

The folk around the table all turn to us. Rou's forehead has gone from a single crease to a collection of deep furrows.

"The Ferinno is Alcoran land," he says in punctuated Moquoian.

An unreadable silence descends over the room—I can't tell if it's hostile or merely attentive. Rou leans forward over the polished table.

"Moquoian soldiers do not have the authority to climb the Ferinno—"

"*Enter*," I amend quickly. "Enter the Ferinno."

"Enter, they don't—damnation." He lapses into Eastern and turns to me, gesturing between us and the rest of the table. "Tell them, Veran. They can't send soldiers into the Ferinno—there are Alcoran citizens that live out along the stage road, and most of the bandits are likely Alcoran anyway. Tell them this kind of action requires authorization by Prime Councilor Itzpin and the Senate *at the very least*, if not—"

"If that's the case, Ambassador," Iano says in crisp Eastern—balls, we've both forgotten again he's perfectly fluent—"why has the Alcoran Senate not put any effort into stemming banditry in the Ferinno up to this point? They've left bandits to their own devices, leaving Moquoia to suffer the consequences."

"Alcoro has been focused on stanching the slave trade," Rou counters, his usual affable diplomacy sharpened into a spearhead. "Which, I am loath to point out, generally flows in one direction. If there's been a rise in bandit activity, it's because Moquoia is bringing more ready targets right to their doorsteps."

Iano's face sours. "The point of this discussion is that the attacks are going beyond just the slavers' wagons—"

"Speak so we might all understand," Kobok booms, cutting through the volley of Eastern.

I chew the inside of my lip—I know what's going on in Iano's mind. He's latching on to the opportunity of hunting bandits to send soldiers to look for whoever he's being blackmailed with, though I can't think why he wants to start in the Ferinno and not within his own borders. I'm not sure how to adequately navigate this—not with Rou practically steaming out his ears next to me. But I think I'm probably the only one with all the pieces.

I clear my throat and say in Moquoian, "The ambassador is concerned about the legality of sending Moquoian soldiers over Alcoran borders. There may be impacts to Alcoran citizens."

Kobok waves a hand. "There has already been a greater impact to Moquoian citizens. The quarries themselves are worked by Moquoian labor."

I start to translate for Rou, but he shakes his head—he's understood the minister. "The quarries are on Alcoran soil, and they're worked by *slave labor*," he spits in Eastern. He jabs me in the ribs. "Tell them we're done dancing around this subject. Time's up."

Oh, by the Light. "The ambassador is concerned about the ownership of the quarries, and the, um, nature of employment of your workers—"

"The recruitment of contract workers is not the concern of this conversation," Iano says. "A wagon and its occupants, bound for Moquoia, have been attacked and killed just outside our borders, and there's nothing to suggest it won't happen again."

I try not to flick my gaze around the table full of Moquoian ministers. "Prince Iano, I understand the distress of your situation. But consider that this is an excellent reason to open the partnership with Alcoro and the rest of the East that we've spent so long discussing—"

"There *is no partnership*," Iano says sharply, his gaze boring into mine. "There *will be no partnership* until the threat to this court stops."

He's not talking about the damn wagon. But nobody else

knows that—certainly not Rou, who blinks in consternation at the Moquoian prince. I can tell from his expression that he doesn't need this latest statement translated, either.

"Did he just—look here, young man, we did not spend weeks of travel and hundreds of silvers for you to treat Alcoran territory as your own!"

"*Speak Moquoian*, by the colors!" Kobok demands.

Iano's next words are in the language of the room, and they fall like a gavel. "Then *leave*. Go back to the East, and take no goodwill from our court to yours."

Rou stares at him momentarily, and then twists in his seat to me, his thumb jerked toward the prince. "*Did he just—?*"

"I think we should go," I say quickly, shoving back my chair. I nod to Prince Iano. "Allow me to speak to the ambassador and Princess Eloise and see if we can come to an accord."

Rou tries to shake off my tug on his arm. "I'm not done here—"

"I need to talk to you," I whisper. "It's important."

He frowns at me but rises to his feet. He turns momentarily back to the prince and raps on the table. "We are *not finished* here."

I offer a vague bow to the room and proceed to drag him out the door of the ministerial chamber.

We're barely through the two guards outside the door when Rou flicks his arm out of my grip. "All right, what is this about?"

"Okay, stay with me," I say, beckoning him to keep moving —I want to get up to Eloise's room to get her input as well. "Iano doesn't want to get out in the desert to hunt bandits. He wants soldiers out there to look for someone he's lost—and I think it's the previous *ashoki*."

"So . . . nope, you've lost me."

We reach the main staircase, which I take with speed—I'm wearing Moquoian shoes again today, and the hobnails echo off the steps. "You know how the *ashoki* before Kimela died before we got here? There's a rumor in court that the Sunshield Bandit was the one to attack her stagecoach. But just yesterday I over-heard Iano taking a message from one of the servants. It sounded like he's being blackmailed with the safety of somebody."

"Blackmailed into what?"

"I don't know, but it might have something to do with his drastic switch in politics. At least, that's the only thing that makes sense to me." We reach the landing in the atrium and cut a line down the guest wing.

"Why hasn't he told anybody?" Rou's voice has a puff to it as he matches my stride.

"I don't think he knows where the threats are coming from, or how to stop them, short of just doing what they're demanding."

"Why is this the first I'm hearing of it, five weeks into this thrice-cursed attempt at diplomacy?"

"Because I've only just found out, and, well . . . you've been so busy with Eloise . . ."

Rou sighs. "You're right—I've been neglecting one duty for another. Okay, I'm listening now. And what you're saying is that Iano wants to use banditry as an excuse to send troops onto Alcoran soil?"

"That's what it sounds like."

"This despite the fact that part of our negotiations was sup-posed to revolve around ownership of the quarries? That's going to look an awful lot like a border expansion back in Callais, and I can't say I'd blame them for the assumption." He shakes his head as we approach Eloise's door. "And why is he homing in on the Ferinno in the first place? Wouldn't a Moquoian captive be held somewhere in Moquoia? Has he checked the forests? The islands? Why's he got his eye on the desert?"

I'm about to answer that I don't know that, either, readying myself to bring this into Eloise's room and hash it out with her, when the answer suddenly hits me, plain as day.

"Oh," I say. "It's probably . . ."

"What?"

"It's probably because he thinks we're doing the blackmailing."

Rou's hand pauses on the doorknob, and he stares at me. His lips move wordlessly for a moment.

"Blazes, *why*?" he asks.

"Well . . . probably first because he's desperate and panicking. And probably because it all happened around our arrival, and because he knows we're after the slave trade, and because the first he heard of the attack, it was all tied up with the Sunshield Bandit—though I'm not entirely sure she had anything to do with it."

He waves a hand as if swatting a fly. "This is all walnuts, and what's more, it's insulting. I've dealt with some wild card politicians in my time, but this is just plain dangerous. If he's not careful, he'll be starting his reign with a full-fledged declaration of enmity instead of an alliance."

I'm worried that's exactly what he's already done. "What if I can talk to him?" I ask. "If I approach him frankly, tell him what I know—"

"Based on what you just told me, if he hasn't told anybody else, it'll only confirm that we're somehow behind it. Fire and *smoke*, what a nightmare." He jerks the doorknob and storms into Eloise's parlor. I follow, my thoughts a thundercloud.

"Eloise?" Rou calls. "How're you feeling, lolly?"

I'm so wrapped up in my thoughts, it takes me a moment to realize Eloise hasn't answered with her usual exasperated affirmation. I snap back to reality when Rou's voice rings out in a bark.

"Ellie, baby! What's wrong?"

I spring for the bedroom door. Rou is swooping down to Eloise's bedside, where she's slumped over with one hand on the side table, as if she'd been reaching for the water jug just out of reach. Her breath sounds like a stone caught in a milling wheel, thick and rocky. Her skin has a grayish pallor to it, filmed by sweat, and her bonnet's askew. Several dark curls cling to her damp forehead.

"Oh, blessed Light, she's on fire." Rou flings an arm toward the door. "Get the physician—get *somebody*!"

Without a pause I scramble back for the parlor, my heart in my throat. Halfway across, I shuck off my shoes and run barefoot into the hall. I fly down the corridor and take the staircase three steps at a time, angling for the physician's ward. She's at her counter rolling pills when I burst into her office.

"Come quick, please—it's Princess Eloise."

*Ten minutes later, I'm hovering behind Rou, who's hovering be-*hind the physician. She has an ear cone to Eloise's chest, her lips in a thin line.

"Rainshed," she says, leaning back.

"What'd she say?" Rou looks over his shoulder at me, almost like he's choosing not to understand.

"It's rainshed fever," I confirm, my stomach left somewhere down on the third floor.

Rou inhales, his face gray. He goes to Eloise's bedside and closes his fingers around hers.

"What's it usually like?" he asks, his voice gravelly.

I translate for the physician.

"High temperature, lethargy, low appetite, a thick cough," she replies. "In about half the cases, it runs its course in ten to twelve days, usually with persisting weakness afterward."

"And—the other half?" Rou prompts when I've finished the translation.

The physician pinches her lips. A sick sense of dread fills my stomach. *Please don't make me tell him that.*

"There's a higher survival rate with the first case," the physician says tactfully. "A relapse would be more dangerous. Has she taken feather-plant before?"

"Has she ever taken yarrow?" I ask Rou. "It grows along the western edge of the Stellarange." Mama sometimes uses it in her scout kits to stanch blood flow.

He shakes his head. "I don't think so. She has some allergies. Her physician at home often uses poultices."

"I'm going to start her on feather-plant, and a small measure of skunk cabbage to help control her cough," the physician says, rising from her chair. "I'll send someone to bring more firewood in case she gets the chills."

Whatever Rou's about to say next is cut short as Eloise breaks into another bout of coughing. He turns back to her bedside, and the physician slips out the door to the hall.

Eloise's cough gets deeper and sharper, her shoulders

shaking. Rou strokes her forehead, tucking a few curls back under her bonnet.

"Papa?" she whispers hoarsely.

"Hi, lolly," he replies with hollow cheerfulness.

"What did—" She coughs again. "What did they say at the meeting?"

"Nothing important. Just odds and ends." He brushes her sweaty forehead. "You rest, okay? We're getting something to help with your cough."

"I wanted to make notes."

"I'll jot some things down for you later. You rest now."

"No, I want—" She clears her groggy throat. "I want to stay caught up—the exchequer is supposed to be at dinner tomorrow—"

"Sweetheart—you're not going to dinner tomorrow. None of us are. We're leaving."

My insides freeze. "What?"

Her fluttering eyelids snap open. "*What?*"

"We're going home," Rou says, his face set. "We're chartering a coach and team to take us back across the Ferinno. This trip has been a failed effort—it's time to cut our losses."

"Wait, no—we can't. Papa . . ."

"We're just starting to make progress," I say.

"No, we're moving backward." He gestures to the door to the hall. "For weeks we've been handled and danced around and put off, only to find out we're potentially being blamed for political blackmail nobody knows about."

Eloise's startled gaze jumps from him to me. "We're being blamed for blackmail?"

"I don't know," I say quickly. "I only said it's a possibility—"

Rou shakes his head with force. "Even if it's not, you've caught the fever everyone's been worried about, Eloise, and I refuse to take risks where your health is concerned."

"How could I have caught it?" she whispers, her eyelids heavy. "I've done everything they told us to do."

"It doesn't matter so much how," he says. "The point is, you've got it, and we know almost nothing about it, and the physician says it could be worse if you were to relapse. I know it's a disappointment—for all of us—but nothing worked out the way we expected."

"Let me talk to Iano," I say, trying to keep from wringing my hands. "Let me just sit down with him—"

"And what, Veran? You had the chance to talk a few nights ago at the ball, but I hear rumors it didn't exactly go well." I drop my gaze. "I'm not saying that to make you feel bad—I need you to understand how the deck is stacked against us. Diplomacy was apparently not the intent of our visit for Prince Iano. I'll be damned if I understand why, but he's not interested in talking policy. And part of good diplomacy is knowing when a graceful retreat is best."

"But . . . but . . ." I get a vision of me arriving back home, rejoining my family dragging such a monumental failure behind me. They'll expect me to tell them everything, every twist and turn and nonevent. I'll have to tell them—Vynce in his new Woodwalker boots, Ida bristling with stripes on her uniform, Susi with a blue-zillion new silver bells on her fringe . . . and Viya, sitting silently, probably keeping a mental tally of all the things she could have done better in her sleep. Papa and Mama, he with a sympathetic smile, she with a few punctuated remarks meant to lighten the weight of my defeat, but both sharing that silent conviction—*he shouldn't have gone. He was never up to it.*

"We can't," I croak to Rou. "This could be the only chance—"

"It's *not* our only chance, V. Diplomacy is a long game."

"I want to keep trying," Eloise says, her words shallow as she tries to hold off her cough. "I'll be okay in a few days."

"No, you probably won't, Ellie. You hold on to even a chest cold longer than most folk, and this is much worse."

"But we can do it," I insist. "I know we can make it work—"

"Veran—"

"Moquoia is the key to everything we've worked for." I press despite the palpable sparks in the air. "Too much is at stake—we just need more *time*—"

I've gone too far. Something in Rou's posture snaps, throwing every line rigid. He leans toward me. "I am not hanging around, working a cold forge, so Eloise can die twelve hundred miles from her mother in the country that *already took her sister away from us.*"

My mouth slams shut, something it should have done about half a minute ago. Eloise's lips scrunch up, her gaze flicking down to the coverlet. Rou's face has gone from weary to uncharacteristically fierce. He takes a sharp breath, looking between the two of us.

"Take a second to get your head around things—both of you. This isn't debate team or philosophy class. I know you both feel like eighteen years old is the height of maturity, but bellringer—*it's not.* And you *both* have more cause to be concerned about your health than most folk. Eloise—you're the single direct heir to Lumen Lake." His voice gets a little rockier. "Since we lost your sister, and since the miscarriages, you're all we have. Veran, you're not any less important. And if this is all just some kind of ego boost for you, then maybe you need the failure to reorient yourselves."

I don't know how his words are affecting Eloise, but they hit me like hammer blows, shuddering my chest with each one. Rou's never harsh. He never snaps. Where Queen Mona is brisk, Mama rough, and Papa calm, Rou's always the one to lighten the mood, to provoke a laugh, to ease the tension among quarreling parties. The fact that I've been callous enough to spark such a reaction from him makes me feel worse than I have so far in this whole five-week debacle.

"I'm sorry," I mumble. "I—I wasn't thinking."

Rou lets out another breath, and he rubs his face. "I know it's not what we hoped for. I'm disappointed, too. It's going to be hard to explain at home, and it complicates our next attempts with Moquoia. But it's for the best. You can see that, can't you?"

"Yes, sir," I say instantly.

"Ellie?"

"Yes, Papa." Her gaze is still lowered, but it's not with the same cut-edged mortification I feel. Rather, she seems to be thinking.

"Good." He rises heavily from Eloise's bed. "I'm going to look into chartering a coach, or at least traveling with a caravan. And I'll have to start making the case for our exit. Veran, you go ahead and start packing."

"Yes, sir."

Eloise plucks a handkerchief off the bedside table and holds it to her mouth in time to cover a few short coughs. Rou tucks a few damp curls back under her lavender bonnet. He stoops and kisses her forehead.

"Get some rest. I'll be back as soon as I can." With one more sigh, he heads out into the parlor. Only when the hall door closes behind him do I let out my breath.

"I'm sorry, Eloise. That was so stupid of me." I wave to the bedside table. "Do you need anything? A drink? I can heat up the kettle . . ."

She drops the handkerchief from her lips. "Okay, so we're potentially being blamed for blackmail?"

My hand halts halfway to the kettle. "Uh, what?"

"Hurry—I need answers if we're going to get anything done." Her voice is whispery and raw. "Who's blackmailing whom?"

"Your pa said you should rest."

"Papa . . ." she begins, and then takes a short breath, pressing her palm to her chest. A cough escapes her. "I won't go against Papa. If he thinks we should leave, then we're leaving. But by my guess the earliest we could leave is tomorrow morning, which means we don't have a lot of time—but we have some."

"Time for what? What can you possibly do in less than twelve hours when you can barely get out of bed?"

"Not much—that's why you're going to have to do most of the heavy lifting. It may be a long night for you. Are you up for it?"

"I don't know," I say warily, thinking back to my string of failures, and my hopes that she wouldn't ask me to take on anything else without her. "What am I agreeing to?"

"First, to answer my questions." She settles her head against her pillow, her eyes underlined with shadows, but her expression set. "Tell me about the blackmail."

Quickly—a little hesitantly, given Rou's admonition a moment ago—I fill her in on what I learned during *Kualni An-Orra* the day before. The threats by way of Fala, the likely connection to the *ashoki*, Iano's anger during the meeting earlier.

"He wants to send soldiers into the Ferinno," I say. "Supposedly to root out bandits, but I'm sure it's to find the *ashoki*. But that kind of military presence crossing a border . . ."

"Would be clear grounds for a defensive show from Alcoro," Eloise murmurs. "Which would ripple out to the rest of the East and set a clear pretext for war—which would be the greatest strain on the Eastern Alliance since it was founded." She coughs into her handkerchief again and rubs her chest. "All right. Priority one, then, has to be clearing our name—we can't leave with him thinking we're behind everything. It's only going to snowball into something we can't control."

"I tried that at *Bakkonso*, but he barely gave me a chance to get started."

She frowns, but before she can respond, there's an almighty thump at the window. We both jump.

"What was that?" she asks.

My stomach curls. "A bird." I get up and go to the window, craning my head to look down, where a little body lies on the ledge, its head bent like the ones I saw along the palace foundation. I start to turn back to Eloise, but then I pause—there's a small drift of moving air. Did the bird break the glass? There are no cracks above it. Curious, I twitch the curtain aside. The main window is made of one giant sheet, but where the drapes hide the edges, they transition to less opulent panes, each just a few inches wide.

In the very corner of the window, where the casing meets solid wall, one small pane has been broken out, hidden by the thick folds of the drapes. I frown—there are no glass fragments inside, but the curtain is soaking wet—it's been broken for some time. I lean right up against the casing and look down at the outside sill, wondering if it was somehow cracked from the inside.

There's no glass on the sill, but there is something else—a small bowl full of rainwater. Tucked into the corner of the window, it's protected from the weather beyond. Puzzled, I bend closer.

And see the hundreds of mosquito larvae writhing in the water.

I straighten so quickly the curtain drags on its rod. My fingers shoot impulsively through the missing pane—not broken, I realize, but purposefully removed—and push the bowl off the sill. It sails into open air, spilling its infested water as it drops away.

"What are you doing?" Eloise asks.

I stand immobile, clutching the curtain. My breath is shallow and quick.

"Eloise," I finally say. "Did you know a windowpane over here is missing?"

"No. Is it broken?"

"It . . . it looks like it was taken out. There's no jagged glass."

I hear the frown in her voice. "That doesn't make sense."

I swallow. "There was . . . a little bowl of water just outside it. With mosquitoes in it."

There's silence behind me. It stretches out until it fills the room, thick with impossibility. At long last, I turn around to face her. Her face is tense, her forehead creased.

She adjusts her position on her pillows. She refolds her hands. The silence sticks a few seconds longer.

"Well," she says.

"Do you . . . do you think someone put it there?" I ask.

"I can't think of many other options," she replies evenly.

We fall silent again.

"Though it seems like an unreliable way to make me sick," she says. "Just hoping an infected mosquito might find its way in. Why not just slip me poison?"

I gesture to the window. "Nobody could say this wasn't an accident."

She purses her lips, but she doesn't say anything. Stiffly, she smooths the quilt over her lap.

"Don't tell Papa," she says. "He's already made up his mind about leaving, and if he starts accusing the Moquoian court of deliberately infecting me with rainshed fever, he'll look like a fool at best and make himself a target at worst. I'll tell him when we've gotten out of the country. Until then, keep your door locked, all right?"

"What about Iano?" I ask.

She shakes her head. "I suppose I'll have to write him a letter and hope it will be enough to convince him not to invade the Ferinno. I'd thought about sending you to make a plea at his door, but if we have an enemy in the palace, I don't think that's a good idea anymore."

I turn back to the window, hoping to hide my disappointment. My gaze falls again on the dead bird on the sill. Iano being blackmailed, but not by us; Eloise being infected, but we don't know by whom—and all the while this *ashoki*, her conspicuous death hovering at the edge of the court, altering the tide of diplomacy, breaking alliances. If only Iano could make his search without threatening war on the East and alerting the wrong people in court. If only we had someone we knew for certain we could trust, someone we *knew* didn't have a hand in this mess of politics.

My gaze roves over the bird, finally recognizing its patterned feathers, speckled black and white above a shock of yellow. It's a western bird, not a Silvern one, but I remember it from the canyon rim around the university, piping its sweet fluty song. A meadowlark.

A lark.

My mind sputters over several things at once.

A captive in the Ferinno. A puzzling account of the attack. A confirmed attack on Colm's stage, a day's ride in the other direction, happening right around the same time.

The need for someone to trust.

I did find out one significant thing—her name.

It's Lark.

I lean back from the window, my heart pounding.

"I need to talk to Iano," I say quickly, staring out at the rain.

"Fetch me some parchment—if you tell me what you want to say, I'll include it in the letter."

"No," I say. "You don't have to write a letter. I'll talk to him face-to-face."

"Veran, if someone purposefully broke my window to let in mosquitoes, I don't think it's a good idea for you to make too much noise on the eve of our departure."

"I can do it without the court finding out." I search for a fast lie. "There's . . . a cocktail party on one of the terraces tonight. I can talk to him there."

"Privately?"

"Yes."

I can feel her gaze boring into the back of my head. "It doesn't involve anything . . . I don't know, excessively risky, does it?"

"Of course not—you know my pa's rules."

"I also know now that you squirreled through a mess of trees yesterday to spy on a foreign monarch. Turn around and tell me to my face that you're not going to take stupid risks."

I turn around, trying to force all emotion out of my expression. Solemnly, I raise a hand. "I swear with a scout's honor I'm not going to take stupid risks."

She squints at me, frowning. "All right, then." She doesn't sound at all like she believes me, so I turn for the door as nonchalantly as I can.

"I'm going to go pack," I say. "For the trip home."

She doesn't reply. I feel her gaze follow me until I'm out of the room. Once in the hall, I take a deep, shaky breath.

I didn't lie to her. I'm not going to take stupid risks.

I'm going to take necessary ones.

Also, I'm not a scout.

TAMSIN

My thumbtack is starting to die. The point has blunted to a rounded nub. I've tried sharpening it on the wall, but the adobe just crumbles. Instead I take to wiggling the second metal band on my waste bucket. After much clawing and cursing, I manage to loosen a second thumbtack. It's born from the wood brand-new and virile, its end hard and pointy.

I move to the door again to start on the fourth letter.

H

I

R

LARK

Rose has a fever.

In the time since the wagon disaster, she's gone from being in constant pain to living in a drifting stupor, her skin fiery hot to touch. Sedge will barely leave her side. He changes the bandage on her knee twice a day, making guesses as to when to elevate it and when to let it air. The ragged end is a sickly black now, crusted with pus and blood that won't stop leaking.

Lila, too, has been especially attentive, mopping Rose's forehead, trickling water into her mouth, and helping change the wrappings underneath her when they get soiled. Her face, often arranged into cool disdain, is creased with worry. She might be in love with Rose, too, come to think of it.

I jog up the final slope of the grassy drainage at the base of Three Lines. Rat trots at my heels—he tweaked a paw in the chase with the oxen, but already he's moving normally again. From my fist swings a skinny jackrabbit, the only game in any of our nearby traps today. It'll make a poor stew, gamey and tough, but at least the bones should make a good broth both Rose and the little ones can drink. I'd make the longer trek down to check the deadfalls along the river, but I'm hesitant to leave the others in camp that long. For the thousandth time in the last hour, I release a breath I've been holding in.

I shift the bundle of wood on my shoulder. I wouldn't have even made the trek down to the drainage this morning, but with the ax head still buried in the stupid pine block, we need the firewood, and the half-mile radius around our camp is picked clean. I've given up thoughts of taking the ox to drag one of the cottonwoods up from the river, at least for the moment. Even if I thought I could leave camp that long, the others are in no shape to help me. Sedge can't bring himself to leave Rose's side. And Saiph . . . Saiph is grieving Pickle hard. They were closest in age, and they'd been friends for years. Now he wanders around camp like a ghost, doing things I ask him to in a hazy, silent stupor. I'm not sure he could focus on hitching up a fallen tree, or whether he'd just drift uselessly along beside us. I haven't had the time to sit him down and talk about what happened because I've been running around to supply camp and care for our newest member.

Moll.

I have no idea what her real name is, because she hasn't uttered a single word since she arrived. Not one. We've called her that after the four letters printed on her dirty cornmeal sack, probably the beginning of MOLLIN'S MILLING SERVICE. She won't part with the sack—Lila and I gently lifted it off her to sponge her down, but when we tried to take it away, she clutched it to her chest and wouldn't let go. I asked her if we could call her the name printed on the burlap. She didn't answer, only sat and shook from head to toe like an aspen in a high wind.

We dressed her in Pickle's spare shirt—it hangs off her little shoulders like a tent. She's a tiny thing, less fragile than Whit but even smaller. Her massive eyes are jewel green and set in a round, copper-skinned face. At some point, someone cut her dark brown hair off in hanks, but it's grown out to hang unevenly by her chin. My guess is that she might be Paroan, which makes my spirits sink even lower—if Cyprien is far away, Paroa might as well be the moon. And she's so little, there's no telling if she can recall anything of her family, or where on the coast she's from. If she ever decides to talk to us at all.

I know she can speak, at least a little, because she does it in her sleep, mumbling and crying. But she won't answer any questions—not where she's from, or what she remembers, or if she's hungry. So we've been caring for her like we've been caring for Rose, spooning broth and corn mush and water into her mouth. I've tried to take her with me a few times, to get her to walk up to the seep, or down to the horses, or even just over to the cookfire, but she clings to Pickle's old sleeping mat like a tick. So I've had to just leave her, charging Whit with checking to see if she needs water and whether she's peed on her blanket. I have noticed she shakes less when Rat sits beside her, but he whines if I take off somewhere without him. Which is why I'm now jogging back up the drainage, chased by the worry that I need to get back in camp as soon as possible. Rat lopes along with me.

I crest the rise on the drainage to find Andras drooped on a rock near the grazing ox. He's been put in charge of the animals for the time being. We're down a horse—I had to shoot poor Scrub after it took the quarrel. Saiph's mule, Weed, will probably survive, but he won't be able to carry loads for a while.

Taking the remaining ox from the wagon was as much to get our wounded, ragtag group back to Three Lines as it was to scavenge something from the wreckage. We've lost my crossbow—that leaves only two, with Rose's still acting up. We salvaged some quarrels, though the ones from the guards are too long to use in our remaining bows, and theirs were broken in the crash as well. We were able to collect Pickle's staff and a few metal bits and pieces from the wagon, but without Scrub and Weed, we couldn't afford to tote anything else. We bundled Pickle and the other bodies inside the wagon. There was no time to say lengthy good-byes. Rose was already in and out of consciousness. I ushered everybody away from the wagon, shot the injured ox, and set a fire under the entire wreck. It went up like kindling, a blazing torch to my failure.

I watch Andras shoo the ox back up the slope. I'm not sure what I plan to do with the animal. It can carry loads, but until I can get down to the cottonwoods, there's nothing for it to carry. I could sell it in Pasul, if I can get it there, but that would take days, and I'd have to take someone with me. That someone would have to be Saiph, and it would leave only one horse in camp.

Andras trudges up the slope after the ox, and then he stumbles over a pile of gravel. I bite my lip. He hasn't seen me coming yet. His eyes are only getting worse, reminding me that Cyprien is clear in the other direction from Pasul. If getting an ox a day's ride west is questionable, getting a boy a month's scramble east is getting more and more impossible.

I pick up my pace.

I'd very much like to collapse and scream, but I don't have the time.

VERAN

Iano moves slowly in the darkness, fumbling for the knob on his lamp. He turns it up, throwing his pale face into sharp relief. With a sigh he unhooks his bright capelet, tosses it on the settee, and slumps into the armchair by the fireplace.

"Is this her?" I ask.

He yelps and vaults from the chair, overturning the end table. A book and an inkwell go flying. And suddenly that pretty rapier that's always on his waist is bare and pointed straight at my chest, steady and extremely real.

He *does* know how to use it.

I throw up my hands.

He stares through the dim light. "You! What are you . . . how did you get in here?"

I scoot back on the window seat a few inches, putting some space between my heart and that unwavering swordpoint, uncrossing my soft-soled boots. "I walked around the terraces."

"It's three stories to the nearest public terrace!"

I point generally toward the floor. "There's scaffolding on each story, so servants can clean the glass. One of the ladders goes right past your terrace."

"It's raining!"

"Yes."

He recovers enough to be upset. "I have guards."

"I threw a rock," I say, still eyeing the rapier. "She went to check the noise. I snuck past."

"My doors are all locked."

"I can pick a lock," I say. Eloise's uncle Arlen showed us both how before we were ten. I used to do it to get into the scout supply room, to sneak things for clandestine trips into the forest.

"Well, get out," he snarls. "Before I have you arrested and deported." He places his palm halfway up his rapier, to steady the drive when he skewers me through the heart. But then his face takes on a wary cast. "What did you say first?"

I hold up the little charcoal sketch, a study, it looks like, perhaps for a full-blown portrait. Though rough, it shows a woman with an almost perfectly round face, her long hair wound into an intricate bun and threaded with strands of jewels. She has a small nose and small, round lips, and she's looking sidelong at the artist, as if she knows something they don't.

"Where did you get that?" Iano demands, panic rising in his voice.

"It was propped against the water jug on your bedside table," I say.

He shakes himself. "Get out!" he says again, and the sword-point catches the edge of my firefly pin. "Get out now, and don't speak to me again."

I lower the sketch, trying to reassure myself that he won't

actually kill me. My nerves don't believe me. "Iano, the previous *ashoki* didn't die in that stagecoach attack, did she? She's alive somewhere. And someone's using her safety to blackmail you."

He stands very still, but for the first time, the point of the rapier wobbles, as if his hand suddenly shook. His eyebrows snap down.

"And just how do you know that, I wonder?" he asks.

"I followed you into the cedar grove during the *Kualni An-Orra* the other day," I say—I've decided truth will be the best route here. "I heard you talking to Mistress Fala."

His face darkens. "You *spied* on me."

"*You've* been spying on *me*," I point out.

His anger flickers into confusion. "When?"

"You told me on the first day of *Mokonnsi*—you said you have people watching us."

The confusion lingers on his face before realization kicks in. "Oh. Right."

I quirk one eyebrow. "Or was that just a threat?"

"Well . . ." He looks sheepish for the briefest moment before remembering his anger. He readjusts his grip on his rapier. "Even if it was, it doesn't matter—you just admitted to eavesdropping on my private affairs."

"I had to do *something*—otherwise Eloise and I were afraid you'd blame us for whatever this blackmail is about."

"And why shouldn't I?" he asks harshly. "What little evidence I have all points to you."

"What evidence?" I spread my hands. "Why would we exchange detailed diplomatic correspondence for a year, only to stage an elaborate false attack on a person we didn't know, and then bully your servants into blackmailing you?"

He hesitates. "I admit . . . I haven't been able to determine what your motive is."

"There *isn't* a motive, Iano. We're desperate for this diplomacy to go through. And anyway, Fala said something about a big fellow in a cloak—I'm not exactly what you'd call big, and unless he spoke broken Moquoian with a spectacular Cypri accent, I'm not sure who in our party you're trying to pin this on."

He glares for a moment, tight-lipped. Then, with a broken sigh, the swordpoint falls. He sets it cockeyed against the end table and collapses back into his armchair like a candlestick in a furnace blast. He grips his head in his hands, mussing hair out of his golden pin.

"I don't know what to do," he murmurs.

I move from the window to the fireplace. I slide the sketch into his lap, and he stares down at it.

"What's her name?" I ask.

"Tamsin," he says. "Tamsin Moropai in-Ochre."

"Is that her empty pedestal in the Hall of the *Ashoki*?"

He nods wearily. "Yes."

"What was her instrument?"

"The lap dulcimer—an old folk instrument. Her voice is the real marvel, though, and her skill with words."

"Fala told me there's been some debate about what lyrics to put on her memorial."

"There's no debate," he says darkly, looking up at me. "I was told in one of the letters to use some throwaway phrase—something benign and harmless to sanitize her memory. But it doesn't matter, because there shouldn't even *be* a memorial—she's not dead, and I'm determined to keep it that way."

I move to the second armchair and settle into it. "How long has this been going on?"

"Four weeks," he says. "That's when I got the first letter. It told me to appoint Kimela as *ashoki* upon my coronation, and to follow her advice to the court."

"Or else?" I ask.

"Or else they kill Tamsin."

"And you're sure they truly have her?"

"Yes," he says. He fishes in his pocket and withdraws a small chain hung with a few keys and one other item—a gold bracelet, set with amber cabochons. "They sent her *si-oque* back with the first letter."

"You're sure this is hers? They didn't forge one?"

"No." He turns it over. Next to the clasp, incongruous among the intricate gold and gleaming amber, are three scratched glass beads, similar to the common ones I saw on Mistress Fala's bracelet—one green, one light blue, and one yellow. "Tamsin was granted the right to a *si* by my father, but rather than adopt a new one, she kept the childhood color her parents gave her. A jeweler might forge the amber, but they could never exactly replicate the glass chips common folk wear." He closes his fingers protectively over the bracelet. "And besides that, her signature is on all the letters."

"May I see the first one?" I ask.

"No," he says, looking up at me. His voice is hard. "It's gone."

"You destroyed it?"

"No, it's *gone*. Someone took it. I receive the letters, and I have them for perhaps a day, and then they disappear. Some-one takes them away. I thought I misplaced the first one, and I searched for hours. Then the second one disappeared out of my bedside drawer overnight. The third I hid." He gestures to an elegant quiver on the wall, one of several, with sleek embroidery and a full fleet of blue-and-black fletched arrows. "It stayed there for three days, and then it disappeared. Someone comes in and takes them from my room. My servants have no idea who." His face is white as a birch. "But not this time. I'm going to sit up. I'm going to wait all night with it in my hand and my sword in the other." He reaches into his silk jacket and pulls out an envelope, creased in his tight grip.

"That's the most recent one?"

He nods stoically. "It came during *Bakkonso*."

I recall the note he was reading just before I approached him—no wonder he lost it when I prodded him. "May I see?"

He considers for a moment, and then hands it to me. His name is written on the cover in a rough, blocky hand. A water spot has blurred the last few letters. I pull out the parchment. It's stained, with just two lines in that same hand.

The appointment of an ashoki *cannot be undone.*
See it through.

And below it, in a different hand, perhaps a bit uneven—
Tamsin Moropai

The *M* of her last name is scrabbled with a spiky flourish, as if her hand had shaken while writing it.

As if, maybe, she was in pain.

"You're sure this is her handwriting?" I say, looking up at him. "They're not forging her name?"

"Yes. No . . . I don't . . ." He palms his eyes again. "Does it matter? Would I take that risk?"

He seems to be asking himself rather than me. The fire pops

in the grate, the dancing flames reflecting off the gold pin in his knot of hair, on the lapis in his heirloom *si-oque*, on the amber of Tamsin's bracelet he's still worrying in his fingers.

"Is she more than just a friend?" I ask.

He's silent, his eyes still covered by his hand.

"I've been a fool," he says.

I look at the letter again, and then back to him.

"Iano. May I speak in Eastern? I need to make sure I have things perfectly straight."

"*Rä*," comes his cracked reply, his Eastern consonant perfectly rolled.

"*Et'ûli*," I thank him. "Tell me if I've gotten things wrong. This woman Tamsin was the previous *ashoki*, a truth teller of significant skill."

"Yes."

"And you fell in love with her—when?"

He sighs and drops his hand, his gaze on the ceiling. "Two years ago. When I first heard her sing at Sun and Rain, just before she came to the palace to be appointed *ashoki*. But I kept it quiet, because she was so . . . she made me so . . . *kuas* . . ." He swears and rubs his face, mussing his hair. "The previous *ashoki*, the one I'd grown up listening to, sang songs about a powerful Moquoia, a champion of industry, being the greatest nation of the ocean west. My grandmother appointed him before I was born. Then she died, and then several years later the *ashoki* died as well, so my father appointed Tamsin. And she sang . . . things I had never heard."

"About the slave trade?"

"Later, yes. The first year her message was more general. Things like the dangers of blinding ourselves with our perceived success, of lying to ourselves, of reveling in our own propaganda. I'd never heard such things. It was like . . ." He passes a hand over his face, mimicking a veil being lifted.

"How did the court take that?" I ask.

"Some, very well. People who deal with businesses in Tolukum, who trade with antislave countries, who provide assistance to the poor in our country, who fund orphanages, shelters—they felt Tamsin was finally speaking a truth the last *ashoki* had always left out. But others, of course, especially those whose industry relies on bond servants . . ." Minister Kobok flashes through my mind. "She started making enemies in court. Every *ashoki* has them, of course, but hers started becoming more vocal. I was reluctant to confess my feelings because I didn't want to—you have a phrase, I think. *Sink the boat?*"

"Rock the boat," I offer, nodding. "When did things change between you and Tamsin?"

"Perhaps a year ago, during *Kualni An-Orra*. Folk were rushing to the terraces to see the rainbow, everyone murmuring the Prayer of the Colors. And I was doing the same, standing at the rail, and then it struck me that the person next to me wasn't. And I turned and it was her." He tilts the amber *si-oque*, gazing at the light flickering on its gems. "She was looking up at the sky, and she smiled and said, 'Funny, how we break it down into twelve parts. It's so very like people to simplify, when instead the truth is a . . .' Forgive me, I can't recall the word. *Opohko*—when all the colors run together, with no breaks between?"

"A spectrum," I suggest.

"Yes, spectrum. And I said, '*Uah*, yes, I feel the same, how simplistic we make it,' and we started talking. And I found she was not nearly so frightening as I'd made her out to be. Brilliant, *uah*, and so sure, but friendly and casual, too."

"And things took off?" I say.

"Things . . . took . . ."

I adjust my wording. "You developed a relationship."

"Well, yes—accidentally. *Ikuah*." He stumbles for words in Eastern. "We kept it quiet, or at least, we thought we did. We were so careful, I still don't understand how . . . how someone found out." He rubs his eyes with vigor. "It's not customary, you see, for an *ashoki* and a monarch to fall in love. Many *ashoki* choose not to marry, to avoid forging one-sided alliances. Certainly no king or queen has ever married their *ashoki*. It's not illegal, just . . . not wise. Too much potential for bias. We knew there would be an uproar in court, so we agreed to proceed slowly, with care, letting things unfold for a few years, before we made any big decisions. We treated each other as casual acquaintances in public, we kept all our correspondences hidden . . . the only times we were alone was during weekly policy meetings, when she helped me write the letters to Princess Eloise."

"Could someone have observed you during those?" I ask.

His ears redden, and I expect my guess was correct—that more went on during those policy meetings than simply drafting a few letters.

"I don't see how," he says firmly. "I meet with all kinds of people privately, and we were no more or less secretive when scheduling them. I don't see why someone might suspect we were up to anything extraordinary." He shakes his head. "But it doesn't matter how we . . . let the weasel out of the box, or however that saying goes. The point is, someone found out—someone who feared Tamsin's influence on me. Which is why I don't know who to trust—it could be anyone, it could be *every-one*. If I appeal to the wrong person for help, or if I confront the wrong person, they could very well turn around and tell whoever's keeping her to murder her, and I can't . . . I can't *do anything*, can't find . . . *ekho*, see . . ."

He's losing his grip on Eastern again, but the frustration in his voice makes it clear. His fingers have strayed unconsciously to the hilt of his rapier on the end table, as if wishing he could introduce it to his secret enemy.

I spread my hands on my knees and switch back into Moquoian. "I'm sorry to hear all this, Iano, really I am—and I'm sorry that it's created such a fiasco for you. But *I* don't have anything to do with it, and neither does the ambassador or the princess. Which is why I want to set a few things right before we leave."

He picks his head up from the back of the chair. "Leave? Why are you leaving?"

"Well, a variety of reasons, one of which is our negative progress in the negotiations for the Ferinno Road. But the other is that Princess Eloise is sick—she's come down with rainshed fever."

"Oh," he says, startled. "I'm sorry to hear that." And he sounds sincere. "Can she not recover here? My personal physician is highly qualified."

"It's complicated," I say. "Rou would rather get her back east, to be closer to her mother, and I don't blame him. He's . . . protective of her." I'm not sure whether to get into the case of Moira Alastaire at the moment—there are so many other moving parts to this. "Besides that, I have my suspicions that someone deliberately exposed her to the fever. One of her windowpanes was removed, and a bowl of water left on the sill to breed mosquitoes. I think your enemy in court is against us, as well."

His eyes widen in shock, and then his gaze drifts to the fire, his fingers clenched on the arms of his chair. "I'm sorry that my court has put her at risk. I respect her a great deal—I wish these circumstances had been different. If it's any consolation, people often recover from rainshed fever the first time around."

"It's not a risk Eloise or Rou is willing to take—particularly not if it was deliberate," I say. "Both of them want to leave now, and I'm not going to try to stop them. But before we go, I just wanted you to understand that you don't need to home in on the Ferinno to search for Tamsin. We haven't got her. And sending soldiers over the border is only going to make things worse for you."

"I'm not sending them into the Ferinno because of you," he says, his eyebrows raised. "Or at least, not anymore. I admit I couldn't think what your motive might be for all this, but like I said, every clue I can find points to the desert. It's where the Sunshield Bandit attacked her stage, and it's where her letters are coming from."

"I'm not so sure the Sunshield Bandit—wait, how do you know it's where her letters are coming from?" My brow furrows. "I thought you didn't know who's sending them."

"I don't. But I can tell *where* they're coming from." He tilts the envelope toward the firelight and taps the writing—specifically on the water spot over his name. "Water-soluble ink, and paper, not parchment, made from some kind of reed—no one in Moquoia would use materials like this. Our ink is gum based, to withstand the rain, and our parchment is all sheep or goatskin."

He gropes for a random piece of correspondence on the side

table and hands it to me to compare. I take both it and the envelope, running my thumb over the parchment. Sure enough, the blackmail letter is noticeably more lightweight, with a rough grain, and the ink is thinner.

"I've compared it to a few other pieces of correspondence from the stage road in the Ferinno, including your letters," he says with determination. "The ink is the same, the paper is similar. The letters are coming from the desert. And that's not even considering the report that the Sunshield Bandit was the one to turn over her stage. If you're not behind it, then she must have a hand in it somehow." He clenches his fingers on his trousers. "She must have contacts in our court. Maybe even people in her pay. The servants seem to think so."

"Why?" I ask. "Why would she want this kind of leverage over you?"

"By the colors, I don't know—power, money. Control."

"But she's not harassing you for that kind of thing. She—or whoever—is focused on appointing Kimela to *ashoki*."

"So?"

"So—why would the Sunshield Bandit want Kimela to be *ashoki*, or care about the *ashoki* at all?"

He's quiet. Then, hurriedly, "There could be some motive we don't know about."

I shake my head. "I really don't think it was her."

"Why?" he asks. "Why are you so ready to believe in the virtue of a notorious outlaw?"

"I don't know that I'd call it *virtue*, but if my dates are correct, I think on the day she was allegedly turning over Tamsin's stage, she was actually robbing a different stage outside Snaketown."

He frowns. "Why? How do you know?"

"Fala told me Tamsin was attacked at the start of *Iksi*?"

"You seem very familiar with my servants," he says shortly.

"No one else was giving me any answers," I point out.

He sighs with some irritation. "I suppose. Yes, the attack was at the start of *Iksi*."

"Do you remember the exact day?"

"We got the news on the fifth. It happened three days before."

I reach into my tunic and pull out the letter Colm sent me a week and a half ago. "We traveled across the desert with one of my professors, Eloise's uncle. He had business to conduct in Pasul while we continued on to Tolukum. He broke camp for Snaketown on the first of *Iksi* and was attacked that day by the Sunshield Bandit." I tap the date written in his cramped hand. "Unless she's developed the ability to manifest out of the sun itself, I don't see how she could be outside Snaketown on the first and ninety miles away in Vittenta on the second."

He takes Colm's letter and scans it himself.

"What's this bit down here—who's Moira? Is this about that missing princess from way back when?"

"No—well, sort of, but not at the moment." By the Light, this is getting complicated—fake murders and desert hostages and long-lost princesses. "What's more important is that the story about the attack on Tamsin's stage was deliberately false."

"That doesn't tell me anything—I already know I'm being misled."

"*But not by the Sunshield Bandit.* You're looking for someone to trust. You're also looking for someone being held captive, by all evidence in the Ferinno." I circle my hands, trying to stir up his comprehension, to guide him to the same lightning strike

I had at Eloise's window a few hours earlier. "Who better to find an antislavery prisoner in the desert than someone who deliberately roots out slavers?"

He stares at me a moment, and then he throws his head back and gives the first laugh I've heard out of him in five weeks. "So far in your stay you have struck me as a little perplexed, a little overeager, but not a joker."

"I'm not joking," I say, my cheeks reddening. "I'm serious. If Tamsin comes back before your coronation, she can resume her post as *ashoki*. You won't have to appoint Kimela."

"I've already made the announcement," he says, gesturing to the blackmail letter.

"But *ashoki* is a lifelong position, isn't it? If Tamsin's still alive, then she's still the *ashoki*, isn't she? You wouldn't be able to appoint Kimela—there's no vacancy to fill."

He stares. "Yes, I suppose . . . you're correct. I've been so worried about finding her that I haven't considered that she negates a new *ashoki*." He brightens considerably, but the expression is instantly replaced by dismay. "Which is why I need to find her before my coronation—they'll keep her alive until then, but once Kimela is appointed, they won't want there to be anything that might undo her position."

I nod. "You need to find her as quickly as possible. If you can do that, and pinpoint who's threatening you, then we avoid war, and we can begin diplomacy again, which means there's a real chance we can stamp out the slave trade—if Tamsin's as set against trafficking as you say she is."

"She is," he says firmly. "She was *dokkua-ti* into working for slavers after her mother died, to copy manifestos and sale papers for them."

"Sorry—she was what? I don't know that word."

"She was . . . recruit . . . er, f-forced? *Uah*, forced. Into a bond."

"She was captured?" I nearly squawk. "She was a slave?"

"She was a bond-servant. It's different. Many people work for bonds, there are some in the palace . . ."

"*It's still . . .*"

He tosses up his hands defensively. "Slavery, I know. I understand. Tamsin helped me realize that. I don't pretend to justify it to you, though it is a more complex system than I think your Eastern courts comprehend. There are many who would not be able to survive without the room and board provided on bond."

"I expect most of them would prefer a livable wage," I say flatly.

He sighs. "Yes. I am aware. And I was working on it. We both were—like I said, Tamsin helped draft all my letters to you. She had the ideas about leasing the quarries, about partnering with Alcoran engineers to mechanize part of the process to cut down the need for human labor. She's—she's incredible, she has such a sense on economy and society and how the two intersect . . . how to sway people, how to communicate . . . it made her an astonishing *ashoki*. It will be a difficult transition—expensive, possibly recessive, and heavily opposed by many influential people in court. But I was so sure, with her at my side . . ."

"Well, that only proves my point about the Sunshield Bandit," I say, trying to steer him back to my earlier thought. "Getting Tamsin back could be *extremely* enticing to her—dismantling the slave trade means no more need to pursue slave wagons."

His eyebrows knit, and I suspect he's suppressing an eye roll. "I think you overestimate her sense of goodwill."

"Well, we'll probably have to offer a reward, too," I acknowledge. "But she's stealing shoes and pocket change—I think we could come up with a sum she'd be willing to accept."

He spreads his hands, half slouched in his chair with one boot up on the cushion. "And how exactly do I pitch this idea to her? Ride out into the desert and hope she attacks me?"

I fidget a moment, silent.

"Oh, colored Light," he says in realization. "That's exactly your plan, isn't it? Veran, she *set fire to a stage* a few days ago."

"She set fire to a slave wagon, not a stage, and the report said there were multiple patches of blood in the sand," I point out. "There was probably some kind of struggle. I don't think she would have attacked the wagon just to torch everyone inside. Something probably went wrong."

He groans and rubs his eyes. "None of this is making it sound any more sensible. She's a notorious outlaw, and an enigma. And anyway—not to sound conceited, but I am a rather important member of court. I'm the only direct heir—should I die, I leave a vacuum. That won't help either of our causes in the least—I'm just as likely to be replaced by a pro-slavery minister."

I ponder a moment, staring at the fire, making mental calculations, guesses, estimations, stretches of imagination.

"I'll go, then," I say.

He arches a sculpted eyebrow. "I thought you were leaving."

"We are—rather conveniently for Pasul." My heart quickens in my chest, blurry details coming together. "I could leave tonight. I'll move fast on horseback, much faster than the coaches. And I won't have to make scheduled stops like they will. I'll camp along the road. It'll take a week for a coach to reach Pasul, but I can make it in half that. I can charter a stage to take me into the desert and draw the Sunshield Bandit's attention. I'll get the information from her, and then, if I'm lucky, I might even be back in Pasul by the time the ambassador and Princess Eloise get there."

Rou will be *livid*.

Iano is staring at me as if I'm in the process of sprouting another head.

"What would the princess think of this?" he asks.

"She'd understand," I lie, my gut twinging. She'll be angry with me, too, but it's a price I'm going to have to pay, and grovel later. Iano's inscrutable gaze remains locked on mine, and I silently pray that he won't ask about Rou. I don't think I can lie that big.

"Why?" he finally asks. "You've given me firm evidence you're not behind the blackmail—why stay tangled up in this?"

"I want to end the slave trade."

He narrows his eyes at me. "That's not why. Or, at least, that's not the main reason."

I swallow. "I . . . listen, this trip, this alliance—this is the first real thing I've ever been trusted with. You know about my parents?"

"King and queen of the Silverwood Mountains?" he asks. "Didn't your mother reinstate Queen Mona Alastaire to the throne of Lumen Lake and facilitate the Eastern Alliance?"

"More or less. My father had nearly as much a role as she did, and my siblings sort of inherited their tendency toward greatness. Of the five of us, I'm the only one who hasn't done anything remotely noteworthy."

"You're eighteen," he says sagely, as if he's not merely a year older than me.

"My little sister is fifteen, and she's already considered one of the greatest dancers the Silverwood has ever seen," I say. "And my brother is nineteen and nearly ready to be a Wood-walker. My older sisters are no different. It's not so much that I want a victory to call my own, it's that I *don't want a colossal failure*. This trip, being here, alongside Rou and Eloise, who have their own status—this has been my first real chance to actually *do* something. My parents weren't keen on me coming. I worked my ass off at the university to make sure I had the highest marks in Moquoian that anyone in the East has ever had." My hands fall open in my lap. "I can't just walk away, knowing what I know, and leave things to only get worse. It could be years before another diplomatic trip can be arranged. I *know* we can make this work, if we can only straighten out what's gone wrong."

"And you're obsessed with the Sunshield Bandit," he says wryly. "Aren't you?"

"I'm not obsessed. But—she does fascinate me. The fact that she's made herself into a . . . a . . ."

"Terror of the desert," he supplies.

"Or queen of the desert, if you will. I really do think she can help us. But—and maybe I'm deranged—but I also just want to see her myself, to see if all the tales are true. And if they're *not* true, then I want to know how she's managed to build and keep such a name for herself." I shrug. "You said it yourself—she's an enigma, powerful and heroic and free as a breeze. That doesn't make you curious?"

"Not in a way that makes me want to put myself at the

mercy of her sword," he says. "But it would be *very* nice to start stripping away some of the pedestal she's on, especially if she helps us in the process."

That's not exactly what I have in mind, but I nod to keep him going. "I think it's worth a try."

"*I* think it's crazy, but you're the one taking the biggest risk, not me. How are you planning to relay your information to me after you return to Pasul?"

This obvious oversight trips me up. "I suppose . . . I'll have to send a message. Is there someone you trust to station in Pasul until I get back?"

He snorts. "With cloaked figures and secret letters being stolen from my rooms? No." His foot drops from the chair cushion. "I'll come with you."

As if on cue, a crackle of lightning flashes outside the window, streaking the far wall with rain shadows.

"You just said it was too dangerous for you to leave," I say.

"I said it was too dangerous for me to ride out alone into the desert to confront a bloodthirsty outlaw," he replies. "The horse track to Pasul is different. It's lightly used, and what little highway robbery we have generally stays on the coach roads. I'll come with you to Pasul and make inquiries while you're gone."

"Er," I begin. "Are you sure? I'm going to be sleeping on the ground. Outside."

"I'm aware, Prince Veran," he says flatly. "And I'll thank you that I am quite a robust camper." He pauses. "Granted, it's always been with the pavilion during hunting season up in the hills, but that's beside the point. I don't pretend it will be pleasant, but that is not why I am going. What's your people's expression? *An open sky makes trials small*?"

That's an Alcoran expression, but I won't contest it. "If you're sure. I can still try to secure a messenger in Pasul . . ."

"No," he says, and there's a definite hardness in his voice now. "This idea may be crazy, but it's the first hope I've had since Tamsin was attacked. The fewer people who know about it, the fewer chances it may go astray." His sharp black gaze narrows at me. "This isn't politics or curiosity to me, Veran. This is about getting Tamsin back. Her life is at stake, along with this country's throne. You understand that, don't you?"

I nod vigorously. "*Uah*, of course."

"Good." He stands from his chair. "Let me change into traveling clothes and pack a few things, and then we can go. We'll tell the guards we're having an argument about racehorses as we go to the stables—it should hold for a few hours."

By the Light, this is moving fast. There will be no time to relay our hasty plan to Eloise or leave a note begging forgiveness from Rou.

Priorities, I remind myself. If we can keep the alliance from collapsing, there will be plenty of time to plead my case later. And perhaps, if we're successful, I might not need to grovel at all. I get a vision of Rou clapping me on the shoulder, of Eloise smiling at me, of letters sent back home with accounts of my heroics. My stomach warms, and I struggle to keep my expression grim to match the look on Iano's face.

He doesn't see my internal battle. He picks up his rapier. "What's your weapon, by the way?"

It strikes me that *wit* is the incorrect response. "Um, I'm decent at targets, though I've never shot a crossbow."

He heads to his wall of quivers, and too late I notice the dart board off to one side. Vynce has one like it on the wall of his room, and he's driven the staff to the edge of sanity with the collection of pinholes from missed targets. On Iano's, there are no holes in the wall, only six darts clustered near the center of the board, just random enough to suggest they were thrown into that arrangement, not shoved in purposefully.

Iano takes down a bow longer than I am tall, running his fingers along the bone-white limbs.

"Er," I begin, trying to head him off before he asks me to draw it. "But I'm not good enough to waste a longbow on. I'm used to flatbows. And anyway, I don't think meeting the Sunshield Bandit heavily armed is the best strategy. We still don't know how many outlaws she has in her camp, and if I look ready for a fight . . ." *She'll probably fight me.*

"Well, *I'm* not traveling the back roads to Pasul after dark without arms," he says flatly, removing the elegant quiver with the blue-fletched arrows. He rummages in a trunk and emerges with a few coils of bowstring, a box that rattles with arrowheads, and a *bintu* hunting knife with its characteristic curve. He checks the edge on the knife, sheaths it, and tosses it to me. I catch it awkwardly.

"Now you've got something, at least." He removes a leather satchel from the trunk. "Here's another consideration, though. Assuming the Sunshield Bandit cooperates and *does* attack you outside Pasul, what if she doesn't stay to listen? Most of our reports say she strikes fast. What if she runs off before you can convince her to help?"

I worry my lip, pretending to test the heft and handling of the knife to buy myself time. The metal gleams coldly, turning the reflected firelight pale.

My head shoots up.

"Oh . . . I have an idea," I say in a rush. "The beginning of an idea, at least. Can we make a side trip before going to the stables?"

"If it's quick."

"I think it will be." I sheathe the knife with a snap. "She uses the sun as a weapon, but we can go after her *with the night*."

Iano *tsks* as he heads toward his bedroom door.

"There's no need to get dramatic," he says over his shoulder.

But I think, with how fast this is all going, dramatic is the only way this is going to work.

TAMSIN

H
I
R
E
S

VERAN

Iano proves to be a more stalwart travel companion than I would have thought. Our first twenty-four hours of travel are defined largely by being utterly, penetratingly soaked. The rain does not so much fall as simply envelop us, above, around, below, and soon inside as well. Despite my heavy felted cloak, within a half hour even my undergarments are soaked, making my seat squelch in the saddle with every rise of my horse's shoulders.

The few times I steal a glance at Iano, his face is set and grim. He's traded his jeweled hairpin for a kind of gallant horsetail under a black hood, festooned with a golden tassel. Between that, his expensively styled tack, and the graceful longbow and quiver slung over his back, we're clearly marked as some flavor of nobility, but I'm hoping we can pass for merely well-to-do travelers and not two princes off on a highly inadvisable mission.

Our first night of camping finds us in a small clearing off the road, huddled under a questionably rigged tarpaulin. The rain streams through the canopy, collecting in the center of the tarp and making it sag until a steady trickle pours between us and puddles on the ground.

Iano doesn't comment at our miserable shelter, but it's eating away at me. Woodcraft has been a staple of my life since before my first breath, but I'm realizing too late it's not exactly hereditary. I've heard enough of Mama's tales to repeat them in my sleep, and I've read the collection of Woodwalker handbooks more than the average Woodwalker, but there can be no denying that I'm severely lacking in hands-on experience. Climbing trees and knowing birdcalls is one thing, but it's another thing entirely to stand holding a rope, befuddled by cold and stiff fingers, trying to recall which knot is used to lash together a bivouac. Is it a slipknot, and if so, which one? Is it an eight on a bight? For that matter, how does one tie an eight on a bight without a manual?

As I'm gnawing on these intricacies, Iano gives a little start and slaps his neck. He pulls his hand away to reveal a crushed mosquito. When we first left the palace, he produced a jar of oily cream that smelled of lemon balm, but a few intrepid insects haven't been deterred by it.

"How soon does rainshed fever develop after you've been bitten?" I ask.

Iano grimaces and wipes his palm on his cloak. "A few days, usually, but we've gotten a fair distance away from Tolukum—the danger of fever diminishes in the outer hamlets. Nobody really knows why."

Perhaps it's the recent series of events that does it—the dead birds on the ground, Eloise's sickness, the mosquitoes in the window—but the answer strikes me like a lightning bolt. That same curiosity Eloise and I mused over not long ago now seems plain as day. I twist to face him.

"How long have those giant windows been up in the palace?"

"The atriums?" He scratches his new bug bite. "The first went up during my great-grandmother's reign, perhaps seventy, seventy-five years ago. That was when our factories first started producing sheet glass. The next few were added a decade or so later, and then the biggest was completed about fifteen years ago."

"And there's been a rise in rainshed fever since then?"

"Only around Tolukum," he says.

"Right. Iano—has anyone noticed how many birds strike the glass of the palace?"

His face creases with confusion. "Well, that's unavoidable, I suppose. One does hear them occasionally—"

"Not occasionally," I say. "*All the time.* All day long, every day. Do you know how many dead birds I saw along the palace foundation?"

"What were you doing at the foundation?"

"Wallowing in despair, thanks to our interaction at *Bakkonso*. There were *dozens*, Iano, just in that little section, and I'm sure there are more all over the terraces and windowsills."

"Well, what of it?" he asks. "That's the responsibility of the staff—to clean up refuse like that. What does it have to do with rainshed fever?"

Something very Silvern is waking up inside me, and ethnocentric bias be damned, I *know* my folk would have made this connection before now. "Those songbirds *eat mosquitoes*, Iano. As you've put up more and more glass in the city, you're killing off more and more birds. Fewer birds means more mosquitoes, which means higher chances of a person being bitten by one that's infected. That's why it's only in the city, not the villages. It's your *glass*, Iano."

He stops scratching, his gaze going unfocused. He stares blankly at the trickle of water streaming from our drooping tarpaulin.

"That seems . . ." he begins. "I mean, how can we really know for sure?"

"I know that killing off a single type of animal in those numbers is going to tip nature's balance," I reply. "That's something my folk would never overlook."

A flicker of disdain crosses his face. "Well, we can't all be *your folk*," he snaps, mimicking my antiquated phrase. "And I'll have you know Moquoia has its own foresters, not so different from your fabled Woodwalkers." He pauses, thoughtful, while I hold back the biggest scoff of my life.

"Though," he adds after a moment, "I'll mention it to the staff when we get back to Tolukum. Perhaps they'll have a more definite estimate of how many birds they collect."

"You should cover the glass," I say. "Or at least string mirrors inside."

"That will be a difficult expense to justify."

"Even if it brings down the cases of rainshed fever?"

He gives me a resigned look. "If," he says. "That's a very big if."

We lapse into silence for the remainder of the evening, listening to the shifting timbre of the rain on our tarp. There's little opportunity for sleep, wet and uncomfortable as we are, and the night passes agonizingly slowly. When the first gray slips of light start to show through the trees, we get up without comment. We share some soggy walnut bread, I roll up our sodden tarp, and then we mount and continue on.

Fortunately—blessedly—we travel as quickly as I'd hoped.

The coach road, by necessity, runs parallel to the coastline below the western spine of the mountains, forced to make a few lengthy detours over bridges stout enough to support heavy loads. Our track, however, splits from the main road early on our second day and takes a more direct line toward Pasul, leading us up and down steep valley sides carpeted with growth so thick you could burrow inside it. Gnarled hardwoods arch over the track, their green-hung boughs made monstrous with ferns and mosses. In the late afternoon, after a long, slippery climb over a misty ridgeline, we cross a tangible border—the fir and hemlock trees transition into aspen and ponderosa pine, the lush moss gives way to tougher lichens, and the skies ease from moody gray to hazy blue.

We've reached the rainshadow.

It's bitterly cold, especially since we've hardly had a chance to dry out before night falls, and there's a confident wind gusting over the ridgeline. In the last slips of daylight, we set up a hasty camp in a stand of boulders that act as a windbreak. There are no sturdy trees to lash up the tarp, but given how well that went the first night, I put my effort instead into collecting splintery lengths of tough mountain juniper for a fire. Fortunately, my firelighting skills are something I could always easily work on from Lampyrinae, and soon Iano and I huddle into our damp bedrolls on either side of a steady blaze.

I'm tired enough from forty-eight hours of hard travel and no sleep that I don't wake at all to stoke the fire, and by morning it's stone cold. Puffing and chilled through, limbs aching, we slap ourselves, stomp our frozen feet, and clumsily pack up camp. Our horses watch, their breath misting around their noses, probably amused at our pitiful attempts to warm up before we fling ourselves into their saddles and urge them downhill, toward warmer air.

The one bad thing about this route, I muse as we start to thaw out, is that we're missing the redwoods. The groves of giants are all on the western slopes, south of Tolukum, where the soil is sea-breeze damp but not drenched. But it's clear as we descend the eastern slopes of the Moquovik Mountains that the soil is now too dry and nutrient-poor to support such mammoth plant life, devoid of the fertile foothills fed by constant rainfall on the other side of the ridge. Our way is instead buffeted by pine, ash, and a heinous amount of scrub oak, choking the path and scratching our calves as our horses push through it.

"Amazing that the landscape can be so different after just a few hours of riding," I say to Iano around midmorning. "Too bad we have to rush through it."

"We're not here to admire the scenery," he says grimly.

I shut up for the rest of the morning.

By afternoon, the last of the moisture finally wicks away from my clothes, just in time for the sun to gain its full fever pitch. My absent-minded observation from earlier becomes a serious consternation. I drag my rolled-up sleeve over my forehead, marveling that in twenty-four hours I've gone from feeling like I'd never be warm and dry again to sweating out all the rain Moquoia has to offer.

Our third night's camp is the easiest, with only a few requisite discomforts, and after another long morning of riding, we crest the head of a drop-off to see the border town of Pasul below. The land changes dramatically before us, the dimpled hills giving way to sagebrush flats as suddenly as if someone had taken a giant rolling pin right up to our feet, leaving us perched on a rocky cliff. This is the final hindrance to a sturdy coach road—even if a coach managed to get this far, over and through the steep, tangled slopes, it could never manage the switchbacking trail down the final incline to the flats below. We take it slowly, our horses patiently plodding around each tight turn, bringing us finally into town as the sun drops behind the cliff at our backs.

Pasul is a place that seemingly can't decide what it wants to be, waffling between a rural outpost and bustling city. It's too far out to support any industry beyond the mail line and quarry camps, but it's the only bit of civilization for miles, and full of transients—ranchers bringing cattle to market, homesteaders laying in supplies, free quarriers on leave, and the odd businessperson cleaving carefully to the small reputable quarter. The main street is wide and well-kept, flanked by inns and public houses, but the alleys that lead off it are narrow and dark, with signs for less luxurious accommodations for the short on change—work-for-rent, copper hangs, and the ominous ROOF COTS—TETHER INCLUDED.

Iano and I make our way past the less savory alleys and head for the Sweet Pine, where Rou and Eloise and I stayed with Colm upon our arrival. It's a grand little building, a clear mashup of Moquoian design and Alcoran building material—rounded walls of white adobe and red tile, with generous windows throughout, though the glass is made of small cut panes, not the endless panels of Tolukum Palace. There's a clean public room below, mostly filled with well-to-do travelers and business folk. The girl at the bar asks for our names.

Partway through giving my name, I decide to lie. "V-vvvynce," I stammer unconvincingly, my brother being the first

V that pops to mind, though I suppose I could have gone with my father. "Vyncet Whitetail. And—" I glance at Iano.

"Escer Gee," he says.

It must be glaringly obvious that we're lying, but she writes them down anyway, making me spell out my foreign vowels. Most folk in town speak at least a little of both Eastern and Moquoian, but the Silverwood is a long way off, and nobody in Alcoro takes epithets like we do. She hands us a key and directs us to the second floor.

The room is small and neat, with two narrow rope beds and a potted agave plant in the window. I want to fling my bruised, achy body onto the mattress and sleep for a day, but we both have things to do if I'm going to ride out into the desert tomorrow morning. We deposit our bags and head back out—he to inquire about a coach and driver willing to travel alone into bandit country, me to clean out the town's general store of its nonperishable goods.

Before the sun rises the following morning, Iano helps me get dressed in the fanciest Moquoian ensemble I've been gifted. It's a rather offensive shade of raspberry, with long tails on the jacket and cabochon buttons the size of my thumbnail along the calves. I suck in my stomach as I fight to fasten the jacket over the waistcoat.

"I must admit," I say breathlessly as Iano fruitlessly twists my hair into something that will hold a pin, "I find your clothing very restrictive."

"You walk too loosely," he says, tugging at my scalp, as if it might make my hair grow. "You walk like you have saplings for legs. The silk is meant to allow the wearer to walk gracefully with minimal effort—it creates the posture for you." He stabs the pin through the knot he's managed to fuss up and stands back, looking unsatisfied. "It looks a bit like a toddler got into his father's jewelry box."

"Well, let's hope the Sunshield Bandit isn't up on her court hairstyles." I pick up the walking cane. "Can you carry the box? I'm going to have a hard enough time getting down the stairs in one piece."

He hefts the crate of our supplies. "Don't roll your feet like that."

"Like what?"

"That way you arch your feet around—I'm surprised you haven't broken an ankle."

"That's the way I was taught to walk," I say snippily. "It lets you walk quietly."

"Maybe in buckskin boots, but not wooden heels. Anyway, who are you trying to sneak up on? Try kick walking instead." He demonstrates as he walks to the door, jutting out a foot before laying it down. "*Kick walk, kick walk.*" He heads through the door with the heavy crate, loud as a rockslide and perfectly balanced.

I grumble about namby Moquoians and how they wouldn't last an hour on a scout march, ignoring Colm hissing about bias and my mother laughing that *I've* never been on a scout march, before following him out the door, kicking my heels upward and laying them down straight.

It does seem to lessen the likelihood of ankle-breaking.

That only pisses me off more.

The driver is waiting in front of her thoroughbrace coach,

the luxe private kind afforded by wealthy business folk. There are several seats for armed guards along the driver's bench and roof, but they're all empty. The two horses up front stamp in their expensive leather braces. The horse I borrowed from Iano, a sleek palomino mare named Kuree—the Moquoian word for flax—is hitched alongside, gleaming in the first brush of dawn.

"Is that for the lockbox?" the driver asks, nodding at the crate in Iano's hands. "You know I won't be responsible for the loss of anything you're bringing along?"

"We're aware," Iano says, handing her the crate. "You deposited the payment?"

She nods. She'd demanded full payment up front, along with a written statement saying we'd pay for any damages to her coach and team—which were almost certain to occur traveling into the rough territory of a notorious bandit, unarmed and well-furnished.

Suddenly, the reality of our plan hits harder. I swallow and finger my firefly pin—I considered leaving it behind, but it's giving me courage, and I've hidden it under the knot of my cravat. Unless the Sunshield Bandit strips me of my clothes, she won't find it.

I don't *think* she'll strip me of my clothes.

Iano wrestles the crate into the lockbox under the interior seat and tacks the fabric back down to hide the door. He steps back and turns to me, and suddenly it's time.

He's grave. "Veran—thank you."

"Sure, anytime."

"No, I'm serious. This could change everything. And listen, I'll make inquiries around here, all right? Maybe someone will have a lead on Tamsin. So if things don't go as planned, don't feel like you have to stay out there. Just come back, and we'll figure something else out. All right?"

I'm jittery, to the point where I want to make a joke to defuse the tension—Mama's influence. *What could possibly go wrong?* But I can tell from his expression this won't go over well.

"I'll be smart about it," I assure him.

"All right." He puffs out his breath. He hands me a drawstring bag, heavy with coin. "Good luck." He opens up a palm and holds it out to me, as if he's offering something. This baffles me at first, before I realize he's trying to mimic my folk's gesture of thanks.

"And you." I mirror the motion. There's a white smudge on my thumb from the drawstring bag.

He steps back, and I clamber awkwardly into the coach, settling onto the velvet cushion. The driver climbs up into her box and clucks to her team. They amble forward, and the carriage swings on its leather bracings. Kuree breaks into a walk on her lead alongside us.

I look back through the window at Iano, but he's lost to the cloud of dust behind us. A needle of red sunlight pierces my eye—dawn is breaking across the rugged flats. I settle back against the cushion, my stomach rocking with the carriage, as we ride toward the sun.

TAMSIN

I started my period this morning!

Honestly, this relieves me. My body's been in such pain and I've been actively ignoring so much trauma that I wouldn't have been surprised if my womb simply resigned in protest. But I felt the first pangs of cramping a few days ago—a welcome, familiar pain amid the worse, squishy pain, and today's the big day.

Of course, I have no bandages and am bleeding all over my trousers, blanket, and reed mat. I sit for a moment upon waking up, simultaneously relieved at the revelation that my body hasn't fully quit on me and fretting about the sticky mess things will be before long. I get to my feet and wobble to the cell door. I close my fist and pound on the wood, shouting through the barred window.

After a few moments of this, I hear swearing down the hall. A lantern flares. Someone stumbles in the dim dawn light.

"What the blazing sun is your problem?" Poia demands through the window. Her eyepatch is off, revealing the milky white of her blind eye. "I swear by the colors if you don't shut up . . ."

Her words die away as she sees my state. My lips twitch at her renewed swearing, and she marches away, taking the lantern with her. She comes back a moment later with a bucket—a new bucket, hello bucket!—filled with cold water, and a rag. She hands me a length of bandages and a clean—cleanish, anyway—set of clothes.

Now would be a good time to sling my waste bucket at her face and run for the open door. But I'm unsure how fast I could move, and I have no idea where I am except not Moquoia, and I imagine I now smell like a sweat-salted steak, grilled bloody rare. I'd be tracked by every predator on the continent. I focus instead on stripping off my clothes while she kneels down and begins scrubbing my mat, cursing. I resist the urge to laugh. Not my fault she didn't give due thought to my menses.

I arrange my new wardrobe—the same as the first, a colorless, shapeless shirt over similar trousers, belted with a bit of twine—and arrange the bandages in my underthings. Poia dunks her rag back in the bucket and wrings it out. She glances up at me and, seeing I'm dressed, suddenly remembers there's a door to the outside world. She checks over her shoulder.

And sees my handiwork on the wood.

HIRES.

I've been carving it a little deeper every day. It's quite distinct, thrown into sharp relief by the angle of the dawn light coming in through the tiny window.

"Damn," I go to say, but it doesn't come out right.

Poia rises on her knees and gets to her feet. I don't have time to duck. With the force of two carriages colliding, she wallops the side of my mouth with the back of her hand. The pain is astounding, bursting into blooms of color behind my eyelids. I drop like a blown-down tree, clutching my exploding head in my arms. She's shouting down at me, but I can't make out her words. I feel a cold shock of water—she empties the wash bucket on me before dropping it next to my head. The water has that faint tang of copper, or maybe it's the blood washing my mouth. Can't tell. Probably it's both.

I hear the cell door slam and the lock turn. I press my elbows against my head, as if physically containing the pain will make it better. Nausea turns my stomach. Great Light, don't vomit, not now, not in this state . . .

I lay curled on the wet dirt floor. After an agonizingly long time, the pounding pain begins to subside, slowly, stubbornly. The colors pulsing behind my eyes fade in intensity, flaming with each heartbeat. The nausea ebbs away. I let out a slow breath.

Carefully, tenderly, I shift my jaw a bit. Right, that hurts a lot, stop it. I loosen my grip on my head. I'm wet now, and so is my mat, and my blanket. I smell like blood. My uterus contracts in a cramp. I lie in the wet dirt. Damn everyone and everything.

At least now I have two buckets.

LARK

I poke morosely at the fire, banking a few of the coals to make them last longer. I sent Saiph and Andras down to the river a few hours ago with the ox to haul up some wood, and I'm actively trying not to wonder where they've gotten to. Sedge is cleaning a rat from one of the snares, as close to Rose's mat as he can work without sullying things with blood and guts. Lila is making a valiant attempt to piece together a few fraying burlap scraps into something big enough to be useful. Moll is napping on her blanket. I had Whit untangling knots from our length of twine, but she's fallen asleep too, her breath wheezing through her cleft lip. She's been sleeping a lot lately, her face pale and thin, her eyes red-rimmed and hooded. Absently I reach out and brush her black hair. It's lanky and dull, falling through my fingers like dry grass.

Rocks clatter from down the canyon. Rat lifts his head but doesn't growl—sure enough, through the sage comes Saiph, puffing from his fast pace.

"Lark," he says.

"What?" I ask. "Where's Andras?"

"He's coming with the ox. But there's something you might want to see, out across the river."

"What?"

"There's a coach," he says, fidgeting with his usual twitchy energy.

I sit back, tired. "I'm not going after a coach."

"It's not a stage," he says. "It's small, just two horses on the team, plus one tethered along the side, all tacked up fancy as a new copper."

"I'm not going after a coach," I repeat. "Who's going to help me turn it over?"

"Me and Sedge can," he says. "There are no guards."

I pause. "None at all?"

He shakes his head. "Just a driver."

"I have a hard time believing they're toting a spare horse with no guards," I say flatly. "Did you get a look inside?"

"I watched it for a while. I think there's just one passenger. They'd drive a little, and then stop, and he'd get out and look around. Then he'd get back in and they'd go a little farther."

"What's he looking for?" I ask.

"I dunno. A ford, maybe?"

"It sounds like they're prospecting," Sedge says. "Looking for mining sites. Maybe they're following that vein of ore along the river."

"Why the spare horse?" I ask.

"Probably to go up the side canyons," Lila says, her stitching in her lap. "So the passenger can ride into the places the coach can't go."

Something squeezes in my gut. A new mine means new hands. More wagons. It means new skin tattooed with a double circle. The scarred skin itches under my sleeve. I look back at Rose. Up the path comes the slow scrabble of the ox's hooves on the rocks.

"You're *sure* there are no guards?" I press Saiph. "Is the driver armed?"

"If they are, it's nothing special," he says excitedly. "Maybe a crossbow, but they'll have a time aiming it while driving, won't they?"

"What about the passenger?"

Saiph is practically bouncing, simmering with an energy that's more raw than before Pickle died. "I didn't see anything on him—and you should see how he's dressed. Head to toe in silk, pink like a berry, with tails and everything."

"Moquoian?"

"Dressed like one, though he looks awfully dark for one— almost as dark as you."

There's a range of skin color among Moquoians, so that's not a good indicator, but nobles of any nationality are few and far between out here. It sounds odd for a prospector to be so finely dressed, but Sedge is right—I can't think of another reason why a wealthy traveler would be ambling along this particular stretch of river, rather than racing to get to Snaketown. Either this passenger has been living with his head in the sand, or he's lost.

Maybe we can point him in the right direction.

Andras comes up the path, tugging on the ox's lead. Its broad back is loaded with firewood.

He looks between Saiph and me excitedly. "Well? Are you

going after it? They're heading closer, and there's still some time before the sun disappears."

I glance at Rose again, and then at Sedge.

We're down a horse, it's true, and the mule is still lame. A strong new horse, with tack and all, could mean a faster route to Pasul.

It could mean getting Rose to a healer. Could mean getting the ox to market for money to get Andras to Cyprien.

"How far?" I ask.

"Maybe a mile west, though we'll have to hurry if we want to ford upstream of them," Saiph says.

Not far at all. We could be back before it's truly dark.

"You can leave us," Lila says. "We'll be fine."

I puff out a breath, but if the coach is really as close as Saiph says, I don't even have to leave Three Lines alone for an hour.

"We'll at least go take a look. If it seems like something we can do between the three of us, maybe we'll give it a shot. But I'm not taking any risks, all right?" I squint at Saiph, trying to make him calm down. "If it looks too chancy, we're turning around."

"I can help," Andras says, mirroring Saiph's excitement. "I can ride behind Sedge—"

"No," I say, fighting another vision of Pickle's broken angles. "You stay here. Unpack the firewood. Help Lila mix something up to eat."

He looks put out, but he doesn't argue. I blow out the last of my breath and look again at Saiph. "Why don't you get Pickle's staff?"

Saiph gives more of a whoop than a reply. He scrambles toward the cache.

I drag a hand over my face and look at Sedge. "You can take the driver?"

He nods. "Let me refill on quarrels."

"All right. Saiph, you'll be responsible for cutting the horse loose." I sigh and beat the dust off my hat. "I'll take the carriage." I settle my hat on my head and pull my bandanna up. "Let's get this over with."

VERAN

I squint out over the sage flats, the Ferinno sun beating down so hard I can practically hear it sear my skin. Behind me, the horse team mouths their bits, snorting to moisten their nostrils.

"It's getting late," the driver calls behind me. "At this point it's going to be smarter to head for Snaketown for the night."

"We'll compensate you the extra night," I say, shading my eyes. I'm growing anxious—I'm certain we've been traveling slowly enough to be seen, but what if nobody's watching? What if the Sunshield Bandit isn't out today? What if she's robbing somebody down on the stage road? What if she's napping in her secret hideaway?

What if this was all just wasted effort?

"Get back in," the driver says suddenly. "There's dust up ahead."

"Where?" I swing to face up the road, wincing at the glare of the sun off the river. The bank is choked with cottonwoods and brush willow, but a patch is obscured by a swirling cloud of dirt.

The driver swears. "There's one behind us, too." She snaps her reins to perk up the team. "Get in the coach!"

I hop back up on the running board, but I don't climb inside just yet. I hold on to the frame and peer behind us, into the sun. The air is suddenly alive with the pounding of hoofbeats.

Damn, that happened fast.

The stagecoach lurches, the carriage swinging on its suspension. The driver slaps her reins on the team's rumps.

"Remember our agreement!" I holler over the squeaking and clattering of the coach.

The driver swears, the precise wording lost to the noise. "I refuse to take a quarrel for your stupid plan!" But she holds the team at a steady trot, not an all-out gallop, the wheels jostling off the rough road.

We hit a rut, and I almost lose my grip. Reluctantly, I swing back inside and latch the door. I pull back the curtain, but the dust obscures most of the activity outside. There's snarling now, like some wild animal, and one of the horses whinnies in response. The carriage weaves—I'm thrown against the door, knocking my forehead on the casing. Now there's shouting, though I can't make it out. Before I can fully push myself upright, the coach slows. The driver's commands to the horses are clipped, as if she's giving them through clenched teeth.

"Standing down!" she shouts. "Standing down."

The jolting slows and then stops, the coach rocking on its straps. I rub the tender spot on my forehead. The driver is exchanging terse words with someone else, their voice too low for me to hear. Is it the Sunshield Bandit? Hurriedly I scramble upright, my heart pounding in anticipation. But before I can move toward the door, there's a singular crunch of bootheels on sand,

and then the carriage rocks. The door swings open of its own accord.

The late-afternoon sun slices inside like an arrow shot, catching me expertly in the eyes. I reel back, shading my face. Through blurry tears, I can make out the dark, hazy shape of someone on the threshold. Slowly, with sinister purpose, she steps up into the stage.

I drag in my breath and hold it.

I don't know what I imagined.

Whatever it was, it didn't come close.

Her eyes are the only things fully visible, and they flick over me and the rest of the coach in a single sweep. The rest of her face is covered by a faded red bandanna and shaded by a broad-brimmed leather hat. She's tall and lean, dressed in calf-high riding boots, brown trousers, a white shirt, and a blue vest. Everything is dusty and worn, but it only makes my heart rage faster. After weeks in the polished, perfumed court of Moquoia, she radiates a sense of purpose and intent. I realize I've shrunk back against the velvet seat cushion.

She lets go of the doorframe, a shiny buckler on one wrist and a wicked-looking hunting knife in her other hand. With the calm, confident manner of someone who's done this a hundred times before, she holds the blade against the apple of my throat. I swallow, and I can feel the tip graze my skin.

She looks me up and down. Her cheeks are smeared with eyeblack, but around it she's a riot of bronzes and coppers and sun-browned sepias. Her eyes are amber in the slanting sunlight, and her dark brown hair is locked in long ropes, pulled back into a thick tail under her hat.

Her bandanna puffs with her breath. "Turn out your pockets."

My throat works again under her knifepoint. "I don't have anything in my pockets."

The point digs a little deeper, bringing a sharp sting. My heart rate spikes. I fumble for my pockets while attempting to continue.

"I didn't bring anything in my pockets," I try again, turning out the cloth linings. "But I did bring you something else." I reach under my cape—slowly, because those eyes could probably sear holes in my flesh if I move too suddenly. I pull out the drawstring bag.

"I came looking for you," I begin. "I brought you money. Thirty keys. But it's a pittance compared to what I'm prepared to offer you, if you'll help me."

Her gaze falls on the bag.

"Open it," she demands without removing the knife.

I do, showing her the glinting coins inside.

"Toss it outside," she says.

I pull the bag tight again and throw it haphazardly—it's hard to maneuver with her blade nicking my skin. It jingles when it hits the ground. For some reason, it sounds like my efforts shattering in the dirt.

"I'm prepared to offer you a sum of two hundred keys," I say quickly, hoping to keep her attention. "Plus the favor of both Moquoia and Alcoro, if you'll help me find someone who's been abducted."

Her eyes flash. "I don't help nobles."

"You're not helping nobles." I can clarify the lie later. "You're helping another trafficking victim, someone stolen away, being held prisoner somewhere here in the Ferinno."

"Ready the horses, Saiph," she calls out. "And pick up that purse outside the stage."

"Wait," I say hurriedly. "Please. I can offer you almost anything you need, as well as the promise of anonymity. This isn't a trick, or a trap. A woman was abducted outside Pasul, near the Moquoian border, a woman named Tamsin Moropai. We believe she's being held prisoner somewhere close by—letters have been sent as blackmail that indicate she's within a few days' ride of the border. She has golden skin, and long black hair—no, wait!"

With no heed to my monologue, the Sunshield Bandit starts to back out the stage door, her knifepoint leaving my neck. Unthinking, I lunge forward and grab her wrist.

Whack.

The world goes blindingly white, and then blurry. I reel backward and slide down the cushion, my head spinning. Vaguely I reach up and touch the throbbing spot where she slammed the edge of her buckler into the side of my forehead.

She stands over me, silhouetted against the open door, the sun making a halo of the little wisps that have frizzed out of her locks. She shifts slightly so the sun beams directly into my eyes. I squeeze them shut.

"I'll use the knife next time," she says evenly. I draw in a ragged breath, hearing the thump of her boots on the running board. "Thanks for the money."

I grab for my last hope.

"Lark," I croak.

She pauses at the sound of her name on my lips. I force my eyes open against the pain and the glare. I shift out of the direct sun. My cape is strewn sideways, the chain pressing against my throat. I unhook it and struggle to sit upright. She's staring at me, her fingers gripping her knife as if she's seriously considering passing it through my sternum and into the seat cushion on the far side.

"Lark," I say again. "I need your help."

"I don't help nobles," she repeats.

"I'm not a noble," I say. "At least, I'm not a Moquoian noble, or an Alcoran one. I'm just trying to save a life, and help a friend." *And facilitate peace between the east and the west, and save my own future from sinking into the mud.* "I dressed like one because I hoped it would draw your attention. I was looking for you—you have to see that. Why else would I come out here with no guards? Please, you're the only person who can help me."

Her gaze rakes over me. To my utter surprise, she steps back inside the stage, and even stranger, she sheathes her knife. But that buckler is still on her arm, glinting dangerously. And when she bends forward and takes my chin in her fingers, my thoughts vanish. I realize I'd been considering myself more or less immune to her mythological powers, since I was actively looking for her, inviting her to rob me. Since I'm not Moquoian, or Alcoran, or otherwise invested in her pursuits.

At present, I feel very much the idiot. She'd kill me whether I was a beggar or the Light incarnate.

She holds my chin still in her fingers. Her eyes are just a few inches from mine. They're shot with gold.

"How do you know my name?" she asks. "Did you get it in Pasul? Are there posters there?"

"I'll tell you," I say, breathless, "if you'll sit down and hear me out."

Her fingers tighten on my chin, and her eyes crease in anger.

The bandanna flutters in front of her mouth. Distantly I wonder if I'm about to meet her buckler again.

She's silent for a long moment, longer, *longer*—it feels like eternity that she simply stares at me from close range, my face locked in her fingers. I tense in the quiet, and then I break the cardinal rule of diplomacy, the one Queen Mona Alastaire drilled into me from childhood.

I rush to break the silence.

"Why do they call you Lark?" I blurt.

It's such a foolish, asinine question—but her name is a misnomer. There's no doubt about it. A lark is a sweet little songbird, lilting and delicate. A bird of poetry and children's rhymes. Of lovers.

It doesn't describe her in the slightest.

Her eyes comb over me again, from my face to my neck and collar and back up. Then she leans even closer, the cloth of her bandanna brushing my lips. My breath catches in a near choke in my throat. Her fingers leave my chin, sliding down to my cravat, close to where her knifepoint was earlier. I clutch the velvet cushion beneath me.

"Because it's how I like to do things," she hisses. "On a lark."

She tilts her chin forward and crushes her lips against mine, the bandanna bunching between us. My heart bursts through my chest. Her fingers twist my cravat so hard the knot cinches against my skin.

And then she's gone.

My eyes fly open—I didn't realize I'd closed them—and I blink as the coach door swings on its hinges. My heart beats around my chest like a bird in a laurel thicket, and at some point,

I remember to breathe again. I resist the urge to put my fingers to my lips, left feeling slightly bruised, with the taste of sand. I've had a string of romantic partners at home and university, but that was in a different galaxy altogether. That felt less like a kiss and more like an attack.

From outside comes the whinny of a horse, a few shouts. The swearing of the driver. Hoofbeats thundering away.

"They took your horse," the driver calls.

My breath streams out through my teeth, and I press my hand to my chest, trying to calm my heartbeat. I slide my fingers to my collar, trying to feel if there's blood there from her knife or fiery burn marks from her fingers. It's the same place she grabbed while she kissed me, leaving my cravat mussed out of its knot.

Suddenly I lurch upright, clutching my collar. Frantically, I run my fingers over the silk, searching my lapels, then my trousers, then the seat cushion beneath me.

Great swarming Light.

It wasn't a kiss.

It was a distraction.

She stole my firefly.

TAMSIN

The bats tonight feel extra loud. I can't lift my head to look at them, because I can barely stand to pick it up off the ground. I've had it clenched between my elbows since this morning. The pain I'd grown used to sharing headspace with has morphed, twisted, pupated into some new creature with wings and spines.

This pain is making it harder for me to keep my thoughts in safe places. Flickers of melodies I'd been writing, turns of phrases, the satisfactory inhalation after a performance, the touch of warm hands—they all bob at the edge of my mind, where I've tried so hard to cloister them. The bricks I've been setting to keep it all walled back keep crumbling.

This captivity has been so much starker, so much plainer than that other stint in my life. There was pain in that one, too, a wrist that burned from twelve-hour days of scribing until I could barely close my fingers, and an emptying dread that I had gotten myself into something far more ugly and dangerous than I thought when I signed the bond. But there was distraction in the slavers' work, an occupation, and one I learned more from than any of my other jobs. Like most people in Moquoia, I was raised with the idea that bond service was just another form of employment, a stopgap for people who had fallen down on their luck.

Maybe that's how the practice started, though I doubt it.

I have very little shame in my life, it's true, but what I do have rests in the recognition that I believed in the benign necessity of bond servitude right up until I was on the wrong end of the system. I assumed it was one of those regretful pillars on which society rested, and that if circumstances were truly terrible for those involved, surely someone would have done something about it by now.

Three months as a cog in the slaving system cured me of that delusion. My nights were spent locked in a windowless room with a roommate, a dulcimer, and little else. But the days were far, far worse, defined by an unending shuffle of frightened Alcoran children stolen out of the Ferinno, resigned Moquoian teenagers forced by necessity into labor bonds, and seasoned workers so sun-beaten and stooped that it was impossible to tell whether they were sixteen or sixty. They had *si-oques* like mine, with beads of worn ancestral glass. My job was to copy down their health assessments, resigning their humanity to quantitative statistics and documenting where they would spend the next period of their lives.

At the beginning, I thought a three-month bond was a fairly good deal—I could survive anything for three months, I reasoned. But I soon came to realize the short term wasn't from a benevolent urge to preserve my future. According to Moquoian law, bond managers had to allow a government inspection every six months to ensure they were respecting bond terms and upholding humanitarian standards. Turns out, moving your base of operations every three months means you can dodge those inspections. Unlike the major bond ports, Port Ree and Port Urskin, which provide clean lodging and transparent record-keeping, the countless smaller black-market rings stage their unregulated business in shop cellars and loading docks, moving as many human bodies through as possible before packing up and leaving before they can be pinned down by suspicious auditors.

I learned this the hard way, when my three-month stint was up. Instead of the meager payout I was expecting, I found myself standing on the street with only the clothes I was wearing, a wrist nearly immovable with scribe's arthritis, an out-of-tune dulcimer, and a head full of haunted faces that I'd quietly consigned to the business of human lives.

That's when I first understood. I hadn't been a victim of the system.

I *was* the system.

I remember looking up from the dirt and trash gusting along the streets of the Blows, the grimy sea-cliff neighborhood where the ephemeral slave ring had been, to where Tolukum Palace rose in the distance, its glassed walls scalding the sky.

I took my first few steps in that direction that night, and I didn't stop.

I roll my wrist now. It twinges, predictably. It's never been quite right since those days, but fortunately after my bond ended, I had to do very little scribing. The slavers had roomed me with the cook, Soe, and that's who the dulcimer came from. I'd already picked up the basics of reading music from my time with Papi, and to pass the time, Soe showed me the fingerings she'd learned from her grandmother down in the redwood forests. I've since learned that her fingerings bear little resemblance to the handful of professional musicians bold enough to play such a humble folk instrument in concert. But I didn't know that at the time—I just knew that music passed the time and that strumming was a welcome relief to my right wrist, stretching out my burning fingers and tendons. Soe gifted it to me after we parted, saying it was too tinny to play and too worthless to sell. I remember clutching it as I staggered, disoriented, toward Tolukum Palace. My treasure.

My weapon.

I wish I had my dulcimer now—an elegant painted model worlds different from that first boxy one with the missing string. I'm not sure I could play it with the pain in my head, but it would be a comfort.

My stomach heaves, and I curl into a tighter ball. I've bled through the bandages Poia so gallantly provided me this morning, but I can't bring myself to stand up and holler at the window again.

Dirt and filth and rags. It seems unreal that I thought I'd left them all behind when I strode boldly onto the stage at Sun and Rain. Word had been spreading that the old *ashoki* was dying, and the palace was hunting for a new one. It wasn't unheard of for monarchs' scouts to discover their new teller on the street corner, or in the tavern. Why not onstage at the Festival of Sun and Rain? I borrowed a dress, used the last of my savings to pay the entry fee, and walked onto the stage knowing if I could just do things right, in front of the eyes of the king and court, no less, it could change things forever.

I was right, but I hadn't imagined my life would turn in a full circle before the end.

LARK

All right, I lied.

About my name, I mean.

I picked the name Lark because I was tired of the rustlers calling me *Nit*, which, as far as I could gather, was the name for little maggots or squirming bug-things. It had been a gritty, washed-out morning, thick with the smell and sound of cows. Cook was banging on the porridge pot to wake us up for breakfast, and I knew there'd be a hide-tanning if I wasn't up quick. I rubbed my face against my threadbare blanket. I didn't want to get up. I was bone-weary from the previous day's branding, and I knew today would only be more of the same, driving the cows through harsh, scrubby territory. I could already taste the dust in my throat, feel the crisping of my skin under the sun.

Somewhere, a bird started singing in the scrub.

I don't know what made me home in on it—it was hardly the first bird I'd ever heard. Maybe I was just trying to ignore

Cook. Maybe I was reaching for the one pretty little thing in that endless stretch of sweat and grime.

"Rose!" Cook called. "Nit! Get your asses out of bed, there's coffee needs straining!"

Rose groaned and rubbed her face. Out past the noise and hustle, the bird still sang.

"Rose," I said quietly. "What bird is that?"

"What bird is what?"

"That one singing in the scrub. Do you know what it is?"

"I'unno," she said sleepily. "A lark?"

It probably wasn't a lark. It was very likely the only bird name she knew, from that sappy song the cowhands sometimes sang off-key around the fire.

It was the only bird name I knew, too.

"A lark," I repeated.

So when I went up to Cook with my tin plate ready for porridge, and he said, "Strain the coffee first, Nit," I responded with, "Lark."

"What'd you call me?" he said.

"My name," I said. "It's Lark." I could still hear the bird singing behind me.

Cook shrugged his big, meaty shoulders. "Strain the coffee first, Lark."

So I strained the coffee. But I did it with a name of my own.

I haven't thought about that moment in a while. I suppose it should be significant, the choosing of a name, but it wasn't really. The work went on. We still had to strain the coffee. We still had to drive the cows across the flats. We still ended up in Utzibor. Rose still lost her leg. We still escaped into this backward half existence. The name didn't change anything.

I stretch my neck and shoulders over the pebbly seep, the sly evening air slinking around the windbreak to lick my wet skin. Maybe it was the jubilation of the others in camp when we arrived with the new horse and the bag of money, but I gave in to extravagance tonight and lit a small fire by the seep, so I could bring my troubled thinking to the water without worrying about the chills. Its crackle adds to the faint, parched murmur of the creek bed. The water in the seep is so low it doesn't even cover the tops of my toes, but instead of brooding on this, my thoughts are stuck on our raid just a few hours ago. Saiph, I imagine, is still crowing. It's been his biggest victory yet—holding up a coach and making off with a gleaming new horse, tack and all. Never mind that the coach stopped on its own, without the need to jam the wheels. Never mind that there were no guards, and the driver didn't pull a crossbow on Sedge. Never mind that the dandy inside literally tossed his money at us.

No, what I minded was that he knew my name.

I clench my fists so hard my knuckles crack. First the old man in the stage outside Snaketown, then the wanted poster in Patzo's general store, and now a Moquoian-dressed dandy poking along the river. My name never seemed that important before, but now it feels like a liability. Like some kind of slippery slope I can't see coming—I know it's there, and I know to be careful, but I can't be sure exactly where it starts, or which step is going to send me over the edge.

Absently, I rub my thumb over the filigree pin I twisted out of the dandy's lapel. It's some kind of bug, and it's a pretty little thing, silver and intricate. The pearl is blue and milky smooth, almost creamy to the touch—I wasn't aware that kind of texture existed in a gem. By my reckoning it could fetch fifty keys, maybe more if I find the right buyer.

Or I might just keep it.

I hang my head, letting the weight of my dreadlocks stretch out the stubborn rod of tension in my neck. We have the horse. We have some money. Now, I suppose, there's no excuse not to try to take Rose into Pasul to be seen by a healer.

No excuse, except that it could be the end of all of us. What if they have my name and face, too? Where else would the dandy have gotten it?

There's a rustle of brush outside, and Rat gives a low growl.

"Lark," Saiph calls beyond the bison-hide windbreak. His voice is high, a little alarmed.

"What?"

"That . . . that noble is here."

I lift my head just an inch, my hair still curtaining my face. "What noble?"

"From the stage. With the purse."

Tension ripples through my muscles like a strummed bow-string. "The dandy from the coach? He's in the canyon?"

"Uh, yeah."

"Where? How did he get here?"

"He, uh, he just walked up the drainage. He has a weird lantern—it's making the ground around him shine. And, the uh, the horse. It's making the horse shine."

I don't know what that means, but if he's near the horses, he's in the grassy bay below the campfire. That damned grit-toothed piece of sod. I grab for my hair tie and clamp it between my teeth, swiping my locks out of my face.

"Where are the others?" I call around the tie.

"Uhh . . ." Why does he sound so shifty? "Not here."

Well, obviously. I only hope they're all together, up at the campfire, and not out gathering twigs or water. I spit out the tie and wind it around my hair. "Can you distract him? Lead him away from camp while I get Sedge and Jema?"

"Uh, well no, actually, because uh . . . 'cause uh . . ."

Rat growls again, and I freeze in place, my hand outstretched to the lantern, realizing exactly why Saiph is being so shifty, exactly why he can't lead the damned dandy noble away from the others up in camp.

Another voice speaks.

"Because I'm already here."

VERAN

There's a long silence from the other side of the ratty bison hide. The boy called Saiph shifts from foot to foot, looking between the hide and me, cradling a crossbow that's much too big for him. It's pointed at me, but his grip is too low on the crank—I could run a circle around him before he had time to get off a shot. Still, no need to worsen my welcome, so I stand as mildly as I can, my hands out to my sides, one still clutching the indigo lamp. Even in the firelight, it's illuminating the *adoh* powder left on my skin.

When the Sunshield Bandit speaks again, her voice is different, cooler and more controlled.

"Get to the others, Saiph," she commands from the other side of the hide. "Tell Sedge to stay on guard. I'll take care of this."

Saiph edges down the track, uncertainty tracing his face. He has a Moquoian look, but like the bandit, he speaks Common Eastern with a rough Alcoran accent. "Are you . . . are you sure?"

"I only want to talk," I say loud enough for both of them to hear. "Here—take my pack, if you want some collateral. Take whatever you need from it." I hold it out to him.

"Go on, Saiph," Lark calls again.

His hand darts forward and takes my pack and, juggling the crossbow in one arm, heads back into the dark scrub.

I move closer to the fire, eyeing the scraggly dog lying on the far side. Its lip is curled, the coarse ruff of fur along its back raised. I keep my gaze on it—I'm not sure how to appear nonthreatening to a dog.

"So," I call out in what I hope is a calm, authoritative manner. She is, after all, huddled on wet rocks behind an old bison skin, and I've caught her camp unawares—if we're honest, I have the upper hand.

And besides that—*besides that*, I'm the son of King Valien and Queen Ellamae Heartwood of the Silverwood Mountains, ambassador to Moquoia, ally to Lumen Lake and Cyprien, student of Alcoro, representative of the allied East.

I am *not no one.*

"I found the Sunshield Bandit," I say with full bravado now. "Years of being a mysterious desert ghost who disappears with the sun, and I've found your camp with a lantern and some glitter. I'm here, and I plan to stay until you hear me out and give me answers. So unless you'd like your position disseminated to the governments of Moquoia and Alcoro alike, I suggest you—"

With no word or warning, a lantern appears above the bison hide. My diatribe fizzles on my tongue. Like a crowned head rising from a throne, the Sunshield Bandit emerges from behind it.

She's naked except for a pair of buttoned shorts, stripped of all the paraphernalia that hid her identity in the close confines of the stagecoach. But if I'd imagined this might make her appear less threatening—and I admit the likelihood of her standing before me wearing hardly a stitch had not crossed even the remotest corner of my mind—I'd have been sorely mistaken. She radiates power, from her crisp, thrown-back posture to the cold, calculating look she's fixing on me. My feet take a full step backward before I can stop myself.

She's holding the lantern aloft in one hand, as if a portable beam of light is just part of her psyche. Its glow highlights the ropy muscles cording her arms and shoulders, and I have just enough time to see a fleet of tattoos along her arms and over her chest before I cut my gaze away, staring unseeing at the darkened sagebrush with the glare of her lantern still spotting my vision. Heat curls through my stomach and along my collar. The last time I saw a naked girl was when I was talked into moonlight dipping in the reservoir outside the university, and then it was just flashes of skin under the dark water. It felt very bold and grown-up two years ago.

It doesn't feel that way now. Now it feels like I've somehow walked into a trap of my own making.

She makes a small sound, something akin to a snort, and steps around the hide. She passes the campfire for a little creek, where a bundle of clothes sits on a rock. I stare intently at my sagebrush, examining its size and shape, the little bald patch on its northward flank, the broken branch near its base. Trying to ignore that persistent curl in my stomach that could be either thrill or fear.

"Like they'd find you," she says.

I go to respond, but it takes a few tries before my throat is clear. "I beg your pardon?"

"You, hollering about telling Moquoia and Alcoro our position." The barest glance out of the corner of my eye shows her toweling off with a bit of sacking. "You're assuming you get out of this situation with your life. I've got your horse, and I've got a handful of desperate folk with enough sharp blades among us to parcel you up neat, plus a half coyote that bites when I say go." My gaze inadvertently flicks again to the feral-looking dog crouched by the fire.

There's a rustle of cloth and the jingle of a belt buckle. "Seems to me, the buzzards are more likely to find you than the crowned heads of either country."

I'm hit with the dawning realization that—yet again—I've gotten myself in over my head. I wonder if I'll ever reach a point where I recognize my stupidity before I blunder into it.

"A lamp and glitter," she continues. "What did you do, coat your horse in the stuff?"

"And my tack, and filled the saddlebags, with perforations along the seams." My gear may never be truly clean again—I'll probably always walk away with a butt that shines under *Bakkonso* light. "The powder streamed out while you led Kuree away. It even stuck to the rocks poking out of the river." I swallow, trying vainly to find that wave of confidence I'd been riding just a moment ago. "Easy."

"Easy," she repeats, a sinister edge in her voice. "What if I hadn't taken your horse?"

"I filled the money bag, too."

A short beat of silence. "You're not lessening my urge to kill you."

I slowly turn back toward her. If she's not concerned about

standing before me half naked, then dammit, I'm not going to let it unbalance me. By now she has her trousers on and is fastening the hooks on a sleeveless breast band.

"I may be tougher to kill than you suspect," I say. "But even if I'm not, killing me would go poorly for you. I'm not some slaver the governments to the east and west would turn a blind eye to. There are folk who know where I've gone, and more who would root you out in a heartbeat if I turned up missing." The image of this bandit facing off with Mama or Vi or Ida flickers briefly in my head. I draw myself up a little more. "I came to talk, and if you think you can hold off roasting me like that wagon last week, you may find I can help you."

She pauses with a shirt in her hands, but both the lantern and the fire are behind her, and I can't see the expression on her face. Her stillness only lasts a heartbeat—in the very next breath, she shrugs the shirt over her tattooed shoulders. Leaving it unbuttoned, she picks up her buckler and moves a few steps to a rock by the fire. With the same incongruous regality as when she emerged from behind the hide, she sinks down onto the rock and crosses her ankle over her knee. She gives a short whistle, and the mangy coydog rises and sits down next to her.

"All right then," she says. "So let's talk."

All my training would suggest that now I physically have the higher ground—I'm standing, and she's sitting. But she's purposefully placed the fire behind her, leaving her little more than a shadowed silhouette, armed with her buckler and attack dog, and now I feel stupid again.

"You took something that belongs to me," I say bitterly.

"Besides the horse?" she asks.

"The pin," I say. "I want it back."

She snorts again. "I want a pillow and a jam biscuit without dirt on it."

"It's *mine*, Lark," I say. "I'm all for you freeing slaves, but you're starting to make enemies you don't want to make."

"Like you?" she says with sarcasm so thick it drips. "I'll take my chances. I've always had enemies—they're just taking more notice of me. And let's get something straight up front—you keep my name out of your mouth."

"Shall I just call you the Sunshield Bandit?" I ask. "And you call me the dandy?"

"Suits me."

"How about we do it this way instead—my name is Veran Greenbrier."

"The balls kind of a name is that?"

"I'm from the Silverwood Mountains, well to the east of here." I eye her as well as I can in the firelight, my cheeks hot. "And before you scoff at my epithet, I'll have you know that where I come from, little birds like you depend on greenbrier thickets."

"So now I know everything," she says testily. "Am I mistaken, or were we supposed to be discussing something important?"

I hesitate, standing awkwardly in the dirt. My thoughts rest briefly on my firefly pin again, but I push them aside. I'll get it from her one way or another, but now isn't the time.

I take one step to my left, away from her dog. She twitches slightly, the firelight glinting on her buckler, but I simply cross my boots at the ankle and sink to the ground. The flames are still behind her, but now they're at an angle, and I can see a little more of her face, enough to see her smoothing away the brief surprise that flickered there. Her hair glows again in a frizzy halo.

"How much do you know about Moquoia?" I begin.

"The inside of a quarry," she says shortly. "Why, is there anything else?"

"So you *were* a slave—that story is true?"

"Hurry up—I still want to kill you."

I force myself not to swallow, trying to match her bravado. "So why don't you?"

She leans forward, a shadow against the light. "Because I want to see if you have anything useful to offer me before I do."

By the Light, this is going to be difficult. "Fine. Here are the basics. Back in June, I traveled from Alcoro to Moquoia, charged with opening diplomatic discussions with Prince Iano Okinot in-Azure—in large part to stem the trafficking trade through the desert, I'll have you know."

"I'm not selling myself out to you," she says flatly.

"I never asked you to, and I don't plan to."

"Then get to the point."

By the *Light*. "Then *listen* instead of interrupting me."

That catches her—and me—off guard. I press on.

"Despite his initial enthusiasm, I made no progress with the Moquoian prince, and now I come to find out it's because he's being blackmailed with the safety of the woman he loves, who's being held somewhere out here in the desert. Have you heard of the Moquoian *ashokis*?"

"No."

"They're performers, singers and musicians, usually, who study the nuances of court and country and tell truths back to the courtiers, wrapped up in stories or parables."

She turns her head and spits into the sand. "That's the most useless thing I've ever heard."

"I couldn't wrap my head around it at first, either—but the position of *ashoki* has more power than I guessed. It's how the court members get their news. It's how they stay connected with the whole length of Moquoia, and the interests at play in politics. It's what they base their decisions on." I spread my hands. "An *ashoki* with certain political leanings could drive the country in an entirely new direction."

She's silent. But I don't think it's a pensive silence—she still seems angry.

"Tamsin was that kind of *ashoki*," I continue, unable to get a read on her. "One who was digging into the roots of the slave trade. She was heading to the quarries outside Vittenta when her stage was attacked. The rumors all said it was you who attacked her."

I expect her to jump to her defense, but she remains still. The hair prickles on the back of my neck.

"It . . . *wasn't* you who attacked her, right?"

"I attack a lot of stages," she says. "You're going to have to be more specific."

Oh! I know this one—Queen Mona schooled me on this. *Folk will take credit for things they didn't do, if you give them the opportunity.*

"You're bluffing to try to scare me," I say. "You weren't anywhere near Vittenta the night Tamsin was attacked, because you were over near Snaketown, turning over my professor's stage and stealing his boots. Do you recall that? A single Lumeni traveler, blond hair and beard?"

She seems to ponder this. "The old man with the ship tattoo?"

"Colm isn't *old*."

"Ancient," she confirms, and now I think maybe we're joking? Am I joking with the Sunshield Bandit?

"You have a mighty low threshold for old if forty-eight means ancient," I say, amused.

"Well, when most folk you know don't see thirty . . ." she retorts.

Oh, we weren't joking.

Uh, backtrack.

"Well—well, you were robbing his stage at the time Tamsin was attacked—"

"I hit him, too," she says almost thoughtfully. "Right in the ear."

She's trying to rile me, she's *purposefully trying to rile me*, and now it's Mama boiling around inside me, not cool, calm Queen Mona. I grip my knees and try to find some middle ground in my father instead. Business. Focus.

"Whoever attacked Tamsin's stage, they dragged her away into the desert," I say through gritted teeth. "Iano and I have pinpointed her position somewhere south of here, perhaps in one of the old mining settlements." I reach into my cloak pocket and produce Iano's latest letter, complete with the water spot. "Long story short, I need to find her and bring her back. Without her, our hope of uniting the East and the West collapses, and with it the chance to stamp out trafficking in the Ferinno for good."

Her gaze drops to the letter, and too late I wonder if I've offended her further by assuming she can read. I can't tell if her eyes are traveling down the page or simply flickering over the words. She focuses in on something, some detail near the bottom of the page, squinting in the dim light. "And you felt the need to root me out for this treasure hunt because . . . ?"

"Because everything I've heard, read, and personally experienced points to you as the most capable person to hunt down a captive in the Ferinno," I say. "And because I think you could probably use the help I can give you. I told you in the stage—I'm prepared to offer you two hundred keys, or the equivalent in Moquoian coin, upon the recovery of Tamsin Moropai, on top of the thirty I've already given you. Besides that, I brought every necessity I could fit in my pack, which your campmates are probably parceling out among themselves right now." I tick off my fingers. "Cornmeal, jerky, dry cherries, pickles, beans, bandages, tonic, skin salve, fever drops, two quilts, a knife, and a cookpot. And I'll get you more, Lark—I'll get you whatever you need with the blessing of the next king of Moquoia, if you'll just help me find Tamsin."

There will be time to try to convince her to meet with the authorities in Alcoro later, after I've gained a modicum of her trust. For now, I suspect, meeting the immediate needs of her camp will be more convincing.

"Please," I add.

She leans back, her gaze fixed on mine again. I can't see any expression in this light. I have no idea if she's warming to me or not. Out of the sun, her bronzes and coppers are darkened into night blacks, like she's made of changing sky.

"No," she says.

The word bounces off my ears. "What?"

"No," she says again. "Thanks for the money and the food, but I'm not running off after your lost princess."

"Why not?"

"Because I don't help folk like you."

My earlier awe is gone, and she's pissing me off now. "Has it occurred to you that *folk like me* may actually be able to do some good out here?"

She uncrosses her leg in a swift motion and leans forward, her face thrown into sharp shadows. The tang of salt and sweat wafts over me. "Has it occurred to *you* that you're the ones who make it rotten for folk like me? You locked me up in a wagon, Veran Greenbrier of the Silver Mountains—you gave me my first tattoo." She hitches up her right sleeve and turns her arm over—the image is of her longsword, but at the end of the point, to all appearances being stabbed by the blade, is a scarred concentric circle. Like a cattle brand. My stomach balls up in a knot.

"And then when you opened the wagon, you dumped me in a rustlers' camp to sweat more of my life away for nothing, and you'd have let me die there if it meant you got to keep your ass walled up safe and sweet in your palaces and universities." She points at me. "You did that, because you didn't care. You care about trafficking *now*, because it's mucking up your parlor games, but you didn't care then. And because of that, me and the rest of us wound up in your glass forges and quarries and ship bilges and rice plantations, and we'll stay there as long as it's convenient for you. So no, Veran. You could offer me a wagon full of gold and I'll still turn you down. I'll keep doing what I do, but I won't be bought and sold by you and your courts in the name of politics."

All I can do is stare, off-balance again.

"I . . . I know it hasn't been easy for you," I start lamely. "And I know people like me are what's put you here. But . . . Lark, for what it's worth, I'm listening now. A lot of us are listening now. You're right—there's nothing anyone can do to change your past. But we might be able to change what tomorrow looks like. We'd like to try to put some of this right."

She stands from her rock throne and turns away, stalking to the rest of her clothes. She pulls on her boots, then buttons up her shirt and slides her arms through her vest. She picks up her longsword and broad-brimmed hat from the ground.

"Lark," I say again. "You go after slavers—you pick off their wagons one by one. But we can stamp out the root—we can stop the wagons altogether. You wouldn't have to rescue kids anymore. Isn't that what you want?"

"No," she says.

"No?" I echo, stunned. "Why on earth not?"

She knots her faded bandanna around her chin. "Because I don't trust for *one second* that you're going to do anything you just said. Take off your boots."

The whirring gears in my head grind to a stop. "What?"

"Take off your boots, now."

My mind jumps back to Colm's letter, how she robbed him of both pairs of boots. But mine aren't tough Alcoran cowhide with a hobnailed sole—mine are soft Silverwood buckskin, with the chevron fringe that matches my father's in his wedding portrait. I made sure to pack my sturdiest pair to change into after peeling off the raspberry silk in the stage.

"I brought you two bags of supplies and the promise of enough money to buy fifty pairs of shoes," I say, angry. "I'm not giving you my boots."

"I'm not asking you to give them to me. I'm taking them." She buckles her longsword onto her hip. "Take them off."

I plant both feet in the dirt and stand facing her. There's

no give in her face, no soft edge of uncertainty or self-doubt. And she might be armed, but I am, too—the hilt of Iano's knife presses into the small of my back. She can posture all she wants, but in the end, I'm determined to be the one walking out of here, leaving her holed away in this graveyard canyon.

"You can't win out here, you know." I want to rattle her, jar some kind of uncertainty out of her. "Folk in both countries are closing in on you, and if I can find you, they will, too, eventually. You won't be queen of the desert for much longer."

It's a quick, efficient movement, and I react too slowly. Without unsheathing her sword more than a few inches, she lunges forward and drives the hilt into my sternum. The breath vanishes from my lungs, and the world tilts—first I double forward, only for her to hook my boot with her toe and give my shoulder a short push. I tip backward like a sawn tree and land hard on my ass in the dirt.

"Rat," she says.

The dog leaps forward. I yelp and throw my arms up, bracing myself for two rows of teeth. But it doesn't come—only a wave of growling and a wash of rancid dog breath. I gasp to find my lungs again—and now my feet are cold.

She gives a short whistle, and the beast slinks away. When I look up, she's tucking my boots under her arm.

"You sleep here tonight," she says to me. "Don't leave this spot or you'll get a quarrel somewhere important. Tomorrow morning I'll tie you up tight and give you a ride to Snaketown. I'll have to leave you a mile or so off the road, though—there's a price on my head. I'm sure you understand."

I scramble to sit up in the dirt, still wheezing, my bare feet scraping on the rocks. "Dammit, Lark, you're making a mistake—"

"Dammit, Veran," she says, turning away. "I've got everything I want from you."

She sets her hat on her head. "Come, Rat."

The coydog lopes to her side. Without another glance in my direction, she strides off through the sagebrush, leaving me with nothing but the coals of the fire and my own idiocy.

I blew it.

Not scouting, not fighting, not socializing. Diplomacy. Politics. The kind of thing Eloise could have done in her bathrobe and slippers. The kind of thing my father glides in and out of on a daily basis. The kind of thing I *should* be successful at, the one role I've ever been allowed, guided and hand-held and humored by the courts of five countries. *Oh, let him try—he can't do anything else.*

I crumple onto my side, fling my arm over my face, and groan into the darkness.

LARK

I storm up the slope toward camp, fuming.

The gall of that man, the sheer nerve of him tracking me here to bribe and extort and assume he could buy my cooperation. How dare he walk right in and act like I belong to him. I should have given him the point end of my sword, not the hilt, but the last thing I need is a posse of crossbows combing the river for their lost dandy. The stagecoach driver could estimate the place she dropped him off. Three Lines isn't safe anymore. I grind my teeth behind my bandanna, slapping sagebrush out of the way. Rat pants along beside me.

I round the boulder at the edge of camp to find everyone huddled around Sedge's blanket. My steps slow until I've come to a full stop just over Saiph's shoulder. Sedge is in the process of organizing the contents of the dandy's pack, in order by size and variety, bless him. The new knife gleams sharp and clean by his knee; the cookpot is bubbling on the fire. Lila is slowly stirring the contents of a packet into the boiling water, releasing a sharp, herby smell. Andras is eagerly chewing a fistful of jerky. Little Whit and Moll are huddled together under one of the quilted blankets, each picking steadily from palms full of plump fruit leathers. I look past them to Rose's mat—she's tucked under the other quilt, her stump peeking out from the edge, wrapped in a fresh bandage.

My legs are suddenly watery, my body crushed with weariness. I listen to the eager smacking of the little ones' lips, gulping down the food they so badly need, bent over their prizes like crows on carrion.

Blazing sun, fire, and dust.

"Saiph," I say.

He turns and looks up at me, his eyes bright and his cheeks bulging with jerky.

"Lark!" he exclaims. "Look!"

"I know. Listen, we're going to need to take watches tonight. You're up first. I'll come get you in a few hours, and Sedge will relieve me. Make sure that noble doesn't leave the seep, okay?"

He swallows forcefully and reaches for a jar of pickles to take with him. "When does he get us out of here? How will he take us all—will he send more horses?"

"What?"

"I mean, I guess we could sort of share horses and walk some—or is he sending a stage?"

Andras's eyes widen. "Are we riding in a stage?"

I look between them. I look at Whit and Moll, absorbed in their fruits. I look at Rose, unconscious. Reluctantly, I look at Lila, who's eyeing me accusingly.

Before I can turn to him, Sedge's hands still on the saddlebags.

Slowly, resignedly, he starts dividing his piles—a little for now.

More for later.

"We'll . . . we'll sort all that out tomorrow," I say to Saiph and Andras. "For now, Saiph, go on—take Rose's crossbow up on the big boulder by the seep. If the dandy tries to leave, fire somewhere close enough to rattle him, and then come get me."

Saiph grabs another handful of jerky and gets up, dragging the crossbow with him as an afterthought. He traipses off through the brush, licking his fingers.

Slowly, I lower down to his vacated spot. I take off my hat and rub my forehead—on top of it all, I had to cut my wash short, and I can feel the grime and dried sweat along my hairline.

"We have to move camp," I say. Sedge looks up from the packs. Lila's spoon stops stirring.

"Whatever for?" she asks.

"Because they've tracked us down." I'd thought that much was obvious. "They've rooted us out. We have to find someplace new. Maybe closer to Pasul, if we can find a draw with a reliable water source."

Sedge is noticeably avoiding my eyes. Lila's not—she's staring hard. A droplet of water jumps from the pot and hisses in the flames. She begins to stir again.

"I take it the negotiations didn't go well?" she asks.

"There were no negotiations," I say. "He wants me to run off and find some court lady in the desert."

"For how much?"

"What does it matter, Lila? We can't eat money, and we can't pop in and out of Pasul for supplies every other week—they'll have all our faces on the outlaw boards within a month." She's giving me that reproachful look, so I untuck the soft leather boots from under my arm and toss them in front of her.

"Here. These will probably fit you, and they're good and soft."

Her gaze falls on them, but she's not the one to move first. Like a shadow come suddenly to life, the quilt drops and Moll reaches forward. Her fingers close on the fringe.

"Pa," she says, dragging one toward her.

Every head swivels to face her.

Lila stops stirring again. "Did she just—"

Andras claps his hands. "Oh, Moll said something!"

I roll forward onto my hands and knees, my heart pounding. I peer into her little round face, her lips stained pink from the cherries.

"Moll—what did you say?"

She hugs the boot to her chest.

"Do you like the boot?"

"Pa's boot," she says. "Pa's dancing boot. Pa and Ma dancing the daisy chain."

"Are you . . . do you mean this looks like your papa's boot?"

"Pa comes back from sivver hole, take off sivver boot, and put on the dancing boot, and dance the daisy chain."

"What kind of boot? A what?"

"Sivver boot." She pets the line of shiny silver beads stitched along the fringe.

"Silver boot," Lila says. "Is that a silver boot?"

"Dancing boot," Moll says to the shoe, cradling it.

Silver—silver boot. My head is too full of buzzing new thoughts. "Wait, that's—the noble came from there. The Silver Mountains."

"Sivverwood," Moll says, rubbing her nose on the leather.

Lila turns back to me. "That man's from the Silverwood Mountains?"

I sit back on my heels, goggling at Moll cuddling the boot and chatting like she's always done it. I hadn't paid attention to where the dandy came from. I assumed the name he dropped was a place in Moquoia or Alcoro, but now I realize I'm wrong.

"That's that country," I begin, my thoughts muddling like shifting clouds. "It's—where? Next to Cyprien?"

"It's *beyond* Cyprien," Lila says. She brushes a patch of dirt by the fire ring and scratches the handle of her spoon into the ground. "Across the big river. Look, here's the Ferinno." She draws an X. "Then the rest of Alcoro, and that mountain range, and then Cyprien." She draws a straggly line. "And then the river, and *then* the Silverwood, with Lumen Lake and the hill country on either side."

I stare at her marks in the dirt, fixing on the scratch representing Cyprien, aware of Andras staring hard at her makeshift map. I look past it at the little patch of the Silverwood Mountains.

"How do you know all this?" I ask.

"It's basic geography, Lark. And I've told you, I think I have family in Lumen Lake. Every chance I've gotten, I've studied the route to get there."

I look at Moll again. She's rocking and humming a tune to herself.

"Moll—is this where you're from? The Silverwood Mountains?"

"Mine house."

"What about your house?"

"*Mines*, Lark," Lila says. "There are silver mines in the Silver-wood. Her father goes into the silver hole—he's a miner. She lives near one of the silver mines."

I stare at the little girl, overwhelmed and suddenly recognizing the copper skin that I thought had been like Pickle's but in reality is darker and richer, recognizing the high round cheeks and bright green eyes—more vivid than the noble's, but I remember their shade from inside the stagecoach. I remember because I've never seen eyes that color before, the color the sage turns after a flush of rain.

Damn, damn, damn, damn.

Lila clears her throat and taps the edge of the shiny pot with her spoon. "Here, tin cups, everybody." She ladles out the fragrant tea and hands a cup to Whit and Moll and Andras. "Careful now, they're very hot. Here, Sedge, and you, Lark. And now—can I have a word?"

She jerks her head over to Rose's mat, and slowly I get up and follow Sedge from the campfire, the hot tin cup burning my fingers—but I'm too numb to care.

Lila settles down at Rose's head and brushes her forehead. "I gave her some of the fever drops," she says. "We'll see if they help."

Sedge takes Rose's hand and strokes it. Lila looks up at me—looks at me hard.

"It's decision-making time," she says firmly.

"I have made decisions," I shoot back. "I'm not leaving you all here alone to run off on some politician's errand—not with Rose like this."

"You would be refusing even if Rose was perfectly healthy,"

Lila accuses. "And you know good and well what she'd say to your decisions. She'd say you're making the wrong ones."

"I'm trying to keep us all safe, Lila. What happens if I'm gone and the folk from town come pouring up Three Lines?"

"If folk from town—" Sedge begins, and then stops.

I whirl on him. "If folk from town *what*, Sedge?"

"If they come looking," he says again, looking uncomfortable but resolved, "they'll come looking for you, Lark, not us."

"You're escaped slaves."

"But you have a price on your head," Lila says. "We're not worth rooting out, but you are. And if you're here in the canyon, they're more likely to arrest us all. But if they find a bunch of kids and a few invalids . . ."

"You go back into the wagons."

"Are you listening to *anyone*, Lark? Folk are trying to *stop* the wagons. I don't pretend there's not the possibility that something might go wrong, but here you are being handed the best opportunity to get us all somewhere safe, and you're turning it down flat. What kind of money is he offering? I'm willing to bet it could buy us each a set of new clothes and a safe, legal ride on a stage out of the desert."

"I'm willing to bet that stage would dump you on a street corner in Snaketown, or Teso's Ford, and you'd be no better off than you are now, only you'd be alone."

"I'd be a little closer to home," she says.

"*This* is home."

"No, it's *not*, Lark." Her brown eyes glitter with the light from the campfire. "This is the heart of the issue for you, isn't it? You've come to think that this dead piece of desert is the only thing in the world left for you. It's not. Do the thing this fellow's asking, take the money, and then build something new for yourself. Or are you too afraid to step off the little hierarchy you've built, where you're the queen of us all?"

I stare at her, her lips twisted up together. "Well, damn, Lila, nobody's making you stay here. If that's how you feel, you're free to go anywhere you like."

"No, I'm not, because I have no money, and because I wouldn't make it past the caprocks." She points angrily at her abdomen. "You know I've been bleeding for eight days now? Not a trickle, *heavy*. Clots. For eight days. I've ruined the spare saddle blanket sleeping with it between my legs."

"Why didn't you tell me?"

"Because what the gall are you supposed to do about it? Nothing. And if I'm angry, it's because you refuse to accept that one of us is going to die next, and probably soon. If not Rose—"

"*Stop it.*"

"—and not little Whit, then it'll be me, Lark," she finishes sharply. "And if you had your way, you'd let it happen."

"That's *not true*."

"Prove me wrong," she hurls back.

The silence rings between us. Over my shoulder, Moll is still humming.

I turn to Sedge. "I suppose you feel the same?"

He looks down at Rose, still holding her hand. "We need help, and it seems like we're being offered the best help we're going to get." He meets my gaze again. "Lila and I can take care of the little ones for a while. Especially with the supplies the noble brought. We'll be okay."

We're not going to be okay. There is no okay. We're all screwed, we're all dead already.

You can't win out here. You won't be queen of the desert for much longer.

I drag my hat off my head and rub my forehead again. For the first time, I think back to what the dandy asked me to do.

A Moquoian woman, being held in the desert. South of here, near the abandoned mines, within a few days' ride of Pasul.

A waterstained letter. Written on rough sawgrass parchment. A blocky hand spelling words I can't sound out, with a scrabbled name at the bottom, complete with that letter that doesn't look like a letter. An *M* with flares on the sides, like wings.

A lot like wings, actually. Not feathered wings—leathery wings.

My brow furrows. I'm hit with the sudden memory of a cloaked figure and the reek of bat droppings.

Oh.

Oh, damn.

I know exactly where she is.

VERAN

Something flumps into the dirt near my head, sending a cloud of dust into my face. I cough, surfacing from the last threads of an unpleasant sleep. Slitting open my eyes, I see one of my boots lying in the dust.

"I have several conditions."

Well, I have a condition, too—what exactly are we talking about? I tilt my head upward and immediately regret it—she's in front of the damned sun again, leaving her little more than a sliver of shadow.

I rub my eyes. "Is standing with your back to the sun just a coincidence, or do you make a conscious decision every time you move around?"

"Sit up and take things seriously. I'd rather not have to stuff you again in front of the little ones."

I open my eyes again, shading them against the glare. She's not alone—there's a small figure practically glued to her side. I scoot until I'm no longer blinded and blink the tears out of my eyes.

Oh, Light, oh earth and sky. She's holding the hand of a tiny woodgirl, who's clutching my other boot like a blanket.

"I rescued this one a week ago," Lark says. "She hasn't said a single word to me until last night, when she recognized your boots. Is she—one of yours?"

The girl peeps at me with one bright green eye—she has the look of the south woods, but she could just as easily be a child of merchants around Lampyrinae. I turn my hands over to her.

"Hello, little sally. Have you got some boots of your own?"

"Pa dances the boot . . . dances the daisy chain with Ma . . . with the boots."

"Your pa wears his fringe boots to dance the daisy chain with your ma?"

She nods.

"What did you call her?" Lark asks. "Is her name Sally?"

"It's a baby name—little salamander." We still call Susimae *sally* to annoy her. "What's your name?"

"Hettie," she says.

"Can you dance the daisy chain, Hettie?"

She circles her finger. "No, I go round and round."

"I bet you do." Little kids often run circles around the older folk dancing before they learn the steps themselves. "What's your parents' epithet?"

"Goldfinch."

"*Flash of yellow in the tree, little finch—*"

"*—per-chick-o-ree,*" she finishes.

"I'm a greenbrier," I offer.

"*Tangle in the laurel slicks,*" she recites.

I want to hug her, little lost sally. I open my arms, and she slips her hand out of Lark's and wraps one grimy arm around my shoulder, still clutching my boot with the other.

"She says she's from a mining town," Lark says, her voice oddly strained. "She says her pa's a miner. Do you know her family?"

"They shouldn't be hard to find," I murmur. I tap the little girl's shoulder. "Hettie, is there a bear or a fox in your dancing square?"

"Fox," she says.

"South Mine, then." I tilt my head up to Lark—she's moved out of the sun and is watching us. She's got all her armor on again—thick eyeblack smeared over her cheeks, faded bandanna draped around her chin, black hat pulled low over her forehead.

"How'd she get out here?" she asks, hushed.

I lean back to look the little girl in the face. "Hettie, does your pa travel with the silver shipments down to the coast?"

She plays with the buttons on my tunic. "Yeah, I goed with him last time."

Oh, little sally. I wrap my arms back around her and draw her close, squeezing her tight.

"I'll get you back home, okay? We're going to go back home." My gaze falls on my second boot, flopped over in the dirt. I'm going to need to pry the other one away from her.

I look up at Lark again and extend my hand.

"Give me my firefly," I say.

Without comment—oh, the shock—she reaches under her collar and fumbles with the clasp. She slides the pin out and places it in my outstretched hand.

"Look, Hettie. I need my boot back, but I have something else for you. Recognize this?"

She takes it into her pudgy hand. "Blue ghost."

"That's right. They're flying now, aren't they? I'm going to put it right here on your shirt. I bet the silver came from your Pa's mine."

She strokes it. "And the lantern from the lake."

Oh, sunlight, I love her. "That's right, the pearl in its lantern came from the lake." I give her one more hug and let her go—she's absorbed with the pin.

I beat the dust off my boots and pull them on, savoring the familiar press of the soft soles as I get to my feet. There's a rustle in the bushes, and into the clearing comes Saiph, ruffle haired and probably sore from sitting up on the boulder standing guard on me last night. I heard him spitting sunflower seeds into the brush until I finally dropped off to sleep. He's traded his crossbow for a flat corn biscuit and a dinged cup.

"Here." He holds out his wares to me. "Lila said to ask for more if you want it. Oh—I mean . . ."

Lark is glaring at him, probably for letting slip the name of another campmate, though I don't know what she expects me to do with this information. I take the biscuit and the cup from him.

"Tell Lila I said thank you."

Lark clears her throat and pats Hettie's shoulder. "Why don't you go with Saiph back to the fire, okay?"

"Mmkay." She slips her hand into the older boy's and follows him back into the brush.

I sip from the cup—watery coffee bitter enough to strip paint, but it's nice to have something hot after a night on the rocks. I mull over the cup, eyeing Lark. She's looking none too rested, either.

"Nice night?" I ask innocently.

She frowns at me—she took watch after Saiph. I saw her outlined against the moon the few times I shifted around. Maybe I'm being mean, but my rear still hurts from where she dumped me in the dirt last night—and I'm still pissed about my boots and firefly.

"I've had worse," she says. She seems to be warring over something internally, her lips twisting over her bandanna.

"I believe you were saying something about having a condition," I prompt over the coffee.

"I have several," she says. "But first, let me see the letter again."

Adding the biscuit to my coffee hand, I dig in my cloak pocket and hand it to her. She takes it and studies it again, peering once more at the end of the text.

"They're all like this?" she asks. "The other letters?"

"Yes. We've plotted a handful of abandoned mining towns that it could have come from, but we hadn't narrowed it much past—"

"She's not in one of the mining towns."

I pause over my cup. "How do you know?"

"In Snaketown, I saw a woman buying some odds and ends in the general store. She was getting more ink and parchment—this is the type they make down there, from sawgrass."

"Yes, we'd gotten that far, but—"

"And she was handing over another letter, like this one."

"All right, but that doesn't—"

"And her cloak stank of guano."

Okay, she's really throwing me off now. "Guano?"

"Bat droppings."

"I know what they are. Why is that important?"

"Because your lost princess has been telling you where she

is all along." She taps the parchment, down at Tamsin's name. Specifically, the scribbled *M* at the beginning of her surname, with the little spiky flourishes on either side of the letter.

"I'm not much at writing," she says. "But that doesn't look like any letter I know."

"It's a flourish, a lot of folk use them—"

"It's a bat," she says. "She's been drawing you a bat. The two points on the *M* are its ears, and the flourishes are its wings."

I take the letter from her and stare at the mark. It seems wildly far-fetched.

I look up at Lark again. "Are you saying this could tell us where she is?"

"No," she says. "I'm saying I know *exactly* where she is."

My heartbeat quickens. "What? How? Where is she?"

She regards me, her sharp bronze eyes flicking over my face.

"You have conditions," I say. "Right. Lay them on me. Condition one."

"Condition one is you cut the sass," she says curtly.

I match her sharp tone. "Sorry, it's a defense mechanism. Condition two."

Her lips twist in a frown, but to my surprise the expression doesn't reach her eyes. She doesn't look angry, she looks concerned. Serious.

I try to backtrack. "I'll cut *some* of the sass. Promise."

Another long pause slides by. She draws in a breath.

"You get them all out of here," she says quickly, as if forcing the words out.

"Get what out of where?"

"All . . . all the others, here in camp," she says. "You get them to safety. The ones who have homes get back home. The ones who don't get set up somewhere they're not going to get dumped in a ditch or back in a wagon. The ones who need medicine get medicine. No prison, no slavery, no tricks. You get them all out."

The silence between us is profound, a tangible thing. And suddenly I realize I've only been seeing part of the issue, like seeing a few branches without seeing the rest of the tree. All the viciousness and thievery and no holds barred—here it is. She's got a camp full of lost kids and no way to take care of them.

"How many are we talking about?" I ask.

"Is that a yes or no?"

"It's neither, yet," I say. "I want to do what you're asking, but I need to know the scope. How many do you have here? Five? Twenty? Fifty?"

She's quiet—she still doesn't trust me.

"There are seven of them," she finally says. "One is . . . one is bad." She swallows behind her bandanna. "She needs surgery, probably, or at least full-time care until she recovers. Another needs medicine for his eyes, and one needs to see a lady's healer. The others may get better with good food and proper care."

"And where do they need to go?"

"Alcoro will be all right for most of them, as long as they're safe. One has family in Cyprien. You can get to Cyprien?"

"I can get to Cyprien," I reply as seriously as I can—Cyprien must seem like the other side of the world from here. "I pass through it to get to and from home, and I'm good friends with the ambassador." I keep quiet so as not to give her false hope, but Rou would turn a country over to reunite a child with their family.

"All right. And Moll—er, Hettie, she belongs in the Silverwood."

"Yes. Is that all?"

"Yes. Well—one would like to go to Lumen Lake, but that could be a long shot."

My blood runs cold, and I physically stop myself from grabbing her arms—I don't want another clip from her buckler. "Lumen Lake—you have someone here from Lumen Lake? A girl? A woman?"

"She's . . . I mean, she's not full Lumeni . . ."

"Yes, yes, of course, good." Lumeni and Cypri—Queen Mona and Ambassador Rou. In the excitement about Tamsin, I've completely forgotten the thought of searching for Moira Alastaire. Eloise's fawn-freckled face and fine brown curls flash in my head. "How old? What's her name?"

She leans back—I've made her wary again. "That's not important. I don't even know if she really has family there, or if she'd just as soon settle down here in Alcoro. The point is, there are seven of them, and I've laid out for you what they need. So? Is it a yes or no?"

Oh, dammit, Lark, this *is* important. I breathe heavily, almost desperately, needing answers about this Lumeni girl she has hidden away out here. But she's frowning again, perhaps regretting sharing so much information with me, and I can't lose this opportunity now that I've got it.

"I'll get them all where you want them to go. I promise." I'll have to talk to the Lumeni girl, at any rate, to help her get home. Patience. Patience now. Tamsin has to come first, the alliance has to come first. I exhale, trying to appear less manic. "I have contacts in Alcoro who can help settle your friends in safety, and Cyprien and the Silverwood are no trouble, none at all. Neither is the lake. I'll get them out."

"Good," she says, and then, as if to make herself believe it, she says it again. "Good."

"Though," I say, suddenly realizing, "you've left someone out."

"Who?"

"You, of course. Surely you want something out of this?"

She goes quiet. A warm desert breeze slinks through the sage, bringing a wisp of smoke from her secret campfire with it.

"I'll take the money," she finally says. "Some of it, anyway—whatever's not used to settle the others. And then you leave me alone—you and everyone else. I owe you nothing beyond what you're asking me to do. I get you your lost lady, you get my campmates to safety, and that's the end of it. There's no partnership here, no contract. Our connection ends the moment the job ends. That's what I want out of this."

"Don't you have somewhere to go?" I ask. "Don't you have somewhere you'd rather be than here?"

I've probed too deep. Her face shutters again, and she hitches the bandanna up over her nose.

"I've got dust instead of blood," she says frankly. "Cut me and I bleed desert. Is it a yes or a no?"

"It's a yes. Get me to Tamsin, and I'll do the things you've asked. You really know exactly where she is?"

"Utzibor caverns. There's a massive bat colony that streams out every night from several of the openings. There are a few outbuildings, abandoned, used only by shady folk looking for a place to conduct business. I spent a few weeks there . . . a while back."

I decide not to press her for personal details. "Where is it? How far?"

"About two days' ride from here, southwest."

"All right, then. If you're sure. There's a hitch, though—Prince Iano is in Pasul, and I need to get word to him that I'm going with you."

She stops midturn. "You are *not*."

"I am," I say firmly. I made up my mind—well, just now, actually, but it's been brewing since leaving Tolukum Palace. I've been waffling over whether I can make the trip. But after journeying over the mountains with Iano, my confidence is higher than it's ever been. Two days to Tamsin, one day to Pasul.

I can make it three days.

I try to present my selfish excitement as resolution, nodding at Lark's snarly look. "I can tell you don't trust me. Well, *I* don't trust *you*. This is important—too important for one person. At the very least, Tamsin's prison is probably guarded. I can help you break her out."

"I don't *need* help."

"I don't care. I'm coming." I square up, my weight forward in case she tries to shank me with her hilt again. "I'm coming, or there's no deal—and now I know where your camp is."

"I could still kill you," she snaps behind her bandanna.

"Is that your fallback solution to everything?" I ask.

"Works so far," she replies.

She's lying, it's all lies—she doesn't kill if she can help it. She'll rob and punch and spit and flash her buckler around, but she doesn't kill if she doesn't have to. She showed me that yesterday in the stage, she showed me that last night. *I can see through you, Lark.*

That fiery glare *does* make one think twice, though.

She fumes silently for a moment, while I try to channel

Mama as hard as I ever have, spreading my feet a little wider and crossing my arms. Immovable. A mountain. A greenbrier, latched on tight without a crawdad's chance of letting go.

"Fine," she finally says. "But don't—don't, like, talk to me or anything."

I permit myself a snort. "Deal. But I still need to get a message to Iano."

"Saiph," she says with reluctance. "Saiph can make the ride to Pasul."

"He can be trusted? This is the prince of Moquoia we're talking about."

Her gaze drifts up the path to her campfire, and I catch a glimpse of that same weighty anxiety as before. "Saiph," she says, almost an exhale. "Yes, he can be trusted. He'll be all right. He knows which tracks are safe."

"All right, then. It seems we have a deal." My university training kicks in, and I gesture to her. "Do you want it in writing? Or at least a handshake?"

She scoffs. "You go back on your word, and I'll kill you. Will that do?"

"Again with murder. Most folk would find that unorthodox."

"Get used to it." She turns away. "I hope you're ready to ride out—we can cover good ground before noon."

"I'm ready." I take a bite of the flat corn biscuit—and gag. The thing coats my tongue like sawdust. I choke around my too-big mouthful, pounding my chest.

"By the *Light*," I gasp. I gulp a swig of coffee and spit it into the dust. "What d'you mix into your biscuits, chalk?"

"Cattail pollen," she says as she heads for the brush. "Get used to that, too."

TAMSIN

I've made them nervous. Beskin and Poia.

After Poia hit me yesterday morning, my mouth swelled so much I couldn't close it all the way. I was spitting blood all day and through the night. And there was no way on this sorry little earth I was going to put anything foreign between my teeth besides water. So I didn't eat yesterday. Or this morning. They snarled at me, saying they weren't going to hurry for my sake this afternoon when I was begging for something to eat.

But that swirling nausea is back again, probably from swallowing so much bloody spit, and now this afternoon they've found me in the same place—curled on my dirty mat, my head clamped between my arms. The pressure from my elbows really does seem to alleviate the worst of the pain.

I hear them conversing outside my door, though I can't make out what they're saying.

"Oi," Poia calls through the bars. "Tamsin. On your corn, would you prefer honey to salt?"

I'm just fuzzy enough to be surprised at this new twist of apparent compassion—I've always had a sweet tooth, and I've always been snacky. It was hardly a secret in court—I was always nibbling on glazed walnuts or bits of toffee carried around in my pocket. That Beskin and Poia have only fed me two salty, unchanging meals for weeks on end seems like just another form of torture, but then my brain catches up with reality.

Honey over salt.

It's not compassion.

It's desperation.

I'm no good to them dead.

I scrunch up my nose where it's sandwiched between my elbows. It's the closest thing I can get to a smile. Alive, I'm their tool. I'm their weapon. I'm their leverage. It's the whole reason I'm in this sorry state, in this rotten place.

Finally, something I can use.

I stare at the back of the door, baring my teeth in a painful mockery of a grin.

LARK

Saiph swings his tattered bedroll over his saddle so enthusiastically Blackeye snorts in displeasure.

"You take the northern cattle tracks," I say for the fiftieth time in the past hour. "Remember that you have to cross the South Burr before the mesas, or you'll lose the ford."

"I know, Lark, I know that." His voice drips excitement. "And I know to stay south of the water scrape, and I know not to travel the washes past afternoon. I can do it, Lark, I can. I promise."

I suck in a breath behind my bandanna. He crams a bag of the dandy's jerky into his already-stuffed pannier.

I put my hands on his shoulders and turn him around. "Saiph—be careful."

"I will." He looks up at me, face flushed, eyes bright. "I'm fifteen, Lark, I'm almost as old as Pickle was. I can do it."

"I know you can. Just—just be smart, all right? Don't take stupid risks. Think things through. I need you to come through this in one piece, okay?"

"I will, I will, I will." He slips from my grip and hoists Rose's crossbow up to the hook on the saddle. "What's the guy's name again?"

"Prince Iano Okinot." The dandy comes up behind me—catlike, those fancy boots don't seem to make any noise on the ground. "Though you're not to call him such in town—use the name Escer Gee. You'll find him in the Sweet Pine—tell the landlord you're his errand boy." He holds out a letter, sealed with a bit of tallow from our box of candle nubs. He's pressed the face of his thick silver ring into it, leaving the imprint of a bug like the pin he gave to Moll.

Hettie.

Fire and dust, I'm so mixed up.

The dandy taps the wax. "My parents' seal. Tell Iano that Veran sent you—the rest should be explained in the letter. Can you do that?"

"Yes, sir, I can."

"Safely, quietly? There's a new Alcoran horse in it for you if you do."

Saiph's eyes practically ignite. "Yes, sir! Absolutely I can, yes, sir."

"Excellent." He hands him the letter, and Saiph tucks it deep into his saddlebag. "We'll see you in Pasul."

Saiph nods and eagerly slides his foot into Blackeye's stirrup. He throws his leg over and gathers up the reins.

I can't help it—I snatch his shirttail before he gives her a kick. "Saiph."

He looks down at me, all energy and no brains. "Yeah?"

I don't know what to say that I haven't already said.

I just don't want him to leave.

"Remember to oil the crossbow," I finally conjure. "The crank sticks."

"I will! Bye! Bye, sir!" He twists in his saddle and calls up the canyon. "Bye, Sedge!"

Thundering sky, he's such a moron. I slap Blackeye's rump. She skitters forward and he swings to grab the saddle horn. His crow echoes off the rocks as they clatter down the slope and out of sight.

I blow out a breath so hard my bandanna flies up in the air, and then I make myself turn away. Our two horses are standing saddled and ready—Jema is looking extra matted and burred next to the dandy's sleek palomino mare. Rat crouches at her hooves, ears perked forward and tongue lolling.

"Sedge," the dandy says thoughtfully behind me. "Is that the one with the bad eyes, or the one who needs a lady's healer?"

I huff and start up the slope. I don't like how curious he is about the others here in camp—particularly not how twitchy he got about Lila. Fortunately, she's down in the draw puking, so he's not likely to catch sight of her even if he sashays into camp. "Are you ready?"

"You know I'm going to have to meet your campmates eventually, Lark. You don't have to hide them from me."

Yes, I do, you and everyone else. I reach Jema's side and make a last check of her battered tack. "I hope you don't eat a lot," I say. "I'm leaving most of the supplies here in camp with the others."

"Oh, I have more," he says. "I figured you'd strip everything from my daypack, so I dropped my main bag down at the head of the canyon. There's enough for all three of us for at least a week. We'll pick it up as we head out."

My anger flares, irrationally, I suppose. I inhale through clenched teeth, twisting my fists on Jema's blanket. With a huge amount of effort, I bend my thoughts away from the image of him bouncing on a rope behind his horse and instead to visions of Rose in a clean bed, Andras with a family, little Whit with a plate full of hot food.

There's a call up the slope, and over the rise comes Sedge, holding Moll—Hettie—by the hand.

"Or is *that* Sedge?" asks the dandy.

"Shut up," I say venomously.

Sedge leads Hettie toward us. I'm glad to see he's got our biggest hunting knife sharpened and sheathed on his belt. Between that and the iron ring around his neck and the sheer size of him, he at least looks threatening enough to make somebody think twice.

"She wanted to say good-bye to the nobleman," Sedge explains, releasing Hettie's hand. The girl hurries to Veran, her arms upstretched. He crouches down and wraps her up, cradling the back of her head.

"I'm coming back, little sally, I promise, okay?" He broadens his outlandish accent when he talks to her, twanging his vowels—I can't tell if it's intentional or not. "I've got to take care of a few things with Lark, and then I'm coming back and we'll head on home. We'll be back before the birches turn, all right?"

She mumbles something into his shoulder, and he squeezes her again. "I know, but it'll be okay. You'll even ride back with the queen herself. Would you like to ride with the queen? She'll let you wear her Woodwalker boots."

Hettie peels back, tear-faced, gazing at him with utter devotion. And I know this little spark of jealousy is utter stupidity, but who can blame her? This man practically manifested out of the desert to hand back her name and family. And he's making it sound like he can do the same for Andras, and Lila. Practically overnight, he's done more for each of them than I've ever done, than I'll ever be able to do.

I cough to clear the block in my throat, trying to pass it off as impatience. I nod at Sedge.

"You sure you'll be all right?"

"We'll be fine," he assures me. "You just be careful."

"Do you want me to leave Rat with you?"

"We'd have to tie him down to keep him from chasing after you," he says. "He'll be better with you."

I hold my breath, wanting to remind him that Whit doesn't like her corn mush salty, that Andras shouldn't handle things hot off the fire, that Lila's going to need more bandages than Rose if her bleeding doesn't stop.

He must be reading my mind. He nods.

"I know, Lark. We'll be fine. Take care."

All right. Okay, good. Good. I let out my breath and mount Jema before I can delay any longer.

The dandy mounts his own horse and waves to Hettie. She waves back, not even throwing a glance in my direction.

I give Jema a bump, and she ambles forward, weaving through the rocks. I hear the dandy's horse pick up a trot behind me.

"You shouldn't lie like that to little kids," I call over my shoulder. "She'll believe you."

"I didn't lie. When did I lie?"

"Saying she can ride home with the queen. It may have made her happy now, but she'll be sad about it later."

He gives a short laugh. "My ma is the queen."

My cheeks heat, and I twitch back around to face the canyon, unseeing.

Not just a dandy noble. A be-damned dandy *prince*.

Fire and dust and a hot bed of snakes.

We ride down the canyon in silence, stopping only to pick up the fine bulging saddlebag and cushy quilted bedroll that he'd stowed in a patch of greasewood. Rat lopes along with us, nosing here and there in the rocks, coming up a few times crunching on some unlucky creature who didn't bolt fast enough.

We hit the river flat just as the sun clears the canyon wall and turn eastward. I pull my brim down to shade my eyes. The land here is wide and clear enough for us to ride abreast, which the dandy noble prince apparently takes as an invitation. He clucks to his horse and comes up alongside me.

"Sure is a pain to ride into the sun, isn't it?" he asks with a sly edge to his voice.

I tilt my buckler and give him a quick blaze to his eyes. He swears.

"Will you cut that out?"

"Don't be smart if you don't want a fight."

He huffs. "You know, you'd probably save a lot of energy if you'd quit raring to fight everybody."

"We'll both save a lot of energy if you shut up for the next week."

His expression sours, but I kick Jema ahead and hear him cough satisfyingly on my dust.

We bend away from the main road, crossing the river around noon. It's broad and shallow, enough so that Rat can clamber across without swimming. We stop on the far side to let the horses water. To avoid encouraging the prince to try to strike up conversation, I poke a little way down the bank and win a few early mallow fruits for my search. I munch them while dabbling my fingers in the water. Rat rolls in a muddy wallow, snorting with pleasure.

When we come back, the prince is licking his fingers from his own meal.

"Onion roll?" he asks.

"No, thanks. Jema—come on, out of that bush, or you'll get a rattlesnake up your nose."

"What did you just call your horse?" the prince asks.

I glance over my shoulder. "Why?"

"I thought you said Gemma."

"I did. I heard it a while back in Teso's Ford from some academics."

"You *named your horse*," he squawks, "after *Gemma Maczatl*? The Last Queen of Alcoro? Provost of the university?"

Oh, I like his sudden flare of indignation. I turn back to Jema. "Well, I couldn't ask them what they'd named her as I was stealing her, could I?"

He splutters and chokes. I grin behind my bandanna, hoist myself into the saddle, and ride away while he's still working up a reprimand. Once he catches up with me, we proceed in frosty silence.

The land changes from rocky river bottom to rolling scrub flats, thick with juniper and nettle. A few burrowing owls *coo-cooo* in the brush, and toward afternoon we startle a family of mule deer from a stand of lilies. As the afternoon edges onward, a thunderhead builds on the horizon, but it's well to the south of us, too far away for us to hear its rumbles. It billows into the crisp blue sky like milk dropped into coffee, and as the light begins to turn, the scuds and swirls of the clouds light up pink and gold. With a minimal amount of words passed between us, we stop to make our first camp in a hollow that frames the shining clouds. I unpack Jema, breathing that light in all the while, the cool air that's found me from the falling water underneath. I imagine it seeping into my skin, turning the dust inside me, however briefly, to mud.

Apparently the prince is watching the storm, too. "My ma says thunderstorms are a breath of beauty."

The sweetness of the moment sours a little. His ma's damn right, but I don't want him to know that. I rummage in my saddlebag for the last few matches I won from that old man's stage weeks ago. "I'm sure they seem that way from a palace window."

He's snapping twigs for kindling—I admit I'm a little surprised he's doing this himself—but he stops as I start scuffing out a fire ring. I ignore him and his twigs and start my own tent of kindling.

"Hey, Lark," he says, his voice flatter and more direct than it's been all day. "I'm going to tell you a little about my family."

I add a few thick sticks to my tent of wood. "No, thanks."

"No, really, because I suspect you have a picture of what they're like and what I'm like, and I think you've got things a little wrong."

"If you want to be helpful, get the pot out and fill it with water," I say, breaking a branch over my knee. "Or better yet, go see if there's a seep down in those willows and fill it there."

"My pa and ma are king and queen of the Silverwood, it's true," he continues, like he didn't hear me. "But in addition to that, my ma's a Woodwalker. You know what a Woodwalker is?"

"Are you getting the damn pot, or not?"

"They're foresters," he says, making no move. "Expert Wood-folk whose job it is to know the tick of the mountains and keep them healthy and productive for the couple thousand people in my country. Nobody else in the Eastern World has any office like it. But before she was a Woodwalker, she was an outlaw, like you. Kicked out of the Silverwood by my sadistic granddad for getting up in his face. She spent five years scrounging around in exile before she flushed out Queen Mona of Lumen Lake, dragged her through the mountains, and kicked Alcoro out of the lake to create the alliance between Lumen and the Silverwood. And that was all *before* she became queen."

I stomp to my pack and pointedly yank the pot from inside. I dig for the cornmeal and dump some in the pot, splash it with some water, and mix it around to let it soak.

"My pa grew up sneaking around my crazy granddad," he carries on. "A little anarchy here, a little anarchy there, before conspiring with my ma to set Queen Mona back on her throne. And then they got married and started turning us out. My ma was out on a scout run when she went into labor with my oldest sister Vi—she birthed her right on the forest floor. And Ida—"

"Veran," I say, slapping the pot down next to the wood. "Look, shut up, okay? I don't give half a damn about your family. I don't care what all your parents did, or how many amazing siblings you have. You don't piss me off because your royal parents have a bunch of titles. You piss me off because you seem to think you're some kind of savior. I'm grateful for the help you say you'll give us—or I will be when I see you stick to your word—but I didn't ask you to come handing it out. So quit acting like I should be on one knee in front of you, and just shut up, all right?"

He goes mercifully silent. I busy myself with lighting the fire, coaxing all the flame I can out of the single match so as not to waste another one. The bone-dry wood catches fast, and I puff air until the bigger sticks light. When it's good and strong, I swirl the corn mush and set the pot in the flames.

The prince watches. He shifts.

"You'll warp your pot," he says.

"It's already warped," I shoot back.

He goes quiet again. I feed the fire and stir the mush periodically to keep it from sticking. The clouds overhead lose the last slivers of golden light, giving way to blushy blues and purples.

I tap the spoon on the pot. "Give me your cup."

"You know, some sausage would be good with that."

"I bet it would." I can't keep the snarl out of my voice. "Do you want some or not?"

He doesn't answer. He burrows briefly in his own pack and comes up with a flat, lightweight skillet and a waxed paper packet, which he unwraps to reveal a fat link of smoked sausage. Without a word, he slices a pile of rounds onto the skillet, flicks a few coals out from the heart of the fire, and holds the skillet over them. After a minute or so of sizzling, he turns them over to fry the other side, and then slides half of them into the pot. He spoons some of the corn mush onto his greasy skillet, digs in another bag, and sets a wedge of bread in my pot. The smell of onions rises with the spicy scent of fried sausage.

He takes his own bread and swipes up a scoop of mush and sausage.

"Health and good heart," he toasts and takes a bite.

I look at my own pot. I can't recall the last time I had sausage. Or real bread.

I mimic him, scooping up a pile with the onion bread.

It's devastatingly, deliriously good.

I try to take small bites, but even still, I devour all mine before he's finished. I lick my fingers as quietly as I can, savoring the salty grease left on them.

He sumps his skillet the same as Cook taught us in the rustlers' camp, swirling it with a splash of water and then drinking the dregs. This finished, he sets it by the fire on top of my pot.

The sky deepens. A belt of stars twinkle above a jut of distant caprocks.

"That was tasty," he says.

Yeah, it was.

He unhooks his bedroll from his bag and spreads it out. "I've got a few sweet potatoes and some red beans, too. Maybe tomorrow we can make a stew."

A stew would be good, too.

He wiggles onto his bedroll, his gaze up at the deepening sky.

"My brother likes to sing at the campfire," he says. "Do you sing?"

My cheeks heat again. "No."

"Oh, good. Me neither." He stretches mightily, folds his fingers across his chest, and closes his eyes. "Night."

I stare for a moment, but he doesn't stir or speak again. His hair curls over his forehead, black and glossy as a crow's wing—are nobles just born pretty? Or would we all look that good with proper food and a pillow on every seat?

Rat returns from the brush, licking his chops, and flops down by the fire. I shake myself and retrieve my own ragged bedroll.

I roll it out, settle down on top, and try to think mostly of stew.

VERAN

Sunrise over the sagebrush flats comes quick, with no mountain peaks or tangled canopy to hold it off. I open my eyes to the golden shine, the drumming of a grouse nearby, and the smell of woodsmoke.

I start to sit up, and then flop back down.

"Oh," I say aloud. "I hurt."

There's a humorless snort from near the campfire. I roll onto my side to see Lark pouring hot water through a sack of coffee grounds that looks about as old as I am. I have to squint—she's in front of the sun *again*. Did she purposefully go to sleep on the eastern side of the fire so the sunrise would be behind her?

I put my hands on my bedroll, testing my weight. My elbows are quivery, hollow feeling. A tendril of worry curls through my stomach.

"Ground too hard for you?" she asks, swirling her cup.

I frown and push myself upright, my stomach sliding into place with a sour splash. Ugh.

I shake my head, trying to rattle a little sense into place. "Is there coffee for me?"

"Make it yourself." She tosses her cup back with one throw, her neck arching above her lowered bandanna. Her coyote mutt is flopped against her thigh, its head on its paws. It side-eyes me, one giant triangular ear tilted back.

I grumble in their general direction—I have good coffee, better than whatever swill is in her pouch, but I'm too achy to bother with brewing it at the moment. I dig for a handful of dry cherries and chew them slowly, surreptitiously testing the pain in my neck and shoulders.

"How far to Utzibor?" I ask, trying to focus on our task.

"Another day's ride over the slot canyons to the Middle Porra, and then it's another few hours to the camp," she says.

"And it's a rustlers' camp?" I ask, hunting in my pack for my canteen. "Do you think they were the ones who captured Tamsin?"

"They don't use it all the time," she says, turning her head away. "It's abandoned most of the year. And anyway, rustlers are too stupid and single-minded to plan a complicated political heist. If it's not a cow, they're stumped."

I laugh into my water, though I'm not sure she means to be funny. She's still looking away, into the sunrise.

"What do they use it for?" I ask, wiping my mouth. "The caverns, I mean."

She's quiet for a breath or two, absently scratching Rat behind his ears. The beast is still watching me.

"Branding, mostly," she says. "They don't go inside the caves—there's no good entrance or flat ground to make a camp inside, and they're full of bats, anyway. They've built a few outbuildings against the bluffs, and the rest of the space is used for branding pens. It's got wide stone banks that form natural semicircles—they just add wooden gates and fencing in the gaps. They'll come there with the cows they steal a few times a year to change their brands, and then they drive them to Teso's Ford to sell."

"Don't the buyers know they're stolen?" I ask.

"You'd be surprised how many folk don't care about who owns what," she replies flatly.

I press my lips together, trying vainly to resist the urge to snipe back at her.

I fail.

"You don't have to keep insinuating I'm the reason you were enslaved, Lark."

She shakes her head, still not looking at me. "Just shut up."

"No, I'm serious—"

"Yeah, I am, too, Veran," she says, looking back at me, her eyes narrowed over her eyeblack. "You don't even think about it, do you? I bet this is such a thrill for you—camping on the ground, like a real adventurer. I bet it's real fun, getting to play make-believe survival, knowing you've got a roof and a bed when you get tired of it. Sorry if I keep reminding you of ugly stuff. *You* remind me that there are some folk in this world who can't sleep a night on the ground without aches and pains. You've never had to fight for a day in your life."

Something Mama-like flares up in my chest. "You don't know a damn thing."

She snorts again and pulls her bandanna up over her nose. "Neither do you." She gets to her feet, beating the dust off the seat of her pants. She grinds out the fire with her bootheel, scattering the coals and stomping them individually, like they each have my face.

She turns and stalks toward our horses. "Come on, hurry up. We need to be past the slots before the afternoon storms. Come, Rat."

The dog slinks after her, its ears still cocked back toward me, head down.

I'm simmering, my fists clenched up tight. My head pounds, making the world blur a little. I want to shout, I want to knock her down like she did me. Instead I grind my teeth against the metallic taste in my mouth and stuff my things back in my pack.

I wish Eloise was here, to share my incredulity at the Sunshield Bandit's nerve. But in the next moment I'm glad she's not—I hope she's safe and well and doesn't fully hate me for lying to her.

Though if she does, I suppose I can just add her to the list.

TAMSIN

After the second day, the hunger pangs lessen.

"Tamsin," Poia says. "Listen. You have to eat."

My hands are in their usual place, on top of my head, as my arms are bent around my face. I hook my pinkie finger at the barred window.

"Don't play with me. If we have to force you to eat, it's going to be all the more painful for you."

I have no doubt of that. It's been satisfying, this modicum of control, even as I feel my body palpably deteriorating. I've been holding this fetal position for so long that the few times I've tried to uncurl, my arms and legs sink to the ground. I've got no muscle strength to hold them in the air. It's a fast, fascinating slope. How quickly one little decision flares out through bone and sinew, snuffing out the body's little forge fires.

Poia murmurs to Beskin outside the door. Another fascination—they've ceased bickering for the present. I've given them a common concern. What a powerful thing that is, the setting aside of petty differences to unite against a shared evil. No wonder history is full of leaders bent on splitting and categorizing their followers. A group united is a powerful thing.

My mind lapses for a moment—guttering like a cracked lantern. I wouldn't mind these hazy slips so much if they didn't bring a jumble of all the memories I've been purposefully avoiding these weeks. My final few performances, that last one in particular—the whooshed silence in the hall after my final chord. The glancing of courtiers toward influential people—oh, it's so easy to see where loyalties lie when one is waiting to mimic a response. So easy to pick out the leaders and followers. The pockets of applause, some wild, some reserved. The tide of murmuring through the curtains as I carried my dulcimer into the wings.

The sound of running footsteps, the brush of long-fingered hands, the press of silk and skin against a wall. All our earlier discussions of tact, of subtlety, of strategy—they all dissolved in that moment as Iano caught me up and covered my open mouth with his. I had threaded my fingers through his, dulcimer calluses against bowstring calluses, pulling us both against the wall.

Even in my body's weakened state, it still has the ability to thrum with eagerness.

I squash my elbows harder against my aching jaw, physically trying to stave off those visceral memories. Iano's face fuzzes out of focus, and I grapple to replace it with something else—rain, rock, glass. The flush collapses from my stomach and leaves a hollowness behind. My arms tremble from the effort of keeping pressure on my cheeks.

"Maybe we should let her outside," Beskin says on the other

side of my door—I'd forgotten they were there. "Let her walk around a bit."

"Our orders are to keep her locked up," Poia counters—good old Poia, such a rule follower. Anyway, the time when a walk in the fresh air would have helped was about three weeks ago.

"We're also supposed to keep her alive," Beskin says.

"I *know*," Poia growls.

I'd smile if I could.

What a conundrum.

LARK

We ride through the morning, silent. The dandy's obviously pissed, but I don't care. He can pout all he wants. I'm more concerned with taking the right line through the land in front of us—too far east and we'll hit the slot canyons where they widen out, making us backtrack along them before we can find a place narrow enough to hop over. Too far west and we'll arrive at the Middle Porra in the rapids, where the water's too deep and fast to ford. Both routes would tack an extra half day onto our travel time. As this is Dirtwater Dob's range, I want to keep travel time as short as I can.

Also, I'd really like to be rid of the dandy as quickly as possible.

The sun continues to rise over my left shoulder, raising the dust under Jema's hooves. I tighten my bandanna over my nose and mouth. The few times I glance back, whether to look for Rat or check the landmarks around us, the dandy has his head down and his hood up against the glare.

The first time he speaks is close to noon, when I turn Jema up a bare bulge of sandstone instead of continuing our line around it.

"Where are we going?"

"Water," I say. "For the horses. There won't be much between the slots and the Middle Porra."

"Why are you going *up*?" he grumbles. "Last time I checked, water runs downhill."

I stifle a sigh and spur Jema a little faster, not wanting to waste the breath on a response.

"Lark," he calls. "I don't want to climb over some exposed ridge just to have to lead the horses back down. One of them's going to break a leg."

"Fine," I say over my shoulder. "Stay here, and when your horse drops dead from dehydration, you can walk along with Rat."

He curses under his breath, but I hear the clop of his horse's hooves on the pale stone as he follows me. The climbing sun glares off the rock. I pull my hat lower, grateful for the greasy eyeblack on my cheeks.

"It's too bright," he calls.

"Blazes, *shut up*," I reply.

He does, following me silently as we plod up the slope. I sweep my gaze over the terrain in front of us—I haven't been up this particular ridge before, but it should have a water pocket of some kind. This secret is one of the few things I'm grateful to the rustlers for. Despite being stupid, they do have to know how to keep a herd of cattle alive when driving them cross-country, away from the main roads along the rivers. Cook used to send Rose and me scrambling up the white stone rises, searching for the hidden wells that collect in the channels and basins. We'd take our time when we found one, lying on our stomachs to suck down our fill of rainwater before it could be mucked up by cows. Back when I was called *Nit*. Back when Rose had two legs of flesh and bone.

Before Utzibor.

As we crest the first swell in the rock, I spy what I'm looking for—a natural depression carved out by a thousand years of rain. It's dry up top, but it slopes down to form a little well on the northward side of the ridge, shaded by a lip of stone. Water sparkles clear and still in a pool.

I dismount and lead Jema along the channel. Behind me, the dandy's horse stops.

I glance back to see him staring from the saddle.

"Yeah, water runs downhill," I call, unable to resist. "If you want to dig twelve inches in the dirt to make a mucky seep. This isn't Moquoia."

He doesn't answer, just blinks under his hood.

"Come on, get out your canteen before the horses have their fill."

He slides heavily out of the saddle and walks a little bow-legged toward the well. I pull down my bandanna and lower onto my stomach, the stone warming my skin through my shirt and vest. I dip my lips to the water and drink. It's cool and clear, no grit or leaves or cow crap. These ridges have the best water around.

I drink until my belly groans and slither back, licking my lips. The dandy stiffly settles down and lowers his head, touching his mouth to the water. His face is dusty, his copper cheeks a little pinker than yesterday. Maybe I should offer him some eyeblack.

Maybe I will, if he quits being unbearable.

He dips his palms and splashes his face, making muddy rivulets down his cheeks. I give him some credit for forethought—he makes sure to do this away from the surface, to avoid dripping into the pocket. The water collects on the blunt curve of his nose and his unnecessarily long eyelashes. Up on one eyebrow is a little pink scar splitting it in half. I wonder what luxury athletic event he hurt himself in—hawking or promenading or sparring with those bendy toothpick swords with the nubs on the end.

A flicker of guilt flares in my gut, but I'm not sure why. He seems like the kind to hurt himself reading a book.

Silently—blazes, I've shut him up good—he unstops his canteen and fills it.

Rat is standing a little way from the edge of the pool, which surprises me—normally I have to fight to keep him from wallowing before I can take a clean drink. He's panting and has his ear cocked back, like he's distracted by something. Maybe he still doesn't like the dandy, like me.

"C'mere, Rat." I dabble the water, and he lopes forward, head and tail low. He splashes right in, slurping and snorting in the water until it's cloudy with dirt and dog slime.

We let the horses water. I look out over the ridge and check the land in front of us—we're heading in the right direction. I can see the distant buckles where the slots run, almost directly ahead of us. I study the slope on the far side of the sandstone ridge.

The dandy doesn't come up to look with me. He sits down with his hood up, his head bent over his knees.

"I think we can keep going over the ridge, instead of backtracking," I say, coming back down to the pocket. "We may need to lead the horses, though—it's scrubbier than the other side. There might be loose stone. All right, Rat, you dope, come on."

Rat quits rolling around in the water and stands, shaking happily. The dandy wordlessly gets to his feet, gripping his horse's saddle, almost like he's steadying himself.

As little as I want to indulge his delicacy, I also don't want him passing out from heat exhaustion—it's not even midday yet.

"Hey," I say, gathering up Jema's reins. "You're okay, right?"

He gives some kind of response from behind his horse's withers. When he doesn't say anything more, I assume he's still just rankled from being wrong about the water. I start to lead Jema along the ridgeline.

We head up and over the bump of white rock, the flats spreading out before us like a blanket. This high up, I can see the Middle Porra glinting in the distance, and beyond them, a dark line on the horizon that can only be the rocky breaks of Utzibor caverns. The sheer meanness of this trip hits me again—traveling back to the place I swore I'd never, ever go back to. The place that gives me sick heaves just from its memory. For the hundredth time, I wonder how I was talked into this.

Then I remember Rose, and Andras, and little Whit, and Lila. I remember Sedge's bad back and metal collar, and Saiph's lost potential, and Hettie's faraway family.

I remember Pickle, and how easily any one of them is next.

I pick up my pace. The downward slope is steep and shaley, and my boots slip on the loose pebbles. Jema picks along beside me, weaving among the occasional stands of sage and yucca.

We're wading through such a patch, scratchy and thick, when the dandy speaks for the first time since the bottom of the ridge.

"Uh . . . uh, wait."

I look over my shoulder. He's stopped walking, gripping his horse's reins with an iron fist. His face is wide with something akin to dread.

"Lark, uh, Lark," he says—too loudly, like I'm a quarrel shot away instead of a few feet in front of him. He drops his horse's reins and swats her nose. She tosses her head.

"What are you doing?" I ask. Rat is pressing against my leg, letting out that high-pitched squeaky gate sound he makes when he's anxious.

"I need . . . I need to sit . . ." He waves his arm like a blind man, dragging it through a tangle of sage—he doesn't seem to feel the scratches. His knees start to bend.

"Veran." I turn to face him, which is hard because Rat is practically between my legs. "What's the matter with you?"

His hand is out unseeing for the ground, but he doesn't make it to his seat. He gives a short, sharp groan, and then his body stiffens. Half crouched, he drops like a tree, his face hitting the earth without any move to break his fall.

"What the—Veran!" I untangle myself from Rat and lunge up the slope, leaving Jema behind. Veran's on his stomach, nearly under his horse's hooves, head facing downhill, and he's shaking—writhing, practically bucking off the ground. His arms jerk on either side of him, his legs buckle and release at his knees, kicking up dust. His horse snorts and shies, hooves dancing—I lean hard on her shoulder to push her aside. She sidesteps into the yucca, and I dive down to Veran's side.

"Veran!" I heave on his shoulder. He rolls, rigid, onto his back, still convulsing. His eyes are nothing but whites.

I curse, panicky. I don't know what to do, I don't know

what's going on. His back bows off the ground, thumping again and again, filling the air with dust. He chokes, his lips frothy with spit.

I do the only thing I can think of—I roll him onto his side, trying to brace his head with my thighs. Spittle flies from his mouth. His arms churn the dirt. His body's tight as a wound spring.

"Rat! Here, Rat!" I wave frantically—Rat hovers a few paces away, ears back, head down. I pat the ground behind Veran's bowing back. "Here! Come here, sit!"

He reluctantly slinks forward. I grab his ruff and drag him down to buffer Veran's back.

"Veran!" I clasp his head, trying to keep it from scraping the ground over and over. *What do I do?*

And then, just like that, the shaking slows. His hands twitch on the ground, his feet kick feebly. His back stops heaving, his eyes go half lidded. Spit seeps out of the corner of his mouth. A sour smell fills the air—I look down to see a wet patch spreading across his lap.

Rat heaves a whimper wrapped up in a sigh.

I let out my breath, still clutching his face. His trembling slows, and he inhales—only to suck in a cloud of dust. He coughs, spraying spit, but he doesn't come to. I fumble at the knot to my bandanna and shake it out before draping it over his lips.

He lies, loose-limbed, half in my lap, utterly silent. My heart ricochets around my chest—I have no idea what just happened, or whether it's done. I've seen folk collapse before, from heat or dehydration or just plain exhaustion, but I've never seen someone shake like he just did. The bandanna flutters over his mouth.

He doesn't look at all like a dandy noble right now. He looks fragile and hurt. All his angles are bent and awkward, and he's drooling on my knee. His forehead's bleeding.

It's nearly noon—the sun is practically overhead, blazing down on the both of us. Slowly I ease his head off my lap. I unhook his cloak where it's tangled up around his shoulders and ball it under his head. I drape the hem over his eyes.

"Stay," I say to Rat. He gives a little sigh but stays where he is, propped against Veran's back. I rise to my knees and look over the sage and yucca.

The horses have ambled a short distance away, tearing at a clump of sedge in the rocks. Just past them is a lopsided boulder, its narrow end lifted uphill, leaving a wedge of shadow underneath. It's not much, but it's the only shelter I can see in our immediate vicinity.

I crouch down.

"Veran." I prod his shoulder. He doesn't twitch, his breath still puffing under my bandanna.

Gritting my teeth, I grab his wrists and lift them over my head. I've carried people before, but they're usually kids, smaller than me and whisper-thin from work and bad food. Veran is my size, well-fed, and utterly dead weight. I bow my shoulder almost to the ground and loop my arm through his legs. The wet patch on his trousers seeps into my shoulder, but this shirt's seen worse—the guts of a thousand stew-pot animals, snot and slime from Jema and Rat, and a variety of body fluids from every one of my campmates. I ignore it and grit my teeth.

"Damn you," I grunt, heaving upright. I stagger to my feet. "Damn you, blasted sun-frazzled dandy."

I stumble through the sage, my boots catching on the rocky

slope, until we reach the lee of the boulder. As gently as I can—which isn't much—I slide Veran off my shoulders. He bumps down to the ground.

"Rat," I call. He trots forward, and I pull him down behind Veran's back again, to keep him on his side.

It's not much better than the slope, but at least his head's in the shade, and he's not pointed downhill. Once I'm sure he's stable against Rat, I hurry to bring the horses back, leading them to another clump of tough grasses. I pull Veran's pack off his horse and dig out his canteen, dribbling some water between his lips. Most of it trickles out again. I sit back on my heels.

"Damn," I repeat.

This is not an ideal place to be stuck. Aside from the lack of shelter, we're high up, making us likely targets if an afternoon thunderstorm blows in. I glance at the sky, but it's too early in the day to tell if there will be a cloudburst later. I could try to move Veran to lower ground—maybe drape him across his horse—but we'll go slowly, and in all likelihood we'll reach the slot canyons right when the showers would usually start. Those sluices are notorious for sudden flash floods, so fast and powerful they could sweep a horse and rider away in seconds.

And anyway, what am I supposed to do if he doesn't wake up? Keep toting him across the desert? Leave him flopped over with my pack while I try to find Tamsin at Utzibor?

I look at his slack face again. The blood seeping through the dirt on his forehead is starting to mat. I decide to start with that. I take my bandanna off his mouth and splash a little water onto it. I'm dabbing at his forehead, turning everything to mud, when he stirs.

"Veran?"

He squeezes his eyes a few times, and then opens them, blinking fast.

"Veran—are you . . . are you all right?"

His blinking continues. He shifts and moans, pressing his face to the dirt. Dust swirls around his lips, coating them. Hurriedly I swipe them with the bandanna again.

His blinking slows, and his eyes dart here and there under half lids.

"Ma." His voice is a croak.

I lean over him. "Veran?"

His head shifts, craning to find me. "Lady Queen?"

"Veran, it's me—Lark."

"Lerk."

"Right, Lark, the Sunshield Bandit—we're traveling together? We're going to find Tamsin?"

His eyes flutter and then open wide. He squirms, shifting his arms to brace against the ground. He pushes as if he's trying to sit up. I loop my arms under his neck and shoulders and heave him upright—he leans heavy on me, cockeyed, his forehead mucked with dirt and blood. Bracing against my shoulder, he stares hard at me, his gray-green gaze flicking here and there over my face.

He slurs something, his accent too thick for me to understand. "What?"

He stares again, and his eyes seem to clear a little. He looks out at the sunbaked slope, and then to the horses, and then back to me. He wipes his mouth with a limp hand and glances down at his wet trousers.

He sucks in a breath.

"Sorry," he mumbles.

"What, Veran—" I shift my feet and try to prop him up a little more. "What happened? Are you all right?"

"I'm fine. I'll be fine." He spits, drool crusting the edge of his lips. "Is there . . . water?"

I hand him his canteen. He fumbles with the cork, takes a short swallow, and spits again.

"What happened?" I ask again. "Are you dehydrated? Was it the heat?"

He takes another swallow and bends his head forward over his knees.

"Seizure," he mutters.

"What?"

"A seizure!" he says more forcefully. "I had a seizure. I blacked out."

"You were shaking all over . . ."

"And I pissed myself. Yeah. It was a seizure. I get them."

"Why?"

He scowls at the patches of water and spit on the ground. "If you figure it out, let me know." He wipes his forehead and then frowns at the sticky blood left on his hand. "Oh, damn."

"Yeah—you hit pretty hard." I fold my bandanna to a clean-ish patch and start to work again on the mess.

He shifts and reaches behind him. "Is that Rat?"

"Yeah, I made him lie down to keep you from rolling over. I didn't know what else to do."

He closes his eyes as I keep dabbing with the bandanna. "That's all you really *can* do. How long did I go?"

"I dunno, a minute, maybe less. Then you were out for about five minutes." Time feels like it's only just starting up again.

"Mm." He flinches as I wipe the grit out of the deepest scratch. "Well, that's nice. They used to be longer."

I lean back—his forehead's still a mess, but the blood is clotting itself. "How long have you had them?"

"Forever," he says shortly. He turns his head away, gazing out across the hillside, his nose and mouth scrunched up.

I'm not really sure what to say. I'm not really sure what to do.

But then he continues. "I had the first one when I was a few months old."

He sips again from his canteen, swishing the water through his mouth before swallowing. "Mama says she had me in the sling up on Skullcap Bald when I started convulsing. It was my bad luck that the next two came when I was out in the forest again— the second around eighteen months toddling around the Rooftops, and the third a few months later while I was playing with my sisters in the creek. Viyamae saw me go down and dragged me out of the water and hollered for Ma. And after that, Papa said nope, no more. Mama always let us run after her boot fringe out in the forest, but Pa decided that was too dangerous for me. So while Vi and Ida and Vynce got to go out with Mama on patrols and camp checks, I had to stick to the council room with Papa."

His accent is broad as a valley, even more so than when he was chatting with Hettie. He rubs his forehead, a frustrated movement. "It was the worst when I was ten, twelve years old. Three or four seizures a week during the bad spells, plus the day or so of crappy recovery time after each one, when everything's too bright and loud and I'm full of sand. They had all kinds of folk look at me. The Alcorans call it the Prism's disease, because they used to think it was brought on by the Light. But my folk just call it the bows. Most medical types now think it's got to do with a hitch in the brain." He taps his grubby forehead.

Suddenly, the little scar splitting his eyebrow makes a bit more sense. My guilt rushes back.

"Is there medicine for it?" I ask.

He takes another swig of water and spits again. "Nothing reliable. Ma tinkered with all kinds of herbs and weird powders. Some sort of worked, most just tasted bad. It killed her that I was stuck around the palace—I was good, you know, at woodcraft, even better than my brother. I knew every page in the handbook, I knew every bird, every plant." The mud creases on his forehead, his eyes distant. "But you can't do your two solo nights to earn your scout florets if you could collapse and convulse at any moment. Can't keep night watch up in the canopy platforms, can't run the walkwires, can't timber a tree, can't fight wildfires. Can't hike through bear country if you're going to fall and lie around bleeding for a while. Can't be part of a scouting party if your team has to keep half an eye on you and route around the terrain you're not allowed to tackle. And guess what? Can't be a scout? Can't be a Woodwalker."

I dig around for the significance of that word and remember it's his mother's title, the name of the folk who watch over the forest. It hadn't seemed an especially important job to me back when he mentioned it the first time, but he talks about it with more reverence than I've heard him mention kings or queens or ambassadors.

He silently examines an abrasion on the back of his hand. I stare at the nearest tangle of sage.

"Greenbrier," I say. "You didn't pick it because it's nice for birds, did you?"

"The toughest, most stubborn, hardest-to-kill thing anywhere on the mountain slopes," he says with a harsh note. "Wildfire, blight, hard freeze, landslide, drought—greenbrier will be the first thing growing again. You couldn't pry it off the mountainsides if you set the whole country on it."

We're silent. He's not so much leaning on me now as sitting shoulder to shoulder.

"And yet here you are," I feel obligated to point out.

"Here I am," he agrees. "Running clear away from everybody who's ever watched out for me, all so I can feel like I've got some control over something." He sighs and rubs his eyes. "I should have told you, Lark. I'm sorry. That wasn't fair to you. You should have known what you were getting into when I told you I was coming."

I stop myself from pointing out that I didn't want him to come even before I knew he had seizures. But just as I think it, Rose's voice comes to me unexpectedly.

You act like a person needs to be whole to be considered a person at all. That crap's tiring, Lark.

How easy must it be for people to brush off Veran as being less than whole?

Easy, if my kneejerk reaction is the same as it was for Rose.

"You know yourself best," I say. "And you still chose to come."

"It was selfish. You shouldn't have had to—"

"It's okay," I say. "Really."

He keeps his head in his hand. "I thought I could make it."

"I led us up the slope. You said it was too bright."

"You didn't know. And I was already shaky this morning. The brightness just hurried things along. Being tired makes it worse, more than anything. I just had one a few days ago after staying up half the night, climbing around a bunch of ladders in the rain. I fell out of bed and woke up all woozy. I thought I might have another few weeks before the next spell, but I was wrong." He digs his fingertips into his eyes. "I shouldn't have come."

I don't have a response. An hour ago I would have said the same thing.

You haven't had to fight for a day in your life, I said this morning. Thinking his stiff, slow movements were due to a singular night on the ground.

You don't know a damn thing, he spat back.

Somewhere in the scrub, a bird starts singing. I latch on to it immediately, drawn to its familiar jumble of fluty notes. I hear it all the time, the bird that was whistling that day in the rustlers' camp, the bird I asked Rose about. The bird she guessed about, and the guess I adopted as my name.

I nudge his arm, hoping to distract him. "Hey, that bird singing—what kind is it?"

He picks his head off his hand, listening. His shoulder is a warm weight on mine. Rat stretches against our backs.

"Meadowlark," he says. "I think. I'm not so good with the western birds."

I dunno. A lark?

Meadowlark.

Sweet little song in a mess of rock and dust.

"Oh." My voice sounds more strained than I mean it to—I try to swallow without being obvious about it. "Well. That's good."

He looks at me. "Why?"

I tilt my hat brim. "I fibbed to you, too. About my name."

"You mean when you kissed me in the stage? *'On a lark?'*"

"It wasn't a kiss," I say quickly. Stupidly.

"No," he agrees. "You punched me in the mouth. With *your* mouth."

A snort escapes me, bubbling into a laugh. It's strangled and chokey at first, like it's rusty from disuse. But then it clears, and I have a hard time stopping. He snickers beside me.

It's weird—just to laugh.

"Sorry about that," I say quickly.

"The mouth-punch? You decked me with your buckler and you're apologizing for the mouth-punch?"

"Well, all of it, I guess."

"To be fair, I did come looking for trouble," he says. "Is kissing a tactic you use a lot?"

"Never," I say.

There's a weird half silence.

"Anyway," I say hurriedly.

"Anyway," he agrees. "Lark. Sweet little desert bird?"

"Not very fitting, is it?"

"Well, I'm named after a nigh unkillable forest thorn when I could die in a puddle of my own urine at any moment." He shifts. "Maybe we should switch. Dandy songbird and prickly vine?"

"Probably best to keep folk guessing," I suggest.

"Probably." He rocks a little, gingerly, and sets his feet under him. "I think I'll go change my pants."

I keep my hand a few inches from his sleeve as he slowly rises, gripping the boulder behind us for support. "You're not going to topple over again?" I ask.

"Nah, probably not." He tries to pass it off as a joke.

"Veran," I say as he gathers up his pack. "If it happens again—what do I do?"

"Oh, you know." He waves his hand, clutching his pack close to his waist. "Basically what you did. Roll me on my side, keep me from choking on my own vomit. Count the days until you're rid of me."

His voice is light—but I can tell it's forced. He's embarrassed, and I think he feels bad for not warning me. He wades into the sagebrush. There's a jingle of a belt buckle.

"It's all right, you know," I call. "I'm just glad you're okay."

"Yeah," he mutters. I can see the top of his head bob up and down over the sage. "And—yeah, thanks. Sorry."

"At least now I know."

"Yeah." I hear fabric hit the ground. "Now you know."

VERAN

Useless. Utterly useless.

Worse than useless.

A burden.

Even the short walk into the sage to change out of my piss-soaked trousers leaves me wobbly and dizzy. I haven't felt this off-balance after a seizure since before university, and I haven't had two so close together since before even that. With this one coming on the heels of the one after *Bakkonso* just a few days ago, I'm gnawing on worry. I've pushed my worthless body past its normal limits, and now I'm squandering the precious time we need to get to Tamsin. For nearly an hour after I change clothes, it's all I can do to sit propped against my pack, sipping water.

I ache all over. My wrist twinges where I probably landed on it, and my forehead throbs. I don't want to think about what it must have been like to haul my soiled, malfunctioning body under this rock.

Blazes.

Lark disappears a few times—once to hike back up the rocky rise to refill my canteen, and once to ride down the base of the ridge to find better shelter. She leaves Rat with me both times, stopping every few seconds to order him to stay. He doesn't like it, panting heavily at my side and squeaking anxiously, but he stays put. He stinks, his breath absolutely rancid. Not many of my folk keep pets—a few keep kestrels, or put up gourds for purple martins to keep the bugs down in garden beds. A few have Winderan-bred dogs to guard their turkeys or goats. But I don't know anyone in the Silverwood who keeps an animal companion. I found it a bizarre practice at university, where my roommate kept a gecko in a crate. He'd put the little lizard on his shoulder while he read.

Still—I admit I like having Rat with me. Beyond the fact that I could probably be taken for carrion by any passing scavenger, he's kind of funny. He hums and huffs and flops those big goofy ears every which way. At one point, he drapes his head over my knees and closes his eyes.

"You smell," I say.

He sneezes, blowing snot on my clean trousers. That feels deserved.

A little while later, he lifts his head, ears perked. Up the slope comes the familiar tromp of boots.

"There's a stand of boulders with a little copse," Lark says, rounding the rock, bandanna and hat protecting her face again. "It's low enough that we wouldn't be a lightning target, but not so low we'd have to worry about flooding."

"We can try to keep going," I say, despite feeling unable to do anything of the sort. "We've already lost so much time."

"At this rate, we'll come into the thick of Dirtwater Dob's

territory in the middle of the afternoon. I don't want to make camp where we might be discovered—he and I don't quite see eye to eye. We might as well wait until we can move quickly through his range. Can you ride? I'll lead your horse."

My cheeks heat, but I take her offered hand. Her palm is thick with calluses and incidental scars—I know because I have to hang on to it, steadying myself on her shoulder. I follow her precariously to my horse's side, but once there, I shake my head.

"I don't think I can get up, Lark."

"I'll help you—here, you can step up on my leg . . ."

"I can't stay up." I grip the saddle, hot with embarrassment. "I'll fall off—especially if we're going downhill."

She looks down the slope. "Well . . . all right. Can you walk, if I help you? It's not that far—maybe a half mile."

A half mile sounds like a day's trek, but I nod. "I can try."

"We can stop when you need to."

"Okay."

"First, though—here." She leaves me clinging to my horse and approaches her own, digging through her pack. She comes up with a threadbare bandanna and a little tobacco tin. She pops open the tin to reveal a gob of dark, sooty eyeblack.

She dips her thumb and smears it over my cheeks. She shakes out the handkerchief and ties it over my nose and mouth.

"This smells like blade polish," I say.

"Probably because I use it to clean my sword," she says, knotting it behind my head.

"Urg, Lark."

"It's your own damn fault—who travels into the desert without even a handkerchief? Or a hat, for that matter." She reaches over my shoulder and flips my cloak hood over my head.

"That'll have to serve, for now." She makes one last check of all our gear and then leads my horse around behind hers, tucking the reins under her panniers. She comes back to my side and gathers up her horse's reins.

"You know, I always thought the bandanna and eyeblack were mostly fashion choices, to hide your identity," I say. "But they really help, don't they?"

Her eyes roll so hard over her greasy cheeks I'm afraid they'll pop out. "By the Light, you are an *imbecile*." She takes my right arm and loops it over her shoulders, under her thick ponytail of locks.

Maybe it's the tone of her voice, or her solid weight supporting my whispery body, but the insult sounds less fierce and more familiar than yesterday's. She settles her arm around my waist, clucks to her horse, and starts us all down the slope.

She's a hair taller than me, making her head cant toward mine as she holds my weight. My feet skid in the loose sandstone, and more than once she has to muscle me upright to keep me from falling. We knock foreheads a few times, worsening my headache. I lean hard on her shoulder, panting against the oily bandanna.

"Sorry," I mumble, over and over. "Sorry."

"Knock it off," she finally says. "It's annoying."

"Sorry."

She huffs and adjusts my arm over her shoulders. "What's that bird singing?"

"Which?"

"The buzzy one."

"Are you just trying to distract me?"

"Yes. What is it?"

"A pewee," I say. "A western one. It says its name, hear it? *Pee-wee.*"

"If you say so. What's that growly one?"

I tilt my ear up to the sky. "Harris hawk. They hunt in groups."

"And the cooing?"

"Hopeless dove."

"Hopeless?"

"That's what it says, listen—*No hope. No hope.*"

She snorts, which I'm quickly finding is her idea of a laugh. I strain to hear any other calls, but our party's slipping and crunching drowns everything else out.

"What's that plant?" she asks, nodding to the closest sagebrush.

I *tsk.* "Oh, please."

"Oh, sorry," she says seriously. "I thought you'd know."

"I *do*—"

She snorts again.

"Very funny," I say, using sarcasm as a cover. *The Sunshield Bandit is joking with me.*

We continue. I take a bad skid, grabbing her vest to steady myself. She pauses, tucks her horse's reins into her belt, and takes hold of my wrist to keep me up on her shoulder. With her arm up, her shirtsleeve slides down toward her elbow, revealing the longsword tattooed on the inside of her forearm. The point drives into that scarred concentric circle.

My stomach twists. It's faded and distorted.

She's had it for a while.

My gaze slides up toward her wrist, where the edge of a letter begins.

"What's that word on your wrist?" I ask.

"Strength."

"And the one on your left?"

"Perseverance."

"Why'd you pick those?"

"Because that's what it takes to survive."

"Hm." I maneuver my foot around a desiccated root. "Maybe for you. I'd probably tattoo *don't stand at the top of stairs*."

Her gaze cuts sideways. "Is that how you got that scar?"

"On my eyebrow? No—would you believe it, that didn't come from a seizure. It came from me falling off a walkwire after I snuck out when I was fourteen. I'd never been allowed to run them before. Ma and Vynce make it look easy." I shrug. "I thought I could do it, too. I was determined to do my two nights."

"Two nights—you've said that before."

"Yeah, to go from trainee to scout, you have to spend two nights solo in the forest." I hitch myself a little higher on her shoulder. "You get a cloak and a compass, and nothing else. They ride you out to the middle of the forest and give you an end point. You have two days to get there on your own to earn your florets. All my friends were earning theirs—I must've watched a dozen of them come back all dirty and victorious, kneeling in front of my ma as she swore them in. And even though I was still having one or two seizures a month at that point, I decided I had to try, too. I made it two miles from the palace, when I was defeated by the first walkwire. I fell into a laurel slick twelve feet below and carved up my eyebrow."

I remember that ugly swoop of emptiness as my feet slid off the wire, the brief realization before hitting the branches that I had made a terrible mistake.

"One of the Woodwalkers found me crawling out of the ravine on his way back to headquarters." I step over a rock. "Of course, it was only *after* the tongue-lashing and the embarrassment of it all that I found out that no trainee does their two nights completely alone—one of the older scouts secretly tails them to make sure they don't get into trouble. Like falling off a walkwire."

Lark's bandanna puffs—I can't tell if it's a laugh or not. I glance at her. "That probably sounds completely stupid to you. I'm sure at fourteen you were already taking down slavers."

"I wouldn't know," she says, adjusting my arm on her shoulder. "I don't know how old I am."

Oh.

I . . .

Oh.

"Oh," I say.

"I *feel* like I'm fifty," she says. "'Specially when I get to coughing. But Rose and I both guess I'm twentysomething. I only really started keeping track of time after the wagon. I'd started my bleeding before I left, so I must have been around thirteen or fourteen. After that I was with the rustlers. Ow—you've got my hair."

"Sorry." I try to loosen her locks from my dire grip. "So . . . rustlers. Cows, I take it?"

"Usually. Sometimes goats, but they're a damn nuisance to drive."

"I see. Is that where you learned to fight?"

"It's where I learned most things. They don't teach you much beyond digging in the quarries." She pauses to tug on Jema's lead as the horse noses a clump of grass. "Everybody needed to be able to fight a little—we weren't a big enough posse that we could afford to leave the herds undefended. Rose had the better aim—they gave her the crossbow. I wound up with the long-sword after we found an abandoned cache in the water scrape."

"And the buckler?"

"The buckler . . . I won that after I turned over my first wagon."

I glance at her. "Really? You took up slaver-hunting before you had the sun strategy?"

"It wasn't a conscious decision," she says. "I didn't one day decide to be a bandit known for using the sun. I didn't even decide I was going to be a bandit who went after wagons. It was just a few weeks after we'd left the rustlers, and Rose and I were at a dead end—our original plan had been to try to find work in Teso's Ford, or along the stage road. But there are bounties in all the towns for escaped slaves."

"There are *not*," I blurt in shock.

She cuts her gaze crossways at me. "Yeah, there are."

"Slaving is illegal in Alcoro. There would never be official bounties . . ."

She tuts behind her bandanna. "Come on, Veran. I know it's all law and order for you, but not everything is done by the rulebook. Slavers lose money when slaves run away, so they post bounties. Do you think a half-starved canyonman is going to turn down twenty keys just because his government doesn't condone slavery? That's how Sedge got the ring around his neck. They're rougher on you if you've already escaped once."

I break my gaze away to stare at the ground in front of us.

"I didn't know that," I finally say. "I thought only Moquoia funneled money into the system."

"Everybody's always willing to think it's somebody else's problem," she says.

"Did *you* escape?"

"Obviously."

"But I mean—more than once?"

"No. Just once."

"How?"

She's quiet, scanning the horizon in front of us, watching for storms or bandits or who-knows-what that I'm not aware of.

"Whatever heroic image you've got in mind isn't how it happened," she says. "I didn't battle my way out. I didn't know how to fight at that point, and I was skinny and small. They were moving some of us from Tellman's Ditch to another quarry. There had been rains, and our wagon got stuck in a drainage. There were four of us inside—the guards pulled us out, unlocked our wrist cuffs, and told us to get behind each wheel and push. The driver whipped the oxen, and the two guards switched between pushing at the back and levering the wheels. At one point, they were both on the far side of the wagon. I'm not sure what I was thinking—I certainly knew there was a higher likelihood of a beating than an escape—but I just sort of sank down into the reeds in the drainage and crawled away. It was my luck they were stuck on that one wheel for a while, or they'd have caught me right away."

"Where did you go?" I ask, trying to keep the awe out of my voice.

"Nowhere," she says. "At some point I was smart enough to realize they would search straight up the drainage to find me, so I left the reeds and started walking out into the desert. They started hunting for me not long after—I could hear them shouting. I crawled into a catclaw thicket to hide until night fell, and then I kept walking. I had no water, and I didn't know how to find it. I passed out the following afternoon under a juniper. If Rose and Cook hadn't found me while they were collecting firewood, I'd have just died right there. Cook gave me water and told me there would be more if I helped Rose chop sweet potatoes." She shrugs under my arm. "And so began my life for the next three years, till Rose and I stole a few horses and some supplies and rode off."

"That's amazing."

"It's really not," she says.

"Just walking away?" I say. "Without knowing what's in front of you? That's brave."

"It's no different from what you just did—walking off from something relatively safe into something unknown."

"Except, as you've seen, my decisions were driven by vanity, not bravery."

"Bravery isn't a motive," she says. "You don't choose to do something because of bravery. 'Bravery' is just a by-product of doing something, a word that gets awarded after you succeed. If I'd died under that juniper tree, crawling away from the wagon would have been stupid. But because I survived—out of luck— you say it's brave."

I chew on that for a moment. The slope is leveling out, and a little way ahead of us, I see the boulder copse we're heading for.

"I dunno, Lark," I say. "I know folk who've failed, and they're still considered brave for trying. If my ma goes out to battle a wildfire, but doesn't manage to control it, and it burns that season's timber harvest, is she less brave for trying? That's happened, by the way."

"You're a big fan of your ma, aren't you?"

"You're dodging my question."

She rolls her eyes again. "I'm not going to say your ma's not brave. You'd probably make a show of trying to fight me, and I just want to get you down this hill."

I'm about to reply that I've never had the stamina for fighting, when my foot slides on a loose rock. I pivot toward her and instinctively throw my free arm around her shoulder—she grabs me just as quickly under the armpits, and by the time I've dug my toes into the ground, we're in an awkward, crouched embrace. Our eyes lock for a breath, just inches away from each other. Behind her, Jema throws up her nose at the abrupt halt.

Heat flares in my face—I hadn't thought anything could be more embarrassing than making a fool of myself in a foreign court, but turns out throwing myself into the arms of the Sunshield Bandit tops it.

"Sorry," I gasp, trying to dig my toes farther into the loose soil. I don't know how to push away from her without first pulling myself closer to her face.

Her bandanna pulls toward her mouth as she draws in a breath. She widens her stance, and with a heave, hefts me upright. She plants her palms on my shoulders and locks her elbows, holding me at arm's length.

"There, you see?" she says. "Always trying to pick a fight. I'm warning you—I'm only going easy because you make pretty good sausages."

My cheeks blaze more, but I'm grateful for the banter. Finally steady, I drop my grip around her neck. "What happens when the sausages are gone?"

"All bets are off." She doesn't take her palms off my shoulders. Her gaze sharpens over her bandanna. "You're good?"

"No, I'm a mess."

"Well, keep it together for another fifty feet." She rearranges Jema's reins in her back pocket and then threads my arm over her shoulder again. With a last bit of huffing and puffing, we reach the stand of boulders, their flanks overgrown with stubborn catclaw. With a grunt, Lark slides me off her shoulder and into the shade. I wobble to the ground with relief.

"Blazes." She winds her arm and straightens her vest where I yanked it askew. She looks down at me, and her gaze drops to my hands. I've opened my palms toward her—my breath just hasn't caught up.

Or maybe the words just stick.

Thanks. It bubbles up in my chest, and I mean to say it— really I do. *Thanks, Lark. You saved my life a little while longer.*

I pause too long.

"Oh—water?" She digs for the canteen and places it in my upturned hands.

"Thank you," I blurt.

"It's your canteen," she says, shrugging and turning away. "I'm going to settle the horses. Rat, you stay."

Rat yawns and flops down beside me. I close my fingers over the canteen as Lark clucks to the horses and leads them out of the brush. Sighing, I drag my hand over my face before remembering the eyeblack. I gaze wearily at the black smears on my palm.

"I'm an idiot," I say.

Rat thumps his tail once on the dusty ground—probably in agreement.

Resigned, I work the cork out of the canteen.

I know one thing for sure.

I'm pulling out all the stops on dinner tonight.

TAMSIN

I'm woken this morning by the creak of my cell door. I open my bleary eyes and wait to move until the world has stopped spinning. But I don't get the chance. Before I fully latch on to consciousness, Poia takes my shoulder and turns me onto my back. I grunt in surprise, but I'm weakened by lack of food and life in general, and it takes little effort for her to hold me in place. I hear the pop of a cork. Poia kneels over me and grasps my cheeks in her fingers. I cry out, squirming. She tips the contents of a bottle into my mouth.

Great shining colors of the Light, she may as well have dunked me in oil and set me on fire. It splits my head open, blinding me. I writhe under Poia, my back bowing off the ground as I gag on the liquid, spraying bloody droplets.

"Get off," Beskin says suddenly. "She might vomit."

Poia moves off my chest, and I roll onto my side like a dying cockroach, tears and snot streaming down my face as I spew the liquid out. I've once seen a boiled egg burst out of its shell, the gelled albumin blistering in the water. That's how it feels, like everything soft and tender in my head is bursting from my skull only to be seared by boiling water. I shake, blinded.

"That should fight off infection, anyway," Poia says matter-of-factly. "Beskin, change out her mat and blanket." She pokes me in the back as I clutch my head once again, trying to squish the insides of my skull back behind my teeth. "Tamsin, I'm going to bring you some broth later. You'd better drink it, if you don't want your mouth to get worse."

They roll me off my bloody mat and set a new one down. They drop a new blanket over me. I don't even care that it's actually big enough to cover my feet. I curl into a ball, half on the mat, half off. Fetal and on fire, hungry and broken, I've got no strength left to spare for my brain, which happily plunges into self-pity.

Iano.

I squeeze my eyes shut, tears still streaming from them. Great Light, Iano. I miss you. I miss your proud eyes and steady arms and archer-clever fingers. I miss your deep, genuine laugh and your determined sense of right and wrong. I miss the way you threaded my hair loose and kissed my eyes. I miss the way you listened, the way you leaned forward, rapt, as if hungry for each word.

What you would think of me now, hair gone, eyes red, left with no words but the guttural sounds I can spit from my swollen lips. You'd turn away. I know you would—it's only what would be expected. You are the people's prince, the court darling, drawn to lovely, adorned things. You're expected to appreciate strength not in raw form, but carefully polished and presented just right. A pretty woman in pretty silk singing with a pretty voice.

I can't blame you. I was glad I fell so neatly into that box.

Leave it, Iano. The picture you're hanging on to isn't accurate anymore, and it won't be ever again. Don't let them twist you into anarchy over me, because all the things you would have fought for are gone now.

Leave it.

Leave me.

LARK

I shift in my saddle, surreptitiously loosening my belt. I ate too much last night, more than I have in months, though I've been reasoning that *somebody* had to finish the last serving in the pot, or it would've attracted animals during the night. To be fair, I think Veran made an extra helping on purpose. I can still taste the sweet potatoes and fat red beans, mixed up with spicy sausage and garlic and onions fried a little too long. By the Light, that was a good meal.

I wonder what else he has in his pack.

He's less woozy today, after some rest. The bruise on his forehead is a rich berry purple, half covered by a flop of dusty black curls. We've fashioned a kind of cowl out of his cloak, and I gave him another round of eyeblack. He made a fuss about washing out my sword rag before tying it back over his chin. Now he's almost unrecognizable, just a pair of eyes and eyebrows and those obnoxious eyelashes and that little scar. I study him out of the corner of my eye—the horses are picking their way down a crumbly slope, and I don't want him swaying too much.

He catches my glance. "What?"

"Oh, I was just thinking, if it weren't for how clean your tunic is, you could pass for just another desert vagabond. Maybe we can turn over a stage and score you a hat."

He grunts and hitches the handkerchief farther up his nose. "After all this is over, I'm taking you shopping. You'd be amazed how much stuff you can get without violently taking it from other people."

"Oh, don't preach at me. Most of the stuff for camp I *have* bought, fair and square, from Patzo's in Snaketown." Though let's not get into details about where the money came from. "And it's thanks to your nosy old professor that I can't anymore."

"If by nosy you mean *traveling in a private stage across the desert, minding his own business until you attacked him*, then yes, I see what you're getting at."

"He reported me back to Callais! He tripled my bounty and set the reward for my live capture! What does he want, to hang me himself?"

Veran, strangely, looks away, down toward the dark line that's the rock cliffs of Utzibor. Just another hour and we'll be there. "On the contrary, Colm has . . . different reasons for wanting to talk to you."

"Something tells me a hundred fifty keys is a little high for just a conversation."

"Do you know who Colm is?" he asks, looking back at me.

"Well, I know *now* that he's some high hat at the university."

"Well, yeah, he's a dean, and he's married to the provost, Gemma." He throws a dirty look at my horse. "But he's also

the brother of Mona Alastaire, queen of Lumen Lake. And fifteen years ago, Queen Mona and her husband, Rou, and their
twin daughters, Eloise and Moira, were in Matariki with me and
my ma for a diplomatic summit, when Moira disappeared off the
pier. They searched the docks, and then the streets, and then the
whole city. Lumeni divers were rushed in to trawl the harbor. My
ma's entire Wood Guard was sent into the surrounding countryside to search for leads. The Paroan and Cypri navies were sent
out. For months and months they searched. But there was never
a body, or any record of where she might have gone. This was
at the height of the ocean slave routes—after that happened, the
navies started going aggressively after seafaring traffickers."

"Because a princess was stolen," I point out. "Not because
of all the other few hundred folk who suffered the same thing
before her."

"I don't deny it. And the crackdown on ocean trafficking
made for a jump in desert trafficking, and here we are. But that's
not the point—the point is that Queen Mona and Ambassador
Rou, and Colm and the rest of us, have always kept our ears
open for leads on Moira. And your reputation is known more
broadly than you think. So when you appeared in Colm's stage
door . . ." He trails off and shrugs.

"Why does everybody assume I personally know every
slave who's passed through the system?" I ask.

"Well, you know more than the rest of us, for sure." He eyes
me sideways over his handkerchief. "And you told me you have
a Lumeni girl in your camp."

"She's not full Lumeni, though—"

"Neither was Moira. Neither is Eloise. Mona is Lumeni, like
Colm. Ambassador Rou is Cypri. Brown skin, brown eyes, fine

curly hair. Moira and Eloise are a blend of both—light brown skin, freckles, curly golden-brown hair."

I glance down at the back of my hand, sun-crisp and scratched, a dark sepia under the dirt. Lila swims in my vision, her tan skin and long lashes and tendency toward fickleness. If anyone in our camp could be a princess, it's her.

"Lila's hair is sort of dirty blond," I admit. "But it's not curly. And I don't think she has any more freckles than anybody else."

"Well, I don't remember exactly how identical Eloise and Moira were. I was little at the time, and I've only seen one portrait of them together. They could look completely different now. Are Lila's eyes blue or brown?"

"Brown."

"Hm," he says. "You see why I might be interested in the others in your camp? Why Colm might be interested, or Eloise or Ambassador Rou?"

"I'm not going lie, Veran—if she's not dead, she's probably not in the Ferinno. I mean, there's a chance it could be Lila. Or it could be someone still in the quarries. But if she was stolen in Matariki and put on a ship, she was probably sent around the cape. At the very least, she's in Moquoia, but it's more likely she's out on one of the islands. All the slaves who work here in the desert started out here—even the older ones."

He frowns in thought. The sun is edging lower in the sky— once we cleared the slot canyons after lunch, I purposefully put myself on his western side, but unlike the past few days it was more to be sure I could see him clearly in case he started to fall. Now he turns to me again, squinting against the glare behind me.

"This is a big reason we need diplomacy with the Moquoians

to go through," he says. "Creating a strong alliance with them means we can start dismantling the system that took Moira away. We can make sure it doesn't happen again."

I look away. "I get that. But do you understand how it feels to hear you say that, when it didn't matter for the rest of us? Nobody sent out navies after me. Nobody stood on a dock, wondering where I'd gone."

"How do you know they didn't?"

I squint hard at the dark line of Utzibor, my mouth twisting underneath my bandanna. I'd like to tell him off—he has no right to make assumptions about my past. Though, I suppose, that's all I've ever done.

When he continues, his voice isn't smug or barbed. It's soft. "I know your campmates are your family, but if you don't know where or who you came from, who's to say someone *didn't* search for you? Who's to say someone doesn't miss you?"

"I know who I came from," I say, trying to inject warning into my voice. *Stop, beware, turn back now.*

But the idiot doesn't catch it. His face splits with shock. "You do? Do you have names?"

"A name," I say pointedly. "My father's."

"But that's something! That could be *everything*! Have you asked around? Have you checked town registers—"

"No."

"But he could still be alive—by the Light, Lark, he could be in the Ferinno."

"Probably."

He stares at me, squinting hard against the sun. I look out over the terrain—we're starting the gradual descent toward Utzibor.

"Don't you want to find him?" he asks. "He probably looked for you—he might still wonder where you've—"

Finally, I snap and turn back to him. "I know my father's name because it was on my *sale papers*, Veran. I didn't get captured. I was sold by my family."

He goes silent. He goes so silent I can hear the gears grind to a halt in his head, and then the clamoring of questions as they racket around his mind. And I don't want to answer them, but I know if I don't he'll always have this assumption, that a family can only be a unit, a tether—not the knife that cuts your rope.

"Vega Palto, Port Iskon," I say. "That's his name, and where the sale was made. My name is Nit, and that's as much as I know. The rest of the document was just my health records at the time of purchase. I risked my neck to swipe it out of my file—I actually broke my finger on purpose so I had to be brought in for medical examination." I tilt my left hand to show him the little bumpy knit on my knuckle, lost among all the other scrapes and scars. "And that's what it told me—that my Alcoran father sold me for a hundred fifty keys. Funny, that's still what I'm worth, isn't it?"

He's dead quiet. The rocks sound with the dull thud of our horses' hooves. The brush shakes as Rat lunges. A doomed creature gives a death squeal.

"The wild thing," I continue, "is that I remember him a little. I try not to, but I distinctly remember that he liked cinnamon in his coffee. I remember that smell. And if he was Alcoran, then I assume my mother was Cypri, and I remember her braiding my hair. And I remember feeling happy. That's the weirdest part. All the other kids I knew who had been sold came from broken families, desperate families, families willing to sell a spare child on a ten-year bond to try to make ends meet. Not me—I was sold by a happy family, one that could afford a spice like cinnamon, with no bond. No expectation or interest in ever getting me back."

"It . . ." he begins. "It could be a mistake, Lark. Or . . . or . . . you could be remembering it wrong . . ."

"You're right," I say sharply. "I could be inventing the part about being happy—it's the part that makes the least amount of sense. I could search them out and find out that I made up those little details—maybe they're layabouts who just needed extra cash." I mirror his question from a minute ago. "You see why I might not want to make a search for them? At least on my own I know what I have. I know what I am. I'm not interested in my family, Veran. They're not safety or identity to me. It's just blood, and that's less than worthless out here. Family doesn't last."

A rocky bluff has risen to my right, momentarily blocking the red sun as it sinks toward the horizon, so he doesn't have to squint to look at me. He just gazes, his sagebrush eyes wide and sad over his blackened cheeks and my grubby polishing rag.

"Don't pity me," I say.

"I'm not."

"Yes, you are. You're doing it right now. Stop it."

"I'm not pitying you," he says. "I just . . . I wish I could change it."

"Life can't be changed. We're just meant to react to it."

"I don't . . . I don't believe that."

"You wouldn't, would you? You can probably give a single word and your whole world tips to suit you."

"Except that my body gives way and takes my mind with

it," he says, each word slow. "And it endangers my life and restricts those around me, and I won't ever be able to do the things I know I can otherwise do, and I'll probably die a young man."

My breath catches behind my bandanna.

I keep forgetting that.

I look away, just as the bluff to my right disappears. The sun blazes across my eyes. I tip my hat brim down.

"Sorry," I mumble. "I didn't mean that."

"Yeah, you did. But I understand. I've been more privileged than most. I'm certainly more privileged than you. But the idea that life is what it is, and I'm just meant to roll along with it—what's that mean for me, Lark? Do I stay in my room with pillows on the floor for the rest of my life? Because a lot of folk think so."

"There must be something in between pillows on the floor and flirting with every opportunity death throws your way."

"If there is, I'd like to hear it, and fast," he says. "Because so far I've only become acquainted with the two extremes. Honestly, if I could die at any moment, I'd rather it be a death in action rather than on the floor of my bedroom."

Before I can reply, there's a sting on my right wrist. I shake off a horsefly, letting out a breathy curse. It's bitten me right on the *e* of *Strength*. I stare at the tattoo, remembering my comment to him yesterday, that these two things—strength and perseverance—are what it takes to survive.

What if you had both of those things, but they weren't enough?

"So don't pity *me*," he says.

I look up. "I'm not."

"Exactly."

I twist my mouth behind my bandanna, and his cheeks round under the eyeblack. Then he cuts his gaze away, rubbing his eyes.

"You and the be-damned sun, I *swear*."

I glance out at the horizon, about to relent and offer to ride on his other side for a while, when my thoughts freeze in my head. I suck in a breath.

"Veran, stop—hold on, stop."

He eases gently on his horse's reins. I move Jema closer to him, peering hard at the terrain in front of us. He follows my gaze.

About a mile ahead of us lie the buckled caverns of Utzibor, spread with the wide tamped-down branding rings. Already, in the orange sunset, a few black specks are flittering around the cottonwoods, bats roused from their daytime roosts. Soon there will be more, many more. But between us and them are four figures, mounted, picking their way along a brushy draw to keep out of sight of the adobe compound built against the bluffs. Late sunlight flashes off a mattock head strapped to a pannier.

"Who's that?" Veran asks. "Are those Tamsin's guards?"

"It's Dirtwater Dob," I say. "Another outlaw. I had a run-in with him and one of Tamsin's guards a little while ago. They must have found where she's holed away."

"Dammit." Veran's hands tighten on his reins. "Of all the rotten timing—what do you suppose they're trying to do?"

"I don't know, but I'm sure it's no good. Let's dismount and get a little closer—there's a copse over there where we can wait and watch. We have to make sure this really is where Tamsin is, anyway."

We slide off our horses and lead them down the slope, keeping an eye on the little posse creeping toward the compound. I glance over my shoulder a few times, nibbling my lip—I wish we could put the sinking sun more directly behind us, but to do that we'd have to ride nearly even with Dob's group. Fortunately, the approach is studded with rocky upthrusts, like roots of the cavern bluffs. We skulk from cover to cover, trying to keep the horses out of gravel that might slide and give us away.

Finally we reach the shade of a stand of cottonwood trees, thick with scrub willow around their roots. We tether the horses and creep through the thicket. At the edge of the brush, we lie on our bellies, gazing down at the compound.

Dob and his three companions have sheltered themselves by the river and are scoping the compound from the sage. I scan the branding rings and the lumpy adobe buildings pressed up against the cavern bluffs, their desiccated timber-and-reed roofs red in the sunset. One outbuilding looks less abandoned than the others—the windows are uncovered, and the clay chimney is black with new smoke. The dirt leading to the door is tamped down, not windblown and scattered with twigs like a few of the other buildings.

"There are mules," Veran whispers, nodding.

In the shadowed corner by the occupied building is a covered hitching post, where two dun-colored mules and a donkey idly nose the ground.

"I think that bigger one is the one I saw last week," I say. "The one the woman was riding when she ran into Dob's posse."

"What are they looking for?" he wonders, his gaze on Dob. "Do you think they've heard about Tamsin?"

"I can't think what they'd want with her," I reply. "It's not particularly like Dirtwater Dob—he's a poacher and a part-time rustler. He's never had an interest in slavers or the road besides wanting territory closer to the grazing grounds up north. More likely he's here to settle a score—that traveler he jumped had a lot of parcels, which means money and goods. He's probably in the mood for a heist."

Veran blows out his breath. "What do we do?"

"We're going to have to wait," I say. "See what Dob does. Who knows—maybe he'll do some of the work for us."

"You think he'll let Tamsin out?"

"No, you dunce, I think he might kill a few of the guards inside."

He winces. "I was sort of hoping we could avoid killing anybody."

"How did you think we were going to break Tamsin out?"

"I . . . hadn't worked much further past making it out of your camp alive," he admits.

"Blazing Light, you really have absolutely no forethought, do you?"

"None at all," he confirms. "My excuse is that part of my brain is the part that's glitchy."

I shake my head, and he snickers.

"Though I can pick a lock," he says. "I figured that might be useful."

"It might be. But let's wait, and get a sense of what we're up against first. We don't know if there's one guard or twenty. I'd rather Dob do that dirty work, if possible."

He pulls his handkerchief down and settles his chin on his arms. I set my cheek on my fist. Rat lopes out of the underbrush and flumps down between us.

"Your dog stinks," Veran says.

"You would, too, if you lived off carrion."

"I guess so. What a diplomatic worldview. You could make a persuasive politician. Shall we switch jobs?"

I get a sudden vision of him stranded out here, all his soft edges and determined buoyancy eventually sanded raw into sharp weariness. "No," I say quickly. "But only because you'd make a lousy bandit."

"That's true." He adjusts his folded arms. "Ah well, you'd probably start international wars, just for kicks."

"I think I'd prefer to just lie around and eat jam biscuits," I say.

"Without dirt on them."

"Exactly."

"Why jam biscuits?"

"I once snitched a hot plate of them off a windowsill in Bitter Springs when we passed through with the rustlers. Rose and I stuffed our faces with them. They were the most delicious things I've ever eaten."

He turns his head so his ear is resting on his arms and his gaze is on me. There's a funny look on his face, something quiet, like the sound of rain outside a window. A jam biscuit is probably one of the least glamorous things he's ever eaten. To get away from that soft stare, I look back out toward Utzibor.

"That's the ring where Rose lost her leg," I say, nodding to the clearing to the right of the compound. I'd finally filled him in on the rest of my campmates during the morning's ride.

He turns his head to look. "It must have been horrible."

"Yeah. It was. She passed out for most of it. I had to hold her still while they sawed it off. I still . . ." I trail off, fiddling with the edge of my bandanna. "I think about it a lot."

"Do you have nightmares?"

"I dunno, sometimes, I guess." I fidget with my hat. "But Rose has the worst of it, obviously. She lost her leg."

"Just because somebody's suffering is worse doesn't mean yours doesn't hurt, too."

Oh, that's ripe for a snark, something acidic about what a little philosopher he is, how wise and noble an oracle. But I can't make the words come out. They hover just behind my bandanna, my gaze fixed on that place, that precise place, where we sat slumped in the dirt. It's a wonder the ground isn't still red there. Is her blood still mixed into the soil?

I clear my throat. "I hope she's okay."

"Me, too," he says.

We melt into silence again. Dob and his posse are edging along the riverbank, toward the outer edge of the compound.

"Lark," he says.

"What?"

"If you don't mind me asking, how did you end up in the Ferinno when you were sold in Moquoia?"

"I wasn't sold in Moquoia."

"You said Port Iskon."

"Yeah, that was what was on my papers."

"That's not an Alcoran name," he says. "At least—there's no port town I've ever heard of by that name. Alcoro's coastline is too rocky to support much more than Port Juaro and Port Annetaxian."

"And obviously if you've never heard of it, it must not exist."

"I'm serious, though. *Iskon* is the name the Moquoians call the redwood trees. It's the name that the first color of the year comes from, *iskonnsi*."

"But my father's name was Palto."

"Yeah, so . . . how did that happen? How did an Alcoran man sell you in a Moquoian port, only for you to wind up back out here?"

I gaze out at the compound, unable to really process whether this is important, or whether it means anything at all. The more I think about it, the more it needles me—not that I started out in one place and ended up in another, but that I've had the wrong interpretation of one of the few known details about my life. It shouldn't surprise me. Probably most of the other things are wrong—the cinnamon, the braids, the happiness.

Just as I'm about to muse further, there's a familiar whirring. The sky, now a deep blush, is speckled by a rising cloud of black bodies. They shoot from the dark gaps in the rocks like a flash flood. They swirl and swarm, growing thicker and louder, diving after invisible bugs midair. Veran picks his head up off his arms.

"Whoa," he says.

The smell hits me, that wave of ammonia, bringing a familiar churn in my gut. But instead of the usual visions of a bloody bow saw separating Rose's calf from her knee, I glance sideways. Veran's lips are parted, his eyes darting here and there as the bats cloud. His hands twitch and then turn over, palms up. It seems an odd gesture with the way he's lying, strangely solemn. Almost reverent.

I look back up at the bats, now spiraling out of the Utzibor crevices with such force they create a kind of cyclone, like a dust devil kicked up in a wind. A cloud of them races over our heads, swooping for the bugs rising from the heads of the cottonwoods.

"They're amazing," Veran says, hushed.

I never thought of them as more than a timepiece, and a rank one at that. But the more I watch them bank and dance, like a current of water suspended in the air, the more I agree with him.

"Yeah," I say.

He follows a trail of bats as they break off toward the sinking sun, and then his gaze drifts back down toward the compound. He squints in the dying light.

"What are they doing?" he asks.

Dirtwater Dob and his group have left their horses standing in the river. Now on foot, they're creeping toward the outer edge of the compound, where the mules and donkey are tethered.

"They're probably waiting for dark, and then they'll steal the mules," I say.

"That one there is messing with something."

At first it's hard to make out—the sky is so vivid that the little flash in Dob's hands could just be a reflection of sunset. But then the flare grows. It smokes.

"What the *blazes . . .*"

"Is he setting a fire?" Veran pushes himself onto his forearms. "Why?"

We both scramble to our feet. Rat starts upright, ears perked.

One of Dob's group peels off toward the mules. Dob himself takes a few running steps and hurls his flaming bundle at the splinter-dry brush roof of the compound.

Veran jumps forward and then back immediately. His fingers flex. "What—what do we do?"

"Wait a minute, let me think . . ."

"We have to get Tamsin out!"

"We don't even know if she's really in there!" I snatch his arm to keep him from rushing down the slope. "And we can't just run in with Dob attacking—we're going to end up in the crossfire."

"But . . . but . . ."

A tongue of flame shoots up from the roof, and then it runs sideways, licking through the brush. There's a shout from inside. Dob and his companions are running for the door at the far end of the compound, weapons ready in their hands. In the sky, the bats veer from the burning roof, spiraling away across the flats.

Veran shakes my arm. "*Lark!*"

"They set the fire on one end to cause a distraction," I say. "They're going to ransack the place and leave it to burn."

"It's going to spread! We have to get Tamsin out!"

"But if we rush in while they're fighting—"

There's another shout and then a smash of crockery. Part of the roof caves, sending up sparks and a glut of black smoke. It's burning fast.

Faster than they expected, probably.

"Dammit." I pull up my bandanna. "All right. Cover your mouth. Keep your head down. Rat, stay. You *stay*."

We break from the cover of the trees and race down the hill. Off to our left, the fourth bandit is dragging the mules and the donkey back toward the river, hollering to keep them moving.

"What's our plan?" Veran gasps as he keeps pace with me.

"By the Light, I don't know." I'm only just realizing he has absolutely nothing in his hands, no weapon, nothing to defend himself with. But then the bandit with the mules shouts, his face turned toward us. We've been spotted—it's too late to send Veran back.

"You try to find Tamsin," I say, sliding my buckler from my forearm to my fist. "Look in the outside windows. There's a grain storage down at the far end—"

"The end that's burning?"

I don't have time to answer. As we reach the door, it flies open, and out races Dirtwater Dob in a plume of smoke, his arms full of foodstuffs and loot from inside. The distance is too short for Veran and me to dive for cover or veer away—all we can do is skid to a stop. Dob does the same, his eyes creased with outrage over his colorless bandanna.

"*What the—*"

There's a roar from inside, and through the door barrels the one-eyed traveler like a bull out of a pen. Her patch is off, baring a milky blind eye, and her shoulder and sleeve are soaked with blood. Dob wheels from me, dropping his armful of loot unceremoniously onto the ground, and grabs for his mattock. With a mighty swing that's as much luck as aim—the one-eyed traveler doesn't slow down a single click, her sword leveled for his neck—his mattock skips over the top of her attack and catches the side of her face.

Oh, thundering rock, it's horrible, blood and mass and teeth flying. I crouch with my sword and buckler up as if it'll shield us both from the sight of the traveler spinning in place, the side of her head smashed like a pumpkin. She drops to the ground in a heap, surrounded by a neat perimeter of red. Dob spares himself a single moment of shock, staring at the work of his mattock as if he never expected a piece of heavy-duty timbering equipment to wreak such damage to a human face. Veran's breath is ragged behind me.

There's shouting—a quick glance over my shoulder shows the fourth bandit racing up from the river where he's left the mules. From the doorway staggers another, clutching a bundle of jarred goods and rubbing smoke from his eyes.

"Damnation, Dob, Berta's down! And I can't get that last

door open—" He stops, seeing the mangled traveler and Dob and me and Veran and the fourth bandit racing up behind. Dob shakes himself out of his pause and swings on us, his mattock head flinging red droplets.

He lunges. "I'm just about *sick of you!*"

I catch the swing on my buckler—*blazes*, it's heavier than any longsword, and not built to deflect like a regular blade. Instead of glancing off the rounded edge, the pickax head simply punches through the mirrored surface. Pain races through my knuckles from the impact. Gritting my teeth, I swing for his open side, but his companion jumps in with his bundle of jars, throwing the lot at my head. I duck as jars and lids smack off my forehead before shattering around my feet. The smell of pickles swirls together with the scent of blood and smoke and ammonia. My sword connects with something soft, but it's a glancing blow, giving way into open air.

A flare goes up from the roof just behind Dob, sending a thick column of smoke billowing out the door. It buys me a half second—Dob pauses to paw at his tearing eyes. I use that moment to whirl around to look for Veran—I have to get him out of here. But as I turn a complete circle, I realize he's not behind me like I thought he was. I spin back to Dob just in time to raise my buckler again for another swing from the mattock—I dodge—and then I see Veran. Dob's companion is on the ground, clutching his forehead, which is covered with glass splinters and bits of pickled okra, and the fringe of Veran's boots is disappearing into the smoking doorway.

"Veran!" I arc my sword and catch Dob's next lunge on his mattock handle, biting deep into the wood. A follow-through with my buckler is hindered by the giant, unwieldy pickax head—the best I can manage is a heavy kick to his kneecap. He hops away, but by now I hear the approaching footsteps of the fourth behind me. I pivot at the last second and deflect a familiar scythe as it cuts through the air. I catch it under the head and slice the curved blade off its handle. This time the follow-through is clear, and I ram my buckler into the face of the bandit with the missing tooth.

It's the last clean hit I land before Dob jumps back in. A tangle of snarling arms and legs, we topple to the ground, me sandwiched between their two ripe bodies like a sardine in a tin. A box to my ears leaves my head ringing. I plunge my elbow backward and connect with a nose. Warm blood spurts over my shoulder. There's a crash of falling timber, and then we're swamped in smoke, turning the fight into a blind grapple in the dirt. My cheek scrapes raw on the ground. Sand fills my mouth.

Blazes.

This is not how I'd wanted to die.

Or rather, this is not *where* I'd wanted to die.

Fighting, okay.

But not here.

And honestly, not right now.

I throw all my weight to one side. Whoever's on top of me tumbles off, giving me just enough time to use my momentum to arc my sword through the air. It flies downward, and this time, it bites deep, the blade stopping only when it strikes bone. A scream spouts toward the sky.

My shoulder throbs. My brain fixes on the blank need for survival. I grit my teeth and set my feet under me, my sword still wedged in bone.

Not going to die today.

TAMSIN

I open my eyes. The bats are flying, swooping, squeaking. But that's not what roused me. I frown, the world blurring around the edges. There's some other sound, something else that prodded me out of the haze my body and mind are sinking into.

Loud sounds. Loud voices.

Shouting.

I pick my head just slightly off my mat, my muscles protesting. I can't keep it up for very long—I lower my ear again to the ground, my limbs hollow. There's a clang that sounds like two pots clashing together. I wonder if Poia has finally snapped. I wonder if she's laying waste to the kitchen, shattering Beskin's obsessive ordering of the crockery.

Then somebody screams.

Not shouts, as if angry.

Screams. As if hurt.

I pick my head up again, forcing my trembling arms to hold my weight. I squint up at the little barred window in the door.

Standing up to look out seems beyond me—though I doubt I could see anything in the gloom anyway.

As if in response, the dark window flares. A flicker of orange plays against the metal bars—a deeper orange than sunset *dequasi*, the sky hues I've been studying and naming and whispering to the emptiness. An *urksi* orange, the deep mellow color of contentment.

Contentment. I lay my head back down, my gaze still on the little window. It's a beautiful color. Very close to mine, the noble title I gave myself as I walked into Tolukum court three years ago with a new dulcimer. *Tamsin Moropai in-Ochre.*

Perhaps this is the fadeaway. Perhaps this is the final dissolution. A melting into the *opohko* of the Light, a consciousness sliding from flesh into fractured color.

The screaming outside is a little weird, though. I wouldn't have expected there to be screaming.

The orange burns brighter, becoming yellow-gold. A waft of darkness curls past the bars, like the clouds of bats teeming outside.

Smoke.

It's Beskin screaming, I'm sure of it now. It's high and long, and then it cuts off abruptly. There's a crash of falling dishware—now it really does sound like the kitchen is being destroyed. More shouting, harried words in Eastern. Perhaps if my head were clearer I could make them out, but my Eastern has never been as fluent as Iano's, and I doubt I've studied the nature of the commands and invective hurtling up and down the hallway. The smoke grows thicker—it's sliding in between the bars and the gap under the door. My carved letters of *HIRES* dance and haze.

A shadow appears in the little window. The knob on the door rattles violently.

"Locked!"

I understand that word, though not the ones that come after it, the hurried jabbering. The knob rattles harder, followed by a few blows of what sounds like a pickax against the door.

The air is growing warm, and it's only just starting to occur to me that I might want to be alarmed. Something is on fire. Something happened to Beskin. I don't especially care about Beskin's well-being, but if something—someone—has hurt her, then what will happen to me?

It seems a silly thought. Just a moment ago I thought I was finally sliding into death.

The door shudders under the repeated blows, but it doesn't give way. Whoever is hammering at it stops and tries to peer through the bars again. But now the light outside is bright as morning, and the smoke is thick, and I doubt they can see anything inside my lightless cell.

"Help," I say.

But the weak, ill-formed word is lost to a crash—not the fall of crockery, but of timber. The little gap between the rafters and the wall flickers red.

The door shudders a few more times, and then there's an impatient shout outside. A fragment of burning material falls behind the shadowy figure at the door. He curses and disappears. Without his head blocking the window, the air is glittery bright.

I cough on the thickening air. Pain shoots through my head, momentarily blinding me. I crawl forward, my head hanging off my shoulders. My limbs quake, my vision spins. My fingers bump wood and travel upward, up to the blank patch where the doorknob was removed. I curl my fingers, trying to grasp something, but there's nothing to hold, nothing to shake. I press feebly on the wood, hoping it might give way after the beating from outside, but nothing yields. I curve forward against the door.

Timber crashes again. Ash and sparks trickle down from the ceiling. Smoke pours in, burning my lungs. I cough again. I had hoped to die placid and easy on my mat—now I'll be found arched and blackened against the doorframe. The letters I worked so hard on—earned so much pain from—won't be found after all. I slump down, my cheek pressed to the cool earth. I should crawl to the little window to the outside, give the bats my final moments of lucidity, but I realize I've used all my strength.

I thought the bats would save me. Thought for sure Iano would see the strange flourish in my signature and follow it like an X on a treasure map. Bats mark the spot.

I don't blame him, or the bats. It was too much to hope for.

Heat shimmers through the door. I cough again and close my eyes.

My brain numbs. It whispers. It murmurs, quick and urgent. It fumbles, metal scraping metal. It turns. It clicks.

It creaks.

Something nudges my body, something dense and hard. A slice of light beams across my eyes. I slit them open.

The door is open. The door is open and hinging against my rib cage.

In the doorway is a crouched figure, blurred face half covered by a dirty cloth, holding a *bintu* knife and an ornamental hairpin. The jewels gleam red.

"It's okay," he says in Moquoian, though the panicked look in his eyes suggests things are absolutely not okay. "You're okay, Tamsin."

He thrusts the knife and pin into his pockets and stoops down. He loops his arm under my shoulders and lofts me upright.

Oh, blessed colors, my body is not ready to be vertical—my vision gutters, and I sag on watery legs. He wobbles at my fall, spreading his feet wide to keep us upright. He coughs violently.

"It's okay," he croaks, and he takes a few steps forward. My feet drag behind us—I can't make them move. The air is painfully hot, singeing the hair on my arms and legs. A chunk of the roof falls in a shower of sparks—he ducks and staggers to one side to avoid the burning timbers. But he stumbles, and in a lurch of pain and panic we're suddenly crouched on the ground, and Beskin's face is right there in front of mine—only it's half her face, quickly being seared by the line of fire that's already engulfed her torso.

He mutters something, something fast and frantic in Eastern. He places his feet to haul us up again. I try to help but it's all I can do to lean, to hold, to not immediately die. But I'm too heavy for him, and the smoke is too thick, and more of the roof is falling, and we're just not going to make it, my friend—it was a valiant attempt, but we're not making it out of this with our lives. Beskin's face is gone, swallowed by flame.

There's a burst of fiery timber, but it's not from above—it's from ahead of us, just a little way down the hall. A door has been smashed inward, and standing suddenly in our midst is a specter of shadow and flame, a sword and a shield glaring with light, burning eyes set between black hat and black cheeks. But it's not some sun guardian come to guide us to the hereafter—the sword is sheathed, and the figure lunges forward. My world tilts once more, and my feet leave the ground, and then we're running, bounding through the shimmering hall toward the open door.

The blaze of heat shivers away—cool air slides over my skin. My body bounces and jostles like the braces on a stage-coach. There are urgent words, a grappling of arms that bloom new pain, tipping, tilting, sliding. My brain fuzzes into half consciousness. And then there's a new movement—rocking, rollicking. The sound of crackling timber gives way to a cycle of pounding hooves.

I don't know how long this lasts. My vision is still dark. My mind slips and sloshes. Every now and then something prods me—fingers clamped over my wrist, a hand held close to my mouth. Pulse, breath. Checking for life. I can't be sure if they're finding it or not.

I don't realize we've stopped until my body tilts in a different direction. A web of arms are sliding me into open space. I drift to the ground.

The shuffling of fabric. Words in Eastern. Words in Moquoian.

"Tamsin? Tamsin, I'm going to prop you up. I have water here. Can you drink?"

The words are slanted, accented with vowels a little too broad and consonants a little too sharp to truly be from home. Something bumps my lips, and I do my best approximation of swallowing, spilling a generous amount. Even lukewarm, the water soothes my scratched throat and burning mouth.

There's water on my forehead now, too. Someone is sponging me off.

I slit open my eyes. Against a *bakksi*-indigo sky thick with stars are two shadowed figures. One of them is occupied with something—there's a flick and a sizzle, conjuring a flare of light. I squeeze my eyes again. Some murmuring in Eastern, and then the light fades to an ambient glow behind my eyelids.

"Sorry—the candle's lowered. You can open your eyes."

I'm not so sure I can, but I give it a shot anyway. Shadowed in the dancing glow are two faces, one wide with worry, the other sharp as flint. Both are smeared with grease and soot and—on the worried one—bruises. Nearby comes the sound of fast, labored breathing—flopped on the ground is a dog, panting anxiously, tongue lolling from its mouth.

"Hi," greets the worried one a little lamely. He shifts his arm under my head. "Uh—I'm Veran. And this is Lark. We're friends. Iano sent us to find you."

My eyelids flutter. The sharp one says something in Eastern, her voice desert rough. He replies in some kind of affirmative, his voice worried.

"*Rä, isten slo . . .* Tamsin, can you—do you understand me? Do you remember Iano?"

Do you remember Iano? I was trying not to, thanks. It hurt too much. Then I lost the last shreds of self-discipline and I couldn't stop.

The worry on his face deepens at my silence, but I gesture for the water again, my hands mothlike. He holds the canteen to my lips, and I drink with more conviction this time. I wipe my mouth.

The sharp one speaks in Moquoian. "Your mouth hurt?"

I wince. My mind's clearing up, enough so that I can catch the gist of the next exchange.

Of course she is hurt, I'm just trying to figure out—

No, look at her mouth, look how she's drinking. Why isn't she saying anything?

She's probably hallucinating, she probably doesn't know where she is, she might not remember . . .

While they bicker, I inch my fingers along the dirt, to where the single flame dances in the corner of my vision. They both realize what I'm doing as my fingers brush warm wax.

"Do you need the light?" asks the worried one. "Here, Lark—*dit'isponse lell . . .* oh, you want to hold it yourself?"

The sharp one keeps a hold on the candle as I lift it and bring it close to my face. The worried one lifts a hand to push it away.

"Careful, it's dripping—Tamsin, careful, not so close . . ."

I push his fingers away and draw the flame next to my lips. Its heat bathes my skin. While they both stare, their eyes glinting wide, I tilt back my head and yawn.

I watch them react, watch them blanch as the light washes over the split cut neatly into my tongue.

VERAN

Both Lark and I stare at Tamsin. Her tongue has been split in two.

"Blessed earth," I stammer, before switching back in Moquoian. "Tamsin . . . they . . . they cut your tongue?"

She closes her mouth and nods, settling back against the crook of my arm.

"By the Light. I'm—I'm sorry. We'll . . . we'll get you to a healer . . ."

She flutters a hand, in equal parts dismissal and nonchalance. Her meaning is clear—a healer might be able to keep the wounds free of infection, but nothing's going to knit the muscle back together again. I exchange a glance with Lark—her lips are pursed, her brow furrowed.

"There are a few scraps of parchment in my pack," I say. "And some charcoal—can you get them out? She can write down responses instead."

"Let's try to get some food in her first—she looks starved."

Lark sets the candle down and opens up my pack. "Ask her if she's hungry."

"The easiest thing I have is honey . . . but that's not enough." I rack my brain, trying to recall all the passages I've read on reviving someone who's collapsed, all the times Mama described treating ill scouts, all the times I've been roused, aching, from the floor. "She's going to need salt, broth . . . something more substantial . . ."

"And we can get it in Pasul, Veran—right now we just have to do the best with what we have." She pulls out the jar of honey. "Try this for now."

I reach for the honey, but my fingers close on Lark's sleeve instead. It was a blind race in the dark from the collapsing building to this patch of desert, and I'm only just now noticing the tears in her sleeves, the singed edges, the shiny skin below— burns. And—by the Light, that's not a shadow along her shoulder, it's blood.

"You're . . . you're hurt."

Her head is tipped forward, her hat brim hiding her face. "Yeah, it better not have screwed up any of my tats."

I dip my head and catch sight of the dark spatters on her nose, her bandanna. "Lark—"

She shakes my hand off her arm. "Come on, Veran—focus on Tamsin. The stronger she is, the quicker we can get to Pasul. We can be there by tomorrow evening if she can hold up." Her gaze slides from my eyes to around my ear. "And anyway, you're hurt, too."

"I am?"

She brushes her thumb over my temple, bringing a sting with it. I follow her touch and feel a raw patch near my hairline.

She leans forward to examine it, her face just a few inches from mine. The candle flame gleams gold in her eyes. My stomach swoops with the suddenness of one of the Utzibor bats.

Her gaze shifts back to my eyes, and she hurriedly straightens again. "I'll clean it out later. Focus on Tamsin right now."

She goes back to the honey jar and pops the cork off. I look back down at Tamsin slumped in my arms. She's leaning her head against my shoulder, but her eyes are still open. She looks worlds different from the pencil portrait in Iano's room. Her cheeks and eyes are sunken, her skin paled to gray, her lips cracked. Her thick, shiny hair has been shaved off, and not gently, either—there are rough patches where razor cuts have scabbed over. But she's eyeing me with that same wry discernment the artist depicted in her portrait, the gleam of an *ashoki* who has a truth to tell.

I shift into a more comfortable position, easing her upright a little more. Lark rummages in my pack for the cook kit and comes up with my wooden spoon.

"We have some honey here," I say. "Would you like to try to eat some?"

Tamsin nods. Lark dips the spoon and holds it to her lips. She takes it from her and eases it into her mouth. Her gaze flicks over me, squinting a bit as if in thought. With her other hand, she pokes me in the chest.

"What?"

She gestures to me, and then at Lark.

"You want to know more about us?"

She nods, sliding the spoon out of her mouth and dipping it again in the honey pot.

"I'm Veran Greenbrier, son of King Valien and Queen

Ellamae Heartwood of the Silverwood Mountains. I'm the translator for the Eastern delegation. I traveled with Princess Eloise Alastaire and her father from Alcoro to Moquoia."

She nods in understanding and dips the spoon again.

"And Lark . . ." I look to her, unsure of how she wants herself described.

"I am helping," she says in rough Moquoian.

"She's my friend," I say, before I realize I've said *my friend* instead of the generic *a friend* that I had been going for. It hangs in the air for a moment. I wait for Lark to scoff or snort, but she doesn't. Maybe her Moquoian isn't polished enough to have caught the difference.

Tamsin is eyeing Lark, her gaze drifting to the back of Lark's hand. She sets the spoon in the pot and slowly closes her fingers over Lark's wrist. The last time I tried that, I got a buckler to the face, but Lark allows Tamsin to hold the back of her hand to the candlelight. The flame flickers off the rays of her sun tattoo.

Tamsin's eyebrow lifts.

She knows.

"Um . . . so, Lark is known to some as the Sunshield Bandit," I say quickly. "But she didn't attack your stage outside Vittenta."

Tamsin rolls her eyes.

"You knew that already?"

She nods and dips another spoonful of honey. "*Uah.*"

It takes me a moment to realize she's spoken. Her voice is raw and cracked. So she can speak a little—the Moquoian word for yes has no tip-of-the-tongue consonants.

"Do you know, then, who attacked you?" I ask.

"Hire," she says.

I lean forward. "Who?"

She looks pointedly at Lark, cupping her hands to form parentheses. "Hire."

Understanding blooms in Lark's expression. Her jaw clenches.

"I should have known it," she says in Moquoian. "The woman with one eye—when she sees my brand . . . I should have understood."

Tamsin nods, but I'm still lost. "Understood what?" I ask Lark.

She shakes her head and switches back to Eastern. "When I ran into that woman in the desert, she caught sight of my brand, and she immediately went on the attack. I didn't think much about it at the time—a lot of people in the desert don't like me— but now it makes more sense. She was a Hire. They're this crazy group of fanatics—they see people under bond as the lowest members of society, working without the dignity of wages, as if we do it out of laziness, or carelessness." She looks at Tamsin again and asks in Moquoian, "She has the curved tattoo?"

Tamsin nods and points to her ankle.

"Some Hires—not all, mostly the really dedicated ones— get tattoos," Lark says to me. "Two half circles, not quite touching—sort of like the circular brand slaves get, only not complete. Open-ended."

"Not bound," I say, aghast.

"Right."

I goggle at her. "I've never heard of them."

"It's not an affiliation one might want to parade around

court," Lark says, holding the honey pot so Tamsin can dip the spoon again. "They have a lot of swagger when they're among their own kind, but in greater society they tend to be looked down upon."

"That's . . . that's terrible. But—this is good, too. These are answers." I look back at Tamsin, sliding back into Moquoian. "We know who attacked you, and she's dead now. You're safe—Iano's safe. The court . . ."

But Tamsin is shaking her head. Gingerly, she slides the spoon from her mouth and covers one of her eyes with her hand, still shaking her head.

"The woman with the eyepatch?" I ask. "She's dead, we saw the bandit kill her . . ."

"It wasn't her," Lark says in sudden comprehension. "You are saying it wasn't her who attacks you? Who hurts you?"

She lowers her hand and nods.

"No' her," she says, and then winces at her pained words.

"Not her," I repeat, dumbfounded. "What about the other woman—the one we saw in the hallway?" I try not to picture the flames crackling across her skin.

Tamsin shakes her head again.

"Iano was getting threatening messages from a big man with a *bintu* knife," I say. "Was there anyone like that?"

Again, she signals no.

I chew my lip. There goes that brilliant plan of mine—that Tamsin would know who the traitor in court was.

Is.

"That means whoever it is," Lark says in Eastern, voicing my own thoughts. "Whoever's doing all the plotting—"

"They're still out there," I agree.

We're silent a moment. Tamsin sips some more water and eats another spoonful of honey.

"Well . . . we'll figure it out, I suppose," I say. "Iano's waiting for us in Pasul. Maybe he's found some answers. He's going to be beside himself that you're alive . . . what?"

She's closed her eyes in a slow, aggrieved movement. Her brows knit together.

"What's wrong? Don't you want to see Iano?"

She opens her eyes, but she doesn't look at either one of us. She stares past us, up to the starry sky overhead. Her expression is something very close to resignation. Lark and I exchange a glance. This might be more than a yes-or-no conversation.

Lark checks the horizon behind us. "Listen, why don't we get a little farther away? It would be smartest to cover as much ground as we can now and rest once the sun rises. If sparks from the fire hit the flats, it's going to spread in a heartbeat. And I can't be sure Dirtwater Dob won't pick up our trail."

I glance at her. "He got away? I thought I saw bodies . . ."

"He was on the ground when I ran into the compound. He wasn't there when I left." She looks away. "I killed the one with the missing tooth, and I finished off the one you brained with a pickle jar."

Her voice is flat, straightforward, but not entirely steady. I hadn't wanted to kill anyone. Now I realize *she* hadn't wanted to kill anyone, either.

She looks back at me, her face shadowed and smudged with soot and blood. "Let's get out of here."

"Right, okay. Tamsin, we're going to try to go on a little farther. Is that okay?"

She nods and fumbles to put the cork back in the honey. I

finish the job for her. Lark snuffs out the candle and bundles things back into my pack. While she brings the horses over, I unhook my cloak and wrap it snugly around Tamsin.

"Do you mind riding with me?" I ask her.

Tamsin's eyes are closed again, and she gives a slight shake of her head. The fabric of my cloak rumples, and her hand emerges from the folds. She unfurls her palm to me. My folk's gesture of thanks. This must be in some Moquoian primer on Eastern culture somewhere. I clasp it and give her a squeeze.

Lark brings my horse alongside. "You mount. I'll lift her up."

I climb into the saddle, but instead of stooping to Tamsin, Lark rests her hand on my knee.

"Are you okay?" she asks. The moon is half full and low on the horizon, but it slants off her eyes all the same. Like she really is made of sky.

"Yes, I'm fine."

"You're tired," she says. "It was bright in there."

Something stirs in my chest, something other than the shame I might normally feel, something warmer. "I'm okay right now."

"Tell me," she says, her grip tightening. "Tell me if you don't feel okay."

I nod. "I will."

She lets go and crouches down. She cradles Tamsin and straightens, settling her in my arms. She's almost weightless, birdlike. I clutch her close to my chest and take up the reins. Lark mounts her own horse—stiffly, I think, slowly. Light be damned, she'd better not be more hurt than she's letting on.

She situates herself in the saddle and whistles to Rat. With a jerk of her head, she starts us forward into the night.

TAMSIN

We ride through the dark. At some point I fall asleep—I wouldn't have thought it possible, woozy and swaying on the horse's back, but one minute I'm leaning against Veran's chest and the next I open my eyes to a deep midmorning shade.

I shift, testing the aches in my body—I'm on the ground, on somebody's bedroll, with a cloak draped loosely over me. We seem to be under an overhang—the ground is shaded and cool, but the air is starting to warm. Carefully I turn onto my side, wincing.

Lying next to me is the bandit, Lark. She's on her back, her fingers laced over her chest and her head turned toward me. It looks like her hat was propped over her face but has since slid off. I study her for a moment, taking in her sloped nose, her full lips, her dark eyelashes, the spatter of freckles hiding under the grease and dirt and sunburn on her cheeks. She looks tough, it's true, but it's not the mean toughness I might have expected. It's more of a resigned toughness, an armored veneer tacked up out of necessity. There's a crease between her brows, but her lips are relaxed and her breathing is deep. The coydog is flopped over her calves, his paws twitching in sleep. I try to reconcile the placid image with the tales of the notorious bandit who has been plaguing the slave trade for the past four years.

"*Psst.*"

I look away from Lark to the edge of the rock overhang, where Veran is sitting in front of a tiny cookfire. He presses a finger to his lips and then scoots forward, hand extended. I take his arm and let him help me move toward the fire.

"We stopped around dawn," he whispers. "She made me sleep first. I only just managed to make her take a rest herself." He has a shiny burn along his temple, taking a small bite out of his hairline, and the dark copper of his forehead is discolored with a purplish bruise. He hands me a canteen. "How are you feeling?"

I swish water around my mouth and level my hand. So-so. He nods and gestures to the fire, where there's a little pot bubbling.

"I'm boiling some jerky and onions and a few herbs to make a broth. It might help more than the honey." He points down the hill. "There's a little creek in those willows. I can help you get down there if you want to wash."

I nod, and he helps me up. The process is painful and slow—I lean heavily on his arm as we shuffle down to the bank. He helps me dip water and wash my face and hands. I rub weeks of grime off my neck and arms, watching dirt slough away and cloud the water. He guides me to a gnarled old tree trunk to lean against, stepping away while I relieve myself. Once I'm put back together and marginally cleaner than before, he steadies me back up the hill.

"'hang you," I say to him back at the fire, trying not to wince at the tenderness in my mouth and the garbled edges of the words.

"You're welcome. Here." He strains some of the broth into a cup and hands it to me. "See if that's any good. Don't have high expectations."

It's not bad—more nourishing than salted corn mush, anyway. I sip it slowly. He offers a bit of an onion roll. I dip little pieces in the broth to soften them.

He gestures to his pack. "I have some parchment and charcoal. Would you be willing to write? I have some questions."

That sounds like an ordeal, but I have questions for him, too. I beckon for the parchment, and he lays a few sheets on the back of his camp skillet and hands it to me. He waits while I block out some letters, my fingers shaky.

WHERE ARE WE?

"About fifteen miles from Pasul," he says. "Lark thinks we can make it by this evening, though we'll have to stop before that to rest the horses."

And me, I think. I sip some more broth and write another question.

IANO WAS GETTING THE BLACKMAIL LETTERS?

"Yes. They were delivered through the head of staff. Fala. We don't know who was sending them to her. You have no idea who attacked your stage?"

I shake my head. NIGHT. 5 OR 6 RIDERS. BLINDFOLDED, THEN—

I gesture generally to my head, my mouth.

He winces. "I'm sorry, Tamsin."

I go back to my broth, trying to appear unbothered. Because

if I dwell on it too long, I'm going to sink back into that horrific spiral of fevered pain, of shock, of denial. The gutted realization of not only being completely powerless—hands and feet tied, eyes covered—but of losing a power I hadn't considered losable.

The broth swirls warm in my mouth, like blood. My scalp prickles.

I turn a tremor into a hair toss before remembering it's gone. I clutch the charcoal and write a question simply to redirect the conversation.

WHAT IS HAPPENING IN COURT?

"Oh, well—" His face blanches, as if in realization. "Um, there's a new *ashoki*. It's Kimela Novarni."

I had guessed as much—I saw her name specified in the first few blackmail letters, so the news doesn't bother me as much as he seems to think it might.

"He had to go through with it," Veran continues, and I'm oddly touched that he's defending Iano to me. "Appointing Kimela, I mean. He didn't know where the threat was coming from, or how to make it stop, until we decided to seek out Lark. She was the only person I could think of who might be able to find you. And she did—she understood the bat in your signature right away."

It had been a long shot, but it had worked after all. I glance back up at the sleeping bandit.

"Do you think you'll be able to set things right?" he asks. "I mean—obviously you'll need to heal. And I suppose . . . there won't be much you *can* do . . . for a while . . . not that, I mean, that you can't *do* anything, it's just—"

I wave to shut him up. I choose to be slightly offended, because it masks the real emotion simmering just underneath—he's right, if we're being honest. For so long my focus was on first surviving prison, and then dying with some shred of dignity, that I didn't spend much time dwelling on how little I would be able to accomplish if I ever got out.

I sip some broth, wincing as a shred of jerky catches in my teeth.

FIRST THING WILL BE FIGURING OUT WHO AT-TACKED, I write. CAN'T DO ANYTHING WITHOUT KNOWING WHO'S BEHIND IT.

"But we have a lead, don't we?" Veran asks. "The Hires. That's something we didn't know before."

IT'S SOMETHING, I concede. BUT NOT EVERY-THING. JUST BECAUSE POIA WAS A HIRE DOESN'T MEAN THE MASTERMIND IS.

And anyway, the Hires aren't like the philosophers' coalition or mushrooming enthusiasts. They don't advertise public meetings in the town square. Their business is conducted in people's homes and tavern corners, and they're known for protecting their own. Waltzing back into Tolukum and asking around for people affiliated with the group wouldn't just be fruitless—it could turn dangerous.

I close my eyes, thinking of all my enemies in court, everyone I nettled since my career began. I think of all the people who would have an interest in preserving an economy based on slave labor—quarry managers and plantation owners and angry change-averse citizens who mistake personal nostalgia for universal utopia.

It could be—give or take—*anyone.*

"This isn't going to sit well with the Eastern courts," Veran says, more to himself than to me. "Rou and Eloise assumed the alliance would be difficult to secure, but they didn't expect it to deteriorate this much."

I'd forgotten about the Eastern ambassador and Lumeni princess. It suddenly strikes me that he hasn't said anything about them leaving Moquoia.

WHERE ARE THEY NOW? I write.

"Well . . . I'm not entirely sure. If they're not already in Pasul, they're probably close. Why?"

NEED TO BE CAREFUL. IF THERE'S AN ENEMY IN COURT . . .

He frowns at my words, and then at me. "You don't think . . . they might be in trouble?"

I gesture uncertainly. LOTS OF MOQUOIAN DIPLOMATS OPPOSED TO EASTERN ALLIANCE. LOTS OPPOSED TO MEDDLING IN INDUSTRY PRACTICE. YOU DISAPPEARED WITH IANO. IF THE RIGHT PEOPLE THINK YOU'RE SWAYING HIM . . .

He frowns. "Or if this group of fanatics gets wind that he and I set out to find you—if our enemy is a Hire, that is—it could be dangerous for Rou and Eloise. Earth and sky, I didn't think we'd put *them* at risk. . . ."

And maybe they're not. But my fingers are aching, and I can't bring myself to write out a long string of pointless placation. If I know our court—and it was my job, after all—then the Eastern diplomats could very well be in trouble. Difficult questions they probably can't answer, at the very least. Possibly detainment, or deportation.

Or worse.

Veran's chewing on his lip. "Well, now I'm worried. We

should get going. I'll feel a lot better when we can all sit down together and lay this whole thing out. I'll feel better when it's back in Rou and Eloise's hands." He looks up to Lark. "I wish we could let her sleep longer, though."

I drink down the rest of the broth and flex my hand before picking up the charcoal again.

WHY LARK? I write.

He studies the two words for a moment, so I add, FOR RESCUE.

He purses his lips and looks back up to the sleeping bandit. "She was the only person I could conclusively believe didn't have a hand in your abduction. And . . . initially I thought she could help in other ways, but now I'm not sure. I think I've been an idiot."

After a moment's pause, he looks back at me and sees my raised eyebrow. His sunburned cheeks go a little redder, and he shrugs.

"I thought she could help me find Moira Alastaire. You know the story about Queen Mona and Ambassador Rou's daughter? The one who was abducted in Matariki all those years ago?"

"*Uah.*" I've heard the hearsay—especially the rumblings that this whole diplomatic affair was an attempt by the East to slander Moquoia with the Lumeni princess's disappearance.

Veran shakes his head. "I had this stupid, heroic idea that I might be able to find traces of Moira, and that Lark could help me do it. And she still might be able to—she has a part-Lumeni girl hidden away in her camp, and if that's not her, she may be able to help me find her in the quarries." He shifts and pokes the fire. "But now I realize . . . well, all the stories always make the Sunshield Bandit out to be either an untouchable desert deity, or else a wretched assassin out for her own gain. And I guess the smug part of me thought that whichever of those were closer to the truth, I could make use of it—her legendary prowess or her desperation. But she's neither. She's just . . . a person, doing her best. I mean—she's amazing at what she does." He looks back up at her, his expression almost reverent. "But I can't ask her to get tied up in things that aren't her concern anymore. She's got enough of her own battles to fight, and at this point I'd rather make an effort to lighten her burden rather than weigh it down."

I hadn't known I'd prompt a soliloquy, but he seems to be processing his thoughts aloud as much as answering my question. I pat his arm. He looks back at me, still a little red, and then his gaze travels past me, out to the desert. He frowns.

"Looks like rain," he says.

I glance over my shoulder at the western horizon. Above the brushy willows, clouds are billowing, their undersides ominously dark.

"We should get going," he says, but before he gets up, I grab his knee. He looks at me inquiringly.

I hesitate over the parchment.

IANO, I write. HE'S OK?

"He's in Pasul," he says, which doesn't answer my damn question, Veran. "He's worried sick about you. He's been a wreck in court. What?" He ducks his head to see my face. "You keep making that expression when Iano comes up . . . like you don't want to see him. I thought you were for love?"

He means *in love*, but it's the *were* that sticks. Past tense. I blow out a breath. I'm not sure how to articulate this on paper, and Veran's near enough a stranger that I don't know if he'll understand.

Iano wasn't in love with me. He *thought* he was in love with me. I think I always knew the truth, but I was willing to over-look it—he was in love with what I brought with me.

At this point, any scenario I envision of reuniting with Iano ends with a kind but quietly horrified succor, and that's if he doesn't immediately recoil. What am I going to do in that mo-ment, when his eyes flicker in shock, when his hands falter as they reach for me? He and the people around him *might* have ac-cepted the marriage of the king and the *ashoki* if it was presented just right. But now the power *and* the package are gone. He was in love with a pretty singer with good words and a comfortably unfortunate past. Not a ripped-down, maimed heretic flipping all the wrong tables in court.

I adjust my grip on the charcoal, but still I don't write. Ve-ran's gaze flicks between me and the page, waiting.

Out over the willows, thunder crackles.

There's a thrash of boots, and Lark sits up. Her thick eye-black is smeared on one side, and her bandanna droops in front of her lips. Her startled gaze jumps past us to the sky. She swears in Eastern. Veran replies, I think asking if we should sit and wait out the storm.

She gets up and leaves the shelter of the overhang, squinting out at the clouds, and then she turns and scrambles up the rock, disappearing from sight. We hear her boots scattering pebbles over the top.

Suddenly her voice cuts the air, sharp as a whip. Veran's head jerks up. He blurts a reply—both of them are speaking too fast for me to catch on.

I flick his sleeve. "Wha'?"

"The bandit from last night," he says. "Dirtwater Dob—he's picked up our trail." He calls up to the top of the overhang. "How far?"

She responds, and he translates. "A mile or so."

Lark jumps from the top of the overhang, her boots crunching on the ground.

"Have to ride, fast," she says to me. "You okay?"

Does it matter? I take her proffered arm, my fingers closing around the swirling water tattooed over her skin. She hefts me to my feet and waits while I steady myself.

"Ride with me?" she prompts. Her Moquoian is slurry, roughed not so much from translation but from learning it at the edges of society.

I look up at her—she's a foot taller than me, at least. Her face is rugged and sun freckled from life in the Ferinno, creased with squint lines. But those eyes are clear, and I realize what I took for ferocity last night is more akin to dauntlessness, frightening only in her sheer acceptance of bad luck.

I nod, and she breaks away to where the horses are tied. Veran scrambles around our campsite, stomping out the fire and stuffing things back in his pack. I try to be helpful by tottering to the edge of the overhang, steeling myself for another grueling ride. Cool air gusts from the thunderstorm ahead. As I come out into the doomed sun, I squint at the horizon behind us. A figure is stopped about a mile distant, dismounted next to his horse. He's peering at the rocky ground, and then he straightens and turns our way.

Our flight has become a hunt.

LARK

Tamsin sweeps a muddy forefinger in the dirt by her side.

WHY DOES HE FOLLOW? she writes.

It takes me a moment to translate the patchy letters on the ground, and another moment to organize the right response, all compounded by trying to keep the food bag out of the rain. We're crouched in a little stand of pines—the closer we get to Pasul, the more these copses dot the landscape. We're just a few miles from town, but there's a whole bunch of open land between here and there, and we need to let the horses rest before we attempt it—especially Jema. She's strong, and Tamsin weighs so little, but I imagine having the load unbalanced on her saddle is as uncomfortable on her back as it is on my butt. I rub my thighs, sore from leaning back to give Tamsin as sure a seat as possible. Rat, too, is sleeping like he's dead—keeping up with the horses has pushed him almost to his limit.

"Stage road," I explain, offering her the last of Veran's soft onion rolls. She pinches off a little piece, and it takes a good deal of restraint not to scarf down the remainder myself. "Dob wants the road. I make him mad. He knows I am alone."

And wounded, I think grimly. That blow he landed with his mattock is the real reason he's tailing us so confidently. I surreptitiously shift my shoulder again. The blood was easy enough to pass off as somebody else's, but it hurts like fire to lift my buckler. I itch for a crossbow—if I had one, I could wait somewhere and snipe at him as he picks after our trail. I'd like to think we can outlast him, especially in the rain, but if it comes down to another swordfight . . .

Thunder booms. Worriedly I glance up at the sky. It's darkened dramatically in the last ten minutes. I'd hoped this storm would rush through like they often do, perhaps blowing off to one side. But the clouds haven't cleared, and our route is taking us closer and closer to the dark center. So that's what we have—Dob on one end and lightning on the other. Normally I'd choose a fight over a storm, but pain shoots up my shoulder again. I grit my teeth.

Tamsin notices. She reaches up to brush my shoulder, quirking an eyebrow.

"I am okay," I say. More and more of my gutter Moquoian is coming back after our handful of exchanges in the saddle. She drew letters on my back a few times, mostly to ask for water. At one brief stop she finally corrected my inflection with a persistent upward jerk of her thumb—apparently I was saying *you're delicious* instead of *you're welcome*, which makes me wonder about my past few forays into Pasul.

She smooths her palm over the dirt and writes again. VERAN CAN'T FIGHT?

I glance over my shoulder. Veran is at the edge of the copse, keeping an eye on the drainage leading up to us—if Dob still has our trail, that's where he'll come from. In one hand Veran's holding a fancy knife that I would have stolen off him the first day if I knew he had it. His other hand is absently scratching Rat, who's sprawled by his knee.

"He can maybe fight a little," I say. "But not, uh, not mulch." She shakes her head and tips her thumb down. I try again. "Mulch. *Molch. Much.*" She nods and goes back to pinching off the onion roll. "He cannot fight much. He has a—problem." I tap my head. "He falls . . . down, falls asleep very fast, and he shakes." I twitch my hand back and forth.

Miraculously, she seems to understand this garbled explanation. "Ah," she says, nodding.

"I am worry he will not tell me if he is feeling bad," I say. "You will help me see if he needs help?"

She quirks an accusing eyebrow and looks pointedly at my shoulder again.

"I am okay," I say again. "We just get to Pasul, and then I am okay. Not far."

She shakes her head, but her next letters on the ground are familiar by now.

THANK YOU.

"You're del . . . welcome?"

She grins through cracked lips.

"Lark," Veran calls.

I hand Tamsin my canteen and get up, brushing the mud off my knees. I sidle through the pines until I get to his side.

He's peering hard at the drainage. His hood is up, and a

few runaway curls are dripping water onto his cheeks. "I keep thinking I see movement down there, but nobody's come up—shouldn't Dob have cleared that bank by now?"

"He'll have to rest his horse as much as us," I say, settling down beside him. Rat doesn't even twitch—if his sides weren't barely lifting with breath, I'd be worried he'd died. "The movement you're seeing could be water—there's the chance that drainage will flood. All the better for us."

"Hm." He doesn't look convinced. "I wish he hadn't shown up. I don't like being chased like this."

"He's not after you," I say. "He's after me. Once you get into Pasul, you'll be fine."

He turns his searching gaze from the landscape to me. "What do you mean, *you*?"

"What do you mean, *what do you mean*?"

"You're coming into Pasul with us, right? I mean, you have to, if you want me to pay you."

I shift. "I'll come in a little ways. I'm not coming into the upper city."

"That's where Rou and Eloise will be."

"Well, good. You get Tamsin somewhere she's safe and comfortable. I'll probably stay at the posthouse."

"Why?"

"Because they're the least likely to kick me out or turn me over to the authorities," I say more sharply than I mean to. "Fire and sun, you really do make a terrible outlaw."

"I'm not sure I'm technically outside the law yet," he says. "But at any rate, we're going to have to sit down and make arrangements for relocating your campmates."

"Yeah, and we can do it at the posthouse. I'm not coming into the upper quarter, Veran."

He's still looking at me. I use his negligence as an excuse to stare hard at the rainy landscape. He's right—there is movement in the drainage. It doesn't look like water, but it doesn't seem to be getting any closer, either.

"And after you get the money?" he asks.

"I told you back in Three Lines," I say. "I'm done. You go your way, I go mine."

"Back into the Ferinno?"

"Probably."

"You could leave."

"I'm aware."

He pauses, and I feel this tangible buildup, a tightening of emotion, like some thread between us is suddenly pulled taut.

"You could come with me," he says.

I lift an eyebrow, not looking away from the flats. "To find your lost princess?"

"No," he says. "I . . . I know that's what I made it seem like before, but . . . Lark, I don't want you to disappear back into the desert again."

"I'm dust in a hat and vest," I say. "If I step out of the desert, I collapse, and then you'll just have a pile of secondhand clothes to pick through. If you want my hat that badly, I can try to find you one."

He doesn't laugh. The eyeblack I applied to his cheeks this morning has rain tracks through it, slowly sloughing off.

"I just . . . what happens to you out there, without your camp? Will you just live up in that canyon by yourself?"

"No, I have to find a different one now, thanks to you."

He still doesn't smile. His sage-green eyes are crinkled with worry. "I could help you. I know you don't want my charity, but I could help you get set up somewhere. I could help you get a job in Callais, or Teso's Ford. Or you could leave Alcoro, Lark—you could go to Cyprien, or Paroa. You could train to be a ferry boat hand in Bellemere, or a shepherd in Wyddroan. You could run for mayor of Poak. Earth and sky, Lark, come be a scout in the Silverwood. My ma would kill for a recruit like you."

"You forget I have a bounty," I say, something weird and snaky slipping around in my chest at his high expectations. "Something tells me folk won't be too keen to hire a wanted outlaw."

"I can get it lifted. Blazes, I know . . . I know that sounds so conceited, but I can talk to Colm and Gemma, and they can talk to the Senate. My ma can talk to the Senate, Rou or Eloise can talk to the Senate. We can get it lifted. Especially since you helped with this. I think they'd have done it anyway, but now you've helped us, and you've helped me."

"Colm wanted me to find that princess."

"Colm will understand. He was just looking for a chance, that's all."

"No, I don't think he will, Veran, and I don't think you do, either." I shove away images of trees and water and soft boots like his—a difficult thing when surrounded by all three of those things. "Even if somebody did want to hire a beat-up mule like me, you forget that I've been at the mercy of your friends before. That same system that's protected you kept me pinned down in the ditch. I'm not just going to follow you up into the upper crust and pretend it's not all a song and dance on other folk's backs. I'm not going to take a job handed to me because now I have a friend with a crown, and leave everybody else behind."

I know I'm being mean, but I can't help it—what he's asking feels too much like betrayal, too much like cuddling up to the very thing me and Rose and the others have been fighting against for so long.

What makes it all the more agonizing is that it would be *so easy* just to do what he's asking. To trust what he says.

He's looking at me, his curls still dripping over his bruised forehead and eyelashes and making more tracks down his cheeks. I want him to knock it off, stop shedding the vestiges of life in the desert so easily and aesthetically.

"Why is it your job to save everybody else?" he asks.

I shake my head. "You don't understand."

"I know," he says, his voice straight and steady. "I know I don't, Lark. I thought I did before, but I don't. And I'm sorry that I made it seem like I had all the answers, that I could assume exactly what you've gone through. I never considered what my own privilege was built on, and I shouldn't have tried to project my assumptions on you."

My eyebrows lift despite myself, my gaze fuzzy on the landscape.

Hot damn. He *was* listening.

I'm not sure what to say, and as my silence stretches, he streams out a breath and looks down at the muddy toes of his fringed boots. The silver medallions on them bead with water.

"If you don't want my help, I'm not going to make you take it," he says. "But at least let me put you up in Pasul for the night, somewhere quiet where folk won't notice you. And then . . . before we go our separate ways, I'd appreciate you sitting down and helping me figure out what I *can* do with the means I have. It's about all I've got, Lark. Connections. Folk aren't ever going to let me do much else. And I want to do some good with it— not just throw it around at charity cases like a lot of folk do, but actually try to fix a few things."

"You can start with my campmates," I say, my neck hot under my bandanna despite the wet.

"Okay," he says.

A quiet falls between us, whispery with rain. Both of us are looking out at the desert, but I'm not sure either of us are actually seeing anything. My stomach is a tumbleweed, all weightless and unsettled. Lightning flashes, and at the edge of my vision, I see him pass his palm over his eyes to shade them. It's a tiny motion, so natural it would be easy to think nothing of it, but my stomach drops. How many unassuming things must he have to navigate day after day? A flash of light, a flight of stairs, a hot drink in his hand. And suddenly, instead of a picture of me skulking back into the Ferinno alone, I get an image of him sucked back into that insulated world, watching the current of life carry on without him.

He'll be safer there, I reason. Safer where folk can watch out for him, where they can keep him steady and stable when he collapses.

Never mind that's the exact opposite of what he wants.

Suddenly I wonder if a life beyond the Ferinno is as much of a betrayal as I'm banking on.

"You're . . ." I begin, and then stop.

He sets his chin in his hand. "An imbecile," he finishes for me.

"Not an imbecile," I clarify.

He sighs. "That's the nicest thing you've ever said to me."

I snort, and he smiles, his gaze distant. The air is cool and threaded with the scent of water and pine. Thunder rumbles, and he closes his eyes, lazily, as if enjoying the sound. Like with the bats, his easy pleasure in something I usually dodge is infectious. I take a deep breath of rain and lick the droplets off my lips.

Over the patter, there's a familiar click of a crank, followed by a whiz and a thump. A chip of bark jumps from the tree just over Veran's shoulder, where a quarrel lodges, quivering.

I lunge sideways, slamming him to the soggy pine needles. He gasps in my ear, his breath washing my skin. It doesn't quite cover the sound of a curse and the hurried rewind of a crossbow crank. Rat wriggles between us, trying to find his feet.

"Get Tamsin!" I scramble off both of them and haul Veran upright. I push him back through the pine trees, throwing a fast glance over my shoulder. I catch a flash of dirty leather through the trees and the glint of a mattock as Dirtwater Dob brings his crossbow up to sight.

"*Fire and smoke.*" I weave, and the quarrel skips wide. He had the same idea I had, only he actually has a crossbow. I keep my head low, recalling the movement down in the drainage— now that I think of it, it did have the look of a horse casually flicking its tail. Dob dismounted to creep up the side of the copse on foot.

Across the clearing, Tamsin's sitting forward. Veran lets loose a string of frantic Moquoian, and her face blanches. She grabs his proffered arm and struggles to her feet.

"Who should take her?" Veran asks me, holding her upright. "You or me?"

"You," I say grimly, snatching at Jema's saddle. I draw my sword from its sheath in one long motion. "Get into Pasul, both of you."

"What're you . . . you're coming too, right?"

"I dunno, we'll see if I can avoid getting a quarrel through the eye."

"You're not staying here!"

"Go, Veran!" I sling my buckler over my fist. "If we break the trees now, Dob's just going to pick us off." I can hear him scraping through the pines, trying to find a place to shoot where I can't fire back—he doesn't know I don't have my crossbow. I thrust my buckler into the small of Veran's back and shove him toward his horse. "I can hold him off long enough for you both to get out of range. Here, Tamsin." I crouch along Veran's horse and pat my thigh. She steps up and struggles to slither over the saddle. I push her up the rest of the way.

"But you'll come back!" He gasps it as a statement, almost a plea.

"Dammit, Veran, if I live, okay? Get on the horse so I can find a better position."

He grabs my arm. "Tell me you'll come into Pasul." His sage-gray eyes flick back and forth between mine, creased and bright.

I grip his elbow around my hilt, in part to force him into the saddle. "I'll come into Pasul. Wait for me at the posthouse."

He nods and lets me shove him up.

"Get out of range." I step back. "Don't stop—don't wait for me. Just go."

He looks like he wants to argue more, so I lift my sword and bring the flat down with a slap on his horse's wet rump. Kuree startles forward, and Veran swings to grab the saddle horn. And then they're gone, tearing down the pebbly slope into the driving rain.

I don't stay to watch them disappear. I break off to the right, away from Jema—I doubt Dob would shoot a good horse he has a high chance of stealing, but I'm not going to risk it. Rat, though, he would shoot—I'm sure of it.

"Rat, *stay*!" I hiss fiercely over my shoulder. He crouches by Jema, panting agitatedly.

The rain is falling harder, cascading through the waving branches. Timber bends and creaks. Thunder booms. Good. It smothers my footsteps as I run through the pine needles. My best hope is to draw Dob's fire—force him to make a bad shot, and then rush him when he's reloading. My shoulder burns with the weight of my buckler.

I see his dirty jacket through the trunks. He spots me half a breath later. With a yell, he swings his sights onto me. I dodge behind a trunk just as he fires.

"Sunshine!" he roars. "You're mine!"

"Hack off, Dob!" I yell back. "Don't make me cut you up like the other two back at Utzibor."

Please.

But he's crashing through the brush. I hear the rattle of quarrels.

"You took my whole crew away! Berta and Mosset and Goon—"

"You did that yourself, stupid!" I jump from my cover before he can reload and lunge for him—he hasn't managed to wind his crank yet, and he brings the crossbow up to parry my swing. My sword catches the lathe of the bow and snaps the whole thing in two. He swears and throws the pieces to the ground. I follow through with my buckler—half grateful I don't connect, my shoulder's on fire—and then up comes his mattock.

"You're done, Sunshine—you and your sorry bunch of runaways." He heaves his mattock, and I dodge backward to avoid having to block it. "You've been the ratty queen of nowhere for too long."

I duck another swing and make a quick strike of my own, but he wheels his mattock handle down to block it. The impact sends a hornet's nest of pain racing across my shoulders. I skitter back toward the edge of the copse, gritting my teeth.

"What're you going to do with the road, Dob?" I call, hoping to slow him down. "Pick off an ox here or there on the wagon trains?"

"Do you know what I could do if I could move beef from the plains through the water scrape? The Burr is wasted on you." He swings again, expecting me to duck—I bend almost double, and my hat tumbles from my head. I make a strike for his boots, but he hops to one side, skidding in the loose pebbles. We're out of the trees now, the flats rolling away and running with water. Droplets sting my scalp.

"That's the thing about the *sun*, Sunshine," he snarls. "It *sets*, and gives everybody else a fighting chance."

"It always seems to rise again, Dob!" I lunge. He blocks, and with every ounce of grit I can muster I sling my buckler from the other direction. I catch him across the nose, sending a shock through my left shoulder. I gasp; he hollers. Blood spurts over the metal. I pull back, letting my shield arm drop, deadened. I skid down the slope a few paces, gripping my throbbing shoulder.

"Leave me alone, Dob," I croak. "You and I are nothing—neither of us is worth killing."

He swears, spits blood, and charges again. The glint of lightning flashes off his raised mattock. The pickax head arcs down.

In any other scenario, the higher ground might have saved him. I hate myself.

I sling my buckler up again, and just like outside Utzibor, the pointed end of his mattock punches straight into it. The pain that follows is as bright and blinding as the lightning, but unlike last time, I'm ready for the follow-through. With his mattock still buried in my buckler, I wrench my left arm down. He lurches forward, pulled by his grip on the handle. Letting raw pain take the place of regret, I swing my sword in a crisp arc to meet his bared neck.

It's not a clean slice. My blade lodges where the workings of his throat must meet bone. Blood sprays. I turn my face away. My fingers loosen on my buckler at the same time his fists open on his mattock. There's no sound—no moan or cry. My sword slides from my grip as he crumples forward, staining the ground red beneath him. Unable to come to a rest on his stomach, my hilt forces him over on his side, where he lies, motionless, save for a final death tremor in his hands and the still-flowing blood from his nose. It crawls upward along his cheeks, following the downward slope of his body on the hill.

This rotten, nameless hill in the middle of nothing, sucking up his blood and breath and juices. The storm will wash his life down the rills and slots like it never was, and a hundred circles of the sun will bleach him dry, and the horde of teeth and beaks will scatter the rest.

I bend double, my stomach roiling, intending to put my hands on my knees, but my left shoulder gives at the first touch of pressure, and I arc upright. I throw my head back to the sky. Rain thumps off my cheeks, my eyes, my tongue, because my mouth is open and before I realize it, I'm yelling upward. I don't know what. I don't know why. It's just an ugly block inside me that comes billowing out at the raging storm.

The taste of soot washes my tongue—my eyeblack is sloughing off, probably along with the grit of twenty years, making muddy tracks down my skin. It feels like shedding armor. Water seeps under my locks and trickles along my scalp. I want to tear my clothes off, bare all my skin under the deluge, let it saturate the dirt in my veins until I run clear.

But I don't. I have places to be.

Places that aren't here—not anymore.

I look down—the rain has darkened the sand around Dirtwater Dob so his blood is barely distinguishable. My buckler, too, is free of streaks, now with two square holes punched into the curved metal. I almost leave it—drop it alongside my sword embedded in his neck, but that seems premature, and anyway, it's as blatant as carving my name alongside the death wound. I step forward, light-headed, feeling a little drunk, and tug the blade from his neck. He follows the pull, like he's getting ready to get back up again, but finally the sword comes clear, and he falls back to the ground. My stomach bubbles, sour. I wipe the blade on his sleeve.

"Think I'll take your advice, Dob," I say. "You can have the road. Me and the sun, we're going to Pasul, and then we're going east."

I head back up the hill, slowly, unsteadily, because I'm feeling both light as wind and heavy as a rockslide. I pick up my hat along the way, flicking the mud from it and setting it back on my drenched locks. I weave through the waving pines to where Rat is crouched by Jema. I mount and nudge her down the slope.

I tip my hat to Dob's slouched body as we pass, and then I spur Jema toward Pasul without looking back.

TAMSIN

Pasul is blurred and running with mud, as dark as twilight under the billowing clouds. Veran pulls his horse out of its canter at the town signpost, but he doesn't pass under yet. He turns in the saddle and stares back across the flats, looking for Lark. I can feel his heart pounding against my back.

"She'll . . . she'll be okay," he says, his voice shaky. "I mean . . . she'll be okay."

I free one of my hands from inside the cloak and pat his knee. It's the closest thing I can approximate to reassurance—even aside from my mouth, I'm too exhausted to summon more energy.

He shakes himself and turns his horse back under the signpost. Pasul is situated on a slight slope, so the town rises gradually before us, twinkling with lanterns in the downpour. We slosh up the main street. The posthouse for the stage line is the dominating feature of the lower town, surrounded by corrals of droopy workhorses, all pressed together in the rain, their coats slick and gleaming. A line of coaches are parked under a long shed. Nobody would think of setting out in this weather.

Nobody, it seems, except one small mud-coach on the end. The doors are open, and the driver is readying it for travel, prepping the iron wheels for rough roads. They're going out into the desert.

We plod nearer. All the lights in the posthouse are blazing, and shadows hurry in front of the windows, as if people are rushing to and fro inside. But one person is stationary, standing on the porch and looking out into the rain. My head hurts, and Veran is distracted, and so it takes us both until we're nearly even with the front door to recognize who it is.

To be fair, his hair is down, and he's in a dark traveling cloak made colorless by the rain. I can't remember when I've ever seen Iano without colors or hairpins, so I can't be blamed for passing over his silhouette. But the mistake doesn't last long, and I snatch at the reins in Veran's hands, causing his horse to snort and jerk to a stop. Veran shakes himself behind me.

"Iano?" he says.

Iano is staring hard at us through the rain—he leaves the glare of lantern light and steps out into the muddy street.

"Oh . . . *eta*, Iano!" Veran comes to himself and slithers to the ground, landing with a splash in the road. "*Ista* . . . I found her! Look . . . look! Tamsin is here!"

Veran reaches up wildly and starts to pull me from the saddle like I'm a parcel. I wobble when I hit the ground, sinking up to my ankles in muck. Iano has drifted nearer, now a few arm's lengths away. Close enough, I expect, to see the damage that's been done.

Though, perhaps not. He takes a few splashing steps, close

enough that I can see his expression but can't interpret it, just lines of agony, probably shock. Perhaps dismay. Any moment now, he'll stop again and simply stare. He may even argue that Veran brought back the wrong person.

But he doesn't. The nameless expression on his face only intensifies, and now he's running, and it's only as he reaches me that I realize he's crying.

I've *never* seen him cry.

He clamps his hands on my shoulders, and then on my face, holding me close enough so that I can see which rivulets are rain and which are tears.

"Tamsin . . ." His voice is cracked. "Oh, Tamsin . . ."

"Uh!" Veran says suddenly. "Uh, Iano . . . I should mention . . . probably wait on the kissing. They, um, . . . they cut her tongue."

Now, then. Now it's over. Iano's face ripples with shock, and his cold fingers tighten on my cheeks. Numbly, I lean back, out of that intimate space only for whispers and kisses, and open my mouth. I take one of his hands and move it up to the fuzz above my ear, trying to make him realize, to see. To come to his senses. Hair gone. Words gone. Skin and swells and self gone. *I'm not anything for you anymore, my dear. Let's hurry this thing along, I'm tired.*

His fingers brush along my scalp to cradle the back of my neck. And his gaze, instead of fixing on my mangled tongue and cracked lips, locks back on mine again, creased and still spilling tears.

"Oh, Tamsin," he whispers. "Bless the Light you're alive."

I sag, catching both of us by surprise. Be it hunger or exhaustion or the sudden realization that he hasn't stepped away, that he really is here in the mud and excreta of the street . . . we sink to our knees. He folds around me, arms warm, pressing his face into my neck, and I simply lean my aching head on his shoulder.

"Oh, Tamsin," he whispers, and I realize that he, like me, has no other words. His breath hitches in his chest, and he tightens his grip. "Oh, Tamsin."

I hear Veran shift awkwardly, his feet squelching in the mud. His horse blows wetly, champing its bit.

"Were you coming out to find us?" Veran finally asks.

Iano lifts his head from my neck but doesn't look at him, still gazing down at me. "What?"

"That coach—were you riding out to find us?"

"Oh—no. It's not for me." He blanches suddenly and looks up. "No . . . sorry. It's for your ambassador. And the princess. They're inside."

"They are? Eloise, is she—"

"Very sick," Iano replies. "She's very sick. But—Veran, wait!"

But Veran has taken off running toward the posthouse, dragging his horse behind him. Iano calls after him again, but whether it's lost to the rain or Veran's simply ignoring him, it does no good. Iano turns back to me.

"They got here this morning," he says. "They were escorted out—deported. The ambassador is furious. But, Tamsin—the guards are here, in Pasul. They ransacked my room. If I hadn't been out by the crossroads, they'd have taken me in. They've found out about you. Someone . . . someone knows. Someone is against us, someone close. And I don't . . ." His face is slowly paling, as if he's coming to all these realizations now. "I don't think we can go back."

He waits, as usual, expecting me to reply, to carry his thoughts forward. But I don't.

I can't.

He lifts his cold fingers again and brushes my cheek, my lips. He leans forward, but at the last moment aims just to the side, pressing a kiss to the corner of my lips.

He leans back. "But you're here. You're back. And we're together again."

He fishes in his pocket and comes up with my *si-oque*, the amber one I commissioned the day I got my right to title from the king. I turn it over and rub my thumb along the three glass beads—green for my mother, pale blue for my father. Yellow for me. Ochre isn't a popular color among the titled—difficult to match, tricky to flaunt. Too pale and it becomes sickly, too dark and it becomes muddy. But when it hits just the right shade, just the right notes, it soars.

I thought that was poetic when I first decided to keep it.

Now it feels impossibly narrow. A too-small box I built for myself. A mold I don't fit anymore.

I slip it onto my wrist, where it settles, loose, against my skin. Iano folds his fingers around mine.

"Things are . . . they're going to be all right," he says.

I want to make him think rationally, to parse through this step by step. I want to tell him about the Hires, and Poia, and the unanswered questions still casting their shadows on us.

But I can't. So I say the only thing I can.

"*Uah.*"

VERAN

The posthouse is a flurry of light and bustle. I throw Kuree's reins over the hitching post and splash to the door, dripping from head to foot. Inside, porters are hauling luggage out the side door to the carriage shed. Rou is standing in the midst of everything, arguing with the post manager and looking angrier than I've ever seen him. Eloise is past him, curled in a hardback chair by the fireplace, wrapped in a quilt.

By the Light, she's lost weight, her normally appled cheeks hollow. Her skin has paled to chalky beige under her freckles. Her eyes are closed, her chest rising and falling in shallow breaths under the quilt.

I start to creep forward, hoping Rou is too distracted to notice me just yet, but it's no good. His sparking gaze falls on me, and his whole body seems to spasm in shock.

"Veran!" he exclaims. And then, again, in more of a shout. *"Veran!"*

I toss up my hands. "I'm sorry—Rou, I'm sorry, but if you'll let me explain—"

Eloise's eyes slit open, and she lifts her head slightly. "Veran?"

Rou is plowing past the porters, advancing on me, and I can't for all the world tell if he's going to hug me or throttle me.

"What the *blazing, blinding Light were you thinking*?" he yells.

Throttle, then, definitely. I use the hapless interference of a few porters to skitter around the periphery of the room toward Eloise, dashing for her chair like it's a safe zone in a game of Tag the Buck.

Rou doesn't miss a beat, pivoting to follow me. "Running off into the desert alone?" he roars. "Do you have any idea what your mother *will do to us both*?"

"But I'm fine," I gasp, hovering behind Eloise's chair. "I'm fine, and I did it—I got Tamsin back, the *ashoki*, the reason everything was falling apart—"

"Oh, it's *come apart*." He wavers, trying to gauge which way I'm going to circle around the chair, before planting himself firmly in the middle. "It's come apart into an *international incident*—we have been officially deported, and that's not the worst of it. You're being named as a conspirator against the Moquoian throne and an enemy of the court, and it was only by a spark's luck I was able to argue for deportation and not *prison* for all three of us. Did you *think* at all? Did you *think* what running off with the prince just weeks before his coronation with the court on eggshells would *look like*?"

"I thought it would help," I croak—he's rivaling Mama for sheer lung power. I cower behind Eloise. "Eloise and I . . . we thought it would help . . ."

But no, that isn't fair—Eloise had nothing to do with me running away. She rouses a little from the quilt and turns her head toward me. Her voice is soft enough that I think maybe she's going to try to back me up, to calm things down. But in the brief moment that Rou's taking a breath, she whispers, "I am *so angry at you.*"

This seems to inflame Rou all the more. "You put *everyone* in danger, Veran. If you were my son—"

"I'm not, though," I say, straightening a little. "I'm not, and . . . and I did what I thought was right, and I'm not entirely convinced it wasn't. If you would just *listen*, and sit down and let us all talk—Iano and Tamsin, the guards, whoever it is who's tugging all these strings . . ."

"Blessed Light, no," Rou says. "We've been given to the end of the hour to leave Moquoia before we're arrested. We're getting in that coach and we're setting the land speed record across the Ferinno. You can answer to the Alcoran Senate, and then your ma and pa. I've got Eloise to take care of now, and we're lucky enough for that." He stabs the air with his finger. "You *sit down* and don't leave this spot until we're ready to leave."

He storms back toward the porters and out the side door, slamming it so hard behind him a map of the desert jumps from its peg on the wall. I sink miserably into a chair beside Eloise.

"I'm sorry, Eloise—I just . . ."

"I thought you were going to *talk to Iano*," she whispers, clutching the quilt tighter under her chin. Her curls are damp with sweat, darkening the deep golds hidden in the smoky brown. She shakes her head. "I was so worried. What if you had died?"

"I didn't, though, Eloise. I even had a seizure out there, and look, I'm fine."

Her eyes crack open again, and she studies me. "All by yourself?"

"Well, no, I . . . I went to find the Sunshield Bandit. No, listen . . ." I put up a hand to stop Eloise's exclamation. "She's . . . she's my friend now. She figured out where Tamsin was. She got us across the desert, and in and out of Tamsin's prison. And she kept me safe while I was seizing. It was all okay. And she'll be here in just a few minutes." By the Light, as long as she *hasn't died* fighting that bandit. Why had her staying behind been the most logical choice? She should have fled with me.

And then there's the matter of all my promises—the vow to get her campmates to safety, to get her sentence lifted, to help her figure out a new life outside the desert. How am I going to do that if every government from coast to coast is angry at me?

"I'll make it work," I say aloud.

Eloise shakes her head, her shadowed eyes closed again. "I'm not so sure we can," she murmurs.

The door opens again, and in come Tamsin and Iano, their clothes clinging to their skin. Iano helps Tamsin to the closest chair. She slumps for a moment, eyes closed. She must be exhausted. And she needs to see a healer.

Rou comes back in the side door, spattered with rain. "The coach is ready. Veran, go get inside."

This is all happening too fast. "Rou—sir—please, can't we just take a minute, and work some of this out?" I gesture to Tamsin. "At the very least, can we get Tamsin somewhere more comfortable?"

"No, V." His nickname is used more as a warning than a familial term. "We're under royal orders to depart the country by three bells, and I am not letting them put Eloise in a cell, or you, for that matter. Go get in the coach. Iano . . . I don't know what to tell you. Your guards are searching the upper city for you."

I swivel to Iano, my heart racing with desperation. "Can you stand down the order for deportation?"

He shakes his head. "Not if it came from my mother. The throne is still hers."

"You could come with us," I say quickly. "We could talk in the coach—"

"And be accused of taking the Moquoian heir hostage—blazes, Veran, *think, think, think.*" Rou taps his own head angrily. "Think about this stuff! This isn't debate class! This could mean international war. *Go get in the coach.*"

Failure, then. All this to salvage something, and it all led to failure anyway.

Eloise gives a thick, rattly cough. Under her father's furious glare, I get up slowly from my chair. I look to Iano, who's folding his wet cloak around Tamsin, who still has her eyes closed.

"I'm sorry," I say in Moquoian. "I didn't mean to make such a mess. What will you do?"

"I'm not sure," Iano says. Despite the crumbling of the world around us, he looks calmer than he has in days, a resolution in his face that can only be described as *kingly*. "But you helped bring Tamsin back. So things aren't as dark as we think."

Tamsin gives what might be a roll of her eyes behind her eyelids, perhaps at Iano's poetic surety. She opens her eyes and surveys me, lips pursed. She turns gingerly toward the fireplace, looking first at Rou, who is waiting expectantly for me to make a move toward the door. Her gaze moves to Eloise, who is doing her best to stay awake and upright.

Tamsin starts to look back to me, then her gaze stops, and

she sweeps back to Eloise. She sits for a moment, her tired, ema-
ciated body suddenly rigid. Her chapped lips part slightly.

And then she's a flurry of agitation, waving both at me and
Iano, motioning around the room.

"*Aou'ha,*" she says urgently. "*Aou'ha.*"

Iano takes one of her frantic hands. "What? Tamsin—"

"Parchment," I say. "*Daona*—parchment. Here." I lunge for
the map that fell from the wall earlier and scramble for a scattering of quills near a ledger. She snatches the objects from my
hands with urgency, grabbing for the jar of ink even as I'm shaking it. She pries the cork out and dips the quill, slopping spots
across the map in her hurry. They spread and stain, leaving a
trail across the desolate Ferinno.

Iano and I crowd behind her to see her writing. Even Rou,
who is readying Eloise to stand, pauses his work.

I stare in shock at the letters forming on the page.

Outside, thunder rumbles.

LARK

The thunder is accompanied by lightning—the storm is directly overhead, and it's a miracle I wasn't struck dead while cantering across the flats. We slosh under the Pasul signpost. Jema is coated with mud from her shoulders to her hooves, and Rat looks like somebody dunked him in a coat of brown paint. I, ironically, am probably cleaner than I've ever been—my boots are coated, of course, but the rest of me is practically pulverized clean. The rain stings my cheeks where my eyeblack has washed away.

I spy Veran's horse outside the posthouse, and I flush with relief. They made it. I wonder if Saiph is with them, or somewhere else with the Moquoian prince. I guide Jema alongside Kuree and dismount with a splash. Rat hunkers down under her hooves and lies in the mud, panting.

I pull my bandanna down and peel my hat off my head, water streaming from the brim. Wiping flecks of mud from my cheeks—it feels strange not to have them thick with grease—I push open the door.

Veran is there, standing behind Tamsin as she scribbles something on a map. Beside him is a bedraggled Moquoian man, long black hair still dripping with rain. At the far end of the table stands an older man, Cypri, I guess, and behind him a pale figure curled up in a quilt. All five of them stop and look up at me as if I'm an apparition. Tamsin's eyes are the sharpest, practically narrowed at my sudden arrival.

"Uh." I waver in the puddle I'm creating, suddenly aware I'm in a room of aristocratic near strangers, and that my face is still on a bunch of bounty sheets. My stomach turns uncomfortably. I gesture at Veran. "Where's Saiph?"

The attack comes from the back of the room.

I'm distracted, and in pain, and off my guard—serves me right—so I react too slowly. The old Cypri literally throws a chair out of his way—it crashes against a wall—and barrels straight for me. I put my fists up, but not quickly enough. His hands fasten around my throat.

No, not my throat.

My face. He plants both palms on either side of my face.

"*Moira!*"

I jerk backward, out of his reach, leaving his hands clawed on the air. His face is split with a bizarre emotion—he looks downright deranged.

"Light," he croaks. "Oh, Light." He presses forward again, reaching.

I knock one of his arms out of the air. "Don't touch me."

I'm expecting somebody to move, to gently guide this addled stage passenger away so we can carry on our business, but the rest of the room is utterly still. Tamsin is still staring shrewdly, her quill limp in her fingers. The Moquoian man isn't looking at me—he's fixed on the back of the room, at the quilted traveler.

But Veran—he's staring, too. Those two sagebrush eyes are practically popping, the eyebrows and that little scar thrown high, rumpling his bruise. His lips form an almost perfect *o*.

The Cypri man clamps a hand on my wrist, and I twist it away. "I said, *don't touch me*, old man. Veran—what's going on? Where's Saiph? Are we in trouble?"

But this man is all hands—he lifts them toward my face again, stopping just short of my chin when I jerk away.

"I mean it," I warn. "I'm going to start throwing punches."

"Moira," he says again. And then, blazing, burning Light, he starts to cry. This old man, in this room full of people. He goes for one of my hands—I snatch it out of his reach and finally step around him. He turns with me like a pull-along toy.

"Moira," he says for a third time.

"Sun be damned, stop saying that," I snap. "Go sit down. Somebody make him sit down—he's addled."

Still, nobody moves. The man beckons for the back of the room. "Eloise, please, lolly, come here."

The quilted figure rises, dreamlike, from the chair, letting the blanket slip down her shoulders. She has a sickly look to her, her cheeks hollowed and her eyes shadowed, like little Whit back in camp. Still, I can't help but notice the fine cut of her traveling dress, and the pearl droplets in her ears, and the gold thread embroidering the band holding back her tumbling curls. She can probably get all the hair care products she can dream of.

I edge away, hoping she's not going to try to touch me, too, but now the corner of the table is blocking my path. I'm boxed in, and I don't like it—I feel like a rabbit in a snare. The girl stands looking me hard in the face. A handful of freckles spatter her nose and the corners of her eyes.

The old man is still crying, fingers flexing toward me. "Great blessed Light."

"Stop it," I say. "Go sit down. Leave me alone."

I look again at Veran, but in one swift motion, he covers his face with both palms, flattening them over his mouth, nose, and eyes. The Moquoian man is staring, his gaze jumping between me and this soft, pretty girl standing half a pace away. Tamsin is the first one to move—she drops her quill on the table and rises from her chair. She picks up the map, a print of the Ferinno, and holds it firmly outward. In the dead, empty space not far from Three Lines, she's written three words in large, hasty letters.

LARK IS MOIRA

"Moira, darling," the Cypri man says, voice thick. "You're my daughter. You're Eloise's sister. You were stolen from us in Matariki fifteen years ago. Do you remember it at all? We searched for you, your mother and I—we searched for years."

I cut my gaze toward Veran, wondering what's witched everybody to toddle along with this nonsense. Veran, at least, should know the truth. Tamsin's barely known me a day, and she's been half starved and swooning. The rest of these folk have never clapped eyes on me before. But Veran and I traveled together for nearly six days, and he never said a thing to this effect.

Though . . . now I wonder why he was so keen on me coming into Pasul.

And where the *balls* is Saiph?

The hair on the back of my neck rises.

"This is stupid," I say. "Veran, come on, tell them to knock it off. I thought we had things to do."

He finally moves, but not much—only sliding his hands down his face to his mouth, staring at me over the tops of his fingers.

The old man wipes his wet cheeks, and then he does touch me again—he takes my hand in both of his. "Oh, Moira . . . oh, love. You look so much like you did. You look so much like your sister, like your mother. Do you still have that silly circle of freckles on your tummy? We used to practice counting them together."

One, two, three, four, five, six.

He leans closer, and I'm washed suddenly in a rush of coffee and cinnamon.

I pivot on my heel, wrenching my hand from his, and take three long strides back to the door. Folk begin shouting behind me, but I kick it open and shut before anyone can touch me again. I storm across the porch and out into the rain. Rat lifts his head from under Jema's hooves. Next to her, Veran's horse stands idly by the hitching post. He hitched her in a hurry—her reins have slid off the post and lie trailing in a puddle.

A rectangle of yellow light blooms across the mud, throwing my shadow long. A swirl of voices accompanies it, shouting that foreign name, shouting at me to stop. The old man's voice is loudest, but it's underscored by a softer one, a female one, young and sweet without the harsh edges of the desert in it.

I don't stop or turn around. I jerk Jema's reins from the hitching post and swing onto her back.

There's splashing, and a hand grabs my knee.

I'm sick of folk touching me when I don't want to be touched.

I kick out with the hard toe of my boot. Veran snatches his hand away, clutching his elbow.

"Lark—Lark, wait. Please, wait." His eyes are turned up to me, and I can see him still searching, still staring. My gut clenches—I don't want him hunting for their lost princess in my face.

He must understand the emotion on my face better than me, because his flittering gaze locks back on mine.

"I didn't know," he says. "I swear it, Lark."

The old man is out the door, making for me with his hands out. In one quick move, I draw my sword from its sheath, holding it high. Veran flinches and jumps backward.

I swing the sword downward and slap the flat across his horse's rump.

Kuree starts mightily and bolts, cantering up the road toward the upper city, reins flying. Veran turns a full circle, watching her run, before whirling back to me, mouth open.

"Wait!" he blurts.

"No!" I jerk my bandanna back over my nose and give Jema a mighty kick. She jumps forward, throwing up mud. Rat streaks along with me.

"Stop!" Veran shouts behind me. "Lark, stop!"

I don't stop, and he can't follow. Jema puts on a burst of frantic speed, and we race back under the Pasul signpost, out into the desert bowing under a lashing sky.

VERAN

Oh Light.

Oh Light.

Oh blessed Light.

I stop at the signpost, ankle deep in mud, as Lark is swallowed up by the rain. I clutch the wood, drawing great ragged gasps of air. Water sluices off me. Another round of thunder peals. Lightning splits the land beyond, but Lark is gone.

There's splashing behind me, and I turn as Rou comes even with me. I press my back against the signpost, but he doesn't look angry anymore. He looks cut wide open. Mama always uses that phrase—*cut wide open*—and I never had a visual for it until now.

He stares out into the rain. Then he swings to me.

"I didn't know," I gasp. "I didn't realize. I—I never saw her full face. She was always wearing eyeblack, and the bandanna." Or else I was coming out of a seizure . . . or else she was wearing nothing at all. And always that sun, that damned sun . . .

Frantically, I set Eloise's face next to Lark's in my head. One smooth and unscarred, full-cheeked and sparkle-eyed, a gentle tawny brown. And the other . . . rough-edged and chapped, hollowed and sun-dark, with lightning in her eyes. Tumbles of soft curls, long locks streaked with gold. But now I see it—the sloping nose, the scattered freckles, the brown eyes . . . *Rou's eyes*, damnation . . .

I am the biggest fool who ever did breathe.

"Where . . . where did she . . ." Rou's voice sounds disjointed, like none of the words are actually hooked together.

"She ran," I say. "Into the desert."

He takes a few steps forward, as if setting out to follow her on foot. But he stops before I can find anything to say, and then a sound from behind us makes us both turn.

The door to the posthouse is open, and three figures are shadowed against the light. The foremost is nearly at the edge of the porch, her traveling dress whipping in the wind.

Rou does a hard pivot and starts jogging back to the porch. I follow numbly, the mud sucking at my boots. As we get nearer, Rou flaps his hands at Eloise, trying to send her inside, but she doesn't budge. She's hugging herself, shivering.

"Papa . . ." she gasps once we're in earshot.

"Inside," Rou croaks. "Inside, Eloise."

Together we all file back through the door, edging past Iano, who's staring up the street.

"The guards are coming," he says as I draw even with him, nodding up the slope.

I follow his gaze to where a knot of mounted riders are materializing in the rain. Lightning flashes off metal helms.

Tamsin reaches out and grasps his sleeve, dragging him back

inside. We cluster in the doorway. The post manager is righting the chairs that were flung aside just moments ago, but one look at the shock and dismay on our faces, and she seems to think better of making any reprimand.

"I'm riding out after her," Rou says, first to nobody in particular, and then homing in on Eloise. "I'm going after her. You stay here . . ."

"Papa, the guards," she whispers. She's spattered with rain, and still shivering. I remember the threat of prison if we're not out of Moquoia by the end of the hour, and suddenly I'm in agreement about one thing—she needs to get out of Pasul.

"Then you take the coach," Rou says. "You and Veran go as far as you can tonight, and keep going until you reach Callais. Have Colm send a letter to your mother . . ."

"I'll go after her," I say.

"No."

"Rou . . ."

"*No.*" There's pure agony in his voice. His hand jumps to the wall almost involuntarily, as if he suddenly needed to steady himself.

"I know where she's going." I swallow. "I know *exactly* where she's going. You won't be able to find her camp, but I can. And . . . she knows me."

The unspoken meaning hangs in the air.

She knows me.

She doesn't know you.

Something close to horror mixes with the agony on Rou's face. I bite my lip, but I don't break his gaze. I take a shuddering breath. "I'll go. You stay with Eloise and send word to Queen Mona."

"Your parents—"

"Won't know until I'm back," I say. "We'll say I ran away. And I will, if you put me on that coach."

Rou's face spasms—I'm being absolutely wretched, I know it—but before he can reply, Eloise gives a thick burst of coughing that she's clearly been fighting to hold back. She hunches over, her hands over her mouth, struggling to draw a breath. Both Rou and I take one of her shoulders.

Iano's leaning against the window, his anxious face reflected in the panes. "They're at the intersection."

"No," Rou says to nobody, to all of us, almost on principle.

Tamsin leaves our huddle, but instead of going to the window, she heads for the post manager, picking up the quill and inkwell on the table along the way.

Eloise gulps a few breaths and straightens, her hand on her chest. I thread my shoulder under hers and look to Rou entreatingly. "I can do it. I did it once—let me do it again."

This despite the fact that Lark probably hates me and will never trust me again.

"No," he says again. "It's not safe."

Eloise steadies herself and takes her father's hand.

"It's not safe for any of us, Papa," she whispers, siding—to my shock—with me. "I need you for this trip." She takes a difficult breath but presses on. "We should focus on getting to Callais and sending word to Mother. She has to know. Let Veran go."

He mouths the word no again, but no sound comes out. He stares at Eloise as if unable to see her.

Choosing, I realize. Choosing a child. All because I was too stupid to understand what was right in front of me.

Oh, Light.

Tamsin gives a little whistle from her conference with the post manager, half of which is scribbled on a blank page of the ledger. She beckons to Iano, who leaves the window and joins her. She plunges a hand into his inner cloak pocket and withdraws a handful of coin. She dumps them on the post manager's ledger. The manager scrutinizes them, tallying them up.

"Very well," she says. "A single horse."

Tamsin raps the ledger, her face cool and intimidating even without a single spoken word.

"And you weren't here," the manager agrees with a bow. "None of you were, save the two Eastern travelers taking the mud-coach."

Tamsin nods with satisfaction. She scribbles another few lines on the ledger, rips off the bottom of the page, and brings it to me.

SOE URKETT
GIANTESS FOREST TOWNSHIP

"This is where you're going?" I ask.

She nods. I glance at Rou. I haven't made clear—to any of us—whether I'll return to Moquoia or Alcoro. If, of course, I catch up to Lark, and if she doesn't murder me on sight, and if I can think of a single thing that might convince her to come back with me.

The likelihood of success is not high.

"I have to find Lark first," I say. "But then . . ."

There's a new sound with the rain outside—a muddling of horses' hooves in the mud, dim voices. Tamsin nods and claps my elbow, then tugs Iano toward the side door to the corrals.

The post manager turns mildly away, taking the pile of coin to her lockbox and ignoring the rest of us.

Rou seems to have been holding a breath for at least three minutes. I look back to him, and he finally exhales.

"She's my little girl," he says, his voice cracked in a way I've never heard.

"I guarantee you," I say. "She's got more chance of surviving than any one of us. It's not a matter of whether she'll be all right. It's a matter of whether someone can get to her before she goes somewhere we can't find her again. Once she gets to her camp, she won't stay long. Please, Rou. Take care of Eloise, like she said."

He flattens his palm over his chest, as if his heart is literally breaking to pieces.

"I can't say yes," he says, and then his breath hitches. He doesn't go on. And I realize that maybe I'm part of this equation, too—that as mad as he is at me, if something happens to me out there, he'll pile it on his conscience.

"Then don't say yes," I say quickly. "Just get in the coach. Go, before the bells."

He doesn't move, doesn't blink.

There's thumping on the porch, and Eloise suddenly turns for the side door, her arm looped through mine. I stumble alongside her, throwing a glance over my shoulder at Rou's cut-open face, wondering if he's going to stall the Moquoian guard or simply stand as he is now, frozen and wrecked.

Eloise drags me out of the bright posthouse and into the shadowy maze of parked carriages. Her breath is ragged.

"I have to go now, Eloise." I squeeze her arm in mine. "Please take care of yourself."

She squeezes back but doesn't let go—she turns to me and takes a fistful of my sodden tunic. I place my hand over hers, unsure if her grip is aggression or not. Her eyes glint in the slivered lantern light—Lark's eyes. Was I too busy wondering if she was made of sky to see the same set of eyes I've been friends with my whole life?

"I'm still mad at you," she whispers hoarsely. "But I will be *much* madder if you die."

"I won't die."

"You can't promise that," she says. "So don't. Veran. I'm going to be taking care of Papa now, as much as he's going to be taking care of me. I was too little to understand what happened to him after Matariki, but I know enough now. This will kill him, if it goes wrong. If you can't find her, or if one of us dies on the trip . . ."

"Don't, Eloise, please don't say that." Eloise can't die, she can't, she can't.

"It's more than a possibility, Veran—don't pretend like it's not. I've gotten away from fever in the past, and you from the bows, but luck is against us all now." She shakes her head, her fingers trembling on my tunic. "Just come back alive, both of you. *Don't—*" Her other hand jumps to cover my mouth. "Don't promise. You can't promise. Just do it."

I nod behind her fingers just as a door creaks, spilling light among the shadowy carriages. From the posthouse comes a voice arguing in stilted Moquoian, made worse with emotion.

"I go, I go, look—yes, yes. I with my daughter *go*."

Eloise pushes me down the row of dark stagecoaches, turning back for the little mud-coach waiting in the rain. I don't wait to watch them board—I steal among the lines of coaches and into the street on the far side.

There are more guards in town, knocking on the doors of inns and demanding to see their registers. But there's no raised alarm or shouts of discovery, so I can only assume Iano and Tamsin have managed to slip away—for now. As for me, it takes six side streets and a tiptoe across the roof of the general store to locate Kuree, and a breathless run through the rain to get her away from the town center. Bless this storm—it will certainly muddle any rogue tracks and curious sound, if it doesn't drown the lot of us first.

I make a wide circle around the perimeter of Pasul before finally reaching the edge of town. I'm cramped with cold and dogged by fatigue, and I can almost hear Mama hollering from here.

Listen to your body, she shouts, she whispers, my face cradled in her palms. *Your body is smarter than your brain. It tells you what it needs. Listen, Veran, listen to it.*

But I can't right now, Mama. And I can't listen to my head, either. I don't know what I'm listening to—the truth about Lark has knocked all sense out of me.

I hope Mama and Papa will understand. I hope they won't blame Rou. I hope he'll be all right—I hope Eloise will be all right.

I hope I haven't used the last of my luck.

And Lark . . .

I have no idea what to hope for her, so with a kick, I urge Kuree forward. She springs over the flooded flats.

We thunder back into the Ferinno.

TAMSIN

Iano reins the horse in on top of the ridge overlooking Pasul. We had almost no time to select a mount from the corrals, and even less to properly saddle it, so we're on an old, bow-backed mare with only a blanket beneath us. But I'm light, and the poor animal so far seems sturdy enough, bringing us to the crest of the trail just as the thunderstorm slackens.

We sit for a moment, watching the dark clouds tumble away into the desert. Every now and again a stray bolt leaps from the sky to connect with the earth.

"By the colors, I hope they'll be all right," Iano says. He's in front of me, his waist a solid trunk for me to cling to. I lean my head on his shoulder blade, gazing out at the open sky and absently worrying the amber beads on my too-loose *si-oque*.

He twists on the mare's back, turning to look me over with anxious eyes. Things are lightening now into an early sunset made brilliant by the streaks of clouds still left in the west. His damp skin and hair are glazed with red and orange.

Tekonnsi. Urksi. Energy. Contentment.

I feel neither of those things.

He reaches back to brush my cheek with his thumb. He runs his fingers through the fuzz of my hair.

"Tamsin . . . I'm sorry."

I am, too. I don't know what this thing looks like now, this bridge between him and me. It feels like every peg and rafter holding it together has gone up in flames, and all that's left is a smoking scaffold waiting to collapse.

How long before this giddy relief at being reunited wears thin?

He takes my hand and presses my fingers to his lips, squeezing his eyes shut. When he opens them again, the light has shifted, as it did so often in my cell window. It slides from the *tekonnsi* reds into *dequasi* golds.

New beginnings.

That one, maybe, is more appropriate, though a beginning, at present, sounds exhausting.

He squeezes my fingers again before letting them go and turning back around.

"It's a day over the ridge, and then another to Giantess," he says. "We'll have to be careful of the crossroads. You're sure Soe still lives there?"

I'm sure. It's been three years since I shared a locked room with her and a dulcimer in the Blows, but I stopped to visit for a day on my way out to Vittenta all those weeks ago, before this disaster came roaring into my life. And anyway, all the other possible refuges I can think of are noble houses in Tolukum, and it's not safe for either of us to depend on those. I nod.

"All right. To Soe's. You'll let me know when we should stop?"

I pat him tiredly in affirmation. He releases a breath and nudges the horse forward.

"I hope . . ." he begins, and then falls silent. We sway with the mare's movement as she steps over a crumbling log.

"I hope we can figure this thing out," he says.

I run my index finger down his spine and trace a few letters on his back.

WE WILL

He straightens. "Sorry, I missed that . . . ?"

Too complex. I revise.

I WILL

LARK

By midnight, the last dregs of the storm have been defeated by the desert as if it never was. The moon beats down in a harsh half slice, just bright enough to catch the big rocks and rough spots in time to weave around them. But not bright enough to track my trail—for that I'm grateful. With any luck someone following will only have a general direction, and not the direct line I'm cutting across the barren flats.

Rat whines from the saddle. He hates being on Jema's back, but he was lagging, and I can't risk slowing down for him. He squirms against my hold on his ruff.

"It's okay." I try to scratch his ears, but I can't lift my hand or else he'll worm off my lap. "It's okay."

It's not okay. Jema has slowed to a plod and is tripping over stones—soon I'll have no choice but to stop and let her rest. I can't stand the thought of stopping, because if I do, that current of memories I'm just managing to outrun will catch up with me, sweep alongside, carry me away. It's like the flash floods in the canyons—they never give any warning. There's just a moment's sound of grinding rock, a wash of rising water, before a torrent of debris eats a path through the earth.

Come with me.

Things could be different.

Jema catches a hoof on a rock, and I lurch to grab the saddle horn. At once, the images I've been staving off prickle my brain—that unhinged Cypri man lunging for me, hands out. The sweet, smooth face of the girl, all freckles and eyelashes and soft curves. Tamsin's sharp, shrewd stare. Veran, utterly aghast, clutching his face. That name, tossed at me over and over, as if hoping it would stick.

That smell, of dark coffee and cinnamon, drunk hot in ceramic mugs rimmed in gold.

I shake, brushing myself, slapping my vest—I can't get that scent off me, can't get rid of it. It overpowers the water-flushed sage and wet dirt, the smell of horse and dog and old leather, the smell of my own skin and hair, the back of my bandanna, which is up even though it's dark and damp, the sooty grease spread thick on my cheeks. Every single thing I've ever been and ever trusted, drowned.

Jema stumbles again, and I kick her harder than I mean to.

"Come on," I urge her. "Please, Jema, just a little farther."

She snorts and plods a little faster, head drooping. My stomach surges with every tired step.

Three Lines. Three Lines is my only chance now. I'll put Rose on the ox, with Sedge leading it, and little Whit with Andras on Pokey. Lila can take Moll on Jema, and I'll walk with Weed. We won't have time to pack, or disassemble the lean-to, or bring coals with us. We'll leave things as they are—the fire rings, the rock walls, the deep, sweet water pocket that never ran dry. We'll head north, into the plains. They'll expect me to go south, or east, into familiar territory, but I won't. We'll find someplace in the endless bison grasslands, or farther, into the wolf-wilds, where the grass turns to talus and the trees disappear. Somewhere nobody will find us, not ever.

For the hundredth time, I wonder where Saiph is—if he's back in Pasul, or if he never made it there at all, or if he got lost or hurt or killed on the road. For the hundredth time, I wonder if Rose is still alive, or if she died because of this disastrous decision to leave my campmates alone.

For the hundredth time, I curse Veran Greenbrier deep in my gut.

Rat whines again. Not far away, a single coyote croons a lone, mournful note, perhaps expecting an answer and receiving none. I shiver at the sound and the slice of wind through still-wet clothes.

"Farther, Jema," I call. "Just a little farther."

EPILOGUE

In Tolukum Palace, this night is not a time of rest.

Queen Isme stands in her parlor, clutching a crimson robe around her throat and listening to her private guard nervously report that there is still no trace of Prince Iano—or the Eastern translator.

Kimela Novarni sits before her mirror, turning her head this way and that as she scrutinizes which jewels to wear for her debut performance—a performance she's determined to give despite the sudden disappearance of the prince.

Minister Kobok paces the rug in front of his fireplace. He's dismissed all his servants and forgone his elaborate evening ritual. Every now and then, his gaze strays to the small box on his mantel, and his pacing quickens.

Many floors below, Mistress Fala tries to concentrate on cataloging the pungent cleaning solutions in the supply closet, but her thoughts keep straying to the halls above. So much in the palace has changed in so short a time, and the work that had seemed so safe now seems fraught with danger around every corner.

Throughout the rest of the palace, the halls bustle with hushed activity. A girl hurries from fireplace to fireplace with her bucket of ashes. A boy scrubs the colored tiles at the roots of the silent cedar trees. Outside, a glass cleaner pauses his precarious ascent to pick up a dead sparrow from a windowsill, tucking it into the bag on his belt with several others.

There is no rest.

The work goes relentlessly on.

ACKNOWLEDGMENTS

If Creatures of Light was my first dip into the waters of publication, The Outlaw Road has been my cannonball. I've wanted to write this story for at least a decade, even if I didn't quite realize it. The story and characters were first born while I was a ranger in Yellowstone National Park, and fittingly, the finishing touches were put on it while I was back in the same park, wearing the same hat, four years down the line.

The first big thank you goes to my agent, Valerie Noble, for latching on to this story right away and championing Lark, Veran, and Tamsin with as much enthusiasm as she did Mae, Mona, and Gemma. Thank you to my editor, David Pomerico, who believed in this story from the very first synopsis, and who attended to it with his usual precision and discernment, making the story as strong and shiny as it could be. And thank you to Mireya Chiriboga, Laurie McGee, Lauren Grange, Paula Szafranski, and the rest of the publication team at Harper Voyager.

Thank you to my parents, who continued to answer weird plot questions and chided me to write a more satisfactory ending. Thank you to the rest of my family and in-laws for always supporting this effort, without fail. Thank you to Caitlin, for taking this journey with me and always being by my side. And thanks to Eliza Gallagher, Josh Frye, and Whitney Lessem for helping me name Jema, Lark's horse.

As usual, I have to thank the ranger crew that was subjected to working with me while under deadline—the Grant Village rangers of Yellowstone National Park, 2019. Thanks for buoying me through edits and giving me great fodder for future projects. West Thumb, Best Thumb.

And finally, thanks to my husband, Will, for pushing me to pursue a career as an author and for weathering the rollercoaster ride that's come with it. And thanks to my girls, Lucy and Amelia, who are the best cheerleaders I could hope for, and my constant inspiration.

The character of Tamsin is written in memory of ranger and mentor Lisa Free, who taught me how to play the mountain dulcimer.

EXPERIENCE THE WORLDS OF EMILY B. MARTIN

WOODWALKER
Creatures of Light, Book 1

Exiled from the Silverwood and the people she loves, Mae has few illusions about ever returning to her home. But when she comes across three out-of-place strangers in her wanderings, she finds herself contemplating the unthinkable: risking death to help a deposed queen regain her throne.

ASHES TO FIRE
Creatures of Light, Book 2

An adult fantasy tale that will surely resonate with young adult readers, *Ashes to Fire* is the story of a queen's desperate journey to secure peace, and the even greater journey to discover herself. *Ashes to Fire* is the captivating and adventurous follow-up to *Woodwalker*—once more with cover art by the author!

CREATURES OF LIGHT
Creatures of Light, Book 3

Queens, countries, and cultures collided in *Woodwalker* and *Ashes to Fire*, the first two books in Emily B. Martin's Creatures of Light series. From Mae's guidance to retake Lumen Lake to Mona's eye-opening adventure in Cyprien, we now see things from Gemma's perspective—a queen in disgrace...and symbol of the oppressive power of Alcoro.

SUNSHIELD
A Novel

A lawless wilderness. A polished court. Individual fates, each on a quest to expose a system of corruption.

Separated by seas of trees and sand, the outlaw, a diplomat, and a prisoner are more connected than anyone realizes. Their personal fates might just tip the balance of power in the Eastern World—if that very power doesn't destroy them first.

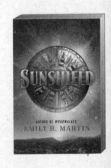

HarperCollins*Publishers*

DISCOVER GREAT AUTHORS, EXCLUSIVE OFFERS, AND MORE AT HC.COM.

THE JESUS LIBRARY
Michael Green, series editor

The Hard Sayings of Jesus

F. F. Bruce

InterVarsity Press
Downers Grove
Illinois 60515

© 1983 by F. F. Bruce

Published in the United States of America by InterVarsity Press, Downers Grove, Illinois, with permission from Hodder and Stoughton Limited, London.

InterVarsity Press is the book-publishing division of Inter-Varsity Christian Fellowship, a student movement active on campus at hundreds of universities, colleges and schools of nursing. For information about local and regional activities, write IVCF, 233 Langdon St., Madison, WI 53703.

Cover illustration: Janice Skivington

ISBN 0-87784-927-7
ISBN 0-87784-933-1 (Jesus Library set)

Printed in the United States of America

Library of Congress Cataloging in Publication Data
Bruce, F. F. (Frederick Fyvie), 1910-
    The hard sayings of Jesus.

    (The Jesus Library)
    Bibliography: p.
    Includes index.
        1. Jesus Christ—Words.   2. Jesus Christ—Teachings.
I. Title.   II. Series.
BT306.B77   1983   232.9'54   83-10793
ISBN 0-87784-927-7

---

17   16   15   14   13   12   11
96   95   94   93   92   91   90

To my students
in the University of Manchester
1959–1978

Abbreviations

AV	Authorised (King James) Version of the English Bible
L	Material peculiar to the Gospel of Luke
M	Material peculiar to the Gospel of Matthew
NEB	New English Bible
NIV	New International Version
Q	Material common to the Gospels of Matthew and Luke but not found in the Gospel of Mark
RSV	Revised Standard Version (1946-1952)
RV	Revised Version (1881-1885)

Editor's Preface

Jesus of Nazareth remains the most important individual who has ever lived. Nobody else has had comparable influence over so many nations for so long. Nobody else has so affected art and literature, music and drama. Nobody else can remotely match his record in the liberation, the healing and the education of mankind. Nobody else has attracted such a multitude not only of followers but of worshippers.

And nobody else has been subjected to such intense and prolonged critical study. After more than two hundred years of detailed examination and argument, many of the critical issues remain astonishingly open. The high-water mark of scepticism has receded somewhat. It is no longer assumed without question that nothing orthodox can be true. But certain emphases, methodologies and presuppositions, common in New Testament studies, are widely held to militate against the reliability of the picture of Jesus presented to us by the documents. There is a rumour abroad that in these days of redaction criticism it is neither proper nor necessary to ask what actually happened, and that the Jesus of history is indistinguishable behind the Christ of faith. This series will address itself to the task of re-examining Jesus.

During the 1970s Hodder put out a series of books on controversial issues within the Christian religion. They were published in various countries, and were written by a variety of authors who were united in the belief that good scholarship and orthodox belief were not incompatible. During the 1980s the same publishers hope to produce a comparable series concentrating on the supremely controversial storm-centre of Christianity, Jesus Christ himself. Various aspects of the Jesus story will be looked at: his teaching, his example, his death and resurrection, his uniqueness. In this, the first volume of the series, Dr. F. F. Bruce, recently retired as Rylands Professor of Biblical Criticism and Exegesis at Manchester, and one of the most distinguished of British New Testament scholars, has set the tone to which other writers in the series will aspire. His book is characterised by clarity, honesty, scholarship, intelligibility and faith.

Those who have heard Professor Bruce answer questions, without a note, on the most abstruse New Testament problems will be delighted that he has agreed to tackle seventy of the most difficult sayings of Jesus. I know of no book like this, and I am confident that it will reach a very wide circle of readers. The considered fruits of his research and reflection will afford both understanding and confidence to many, and will bring the person of Jesus into clearer focus for every reader.

Michael Green

Author's Preface

When Michael Green, in his friendly and persuasive way, invited me to contribute to this series and allowed me a choice of titles, I told him I would play for safety and opt for *The Hard Sayings of Jesus*. What I meant by 'playing for safety' was, I think, that this subject would confine me mainly to exposition, an exercise in which I feel comfortably at home.

I quickly found that the exposition of the hard sayings of Jesus is a difficult and responsible task; yet I am glad that I undertook it, for it has proved specially rewarding. His yoke is easy and his burden is light, but his sayings are often hard because they run counter to well-entrenched presuppositions and traditional assumptions about life and human relations. When they are hard for this reason, I hope I have not made them easier, for that would be to obscure their meaning. But the exposition of seventy of his sayings in the following pages may help readers to see what the main emphases of his teaching were.

F. F. B.

Introduction

Many of those who listened to Jesus during his public ministry found some of his sayings 'hard', and said so. Many of those who read his sayings today, or hear them read in church, also find them hard, but do not always think it fitting to say so.

Our Lord's sayings were all of a piece with his actions and with his way of life in general. The fewer preconceptions we bring from outside to the reading of the Gospels, the more clearly shall we see him as he really was. It is all too easy to believe in a Jesus who is largely a construction of our own imagination – an inoffensive person whom no one would really trouble to crucify. But the Jesus whom we meet in the Gospels, far from being an inoffensive person, gave offence right and left. Even his loyal followers found him, at times, thoroughly disconcerting. He upset all established notions of religious propriety. He spoke of God in terms of intimacy which sounded like blasphemy. He seemed to enjoy the most questionable company. He set out with open eyes on a road which, in the view of 'sensible' people, was bound to lead to disaster.

But in those who were not put off by him he created a passionate love and allegiance which death could not destroy. They knew that in him they had found the way of acceptance, peace of conscience, life that was life indeed. More than that: in him they came to know God himself in a new way; here was the life of God being lived out in a real human life, and communicating itself through him to them. And there are many people today who meet Jesus, not in Galilee and Judaea but in the gospel record, and become similarly aware of his powerful attractiveness, entering into the same experience as those who made a positive response to him when he was on earth.

One reason for the complaint that Jesus's sayings were hard was that he made his hearers think. For some people thinking is a difficult and uncomfortable exercise, especially when it involves the critical reappraisal of firmly held prejudices and convictions, or the challenging of the current consensus of opinion. Any utterance, therefore, which invites them to engage in this kind of thinking is a hard saying. Many of Jesus's sayings were hard in this sense. They suggested that it would be good to reconsider things that every reasonable person accepted. In a world where the race was to the swift and the battle to the strong, where the prizes of life went to the pushers and the go-getters, it was preposterous to congratulate the unassertive types and tell them that *they* would inherit the earth or, better still, possess the kingdom of heaven. Perhaps the beatitudes were, and are, the hardest of Jesus's sayings.

For the Western world today the hardness of many of Jesus's sayings is all the greater because we live in a different culture from that in which they were uttered, and speak a different language from his. He appears to have spoken Aramaic for the most part, but with few exceptions his Aramaic words have not been preserved. His words have come down to us in a translation, and that translation – the Greek of the Gospels – has to be retranslated into our own language. But when the linguistic problems have been resolved as far as possible and we are confronted by his words in what is called a 'dynamically equivalent' version – that is, a version which aims at producing the same effect in us as the original words produced in their first hearers – the removal of one sort of difficulty may result in the raising of another.

For to us there are two kinds of hard saying: there are some which are hard to understand and there are some which are only too easy to understand. When sayings of Jesus which are hard in the former sense are explained in dynamically equivalent terms, then they are likely to become hard in the latter sense. Mark Twain spoke for many when he said that the things in the Bible that bothered him were not those that he did not understand but those that he did understand. This is particularly true of the sayings of Jesus. The better we understand them, the harder they are to take. (Perhaps, similarly, this is why some religious people show such hostility to modern versions of the Bible: these versions make the meaning plain, and the plain meaning is unacceptable.)

If the following pages explain the hard sayings of Jesus in such a way as to make them more acceptable, less challenging, then the probability is that the explanation is wrong. Jesus did not go about mouthing pious platitudes; had he done so, he would not have made as many enemies as he did. 'The common people heard him gladly', we are told – more gladly, at any rate, than members of the religious establishment did – but even among the common people many were disillusioned when he turned out not to be the kind of leader they hoped he would be.

Apart from the one archetypal hard saying with which our collection starts, all the sayings treated here come from the synoptic Gospels. The Gospel of John has hard sayings in plenty, but they have a character of their own, and to deal with them would call for another volume of the same dimensions as this.

The view of the interrelatedness of the synoptic Gospels taken in this work does not greatly affect the exposition of the hard sayings, but it will be as well to state briefly here what that view is. It is that the Gospel of Mark provided Matthew and Luke with one of their major sources; that Matthew and Luke shared another common source, an arrangement of sayings of Jesus set in a brief narrative framework (not unlike the arrangement of the prophetic books of the Old Testament); and that each of the synoptic evangelists had access also to sources of information not used by the others.[1] It helps at times to see how one evangelist understood his predecessor by recasting or amplifying his wording.

Some of the sayings appear in different contexts in different Gospels. On this it is often said that Jesus must not be thought incapable of repeating himself. This is freely conceded: he may well have used a pithy saying on a variety of occasions. There is no reason to suppose that he said 'He who has ears to hear, let him hear', or 'Many are called, but few are chosen', once only. But there are occasions when a saying, indicated by comparative study to have been spoken in one particular set of circumstances, is assigned to different contexts by different evangelists or different sources. There are other principles of arrangement than the purely chronological: one writer may group a number of sayings together because they deal with the same subject-matter or have the same literary form; another, because they have a common keyword (like the sayings about fire and salt in Mark 9:43–50).

Where there is reason to think that an evangelist has placed a saying in a topical rather than a chronological setting, it can be interesting to try to decide what its chronological setting in the ministry of Jesus probably was. For example, it has been suggested that the saying 'You are Peter', which Matthew (alone of the synoptic evangelists) includes in the report of Jesus's interchange with the disciples at Caesarea Philippi (see p. 139), may have belonged chronologically to another occasion, such as Jesus's appearance to Peter in resurrection. Even more speculative is the interpretation of some of the sayings as words of Jesus spoken not during his public ministry but later, through the mouth of a prophet in the early church. It has been thought best in this work not to engage in such speculation but to treat the sayings primarily in the contexts provided for them by the evangelists.

Again, this does not seem to be the place for an enquiry into the question whether the sayings examined are authentic sayings of Jesus or not. To help students in answering such a question some scholars have formulated 'criteria of authenticity' for application to the sayings recorded in the Gospels. One scholar, who attached great importance to these criteria, told me a few years ago that he had concluded that among all the sayings ascribed to Jesus in the Gospels, only six, or at most eight, could be accepted as undoubtedly his. The reader of this work will realise that it is written from a less sceptical viewpoint than that. Let this be said, however: the fact that a saying is hard is no ground for suspecting that Jesus did not say it. On the contrary, the harder it is, the more likely it is to be genuine.

The second volume of the *Encyclopaedia Biblica*, published

in 1901, contained a long and important entry on 'Gospels' by a Swiss scholar, P. W. Schmiedel. In the course of this he listed a number of sayings of Jesus and other passages which, to his mind, ran so much counter to the conception of Jesus which quickly became conventional in the Church that no one could be thought to have invented them. He therefore regarded their authenticity as beyond dispute and proposed to treat them as 'the foundation-pillars for a truly scientific life of Jesus'. Several of them will come up for inspection in the following pages for, whether in Schmiedel's sense or otherwise, they are certainly hard sayings.

The biblical version most frequently quoted in this work is the Revised Standard Version. It is for the most part in the wording of the Authorised (King James) Version that the sayings studied have acquired the status of 'hard sayings', and the RSV wording is sufficiently close to that of the AV to retain the same element of 'hardness'. A version like the New English Bible sometimes removes one hardness to replace it by another.

In the interpretation of the sayings quoted I am, of course, indebted to many other interpreters. Some acknowledgment of my indebtedness is made in the following pages. There is one interpreter, however, to whom I am conscious of a special debt: that is the late Professor T. W. Manson, particularly in respect of his two works *The Teaching of Jesus*[2] and *The Sayings of Jesus*.[3] From the latter of these works I take leave to borrow words which will supply a fitting conclusion to this introduction:

> It will simplify the discussion if we admit the truth at the outset: that the teaching of Jesus is difficult and unacceptable because it runs counter to those elements in human nature which the twentieth century has in common with the first – such things as laziness, greed, the love of pleasure, the instinct to hit back and the like. The teaching as a whole shows that Jesus was well aware of this and recognised that here and nowhere else lay the obstacle that had to be surmounted.[4]

Chapter
1

Eating the Flesh and Drinking the Blood of the Son of Man

'Truly, truly, I say to you, unless you eat the flesh of the Son of man and drink his blood, you have no life in you' (John 6:53)

This was the original hard saying: as John reports, 'many of his disciples, when they heard it, said, "This is a hard saying; who can listen to it?"' (John 6:60). The implication is that they not only found it difficult to understand, but suspected that, if they did understand it, they would find it unacceptable. The NEB expresses a different nuance by its rendering: 'This is more than we can stomach! Why listen to such talk?' That implies that they thought Jesus was talking nonsense, and that it was a waste of time listening to it; but that is probably not what John means.

The feeding of the five thousand is one of the few incidents in the ministry of Jesus recorded by all four evangelists. The narrative of Mark 6:31–52 (including the sequel in which Jesus came walking to his disciples across the water) is reproduced substantially in Matthew 14:13–33 and (without the walking on the water) in Luke 9:10–17. John tells the story independently (together with the walking on the water) in John 6:1–21.

In the synoptic Gospels we get the impression that there was more in the feeding of the multitude than met the eye at the time or meets the reader's eye today. Mark in particular makes it plain that the feeding was intended to teach the disciples a lesson which they failed to learn, and that Jesus was surprised at their failure. When Jesus had joined them in the boat on their way back to the other side of the lake of Galilee, and the strong head wind which had made progress so difficult for them stopped blowing, then, says Mark, 'they were utterly astounded, for they did not understand about the loaves, but their hearts were hardened' (Mark 6:51–52). 'Their hearts were hardened' means 'their minds were closed', as the NEB puts it: they were too obtuse to take the lesson in, and the lesson evidently had something to do with the person of their Master.

But the further meaning which lies beneath the surface of the synoptic record is brought up above the surface by John and spelt out in detail. He does this in the form of an address given by Jesus shortly afterwards in the synagogue at Capernaum. The subject of the discourse is the bread of life. It has been suggested that on that sabbath day one of the scripture lessons in the synagogue was Exodus 16:13–36 or Numbers 11:4–9, which tell of the manna, the bread from heaven with which the Israelites were fed during their wilderness wanderings. At any rate, this is the subject with which the address begins.

The manna which their ancestors ate in the wilderness, Jesus tells his hearers, was not the food of immortality: those who ate it died nevertheless – some sooner, some later. Similarly, the bread with which he had recently fed the multitude was but material bread. They wished to make him their leader because he had given them that bread, but really he had come to give them better bread than that. Just as he had offered the Samaritan woman at Jacob's well better water than that in the well, the eternally satisfying water of life, so now he offers these Galileans better bread than the loaves with which the five thousand had been fed, better bread even than the manna which their forefathers had eaten, 'the food which endures to eternal life'. The manna might be called bread from heaven, even the bread of God; but the true 'bread of God is that which comes down from heaven, and gives life to the world' (John 6:27–34). Not only so, but God has one authorised and certified agent to bestow this life-giving bread: that is the Son of man,

Jesus himself. So far, so good: as the Samaritan woman, hearing of the water of life, said, 'Sir, give me this water, that I may not thirst' (John 4:15), so now Jesus's present hearers say, 'Sir, give us this bread always.'

This sets the stage for the next step of the lesson. Jesus not only *gives* the bread of life; he *is* the bread of life. True life, eternal life, is to be had in him alone: 'he who comes to me shall not hunger, and he who believes in me shall never thirst' (John 6:35). Indeed, not only will those who come to him in faith find in him perpetual sustenance and refreshment for their souls' hunger and thirst; they will never die. 'I am the living bread which came down from heaven; any one who eats of this bread will live for ever; and the bread which I shall give for the life of the world is my flesh' (John 6:51).

Now the lesson really begins to be hard. Anyone who has the advantage of reading these words in the context of the whole Gospel of John knows what their purport is. To believe in Christ is not only to give credence to what he says: it is to be united to him by faith, to participate in his life. Up to a point, his words about giving his flesh for the life of the world are paralleled in Mark 10:45, where he speaks of the Son of man as coming 'to give his life a ransom for many'. In the language which Jesus spoke 'my flesh' could be another way of saying 'myself': he himself is the bread given for the life of the world. But the saying in Mark 10:45 makes no reference to the Son of man as food for the souls of the 'many'; this is an additional emphasis, and one which leaves the synagogue congregation out of its depth.

On the lips of people who felt out of their depth, the question 'How can this man give us his flesh to eat?' (John 6:52) was a natural one. But it is John's practice when recording Jesus's discourses or conversations to quote words which have a spiritual meaning and then make the hearers show by their response that they have failed to grasp that meaning; Jesus is thus given an opportunity to repeat his words more fully. So here he repeats himself more fully in reply to the congregation's bewilderment: 'he who eats my flesh and drinks my blood has eternal life, and I will raise him up at the last day. For my flesh is food indeed, and my blood is drink indeed. He who eats my flesh and drinks my blood abides in me, and I in him' (John 6:54–56).

What could he mean? Plainly his language was not to be taken literally: he was not advocating cannibalism. But how was it to be taken? It was not only obscure, they thought: it was offensive. For Jews the drinking of any blood, even the eating of flesh from which the blood had not been completely drained, was taboo. But drinking the blood of a human being was an idea which ought not even to be mentioned. This was a hard saying in more senses than one.

Jesus answered their protest by pointing out that his words were to be understood spiritually. 'It is the spirit that gives life, the flesh is of no avail' (John 6:63). The physical or literal meaning of the words was plainly ruled out. But what was the spiritual meaning?

Again the reader of this Gospel, viewing these words in the context of the whole work, has an advantage over the first hearers, who had no such explanatory context. What we have in Jesus's strange language is a powerful metaphor stating that a share in the life of God, eternal life, is granted to those who in faith come to Jesus, appropriate him, enter into union with him. On this let two doctors of the Church be heard: Augustine of Hippo (at the end of the fourth century) and Bernard of Clairvaux (twelfth century).

The hard saying cannot be taken literally, says Augustine, since it would seem to be enjoining a crime or a vice: 'it is therefore a figure, bidding us communicate in the sufferings of our Lord, and secretly and profitably treasure in our hearts the fact that his flesh was crucified and pierced for us.'[1] Elsewhere he sums the matter up in an epigram: *Crede et manducasti*, 'Believe, and thou hast eaten.'[2]

Bernard expounds the words 'he who eats my flesh and drinks my blood has eternal life' as meaning: 'He who reflects on my death, and after my example mortifies his members which are on earth, has eternal life – in other words, "If you suffer with me, you will also reign with me."'[3]

The question is naturally raised: What relation do these

words of Jesus bear to the communion service, in which believers receive bread and wine as tokens of the body and blood of the Lord? Since John, unlike the other evangelists, does not record the institution of the Holy Communion, it could be said that this discourse represents his counterpart to their accounts of what Jesus did and said in the upper room when he gave his disciples the bread and the cup (see pp. 236-9). In the discourse of John 6 Jesus is not making a direct reference to the Holy Communion, but this discourse conveys the same truth in words as the Holy Communion conveys in action. This truth is summed up in the invitation extended to the communicant in the *Book of Common Prayer*: 'Take and eat this in remembrance that Christ died for thee, and feed on him in thy heart by faith with thanksgiving.' To feed on Christ in one's heart by faith with thanksgiving is to 'eat the flesh of the Son of man and drink his blood' and so have eternal life. (On the phrase 'the Son of man' see pp. 27, 246.)

Chapter
2

The Son of Man Forgiving Sins

'The Son of man has authority on earth to forgive sins'
(Mark 2:10)

When the four friends of the paralysed man broke through the roof of the house in Capernaum where Jesus was teaching, and lowered him on his pallet at Jesus's feet, Jesus appreciated their faith and determination and healed the man. But before he told the man to pick up his pallet and walk out with it, he said to him, 'My son, your sins are forgiven' (Mark 2:5). Nothing is said of the cause of the man's paralysis, but Jesus evidently recognised that the first thing he needed was the assurance that his sins were forgiven. If this assurance were accepted, the physical cure would follow.

His words to the paralysed man constituted a hard saying in the ears of some of the bystanders. Who was this to pronounce forgiveness of sins? To forgive injuries that one has received oneself is a religious duty, but sins are committed against God, and therefore God alone may forgive them. One may say to a sinner, 'May God forgive you'; but by what authority can one say to him, 'Your sins are forgiven'? Probably Jesus's critics would have agreed that a duly authorised spokesman of God might, in the words of the General Absolution, 'declare and pronounce to his people, being penitent, the absolution and remission of their sins'; but they did not acknowledge Jesus as such a duly authorised spokesman, nor was there any evidence, so far as they could see, that repentance was forthcoming or that an appropriate sin-offering had been presented to God. It was the note of authority in Jesus's voice as he pronounced forgiveness that gave chief offence to them: he imposed no conditions, called for no amendment of life, but spoke as though his bare word ensured the divine pardon. He was really arrogating to himself the prerogative of God, they thought.

How could Jesus give evidence of his authority to forgive sins? They could not see sins being forgiven, but they could see the effect of Jesus's further words in the man's response. It is easy to *say* 'Your sins are forgiven', because no one can ordinarily see whether sins are forgiven or not. But if one tells a paralysed man to get up and walk, the words will quickly be shown to be empty words if nothing happens. 'So,' said Jesus to his critics, 'that you may know that the Son of man has authority on earth to forgive sins,' and then, addressing himself to the paralytic, 'rise, take up your pallet, and go home.' When the paralytic did just that, Jesus's power as a healer was confirmed – but more than that, it was the assurance that his sins were forgiven that enabled the man to do what a moment previously would have been impossible, so Jesus's authority to forgive sins was confirmed at the same time.

This is the first occurrence of the designation 'the Son of man' in Mark's Gospel, and one of the two occurrences in his Gospel to be located before Peter confessed Jesus to be the Christ at Caesarea Philippi (the other being the statement in Mark 2:28 that the Son of man is lord of the sabbath; see p. 34). 'The Son of man' was apparently Jesus's favourite way of referring to himself (see pp. 34, 154). Sometimes the 'one like a son of man' who receives supreme authority in Daniel's vision of the day of judgment (Dan. 7:13–14) may provide the background to Jesus's use of the expression (see p. 246), but that son of man is authorised to execute judgment rather than to pronounce forgiveness (one may compare John 5:27, where the Father has given the Son 'authority to execute judgment, because he is son of man'). Here, however, the expression more probably points to Jesus as the representative man – 'the Proper Man, whom God himself hath bidden'. This is how Matthew appears to have understood it: he concludes his account of the incident by saying that the crowds that saw it 'glorified God, who had given such authority to men' – that is, to human beings (Matt. 9:8). The authority so given is exercised by Jesus as the representative man – or, as Paul was later to put it, the 'last Adam' (1 Cor. 15:45). To pronounce, and bestow, forgiveness of sins is the highest prerogative of God, and this he has shared with the Son of man.

Chapter
3

Not the Righteous but Sinners

'I came not to call the righteous, but sinners' (Mark 2:17)

Nineteen centuries and more of gospel preaching and New Testament reading have familiarised us with the idea that Jesus's ministry was specially directed to sinners – not simply to sinners in the sense in which most people will admit that 'we are all sinners', but sinners in the sense that their lives offended the accepted moral code of their community. 'The saying is sure and worthy of full acceptance, that Christ Jesus came into the world to save sinners' (1 Tim. 1:15); this is a great gospel text, and if the writer goes on to speak of himself as first and foremost among sinners, that serves to underline his claim on the saving grace of Christ. But during the ministry of Jesus it gave great offence to many respectable people that a religious teacher as he was should have so little regard for what was expected of him as to consort with those who were no better than they should be. 'If this man were a prophet,' said Simon the Pharisee to himself, when Jesus allowed a woman of doubtful reputation to touch him, 'he would have known ... what sort of woman this is who is touching him, for she is a sinner' (Luke 7:39). But Jesus knew perfectly well what sort of woman she was, and for that very reason would not prevent her from paying him such embarrassing attention (see p. 80).

Among all the traditional designations of Jesus, probably none is more heart-warming than 'the friend of sinners'. But this designation was first given to him by way of criticism: 'a glutton and a drunkard,' they said, 'a friend of tax collectors and sinners!' (Luke 7:34) – tax-collectors occupying the lowest rung on the ladder of respectability, matched only by harlots. It was not that he tolerated such people, as though he did them a favour by taking notice of them, *de haut en bas*: he gave the impression that he liked their company, that he even preferred it; he did not condemn them but encouraged them to feel at home with him. 'This man receives sinners', the scribes said by way of complaint; and more than that, he actually 'eats with them' (Luke 15:2). To accept invitations to a meal in the homes of such people, to enjoy table-fellowship with them – that was the most emphatic way of declaring his unity with them. No wonder this gave offence to those who, sometimes with considerable painstaking, had kept to the path of sound morality. If a man is known by the company he keeps, Jesus was simply asking to be known as the friend of the ne'er-do-wells, the dregs of society. And would not many religious people today react in exactly the same way?

On one occasion when Jesus had accepted a dinner invitation in the home of one of these disreputable people, his disciples were approached by the scribes. The disciples were included in the invitation, but some of them may have had misgivings. 'Why does he eat with tax collectors and sinners?' they were asked. But Jesus interposed with the answer. 'It is sick people, not healthy people, who need the doctor,' he said; 'it is sinners, not righteous people, that I came to call' (Mark 2:17). To call means to invite: he had accepted their invitation, but they received an invitation from him – to take and enjoy the loving mercy of the heavenly Father. It is inevitable that the 'ninety-nine righteous persons who need no repentance' (Luke 15:7) should feel that too much fuss is made over sinners (see p. 170), but since the gospel is for sinners first and foremost – indeed, for sinners only – it cannot be otherwise.

These words of Jesus are reproduced by the two other synoptic evangelists (Matt. 9:13; Luke 5:32), but Luke adds a short explanatory gloss: 'I have not come to call the righteous, but sinners *to repentance*.' Repentance figures more frequently in Luke's Gospel than in the other two (it does not figure at all in the Gospel of John). It has sometimes been suggested that Luke's addition betrays a misunderstanding on his part, but this is not really so. If repentance in the teaching of Jesus implies change of character rather than reformation of behaviour,[1] then Jesus believed in dealing with the root of the disease and not merely with the symptoms. And the root could be dealt with effectively only by the practical assurance and demonstration of outgoing, self-giving love.

Chapter
4

The Sabbath for Man

'The sabbath was made for man, not man for the sabbath; so the Son of man is lord even of the sabbath' (Mark 2:27–28)

This is the second occurrence of the designation 'the Son of man' in Mark's Gospel – one of the two occurrences which he places before the Caesarea Philippi incident. (For the first see p. 26.) The words were the conclusion of Jesus's reply to those who criticised his disciples for plucking ears of grain as they walked through the fields one sabbath and then (according to Luke 6:1) eating the grain when they had rubbed the ears in their hands to separate the kernel from the husk. Harmless enough actions, it might be supposed today (unless the owner of the crop complained that he was being robbed), but plucking the ears was technically regarded by the interpreters of the law as a form of reaping, and rubbing them to extract the kernel as a form of grinding, and reaping and grinding were two kinds of work that were forbidden on the sabbath. Probably, in addition to the expressed criticism of the disciples, there was an implied criticism of Jesus for allowing them to break the law in this way.

Jesus first invoked a precedent: in an emergency David had been permitted by the priest in charge of the sanctuary at Nob (perhaps on Mount Scopus, near Jerusalem) to have some of the holy bread (the 'shewbread' or 'bread of the [divine] presence') for himself and his followers to eat, although it was laid down in the law that none but priests should eat it (1 Sam.

21:1–6). The point of Jesus's argument here seems to be that human need takes priority over ceremonial law; it is relevant to recall that in traditional interpretation (though not in the Old Testament text) the incident from the life of David took place on a sabbath (the day when, according to Leviticus 24:8–9, the old bread was to be removed, to be eaten by 'Aaron and his sons … in a holy place', and replaced by new bread, 'set in order before the Lord').

But Jesus went on to invoke an earlier and higher precedent (see p. 45). The sabbath was instituted by God; what was God's purpose in instituting it? If that can be discovered, then the sabbath law is best kept when God's purpose in giving it is best fulfilled. In Genesis 2:2–3, God is said to have 'rested' on the seventh day when he had finished the creative work of the six preceding days, so he 'blessed the seventh day and hallowed it'. The Hebrew verb translated 'rest' is *shābath*, which is given here as the explanation of the word 'sabbath' (Hebrew *shabbāth*). Neither Jesus nor his critics thought that God needed to rest on the seventh day because he was tired after a hard week's work. He 'ceased' or 'desisted' from his work. Why, then, did he 'bless' the sabbath day and 'hallow' it? Not for his own sake, but for the sake of his creatures who, he knew, would certainly need to rest after a hard week's work. This is implied in the Genesis narrative itself. The fourth commandment, in the form which it is given in Exodus 20: 8–11, bids the Israelites sanctify the seventh day by refraining from work, because God sanctified it by ceasing from his work after the six days of creation. But in the form which this commandment is given in Deuteronomy 5:12–15 it is made explicitly clear that the sabbath was given for the sake of those who need to rest after hard work: 'that your manservant and your maidservant may rest as well as you'.

The sabbath day was instituted, then, to meet a human need, and the day is best sanctified when human need is met on it. Expositors regularly quote as a parallel the words of Rabbi Simeon ben Menasya preserved in a rabbinical commentary on Exodus 31:14: 'The sabbath is delivered to you; you are not delivered to the sabbath.'[1]

But the real problem of Jesus's saying is the significance of the 'so' or 'so that' introducing the next words: 'the Son of man is lord even of the sabbath'. How does it follow from the fact that the sabbath was made for man that the Son of man is lord of the sabbath? In one way, this would not have been so much of a problem for those who first heard Jesus speak the words. Since 'man' was regularly expressed in Aramaic by the idiom 'son of man', the literal translation of the saying would have been: 'The sabbath was made for the son of man, not the son of man for the sabbath; so the son of man is lord even of the sabbath.' The question that would rise in the hearers' minds was: 'In what sense is the son of man lord of the sabbath? Does he mean that humanity in general is lord of the sabbath?' This question confronts us too, but we have a further question to think about: why did Mark use the simple noun 'man' (human being, or the human race) in the first two clauses, but the locution 'the Son of man' in the third? He must have intended the subject of the third clause to mean something more than man in general. If so, what was that something more? Jesus probably meant that he who is lord of the sabbath, he who has the sovereign authority to interpret the sabbath law in accordance with the divine purpose in instituting it, is the representative man, and that is the role which he now discharges. Since the sabbath was made for man, he whom God has ordained to be man's representative before him is authorised to dispose of the sabbath at his own discretion.

Chapter
5

Not Dead but Sleeping

'Why do you make a tumult and weep? The child is not dead but sleeping' (Mark 5:39)

The statement that Jairus's twelve-year-old daughter was 'not dead, but sleeping' appears in all three synoptic narratives (cf. Matt. 9:24; Luke 8:52). But what did Jesus mean when he said so? The girl's death had certainly been reported: as Jesus was on the way to the house where she lived, in response to her father's anguished plea to him to come and lay his healing hands on her, a messenger came to say that she had died; therefore, 'why trouble the Teacher any further?' But Jesus encouraged her father: 'Do not be afraid; only believe', and went on with him to the house. It was then that he rebuked the crowd that had gathered for the noise they were making. Did he mean that she was not dead (as had been reported) but only sleeping in the literal sense of the word? The crowd took him to mean that, but it was perfectly evident to them that she was dead: 'they laughed at him', say all three evangelists; 'knowing that she was dead', Luke adds (and the fact that he says 'knowing' rather than 'supposing' suggests that he believed that she had died). Or did Jesus mean that her state of death, though real, was not to be permanent – that it would prove to be nothing more than a temporary sleep? Did he, in other words, use the word 'sleep' figuratively, as he did when he reported the death of Lazarus to his disciples by saying, 'Our friend Lazarus has fallen asleep, but I go to awake him out of sleep' (John 11:11)? It is beside the point to say that two different Greek words for 'sleep' are used – one in the story of Jairus's daughter and the other in the Lazarus narrative. Both of them can be used figuratively for death in appropriate contexts.

Which way, then, should our Lord's words be taken? We cannot be sure, in the absence of the confirmation which a medical certificate would supply. To the modern reader his words are ambiguous. To the child he used the kind of language which might be used by anyone waking a child up from sleep: *Talitha cumi* is the Aramaic for 'Little girl, get up!' But the mere waking of a child from sleep is not the kind of action which would call for special commemoration: the fact that the evangelists record the incident, coupled with the way in which they record it, implies their belief that she was really (if only temporarily) dead.

Chapter
6

Saltless Salt

'Salt is good; but if the salt has lost its saltness, how will you season it?' (Mark 9:50)

One can use salt to season meat or bread, but if the salt that one might use for this purpose loses its saltness, what can be used to season *it*?

But how can salt lose its saltness? If it is truly salt, of course, it must remain salt and retain its saltness. But probably in the ordinary experience of Galilean life, salt was rarely found in a pure state; in practice it was mixed with other substances, various forms of earth. So long as the proportion of salt in the mixture was sufficiently high, the mixture would serve the purpose of true salt. But if, through exposure to damp or some other reason, all the salt in the mixture was leached out, what was left was good for nothing. As Luke, in his amplified version of the saying, puts it, 'it is fit neither for the land nor for the dunghill' (Luke 14:35). It might have been thought that the dunghill was all that it was fit for, but Jesus may have used a word that meant 'manure': 'it is no good for the land, not even as manure'. Matthew says, 'It is no longer good for anything except to be thrown out and trodden under foot by men' (Matt. 5:13); that is to say, people throw the useless stuff out into the street.

The figure of insipid salt appears in the words of the rabbis, with reference (it seems) to Israel's role as the salt or purifying agency among the nations of mankind. Matthew's version of Jesus's saying begins with the words: 'You are the salt of the earth' (Matt. 5:13) addressed to his disciples. This implies that the disciples have a particular function to perform on earth, and that, if they fail to perform it, they might as well not exist, for all the good they will do. In what respect they are said to be salt is not specified, so the nature of their function has to be inferred from the context and from what is known of the effect of salt. They may be intended to have a preserving and purifying effect on their fellows, or to add zest to the life of the community, or to be a force for peace. The idea of an insipid Christian ought to be a contradiction in terms. One way in which the quality of saltness can be manifested is in one's language. 'Let your speech be always gracious, seasoned with salt', Paul writes to the Colossians (Col. 4:6), where the 'salt' seems to be that ready Christian wit or wisdom (specially apt in the answering of questions about the faith) which is far removed from the slanderous and unsavoury talk deprecated earlier in the same letter (3:7).

Since the disciples are spoken of as the salt of the earth in the same context of the Sermon on the Mount in which they are also spoken of as the light of the world and a city set on a hill (Matt. 5:14), it is evidently their public life that is in view. They must be seen by others as living examples of the power and grace of God, examples which others are encouraged to follow.

Mark adds some other sayings in which salt figures. These 'salt' sayings follow the warning that it is better to enter into life maimed than to be consigned with all one's limbs to the 'Gehenna of fire' (Mark 9:43–48). A transition between that warning and the 'salt' sayings is provided by the sentence: 'For every one shall be salted with fire' (Mark 9:49). The fires which burned continuously in the Gehenna or municipal refuse-tip south of Jerusalem (see p. 51) reduced the risk of disease which might have arisen from the decomposing organic matter; fire had a purifying effect, as salt also had. The point of Jesus's words in this 'transitional' sentence may be that the fire of persecution will have a purifying or refining effect in the disciples' lives (cf. 1 Pet. 1:6–7). Some texts of Mark append here a quotation from Leviticus 2:13 (where the reference is more particularly to the cereal offering): 'and every sacrifice will be salted with salt'. This clause is probably not original in this context, but those who were responsible for inserting it (being moved to do so probably by the common theme of salt) may have intended it to mean: 'Every Christian, by enduring persecution, will be cleansed thereby and so become a more acceptable offering to God.'

Then, after the saying about the salt that has lost its saltness, Mark concludes this series of sayings with 'Have salt in yourselves, and be at peace with one another.' Again, we should understand this injunction better if we knew the situation in which it was originally spoken. 'Have salt in yourselves' might mean 'Have salt among yourselves' and might refer to the eating of salt together which was an expression of fellowship at table and therefore of peaceful relations. If this is so, then 'be at peace with one another' is a non-figurative explanation of 'have salt among yourselves'. But we cannot be sure.

Chapter
7

The Old Is Better

'And no one after drinking old wine desires new; for he says, "The old is good"' (Luke 5:39)

The ancient authorities for the text read variously 'The old is good' and 'The old is better', but even if we accept the authority of those which read 'The old is good', it makes no material difference: anyone who said, with reference to wine, 'The old is good' meant that it was better than the new wine.

This is not so much a hard saying as a misunderstood saying. It is often treated as though it carried Jesus's authority and could be applied to a wide variety of situations in which the old is threatened by the new – an old version of the Bible, an old form of worship, an old method of evangelism, and in short everything that is popularly summed up in the traditional term 'the old-time religion'. But Jesus quotes the saying; he does not necessarily endorse it. The saying is preserved by Luke, who appends it to his version of Jesus's words about new wine and old wineskins. In those words, taken over from Mark 2:22, Jesus compares his message of the kingdom of God to new wine, which cannot be contained in old wineskins that have lost their elasticity. The old wineskins were the rules and forms of traditional religion, which were menaced, as many religious people thought, by Jesus's revolutionary teaching. If, in the saying appended by Luke, the new wine has the same meaning – Jesus's message of the kingdom – then the people who say 'The old is good' or 'The old is better' are expressing their preference for the old, established, familiar ways. New teaching is disturbing; it forces people to think, to revise their ideas and attitudes. Religious people tend to be conservative, to suspect innovations. Job's friends were like this: the wisdom to which they appealed had the sanction of antiquity, and Job's arguments tended to upset it. 'What do you know that we do not know?' asked Eliphaz the Temanite. 'What do you understand that is not clear to us? Both the gray-haired and the aged are among us, older than your father' (Job 15:9-10).

Jesus found that much resistance to accepting his message, on the part not of hostile but of well-intentioned and pious people, arose simply from this attachment to old ways and old ideas. They had stood the test of time; why should they be changed? This was a perfectly natural response, and one which was not totally regrettable: it could be a safeguard against the tendency to fall for anything new just because it was new – to embrace novelty for novelty's sake. But when God does a new thing or imparts a new revelation, as he did in the ministry of Jesus, then this instinctive preference for the old could be an obstacle to the progress of his cause. Ultimately, the question to ask about any teaching is not 'Is it old?' or 'Is it new?' but 'Is it true?' Old wine has a goodness of its own and new wine has a goodness of its own. Personal preference there may be, but there is no room for the dogmatism which says, 'No wine is fit to drink till it is old.'

'The old is good' or 'The old is better', then, far from expressing the mind of Jesus, could well express an attitude which he deplores because it hinders the advance of the kingdom of God.

Chapter
8

One Jot or One Tittle Shall in No Wise Pass

> *'Think not that I have come to abolish the law and the prophets; I have come not to abolish them but to fulfil them. For truly, I say to you, till heaven and earth pass away, not an iota, not a dot, will pass from the law until all is accomplished. Whoever then relaxes one of the least of these commandments, and teaches men so, shall be called least in the kingdom of heaven; but he who does them and teaches them shall be called great in the kingdom of heaven. For I tell you, unless your righteousness exceeds that of the scribes and Pharisees, you will never enter the kingdom of heaven'* (Matt. 5:17–20)

Here is surely an uncompromising affirmation of the eternal validity of the law of Moses. Not the smallest part of it is to be abrogated. The 'jot' (AV) is the smallest letter of the Hebrew alphabet; the 'iota' (RSV) is the smallest letter of the Greek alphabet. The 'tittle' (AV) or 'dot' (RSV) was a very small mark attached to a letter, perhaps to distinguish it from another which resembled it, as in our alphabet 'G' is distinguished from 'C', or 'Q' from 'O'.

What is hard about this uncompromising affirmation? For some readers the hardness lies in the difficulty of recognising in this speaker the Christ who, according to Paul, 'is the end of the law, that every one who has faith may be justified' (Rom. 10:4).

Others find no difficulty in supposing that Paul's conception of Jesus differed radically from the presentation of his character and teaching in the Gospels. The view has indeed been expressed (not so frequently nowadays as at an earlier time) that Paul is pointed to as the man who 'relaxes one of the least of these commandments and teaches men so'. This implies that the saying does not come from Jesus, but from a group in the early Church which did not like Paul. Even where the reference to Paul would not be entertained, it is held by many that these words come from a group in the early Church which wished to maintain the full authority of the law for Christians. The saying, according to Rudolf Bultmann, 'records the attitude of the conservative Palestinian community in contrast to that of the Hellenists'.[1]

There were probably several selections of sayings of Jesus in circulation before the Gospels proper began to be produced, and one of these, which was preferred by stricter Jewish Christians, seems to have been used, along with others, by Matthew. Such a selection of sayings could be drawn up in accordance with the outlook of those who compiled it; sayings which in themselves appeared to support that outlook would be included, while others which appeared to go contrary to it would be omitted. The teaching of Jesus was much more diversified than any partisan selection of his sayings would indicate. By not confining himself to any one selection Matthew gives an all-round picture of the teaching. A saying such as has just been quoted had three successive life-settings: its life-setting in the historical ministry of Jesus, its setting in a restricted selection of Jesus's sayings, and its setting in the Gospel of Matthew. It is only its setting in the Gospel of Matthew that is immediately accessible to us. (In addition to these three settings, of course, it may have acquired subsequent life-settings in the history of the Church and in the course of interpretation. The statement 'I have come not to abolish them but to fulfil them' has been used, for example, to present the gospel as the crown of fulfilment of Hinduism,[2] but such a use of it is irrelevant to the intention of Jesus or of the evangelist.)

To the remark that it is only in its setting in the Gospel of

Matthew that the saying is immediately accessible to us there is a partial exception. Part of it occurs in a different context in the Gospel of Luke. In Luke 16:16–17 (between the parable of the unjust steward and the story of the rich man and Lazarus; see p. 116). Jesus says, 'The law and the prophets were until John; since then the good news of the kingdom of God is preached, and every one enters it violently. But it is easier for heaven and earth to pass away, than for one dot of the law to become void.' The second of these two sentences is parallel to (but not identical with) Matthew 5:18, the saying about the jot and tittle (or the iota and dot).

The selection of sayings which is supposed to have been drawn up in a more legally minded Christian circle, and which Matthew is widely considered to have used as one of his sources, is often labelled M (because it is represented in Matthew's Gospel only). Another, more comprehensive, selection on which both Matthew and Luke are widely considered to have drawn is commonly labelled Q. It may be, then, that the form of the 'jot and tittle' saying found in Matthew 5:18 is the M form, while that found in Luke 16:17 is the Q form. T. W. Manson was one scholar who believed that this was so, and he invited his readers to bear two possibilities in mind. The first possibility was that Luke's form of the saying is closer to the original wording and that the form in Matthew 'is a revision of it to bring it explicitly into line with Rabbinical doctrine'. The other possibility, which follows on from this one, was 'that the saying in its original form asserts not the perpetuity of the Law but the unbending conservatism of the scribes', that it is not intended to be 'sound Rabbinical dogma but bitter irony'. Jesus, that is to say, addresses the scribes and says, 'The world will come to an end before you give up the tiniest part of your traditional interpretation of the law.'[3]

It is plain that Jesus did not accept the rabbinical interpretation of the law. Indeed, he charged the scribes, the acknowledged students and teachers of the law, with 'transgressing the commandment of God for the sake of their tradition' (so the wording runs in Matthew 15:3, in a passage based on Mark 7:9). He said that by their application of the law 'they bind heavy burdens, hard to bear, and lay them on men's shoulders' (Matt. 23:4); by contrast, he issued the invitation: 'Take my yoke upon you, and learn from me; for . . . my yoke is easy, and my burden is light' (Matt. 11:29–30).

But he did not relax the requirements of God's law as such, nor did he recommend a lower standard of righteousness than the 'scribes and Pharisees' required. On the contrary: he insisted that admittance to the kingdom of heaven called for righteousness exceeding that of the scribes and Pharisees. This last statement, found in Matthew 5:20, serves as an introduction to the paragraphs which follow, in which Jesus's account of what obedience to the law involves is given in a succession of hard sayings, at which we shall look one by one. But at the moment we may mention two principles by which he interpreted and applied the law.

First, he maintained that the proper way to keep any commandment was to fulfil the purpose for which it was given. He did this with regard to the law of marriage (see p. 58); he did it also with regard to the sabbath law. On the sabbath day, said the fourth commandment, 'you shall not do any work'. In the eyes of some custodians of the law, this called for a careful definition of what constituted 'work', so that people might know precisely what might or might not be done on that day. Circumstances could alter cases: an act of healing, for example, was permissible if it was a matter of life and death, but if the treatment could be put off to the following day without any danger or detriment to the patient, that would be better. It was precisely on this issue that Jesus collided repeatedly with the scribes and their associates. His criterion for the keeping of this law was to inquire for what purpose the sabbath was instituted. It was instituted, he held, to provide rest and relief for human beings: they were not made for the sake of the sabbath, but the sabbath was given for their sake (see p. 33). Therefore, any action which promoted their rest, relief and general well-being was permissible on the sabbath. It was not merely permissible on the sabbath: the sabbath was the most appropriate day for its performance, because its performance so signally promoted God's purpose in instituting the sabbath. Jesus appears to have cured people by preference on the sabbath day, because such an action honoured the day.

He did not abrogate the fourth commandment: he interpreted it in a different way from the current interpretation. Did his principle of interpretation 'exceed the righteousness of the scribes and Pharisees?' Perhaps it did. There are some people who find it easier to have a set of rules: when a practical problem arises, they can consult the rules and know what to do. But if they have to decide which action best fulfils the purpose of the law, that involves thought, and thought of this kind, with the personal responsibility that accompanies it, is a difficult exercise for them.

Secondly, Jesus maintained that obedience or disobedience to the law began inwardly, in the human heart. It was not sufficient to conform one's outward actions and words to what the law required; the thought-life must be conformed to it first of all. One of the Old Testament psalmists voiced his feelings thus: 'I delight to do thy will, O my God; thy law is within my heart' (Ps. 40:8). This psalm is not quoted by Jesus in the Gospels, but in another place in the New Testament its language is applied to him (Heb. 10:7, 9). It does indeed express very well the attitude of Jesus himself and the attitude which he recommended to his hearers. Where the mind and will are set to do the will of God, the speaking and acting will not deviate from it.

Besides, where this is so, there will be an emphasis on the inward and spiritual aspects of ethics and religion, rather than on the outward and material aspects. The idea that a religious obligation could be given precedence over one's duty to one's parents was one with which Jesus had no sympathy (cf. Mark 7:10–13). This idea was approved by some exponents of the law in his day, but in general Jewish teaching has agreed with him here. Again, Jesus set very little store by details of ritual purification or food regulations, because these had no ethical content. Mark goes so far as to say that by his pronouncements on these last matters 'he declared all foods clean' (Mark 7:19). If Matthew does not reproduce these words of Mark, he does reproduce the pronouncements of Jesus which Mark so interprets (Matt. 15:17–20).

But did the ritual washings and food restrictions not belong to the jots and tittles of the law? Should they not be reckoned, at the lowest estimate, among 'the least of these commandments'? Perhaps so, but in Jesus's eyes 'justice, mercy and faith' were of much greater importance (Matt. 23:23). And what about the sacrificial ceremonies? They were included in the law, to be sure, but Jesus's attitude to such things is summed up in his quotation from a great Old Testament prophet: 'I desire mercy, and not sacrifice' (Hos. 6:6). It is Matthew, and Matthew alone among the evangelists, who records Jesus as quoting these words, and he records him as using them twice (Matt. 9:13; 12:7). The law is fulfilled ethically rather than ceremonially. Jesus confirmed the insistence of the great prophets that punctiliousness in ceremonial observances is worse than useless where people neglect 'to do justice, and to love kindness, and to walk humbly with . . . God' (Mic. 6:8). It is human beings, and not inanimate things, that matter.

The law for Jesus was the expression of God's will. The will of God is eternal and unchangeable. Jesus did not come to modify the will of God; he fulfilled it. The standard of obedience to that will which he set, by his example and his teaching alike, is more exacting than the standard set by the written law. He insisted that the will of God should be done from the heart. But, in so insisting, he provided the means by which the doing of God's will from the heart should not be an unattainable ideal. If Paul may be brought in to interpret the teaching of Jesus here, the apostle who maintained that men and women are justified before God through faith in Jesus and not through keeping the law also maintained that those who have faith in Jesus receive his Spirit so that 'the just requirement of the law might be fulfilled in us, who walk not according to the flesh but according to the Spirit' (Rom. 8:4). The gospel demands more than the law, but supplies the power to do it. Someone has put it in doggerel but telling lines:

To run and work the law commands,
Yet gives me neither feet nor hands;
But better news the gospel brings:
It bids me fly, and gives me wings.

Chapter
9

"You Fool!" Merits Hell Fire

'Every one who is angry with his brother shall be liable
to judgment; whoever insults his brother shall be liable
to the council, and whoever says, "You fool!" shall be
liable to the hell of fire' (Matt. 5:22)

This is the first of a series of statements in which Jesus makes
the requirements of the law more radical than the strict letter
might indicate. Quoting the sixth commandment, Jesus says,
'You have heard that it was said to the men of old, "You shall
not kill; and whoever kills shall be liable to judgment"'. 'But *I*
say to you,' he continues, and then comes the passage above,
ending in the hard saying about the penalty incurred by one
who says to another, 'You fool!'

Murder was a capital offence under Israelite law; the death
penalty could not be commuted to a monetary fine, such as was
payable for the killing of someone's domestic animal. Where it
could be proved that the killing was accidental – as when a
man's axe-head flew off the handle and struck his fellow-
workman on the head – it did not count as murder, but even so
the owner of the axe-head had to take prudential measures to
escape the vengeance of the dead man's next of kin. Otherwise,
the killer was brought before the village elders and on the
testimony of two or three witnesses was sentenced to death.
The death penalty was carried out by stoning: the witnesses
threw the first stones, and then the community joined in, thus
dissociating themselves from blood-guiltiness and expiating

the pollution which it brought on the place.

Jesus points out that the murderous act springs from the angry thought. It is in the mind that the crime is first committed and judgment is incurred. The earthly court cannot take action against the angry thought, but the heavenly court can – and does. This in itself is a hard saying. According to the AV, 'whosoever is angry with his brother without a cause shall be in danger of the judgment', but the phrase 'without a cause' is a later addition to the Greek text, designed to make Jesus's words more tolerable. The other man's anger may be sheer bad temper, but mine is righteous indignation – anger with a cause. Like the prophet Jonah, 'I do well to be angry' (Jonah 4:9). But Jesus's words, in the original form of the text, make no distinction between righteous and unrighteous anger: anyone who is angry with his brother exposes himself to judgment. There is no saying where unchecked anger may end. 'Be angry but do not sin', we are told in Ephesians 4:26; that is, 'If you are angry, do not let your anger lead you into sin; let sunset put an end to your anger, for otherwise it will provide the devil with an opportunity which he will not be slow to seize.'

There seems to be an ascending scale of seriousness as Jesus goes on: 'liable to judgment . . . liable to the council . . . liable to the hell of fire'. The council in question is the Sanhedrin, apparently the supreme court of the nation in contrast to a local court. Evidently, then, to insult one's brother is more serious than to be angry with him. This is clearly so: the angry thought can be checked, but the insult once spoken cannot be recalled and may cause violent resentment. The person insulted may retaliate with a fatal blow, for which in fact if not in law the victim of the blow may be as much to blame as the one who strikes it. The actual insult mentioned by Jesus is the word 'Raca', as it stands in the AV. The precise meaning of 'Raca' is disputed; it is probably an Aramaic word meaning something like 'imbecile' but was plainly regarded as a deadly insult. (Words of abuse are above all others to be avoided by speakers of a foreign language; they can have an unimagined effect on a native speaker of the language.)

But 'whoever says, "You fool!" shall be liable to the hell of fire'. From this we might gather that 'you fool!' is a deadlier insult than 'Raca', whatever 'Raca' may mean. For 'the hell of fire' (RSV) or 'hell fire' (AV) is the most severe penalty of all. The 'hell of fire' is the fiery Gehenna. Gehenna is the valley on the south side of Jerusalem which, after the return from the Babylonian exile, served as the city's rubbish dump and public incinerator. In earlier days it had been the site of the worship of Molech, and so it was thought fit that it should be degraded in this way. In due course it came to be used as a symbol of the destruction of the wicked after death, just as the garden of Eden became a symbol of the blissful paradise to be enjoyed by the righteous.

But was 'You fool!' actually regarded as being such a deadly insult? In this same Gospel of Matthew the cognate adjective is used of the man who built his house on the sand (7:26) and of the five girls who forget to take a supply of oil to keep their torches alight (25:2–3), and Jesus himself is reported as calling certain religious teachers 'blind fools' (23:17). It is more probable that, just as 'Raca' is a non-Greek word, so is the word *mōre* that Jesus used here. If so, then it is a word which to a Jewish ear meant 'rebel (against God)' or 'apostate'; it was the word which Moses in exasperation used to the disaffected Israelites in the wilderness of Zin: 'Hear now, you rebels; shall we bring forth water for you out of this rock?' (Num. 20:10). For these rash words, uttered under intense provocation, Moses was excluded from the promised land.

Whether this was the word Jesus had in mind or not, he certainly had in mind the kind of language that is bound to produce a murderous quarrel: chief responsibility for the ensuing bloodshed, he insisted, lies with the person who spoke the offending word. But behind the offending word lies the hostile thought. It is there that the guilty process starts; and if the hostile thought is not killed off as soon as the thinker becomes aware of it, then, although no earthly court may be in a position to take cognisance of it, that is what will be the first count in the indictment before the judgment-bar of God.

Chapter
10

Adultery in the Heart

'Every one who looks at a woman lustfully has already committed adultery with her in his heart' (Matt. 5:28)

This is another instance of Jesus's making the law more stringent by carrying its application back from the outward act to the inward thought and desire. The seventh commandment says, 'You shall not commit adultery' (Exod. 20:14). In the cultural context of the original Decalogue, this commandment forbade a man to have sexual relations with someone else's wife. To infringe this commandment was a capital offence; the penalty was stoning to death (as it still is in some parts of the Near and Middle East). Another commandment seems to carry the prohibition back beyond the overt act: the second clause of the tenth commandment says, 'You shall not covet your neighbour's wife' (Exod. 20:17), where his wife is mentioned among several items of his property. In a property context one might 'covet' someone else's wife not by way of a sexual urge but because of the social or financial advantages of being linked with her family.

However that may be, Jesus traces the adulterous act back to the lustful glance and thought, and says that it is there that the rot starts: it is there, therefore, that the check must be immediately applied. Otherwise, if the thought is cherished, or fed by fantasy, the commandment has already been broken. There may be significance in the fact that Jesus does not speak of someone else's wife but of 'a woman' in general. Parallels to this saying can be found in rabbinical literature.

Pope John Paul II excited some comment in 1981 by saying that a man could commit adultery in this sense with his own wife. Emil Brunner, in fact, had said something to very much the same effect over forty years before.[1] But there is nothing outrageous about such a suggestion. To treat any woman as a sex object, and not as a person in her own right, is sinful; all the more so, when that woman is one's own wife.

Chapter
11

Plucking Out the Right Eye

> *'If your right eye causes you to sin, pluck it out and throw it away; it is better that you lose one of your members than that your whole body be thrown into hell'* (Matt. 5:29)

This saying is not so hard in the RSV form in which it has just been quoted as it is in some older versions. The AV says, 'If thy right eye offend thee ...', which is generally meaningless to readers today; the verb 'offend' no longer means 'trip up' or anything like that, which in literary usage it still did in 1611. Less excusable is the RV rendering, 'If thy right eye causeth thee to stumble ...', because this introduced an archaism which was long since obsolete in 1881.

The RSV rendering, however, is more intelligible. It means, in effect: 'Don't let your eye lead you into sin.' How could it do that? By resting too long on an object of temptation. Matthew places this saying immediately after Jesus's words about adultery in the heart, and that is probably the original context, for it provides a ready example of how a man's eye could lead him into sin. In the most notable case of adultery in the Old Testament – King David's adultery with the wife of Uriah the Hittite – the trouble began when, late one afternoon, David from his palace roof *saw* the lady bathing (2 Sam. 11:2). Jesus says, 'Better pluck out your eye – even your right eye (as being presumably the more precious of the two) – than allow it to lead you into sin; it is better to enter into eternal life with one eye than to be thrown into Gehenna (as a result of that sin) with two.'

Matthew follows up this saying about the right eye with a similar one about the right hand. This strong assertion seems to have stayed with the hearers; it is repeated in Matthew 18:8–9 (in dependence on Mark 9:43–48), where the foot is mentioned in addition to the eye and the hand.

Shortly after the publication of William Tyndale's English New Testament, the attempt to restrict its circulation was defended on the ground that the simple reader might mistakenly take such language literally and 'pluck out his eyes, and so the whole realm will be full of blind men, to the great decay of the nation and the manifest loss of the King's grace; and thus by reading of the Holy Scriptures will the whole realm come into confusion'. So a preaching friar is said to have declared in a Cambridge sermon; but he met his match in Hugh Latimer who, in a sermon preached the following Sunday, said that simple people were well able to distinguish between literal and figurative terms. 'For example,' Latimer went on, 'if we paint a fox preaching in a friar's hood, nobody imagines that a fox is meant, but that craft and hypocrisy are described, which so often are found disguised in that garb.'[1]

In fact, it is not recorded that anyone ever mutilated himself because of these words in the Gospels. There is indeed the case of Origen, but if the story is true that he made himself a eunuch 'for the kingdom of heaven's sake', that was in response to another saying, at which we shall look later (p. 63).

Chapter
12

Divorce and Remarriage

'Whoever divorces his wife and marries another, commits adultery against her; and if she divorces her husband and marries another, she commits adultery'
(Mark 10:11–12)

This was felt to be a hard saying by the disciples who first heard it; it is no less a hard saying for many of their present-day successors.

Jesus was asked to give a ruling on a point of law which was debated in the Jewish schools. In Deuteronomy 24:1–4 there is a law which says in effect, 'When a man divorces his wife because he has found "some indecency" in her, and she is then married to someone else who divorces her in his turn, her former husband may not take her back to be his wife again.' This law, forbidding a man who has divorced his wife to marry her again after she has lived with a second husband, does not lay down the procedure for divorce; it assumes this procedure as already in being. Nowhere in the Old Testament law is there an explicit command about the divorce procedure, but in this context it is implied that to divorce a woman a man had to make a written declaration that she was no longer his wife: 'he writes her a bill of divorce and puts it in her hand and sends her out of his house' (Deut. 24:1). Elsewhere in the Old Testament divorce is disparaged as something unworthy: 'I hate divorce, says the Lord the God of Israel', according to the prophet Malachi (2:16).

But in Deuteronomy 24 it is assumed that a man may divorce his wife, and that he may do so on account of 'some indecency' or 'something shameful' (NEB) that he has found in her. The interpreters of the law around the time of our Lord, who were concerned not only with deciding what it meant but with applying it to contemporary life, paid special attention to this phrase. What, they asked, might be indicated by this 'indecency' or unseemliness which justified a man in divorcing his wife?

There were two main schools of thought: one which interpreted it stringently, another which interpreted it more broadly. The former school, which followed the direction of Shammai, a leading rabbi who lived a generation or so before Jesus, said that a man was authorised to divorce his wife if he married her on the understanding that she was a virgin and then discovered that she was not. There was, in fact, an enactment covering this eventuality in the law of Deuteronomy (22:13–21), and the consequences could be very serious for the bride if the evidence was interpreted to mean that she had had illicit sexual relations before marriage. This, then, was one school's understanding of 'some indecency'.

The other school, following the lead of Shammai's contemporary Hillel, held that 'some indecency' might include more or less anything which her husband found offensive. She could cease to 'find favour in his eyes' for a variety of reasons – if she served up badly cooked food, for example, or even (one rabbi said) because he found her less beautiful than some other woman. It should be emphasised that the rabbis who gave these 'liberal' interpretations were not moved by a desire to make divorce easy: they were concerned to state what they believed to be the meaning of a particular scripture.

It was against this background that Jesus was invited to say what he thought. The Pharisees who put the question to him were themselves divided over the matter. In Matthew's account of the incident, they asked him, 'Is it lawful to divorce one's wife for any cause?' (19:3). If his answer was 'Yes', they would want to know for what cause or causes, in his judgment, divorce was permissible. He gave them his answer and then, in private, expanded it for the benefit of his disciples who had heard it.

As usual, he bypassed the traditional interpretation of the rabbinical schools and appealed to the scriptures. 'What did Moses command you?' he asked. 'Moses', they replied (referring to Deuteronomy 24:1–4), 'allowed a man to write a certificate of divorce, and to put her away.' They rightly said 'Moses allowed', not 'Moses commanded'; the enactment to which they referred, as we have seen, took for granted the existing divorce procedure, and wove it into a commandment relating to a further contingency. But Jesus told them that it was 'for your hardness of heart' that 'Moses wrote you this commandment'. Then, as with the sabbath law so with the marriage law, he went back to first principles. 'From the beginning of creation', he said, '"God made them male and female." "For this reason a man shall leave his father and mother and be joined to his wife, and the two shall become one." So they are no longer two but one. What therefore God has joined together, let not man put asunder' (Mark 10:2–9).

Jesus reminds them of the biblical account of the institution of marriage. The marriage law must conform with the purpose for which marriage was instituted by God. It was instituted to create a new unity of two persons, and no provision was made for the dissolving of that unity. Jesus does not idealise marriage. He does not say that every marriage is made in heaven; he says that marriage itself is made in heaven – that is, instituted by God. To the question, 'Is it lawful for a man to divorce his wife?' his answer, in effect, is 'No; not for any cause.'

There is a feature of Jesus's answer to the Pharisees which could easily be overlooked. The stringent interpretation of the school of Shammai and the 'liberal' interpretation of the school of Hillel were both given from the husband's point of view. In the stringent interpretation it was the bride's virginity that had to be above suspicion; the bridegroom's chastity before marriage did not enter into the picture. As for the 'liberal' interpretation, it was liberal in the husband's interest, in that it permitted him to divorce his wife for a variety of reasons; so far as the wife's interest was concerned, it was most illiberal, for she had little opportunity of redress if her husband decided to divorce her within the meaning of the law as 'liberally' interpreted. What was true of these interpretations was true of the original legislation which they undertook to expound: it was because of the hardness of *men's* hearts that divorce was conceded. The law was unequally balanced to the disadvantage of women, and Jesus's ruling, with its appeal to the Creator's intention, had the effect of redressing this unequal balance. It is not surprising that women regularly recognised in Jesus one who was their friend and champion.

We may observe in passing that, in referring to the creation ordinance, Jesus combined a text from the creation narrative of Genesis 1 with one from the narrative of Genesis 2. In Genesis 1:27, when 'God created man in his own image', the 'man' whom he so created was humanity, comprising both sexes: 'male and female he created them'. And in Genesis 2:24, after the story of the formation of Eve from Adam's side, the narrator adds: 'This is why a man leaves his father and his mother and cleaves to his wife, and they become one flesh.' That may be the narrator's comment on the story, but Jesus quotes it as the word of God. It is by God's ordinance that the two become one; men are given no authority to modify that ordinance.

When the disciples asked Jesus to clarify his ruling, he reworded it in the two statements quoted at the head of this section. The second of the two statements refers to a situation not contemplated in the Old Testament law, which made no provision for a wife to divorce her husband and marry another man. It has therefore been thought that this second statement is a corollary added to Jesus's original ruling when Christianity had made its way into the Gentile world. In a number of Gentile law-codes it was possible for a wife to initiate divorce proceedings, as it was not under Jewish law. But at the time when Jesus spoke there was a recent *cause célèbre* in his own country, to which he could well have referred.

Less than ten years before, Herodias, a granddaughter of Herod the Great, who had been married to her uncle Herod Philip and lived with him in Rome, fell in love with another uncle, Herod Antipas, tetrarch of Galilee and Perea, when he paid a visit to Rome. In order to marry Antipas (as Antipas also desired), she divorced her first husband. She did so under Roman law, since she was a Roman citizen (like all members of the Herod family). For a woman to marry her uncle was not a breach of Jewish law, as it was commonly interpreted at that time, but it was certainly a breach of Jewish law for her to marry her husband's brother. John the Baptist was imprisoned by Herod Antipas for insisting that it was unlawful for him to be married to his brother's wife. Jesus named no names, but any reference at that time, either in Galilee or in Perea, to a woman divorcing her husband and marrying someone else was bound to make hearers think of Herodias. If the suggestion that she was living in adultery came to her ears, Jesus would incur her mortal resentment as surely as John the Baptist had done.

But it was his words about divorce and remarriage on a man's part that his disciples found hard to take. Could a man not get rid of his wife for *any* cause? It seemed not, according to the plain understanding of what Jesus said. No wonder then that in the course of time the hardness of men's hearts modified his ruling, as earlier it had modified the Creator's original intention.

In Matthew's version of this interchange, Jesus's ruling is amplified by the addition of a few words: 'whoever divorces his wife, *except for unchastity*, and marries another, commits adultery' (Matt. 19:9). The same exception appears in another occurrence of his ruling in this Gospel, in the Sermon on the Mount: 'every one who divorces his wife, *except on the ground of unchastity*, makes her an adulteress; and whoever marries a divorced woman commits adultery' (Matt. 5:32). The ruling in this latter form appears also in Luke 16:18, but without the exceptive clause; the exceptive clause is found in Matthew's Gospel only, and found twice over.

What is to be made of the exceptive clause? Is it an addition reflecting the hardness of men's hearts? Or is it an expansion stating the obvious – that if something is done which by its very nature dissolves the marriage bond, then the bond is dissolved?

Is it an attempt to conform Jesus's ruling to Shammai's interpretation – that if the bride is found to have had an illicit sexual relation before her marriage, her husband is entitled to put her away? All these suggestions have been ventilated. Most probable is the view that the exceptive clause is designed to adapt the ruling to the circumstances of the Gentile mission. If this is so, the term 'unchastity' has a technical sense, referring to sexual unions which, while they might be sanctioned by use and wont in some parts of the Gentile world, were forbidden by the marriage law of Israel. It is a matter of history that the Church's traditional marriage law, with its list of relationships within which marriage might not take place, was based on that of Israel. What was to be done if two people, married within such forbidden degrees, were converted from paganism to Christianity? In this situation the marriage might be dissolved.

Certainly the Gentile mission introduced problems which were not present in the context of Jesus's ministry. One of these problems cropped up in Paul's mission-field, and Paul introduced his own 'exceptive clause' to take care of it, although in general he took over Jesus's prohibition of divorce among his followers. Some of Paul's converts put to him the case of a man or woman, converted from paganism to Christianity, whose wife or husband walked out because of the partner's conversion and refused to continue the marriage relationship. In such a situation, said Paul, let the non-Christian partner go; do not have recourse to law or any other means to compel him or her to return. The deserted spouse is no longer bound by the marriage tie which has been broken in this way (see p. 132). Otherwise, he said, 'to the married I give charge, not I but the Lord, that the wife should not separate from her husband (but if she does, let her remain single or else be reconciled to her husband) – and that the husband should not divorce his wife' (1 Cor. 7:10–16).

Plainly Paul, a considerable time before Mark's Gospel was written, knew what Jesus had laid down on the subject of marriage and divorce, and knew it in the same sense as Mark's account. Like his Master, Paul treated women as persons and not as part of their husbands' property. But the disciples who first heard Jesus's ruling on the subject found it revolutionary, and not altogether welcome; it took them some time to reconcile themselves to it.

Is it wise to take Jesus's rulings on this or other practical issues and give them legislative force? Perhaps not. The trouble is that, if they are given legislative force, exceptive clauses are bound to be added to cover special cases, and arguments will be prolonged about the various situations which are, or are not, included in the terms of those exceptive clauses. It is better, probably, to let his words stand in their uncompromising rigour as the ideal at which his followers ought to aim. Legislation has to make provision for the hardness of men's hearts, but Jesus showed a more excellent way than the way of legislation and supplies the power to change the human heart and make his ideal a practical possibility.

Chapter 13

Eunuchs for the Kingdom of Heaven's Sake

> *'For there are eunuchs who have been so from birth,
> and there are eunuchs who have been made eunuchs by
> men, and there are eunuchs who have made themselves
> eunuchs for the sake of the kingdom of heaven. He who
> is able to receive this, let him receive it'* (Matt.
> 19:12)

This saying occurs in Matthew's Gospel only: it comes immediately after his version of the saying about marriage and divorce, which we have just considered. When their Master ruled out the possibility of their getting rid of their wives by divorce, the disciples suggested that, in that case, it was better not to marry. To this he replied, 'Not all men can receive this precept, but only those to whom it is given' (Matt. 19:11). This means that the only men who can successfully live a celibate life are those who have received the gift of celibacy. This context shows how the following reference to eunuchs is to be understood; it certainly shows how Matthew understood it.

The saying, as reproduced by Matthew, consists of three parts. The first two present no problem. Some men are born eunuchs, and as for being 'made eunuchs by men', that was no unfamiliar practice in the ancient Near East. The hard saying is the third part: what is meant by making oneself a eunuch 'for the sake of the kingdom of heaven'?

It is reported that one eminent scholar in the early Church, Origen of Alexandria (A.D. 185–254), took these words with

literal seriousness in the impetuousness of youth, and
performed the appropriate operation on himself.[1] In later life
he knew better: in his commentary on Matthew's Gospel he
rejects the literal interpretation of the words, while acknowledging that he once accepted it, and says that they should be
understood spiritually and not 'according to the flesh and the
letter'.

What then did Jesus mean? These words are no more to be
taken literally than his words about cutting off the hand or foot
or plucking out the eye that leads one into sin. In the Jewish
culture in which he lived and taught, marriage was the accepted
norm, and celibacy was not held in the high esteem which it
later came to enjoy in many parts of the Church. That men such
as John the Baptist and himself should deny themselves the
comforts of marriage and family life may well have aroused
comment, and here is his answer to unspoken questions. Some
men and women have abstained from marriage in order to
devote themselves more wholeheartedly to the cause of the
kingdom of heaven. The man who marries and brings up a
family incurs special responsibilities for his wife and children:
they have a major claim on his attention. Jesus indicated his
attitude towards the ties of the family into which he was born
when he said that anyone who did the will of God was his
brother, sister or mother (Mark 3:35). It was people like these –
those who had taken on themselves the yoke of the kingdom
which he proclaimed – who constituted his true family. To
incur the more restricted obligations which marriage and the
rearing of children involved would have limited his dedication
to the ministry to which he knew himself called.

At the same time, he made it plain that only a minority
among his followers could 'receive' this course: for most of
them marriage and family life should be the norm.

Twenty-five years later the same teaching was repeated in
different language by Paul. Paul himself found the celibate way
of life congenial, but knew that the consequences would be
disastrous if those who were not called to it tried to follow it.
Hence his advice for the majority of his converts was that 'each
man should have his own wife and each woman her own

husband' – for, as he went on to say, 'each has his own special gift from God, one of one kind and one of another' (1 Cor. 7:2, 7). Those whom God called to the celibate life would receive from him the 'gift' of celibacy – of making themselves 'eunuchs for the sake of the kingdom of heaven'.

Chapter
14

Do Not Swear at All

'But I say to you, "Do not swear at all"' (Matt. 5:34)

Perjury is a serious offence in any law-code. It was so in the law of Moses. Perjury is forbidden in the third commandment: 'You shall not take the name of the Lord your God in vain; for the Lord will not hold him guiltless who takes his name in vain' (Exod. 20:7). To swear an oath falsely in the name of God was a sin not only against the name but against the very person of God. Later the scope of the commandment was broadened to include any light or thoughtless use of the divine name, to the point where it was judged safest not to use it at all. That is why the name of the God of Israel, commonly spelt Yahweh, came to be called the ineffable name, because it was forbidden to pronounce it. The public reader in the synagogue, coming on this name in the scripture lesson, put some other form in its place, lest he should 'take the name of the Lord his God in vain' by saying 'Yahweh' aloud. But originally it was perjury that was in view in the commandment, and in other injunctions to the same effect from Exodus to Deuteronomy. Summing up the sense of those injunctions, Jesus said, 'You have heard that it was said to the men of old, "You shall not swear falsely, but shall perform to the Lord what you have sworn"' (Matt. 5:33).

Realising the seriousness of swearing by God if the truth of the statement was not absolutely sure, people tended to replace the name of God by something else – by heaven, for example – with the idea that a slight deviation from the truth would then be less unpardonable. From another passage in this Gospel

(Matt. 23:16–22) it may be gathered that there were some casuists who ruled that vows were more binding or less binding according to the precise wording of the oath by which they were sworn. This, of course, would be ethical trifling.

It was necessary that people should be forbidden to swear falsely, whether in the name of God or by any other form of words. 'Pay what you vow', says the Preacher whose practical maxims enrich the Old Testament Wisdom literature; 'it is better that you should not vow than that you should vow and not pay' (Eccles. 5:4–5). But Jesus recommends a higher standard to his disciples. 'Do not swear at all,' he says; 'let what you say be simply "Yes" or "No"; anything more than this comes from evil' (Matt. 5:37). An echo of these words is heard in a later book of the New Testament: 'But above all, my brethren, do not swear, either by heaven or by earth or with any other oath, but let your yes be yes and your no be no, that you may not fall under condemnation' (James 5:12).

The followers of Jesus should be known as men and women of their word. If they are known to have a scrupulous regard for truth, then what they say will be accepted without the support of any oath. This is not mere theory; it is well established in experience. One body of Jesus's followers, the Society of Friends, has persisted in applying these words of his literally. And such is their reputation for probity that most people would more readily trust the bare word of a Friend than the sworn oath of many another person. 'Anything more than this', said Jesus, 'comes of evil'; that is to say, the idea that a man or woman can be trusted to speak the truth only when under oath (if then) springs from dishonesty and suspicion, and tends to weaken mutual confidence in the exchanges of everyday life. No one demands an oath from those whose word is known to be their bond; even a solemn oath on the lips of others tends to be taken with a grain of salt.

Chapter
15

Turning the Other Cheek

'If any one strikes you on the right cheek, turn to him the other also' (Matt. 5:39)

This is a hard saying in the sense that it prescribes a course of action which does not come naturally to us. Unprovoked assault prompts resentment and retaliation. If one wants to be painfully literal, the assault is particularly vicious, for if the striker is right-handed, it is with the back of his hand that he hits the other on the right cheek.

This is one of a number of examples by which Jesus shows that the life-style of the kingdom of God is more demanding than what the law of Moses laid down. 'You have heard that it was said, "An eye for an eye and a tooth for a tooth"' (Matt. 5:38). This was indeed laid down in Israel's earliest law-code (Exod. 21:24), and when it was first said it marked a great step forward, for it imposed a strict limitation on the taking of vengeance. It replaced an earlier system of justice according to which, if a member of tribe X injured a member of tribe Y, tribe Y was under an obligation to take vengeance on tribe X. This quickly led to a blood feud between the two tribes and resulted in suffering which far exceeded the original injury. But incorporated into Israel's law-code was the principle of exact retaliation: one eye, and no more, for an eye; one life, and no more, for a life. When wounded honour was satisfied with such precisely proportionate amends, life was much less fraught with hazards. The acceptance of this principle made it easier to regard monetary compensation as being, in many cases, a reasonable replacement for the infliction of an equal and opposite injury on the offending party.

But now Jesus takes a further step. 'Don't retaliate at all', he says to his disciples. 'Don't harbour a spirit of resentment; if someone does you an injury or puts you to inconvenience, show yourself master of the situation by doing something to his advantage. If he gets some pleasure out of hitting you, let him hit you again.' (It should not be necessary to say that this saying is no more to be pressed literally than the saying about plucking out one's right eye and throwing it away – see p. 54; it is not difficult to envisage the other cheek being turned in a very provocative manner.) If a soldier or other government official conscripts your services to carry a load for him so far, you are under compulsion; you are forced to do it. But, when you have reached the end of the stipulated distance, you are a free person again; then you can say to him, 'If you'd like it carried farther, I will gladly carry it for you.' The initiative has now become yours, and you can take it not by voicing a sense of grievance at having been put to such inconvenience but by performing an act of grace. This way of reacting to violence and compulsion is the way of Christ.

To have one's services conscripted to carry a soldier's pack for him is not an everyday experience in the Western world. How, in our situation, could this particular injunction of Jesus be applied? Perhaps when a citizen is directed by a policeman to assist him in the execution of his duty. But if (say) it is a matter of helping him to arrest a larger number of suspicious characters than he can cope with single-handed, would they not also come within the scope of duty to one's neighbour? This simply reminds us that Jesus's injunctions are not usually of the kind that can be carried out automatically; they often require careful thought. Whatever sacrifices he expects his followers to make, he does not ask them to sacrifice their minds. What they are urged to do is to have their minds conformed to his, and when careful thought is exercised in accordance with the mind of Christ, the resulting action will be in accordance with the way of Christ.

Another parallel might be the Christian's reaction to his

income tax demand. (Some followers of Christ have taken his teaching about property so seriously that they have no income on which tax can be paid – see p. 174.) The tax demanded must be paid; no choice can be exercised there. But suppose the Christian taxpayer, as an act of grace, pays double the amount demanded, or at least adds a substantial amount to it: what then? The computer would probably record it as tax overpaid, and the surplus would come back to him as a rebate. Perhaps it would be wisest if he were to send it direct to the Chancellor of the Exchequer, and send it anonymously – not only so as not to let his left hand know what his right hand was doing, but to forestall unworthy suspicions and enquiries. Once again, the carrying out of the simple injunctions of Jesus in a complex society like ours is not so easy. But where the spirit which he recommended is present, the performance should not go too far astray.

The admonition to turn the other cheek is given by Jesus to his disciples. It belongs to the sphere of personal behaviour. There are many Christians, however, who hold that this teaching should be put into practice by communities and nations as well as by individuals. Where Christian communities are concerned, we may well agree. The spectacle of the Church enlisting the aid of the 'secular arm' to promote its interests is rarely an edifying one. 'It belongs to the church of God', someone once said, 'to receive blows rather than to inflict them – but,' he added 'she is an anvil that has worn out many hammers.'[1] But what about a political community?

The situation did not arise in New Testament times. The first disciples of Jesus did not occupy positions of authority. Joseph of Arimathea might be an exception: he was a member of the Sanhedrin, the supreme court of the Jewish nation, and according to Luke (23:50–51), he did not go along with his colleagues' adverse verdict on Jesus. As the gospel spread into the Gentile world, some local churches included in their membership men who occupied positions of municipal responsibility, like Erastus, the city treasurer of Corinth (Rom. 16:23); but neither Paul nor any other New Testament writer finds it necessary to give special instructions to Christian rulers corresponding to those given to Christian subjects. But what was to happen when Christians became rulers, as in due course some did? Can the Christian magistrate practise non-retaliation towards the criminal who comes up before him for judgment? Could the Christian king practise non-retaliation towards a neighbouring king who declared war against him?

Paul, who repeats and underlines Jesus's teaching of non-retaliation, regards retaliation as part of the duty of the civil ruler. 'Would you have no fear of him who is in authority?' he asks. 'Then do what is good, and you will receive his approval, for he is God's servant for your good. But if you do wrong, be afraid, for he does not bear the sword in vain; he is the servant of God to execute his wrath on the wrongdoer' (Rom. 13:3–4). For Paul, the ruler in question was the Roman emperor or someone who held executive or judicial authority under him. But his words were relevant to their chronological setting. The time had not yet come (although it did come in less than ten years after those words were written) when the empire was openly hostile to the Church. Still less had the time come when the empire capitulated to the Church and emperors began to profess and call themselves Christians. When they inherited the 'sword' which their pagan predecessors had not borne 'in vain', how were they to use it? The answer to that question cannot be read easily off the pages of the New Testament. It is still being asked, and it is right that it should; but no single answer can claim to be the truly Christian one.

Chapter
16

Love Your Enemies

'But I say to you, "Love your enemies and pray for those who persecute you"' (Matt. 5:44)

Agreed, then: we should resist the impulse to pay someone who harms us back in his own coin, but does that involve *loving* him? Can we be expected to love to order?

Jesus's command to his disciples to love their enemies follows immediately on his words: 'You have heard that it was said, "You shall love your neighbour and hate your enemy"' (Matt. 5:43). 'You shall love your neighbour' is a quotation from the Old Testament law; it is part of what Jesus elsewhere referred to as the second of the two great commandments: 'You shall love your neighbour as yourself' (Lev. 19:18). On this commandment, with its companion 'You shall love the Lord your God ...' (Deut. 6:5), which he called 'the great and first commandment', Jesus said that all the law and the prophets depend (Matt. 22:36–40). But the commandment does not in fact go on to say 'You shall hate your enemy.' However, if it is only our neighbours that we are to love, and the word 'neighbours' be defined fairly narrowly, then it might be argued that we are free to hate those who are not our neighbours. But Jesus said, 'No; love your enemies as well as your neighbours.'

One difficulty lies in the sentimental associations that the word 'love' has for many of us. The love of which the law and the gospel alike speak is a very practical attitude: 'Let us not love in word or speech [only] but in deed and in truth' (1 John 3:18). Love to one's neighbour is expressed in lending him a helping hand when that is what he needs: 'Right,' says Jesus, 'lend your *enemy* a helping hand when that is what *he* needs. Your feelings towards him are not the important thing.'

But if we think we should develop more Christian feelings towards an enemy, Jesus points the way when he says 'Pray for those who persecute you' (or, as it is rendered in Luke 6:28, 'Pray for those who abuse you'). Those who have put this injunction into practice assure us that persistence in prayer for someone whom we don't like, however much it goes against the grain to begin with, brings about a remarkable change in attitude. Alexander Whyte quotes from an old diary the confessions of a man who had to share the same house and the same table with someone whom he found unendurable. He betook himself to prayer, until he was able to write, 'Next morning I found it easy to be civil and even benevolent to my neighbour. And I felt at the Lord's Table today as if I would yet live to love that man. I feel sure I will.'[1]

The best way to destroy an enemy is to turn him into a friend. Paul, who in this regard (as in so many others) reproduces the teaching of Jesus, sums it up by saying, 'Do not be overcome by evil, but overcome evil with good' (Rom. 12:21). He reinforces it by quoting from Prov. 25:21–22: 'If your enemy is hungry, feed him; if he is thirsty, give him drink; for by so doing you will heap burning coals upon his head'. Whatever that proverb originally meant, Paul adapts it to his purpose by omitting the self-regarding clause which follows those he quotes: 'and the Lord will reward you'. In this new context the 'burning coals' may mean the sense of shame which will be produced in the enemy, leading to a change of heart on his side too. But first do him a good turn; the feelings can be left to their own good time.

Chapter
17

'You, therefore, must be perfect, as your heavenly Father is perfect' (Matt. 5:48)

Some students of Christian ethics make a distinction between the general standards of Christian conduct and what are called 'counsels of perfection', as though the former were prescribed for the rank and file of Christians while the latter could be attained by real saints (see p. 174).

Such a distinction was not made by Jesus himself. He did make a distinction between the ordinary standards of morality observed in the world and the standard at which his disciples should aim; but the latter was something which should characterise all his disciples and not just a select few. For example, the principle that one good turn deserves another was observed by quite irreligious people and even by pagans. For anyone to repay a good turn with a bad one would be regarded as outrageous. But Jesus's followers were not to remain content with conventional standards of decent behaviour. According to conventional standards one good turn might deserve another, but according to the standards which he laid down for his disciples one bad turn deserves a good one – except that 'deserves' is not the right word. One bad turn may deserve a bad one in revenge, but one bad turn done to his disciples should be repaid by them with a good one. They must 'go the second mile'; they must do more than others do if they are to be known as followers of Jesus. If you confine your good deeds to your own kith and kin, he said to them, 'what more are you doing than others? Do not even the Gentiles do the same?' (Matt. 5:47). It is immediately after that that the words come: 'You, therefore, must be perfect, as your heavenly Father is perfect.'

This indeed sounds like a 'counsel of perfection' in the most literal sense. 'Be perfect like God.' Who can attain perfection like his? Is it worthwhile even to begin to try? But the context helps us to understand the force of these words. Why should the disciples of Jesus, the heirs of the kingdom of God, repay evil with good? The ancient law might say, 'You shall love your neighbour as yourself' (Lev. 19:18), but the fulfilment of that commandment depends on the answer given to the question, 'Who is my neighbour?' (Luke 10:29). When Jesus was asked that question, he told the story of the good Samaritan to show that my 'neighbour' in the sense intended by the commandment is anyone who needs my help, anyone to whom I can render a 'neighbourly' service. But those Israelites to whom the commandment was first given might not have thought of a Canaanite as being a 'neighbour' within the meaning of the act, and their descendants in New Testament times might not have thought of a Roman in this way.

Most systems of ethics emphasise one's duty to one's neighbour, but progress in ethics is marked by the broadening scope indicated in the answer to the question 'Who is my neighbour?' Why should I be neighbourly to someone who is unneighbourly to me? If someone does me a bad turn, why should I not pay him back in his own coin? Because, said Jesus, God himself sets us an example in this regard. 'Your Father who is in heaven ... makes his sun rise on the evil and on the good, and sends rain on the just and on the unjust' (Matt. 5:45). He bestows his blessings without discrimination. The followers of Jesus are children of God, and they should manifest the family likeness by doing good to all, even to those who deserve the opposite. So, said Jesus, go the whole way in doing good, just as God does.

The same injunction appears in a similar context, but in slightly different words, in Luke 6:36, 'Be merciful, even as your Father is merciful.' When we find one and the same saying preserved in different forms by two evangelists, as we do here, the reason often is that Jesus's Aramaic words have been translated into Greek in two different ways. We do not know the precise Aramaic words that Jesus used on this occasion, but they probably meant, 'You must be perfect (that is, all-embracing, without any restriction) in your acts of mercy or kindness, for that is what God is like.'

When the books of the law were read in synagogue from the original Hebrew, the reading was accompanied by an oral paraphrase (called a *targum*) in Aramaic, the popular vernacular. There is a passage in the law (Lev. 22:26–28) which prescribes kindness to animals. In one of the Aramaic paraphrases, this passage ended with the words: 'As our Father is merciful in heaven, so you must be merciful on earth.' Perhaps, then, some of Jesus's hearers recognised a familiar turn of phrase when this 'hard saying' fell from his lips. It is not, after all, hard to understand; it is sometimes hard to practise it.

Chapter
18

If You Do Not Forgive Your Brother

*'So also my heavenly Father will do to every one of you,
if you do not forgive your brother from your heart'*
(Matt. 18:35)

This is a very hard saying. The 'so' which introduces it refers to
the severe punishment which the king in a parable inflicted on
an unforgiving servant of his. The parable arises out of a
conversation between Jesus and Peter. Jesus repeatedly
impressed on his disciples the necessity of forgiveness: they
were not to harbour resentment, but freely forgive those who
injured them. 'Yes, but how often?' Peter asked. 'Seven times?'
– and probably he thought that that was about the limit of
reasonable forbearance. 'Not seven times,' said Jesus, 'but
seventy times seven' (Matt. 18:21–22). Perhaps by the time one
had forgiven for the seventy-times-seventh time, forgiveness
would have become second nature to one.

Some commentators have seen an allusion here to the war-
song of Lamech in Genesis 4:24. Lamech was a descendant of
Cain, who (surprisingly, it may be thought) was taken under
God's protection. 'If any one slays Cain,' said God, 'vengeance
shall be taken on him sevenfold.' Lamech boasted in his war-
song that no one would injure him and get away with it: 'If Cain
is avenged sevenfold, truly Lamech seventy-sevenfold' (or
perhaps 'seventy times sevenfold'). Over against seventy-times-
sevenfold vengeance Jesus sets, as the target for his followers,
seventy-times-sevenfold forgiveness.

The gospel is a message of forgiveness: it could not be otherwise, because it is the gospel of God, and God is a forgiving God. 'Who is a God like thee, pardoning iniquity?' said one Hebrew prophet (Mic. 7:18). 'I knew', said another (protesting against God's proneness to forgive those who, he thought, did not deserve forgiveness), 'that thou art a gracious God and merciful, slow to anger, and abounding in steadfast love' (Jonah 4:2). It is to be expected, then, that those who receive the forgiveness which God holds out in the gospel, those who call him their Father, will display something of his character and show a forgiving attitude to others. If they do not, what then?

What then? Jesus answers this question in the parable of the unforgiving servant, which he told to confirm his words to Peter about repeated forgiveness 'until seventy times seven'. A king, said Jesus, decided to settle accounts with his servants, and found that one of them (who must have been a very high officer of state) had incurred debts to the royal exchequer which ran into millons. The king was about to deal with him as an oriental potentate might be expected to do, when the man fell at his feet, begged for mercy, and promised that, if the king would be patient with him, he would make full repayment. The king knew perfectly well that he could never repay such a debt, but he felt sorry for him and remitted the debt. Then the man found someone else in the royal service who was in debt to him personally (not to the king): his debt amounted to a few pounds. He demanded prompt repayment, and when this debtor asked for time to pay he refused and had him consigned to the debtors' prison. The king got to hear of it, and summoned the man whom he had pardoned back into his presence, revoked the pardon, and treated him as he had treated the other: 'In anger his lord delivered him to the jailers, till he should pay all his debt'. 'So,' said Jesus, 'in this way my heavenly Father will deal with any one of you if you do not forgive your brother (or sister) from your heart.' Revoke a pardon once granted? God would not do a thing like that, surely? Jesus said he would. A hard saying indeed!

That this emphasis on the necessity of having a forgiving

spirit had a central place in the teaching of Jesus is evident from
the fact that it is enshrined in both versions of the Lord's
Prayer. In Luke 11:4 the disciples are told to pray, 'Forgive us
our sins, for we ourselves forgive every one who is indebted to
us.' It is difficult to believe that anyone could utter this prayer
deliberately, knowing at the same time that he or she cherished
an unforgiving spirit towards someone else. In the Aramaic
language which Jesus spoke the word for 'sin' is the same as the
word for 'debt'; hence 'every one who is indebted to us' means
'everyone who has sinned against us'. In the parallel petition of
Matthew 6:12 this use of 'debt' in the sense of 'sin' occurs twice:
'Forgive us our debts, as we also have forgiven our debtors'
means 'Forgive us our sins, as we for our part have forgiven
those who have sinned against us.' This wording implies that
the person praying has already forgiven any injury received;
otherwise it would be impossible honestly to ask God's
forgiveness for one's own sins. Immediately after Matthew's
version of the prayer this is emphasised again: 'For if you
forgive men their trespasses, your heavenly Father also will
forgive you; but if you do not forgive men their trespasses,
neither will your Father forgive your trespasses' (Matt.
6:14–15).

The meaning is unambiguous, and it is unwise to try to avoid
its uncomfortable challenge. One well-known annotated
edition of the Bible had a comment on the clause 'as we forgive
our debtors' which ran as follows: 'This is legal ground. Cf.
Eph. 4.32, which is grace. Under law forgiveness is conditioned
upon a like spirit in us; under grace we are forgiven for Christ's
sake, and exhorted to forgive because we have been forgiven.'[1]
But forgiveness is neither given nor received on 'legal ground';
it is always a matter of grace. What Paul says in Ephesians 4:32
is this: 'Be kind to one another, tenderhearted, forgiving one
another, as God in Christ forgave you.' But if some of those to
whom this admonition was addressed (and it is addressed to all
Christians at all times) should persist in an unforgiving attitude
towards others, could they even so enjoy the assurance of
God's forgiveness? If Jesus's teaching means what it says, they
could not.

Jesus told another parable about two debtors to illustrate another aspect of forgiveness. This was in the house of Simon the Pharisee, who neglected to pay him the courtesies normally shown to a guest, whereas the woman who ventured in from the street lavished her grateful affection on him by wetting his feet with her tears (Luke 7:36–50; see p. 29). The point of the parable was that one who has been forgiven a great debt will respond with great love, whereas no great response will be made by one whose sense of having been forgiven is minimal. (It might be objected that the man who had been forgiven a colossal debt in the parable in Matthew 18:23–35 showed little love in return, but the two parables are addressed to two different situations, and forgiveness and love are not subject to cast-iron rules of inevitable necessity.) Where there is a genuine response of love, there will be a forgiving spirit, and where there is a forgiving spirit, there will be a still greater appreciation of God's forgiving mercy, and still greater love in consequence. Some commentators find difficulty with Jesus's words about the woman, 'Her sins, which are many, are forgiven; for she loved much': the logic of the parable would suggest 'She loves much, for her sins have been forgiven'. But if that had been the meaning, that is what would have been said. Love and forgiveness set up a chain reaction: the more forgiveness, the more love; the more love, the more forgiveness.

Chapter
19

Lead Us Not into Temptation

'And lead us not into temptation' (Matt. 6:13; Luke 11:4)

The traditional rendering of the Lord's Prayer in English contains as its second-last petition, 'And lead us not into temptation'. It is a petition which has puzzled successive generations of Christians, for whom the word 'temptation' ordinarily means temptation to sin. Why should we ask God not to lead us into this? As if God would do any such thing! 'God cannot be tempted with evil and he himself tempts no one' (James 1:13).

Perhaps this was absolutely the last petition in the original form of the Lord's Prayer, as it is to this day in the authentic text of Luke's version. The petition which follows it in the traditional rendering, 'but deliver us from evil', found in Matthew's version, was perhaps added to help to explain the preceding one – whether the added petition means 'Deliver us from what is evil' or 'Deliver us from the evil one'. Is God asked to deliver his children from evil by preserving them *from* temptation or by preserving them *in* temptation? By preserving them *in* temptation, probably. It is appropriate to be reminded of a very similar petition which occurs in the Jewish service of morning and evening prayer: 'Do not bring us into *the power of* temptation.' That seems to mean, 'When we find ourselves surrounded by temptation, may we not be overpowered by it.'

Temptation, when the word occurs in the older versions of the Bible, means more than temptation to sin: it has the wider sense of testing. God 'tempts no one', according to James 1:13; yet the same writer says, according to the AV, 'Count it all joy when ye fall into divers temptations' and 'Blessed is the man that endureth temptation' (James 1:2, 12). What he means is simply brought out by the RSV: 'Count it all joy ... when you meet various trials, for you know that the testing of your faith produces steadfastness' and 'Blessed is the man who endures trial, for when he has stood the test he will receive the crown of life which God has promised to those who love him.' To the same effect other Christians are assured in 1 Peter 1:6-7 that the purpose of their being called to undergo various trials – 'manifold temptations' in the AV – is 'so that the genuineness of your faith ... may redound to praise and glory and honour at the revelation of Jesus Christ'. That is to say, when faith is tested it is strengthened, and the outcome is reinforced stability of character.

It was so in Old Testament times. When the AV of Genesis 22:1 says that 'God did tempt Abraham', the meaning is that he *tested* him – tested his faith, that is to say. An untested faith is a weak faith, compared with one that has passed through a searching test and emerged victorious.

Jesus himself was led into 'temptation'. So Matthew implies when he says (4:1) that 'Jesus was led up by the Spirit into the wilderness to be tempted by the devil'. Mark (1:12) uses an even stronger verb: after Jesus's baptism, he says, 'the Spirit immediately drove him out into the wilderness'. What was the nature of his 'temptation'? It was the testing of his faith in God, the testing of his resolution to accept the path which he knew to be his Father's will for him in preference to others which might have seemed more immediately attractive. It was from that testing that he returned – 'in the power of the Spirit', says Luke (4:14) – to undertake his public ministry.

So, whatever is meant by the petition, 'Lead us not into temptation', it is highly unlikely that it means 'Do not let our faith be tested' or, as the NEB puts it, 'Do not bring us to the test'. 'Do not bring us to the test' is at least as obscure as 'Lead us not into temptation'. It invites the question: 'What test?' Perhaps Paul had this petition in his mind when he says to his friends in Corinth, 'No temptation has overtaken you that is not common to man. God is faithful, and he will not let you be tempted beyond your strength, but with the temptation will also provide the way of escape, that you may be able to endure it' (1 Cor. 10:13). This could well be regarded as an expansion of our problem petition, which unpacks its concentrated meaning. It was evidently so regarded by those whose thought lies behind the fifth-century Eastern *Liturgy of St. James*. In this liturgy the celebrant, after reciting the Lord's Prayer, goes on:

> Yes, O Lord our God,
> lead us not into temptation which we are not able to bear,
> but with the temptation grant also the way out,
> so that we may be able to remain steadfast;
> and deliver us from evil.

This implies something like the following as the intention of our petition. We know that our faith needs to be tested if it is to grow strong; indeed, the conditions of life in this world make it inevitable that our faith must be tested. But some tests are so severe that our faith could not stand up to the strain; therefore we pray not to be brought into tests of such severity. If our faith gave way under the strain, that might involve us in moral disaster; it would also bring discredit on the name of the God whom we call our Father.

When we use the prayer, we may generalise this petition along these lines. But in the context of Jesus's ministry and his disciples' association with him, the petition may have had a more specific reference. What that reference was may be inferred from his admonition to some of his disciples in Gethsemane just before his arrest: 'Watch and pray that you may not enter into temptation' (Mark 14:38). When some regard is paid to the Aramaic wording which probably lies behind the evangelist's Greek rendering of the admonition, there is much to be said for the view of some scholars that it meant, 'Keep awake, and pray not to fail in the test!' The disciples had no idea how crucial was the test which was almost upon them. It was the supreme test for him; what about them? Would they, who had continued with their Master in his trials thus far, stand by him in the imminent hour of ultimate trial, or would they fail in the test? We know what happened: they failed – temporarily, at least. Mercifully (for the world's salvation was at stake), he did not fail. When the Shepherd was struck down, the sheep were scattered. But he endured the ordeal of suffering and death and, when he came back to life, he gathered his scattered followers together again, giving them a new start – and this time they did not fail in the test.

Our perspective on the events of Gethsemane and Calvary, even when our lives are caught up into those events and revolutionised by them, is necessarily different from theirs at that time. Jesus was prepared for the winding up of the old age and the breaking in of the new – the powerful coming of the kingdom of God. The transition from the old to the new would involve unprecedented tribulation, the birthpangs of the new creation, which would be a test too severe even for the faith of the elect, unless God intervened and cut it short. This tribulation would fall pre-eminently on the Son of man, and on his endurance of it the bringing in of the new age depended. He was ready to absorb it in his own person, but would he find one or two others willing to share it with him? James and John had professed their ability to drink his cup and share his baptism, but in the moment of crisis they, with their companions, proved unequal to the challenge.

Going back, then, from our Lord's admonition in Gethsemane to the problem petition which we are considering, we may conclude that in the context of Jesus's ministry its meaning was, 'Grant that we may not fail in the test' – 'Grant that the test may not prove too severe for our faith to sustain.' The test in that context was the crucial test of the ages to which Jesus's ministry was the immediate prelude. If we adopt the rendering of the petition followed in the Series 3 Anglican Order for Holy Communion, 'Do not bring us to the time of trial', or the variant proposed by the International Consultation on English Texts, 'Save us from the time of trial', then the 'time of trial' originally intended was one against which the disciples who were taught to use the petition needed to be forearmed. But the force of the petition would be better expressed by rendering it, 'May our faith stand firm in the time of trial' or 'Save us *in* the time of trial.' Through *that* trial we can no longer pass; the Son of man passed through it as our representative. But the time of trial which will show whether we are truly his followers or not may come upon any Christian at any time. Those who have confidence in their ability to stand such a test may feel no need of the petition. But those who know that their faith is no more reliable than that of Peter and James and John may well pray to be saved from a trial with which their faith cannot cope or, if the trial is inescapable, to be supplied with the heavenly grace necessary to endure it: 'Grant that we may not fail in the test.'

Chapter
20

Pearls before Swine

'Do not give dogs what is holy;
and do not throw your pearls before swine,
lest they [the swine] trample them under foot
and [the dogs] turn to attack you' (Matt. 7:6)

The construction of this saying seems to be chiastic. It is the swine that will trample the pearls beneath their feet and the dogs that will turn and bite the hand that fed them, even if it fed them with 'holy' flesh.

The general sense of the saying is clear: objects of value, special privileges, participation in sacred things should not be offered to those who are incapable of appreciating them. Pearls are things of beauty and value to many people – Jesus himself in one of his parables compared the kingdom of God to a 'pearl of great price' (Matt. 13:45–46) – but pigs will despise them because they cannot eat them. Holy flesh – the flesh of sacrificial animals – has a religious value over and above its nutritive value for worshippers who share in a 'peace offering', but pariah dogs will make no difference between it and scraps of offal for which they battle in the street; they will not feel specially grateful to anyone who gives it to them.

But has the saying a more specific application? One could imagine its being quoted by some more restrictive brethren in the Jerusalem church as an argument against presenting the gospel to Gentiles, certainly against receiving them into full Christian fellowship. At a slightly later date it was used as an argument against admitting unbelievers to the Lord's Supper:

thus the *Didache (Teaching of the Twelve Apostles)*, a manual of Syrian Christianity dated around A.D. 100, says: 'Let none eat or drink of your Eucharist except those who have been baptised in the name of the Lord. It was concerning this that the Lord said, "Do not give dogs what is holy."' [1]

It would be anachronistic to read this interpretation back into the ministry of Jesus. It is better to read the saying in the context given it by Matthew (the only Gospel-writer to report it). It comes immediately after the injunction, 'Judge not, that you be not judged' (Matt. 7:1), with two amplifications of that injunction: you will be judged by the standard you apply in the judgment of others (7:2); and you should not try to remove a speck of sawdust from someone else's eye when you have a whole plank in your own (7:3–5). Then comes this saying, which is a further amplification of the principle, or rather a corrective of it: you must not sit in judgment on others and pass censorious sentences on them, but you ought to exercise discrimination. Judgment is an ambiguous word, in English as in Greek: it may mean sitting in judgment on people (or even condemning them), or it may mean exercising a proper discrimination. In the former sense judgment is deprecated; in the latter sense it is recommended. Jesus himself knew that it was useless to impart his message to some people: he had no answer for Herod Antipas when Herod 'questioned him at some length' (Luke 23:9).

With this saying the paragraph on judging in the Sermon on the Mount is concluded; the next paragraph, with its encouragement to ask, seek and knock, turns to another subject.

Chapter 21

The Sin against the Holy Spirit

'Truly, I say to you, all sins will be forgiven the sons of men, and whatever blasphemies they utter; but whoever blasphemes against the Holy Spirit never has forgiveness, but is guilty of an eternal sin' (Mark 3:28–29)

'And every one who speaks a word against the Son of man will be forgiven; but he who blasphemes against the Holy Spirit will not be forgiven' (Luke 12:10)

The person who has committed the unpardonable sin figures powerfully in literature. There is, for example, Bunyan's man in the iron cage. There is the Welsh preacher Peter Williams, breaking the silence of night in George Borrow's *Lavengro* with his anguished cry: 'Pechod Ysprydd Glan! O pechod Ysprydd Glan!' ('Oh, the sin against the Holy Spirit!') – which he was persuaded he had committed. Or there is Mr. Paget, in Edmund Gosse's *Father and Son*, who

> had thrown up his cure of souls because he became convinced that he had committed the Sin against the Holy Ghost. ... Mr. Paget was fond of talking, in private and in public, of his dreadful spiritual condition, and he would drop his voice while he spoke of having committed the Unpardonable Sin, with a sort of shuddering exultation, such as people sometimes feel in the possession of a very unusual disease. ... Everybody longed to know what the exact nature had been of that sin against the Holy Ghost

which had deprived Mr. Paget of every glimmer of hope for time or for eternity. It was whispered that even my Father himself was not precisely acquainted with the character of it.[1]

Of course not, because the 'sin' existed only in Mr. Paget's imagination.

In real life there are few more distressing conditions calling for treatment by physicians of the soul than that of people who believe they have committed this sin. When they are offered the gospel assurance of forgiveness for every sin, when they are reminded that 'the blood of Jesus ... cleanses us from all sin' (1 John 1:7), they have a ready answer: there is one sin which forms an exception to this rule, and they have committed that sin; for it, in distinction from all other kinds of sin, there is no forgiveness. Did not our Lord himself say so? And they tend to become impatient when it is pointed out to them (quite truly) that the very fact of their concern over having committed it proves that they have not committed it.

What then did Jesus mean when he spoke in this way? His saying has been preserved in two forms. Luke records it as one of a series of sayings dealing with the Son of man or the Holy Spirit, but Mark gives it a narrative context. (The Marcan and Lucan forms are combined in Matthew 12:31-32.)

According to Mark, scribes or experts in the Jewish law came down from Jerusalem to Galilee to assess the work which, as they heard, Jesus was doing there, and especially his ministry of exorcism – expelling demons from the lives of those who suffered under their domination. (This language indicates a real and sad condition, even if it would commonly be described in different terms today.) The scribes came to a strange conclusion: 'He is possessed by Beelzebul, and by the prince of demons he casts out the demons' (Mark 3:22). (Beelzebul had once been the name of a Canaanite divinity, 'the lord of the high place', but by this time it was used by Jews to denote the ruler of the abyss, the abode of demons.) When Jesus knew of this, he exposed the absurdity of supposing that Satan's power could be overthrown by Satan's aid. Then he went on to charge those who had voiced this absurd conclusion with blaspheming against the Holy Spirit. Why? Because they deliberately ascribed the Holy Spirit's activity to demonic agency.

For every kind of sin, then, for every form of blasphemy or slander, it is implied that forgiveness is available – presumably when the sin is repented of. But what if one were to repent of blasphemy against the Holy Spirit? Is there no forgiveness for the person who repents of this sin?

The answer seems to be that the nature of this sin is such that one does not repent of it, because those who commit it and persist in it do not know that they are sinning. Mark tells his readers why Jesus charged those scribes with blaspheming against the Holy Spirit: it was because 'they had said, "He has an unclean spirit"' (Mark 3:30). Jesus was proclaiming the kingly rule of God, and his bringing relief to soul-sick, demon-possessed mortals was a token that the kingly rule of God was present and active in his ministry. 'If it is by the finger of God that I cast out demons,' he said, 'then the kingdom of God has come upon you' (Luke 11:20; in Matthew 12:28, where these words also appear, 'finger of God' is replaced by 'Spirit of God'). If some people looked at the relief which he was bringing to the bodies and minds of men and women and maintained that he was doing so with the help of their great spiritual oppressor, the prince of the demons, then their eyes were so tightly closed to the light that for them light had become darkness and good had become evil. The light is there for those who will accept it, but if some refuse the light, where else can they hope to receive illumination?

Was Paul sinning against the Holy Spirit in the days when he persecuted Christians and even (according to Acts 26:11) 'tried to make them blaspheme'? Evidently not, because (as it is put in 1 Timothy 1:13) he 'acted ignorantly in unbelief' and therefore received mercy. But if, when he had seen the light on the Damascus road and heard the call of the risen Lord, he had closed his eyes and ears and persevered on his persecuting course, that would have been the 'eternal sin'. But he would not have recognised it as a sin, and so would not have thought of seeking forgiveness for it; he would have gone on thinking that he was doing the work of God, and his conscience would have remained as unperturbed as ever.

Luke, as has been said, gives his form of the saying a different context. He does record the charge that Jesus cast out demons with Beelzebul's aid, but does so in the preceding chapter (Luke 11:14-26) and says nothing there about the sin against the Spirit. His report on Jesus's words about this sin comes in Luke 12:10, immediately after the statement: 'I tell you, every one who acknowledges me before men, the Son of man also will acknowledge before the angels of God; but he who denies me before men will be denied before the angels of God' (Luke 12:8-9). (The second half of this statement is paralleled in Mark 8:38, where it is located in the aftermath to Peter's confession near Caesarea Philippi.) Then, after the words about the sin against the Spirit, Luke quotes the injunction: 'And when they bring you before the synagogues and the rulers and the authorities, do not be anxious how or what you are to answer or what you are to say; for the Holy Spirit will teach you in that very hour what you ought to say' (Luke 12:11-12). This injunction has a parallel in Mark in his version of the Olivet discourse (Mark 13:11); the parallel is taken over in Luke's version of the discourse, where however it is not the Spirit but Jesus who will give his disciples 'a mouth and wisdom' to reply to their inquisitors (Luke 21:15). Matthew has a parallel in his account of the sending out of the twelve apostles: 'What you are to say will be given you in that hour; for it is not you who speak, but the Spirit of your Father speaking through you' (Matt. 10:20).

Luke, then, places the saying about blaspheming the Holy Spirit between a saying about the Spirit's heavenly role as counsel for the defence of those who confess the Son of man (that is, Jesus) and a saying about the Spirit's enabling confessors of Jesus before an earthly tribunal to say the right word at the right time. In this context a different emphasis is given to the matter of blasphemy against the Spirit from that given to it by Mark. It is suggested by Luke that the blaspheming of the Spirit involves a refusal of his powerful help when it is available to save the disciples of Jesus from denying him and so committing apostasy. If so, blasphemy against the Spirit in this context is tantamount to apostasy, the deliberate and decisive repudiation of Jesus as Lord. This is not the only New Testament passage which warns against the irremediable evil of apostasy: another well-known example is Hebrews 6:4–6, where it is said to be impossible to renew apostates to repentance, since they have repudiated the only way of salvation.

But Luke couples with the warning against the unpardonable sin of blasphemy against the Spirit the affirmation of Jesus that there is forgiveness for everyone who speaks a word against the Son of man. On this there are two things to be said.

First, in Jesus's language (Aramaic), the phrase 'the son of man' normally meant 'the man'; only the context could indicate when he intended the phrase to have the special sense which is conveyed by the fuller translation 'the Son of man'. Moreover, in the phrase 'the man' the definite article could, on occasion, have generic force, referring not to a particular human being but to man in general (in English this generic force is best conveyed by using the noun without any article, as in 'Man is born unto trouble, as the sparks fly upward'). So Jesus may have meant, 'To speak against (a) man is pardonable, but to speak against the Spirit is not.'

Secondly, if that is what Jesus meant, he included himself as a man, if not indeed as the representative man (see p. 27). Luke understands him to refer to himself in particular; otherwise he would have said 'everyone who speaks a word against a man' and not (as he does) 'every one who speaks a word against the Son of man'. Why would it be so much more serious to slander the Holy Spirit than to slander the Son of man? Perhaps because the identity of the Son of man was veiled in his humility; people might easily fail to recognise him for who he was. There was nothing in the designation 'the Son of man' in itself to express a claim to authority. The Son of man, at present operating in lowliness and liable to be rejected and ill-treated, might indeed be despised. But if those who had begun to follow him were afraid that, under stress, they might deny him, they were assured that the Spirit's aid was available. If, however, they resisted the Spirit and rejected his aid, then indeed their case would be desperate.

Peter, through fear, denied the Son of man, but he found forgiveness and restoration: his lips had momentarily turned traitor but his heart did not apostatise. His repentance left him wide open to the Spirit's healing grace, and when he was restored, he was able to strengthen others (Luke 22:31–32). Why then, it might be asked, did he not strengthen Ananias and Sapphira when they came to him with part of the proceeds of the sale of their property, pretending that it was the whole amount (see p. 144)? Presumably because, as he said, they had consented to the satanic suggestion that they should 'lie to the Holy Spirit', because they had 'agreed together to tempt the Spirit of the Lord' (Acts 5:3, 9). Thus, in Peter's reckoning, they had sinned beyond the point of no return. How Jesus would have regarded their offence is another question.

In Mark's context, then, the sin against the Holy Spirit involves deliberately shutting one's eyes to the light and consequently calling good evil; in Luke (that is, ultimately, in the sayings collection commonly labelled Q) it is irretrievable apostasy. Probably these are not really two conditions but one – not unlike the condition which Plato described as having the lie in the soul.[2]

Chapter
22

No Sign

*'Why does this generation seek a sign? Truly, I say to
you, no sign shall be given to this generation'* (Mark
8:12)
*'This generation is an evil generation; it seeks a sign,
but no sign shall be given to it except the sign of Jonah.
For as Jonah became a sign to the men of Nineveh, so
will the Son of man be to this generation'* (Luke
11:29–30)

Formally, these two sayings appear to contradict each other:
'no sign at all' does not seem to mean the same as 'no sign
except the sign of Jonah'. Materially, however, there is little
difference in sense between the two, as we shall see when we
consider what the sign of Jonah was. In fact, we may be dealing
not with two separate sayings but with two variant forms which
the same original saying has acquired in the course of
transmission. The form preserved by Luke was probably
derived from the collection of sayings of Jesus which is
conventionally labelled Q. Mark's form reappears in Matthew
16:1–4; the Q form is reproduced in Matthew 12:38–40. Both
forms are amplified in Matthew's text and assimilated to one
another.

According to Mark, the refusal to give a sign was Jesus's
response to some Pharisees who, in the course of debate, asked
him to supply 'a sign from heaven'. Jesus spoke and acted with
evident authority; what was his authority for speaking and
acting as he did? His practice on the sabbath day set at defiance

the traditional interpretation of the sabbath law which had
been built up over the generations; what was his authority for
refusing to accept the 'tradition of the elders'? Whereas the
great prophets of the past had prefaced their proclamation
with 'Thus says the Lord', Jesus was content to set over against
what 'was said to the men of old' his uncompromising 'But *I* say
to you.' What was the basis for this claim to personal
authority?

How can such authority be vindicated? When Moses
approached Pharaoh as the spokesman of the God of Israel
and demanded that his people be allowed to leave Egypt, he
demonstrated the authority by which he spoke in a succession
of signs, such as turning his rod into a serpent and changing
Nile water into blood (Exod. 7:8–24). No doubt Pharaoh was
the sort of person who would be impressed by such signs, but
Moses' enduring right to be recognised as a prophet of the
living God rests on a firmer foundation than such signs. When
Elijah entered the presence of Ahab to denounce his toleration
of Baal-worship in Israel, he confirmed his denunciation with
the announcement of three years' drought (1 Kgs. 17:1). Baal,
the rain-giver, was to be hit in the one place where he could be
hurt – in his reputation. This particular sign was thus highly
relevant to Elijah's message. If Moses and Elijah, then, had
confirmed their authority as messengers of God by signs such
as these, why could not Jesus confirm his authority in a similar
way?

First, what sort of sign would have convinced them?
External signs might have been necessary to convince a
heathen Egyptian or an apostate king of Israel, but why should
they be necessary for custodians and teachers of the law of the
true God? They should have been able to decide without the aid
of signs whether Jesus's teaching was true or not, whether it
was in line or not with the law and the prophets.

Secondly, would the kind of sign they had in mind really
have validated the truth of Jesus's words? Matthew Arnold
remarked, in the course of a nineteenth-century controversy,
that his written statements were unlikely to carry greater
conviction if he demonstrated his ability to turn his pen into a

penwiper.[1] It may be suspected that it was some similarly extraordinary but essentially irrelevant sign that was being asked from Jesus. If, for example, he had thrown himself down in public from the pinnacle of the temple into the Kidron gorge and suffered no harm, that would have done nothing to confirm his teaching about the kingdom of God, even if it would have silenced the demand for a sign.

In the third place, what about the signs he actually performed? Why were they not sufficient to convince his questioners? One Pharisee, indeed, is reported as saying to him, 'Rabbi, we know that you are a teacher come from God; for no one can do these signs that you do, unless God is with him' (John 3:2). Jesus himself affirmed that if it was by the power of God that he relieved those who were demon-possessed, that was a sign of the arrival of the kingdom of God (Luke 11:20; see p. 90). But some of those to whom these words were spoken chose to believe that it was not by the power of God but by the power of the prince of demons that he healed the demon-possessed. If the restoration of bodily and mental health could be dismissed as a work of Satan, no number of healing acts would have established the divine authority by which they were performed.

In his comments on the 'pillar passages' for a scientific life of Jesus, P. W. Schmiedel included Mark 8:12 as the first of four such passages which had a special bearing on the miracles of Jesus. The saying 'No sign shall be given to this generation' was an absolutely authentic one, he maintained, and implied that the miracle stories of the Gospels were secondary constructions. To this it might be said that, while the healing miracles did serve as signs of the kingdom of God to those who had eyes to see, they did not *compel* belief in those who were prejudiced in the opposite direction. The Pharisees mentioned in this incident may have wanted a sign that would compel belief, but can genuine belief ever be compelled? While the miracles served as signs, they were not performed in order to be signs. They were as much part and parcel of Jesus's ministry as was his preaching – not, as it has been put, seals affixed to the document to certify its genuineness but an integral element in the very text of the document.[2] No sign would be given which was not already available in the ministry itself; to ask for more was a mark of unbelief.

What, now, of the sign of Jonah? Jonah, it is said, was 'a sign to the men of Nineveh'. How? By his one-sentence message of judgment. That was all the 'sign' that the people of Nineveh had; it was sufficient to move them to belief and repentance. Schmiedel illustrates that there is no real contradiction between 'no sign' absolutely and 'no sign except the sign of Jonah' by the analogy of an aggressor who invades a neighbouring country without provocation. When asked what justification he can give for his action, he replies, 'I shall give you no other justification than that which my sword gives' – which is as much as to say 'no justification'. As Jonah's ministry in Nineveh was sign enough, so Jesus's ministry in Palestine is sign enough. No other sign would be given.

In the Q collection the refusal to give any sign but the sign of Jonah was followed by a comparison between the people to whom Jesus ministered and those to whom Jonah preached. Jesus's hearers shared the rich heritage of divine worship and revelation which had been enjoyed over the centuries by the people of Israel; Jonah preached to pagans. Yet Jonah's hearers made a swift and positive response to his message; the reaction on the part of the majority of Jesus's hearers was quite different. Therefore, he said, 'The men of Nineveh will arise at the judgment with this generation and condemn it; for they repented at the preaching of Jonah, and behold, something greater than Jonah is here' (Matt. 12:41; Luke 11:32). The 'something greater' was Jesus's proclamation of the kingdom of God, which was more important and far-reaching than Jonah and his preaching. Yet Jonah and his preaching were enough to bring the people of Nineveh to repentance; Jesus's proclamation of the kingdom made no such large-scale impact on his generation. On the day of judgment, therefore, the people of Nineveh would compare very favourably with the Galileans to whom Jesus preached; indeed, they would serve as tacit, if not as vocal, witnesses against them. Whether these words of Jesus were spoken on the same occasion as the saying about the sign or on another occasion, their relevance to it is unmistakable.

Matthew, for his part, adds a further analogy between Jonah's situation and that of Jesus: 'As Jonah was three days and three nights in the belly of the whale, so will the Son of man be three days and three nights in the heart of the earth' (Matt. 12:40). This is commonly supposed to be a later insertion among the Jonah sayings. T. W. Manson, however, suggests that no one after the resurrection of Jesus, which by common Christian consent took place on 'the third day', would have represented him as being buried for a much longer period[3]. This would point to a life-setting for the Matthaean saying before Jesus's death and resurrection. In any case, it would be unwise to press 'three days and three nights' to mean 72 hours, neither more nor less. Jonah's experience in the Mediterranean was not a sign to the people of Nineveh, any more than Jesus's resurrection on Easter Day after his entombment on Good Friday was a public spectacle. In Matthew 12:40 we simply have an analogy traced between two servants of God, who were both brought up by God 'from the Pit' (Jonah 2:6; cf. Ps. 16:10, quoted with reference to Jesus in Acts 2:27; 13:35).

Chapter
23

Seeing and Not Perceiving

*'To you has been given the secret of the kingdom of
God, but for those outside everything is in parables; so
that they may indeed see but not perceive, and may
indeed hear but not understand; lest they should turn
again, and be forgiven'* (Mark 4:11–12)

This saying comes in Mark's record between the parable of the
sower (or parable of the four soils, as some prefer to call it)
and the explanation of that parable. The parable, the
explanation, and the saying quoted above are all ascribed to
Jesus himself. But if the saying means what it seems to mean,
then Jesus tells his disciples that the purpose of his use of
parables is that his hearers in general (those who are not his
followers) may hear him but not understand him; and it is
difficult to believe that this was so.

Matthew alters the sense by using the conjunction 'because'
instead of 'so that': 'This is why I speak to them in parables,
because seeing they do not see, and hearing they do not hear,
nor do they understand' (Matt. 13:13). That is to say, because
the general public was slow to grasp the sense of Jesus's
teaching, he embodied it in parables to make it more
immediately intelligible. The hardness of the saying is thus
mitigated; it is readily accepted that:

> Truth embodied in a tale
> Shall enter in at lowly doors.[1]

Luke 8:10 follows Mark's construction, with some abbreviation.

But what is the point of Mark's construction? One suggestion is that the saying was entirely Mark's creation. The parable, it is said, was told by Jesus; the explanation received its shape in the primitive Church, but the hard saying is Mark's own contribution: it expresses his view (or the view of the school of thought to which he belonged) about the purpose of Jesus's parables. But is it out of the question that the saying represents something spoken by Jesus himself?

It is plain that the saying is an adaptation of an Old Testament text, Isaiah 6:9-10. When Isaiah received his call to the prophetic ministry, in the well-known vision that he saw in the temple 'in the year that King Uzziah died', the voice of God said to him, 'Go, and say to this people: "Hear and hear, but do not understand; see and see, but do not perceive." Make the heart of this people fat, and their ears heavy, and shut their eyes; lest they see with their eyes, and hear with their ears, and understand with their hearts, and turn and be healed.'

Should this commission be pressed to mean that Isaiah was ordered to go and tell the people to pay no heed to what they heard him say? Was it his prescribed duty to prevent them from hearing and understanding his message, and thus make it impossible for them to repent and so escape the destruction that would otherwise overtake them? No indeed; if that impression is given, it is simply due to the Hebrew tendency to express a consequence as though it were a purpose. Isaiah volunteers to be God's messenger to his people, and God takes him at his word, but says to him in effect, 'Go and deliver my message, but don't expect them to pay any attention to it. The effect of your preaching will be their persistent refusal to accept what you say, to the point where they will have rendered themselves incapable of accepting it.' In the event, this is exactly what Isaiah was to experience for the next forty years.

Isaiah's experience was reproduced in Jesus's ministry. For all the enthusiasm which greeted his ministry in its earlier phase, he had later on to lament the unbelief with which he met in the very places where most of his mighty works had been done. He might well have applied the words of Isaiah 6:9–10 to the effect (not, of course, to the purpose) of his own ministry. Certainly this text became one of the commonest Old Testament 'testimonies' in the early Church on the subject of Jewish resistance to the gospel. Apart from the allusion to it in the context of the parable of the sower in all three synoptic Gospels, it is quoted in John 12:40 at the end of Jesus's Jerusalem ministry and in Acts 28:26–27 at Paul's meeting with the Jewish leaders in Rome, while there is an echo of it in Romans 11:8. Its pervasiveness in this sense could well be due to Jesus's application of it to his own experience. 'As in its original setting in the Book of Isaiah, so here, it is most naturally taken as an arresting, hyperbolical, oriental way of saying, "Alas! many will be obdurate."'[2]

At the end of the Isaiah quotation the verb used is 'be healed'. It is so in the Hebrew text and it is so in the Greek version (the Septuagint). But in the corresponding position in Mark 4:12 the verb is 'be forgiven'. This might be set down as a free paraphrase on the evangelist's part, were it not that the Aramaic Targum on the Prophets has 'be forgiven'. The date of the written Targum on the Prophets is considerably later than the date of Mark, but behind the written Targum lies an oral tradition: the Aramaic paraphrase of the Hebrew lesson was originally given in the synagogue by word of mouth. Perhaps, then, 'be forgiven' is due not to Mark but to Jesus: speaking in Aramaic, he alluded to the Aramaic wording of the Isaiah passage.

Recognising this, T. W. Manson went on to make a further suggestion.[3] If Jesus had the Aramaic version of the text in mind, then it is relevant to consider that in Aramaic one and the same form does duty for 'so that' and 'who', while the expression for 'lest' may also mean 'perhaps'. The meaning of Jesus's saying would then be: 'For those outside everything is in parables, (for those, namely) who see indeed but do not perceive, who hear indeed but do not understand; perhaps they may turn again and be forgiven'.

This certainly removes most of the hardness from the saying, making it mean that Jesus imparted the 'mystery' of the kingdom of God to the disciples but spoke in parables to those outside their circle in hope that they would grasp sufficient of his teaching to repent and receive forgiveness. But if this is what the saying meant, Mark (or his source of information) has misunderstood it and made it hard.

If we remember that in the idiom of Jesus and his contemporaries a result might be expressed as though it were a purpose, the saying remains hard, but not intolerably hard. It is helpful also to realise that in Hebrew and Aramaic the word for 'parable' might also mean 'riddle'.

Jesus proclaimed the kingdom of God and made plain the far-reaching implications of its arrival. This was a 'mystery' in the sense that it had not been disclosed in this form before: Jesus revealed it in his ministry. Among his hearers there were some whose minds were open to his teaching; they grasped its meaning and appreciated the point of his parables. There were others whose minds were closed. Even if at first they thought that he was the teacher and leader for whom they had been waiting, they soon changed their minds. His parables, luminous to those who had eyes to see and ears to hear, were but riddles to them. They could not take his message in, and so they could not profit by it. The more he spoke and acted among them, the less responsive they became. And they were in the majority. Only a few, relatively speaking, embraced the good news of the kingdom, but for their sake it was worthwhile making it known.

If the saying is understood in this sense, its relevance to the context, immediately after the parable of the sower, should be clear. The sower scattered the good seed broadcast, but only a quarter of it yielded a crop, because of the poor soil on which the rest of it fell – the hard-beaten path, the thorn-infested ground, the shallow skin of earth on top of the rock. But the harvest that sprang up from the good and fertile ground meant that the labour of sowing was by no means in vain – quite the contrary. The gain derived from those 'who hear the word and accept it' more than outweighs the loss incurred through those who turn away.

Chapter 24

Go Nowhere among the Gentiles

'Go nowhere among the Gentiles, and enter no town of the Samaritans, but go rather to the lost sheep of the house of Israel' (Matt. 10:5-6)

These words occur in Matthew's account of Jesus's sending out the twelve apostles two by two at a fairly early stage in his Galilean ministry, in order that the proclamation of the kingdom of God might be carried on more extensively and more quickly than if he had done it by himself alone. The message they were to preach was the same as he preached: 'The kingdom of heaven is at hand.' The works of healing that were to accompany their preaching were of the same kind as accompanied his.

Mark (6:7-13) and Luke (9:1-6) also report the sending out of the twelve, but more briefly than Matthew does. Matthew is the only evangelist to include these 'exclusive' words in his account. 'The lost sheep of the house of Israel' is an expression peculiar to his Gospel (although it is not dissimilar to 'sheep without a shepherd' in Mark 6:34); it occurs again in his account of the healing of the Canaanite woman's daughter (Matt. 15:24).

Since Matthew is the only evangelist to report these words, it might be argued that they were not originally spoken by Jesus, but were ascribed to him by the evangelist or his source. We cannot make Matthew responsible for inventing them: there is no reason to think that Matthew had an anti-Gentile bias or entertained a particularist view of the gospel. At the beginning of his record he brings the Gentiles in by telling how the wise men came from the east to pay homage to the infant king of the Jews – the occasion traditionally referred to as the 'epiphany' or 'manifestation' of Christ to the Gentiles. In the course of his report of Jesus's teaching he quotes him as saying that, before the end comes, 'this gospel of the kingdom will be preached throughout all the world, as a testimony to all nations' (Matt. 24:14). At the end of the book (Matt. 28:19) he tells how the risen Christ commissioned the apostles to 'go ... and make disciples of all nations' (that is, among all the Gentiles). And in the course of his record he tells of Jesus's praise for the Roman centurion of Capernaum, in whom he found greater faith than he had found in any Israelite (Luke 7:2–10), and of his following assertion that 'many will come from east and west and sit at table with Abraham, Isaac and Jacob in the kingdom of heaven', while some of the descendants of Abraham, Isaac and Jacob would find themselves excluded from the feast (Matt. 8:5–13; cf. Luke 13:28–29; see p. 200.) Those last words would certainly be a hard saying for Jewish hearers, just as hard as 'Go nowhere among the Gentiles' might be for Gentile readers.

Matthew probably did derive some of the material peculiar to his Gospel from a source marked by a Jewish emphasis – perhaps a compilation of sayings of Jesus preserved by a rather strict Jewish-Christian community. 'Go nowhere among the Gentiles' may well have been found in this source.[1] But the source in question probably selected those sayings of Jesus which chimed in with its own outlook; that is no argument against their genuineness.

When Jesus sent out the twelve, the time at their disposal was short, and it was necessary to concentrate on the people who had been specially prepared for the message of the kingdom. Even if the twelve did confine themselves to the 'lost sheep of the house of Israel', they would not have time to cover all of these. This had sometimes been thought to be the point of the words: 'you will not have gone through all the towns of Israel, before the Son of man comes' (Matt. 10:23), cryptic words which must be considered by themselves – see p. 107.

Moreover, it is taught in the prophetic writings of the Old Testament, and nowhere more clearly than in Isaiah 40–55, that when Israel grasps the true knowledge of God, it will be her privilege to share that knowledge with other nations. Nearly thirty years later, Paul, apostle to the Gentiles though he was, lays down the order of gospel presentation as being 'to the Jew first and also to the Greek' (Rom. 1:16) – the 'Greek' here standing for the Gentile. This statement of primitive evangelistic policy was evidently founded on Jesus's own practice. Even so, there are hints here and there in the synoptic Gospels that the Gentiles' interests were not forgotten. The incident of the Roman centurion of Capernaum has been mentioned; the healing of the Canaanite woman's daughter will receive separate treatment – see p. 110. Such occasions, isolated and exceptional as they were during Jesus's ministry, foreshadowed the mission to the Gentiles which was launched a few years after his death. The Fourth Gospel emphasises this by relating an incident which took place in Jerusalem during Holy Week, only two or three days before Jesus's arrest and crucifixion. Some Greeks who were visiting the city approached one of the disciples and asked for an interview with Jesus. His reply, when he was told of their request, was in effect 'Not yet, but after my death' – 'when I am lifted up from the earth, I will draw all men to myself', all without distinction, Gentiles and Jews alike (John 12:20–32). That is exactly what happened.

The ban on entering any town of the Samaritans is to be understood in the same way. Samaritans were not Jews, but neither were they Gentiles. Jesus did not share his people's anti-Samaritan bias (although the evidence for this is supplied by Luke and John, not by Matthew), and after his death and resurrection his message of salvation was effectively presented to Samaritans even before it was presented to Gentiles (Acts 8:5–25).

Chapter
25

*'When they persecute you in one town, flee to the next;
for truly, I say to you, you will not have gone through
all the towns of Israel, before the Son of man comes'*
(Matt. 10:23)

This saying, found in Matthew's Gospel only, comes at the end
of Jesus's commission to the twelve apostles when he sent them
out two by two. It was brought to public attention early in the
twentieth century when the great Albert Schweitzer made it the
foundation of his interpretation of the ministry of Jesus. Jesus,
he believed, expected the kingdom of God to dawn with power
and glory at harvest time that year, before the twelve had
completed their mission. 'He tells them in plain words . . . that
He does not expect to see them back in the present age.'[1] Jesus
would be supernaturally revealed as the Son of man, in a
manner involving his own transformation, as well as the
transformation of his followers, into a state of being suited to
the conditions of the resurrection age. But the new age did not
come in; the twelve returned from their mission. Jesus then
tried to force its arrival. He 'lays hold of the wheel of the world
to set it moving on that last revolution which is to bring all
ordinary history to a close. It refuses to turn, and He throws
Himself upon it. Then it does turn; and crushes Him.'[2] Yet in
the hour of his failure he released a liberating power in the
world which is beyond description.

The teaching of the Sermon on the Mount and related passages in the Gospels was understood by Dr. Schweitzer to be an 'interim ethic' to guide the lives of Jesus's disciples in the short interval before the manifestation of the Son of man in power and glory. When, on Dr. Schweitzer's reading of the evidence, the hope of that manifestation was disappointed, what happened to the interim ethic? Logically, it should have been forgotten when its basis was removed. Actually, the interim ethic survived in its own right, as is magnificently evident from Dr. Schweitzer's own career. It was the driving force behind his life of service to others in West Africa. What, on his understanding, was but the prologue to the expected drama 'has become the whole drama . . . the ministry of Jesus is not a prelude to the Kingdom of God: it *is* the Kingdom of God.'[3]

The commission to the twelve, as given in Matthew 10:5–23, has two parts, each with its own perspective. The first part (verses 5–15) deals with the immediate situation, within the context of Jesus's own Galilean ministry. The second part (verses 16–23) envisages a later period, when the apostles will be engaged in a wider ministry – the kind of ministry in which in fact they were engaged in the period *following* the resurrection of Jesus and the coming of the Spirit. Think of the warning: 'Beware of men; for they will deliver you up to councils, and flog you in their synagogues, and you will be dragged before governors and kings for my sake, to bear testimony before them and the Gentiles' (Matt. 10:17–18). This reference to the Gentiles presents a contrast with the reference to them in verse 5, where they are excluded from the scope of the earlier preaching tour. The warning just quoted has a close parallel in Mark 13:9–10, where the situation is that leading up to the destruction of Jerusalem in A.D. 70. And in both places the warning is followed by an assurance that, when the disciples are put on trial and required to bear witness to their faith, the Holy Spirit will put the right words into their mouths. It is this second part of the commission in Matthew 10 that is rounded off with the saying of verse 23: 'You will not have gone through all the towns of Israel, before the Son of man comes.'

What, then, does the saying mean in *this* context? It means, simply, that the evangelisation of Israel will not be completed before the end of the present age, which comes with the advent of the Son of man. The parallel passage in Mark has a similar statement, which however takes more explicit account of Gentile as well as Jewish evangelisation: before the end-time, 'the gospel must first be preached to all the nations' (Mark 13:10). (This statement is reproduced in slightly amplified form in Matthew 24:14: 'This gospel of the kingdom will be preached throughout the whole world, as a testimony to all the nations; and then the end will come'.) Paul, from his own perspective, expresses much the same hope when he foresees the salvation of 'all Israel', the sequel to the ingathering of the full tale of Gentile believers, being consummated at the time when 'the Deliverer will come from Zion' (Rom. 11:25–27).

The wording of Matthew 10:23 is earlier in its reference than that of the other passages just mentioned: here witness-bearing to the Gentiles receives a brief mention, but all the emphasis lies on the mission to the Jews. This mission, as we know from Galatians 2:6–9, was taken seriously by the leaders of the Jerusalem Church in the early apostolic age, and they carried it out with some sense of urgency. For anything they knew to the contrary, the Son of man might come within their own generation. We must not allow our understanding of their perspective to be influenced by our own very different perspective. We know that their mission, in the form in which they pursued it, was brought to an end by the Judaean rebellion against Rome in A.D. 66, but it would be unwise to say that *that*, with the fall of Jerusalem four years later, was the coming of the Son of man of which Jesus spoke.

Chapter
26

Let the Children First Be Fed

'Let the children first be fed, for it is not right to take the children's bread and throw it to the dogs' (Mark 7:27)

This was Jesus's response to the plea of a Gentile woman that he would cure her demon-possessed daughter. The woman was a Syrophoenician according to Mark, a Canaanite according to Matthew, who also records the incident (Matt. 15:21-28). The incident took place during a brief visit paid by Jesus to the territory of Tyre and Sidon, north of Galilee.

The saying was a hard one in the first instance to the woman, yet not so hard that it put her off: if Jesus's healing ministry was for Jewish children and not for Gentile dogs, yet she reminded him that the dogs commonly get what the children leave over, and that was what she was asking him to give her and her daughter. To the modern reader it is hard because it seems so inconsistent with the character of Jesus. Its hardness is put in blunt terms by one writer: 'Long familiarity with this story, together with the traditional picture of the gentleness of Jesus, tends to obscure the shocking intolerance of the saying.'[1]

Jesus's Palestinian ministry was directed to the Jewish people: Matthew, in his account of the present incident, represents him as saying to the woman, 'I was sent only to the lost sheep of the house of Israel' (Matt. 15:24). There are suggestions here and there in the record of the ministry that, as a sequel to it, blessing would be available for Gentiles too, but very few instances of direct blessing to Gentiles appear within the context of the ministry itself.

Why did the woman not take offence at such an unpromising reply to her request? One obvious reason was that she was determined to get what she wanted for her daughter. In addition, what if there was a twinkle in his eye as he spoke, as much as to say, 'You know what we Jews are supposed to think of you Gentiles; do you think it is right for you to come and ask for a share in the healing which I have come to impart to Jews?' The written record can preserve the spoken words; it cannot convey the tone of voice in which they were said. Maybe the tone of voice encouraged the woman to persevere.

Again, what are we to say of the term 'dogs'? That is a term of abuse, if ever there was one. The pariah dog was not an estimable animal in Near Eastern culture then, any more than he is today. But it is not the pariah dogs that are intended here, like those at the door of the rich man in the parable, whose attentions added to Lazarus's afflictions. It is the dogs beneath the table. That in itself might suggest that they are household pets, the children's playmates; and this is confirmed by the fact that the word for 'dogs' used by both Jesus and the woman is a diminutive. Since the woman is said by Mark to have been a Greek (i.e. one who spoke Greek), the Greek diminutive used by Mark may have been the word actually used in the conversation.

The woman was quick-witted enough to deduce from Jesus's words the kind of reply to him that would win the granting of her request: 'Sir, even the little dogs under the table eat the children's left-overs!' The word 'faith' is not mentioned in Mark's account of the incident (as it is mentioned in Matthew 15:28), but the woman's reply expresses just the kind of faith that Jesus so greatly appreciated and that never failed to receive what it asked from him. Jesus was aware of a greater rapport with him on her part than he too often found among his own people. Her daughter was healed immediately, and healed, as in the other instance of Gentile faith in the synoptic Gospels (that of the Capernaum centurion and his sick servant – see p. 105), not by direct contact but at a distance.

Chapter
27

Who Is Greater Than John the Baptist?

'I tell you, among those born of women none is greater than John; yet he who is least in the kingdom of God is greater than he' (Luke 7:28; cf. Matt. 11:11)

With minor variations, this saying is reproduced by both Matthew and Luke in the same context. Matthew's wording is slightly fuller and, as usual, he has 'kingdom of heaven' where his parallel has 'kingdom of God'. (The two expressions are completely synonymous; then as now there were some who used 'heaven' as a substitute for the name of God.)

The saying is paradoxical: if John was not surpassed in greatness by any human being, how could anyone be greater than he? The paradox was certainly deliberate: we may wonder if any of Jesus's hearers grasped the point more readily than we do today.

In both Gospels the saying comes in the sequel to the account of the deputation of disciples which John, who was then imprisoned by Herod Antipas, tetrarch of Galilee and Perea, sent to Jesus. In his preaching in the lower Jordan valley John had called on his hearers to amend their ways in preparation for the Coming One, who would carry out a judgment symbolised by wind and fire (Luke 3:17; Matt. 3:12; see p. 123). Judgment involved the separation of the good from the worthless, the wheat from the chaff. The chaff, blown away by the wind, would be swept up and thrown into the fire.

After the baptism of Jesus, John recognised him as the

Coming One of whom he spoke, but now he was not so sure. Jesus had begun his own ministry, but from the reports of it which reached John in prison, it bore little resemblance to the ministry of judgment which John had foretold for the Coming One. Hence he sent his disciples to ask Jesus, 'Are you the Coming One, or must we look for someone else?'

Jesus might have told the messengers to go back and say to John that the answer to his question was, 'Yes, I am the Coming One; there is no need to look for anyone else.' But that would not have been very satisfactory. John might have said, 'Ah! but he might be mistaken himself.' Instead, Jesus kept the messengers with him for some time, and they heard and saw what was actually happening in his ministry. Then, when he judged that they had heard and seen enough for his purpose, he sent them back to tell John all about it – how the blind had their sight restored, the lame were walking, the deaf were enabled to hear and so forth, and how the good news was being proclaimed to the poor. 'Tell him this too,' he added: 'Blessed is the man who does not feel that I have let him down' (Matt. 11:2–6; Luke 7:19–23).

Jesus knew what John would make of his disciples' report. Jesus was doing the very things which, according to the prophets, would mark the inbreaking of the new age: 'Then the eyes of the blind shall be opened, and the ears of the deaf unstopped; then shall the lame man leap like a hart, and the tongue of the dumb sing for joy' (Isa. 35:5–6). Above all, he was actively fulfilling, and indeed embodying, the prophetic word which said, 'The Spirit of the Lord God is upon me, because the Lord has anointed me to bring good tidings to the poor ...' (Isa. 61:1). This should convince John that Jesus was indeed the Coming One: John had not been mistaken about him and need not feel that Jesus was letting him down by not doing the kind of thing John had said he would do.

When the messengers had departed, Jesus began to speak to the crowd about John in terms of unqualified commendation. John was nobody's yes-man, no weather-vane; he stood four-square to every wind that blew and declared the message of God without fear or favour, to peasant and prince. And when

Jesus asked them if they went out to the wilderness to see 'a man clothed in soft raiment', they must have laughed, as they remembered John's rough coat of camel's hair. No, said Jesus, for people who wear fine clothes and eat more luxurious food than John's diet of locusts and wild honey you have to go to royal courts – and John was not at the royal court but in the royal jail. John was a prophet, as most people thought; yes, said Jesus, and more than a prophet; he was God's special messenger sent to prepare his way, foretold in Malachi 3:1; he was, in fact, unsurpassed by any other. 'Among those born of women none is greater than John.' John spoke of the Coming One as 'he who is mightier than I', but here is the Coming One, himself born of a woman, paying a remarkable tribute to John. Then why did he add, 'yet he who is least in the kingdom of God is greater than he'?

I think we can ignore the suggestion that 'the least in the kingdom of God' was a reference to Jesus himself. 'The least in the kingdom of God' is the most insignificant person who enjoys the blessings of the new age of salvation which Jesus was bringing in. John was like Moses, who viewed the promised land from the top of Mount Pisgah, but did not enter it; he was the last of the heroes of Hebrews 11 who, 'though well attested by their faith, did not receive what was promised'. It is not in moral stature or devotion or service, but in privilege, that those who are least in the kingdom of God are greater than John – greater not for what they do for God (in this John was unsurpassed) but for what God does for them. On another occasion Jesus congratulated his disciples because they lived to see and hear what many prophets and kings had longed in vain to see and hear (Luke 10:23–24). It was not because of any superior merit of theirs that the disciples enjoyed these blessings: it was because they lived at the time when Jesus came and were called by him to share the life and service of the kingdom of God. Even to be his herald and forerunner, as John was, was not such a great privilege as to participate in the ministry of the Coming One, to be heirs of the kingdom which John, as the last of the prophets of old, foresaw and foretold.

Chapter
28

Violence and the Kingdom

'From the days of John the Baptist until now the kingdom of heaven has suffered violence, and men of violence take it by force' (Matt. 11:12)
'The law and the prophets were until John; since then the good news of the kingdom of God is preached, and every one enters it violently' (Luke 16:16)

Matthew and Luke appear to present us here with two versions of one and the same original saying. We have to try to determine what each of the two versions means in the context in which either evangelist has placed it; then, if possible, we have to determine what the original saying meant in the context of Jesus's ministry.

Both versions agree on this: the ministry of John the Baptist was an epoch marking the end of one age and the approach of a new. 'All the prophets and the law prophesied until John' (Matt. 11:13). John himself belonged rather to the old age than to the new. He is viewed as being the last and greatest of the 'goodly fellowship of the prophets'; while he was the herald of the new order he did not actually participate in it. When his public ministry was forcibly ended by his imprisonment, that was the signal for Jesus to embark on *his* ministry in Galilee, with the proclamation that the kingdom of God had drawn near.

'Since then', says Jesus in Luke's version of his words, 'the good news of the kingdom of God is preached.' That was a statement of fact, which his hearers must have recognised. But in what sense does everyone enter it violently?

Luke includes his version in a series of sayings inserted between the story of the dishonest steward and the story of the rich man and Lazarus and linked together by the general theme of law. 'Everyone forces his way in', says the NEB; the Good News Bible has the same wording. This might suggest something like a universal gate-crashing, which does not tally too well with some other sayings of Jesus on the relative fewness of those who enter the kingdom, such as 'Strive to enter by the narrow door; for many, I tell you, will seek to enter and will not be able' (Luke 13:24; cf. Matt. 7:13-14). But perhaps the meaning is, 'Everyone who enters must force his way in', which implies the same kind of determined and vigorous action as 'Strive to enter'. So far as the Lucan version of the saying goes, this could well be its meaning. It was no doubt this interpretation of it that moved an eighteenth-century hymn-writer to say, in language which probably sounded less strange in his contemporaries' ears than it does in ours:

> O may thy mighty word
> Inspire each feeble worm
> To rush into thy kingdom, Lord,
> And take it as by storm!

But Matthew's version now demands our attention. Where Luke says 'The good news of the kingdom of God is preached', Matthew says 'The kingdom of heaven has been suffering violence'. But there is an ambiguity in the particular form of the Greek verb in this clause: it may have passive force, meaning 'has been treated with violence' or 'has been suffering violence', or it may have intransitive force, meaning 'has been acting violently' or 'has been forcing its way in'. It could be said in favour of this last interpretation that in the ministry of Jesus the kingdom of heaven was on the march, taking the field against the forces of evil that held the souls and bodies of men and women in bondage. The mighty works that were an essential part of his ministry were the 'powers of the age to come' invading the present age and establishing a beach-head on its territory which was destined to expand until nothing of the old order was left.

If the passive force of the verb be preferred, then Jesus says that from the time of John the Baptist the kingdom of heaven has been violently attacked. This meaning too could fit the setting of the words. Matthew records them among several of Jesus's sayings about John (including the description of him as unsurpassed among those born of women) which he appends to the incident of John's messengers who were sent to question Jesus. It could be said that the imprisonment of John the Baptist (with his ensuing execution) was one instance of a violent attack on the kingdom of heaven by forces opposed to it – whether one thinks of human forces or demonic forces using men as their instruments. Further attacks were to be experienced until they reached their climax in the arrest and crucifixion of Jesus himself. The same meaning could be attached to the following clause: 'and men of violence take it by force' or 'men of violence seize it'. In that case, the two clauses say very much the same thing.

But the 'men of violence' need not be those who violently attacked the kingdom which Jesus proclaimed. There were other 'men of violence' around at the time – those who came later to be known as the party of the Zealots. They were passionately devoted to the bringing in of the kingdom of God, but their methods were clean contrary to those which Jesus practised and recommended. The kingdom of God, as they understood it, was a new order in which the Jewish people would live in freedom from Gentile rule, subject to no king but the God of their fathers. This new order could be introduced only by the forcible expulsion of the occupying Roman power from Judaea. Many of Jesus's hearers could remember the revolt of one such 'man of violence', Judas the Galilean, in A.D. 6. That revolt was crushed by the Romans, but the spirit which inspired it lived on. It could be said that men of this outlook were trying to take the kingdom of God by force, and on the whole it seems most probable that Jesus was referring to them.

Matthew's wording, then, seems to mean that, despite the

setback which the cause of God might have seemed to suffer by the imprisonment of John the Baptist, his kingdom has in reality been advancing irresistibly ever since. Men of violence may attempt to speed its progress by armed force, but that is not the way in which its triumph will be assured.

When Luke's account and Matthew's are compared, it appears that Matthew's wording is more relevant to the immediate circumstances of Jesus's ministry, while Luke's wording generalises the application of the saying, showing how its principle continued to work itself out in the world-wide proclamation and progress of the gospel. The good news was still being made known, and it still called for courage and resolution to enter the kingdom of God.

Chapter
29

Hating One's Parents

'If any one comes to me and does not hate his own father and mother and wife and children and brothers and sisters, yes, and even his own life, he cannot be my disciple' (Luke 14:26)

This is a hard saying in more senses than one: it is hard to accept and it is hard to reconcile it with the general teaching of Jesus. The attitude which it seems to recommend goes against the grain of nature, and it also goes against the law of love to one's neighbour which Jesus emphasised and radicalised. If the meaning of 'neighbour' must be extended so as to include one's enemy, it must not be restricted so as to exclude one's nearest and dearest.

What does it mean, then? It means that, just as property can come between us and the kingdom of God (see p. 174), so can family ties. The interests of God's kingdom must be paramount with the followers of Jesus, and everything else must take second place to them, even family ties. We tend to agree that there is something sordid about the attitude which gives priority to money-making over the nobler and more humane issues of life. But a proper care for one's family is one of those nobler and more humane issues. Jesus himself censured those theologians who argued that people who had vowed to give God a sum of money which they later discovered could have been used to help their parents in need were not free to divert the money from the religious purposes to which it had been vowed in order to meet a parental need. This, he said, was a violation of the commandment to honour one's father and mother (Mark 7:9–13).

Nevertheless, a man or woman might be so bound up by family ties as to have no time or interest for matters of even greater moment, and there could be no matter of greater moment than the kingdom of God. The husband and father was normally the head of the household, and he might look on his family as an extension of his own personality to the point where love for his family was little more than an extended form of self-love. Jesus strongly deprecated such an inward-looking attitude and used the strongest terms to express his disapproval of it. If 'hating' one's relatives is felt to be a shocking idea, it was meant to be shocking, to shock the hearers into a sense of the imperious demands of the kingdom of God. We know that in biblical idiom to hate can mean to love less. When, for example, regulations are laid down in the Old Testament law for a man who has two wives, 'one beloved and the other hated' (Deut. 21:15), it is not necessary to suppose that he positively hates the latter wife; all that need be meant is that he loves her less than the other and must be prevented from showing favouritism to the other's son when he allocates his property among his heirs. The RSV indicates that positive hatred is not intended by speaking of the one wife as 'the loved' and the other as 'the disliked', but the Hebrew word used is that which regularly means 'hated', and it is so rendered in the AV.

That hating in this saying of Jesus means loving less is shown by the parallel saying in Matthew 10:37: 'He who loves father or mother more than me is not worthy of me; and he who loves son or daughter more than me is not worthy of me.' In Matthew's Gospel these words are followed by the saying about taking up the cross and following Jesus (see p. 150): the implication of this sequence is that giving one's family second place to the kingdom of God is one way of taking up the cross.

We can perhaps understand more easily the action of those who choose a celibate life to devote themselves more unreservedly to the service of God, those who, as Jesus said on another occasion, 'have made themselves eunuchs for the sake of the kingdom of heaven' (Matt. 19:12; see p. 63). But the saying with which we are at present concerned refers to those who are already married and have children, not to speak of dependent parents. That Jesus's followers included some who had dependents like these and had left them to follow him is plain from his own words: 'There is no one who has left house or brothers or sisters or mother or father or children or lands, for my sake and for the gospel, ... who will not receive a hundredfold now in this time, ... and in the age to come eternal life' (Mark 10:29–30). Might this not involve the abandonment of natural responsibilities? Who, for example, looked after Peter's family when he took to the road as a disciple of Jesus? We are not told. Clearly his wife survived the experience, and her affections apparently survived it also, for twenty-five years later he was accustomed to take her along with him on his missionary journeys (1 Cor. 9:5).

Later in the New Testament period, when family life was acknowledged as the norm for Christians, it is laid down that, 'If any one does not provide for his relatives, and especially for his own family, he has disowned the faith and is worse than an unbeliever' (1 Tim. 5:8). There is no evidence in the Gospels that this conflicts with the teaching of Jesus. But this needed no emphasising from him: it is natural for men and women to make what provision they can for their nearest and dearest. Jesus's emphasis lay rather on the necessity of treating the kingdom of God as nearer and dearer still. Because of the natural resistance on the part of his hearers to accepting this necessity with literal seriousness, he insisted on it in the most arresting and challenging language at his command.

Chapter
30

Casting Fire on Earth

*'I came to cast fire upon the earth; and would that it
were already kindled!'* (Luke 12:49)

This saying is hard in the sense of being difficult to understand,
mainly because it is not obviously related to the context in
which it appears. It may be thought probable that it is
somehow connected with the saying immediately following
(see p. 125), about the baptism which Jesus had to undergo
before current restraints were removed, but this cannot be
taken for granted: each of the two sayings must first be
examined by itself.

It is natural to link the 'fire' in this saying with the 'fire'
mentioned in John the Baptist's description of the work to be
accomplished by the one whose way he was preparing: 'He who
is mightier than I is coming, the thong of whose sandals I am
not worthy to untie; he will baptize you with the Holy Spirit
and with fire' (Luke 3:16). The fire is closely associated here
with the Holy Spirit. A shorter form of John's words is found
in Mark 1:8; there, however, there is no mention of fire: 'He will
baptise you with the Holy Spirit'. Matthew, like Luke, adds the
words 'and with fire' (Matt. 3:11), and both Matthew and Luke
go on to report further words of John about the Coming One:
'His winnowing fork is in his hand, and he will clear his
threshing floor and gather his wheat into the granary, but the
chaff he will burn with unquenchable fire' (Matt. 3:12; Luke
3:17). It is worth bearing in mind that the same word is used in
Greek, the language of the Gospels, for 'Spirit', 'breath' and

'wind'; similarly in the language normally spoken by John and Jesus one and the same word did duty for all three concepts. The picture John draws is of the grain and the chaff lying piled up on the threshing floor after the harvest. The mixture of grain and chaff is tossed up into the air with the winnowing fork or shovel; the light chaff is blown away by the wind and the heavier grain falls back on the floor, from which it is collected to be stored in the granary. The chaff is then swept up and burned. Both the wind and the fire are symbols of the Holy Spirit; they depict the work that the Coming One is to do by the power of the Spirit, separating the true children of the kingdom from those who were only nominally so. (The figure of chaff is an ancient one in this kind of context: according to Psalm 1:4, 'The wicked ... are like chaff which the wind drives away'.)

Jesus's ministry was not exactly the ministry of judgment which John envisaged, but a ministry of sifting and separating it certainly was. Yet Jesus plainly looked for something further when he said, 'I came to set the earth on fire, and how I wish the fire had already broken out!'

One suggestion links these words with the hard saying which comes shortly afterwards in Luke 12:51–53, where Jesus says that he did not come to give peace on earth but rather division (see p. 150). We shall have to consider this hard saying also, but the difficulty about understanding his words about setting the earth on fire in the sense of the division and strife which he foresaw as the effect of his ministry lies in his earnest wish that the fire 'were already kindled'. He foresaw the division and strife indeed as the effect of his ministry, but he did not desire it. It is more satisfactory to take these words as the expression of a longing for an outpouring of the Spirit in power the like of which had not yet been seen.

Jesus himself experienced a personal outpouring of the Spirit at his baptism in the Jordan. A pictorial account of this outpouring in terms of fire is preserved in the second-century Christian writer Justin Martyr: 'When Jesus went down into the water a fire was kindled in the Jordan.'[1] The same figure appears in a saying ascribed to Jesus in the *Gospel of Thomas* and elsewhere: 'He who is near me is near the fire, and he who is far from me is far from the kingdom.'[2] The fire was there in Jesus's ministry, but the earth had not yet caught fire. One day it would catch fire in earnest, with the descent of the Holy Spirit at Pentecost; but Jesus himself had to die before this consummation could be realised, and while his death is not explicitly mentioned in these words about the fire, it is probably implied as a prospect beneath their surface. Hence the note of poignancy which can be discerned.

Chapter
31

How I Am Constrained Until It Is Accomplished!

'I have a baptism to be baptised with; and how I am constrained until it is accomplished!' (Luke 12:50)

There is nothing in the immediate context of this saying, which is found only in Luke's Gospel, to throw light on its meaning. It must be read in the wider context of Jesus's whole teaching and ministry. In form it resembles the saying which precedes it, in which Jesus longs that the fire which he came to start were already kindled, but in sense it has much in common with those sayings in which the kingdom of God is seen to be subject to temporary limitations until something happens to unleash its full power. Here it is Jesus himself who is subject to a temporary limitation. As the NEB renders the saying: 'I have a baptism to undergo, and what constraint I am under until the ordeal is over!'

Two questions are raised by the saying:

1. What was the baptism which Jesus had to undergo? and

2. What was the constraint under which he had to work until this baptism had taken place?

1. There is little doubt that by his baptism he meant his impending death. This is confirmed by the record of another occasion on which he used similar language. On Jesus's last journey to Jerusalem, Mark tells us, he was approached by James and John, the two sons of Zebedee, who asked that they might be given the two positions of chief honour when his kingdom was established – the one at his right hand and the

other at his left. Their request betrayed an almost ludicrous misconception of the nature of the kingdom of which Jesus spoke, but he began to set them right by asking a question which at first did not seem to have much bearing on what they had said. 'Tell me this', he replied: 'Are you able to drink from my cup and be baptised with my baptism?' When they said, 'We are', he replied, 'You shall – but even so that will not guarantee you the two chief places for which you ask.' When he asked, 'Are you able to drink from my cup and be baptised with my baptism?' (Mark 10:38), he meant, simply, 'Are you able to share my suffering and death?' In fact, they did not share his suffering and death – not, at least, at the time when he was crucified. If things had turned out otherwise, if the crosses which flanked the cross of Jesus had been occupied not by the two robbers but by James and John, would they not have secured there and then the two positions of chief honour – the one at his right hand and the other at his left? In all subsequent Christian memory this high glory would have been exclusively theirs.

For our present purpose, however, we note that Jesus spoke then of his impending suffering and death as his 'baptism', and that supports the suggestion that the baptism to which he looked forward in the saying now under consideration bears the same meaning. If that is so, a further question arises: why did he speak of his suffering and death as a baptism? He had undergone one baptism at the beginning of his ministry, his baptism in the Jordan. Was there some feature of that baptism, administered by John the Baptist, which lent itself to this figurative use?

John's baptism is said to have been 'a baptism of repentance for the forgiveness of sins' (Mark 1:4). That is to say, people who were convicted of sin under John's preaching were invited to give public proof of their repentance by accepting baptism at his hands. Thus their sins would be forgiven and they would be 'a people prepared for the Lord' (Luke 1:17), ready for the moment when he would begin to execute his judgment through the agency of a person whom John denoted as the 'Coming One'. Jesus recognised John's ministry to be a work of God, and associated himself with it publicly by asking John to baptise him. True, Jesus at no time betrays any awareness of sin, any sense of repentance, any need for forgiveness. Yet he was never unwilling to associate with sinners: indeed, he was written off by some godly people as a 'friend of sinners' (and therefore, by implication, no better than the company he kept – see page 29). So his association with repentant sinners in receiving John's baptism was in keeping with his later practice.

Even so, some difficulty was felt about Jesus's undergoing a 'baptism of repentance for the forgiveness of sins'. Matthew in his account tells how John himself demurred at Jesus's request, saying, 'It would be more fitting that I should be baptised by you; why do you come to me?' Jesus's response to John's protest is excellently rendered in the NEB: 'Let it be so for the present; we do well to conform in this way with all that God requires' (Matt. 3:15). These words are recorded by Matthew only, but they express perfectly the spirit in which Jesus sought and received John's baptism. That this is so is confirmed by his experience when he came up from the river: he saw heaven split in two and the Spirit of God descending on him in the form of a dove, while a voice addressed him from heaven: 'You are my beloved Son; with you I am well pleased' (Mark 1:10–11). It was as though God said to him, 'You dedicate yourself to the doing of my will? You conform in this way with all that I require? I tell you this, then: you are my Son, my chosen one, the one in whom I delight.'

Jesus's period of testing in the wilderness, which followed immediately after his baptism, reinforced the strength of his commitment to do the will of God without deviation.

But what had this to do with the baptism to which he looked forward? He could, no doubt, have referred to his death, with the events leading up to it, as his baptism in the sense of a sea of troubles that threatened to overwhelm him. But in the light of the baptism which inaugurated his public ministry, we can see more in his language than that. His baptism in the Jordan gave visible expression to his resolution to fulfil the will of God, and it involved at least a token identification of himself with sinners. The ministry thus inaugurated manifested his

constant devotion to the will of God and was marked by
unaffected friendship with sinners. His death, which crowned
that ministry, consummated his embracing of the will of God
as the rule for his life, and it involved a real and personal
identification of himself with sinners, on the part of one sinless
himself. In this way he embodied the Old Testament picture of
the obedient and suffering Servant of the Lord who 'bore the
sin of many, and made intercession for the transgressors' (Isa.
53:12).

It is not for nothing that one of the latest New Testament
documents voices the Christian confession in these words:
'This is he who came by water and blood, Jesus Christ – not
with the water only, but with the water and with the blood'
(1 John 5:6) – or, as we might say, not only with the baptism of
water, but with the baptism of water and the baptism of death.
The baptism of water, which inaugurated his ministry, was a
faint anticipation of the baptism of death, which crowned his
ministry.

2. What, then, was the constraint to which he was subject
until he underwent this impending baptism? The answer to this
part of our question is closely bound up with the meaning of
another of Jesus's sayings at which we shall look (p. 153) –
his saying about the kingdom of God coming with power
(Mark 9:1). While Jesus was amply endowed with the Spirit of
God for the messianic ministry which began at his baptism in
the Jordan and continued until his death, his death and
resurrection unleashed a power which was previously unparalleled. The limitation of which he was conscious during his
ministry was due to the fact that, as it is put in the Fourth
Gospel, 'As yet the Spirit had not been given, because Jesus
was not yet glorified' (John 7:39).

We have spoken of his messianic ministry as lasting from his
baptism in the Jordan to his death on the cross, but it would be
more accurate to speak of that as the first phase of his ministry.
His ministry did not come to an end with his death; he resumed
it when he rose again, and continues it until now, no longer in
visible presence on earth but by his Spirit in his followers. We
should not think of the apostles as taking up the task which

Jesus left unfinished at his death; we should think of them rather as called to share in his still very personal ongoing ministry. This is the perspective of the New Testament writers. Luke, for example, opens the second volume of his history of Christian beginnings – the volume which we call the Acts of the Apostles – by referring back to the first volume as the record of 'all that Jesus began both to do and to teach until the day in which he was taken up' (Acts 1:1–2). The implication is that the new volume is going to tell of what Jesus *continued* to do and teach *from* the day in which he was taken up. To the same effect Paul, looking back on the major phase of his apostolic career, speaks of its very considerable achievements as 'what Christ has wrought through me to win obedience from the Gentiles, by word and deed, by the power of signs and wonders, by the power of the Holy Spirit' (Rom. 15:18–19).

The scale of the Christian achievement within a few years from the death and resurrection of Christ was out of all proportion to that of his personal achievement during his Palestinian ministry. The limitation was removed by the outpouring of the Spirit as the sequel to Christ's saving work. But without the Palestinian ministry, crowned by his death and resurrection, there would have been no such sequel, and the achievement which followed the outpouring of the Spirit was still Christ's personal achievement. He had undergone his baptism of death, and now worked on free of all restraint.

Chapter
32

Not Peace but a Sword

*'Do not think that I have come to bring peace on earth;
I have not come to bring peace, but a sword'* (Matt.
10:34)

This is a hard saying for all who recall the message of the angels
on the night of Jesus's birth: 'Glory to God in high heaven, and
peace on earth among human beings, the objects of God's
favour' (as the message seems to mean). True, the angels'
message appears only in Luke (2:14) and the hard saying, in the
form in which we have quoted it, comes from Matthew. But
Luke records the same hard saying, except that he replaces the
metaphorical 'sword' by the non-metaphorical 'division' (Luke
12:51). Both evangelists then go on to report Jesus as saying,
'For I have come to set a man against his father, and a daughter
against her mother, and a daughter-in-law against her mother-
in-law' (Matt. 10:35; Luke 12:53), while Matthew rounds the
saying off with a quotation from the Old Testament: 'a man's
foes will be those of his own household' (Mic. 7:6).

One thing is certain: Jesus did not advocate conflict. He
taught his followers to offer no resistance or retaliation when
they were attacked or ill-treated. 'Blessed are the peace-
makers,' he said, 'for they shall be called sons of God' (Matt.
5:9), meaning that God is the God of peace, so that those who
seek peace and pursue it reflect his character. When he paid his
last visit to Jerusalem, the message which he brought it
concerned 'the things that make for peace', and he wept
because the city refused his message and was bent on a course

which was bound to lead to destruction (Luke 19:41–44). The message which his followers proclaimed in his name after his departure was called the 'gospel of peace' (Eph. 6:15) or the 'word of reconciliation' (2 Cor. 5:19). It was called this not merely as a matter of doctrine but as a fact of experience. Individuals and groups formerly estranged from one another found themselves reconciled through their common devotion to Christ. Something of this sort must have been experienced even earlier, in the course of the Galilean ministry: if Simon the Zealot and Matthew the tax-collector were able to live together as two of the twelve apostles, the rest of the company must have looked on this as a miracle of grace.

But when Jesus spoke of tension and conflict within a family, he probably spoke from personal experience. There are indications in the gospel story that some members of his own family had no sympathy with his ministry: the people who on one occasion tried to restrain him by force because people were saying 'He is beside himself' are called 'his friends' in the RSV but more accurately 'his family' in the NEB (Mark 3:21). 'Even his brothers did not believe in him', we are told in John 7:5. (If it is asked why, in that case, they attained positions of leadership alongside the apostles in the early Church, the answer is no doubt to be found in the statement of 1 Cor. 15:7 that Jesus, risen from the dead, appeared to his brother James.)

So, when Jesus said that he had come to bring 'not peace but a sword', he meant that this would be the *effect* of his coming, not that it was the *purpose* of his coming. His words came true in the life of the early Church, and they have verified themselves subsequently in the history of Christian missions. Where one or two members of a family or other social group have accepted the Christian faith, this has repeatedly provoked opposition from other members. Paul, who seems to have experienced such opposition in his own family circle as a result of his conversion, makes provision for similar situations in the family life of his converts. He knew that tension could arise when a husband or a wife became a Christian and the other spouse remained a pagan. If the pagan spouse was happy to go on living with the Christian, that was fine; the whole family might become Christian before long. But if the pagan partner insisted on walking out and terminating the marriage, the Christian should not use force or legal action, because 'God has called us to peace' (1 Cor. 7:12-16) – see page 61.

In these words, then, Jesus was warning his followers that their allegiance to him might cause conflict at home, and even expulsion from the family circle. It was well that they should be forewarned, for then they could not say, 'We never expected that we should have to pay *this* price for following him!'

Chapter
33

The Fall of Satan

'I saw Satan fall like lightning from heaven' (Luke 10:18)

When we think of the fall of Satan, we tend to be more influenced by John Milton than by the Bible. In *Paradise Lost* Milton describes Satan and his angels being ejected from heaven and falling down to hell back in the primeval past, before the creation of the human race.

> Him the Almighty Power
> Hurl'd headlong flaming from th' Ethereal Skie
> With hideous ruin and combustion down
> To bottomless perdition, there to dwell
> In Adamantine Chains and penal Fire,
> Who durst defie th' Omnipotent to Arms.

It would be difficult to find biblical authority for this picture, however. The reader of the AV may think of Isaiah 14:12, 'How art thou fallen from heaven, O Lucifer, son of the morning!' And in truth the poetic imagery in which Lucifer's fall is depicted has been borrowed by the traditional concept of the fall of Satan. But Lucifer, son of the morning, is 'Day Star, son of Dawn' (RSV). The prophet is proclaiming the downfall of the king of Babylon, who occupied such a high place in the firmament of imperial power that his overthrow can be compared to the morning star being toppled from heaven. In the Old Testament Satan, or rather 'the satan' (the adversary), is chief prosecutor in the heavenly court, and when he fills this role he does so in the presence of God and his angels (Job 1:6–2:7; Zech. 3:1–5). See p. 147.

So when Jesus speaks of seeing Satan's fall from heaven he is not thinking of an event in the remote past. He is thinking of the effect of his ministry at the time. He had sent out seventy of his disciples to spread the announcement that the kingdom of God had drawn near, and now they had come back from their mission in great excitement. 'Why,' they said, 'even the demons are subject to us in your name!' To this Jesus replied, 'I watched how Satan fell, like lightning, out of the sky' (NEB). It is implied that he was watching for this when suddenly, like a flash of lightning, it happened; Satan plummeted – whether to earth or down to the abyss is not said.

Jesus may be describing an actual vision which he experienced during the mission of the seventy – not unlike the vision seen by John of Patmos, when, as he says, war broke out in heaven 'and the great dragon was thrown down, that ancient serpent, who is called the Devil and Satan, the deceiver of the whole world' (Rev. 12:9). When Jesus's messengers found that the demons – malignant forces that held men and women in bondage – were compelled to obey them as they commanded them, in Jesus's name, to come out of those people in whose lives they had taken up residence, this was a sign that the kingdom of God was conquering the kingdom of evil. Many of the rabbis held that, at the end of the age, God or the Messiah would overthrow Satan: the report of the seventy showed that Satan's overthrow had already taken place; and Jesus's vision of his fall from heaven confirmed this. John's Patmos version of Satan being ejected similarly indicates that his downfall was the direct result of Jesus's ministry. So too, when Jesus says in John 12:31 'Now shall the ruler of this world be cast out', the adverb 'now' refers to his impending passion, which crowned his ministry.

The downfall of Satan may be regarded as the decisive victory in the campaign; the campaign itself goes on. Hence Jesus's further words to the exultant disciples: 'I have given you authority to tread upon serpents and scorpions, and over all the power of the enemy; and nothing shall hurt you' (Luke 10:19). The 'serpents and scorpions' represent the forces of evil: thanks to the work of Christ, his people can trample them underfoot and gain the victory over them. The imagery may be borrowed from Psalm 91:13, where those who trust in God are promised that they 'will tread on the lion and the adder'. Paul uses a similar expression when he tells the Christians in Rome that, if they are 'wise as to what is good and guileless as to what is evil,' then the God of peace will soon crush Satan under their feet (Rom. 16:19–20). The wording here harks back not so much to Psalm 91 as to the story of man's first disobedience, where the serpent of Eden is told that its offspring will have its head crushed by the offspring of the woman (Gen. 3:15).

Finally, the seventy are directed not to exult in their spiritual achievements (that way lie pride and catastrophe) but to exult rather in what God has done for them.

> Rejoice not ye that sprites of ill
> Yield to your prowess in the fight;
> But joy because your Father God
> Hath writ your names elect for life.

To have one's name 'written in heaven' is to have received God's gift of eternal life.

Chapter
34

The Father and the Son

'All things have been delivered to me by my Father; and no one knows the Son except the Father, and no one knows the Father except the Son, and any one to whom the Son chooses to reveal him' (Matt. 11:27; cf. Luke 10:22)

No one would have been surprised had this saying appeared somewhere in the Gospel of John. The language is characteristically Johannine; the saying has been called 'an aerolite from the Johannine heaven' or 'a boulder from the Johannine moraine'. For all its Johannine appearance, it does not come in the Gospel of John but in the non-Markan material common to the Gospels of Matthew and Luke, drawn (it is widely supposed) from the Q collection of sayings of Jesus, which may have been in circulation not long after A.D. 50. The nearest thing to it in the synoptic Gospels is the utterance of the risen Christ at the end of Matthew's Gospel: 'All authority in heaven and on earth has been given to me' (Matt. 28:18).

In both Matthew and Luke (and therefore presumably also in the source on which they drew), the saying follows on immediately from words in which Jesus thanks God that things hidden from the wise and understanding have been revealed to 'babes' – that is, apparently, to the disciples. The one who has revealed those things is Jesus himself; indeed, he is not only the revealer of truth; he is the Son who reveals the Father. In this context the 'all things' which have been delivered to him by the Father would naturally be understood of the content of his teaching or revelation. But the content of this teaching or revelation is not an abstract body of divinity; it is personal, it is God the Father himself. Jesus claims a unique personal knowledge of God, and this personal knowledge he undertakes to impart to others. Unless it is imparted by him, it is inaccessible. He is the one who at his baptism heard the Father acclaim him as his Son, his beloved, his chosen one (Mark 1:11). He enjoys a special relation and fellowship with the Father, but that relation and fellowship is open to those who learn from him. As he calls God 'Abba, Father', they may know him and call him by the same name. All the other gifts which the Father has to bestow on his children come with this personal knowledge, which is mediated by Jesus.

Matthew and Luke give the saying two different literary contexts; if we look for a historical context, we might think of some occasion when the disciples showed that they had grasped the heart of his teaching to which the minds of others remained closed, as at Caesarea Philippi.

There is nothing hard in this except to those who cannot accept the claim to uniqueness, the 'scandal of particularity', implicit in the gospel. But to those who accept the presuppositions current in a plural society this can be hard enough.

But what of the statement that 'no one knows the Son except the Father'? One line of traditional interpretation takes this to mean that the union of the divine and human natures in the one person of the Son of God is a mystery known only to the Father. But it is anachronistic to impart later christological teaching into the context of Jesus's ministry. More probably the two clauses 'no one knows the Son except the Father' and 'no one knows the Father except the Son' constitute a fuller way of saying 'no one except the Father and the Son know each other'. It has been suggested, indeed, that there is an argument from the general to the particular here – that a saying to the effect that 'only a father and a son know each other' (and therefore only the son can reveal the father) is applied to the special relation of Jesus and God: 'only the Father and the Son know each other' (and therefore only the Son can reveal the

Father). Whatever substance there may be in this suggestion, it is clear that a reciprocity of personal knowledge between the Son of God and his Father is affirmed. As none but the Father knows the Son, so none but the Son knows the Father, but the Son shares this knowledge with those whom he chooses, and in the present context that means his disciples.

There is a fascinating collection of variant readings in the textual transmission of this saying; they bear witness to difficulties which early scribes and editors found in it. The only variation at which we need to look is that between Matthew's wording and Luke's: whereas Matthew says 'knows the Son... knows the Father', Luke says 'knows who the Son is... or who the Father is'. Luke's wording might appear to weaken the emphasis on direct personal knowledge expressed by Matthew's wording, but this was probably not Luke's intention. If consideration be given to the Semitic construction behind the Greek of the two Gospels, Matthew's wording can claim to be closer to what Jesus actually said.

Chapter
35

You Are Peter

'And I tell you, you are Peter, and on this rock I will build my church, and the powers of death shall not prevail against it. I will give you the keys of the kingdom of heaven, and whatever you bind on earth shall be bound in heaven, and whatever you loose on earth shall be loosed in heaven' (Matt. 16:18–19)

Why should this be reckoned a hard saying? It does, to be sure, contain some figures of speech which require to be explained – 'the gates of Hades' (which RSV has interpreted for us as 'the powers of death'), 'the keys of the kingdom', 'binding' and 'loosing'. But it is not because of these figures of speech that the saying is widely reckoned to be hard – so hard, indeed, that some interpreters have tried not only to explain it but to explain it away.

One reason for regarding it as a hard saying is that Peter in the Gospels is too unstable a character to serve as the foundation for any enterprise or to be given such authority as is conveyed in these words. But the main reason for finding a difficulty in the text is strictly irrelevant to its straightforward reading and interpretation. Few Protestants, asked to name their favourite text, would think of quoting this one. It has been invoked to support the supremacy of the Roman Church over other Churches – more precisely, to support the supremacy of the bishop of Rome over other bishops – and those who do not acknowledge this use of it as valid have sometimes reacted by trying to make it mean something much less positive than it appears to mean. Some have suggested, with no manuscript evidence to justify the suggestion, that the text has been corrupted from an original 'you have said' (instead of 'you are Peter'); others have argued that the Greek wording is not an accurate translation of the Aramaic form in which the saying was cast by Jesus – that what he said was, 'I tell you, Peter, that on this rock I will build my Church.' But this too is conjecture. If we can get rid of the idea that the text has any reference to the Roman Church or to the Papacy, we shall lose interest in such attempts to remove what has been felt to be its awkwardness.

Certainly there is nothing in the context to suggest Rome or the Papacy. But the context of the saying presents us with a problem of a different kind. All three synoptic evangelists record the incident in the neighbourhood of Caesarea. All of them tell how Jesus, after asking his disciples what account people were giving of him, asked them next what account they themselves gave: 'Who do you say that I am?' To this question Peter, acting as their spokesman, replied 'You are the Messiah' (that is the form of his answer in Mark 8:29; the other Gospels have variations in wording). All three evangelists add that Jesus strictly forbade them to repeat this to anyone. But Matthew inserts, between Peter's answer and Jesus's charge to the disciples not to repeat it, a personal response by Jesus to Peter. This response begins, 'Blessed are you, Simon Bar-Jona! For flesh and blood has not revealed this to you, but my Father who is in heaven.' It then continues with the words we have quoted as our hard saying.

How are we to account for the fact that the saying, with its introductory benediction, does not appear in Mark's or Luke's record of the occasion? If Matthew were the source on which Mark and Luke depended, then we could say that they abridged his record for purposes of their own, and we should try to determine what those purposes were. If, however, we are right in thinking that Mark was one of the sources on which Matthew drew, then we have to say that Matthew has amplified Mark's record by incorporating material derived from elsewhere. This is not the only place where Matthew expands Mark's record by the inclusion of material about Peter not found in our other Gospels. We may think, for example, of the episode of Peter's getting out of the boat and beginning to sink when he tried to walk to Jesus on the water (Matt. 14:28-31).

It has been argued that the passage we are considering belongs to a later period in Christian history rather than that to which Matthew assigns it. Some have seen in it the report of words spoken by Jesus to Peter when he appeared to him in resurrection – words which Matthew transferred to the Caesarea Philippi context because of the aptness of the subject-matter. Others would date them later still: is it likely, they ask, that the historical Jesus would speak of his 'church'? Certainly it is not likely that he used the word in the sense which it usually bears for us, but it is not unlikely that he used an Aramaic word which was represented in Greek by *ekklesia*, the term regularly rendered 'church' in the New Testament. And if he did, what did he mean by it? He meant the new community which he aimed to bring into being, the new Israel in which the twelve apostles were to be the leaders, leading by service and not by dictation.

A helpful analogy to Jesus's words to Peter is provided by an allegory found in rabbinical tradition setting forth God's dealings with humanity from the beginning to the time of Abraham. The written documents in which this allegory is found are later than our Gospels, but behind the written form lies a period of oral transmission. In Isaiah 51:1 Abraham is called 'the rock from which you were hewn', and the allegory undertakes to explain why Abraham should be called a 'rock'. It tells how a certain king wished to build a palace, and set his servants to dig to find a foundation. They dug for a long time, and took soundings twice, but found nothing but morass. (The soundings were taken first in the generation of Enosh, Adam's grandson, and then in the generation of Noah.) After further digging they took soundings again, and this time they struck rock (*petra*). 'Now', said the king, 'at last I can begin to build.'[1]

In the allegory the king, of course, is God; the palace which he planned to build is the nation of Israel, and he knew that he could make a beginning with the project when he found Abraham, a man ready to respond to his call with implicit faith and obedience. It would be precarious to envisage any direct relation between this allegory and Jesus's words to Peter, as recorded by Matthew, but there is a notable resemblance.

According to John's account of the call of the first disciples, it was during John the Baptist's ministry in Transjordan that Peter heard his brother Andrew say, with reference to Jesus, 'We have found the Messiah' (John 1:41). Evidently Peter then believed Andrew's testimony, but that would have been an instance of what Jesus now described as 'flesh and blood' (a human being) telling him. There were various ideas abroad in the popular mind at that time regarding the kind of person the Messiah was and the kind of things he would do, but Jesus's character and activity, as his disciples had come to know them, probably corresponded to none of those ideas. If Peter believed Jesus to be the Messiah when he first received his call, and now confessed him to be the Messiah a year or more later, the concept 'Messiah' must have begun to change its meaning for him. Not long before, he had seen his Master repel the attempt of a band of eager militants, five thousand strong, to make him their king so that he might lead them against the occupying forces of Rome and their creature, Herod Antipas (John 6:15). The Messiah as popularly conceived ought surely to have grasped such an opportunity. Some at least of the disciples were disappointed that he refused to do so.

The fact that Peter, even so, was prepared to confess Jesus as the Messiah was evidence that a change had at least begun to take place in his thinking – that he was now coming to understand the term 'Messiah' in the light of what Jesus actually was and did, rather than to understand Jesus in the light of ideas traditionally associated with the term 'Messiah'. Hence the pleasure with which Jesus greeted his response: hence the blessing which he pronounced on him. For, like the king in the Jewish parable, Jesus said in effect, 'Now at last I can begin to build!'

It is well known that 'You are Peter, and on this rock I will build my church' involves a play on words. In Greek 'Peter' is *petros* and 'rock' is *petra* (the difference being simply that between the masculine termination -*os*, necessary in a man's name, and the feminine termination -*a*). In the Aramaic which Jesus probably spoke, there was not even such a minor grammatical distinction between the two forms: 'You are *kēphā*,' he said, 'and on this *kēphā* I will build my church.' The form *kēphā*, as applied to Peter, appears in many of our New Testament versions as Cephas (e.g. in John 1:42; 1 Cor. 1:12), an alternative form of his name. As a common noun, the Aramaic *kēphā* means 'rock'; the Hebrew equivalent *kēph* is used in this sense in Job 30:6 and Jeremiah 4:29. In some modern languages the play on words can be exactly reproduced: thus in most editions of the French New Testament Jesus says to Peter, 'Tu es *Pierre*, et sur cette *pierre* je bâtirai mon église.' But this cannot be done in English; if the play on words is to be brought out, a rendering like that of the NEB has to be adopted: 'You are Peter, the Rock; and on this rock I will build my church.' Now that someone has been found who is prepared to confess Jesus as what he really is, and not try to fit him into some inherited framework, a start can be made with forming the community of true disciples who will carry on Jesus's mission after his departure.

Peter personally might be thought too unstable to provide such a foundation, but it is not Peter for what he is in himself but Peter the confessor of Jesus who provides it. In that building every other confessor of Jesus finds a place. What matters is not the stature of the confessor but the truth of the confession. Where Jesus is confessed as the Messiah or (as Matthew amplifies the wording) as 'the Christ, the Son of the living God', there his Church exists. It is in the one who is thus confessed, and not in any durable quality of her own, that the Church's security and survival rest. While she maintains that confession, the gates of the prison-house of Hades (i.e. death) will never close on her.

And what about the 'keys of the kingdom'? The keys of a royal or noble establishment were entrusted to the chief steward or major domo; he carried them on his shoulder in earlier times, and there they served as a badge of the authority entrusted to him. About 700 B.C. an oracle from God announced that this authority in the royal palace in Jerusalem was to be conferred on a man called Eliakim: 'I will place on his shoulder the key of the house of David; he shall open, and none shall shut; and he shall shut, and none shall open' (Isa. 22:22). So in the new community which Jesus was about to build, Peter would be, so to speak, chief steward. In the early chapters of Acts Peter is seen exercising this responsibility in the primitive church. He acts as chairman of the group of disciples in Jerusalem even before the coming of the Spirit at the first Christian Pentecost (Acts 1:15-26); on the day of Pentecost it is he who preaches the gospel so effectively that three thousand hearers believe the message and are incorporated in the church (Acts 2:14–41); some time later it is he who first preaches the gospel to a Gentile audience and thus 'opens a door of faith' to Gentiles as well as Jews (Acts 10:34–48). Both in Jerusalem at Pentecost and in the house of Cornelius at Caesarea, what Peter does on earth is ratified in heaven by the bestowal of the Holy Spirit on his converts. This divine confirmation was specially important in his approach to Gentiles. As Peter put it himself, 'God who knows the heart bore witness to them, giving them the Holy Spirit just as he did to us; and he made no distinction between us and them, but cleansed their hearts by faith' (Acts 15:8–9).

'Binding' and 'loosing' were idiomatic expressions in rabbinical Judaism to denote the promulgation of rulings either forbidding or authorising various kinds of activity. The authority to bind or loose given to Peter in our present context is given to the disciples as a body in Matthew 18:18, in a saying of Jesus similarly preserved by this evangelist only. Again, the record of Acts provides an illustration. Where church discipline is in view, Peter's verbal rebuke of Ananias and Sapphira received drastic ratification from heaven (Acts 5:1–11) – see p. 93. And Paul for his part, though he was not one of the disciples present when Jesus pronounced these words of authorisation, expects that when judgment is pronounced by the church of Corinth on a man who has brought the Christian name into public disrepute, at a meeting 'when you are assembled, and my spirit is present, with the power of our Lord Jesus,' the judgment will be given practical effect by God (1 Cor. 5:3–5). Again, when 'the apostles and the elders' came together in Jerusalem to consider the conditions on which Gentile believers might be recognised as fellow-members of the Church, their decision was issued as something which 'has seemed good to the Holy Spirit and to us' (Acts 15:28). Here, then, Luke may be held to provide a commentary on Matthew's record by showing how, in pursuance of Jesus's words, the keys of the kingdom were used and the power of binding and loosing was exercised in the primitive Church in preaching, discipline and legislation.

This may be added. The words in which Peter is singled out for special commendation and authority were probably handed down in a community where Peter's name was specially esteemed. The church of Antioch in Syria was one such community. There are other reasons for envisaging a fairly close association between the church of Antioch and the Gospel of Matthew, and it may well have been from material about Peter preserved at Antioch that Matthew derived these words which he incorporates into his account of what Jesus said at Caesarea Philippi.

Chapter
36

Get behind Me, Satan!

*But turning and seeing his disciples, he rebuked Peter,
and said, 'Get behind me, Satan! For you are not on the
side of God, but of men'* (Mark 8:33)

Why did Jesus address Peter with such severity?

When, in the neighbourhood of Caesarea Philippi, Peter
confessed Jesus to be the Messiah, Jesus laid a strict charge on
him and his fellow-disciples not to mention it to a soul. Why?
Probably because the title 'Messiah' (the anointed king) was
bound up in the minds of most people, and to some extent even
yet in the disciples' minds, with ideas of political rule and
military conquest, which were very far from his own
understanding of his mission in the world. If the people of
Galilee learned that Jesus's disciples considered him to be
the Messiah, their own convictions about him, which he had
done his best to dispel at the time of the feeding of the
multitude (see p. 142), would be reinforced, and this might
have disastrous results.

As for the disciples, they had to learn that, far from victory
over the Romans and a royal throne awaiting him, he faced
suffering and violent death. If they believed that he was the
Messiah, they must know what kind of Messiah he was; if they
were still minded to follow him, they must realise clearly what
kind of leader they were following, and what lay at the end of
the road he was pursuing. The revelation shocked them; this
was not what they expected. Their common sense of shock was
voiced (as usual) by Peter, who in his concern took Jesus by the

arm in a friendly gesture and began to expostulate with him: 'Mercy on you, Master! Don't speak like that. This is never going to happen to *you*!' It was to this expostulation that Jesus made his severe reply.

The words of his reply recall those with which he repelled the tempter in the wilderness, and indeed they have much the same sense here as they had there. It should be understood that 'Satan' is not primarily a proper name. It is a Hebrew common noun meaning 'adversary'. When it appears in the Old Testament preceded by the definite article, it means 'the adversary'. In the story of Job, for example, where Satan (better, 'the satan') is said to have presented himself at a session of the heavenly court (Job 1:6), the expression means 'the adversary' or, as we might say, 'counsel for the prosecution'. This is the regular function of this unpleasant character in the Old Testament. Every court must have a prosecutor, but this prosecutor enjoys his work so much that, when there are not sufficient candidates for prosecution, he goes out of his way to tempt people to go wrong, so that he may have the pleasure of prosecuting them (cf. 1 Chron. 21:1). His role as tempter is thus secondary to his role as prosecutor. The Greek word corresponding to Satan is *diabolos*, meaning 'accuser' (it is the word from which our 'devil' is derived). In Revelation 12:10, where the devil is thrown down from heaven (not at the beginning of time, as in Milton's *Paradise Lost*, but in consequence of the redemptive work of Christ – see p. 134), the holy ones in heaven rejoice because, they say, 'the accuser of our brethren has been thrown down, who accuses them day and night before our God.'

In his character as tempter he encountered Jesus in the wilderness. Jesus had just been baptised by John the Baptist and had received the assurance from God that he was his Son, his beloved one in whom he found pleasure. The language addressed to him by the voice of God (Mark 1:11) bears a fairly close resemblance to the words of Isaiah 42:1 in which God introduces the one whom he calls his servant: 'Behold my servant, whom I uphold; my chosen, in whom my soul delights.' If Jesus learned from the heavenly voice that he was to fulfil his life-mission in terms of the portrayal of the Servant of the Lord in Isaiah 42:1-4 and other passages of the same book (especially Isaiah 52:13-53:12, which similarly begins with 'Behold my servant'), then it was clear to him that the common expectation of a conquering Messiah was not going to be realised through him. Humility, obedience, suffering and death marked the way of the Father's will for him. The temptations to which he was exposed in the wilderness were calculated by the adversary to weaken his trustful obedience to God, and included the temptation to fulfil his destiny along the line of common expectation and not in accordance with what he knew to be his Father's will. We recall in particular the temptation to accept world dominion on the adversary's terms. 'It will all be yours', said he to Jesus, 'if you will fall down and worship me.' Many an ambitious man before then had yielded to that temptation, and many have yielded to it since. But Jesus repudiated the adversary's offer, and it was in his repudiation of this temptation, according to Matthew 4:10, that he said, 'Begone, Satan!' or, as many manuscripts have it, 'Get behind me, Satan!'

And now, from the lips of Peter, Jesus heard what he recognised to be the same temptation again. Peter, in effect, was trying to dissuade him from obeying his Father's will. Peter had no idea that this was what he was doing; he was moved only by affectionate concern for his Master's well-being and did not like to hear him utter such ominous words: 'The Son of man must suffer many things and be rejected' (Mark 8:31). But he was, for the moment, playing the part of an adversary, however inadvertently, for as Jesus told him, 'you are not on the side of God, but of men' (Mark 8:33).

In reproducing these words, Matthew inserts a clause not found in Mark: 'Get behind me, Satan! *You are a stumbling-block to me*, for you are not on the side of God, but of men' (Matt. 16:23). It is noteworthy that Matthew adds this reference to Peter's being a stumbling-block, since it is he alone who, in the preceding paragraph, reports Jesus's words about the rock. There are two kinds of rock here: there is a kind of rock which provides a stable foundation, and there is the kind of rock which lies in the way and trips people up. Indeed, one and the same rock can sometimes fulfil both functions. There is an oracle in Isaiah 8:13–15 where God himself is a rock which offers safe sanctuary to those who seek refuge on it in time of flood, but which will become 'a stone of offence and a rock of stumbling' to those who are swept against it by the swirling waters. Peter had it in him to be either a foundation-stone or a stumbling-block. Thanks to the intercession which his Master made for him in a critical hour, he strengthened his brethren (Luke 22:32) and became a rock of stability and a focus of unity.

Chapter
37

Taking Up the Cross

*'If any one would come after me, let him deny himself
and take up his cross and follow me'* (Mark 8:34)

As commonly applied, this is not a very hard saying. As
originally intended, it is very hard indeed; no saying could be
harder.

As commonly applied, the expression is used of some bodily
disability, some unwelcome experience, some uncongenial
companion or relative that one is stuck with: 'This is the cross I
have to bear', people say. It can be used in this watered-down
way because its literal sense is remote from our experience. In a
country where capital punishment is a thing of the past it is
difficult even to paraphrase it in terms of ordinary experience.

There was a time when capital punishment was not only
carried out in Britain, but carried out publicly. The condemned
criminal was led through the streets on foot or dragged on a
cart to the place of execution, and the crowds who watched this
grim procession knew what lay at the end of the road. A person
on the way to public execution was compelled to abandon all
earthly hopes and ambitions. At that time these words of Jesus
might have been rendered thus: 'If anyone wishes to come after
me, let him be prepared to be led out to public execution,
following my example.'

In all three synoptic Gospels these words follow the account
of Peter's confession at Caesarea Philippi, Jesus's first warning
about his impending passion, Peter's expostulation and the
rebuke which it drew forth from Jesus. It is as though Jesus

said to them, 'You still confess me to be the Messiah? You still wish to follow me? If so, you should realise quite clearly where I am going, and understand that, by following me, you will be going there too.' The Son of man must suffer; were they prepared to suffer with him? The Son of man faced the prospect of violent death; were they prepared to face it too? What if that violent death proved to be death on a cross? Were they prepared for that?

The sight of a man being taken to the place of public crucifixion was not unfamiliar in the Roman world of that day. Such a man was commonly made to carry the crossbeam, the *patibulum*, of his cross as he went to his death. That is the picture which Jesus's words would conjure up in the minds of his hearers. If they were not prepared for that outcome to their discipleship, let them change their minds while there was time – but let them first weigh the options in the balances of the kingdom of God: 'for whoever would save his life will lose it; and whoever loses his life for my sake and the gospel's will save it' (Mark 8:35).

Many, perhaps most, of those who heard these words proved their truth. Not all of them were actually crucified. This, we know, was Peter's lot; the first of those present to suffer death for Jesus's sake, James the son of Zebedee, was beheaded (Acts 12:2). But this is what is meant by 'taking up the cross' – facing persecution and death for Jesus's sake.

When Luke reproduces this saying he amplifies it slightly: 'let him deny himself and take up his cross *daily*' (Luke 9:23). A later disciple of Jesus, one who was not present to hear these words in person, entered fully into their meaning and emphasises this aspect: 'I die every day', Paul writes (1 Cor. 15:31), meaning 'I am exposed to the risk of death every day, and that for Jesus's sake.' He speaks of himself and his fellow-apostles as 'always carrying in the body the dying of Jesus' and explains himself by saying that 'while we live we are always being given up to death for Jesus' sake, so that the life of Jesus may be manifested in our mortal flesh' (2 Cor. 4:10–11). In another place he refers to 'the surpassing worth of knowing Christ Jesus my Lord' for whose sake he has suffered the loss of everything, and tells how his consuming ambition is 'that I may know him and the power of his resurrection, and may share his sufferings, becoming like him in his death' (Phil. 3:8, 10). As a Roman citizen, Paul was not liable to be crucified, but he knew by experience what it meant to 'take up his cross daily' and follow Jesus.

Jesus's words about the necessity of denying oneself if one wishes to be his disciple are to be understood in the same sense. Here too is a phrase that has become unconscionably weakened in pious phraseology. Denying oneself is not a matter of giving up something, whether for Lent or for the whole of life: it is a decisive saying 'No' to oneself, to one's hopes and plans and ambitions, to one's likes and dislikes, to one's nearest and dearest (see p. 121), for the sake of Christ. It was so for the first disciples, and it is so for many disciples today. But if this is how it is to be taken – and this is how it was meant to be taken – it is a hard saying indeed.

Yet to some disciples it might be encouraging at the same time – to those actually being compelled to suffer for their Christian faith. The Gospel of Mark was probably written in the first instance for Christians in Rome who were enduring unforeseen and savage persecution under the Emperor Nero in the aftermath of the great fire of A.D. 64. For some of them this persecution involved literal crucifixion. It was reassuring for them to be reminded that their Lord himself had said that this kind of experience was only to be expected by his disciples. If they were suffering for his name's sake, this meant that they were sharers in his suffering; it meant also that they were truly his disciples and would be acknowledged as such by him in the presence of God.

Chapter
38

The Kingdom Coming with Power

'Truly, I say to you, there are some standing here who will not taste death before they see that the kingdom of God has come with power' (Mark 9:1)

To say that some who are now present will not die before a certain event takes place is the same thing as saying that the event will take place within 'this generation' (see p. 225). What, then, is the event in question – the coming of the kingdom of God, 'with power'?

The kingdom of God, the new order which Jesus came to inaugurate, had drawn near when he began his public ministry in Galilee: this was the burden of his preaching at that time (Mark 1:14–15). Its presence was manifested by his works of mercy and power, especially by his healing of the demon-possessed: 'If it is by the finger of God that I cast out demons,' he said, 'then the kingdom of God has come upon you' (Luke 11:20). But evidently it had not yet come 'with power' as it would come one day in the foreseeable future. At present it was subject to limitations, but the time would come when those limitations would be removed and it would advance unchecked (see p. 128).

What, we may ask, had Jesus in mind when he made this prediction? And can we recognise its fulfilment in any event or development recorded in the New Testament? We can; but before we try to do so, let us think of a parallel set of sayings. Jesus sometimes spoke of the kingdom of God; he sometimes spoke of the Son of man. He rarely used the two expressions together, but each implies the other. It is the Son of man who introduces the kingdom of God, the Son of man being Jesus himself. There are two sets of sayings about the Son of man in the Gospels which stand in contrast to one another. In the one set the Son of man is exposed to humiliation and suffering; in the other he is vindicated and glorified. His vindication is sometimes described pictorially as his being enthroned at the right hand of God. This expression is derived from Psalm 110:1, where the divine invitation is extended to a royal personage: 'Sit at my right hand' – the right hand of God being the position of supreme honour and power. Thus, standing before his judges, on the point of receiving the death sentence from them, Jesus assures them that 'from now on the Son of man shall be seated at the right hand of the power of God' (Luke 22:69; see p. 247).

His death marked the end of his humiliation and suffering and, with his resurrection, ushered in his vindication. As a later Christian confession put it, he 'was manifested in the flesh, vindicated in the Spirit' (1 Tim. 3:16). And this transition from the Son of man's humiliation to his vindication corresponds exactly to the transition from the kingdom of God subject to temporary limitations to the kingdom of God now present 'with power'. The same phrase 'with power' (or 'in power') is used by Paul when he speaks of Jesus as 'descended from David according to the flesh' but 'designated Son of God in power according to the Spirit of holiness by his resurrection from the dead' (Rom. 1:3–4).

With the death and exaltation of Jesus and the coming of the Spirit on the day of Pentecost following, some of those who were witnesses of his mighty works in Galilee and elsewhere saw the power of the kingdom of God manifested on a scale unmatched during his ministry. Within a few weeks, the number of his followers multiplied tenfold; his kingdom was visibly on the march.

This, at any rate, is an interpretation of his saying about the kingdom of God having come with power which makes it intelligible to us. Whether or not this interpretation coincides with his intention when he spoke in this way is a question to which it is best not to give a dogmatic answer.

The three evangelists who record the saying (in varying terms) go on immediately to describe Jesus's transfiguration, as though that event bore some relation to the saying (Matt. 17:1–8; Mark 9:2–8; Luke 9:28–36). It cannot be said that the transfiguration was the event which Jesus said would come within the lifetime of some of his hearers: one does not normally use such language to refer to something that is to take place in a week's time. But the three disciples who witnessed the transfiguration had a vision of the Son of man vindicated and glorified: they saw in graphic anticipation the fulfilment of his words about the powerful advent of the kingdom of God. Matthew, strikingly, in his report of the words speaks of the Son of man instead of the kingdom of God: 'there are some standing here who will not taste death before they see the Son of man coming in his kingdom' (Matt. 16:28). This is an interpretation of the words, but a true interpretation. And Matthew follows Mark in saying that, when the disciples had seen the vision, Jesus forbade them to speak about it to anyone 'until the Son of man should have risen from the dead' (Mark 9:9). His rising from the dead would inaugurate the reality which they had seen in vision on the mount of transfiguration, and would at the same time herald the coming of the kingdom 'with power'.

One final point: the coming of the kingdom of God is essentially the coming of God himself. In the Targum (the Aramaic rendering of the Hebrew Bible used in synagogue services) the wording at the end of Isaiah 40:9 is changed from 'Behold your God!' to 'The kingdom of your God is revealed.' The documentary evidence for this rendering is much later than the New Testament period, but it reflects rabbinical usage. When the God of Israel overruled the course of events so as to bring his people home from exile, it might be said that his sovereign power (his 'kingdom') was manifested, but what the prophet said was more direct: 'Behold your God!' In the course of events which led to Israel's return from exile, God himself was to be seen. So again, when the new deliverance was fully accomplished by the death and triumph of Jesus, the sovereign power of God was manifested – God himself came with power.

Chapter
39

For or Against

'He who is not with me is against me, and he who does not gather with me scatters' (Matt. 12:30; Luke 11:23)
   'He that is not against us is for us' (Mark 9:40; cf. Luke 9:50)

There is no formal contradiction between 'He who is not with me is against me' and 'He that is not against us is for us' (or, as Luke has it, 'he that is not against you is for you'). In a situation where no neutrality is possible, people must be either on one side or on the other, so that those who are not for are against, and those who are not against are for. But there is a difference in emphasis between the two ways of expressing this.

The former saying comes in a context where Jesus is speaking of the conflict between the kingdom of God and the forces of evil. This is a conflict in which no one should be neutral. Since Jesus is the divinely appointed agent for leading the battle against the forces of evil, those who wish to see the triumph of God's cause must follow him. If they do not, then whatever they may think themselves, they are effectively on the enemy's side. As for the added words about gathering and scattering, gathering is the work of God, while scattering is the work of Satan. God is the God of peace; Satan is the author of strife. 'The Kingdom of God is the one constructive unifying redemptive power in a distracted world; and every man has to choose whether he will take sides with it or against it.'[1]

The latter saying is related to the same subject, although it comes in the course of a narrative, as the punch-line in what is sometimes called a 'pronouncement story'. The story is told, that is to say, for the sake of the pronouncement to which it leads up. Here, then, we have such a punch-line. John, one of the two 'sons of thunder' (as Jesus called him and his brother James because of their stormy temperament), tells Jesus that he and his companions saw someone casting out demons in Jesus's name, 'and we forbade him, because he was not following us' (Mark 9:38). In other words, he was not one of the regularly recognised disciples of Jesus. But he was showing clearly which side he was on in the spiritual warfare; moreover, he was acknowledging the authority of Jesus, because it was in his name that he was casting out demons. This was a far cry from the spirit that ascribed Jesus's demon-expelling power to the aid of Beelzebul. By his words and actions he was showing himself to be on Jesus's side.

John was no doubt concerned lest his Master's name might be taken in vain, if it was invoked by a man who had not been authorised by Jesus to speak or act in his name. But Jesus did not share his well-meant concern. John has always had his successors in the Church, who feel unhappy when things are done in Jesus's name by people whose authority to do them they cannot recognise. But Jesus's reply remains sufficient to silence this attitude: 'no one who does a mighty work in my name will be able soon after to speak evil of me' (Mark 9:39).

Chapter
40

The Son of Man Has Nowhere to Lay His Head

'Foxes have holes, and the birds of the air have nests; but the Son of man has nowhere to lay his head'(Matt. 8:20; Luke 9:58)

This saying comes in the first of a series of interviews (two in Matthew, three in Luke) between Jesus and would-be disciples. It can be called a hard saying only in the sense that it warned the would-be disciple of the hardships that would be involved in following Jesus. For the man – a scribe, or expert interpreter of the law, according to Matthew – was not volunteering to become a follower of Jesus in the general sense of following his teaching; he proposed to join his company on a permanent footing: 'I will follow you wherever you go', he said. Jesus warned him that, while wild animals have places where they can rest by night (the foxes in their dens and the birds in their nests), he himself did not know from day to day as he moved around the country where he would find shelter, or even if he would find shelter, for the next night; and his companions must be prepared to share the same uncertain lot. This lack of any place which he could call his own was only one aspect of the humiliation of the Son of man – a humiliation which many of the disciples found it hard to accept.

The saying has been made harder than it really is by attempts to understand the phrase 'the Son of man' as something more (or less) than a way of referring to Jesus himself. One suggestion is that the phrase here simply means 'man' in general, and that its application to Jesus is secondary. That is to say, the saying is in origin a proverb meaning that wild animals have their natural resting-places but man is homeless. There is no evidence for the currency of such a proverb, and in any case it would not be true.

Another suggestion was made by T. W. Manson, in line with his view that 'the Son of man' in the teaching of Jesus primarily denoted God's elect community, the true believing Israel, which Jesus was constituting around himself (and which, in the crucial hour, was embodied in Jesus himself). If 'the Son of man' has this corporate sense in the present saying, then the foxes and the birds might be expected to have a comparable sense. He proposed therefore, tentatively, to understand the saying thus: 'everybody is at home in Israel's land except the true Israel. The birds of the air (the Roman overlords), the foxes (the Edomite interlopers), have made their position secure. The true Israel is disinherited by them: and if you cast your lot with me and mine you join the ranks of the dispossessed, and you must be prepared to serve God under those conditions.'[1] (The 'Edomite interlopers' were the Herods; Herod Antipas, the ruler of Galilee, is described by Jesus as 'that fox' in Luke 13:32.) But it is unlikely that the would-be disciple would have understood those allusions; it is best to take the words about the Son of man as referring to Jesus himself. 'The saying refers to the continuing hardship and loneliness involved in *following* the Son of Man'.[2]

Chapter
41

Let the Dead Bury Their Dead

'Leave the dead to bury their own dead; but as for you,
go and proclaim the kingdom of God' (Luke 9:60)

These words belong to the second in the group of three
incidents in which Jesus impresses on potential followers the
absolute priority of the claims of the kingdom of God over
everything else. Here he calls on a man to come along with him
as his disciple. The man is not unwilling, but says, 'let me first
go and bury my father'. A reasonable request, one might have
thought: burial took place very soon after death, so, if his
father had just died, he would probably be buried the same day.
The man would then be free to follow Jesus. If he was the eldest
son, it was his responsibility to see to his father's burial. It may
be, however, that he meant, 'Let me stay at home until my
father dies; when I have buried him, I shall be free of family
obligations, and then I will come and follow you.' This is not
the most natural way to take his words, although it makes
Jesus's response less peremptory. But an interpretation which
makes Jesus's demands less peremptory than they seem to be at
first blush is probably to be rejected for that very reason. His
demands *were* peremptory.

Who then are 'the dead' who are to be left to bury the dead?
One suggestion is that Jesus's Aramaic words have been
mistranslated into Greek – that he actually meant, 'Leave the
dead to the burier of the dead.' That is to say, there are people
whose professional work it is to bury the dead; they can be left

to look after this business, but there is more important work
for you to do. But this again detracts from the rigorous
peremptoriness of Jesus's words. They are best taken to mean,
'Leave the (spiritually) dead to bury the (physically) dead' –
there are people who are quite insensitive to the claims of the
kingdom of God, and they can deal with routine matters like
the burial of the dead, but those who are alive to its claims must
give them the first place. T. W. Manson thought that Jesus's
reply was a vivid way of saying, 'That business must look after
itself; you have more important work to do.'[1]

The burial even of dead strangers was regarded as a highly
meritorious work of piety in Judaism; how much more the
burial of one's own kith and kin! Attendance to the duty of
burying one's parents was held to be implied in the fifth
commandment: 'Honour your father and mother.' It took
precedence over the most solemn religious obligations. But so
important in Jesus's eyes was the business of following him and
promoting the kingdom of God that it took precedence even
over the burial of the dead.

The added words in Luke 9:60, 'but as for you, go and
proclaim the kingdom of God', are absent from the parallel in
Matthew 8:22. The proclamation that the kingdom of God had
drawn near was part of the charge which Jesus laid on his
disciples (Luke 9:2; 10:9). The direct sense of his injunction to
this man is related to the circumstances of his Galilean
ministry, but it retained its relevance after his death and
resurrection, and a situation may arise in which it proves still to
be strikingly relevant.

John McNeill, a well-known Scottish preacher of a past
generation, used to tell how he found this saying directly
relevant to him. When his father died in Scotland, towards the
end of the nineteenth century, he was in the English Midlands,
and was advertised to address an evangelistic meeting in a
certain city on the very day of his father's funeral. People
would have understood had he sent a message to say that he
was compelled to cancel his engagement. 'But I dared not send
it,' he said, 'for this same Jesus stood by me, and seemed to say,

"Now, look, I have you. You go and preach the gospel to those people. Whether would you rather bury the dead or raise the dead?" And I went to preach.'[2]

Chapter 42

Looking Back

'No one who puts his hand to the plough and looks back is fit for the kingdom of God' (Luke 9:62)

This is the third response of Jesus to a would-be disciple: Luke has brought the three together into one context. There is no parallel to this response in Matthew's record, as there is to its two predecessors.

'I will follow you, Lord,' said this man, 'but let me first say farewell to those at my home.' The words 'I will follow you, *but ...*' have served as the text for many a powerful sermon, but in the present instance the 'but' was not unreasonable and could indeed claim a venerable precedent. Over 800 years before, the prophet Elijah was divinely commanded to enlist Elisha the son of Shaphat to be his colleague and successor. As Elijah went to do so, he found Elisha ploughing with oxen. He said nothing, but threw his cloak over the young man as he passed. The young man knew immediately what the prophet's gesture meant, ran after him and said, 'Let me kiss my parents goodbye; then I will come with you.' 'Go back', said Elijah; 'what have I done to you?' But Elisha would not be put off; he knew that Elijah had called him to go with him, but did not wish to put any pressure on him; the response to his gesture must be Elisha's spontaneous choice. So Elisha went back and not only said goodbye to his father and mother, but made a sumptuous farewell feast for all who lived or worked on their family farm; he killed two oxen, cooked their flesh on a fire made with the wood of their yoke, and after he had entertained the people in this way he 'went after Elijah, and ministered to him' (1 Kgs. 19:19–21).

Elijah was a very important person, outstandingly engaged in the service of the God of Israel, but he offered no objection to Elisha's taking time to bid his family and friends farewell in a suitable manner. But the business of the kingdom of God, on which Jesus was engaged, was much more urgent than Elijah's business, and brooked no such delay. Once again it is evident that, in Jesus's reckoning, family ties must take second place to the kingdom which he proclaimed.

Jesus's reply, like the story of Elisha's call, has a reference to ploughing, but this is probably coincidental. In any agricultural society we might expect a proverbial saying about the importance of looking straight ahead when one's hand has been put to the plough: the ploughman who looks back will not drive a straight furrow. Jesus may well have adapted such a saying: the ploughman who looks back is unfit for the kingdom of God. Here the ploughman who looks back is the would-be disciple whose mind is still partly on the life he left to follow Jesus. The work of the kingdom of God requires singleness of purpose.

Sometimes a reference has been detected here to Lot's wife, whose backward look as she and her family fled from the destruction of Sodom was her undoing (Gen. 19:26). This reference is unlikely in the present context. On another occasion Jesus did say 'Remember Lot's wife' (Luke 17:32), but that was when he was warning his hearers to flee from a future destruction comparable with that which overtook Sodom.

Chapter
43

I Will Warn You Whom to Fear

'I tell you, my friends, do not fear those who kill the body, and after that have no more that they can do. But I will warn you whom to fear: fear him who, after he has killed, has power to cast into hell; yes, I tell you, fear him!' (Luke 12:4–5; cf. Matt. 10:28)

The first part of this saying presents no difficulty. Jesus faced violent death himself, and warned his disciples more than once that they might expect no less. 'Brother will deliver up brother to death,' he said, '. . . and you will be hated by all for my name's sake' (Matt. 10:21–22). In a counterpart to these words in the Fourth Gospel he tells them that 'the hour is coming when whoever kills you will think he is offering service to God' (John 16:2). But those who put them to death could do them no more harm. Stephen might be stoned to death, but his eyes were filled with the vision of the Son of man standing to welcome him as his advocate and friend at the right hand of God (Acts 7:55–60). So too Paul, on the eve of execution, could say with confidence, 'The Lord will rescue me from every evil and save me for his heavenly kingdom' (2 Tim. 4:6–18).

It is the second part of the saying that raises a question. Whereas in both Gospels 'those who kill the body' are referred to in the plural, the person who is really to be feared is mentioned in the singular: it is he 'who, after he has killed, has power to cast into hell' or, as it is put in Matthew's version, 'who can destroy both soul and body in hell' (Matt. 10:28). Who is he?

There are those who 'kill the body but cannot kill the soul', as it runs in Matthew; there are others who do serious damage to the souls of men, women and children by reducing them to obedient automata, by leading them into sin, or in other ways. Are such people more to be feared than ordinary murderers? Perhaps they are. The singular pronoun 'him' in 'fear him!' could mean 'that sort of person'. But it is more probable that Jesus meant, 'Be more afraid of the condemnation of God than of the death-sentence of human beings.' This sense is not unparalleled in Jewish literature of the period. In a document from Jewish Alexandria, the fourth book of Maccabees (which quite certainly has not influenced the present saying of Jesus or been influenced by it), seven brothers about to be martyred because of the refusal to renounce their faith encourage one another in these words: 'Let us not fear him who thinks he is killing us; for great conflict and danger to the soul is laid up in eternal torment for those who transgress the commandment of God' (4 Macc. 13:14–15). If they are put to death for their fidelity to God, they have the sure hope of eternal life; if through fear of physical death they prove unfaithful to him, certain retribution awaits them. The sense is more or less the same in Jesus's present saying. The one who has power to cast into hell is not, as some have suggested, the devil; if he is resisted, he can do no real harm to the follower of Jesus. It is God who is to be feared:

> Fear him, ye saints, and you will then
> Have nothing else to fear.

The 'hell' mentioned here is Gehenna, the place of eternal destruction after death. There are Jewish parallels for the belief, attested in Matthew's form of the saying, that soul and body alike are consumed in the fire of Gehenna.

It is noteworthy that in both Gospels, immediately after the warning that the condemnation of God is to be feared, comes the encouragement that the protecting love of God is to be trusted: the God who takes note of the fall of a single sparrow knows every hair of his children's heads (Luke 12:6–7; Matt. 10:29–31).

Chapter
44

The Elder Brother

'Now his elder son ... was angry and refused to go in'
(Luke 15:25–28)

The prodigal's elder brother deserves our sympathy. He had never given his father a moment's anxiety, but no fuss was ever made over him. Of course not; no one makes a fuss over people who are always at hand and always dependable. The tendency is rather to take them for granted, and those who are always being taken for granted become aware of the fact and do not like it.

How different it was with the younger son! His original request was reasonable: for the two sons to share the family smallholding would probably not have worked. It was better that he should get his share of the inheritance in cash, and seek his living elsewhere. His was in any case the smaller share; the elder son would get his double portion in land.

The trouble arose when the younger son squandered his money instead of investing it wisely. The day of reckoning was bound to come for him. For a Jew to be reduced to looking after a Gentile's pigs was degradation indeed; yet he would gladly have joined the pigs at the feeding-trough for a share in the carob-bean pods which they munched, so hungry was he. To go back and beg for employment as a casual labourer on his father's land was humiliating, but he could think of nothing better. Casual labourers might earn but a denarius a day (see p. 196), but that was probably more than he was getting from the pig-owner; and while they were there, they could eat as much as they wanted. So he swallowed his pride and went back.

The father might have said, 'That's all very well, young man; we have heard fine speeches before. Now you buckle to and get down to work as you have never worked before, and if we see that you really mean what you say, we may let you work your passage. But you can never make good the damage you have done to the family's good name and property.' That in itself would have been an act of grace; it might have done the young man a world of good, and his elder brother would probably not have objected. But – and this is the point of the parable – that is not how God treats sinners. He does not put them on probation first, to see how they will turn out. He welcomes them with overflowing love and generosity. And Jesus, in befriending such undesirable types as he did, was displaying the generous love of God (see p. 30).

Those who entered into theological controversy with Jesus would not have denied that God was like that. In a later rabbinical work God is represented as saying to the Israelites, 'Open to me a gateway of repentance only as wide as the eye of a needle, and I will drive chariots and horses through it.'[1] But it is not always easy to put theological theory into practice. They might magnify the grace of God, as we may do, but does it not seem prudent to put repentant sinners on probation first? Can they be admitted to the holy table, not to speak of our own tables at home, without more ado?

That is how the prodigal's elder brother felt. He had stayed at home all the time, led a blameless life, worked on the farm, carried out his father's direction. It had not occurred to him to expect much in the way of appreciation until the black sheep of the family turned up with his hard-luck story and the occasion was celebrated with an evening's feasting and jollification – the fatted calf killed, the neighbours invited in, music and dancing and no expense spared!

But life is like that. As the parables of the lost sheep and the lost coin showed, more fuss is made over the recovery of something that was lost than over the safe keeping of what has been there all the time, and where human beings are concerned, this is even more so.

There are young people who have come up through Sunday School and Bible Class, who join the church and are present week by week at all the meetings – perhaps notice is taken of them, perhaps not. But here is a rank outsider – a Borstal alumnus, maybe – who has been dragged along to a Billy Graham meeting or something of the sort and has gone forward when the appeal was made; and what a fuss is made of him! He is billed at every youth rally, invited to give his testimony at every opportunity (and it must be admitted that his testimony is rather more colourful than that of someone who has never strayed from the straight and narrow) – but if some people feel that it is all really sickening one can understand their point of view.

No blame is attached to the elder brother; he remains sole heir to all his father's property. He simply does not feel the way his father does about the prodigal's return. A human father feels that way, and the heavenly Father feels that way. 'There will be more joy in heaven over one sinner who repents than over ninety-nine righteous persons who need no repentance' (Luke 15:7). No blame attaches to the ninety-nine; of course not. But they were never lost; that is what makes the difference.

Chapter
45

Why Do You Call Me Good?

'Why do you call me good? No one is good but God alone' (Mark 10:18; Luke 18:19)

This is not a very hard saying. Schmiedel, however, included it in his list of pillar texts, arguing (quite cogently) that it is most likely to come from Jesus himself, since no one else was likely to put into his mouth words which seemed to cast doubt on his goodness. A would-be disciple (a rich man, as the sequel shows, but that is irrelevant at this point) ran up to Jesus once and said, 'Good Teacher, what must I do to inherit eternal life?' Before answering his question, Jesus took him up on his use of the epithet 'good'. A word which in its proper sense belonged to God alone should not be used lightly as a mere expression of courtesy, and Jesus suspected that it was simply as a polite form of address that the man used it. He himself did not refuse to describe people as good when he really meant 'good'. If it be asked how such language squares with his assertion here that 'No one is good but God alone', the answer is plain: no one is altogether good, as God is, but men and women are good in so far as they reflect the goodness of God.

It appears, indeed, that the form in which Mark (followed by Luke) preserves these words of Jesus was felt to present a difficulty at quite an early stage in the formation of the Gospels. In the parallel passage in Matthew 19:16–17 the weight of the textual evidence favours the recasting of the man's question as 'Teacher, what good deed must I do, to have eternal life?' – to which Jesus replies, 'Why do you ask me about what is good? One there is who is good.' This recasting of the question and answer, however, was not perpetuated. Whereas normally, in the process of transmitting the Gospel text, the tendency is for the wording of the other evangelists to be conformed to that of Matthew, here the Matthaean wording has been conformed to that of Mark and Luke in the majority of later manuscripts, followed by the AV: '"Good Master, what good thing shall I do, that I may have eternal life?" ... "Why callest thou me good? there is none good but one, that is, God."' If the saying had been felt to be insuperably hard, the Matthaean form would have prevailed throughout the synoptic record of the incident.

Chapter
46

Sell What You Have

'You lack one thing; go, sell what you have, and give to the poor, and you will have treasure in heaven; and come, follow me' (Mark 10:21)

The man to whom these words were spoken certainly found them hard. He was the rich man who came to Jesus and asked what he should do to inherit eternal life. Jesus said, 'Well, you know the commandments', and mentioned those which sum up one's duty to a neighbour. That keeping the commandments was the way to life is stated in the law itself: 'You shall therefore keep my statutes and my ordinances, by doing which a man shall live: I am the Lord' (Lev. 18:5). The man answered that he had kept all these from early days – presumably ever since the age of thirteen, when he became *bar mitzvah*, personally responsible to keep the commandments.

But he plainly expected Jesus to say something more: he did not come to him just to learn that keeping the commandments was the way to life. And the something more that he waited for came quickly: 'There is one thing you haven't done', Jesus said, 'and you can do it now: sell your property, give the poor the money you get for it, and come and join my disciples. You will get rid of the burden of material goods, and you will be laying up treasure in heaven.' But the man, an honest and attractive character evidently, found this counsel too hard to accept. It is sometimes called a counsel of perfection, from the way in which another evangelist phrases it: 'If you would be perfect, go, sell what you possess and give to the poor' (Matt. 19:21).

But this does not mean that keeping the commandments is the duty of all, whereas giving all their goods to feed the poor is the privilege of those who would attain a higher level of devotion. Paul reminds us that even giving all our goods to feed the poor is worthless without love in the heart (1 Cor. 13:3). Matthew's wording might be rendered: 'If you want to go the whole way in fulfilling the will of God, this is what you must do.'

For those who wish to treat the teaching of Jesus seriously and make it, as far as possible, their rule of life, this is still a hard saying. It is easy to say, 'This is how he tested one man's devotion, but he did not ask all his hearers to give away their property in the same way.' It is true that those who joined his company and went around with him as his disciples appear to have left all to follow him. But what of those friends by whose generosity they were maintained – those well-to-do women who, as Luke tells us, 'provided for them out of their means' (Luke 8:3)? They were not asked to make the sacrifice that our rich man was asked to make; it might be said, of course, that they were doing something of the same kind by supplying Jesus and the twelve out of their resources. When Jesus invited himself to a meal in the house of the chief tax-collector of Jericho, no pressure apparently was put on Zacchaeus to make his spontaneous announcement: 'Behold, Lord, the half of my goods I give to the poor' (Luke 19:8). It is usually inferred that this was to be his practice from that time on; it is just possible, however, that he meant that this was what he regularly did. Either way, Jesus recognised him as a 'son of Abraham' in the true sense, a man of faith. But he did not tell him to get rid of the other half of his goods as well, nor did he suggest that he should quit his tax-collecting and join his company, as another tax-collector had done in Capernaum at an earlier date.

Even so, Jesus's advice to the rich man is by no means isolated; it is a regular feature of his teaching. The same note is struck in words appearing without a narrative context in Luke 12:33–34: 'Sell your possessions, and give alms; provide yourselves with purses that do not grow old, with a treasure in the heavens that does not fail, where no thief approaches and no moth destroys. For where your treasure is, there will your heart be also.' Matthew includes the same message in his version of the Sermon on the Mount (Matt. 6:19-21), in a rhythmical form which may have been designed for easy memorising:

> Do not lay up for yourselves treasures on earth,
>   where moth and rust consume,
>   and where thieves break in and steal;
> but lay up for yourselves treasures in heaven,
>   where neither moth nor rust consumes,
>   and where thieves do not break in and steal.
>   For where your treasure is,
>   there will your heart be also.

(If an attempt is made to turn these words from the Greek in which the evangelist has preserved them back into the Aramaic in which they were spoken, they display not only poetical rhythm but even rhyme.)

This teaching was not given to one special individual; it was intended for Jesus's followers in general. He urged them to have the right priorities, to seek God's kingdom and righteousness above all else (Matt. 6:33). But it is very difficult to do this, he maintained, if one's attention is preoccupied by material wealth. Experience shows that some wealthy men and women have promoted the kingdom of God above their worldly concerns – that they have, indeed, used their worldly concerns for the promotion of his kingdom. But experience also shows that their number is very small. There is something about concentration on material gain which not only encroaches on the time and energy that might otherwise be devoted to the interests of the kingdom of God; it makes one less concerned about those interests, less disposed to pay attention to them. Naturally so: Jesus was stating a law of life when he said that where one's treasure is, there the heart will be also. He would clearly have liked to enrol the rich man among his disciples, and up to a point the rich man was not unwilling to become one of them. But the sticking point came when he was asked to unburden himself of his property.

Fulness to such a burden is
That go on pilgrimage.[1]

But he decided that he would sooner go on bearing his burden than become a pilgrim. Jesus's words to him were not intended for him alone; they remain as a challenge, a challenge not to be evaded, for all who wish to be his disciples.

Chapter
47

Give for Alms What Is Within

'But give for alms those things which are within; and behold, everything is clean for you' (Luke 11:41)

This is a hard saying in the sense that it is not easily understood. Other sayings about giving alms are hard in the sense that, while their meaning is all too plain, it goes against the grain to put them into action. 'Sell your possessions, and give alms' (Luke 12:33) is one of these; not even the assurance that this is a way of laying up treasure in heaven makes it altogether easy to comply with it. But what are the 'things which are within' that are to be given for alms?

This saying comes in a context where Jesus rebukes some religious people for insisting on the external forms of religious practice while overlooking the inward and essential realities. No amount of ritual washing of the hands or other parts of the body will be of any avail if the heart is not pure. Only a foolish person would be careful to wash the outside of a cup or dish after use and pay no attention to the inside; the inside generally requires more careful washing than the outside. It is even more foolish to pay meticulous heed to external observances when inwardly one is 'full of extortion and wickedness'. What, then, is the point of the immediately following exhortation, 'But give the things inside for alms'? How will that make 'everything . . . clean for you'?

If one looks at the Greek text, the first clause of Luke 11:41 could be translated differently: 'But give for alms those things that are within your control (or at your disposal)'. Could this go well with the next clause: 'and behold, everything is clean for you'? It might: this would not be the only text in the Bible to imply that almsgiving is a means of ethical purification. Daniel, impressing on King Nebuchadnezzar the urgent necessity of mending his ways, advised him: 'break off your sins by practising righteousness [which may well mean almsgiving], and your iniquities by showing mercy to the oppressed' (Dan. 4:27).

But could the rendering 'give for alms those things that are within your control' go well with what precedes? It might be argued that, since Jesus had just mentioned extortion as one of the things which pollute a person's inner life, almsgiving, which is the opposite of extortion, would have a cleansing instead of a polluting effect. Even so, the flow of thought is not smooth.

Luke's form of the saying, however, cannot be considered in isolation from the parallel text in Matthew 23:26. There too the words come in the course of criticism of those Pharisees who, as Jesus says, 'cleanse the outside of the cup and of the plate, but inside . . . are full of extortion and rapacity'. Then comes his direction: 'first cleanse the inside of the cup and of the plate, that the outside also may be clean'. First things first, in other words. But the difficulty raised by Luke's form of the saying has disappeared: 'first cleanse the inside' is much more intelligible than 'give what is inside for alms'.

Has Matthew eased a difficult construction which Luke left unchanged, as he found it? That is possible. But another possibility is pointed out by some scholars. Whereas Matthew and Luke seem at times to use the same Greek translation of the Q sayings, there are other times when they use different translations of one Aramaic original. Here 'cleanse' and 'give alms' could be translations of two quite similar Aramaic verbs; they could even be alternative translations of one and the same Aramaic verb, in two different senses. This could be the explanation of the difference between the versions of Matthew and Luke, but since the original Aramaic wording of the saying has not survived, the explanation must remain speculative.

Chapter 48

The Camel and the Eye of a Needle

*'It is easier for a camel to go through the eye of a needle
than for a rich man to enter the kingdom of God'*
(Mark 10:25)

This saying is paralleled in Matthew 19:24 and Luke 18:25. In
all three synoptic Gospels it follows the incident of the rich man
who was anxious to know how to inherit eternal life – and, in
the idiom of the Gospels, inheriting eternal life is synonymous
with entering the kingdom of God. His record in keeping the
commandments was unimpeachable – he assured Jesus that he
had kept them all ever since he came to years of discretion, and
Jesus said nothing to suggest that his claim was exaggerated.
But, to test the strength of his commitment, Jesus bade him sell
his property and distribute the proceeds among the poor.
'Then', he said, 'you will have treasure in heaven; and come,
follow me.' At that the rich man's face fell: this sacrifice was
more than he was prepared to make. The incident brings out
the radical nature of the discipleship to which Jesus called
people.

Then, to illustrate 'how hard it is for those who have riches to
enter the kingdom of God' he used this striking figure of
speech. His hearers recognised it immediately to be a hard
saying. It is not merely difficult, it is impossible for a rich man
to get into the kingdom of God, just as it is not merely difficult
but impossible for a camel to pass through the eye of a needle –
even a needle of the largest size. The listeners were dismayed:
'Then who can be saved?' they asked. (Being saved in the

Gospels is a further synonym for entering the kingdom of God and inheriting eternal life.) The disciples themselves were not affluent: Peter spoke for the others when he said, 'we have left everything and followed you' (Mark 10:28). But they had not realised, perhaps, just how stringent the terms of entry into the kingdom were – and are.

Not only those who heard the words when they were first spoken, but many others since, have found the saying to be a hard one. Attempts have been made to soften it somewhat. The eye of a needle, we are sometimes assured, is a metaphor: the reference is to a small opening giving independent access or egress through a much larger city gate. Visitors are sometimes shown such a small entrance in one of the city gates of Jerusalem or another Eastern city and are told that this is what Jesus had in mind. If a man approaches the city gate on camel-back when it is closed, he can dismount and get through the small entrance on foot, but there is no way for a camel to do so, especially if it is loaded: it must wait for the main gate to be opened to let it through. Even if a small camel, unloaded, tried to get through the small entrance, it would be in danger of sticking half-way. It is ordinarily impossible for a camel to get through such a narrow opening, but not so ludicrously impossible as for anyone to try to get it through the eye of a needle. But this charming explanation is of relatively recent date: there is no evidence that such a subsidiary entrance was called the eye of a needle in biblical times.

Others point out that there is a Greek word (*kamilos*) meaning 'cable' very similar in appearance and sound to the word (*kamēlos*) meaning 'camel'. In fact the word meaning 'cable' appears in a few late witnesses to the gospel text. Their reading is reflected in a version of the English New Testament entitled *The Book of Books*, issued in 1938 to mark the quatercentenary of Henry VIII's injunction requiring a copy of the English Bible to be placed in every parish church in England: 'It is easier for a rope to go through the eye of a needle than for a rich man to enter the kingdom of God'. The editors of *The Book of Books* did not commit themselves to the view that the word meaning 'rope' or 'cable' stood in the original text: they simply remarked that while the familiar form with 'camel' would 'doubtless be preferred by Eastern readers', their own chosen reading 'makes a more vivid appeal to the West'. This is doubtful. In any case, the substitution of 'cable' or 'rope' for 'camel' should probably be recognised as 'an attempt to soften the rigour of the statement'.[1] 'To contrast the largest beast of burden known in Palestine with the smallest of artificial apertures is quite in the manner of Christ's proverbial sayings.'[2] In Jewish rabbinical literature an *elephant* passing through the eye of a needle is a figure of speech for sheer impossibility.[3]

No doubt Jesus was using the language of hyperbole, as when he spoke of the man with a whole plank sticking out of his eye offering to remove the splinter or speck of sawdust from his neighbour's eye (Matt. 7:3–5; Luke 6:41–42). But the language of hyperbole was intended to drive the lesson home: it is impossible for a rich man to enter the kingdom of God – humanly impossible, Jesus concedes, for God, with whom nothing is impossible, can even save a rich man. But if so, then the rich man's heart must be changed, by having its attachment to material riches replaced by attachment to the true riches, 'treasure in heaven'.

It is not easy for anyone to enter the kingdom of God – 'the gate is narrow and the way is hard' (Matt. 7:14) – but it is most difficult of all for the rich. Jesus's absolute statement in Mark 10:24, 'how hard it is to enter the kingdom of God!' has been expanded in later witnesses to the text so as to read: 'how hard it is *for those who trust in riches* to enter the kingdom of God!' This could be another attempt to soften the hardness of his words, making it possible for a reader to comfort himself with the thought: 'I have riches, indeed, but I do not trust in them: I am all right.' But, according to Jesus's teaching, it was very difficult for people who had riches not to trust in them. They would show whether they trusted in riches or not by their readiness to part with them. But the inserted words, 'for those who trust in riches', are not so wide of the mark. What was it about riches that made Jesus regard them as an obstacle to entrance into the kingdom? Simply the fact that those who had them relied on them, like the rich farmer in the parable (Luke

12:16–21; see p. 185), who encouraged himself with the thought of the great wealth which he had stored up for a long time to come, or his counterpart today whose investments are bringing in a comfortable, inflation-proof income.

There is probably no saying of Jesus which is 'harder' in the Western mind today than the saying about the camel and the needle's eye, none which carries with it such a strong temptation to tone it down.

Chapter
49

Serving God and Mammon

'You cannot serve God and mammon' (Matt. 6:24;
Luke 16:13)

'Mammon' is a term that Jesus sometimes used to denote
wealth. He was not the only teacher in Israel to use it, and
whenever it is used it seems to indicate some unworthy aspect
of wealth – not so much, perhaps, the unworthiness of wealth
itself as the unworthiness of many people's attitudes to it. The
derivation of the word is uncertain. Some think that it
originally meant that in which men and women put their trust;
others, that it originally meant 'accumulation', 'piling up'. But
the derivation is not very important; it is the use of a word, not
its derivation, that determines its meaning.

Since the service of mammon is presented in this saying as an
alternative to the service of God, mammon seems to be a rival
to God. Service of mammon and service of God are mutually
exclusive. The servant of mammon, in other words, is an idol-
worshipper: mammon, wealth, money has become his idol, the
object of his worship.

The man who depended on finding enough work today to
buy the next day's food for his family could pray with feeling,
'Give us this day our daily bread' (Matt. 6:11) or, as Moffat
rendered it, 'give us to-day our bread for the morrow'. But the
man who knew he had enough laid by to maintain his family
and himself, whether he worked or not, whether he kept well or
fell ill, would not put the same urgency into the prayer. The
more material resources he had, the less whole-hearted his

reliance on God would tend to become. The children of the kingdom, in Jesus's teaching, are marked by their instant and constant trust in God; that trust will be weakened if they have something else to trust in.

In the Western world today we are cushioned, by social security and the like, against the uncertainties and hardships of life in a way that was not contemplated in New Testament times. It was in a society that did not provide widows' pensions that the words of 1 Tim. 5:5 were written: 'She who is a real widow, and is left all alone, has set her hope on God and continues in supplications and prayers night and day.' This is not a criticism of social security (for which God be thanked); it is a reminder of the difficulty we find in applying the sayings of Jesus and his apostles to our own condition. But when we view the starving Karamajong in Uganda, or the uprooted Boat People of Vietnam, we can try to imagine what it must be like to be in their situation, and consider what claim they have on our resources. This will not get us into the kingdom of God, but at least it may teach us to use material property more worthily than by treating it as something to lay our hearts on or rest our confidence in.

A covetous person, says Paul, is an idolater (Eph. 5:5), and in saying so he expressed the same idea as Jesus did when he spoke about mammon. 'Take heed, and beware of all covetousness,' said Jesus on another occasion, 'for a man's life does not consist in the abundance of his possessions' (Luke 12:15). That should teach us not to say 'How much is So-and-so worth?' when we really mean 'How much does he possess?' Luke follows this last saying with the parable of the rich fool, the man who had so much property that he reckoned he could take life easy for a long time to come. He went to bed with this comforting thought, but by morning he was a pauper – he was dead, and had to leave his property behind. He had treated it as mammon, the object of his ultimate concern, and in his hour of greatest need it proved useless to him. If he had put his trust in God and accumulated the true and lasting riches, he would not have found himself destitute after death.

Chapter 50

Using Unrighteous Mammon to Make Friends

'And I tell you, make friends for yourselves by means of unrighteousness mammon, so that when it fails they may receive you into the eternal habitations' (Luke 16:9)

This is the 'moral' of the parable of the dishonest steward, a story which presents problems of its own. The steward looked after his master's estate, dealt with the other employees and tenants, and in general should have relieved his master of all concern about the day-to-day running of his affairs. But he mismanaged the estate, and not simply (it appears) through incompetence or negligence, until the time came when his master discovered that his affairs were in bad shape and ordered the steward to turn in his books, since his employment was terminated.

Before he turned in his books, the steward took some hasty measures with an eye to his future interests. In particular, he summoned his master's debtors and reduced their debts substantially, altering the entries accordingly. Perhaps we are to understand that he made good the difference out of his own pocket: if he did, his money was well invested. He wanted to be sure of bed and board when he was dismissed from his employment with no severance benefit. No one would take him on as steward (his master was not likely to give him the kind of testimonial that would encourage any other landowner to employ him); the alternatives were casual labour (digging, for example) or begging. He did not feel strong enough for the former, and to be a beggar would be insufferably disgraceful. But if he made some friends now by a judicious expenditure of his means, they might give him shelter when he was evicted from his tied cottage.

His master got to know of his action and called him a clever rascal. No more than this need be understood of Jesus's remark that 'The master commended the dishonest steward for his prudence' (Luke 16:8). The master may well have recognised some analogy between the steward's conduct and the methods by which his own wealth had been amassed. 'You see,' said Jesus, 'worldly people, with no thoughts beyond this present life, will sometimes behave more sensibly and providently than other-worldly people, "the children of light". *They* will use material wealth to prepare for their earthly future; why cannot the children of light use it to prepare for their eternal future? Use the "unrighteous mammon" to win yourselves friends in the world to come.' It is called 'unrighteous mammon' because it is too often acquired unjustly and used for unjust ends. It is ethically neutral in itself; it is people's attitudes to it and ways of dealing with it that are reprehensible. As has often been pointed out, it is not money as such but 'the love of money' which scripture affirms to be 'the root of all evils' (1 Tim. 6:10).

But how can material wealth be used to procure friends who will receive one 'into the eternal habitations' when it is no longer accessible? This parable is followed by a collection of isolated sayings several of which are concerned with the subject of wealth, and then comes another story – the story of the rich man and Lazarus. In it we meet a man who had plenty of the 'unrighteous mammon' and used it all to secure comfort and good cheer for himself in this life, giving no thought to the life to come. The time came when he would have been very glad to have even one friend to welcome him into the 'eternal habitations', but he found none. Yet he had every opportunity of securing such a friend. There at his gate lay Lazarus, destitute and covered with sores, only too glad to catch and eat the pieces of bread which the rich man and his guests used to wipe their fingers at table and then threw to the dogs outside. If the rich man had used a little of his wealth to help Lazarus, he would have had a friend to speak up for him on the other side. 'This man', Lazarus might have said to Abraham, 'showed me the kindness of God on earth.' But Lazarus had been given no ground to say any such thing. The rich man in Hades found himself without a friend when he needed one most – and he had no one to blame but himself.

Chapter
51

The Great Gulf

'Between us and you a great chasm has been fixed, in order that those who would pass from here to you may not be able, and none may cross from there to us' (Luke 16:26)

These words are part of Abraham's reply to the rich man, explaining why Lazarus could not go and cool his tongue with a drop of water and so relieve his anguish.

In view of what has been said about the rich man's failure to make friends by means of his wealth, there may be a problem here. Even if he had used some of his wealth to help Lazarus on earth, and Lazarus had therefore been willing to do something for him in the afterworld, how could Lazarus have crossed the great gulf or chasm that lay between them? But the chasm is not a geographical one, whose width and depth could be measured. When the story is read nowadays in the AV, a wrong impression may be given by the statement that, when the rich man died and was buried, 'in hell he lift up his eyes, being in torments' (Luke 16:23). As our more recent versions indicate, 'hell' means Hades, the undifferentiated abode of the dead. It was not because he was in Hades that the rich man was in pain, but because of his past life. Had he made a friend of Lazarus by helping him in his wretchedness, there would not have been the impassable gulf which prevented Lazarus from coming to help him. The impassable gulf, in fact, was of the rich man's own creating. This may mean more or less what C. S. Lewis expressed by a different metaphor when he suggested that 'the doors of hell' (and he meant the abode of the damned, not just the abode of the dead) 'are locked on the *inside*'.[1]

The story of the rich man and Lazarus appears to have a literary and oral prehistory, and it is interesting to explore this. But such exploration will not help us much to understand it in the context which Luke has given it (and Luke is the only evangelist to record it).

The rich man, hearing that it is impossible for Lazarus to come and help him, turns his mind to something else. Let Lazarus be sent back to earth to warn the rich man's five brothers to mend their ways, lest they find themselves after death sharing his own sad lot. Perhaps there is the implication here: 'If only someone had come back to warn me, I should not have found myself in this plight.' But Abraham replies that they have all the warning they need: 'They have Moses and the prophets', that is, the Bible. If the rich man himself had paid heed to what Moses and the prophets say about the blessedness of those who consider the poor – a theme so pervasive that it cannot well be overlooked – it would have been better for him.

But Moses and the prophets are not enough, argued the rich man. Let them have an exceptional sign that will compel their repentance. Abraham's response has special relevance to what was happening in the course of Jesus's ministry. People asked him to validate his claim that the kingdom of God had approached them in his ministry by showing them a sign from heaven – something spectacular that would compel them to acknowledge his authority to speak and act as he did. He refused to grant their request: if his works and words were not self-authenticating, then no external sign, however impressive, could be any more persuasive (see p. 96). Moses and the prophets, pleads the rich man, are not persuasive enough, 'but if some one goes to them from the dead, they will repent'. But Abraham has the last word: 'If they do not hear Moses and the prophets, neither will they be convinced if some one should rise from the dead' (Luke 16:31). Or, as James Denney paraphrased it, 'If they can be inhuman with the Bible in their hands and Lazarus at their gate, no revelation of the splendours of heaven or the anguish of hell will ever make them anything else.'[2]

Is it a pure coincidence that another of the evangelists tells of a Lazarus who did come back from the dead? His restoration to life was certainly a very impressive sign, which strengthened the faith of those who already believed in Jesus, or were disposed to believe in him, but according to John it strengthened the determination of those who were convinced that the safety of the nation demanded Jesus's death – indeed, they 'planned to put Lazarus also to death, because on account of him many of the Jews were going away and believing in Jesus' (John 12:10–11).

But by the time Luke wrote his Gospel a greater than Lazarus had risen from the dead. The proclamation that Christ had been raised 'in accordance with the scriptures' (1 Cor. 15:4) led many to believe in him, but it did not compel belief; even his resurrection did not convince those who had made up their minds not to believe.

Chapter
52

Will the Son of Man Find Faith on Earth?

*'Nevertheless, when the Son of man comes, will he find
faith on earth?'* (Luke 18:8).

This is a hard saying in the sense that no one can be quite sure
what it means, especially in relation to its context. When a
question is asked in Greek, it is often possible to determine,
from the presence of one particle or another, whether the
answer expected is 'Yes' or 'No'. But no such help is given with
this one. Many commentators assume that the answer implied
here is 'No', but in form at least it is a completely open
question.

Luke is the only evangelist who records the question, and he
places it at the end of the parable of the persistent widow – the
widow who refused to take 'No' for an answer. Jesus told this
parable, says Luke, to teach his disciples that 'they ought
always to pray and not lose heart' (Luke 18:1). But what has
this purpose to do with the Son of man's finding faith on earth
when he comes?

The widow in the parable showed faith of an unusually
persevering quality – not personal faith in the unjust judge
whom she pestered until he granted her petition to keep her
quiet, but faith in the efficacy of persistent 'prayer'. The point
of the story seems to be this: if even a conscienceless judge, who
'neither fears God nor regards man', sees to it that a widow gets

her rights, not for the sake of seeing justice done but to get rest from her importunity, how much more will God, who is no unjust judge but a loving Father, listen to his children's plea for vindication! It is vindication that they seek, just as the widow insisted on getting her rights, of which someone was trying to deprive her.

Then comes the question: 'when the Son of man comes, will he find faith on earth?' It is possible indeed that it is Luke who attaches the question to the parable, and that in Jesus's teaching it had some other context which is no longer recoverable. T. W. Manson leant to the view that 'the Son of man' does not bear its special meaning here – that the sense is: 'Men and women ought to have implicit faith that God will vindicate his elect people, that righteousness will triumph over evil. But when one comes and looks for such faith – when, for example, I come and look for it – is it anywhere to be found?' The answer implied by this interpretation is 'No' – people in general, it is suggested, do not really expect God to vindicate his chosen ones, nor do they at heart desire the triumph of righteousness over evil.[1]

But perhaps we should look at a wider context than this on. parable. The coming of the Son of man is a major theme in the preceding section of Luke's record, in the discourse of Jesus about 'the day when the Son of man is revealed' (Luke 17:22–37). The lesson impressed by this discourse on the hearers is that they must keep on the alert and be ready for that day when it comes. When it comes, God will vindicate his righteous cause, and therewith the cause of his people who trust in him. But they must trust him and not lose heart; they must here and now continue faithfully in the work assigned to them. (This is the lesson also of the parable of the pounds in Luke 19:11–27.) The Son of man, whose revelation will be like the lightning, illuminating 'the sky from one side to the other' (Luke 17:24), will be able to survey the earth to see if there is any faith on it, any 'faithful and wise steward' whom his master when he comes will find loyally fulfilling his service (Luke 12:42–44).

So the question 'will he find faith on earth?' remains an open one in fact as it is in form: its answer depends on the faithful obedience of those who wait to render an account of their stewardship when he calls for it.

Chapter
53

The Rate for the Job?

'Take what belongs to you, and go; I choose to give to this last as I give to you. Am I not allowed to do what I choose with what belongs to me? Or do you begrudge me my generosity?' (Matt. 20:14–15).

One of the complaints that right-living and religious people made about Jesus arose from his treatment of the more disreputable members of society. They might have agreed that such persons should not be entirely excluded from the mercy of the all-loving God. Even for them there was hope, if they showed that they were not beyond redemption by practical repentance and unquestionable amendment of life. But not until such evidence had been given could they begin to be accepted as friends and neighbours.

Jesus, however, accepted them immediately; he did not wait to see the outcome before he committed himself to them. This was disturbing; it was even more disturbing that he seemed to think more highly of them than of those who had never blotted their public copy-book. He gave the impression that he actually preferred the company of the rejects of society: he not only made them feel at home in his company, so that they felt free to take liberties with him that they would never have thought of taking with an ordinary rabbi, but he even accepted invitations to share a meal with them and appeared genuinely to enjoy such an occasion. When he was challenged for this unconventional behaviour, his reply was that this was how

God treated sinners; and he told several parables to reinforce this lesson.

One of these parables tells of the man who hired a number of casual labourers to gather the grapes in his vineyard when the appropriate time of year came round. It is a disconcerting parable on more levels than one. A highly respected trade union leader of our day is said to feel very unhappy when he is asked to read this parable as a scripture lesson in church, because it seems to defend the unacceptable principle of equal pay for unequal work.

There are certain seasons when a farmer or a vine-grower requires a large supply of labour for a short period. Until recently the autumn mid-term school holiday was known in Scotland as the 'potato-lifting' holiday, because it fell at the right time to release an ample supply of cheap juvenile assistance for gathering the potatoes from the fields. In the economic depression from which most of Palestine suffered in the time of Jesus anyone who wanted a short-term supply of labour for this kind of purpose was sure of finding it. The vine-grower in the parable had only to go to the market-place of the village and there he would find a number of unemployed men hanging around in hope that someone would come and offer them a job.

At daybreak, then, this vine-grower went to the market-place and hired several men to do a day's work for him gathering grapes. The agreed rate for such a day's work was a denarius, which was evidently sufficient to keep a labourer and his family at subsistence level for a day. Apparently the vine-grower wanted the job completed within one day. As he considered the amount of work to be done and the speed at which the men were working, he decided that he would need more hands, so at three-hourly intervals he went and hired more. He did not bargain with them for a denarius or part of a denarius: he promised to give them what was proper. Then, just an hour before sunset, in order to ensure that the work would not be left unfinished, he went back and found a few men still unemployed, so he sent them to join the others working in the vineyard.

An hour later the work was finished, and the workers queued up to receive their pay, the last-hired being at the head of the queue. They had no idea what they would get for an hour's work; in fact, each of them received a denarius. So did the men who had worked three hours, six hours and nine hours. At last came those who had been hired at daybreak and had done twelve hours' work: what would they get? Each of them similarly got a denarius. They complained, 'Why should these others get as much as we have done? Why should not we get more after a hard day's work?' But the vine-grower told them that they had no cause for complaint. They had agreed to do a day's work for a denarius, and he had kept his promise to give them that. It was no business of theirs what he gave to others who had entered into no agreement with him for a fixed sum. He might have said, 'They and their families have to live.' But he did not: he simply said, 'Can't I do what I like with my own money?'

The law-abiding people whom Jesus knew tended to feel that they had made a bargain with God: if they kept his commandments, he would give them the blessings promised to those who did so. They would have no reason to complain if God treated them fairly and kept his promises. But what about those others who had broken his commandments, who had started to do his will late in the day after their encounter with Jesus and the way of the kingdom? They were in no position to strike a bargain with God: they could do nothing but cast themselves on his grace, like the tax-collector in another parable who could only say, 'God have mercy on me, sinner that I am!' (Luke 18:13). What could they expect? The lesson of the parable seems to be this: when people make a bargain with God, he will honour his promise and give them no cause for complaint; but there is no limit to what his grace will do for those who have no claim at all on him but trust entirely to his goodness. If it be said that this gives them an unfair advantage, let it be considered that they were terribly disadvantaged to begin with. If it be urged that their rehabilitation should involve some payment for their past misdeeds, the truth may be that they have paid enough already. Should those who have turned to God at the eleventh hour and given him only the last twelfth of life get as much of heaven as those who have given him a whole lifetime? If God is pleased to give them as much, who will tell him that he should not? If God did not delight in mercy, it would go hard with the best of us:

> Though justice by thy plea, consider this,
> That, in the course of justice, none of us
> Should see salvation.[1]

The first arrivals might not have complained if the last comers had been paid only a small fraction of what they themselves received. There was in fact, as T. W. Manson points out in his treatment of this parable, a coin worth one-twelfth of a denarius: 'It was called a *pondion*. But there is no such thing as a twelfth part of the love of God.'[2]

Chapter 54

The First Will Be Last

'But many that are first will be last, and the last first'
(Mark 10:31; Matt. 19:30; cf. Luke 13:30; Matt. 20:16).

The saying about the first being last and the last first is not peculiar to the teaching of Jesus; it is a piece of general folk wisdom, which finds memorable expression in Aesop's fable of the hare and the tortoise. But in the Gospels it is applied to the living situation during Jesus's ministry.

The saying occurs in two contexts in the Gospels. The first context (in Mark 10:31 and the parallel in Matthew 19:30) is the sequel to the incident of the rich man who could not bring himself to sell his property and give the proceeds to the poor. Jesus commented on the difficulty experienced by any rich man who tried to get into the kingdom of God, and Peter spoke up: 'Well, we at least are not rich; we have given up everything to be your followers' (see pp. 180–3). To this Jesus replied that, even in this age, those who had given up anything for him would receive more than ample compensation, over and above the persecutions which would inevitably fall to the lot of his followers, while in the age to come they would receive eternal life. Then he added, 'But many that are first will be last, and the last first.'

What is the point of the saying in this context? It seems to be directed to the disciples, and perhaps the point is that those who have given up most to follow Jesus must not suppose that the chief place in the kingdom of God is thereby guaranteed to them. It is possible to take pride in one's self-denial and suppose that by its means one has established a special claim on God. 'No amount of exertion, not even self-denial or asceticism, can make one a disciple. Discipleship is purely a gift of God.'¹ Even those who have made great sacrifices for God are not justified in his sight for that reason; and even Peter and his companions, who gave up all to follow Jesus, may get a surprise on the day of review and reward by seeing others receiving preference over them.

In Luke 13:30 the words (but in the reverse order: 'some are last who will be first, and some are first who will be last') are added to Jesus's affirmation that 'men will come from east and west, and from north and south, and sit at table in the kingdom of God' (in Matthew 8:11 this affirmation is attached to the incident of the centurion's servant). Those who come from the four points of the compass are plainly Gentiles, whereas some of Jesus's Jewish hearers, who looked forward confidently to a place in the kingdom, along with 'Abraham and Isaac and Jacob and all the prophets', would find themselves shut out. The free offer of the gospel might be extended 'to the Jew first' (Rom. 1:16), but if those to whom it was first extended paid no heed to it, then the Gentiles, late starters though they were, would receive its blessings first (see p. 105).

In Matthew 20:16 the parable of the labourers in the vineyard (see p. 196) is rounded off with these words: 'So the last will be first, and the first last.' In the parable the last-hired workmen received the same wage at the end of the day as those who were hired at dawn. It might be said indeed that in that situation there was neither first nor last: all were treated equally. But the words had a wider fulfilment in Jesus's ministry. Those who were far ahead in understanding and practice of the law found themselves falling behind those whom they despised in receiving the good things of the kingdom of God. The son who said 'I will' to his father's command but did nothing about it naturally yielded precedence to the son who, having first said 'I will not', later repented and did it. Similarly, said Jesus to the chief priests and elders in Jerusalem, 'the tax collectors and the harlots go into the kingdom of God before you' (Matt. 21:28–32). This was a hard saying to those who heard it, who must indeed have regarded it as an insult – as many of their present-day counterparts equally would. But the work of Jesus brings about many reversals, and the day of judgment will be full of surprises.

Chapter 55

Many Are Called, but Few Are Chosen

'For many are called, but few are chosen' (Matt. 22:14).

In the original text of the Gospels, these words appear once – as a comment on Matthew's parable of the marriage feast. In the course of transmission of the text it came to be attached to the parable of the labourers in the vineyard also (Matt. 20:16), where it appears, for example, in the AV, but it is not really relevant there.

In form this seems to be a proverbial saying; other sayings with the same construction are found elsewhere in ancient literature. Plato quotes one with reference to the mystery religions: 'many are the wand-bearers, but few are the initiates'[1]; that is to say, there are many who walk in the procession to the cult-centre carrying sacred wands, but only a few are admitted to the knowledge of the innermost secret (which confers the prize of immortality). Two sayings with this construction are ascribed to Jesus or his disciples in the second-century *Gospel of Thomas*. In Saying 74 one of the disciples says to him, 'Lord, there are many around the opening but no one in the well.' (The well is the well of truth: many approach it without getting into it. In this form the saying has a gnostic flavour; in fact, Celsus, an anti-Christian writer of the second century, quotes it from a gnostic treatise called the *Heavenly Dialogue*.[2]) Jesus's reply to the disciple is given in Saying 75: 'Many stand outside at the door, but it is only the single ones who enter the bridal chamber.' (In gnostic terminology the bridal chamber is the place where the soul is reunited with its proper element and the 'single ones' are those who have transcended the distinctions of age and sex. Hence Saying 49 makes Jesus say, 'Happy are the single and the chosen ones, for you will find the kingdom.')

The gnostic ideas of the *Gospel of Thomas* will give us no help in understanding the saying as it appears at the end of the parable of the wedding feast. There the 'called' are those who were invited to the wedding feast; the 'chosen' are those who accepted the invitation. The king invited many guests to the feast, but only a few, if any, of those who were invited actually came to it. The feast is a parable of the gospel and the blessings which it holds out to believers. The invitation to believe the gospel and enjoy its blessings goes out to all who hear it. But if all receive the call, not all respond to it. Those who do respond show by that very fact they are 'chosen'. Protestant theologians used to distinguish between the 'common call', addressed to all who hear the gospel, and the 'effectual call', received by those who actually respond. In part 2 of Bunyan's *Pilgrim's Progress* Christiana and her family are taught this lesson in the Interpreter's house by means of a hen and her chickens: 'She had a common call, and that she hath all day long. She had a special call, and that she had but sometimes.' The only way in which the effectual call can be distinguished from the common call is that those who hear it respond to it. 'Effectual calling is the work of God's Spirit, whereby, convincing us of our sin and misery, enlightening our minds in the knowledge of Christ, and renewing our wills, he doth persuade and enable us to embrace Jesus Christ, freely offered to us in the gospel.'[3]

Paul insists that 'it is not the hearers of the law who are righteous before God, but the doers of the law who will be justified' (Rom. 2:13), and it is those who live 'according to the Spirit' in whom 'the just requirement of the law' is fulfilled. James, to the same effect, urges his readers to 'be doers of the word, and not hearers only' (James 1:22).

The gnostic teachers whose ideas are reflected in the *Gospel of Thomas* rather liked the idea that 'the single and the chosen ones' were a small minority, provided they themselves were included in that élite number. On one occasion the disciples tried to make Jesus commit himself on the relative number of the called and the chosen, asking, 'Lord, will those who are saved be few?' (Luke 13:23). But he refused to gratify their curiosity: he simply told them to make sure that they themselves entered in through the narrow gate, 'for many, I tell you, will seek to enter and will not be able.'

It has frequently been taken for granted that Jesus's words about the relative fewness of the saved had reference not only to the period of his ministry but to all time. William Fisher, elder of the parish of Mauchline, Ayrshire, in the later part of the eighteeenth century, estimated the proportion as one to ten; but that may have been a piece of speculation on the part of a man who, convinced that he himself was one of the chosen, preferred to keep the number small and select. In any case, his estimate has been immortalised by the national poet of Scotland.[4] More recently, and more seriously, Mr. Enoch Powell has interpreted Jesus's words, 'few are chosen', as an assertion 'that his salvation will not be for all, not even for the majority', and has insisted that 'ignorance, incapacity, perversity, the sheer human propensity to error are sufficient to ensure a high failure rate'.[5] They are sufficient, indeed, to ensure a hundred-per-cent failure rate, but for the grace of God. But when divine grace begins to operate, the situation is transformed.

It may well be that Jesus was speaking more particularly of the situation during his ministry when he spoke of the few and the many. Even the casual reader of the New Testament gathers that there was a great and rapid increase in the number of his followers after his death and resurrection. Within a few months from his crucifixion, the number of his followers in Palestine was ten times as great as it had been during his ministry. And Paul, the greatest theologian of primitive Christianity, speaks of those who receive the saving benefit of the work of Jesus as 'the many' (Rom. 5:15, 19). No reasonable interpretation can make 'the many' mean a minority for, as John Calvin put it in his commentary on those words of Paul, 'if Adam's fall had the effect of producing the ruin of many, the grace of God is much more efficacious in benefiting many, since admittedly Christ is much more powerful to save than Adam was to ruin.'[6]

Chapter
56

The Wedding Garment

'"Friend, how did you get in here without a wedding garment?"' (Matt. 22:12)

The incident of the man who had no wedding garment is attached in Matthew's Gospel to the parable of the wedding feast (Matt. 22:1-10). The parable of the wedding feast has a parallel in the parable of the great banquet in Luke 14:16-24. There are differences of detail between the two parables, but the main outline of the story is the same: the host (a king, in Matthew's version) invites many guests, but on the day of the feast they excuse themselves for various reasons. But all the preparations have been made: the food (and plenty of it) is waiting to be eaten. The host therefore sends his servants out into the streets and lanes to round up those whom they find there and bring them to the banqueting hall. All the empty places are filled, and filled by people who are only too glad to be set down face to face with a square meal. They do full justice to what has been provided, even if those who were originally invited are not interested.

This is readily understood as a parable of Jesus's proclamation of the kingdom of God. The religious people, those who attended synagogue regularly, were not really interested in what he had to say and despised the good news which he brought. But the outcasts of society recognised his message as just what they had been waiting for. The blessings of the gospel, the Father's loving forgiveness, exactly suited their need and they eagerly seized what Jesus had to give.

But the wedding garment presents a problem. How could people who had been swept in from the streets be expected to have suitable clothes for a festive occasion? One man was asked how he got in without a wedding garment, but they might all have been expected to be similarly unprovided with suitable attire. It would have been more surprising if one of them had come in actually wearing a wedding garment. It may be suggested that the royal host thoughtfully provided them with suitable clothes, but this is not said in the parable, and the implication is that the man who was improperly dressed could have come properly clad. When taxed with his failure he had no excuse: he was 'speechless'.

It is most probable that this was originally a separate parable. If the host was a king, he would expect those whom he invited to a banquet to honour him by coming appropriately dressed: failure in this respect would be a studied insult to him. The culprit in this case might count himself fortunate if nothing worse befell him than to be trussed up and thrown out into the darkness, to grind his teeth in annoyance with himself for having been so foolish. The requirement of a wedding garment, unsuitable for people peremptorily conscripted from the streets to come and enjoy a free supper, was eminently suitable for the guests whom a king or magnate would normally invite to dine with him. What then is the point of the garment in the parable, if it was originally a parable on its own? Clothes are not infrequently used in the Bible as a symbol of personal character, and it is possibly implied that some might think themselves entitled to be counted among the 'children of the kingdom' or the followers of Jesus whose character was out of keeping with such a profession. If so, then the parable of the wedding garment would be a warning against false discipleship: it is not saying 'Lord, lord' that admits one to the kingdom, but doing the heavenly Father's will (Matt. 7:21).

Chapter
57

The Cursing of the Fig Tree

'May no one ever eat fruit from you again' (Mark 11:14)

This incident is related by Mark and, in a more compressed form, by Matthew. According to Mark, Jesus and his disciples spent the night following his entry into Jerusalem in Bethany. Next morning they returned to Jerusalem. On the way he felt hungry, 'and seeing in the distance a fig tree in leaf, he went to see if he could find anything on it. When he came to it, he found nothing but leaves, for it was not the season for figs.' Then come the words quoted above. They continued on their way into Jerusalem, where that day he cleansed the temple; in the evening they returned to Bethany. Next morning, as they passed the same place, they saw the fig tree withered away to its roots. And Peter remembered and said to him, 'Rabbi, look! The fig tree which you cursed has withered' (Mark 11:20–21).

Was it not unreasonable to curse the tree for being fruitless when, as Mark expressly says, 'it was not the season for figs'? The problem is most satisfactorily cleared up in a discussion of 'The Barren Fig Tree' published many years ago by W. M. Christie, a Church of Scotland minister in Palestine under the British mandatory regime. He pointed out first the time of year at which the incident is said to have occurred (if, as is probable, Jesus was crucified on April 6th, A.D. 30, the incident occurred during the first days of April). 'Now,' wrote Dr. Christie, 'the facts connected with the fig tree are these. Towards the end of March the leaves begin to appear, and in about a week the foliage coating is complete. Coincident with [this], and sometimes even before, there appears quite a crop of small knobs, not the real figs, but a kind of early forerunner. They grow to the size of green almonds, in which condition they are eaten by peasants and others when hungry. When they come to their own indefinite maturity they drop off.'[1] These precursors of the true fig are called *taqsh* in Palestinian Arabic. Their appearance is a harbinger of the fully formed appearance of the true fig some six weeks later. So, as Mark says, the time for figs had not yet come. But if the leaves appear without any *taqsh*, that is a sign that there will be no figs. Since Jesus found 'nothing but leaves' – leaves without any *taqsh* – he knew that 'it was an absolutely hopeless, fruitless fig tree', and said as much.

But if that is the true explanation of his words, why should anyone trouble to record the incident as though it had some special significance? Because it did have some special significance. As recorded by Mark, it is an acted parable with the same lesson as the spoken parable of the fruitless fig tree in Luke 13:6–9. In that spoken parable a landowner came three years in succession expecting fruit from a fig tree on his property, and when year by year it proved to be fruitless, he told the man in charge of his vineyard to cut it down because it was using up the ground to no good purpose. In both the acted parable and the spoken parable it is difficult to avoid the conclusion that the fig tree represents the city of Jerusalem, unresponsive to Jesus as he came to it with the message of God, and thereby incurring destruction. Elsewhere Luke records how Jesus wept over the city's blindness to its true well-being and foretold its ruin 'because you did not know the time of your visitation' (Luke 19:41–44). It is because the incident of the cursing of the fig tree was seen to convey the same lesson that Mark, followed by Matthew, recorded it.

Chapter
58

Faith That Removes Mountains

'Truly, I say to you, whoever says to this mountain, "Be taken up and cast into the sea", and does not doubt in his heart, but believes that what he says will come to pass, it will be done for him' (Mark 11:23)
   'If you had faith as a grain of mustard seed, you could say to this sycamine tree, "Be rooted up, and be planted in the sea", and it would obey you' (Luke 17:6)
   'For truly, I say to you, if you have faith as a grain of mustard seed, you will say to this mountain, "Move hence to yonder place", and it will move; and nothing will be impossible to you' (Matt. 17:20)

Of these sayings, or varieties of an original saying, emphasising the limitless possibilities open to faith, Mark's form (followed in Matthew 21:21) has a life-setting in the neighbourhood of Jerusalem, during Holy Week; Luke's form may be from the Q collection, in which case the form in Matthew 17:20 (an amplification of Jesus's words to the disciples after the healing of the epileptic boy at the foot of the mountain of transfiguration) combines features from Mark and Q.

In any case, Jesus illustrates the power of faith by analogies from the natural world. If faith is present at all, even if it is no bigger than a mustard seed, it can accomplish wonders: think what a large plant springs from something as tiny as a mustard seed. 'We are not afraid when the earth heaves and the mountains are hurled into the sea': so Psalm 46:2 (NEB) describes a real or figurative convulsion of nature which leaves

men and women of God unshaken because he is their refuge
and strength. It may be that Jesus is using such a form of words
figuratively to describe the incalculable effects of prevailing
faith.

But in Mark's account there may be some more explicit
point in the form of words. In that account the words are
addressed to the disciples after the incident of the cursing of the
fig tree. There may not seem to be much to connect that
incident with a lesson on the power of faith. The connection,
however, may be provided by the place where, according to
Mark, the words were spoken. They were spoken in the
morning, as Jesus and his disciples made their way from
Bethany to Jerusalem, crossing the Mount of Olives. So, in
Mark's account, 'this mountain' in the saying would be the
Mount of Olives.

Now, in current expectation regarding the time of the end,
the Mount of Olives played a special part. It would be the scene
of a violent earthquake on the Day of the Lord. 'On that day',
said one of the prophets (referring to the day when the God of
Israel would take final action against the enemies of his
people), 'his feet shall stand on the Mount of Olives which lies
before Jerusalem on the east; and the Mount of Olives shall be
split in two from east to west by a very wide valley; so that one
half of the Mount shall withdraw northward, and the other half
southward' (Zech. 14:4). If Jesus had this and related Old
Testament prophecies in mind on his way across the Mount of
Olives, his meaning might have been, 'If you have sufficient
faith in God, the Day of the Lord will come sooner than you
think.' (For this suggestion indebtedness should be acknowledged to a work by Professor William Manson, published in
1943.[1])

Chapter
59

Neither Will I Tell You

'Neither will I tell you by what authority I do these things' (Mark 11:33; Matt. 21:27; Luke 20:8)

Why did Jesus refuse to give a straight answer to those who asked him why he acted as he did?

It was during Holy Week, while he was walking in the temple precincts in Jerusalem, that some representatives of the Sanhedrin, Israel's supreme court (comprising chief priests, scribes and elders, as Mark tells us in verse 27), came to Jesus and asked him, 'By what authority are you doing these things, or who gave you this authority to do them?' By 'these things' they meant not so much his teaching in the outer court but his cleansing of the temple, which had taken place the previous day. What right had he to put a stop to buying and selling within the bounds of the temple, or to forbid 'any one to carry anything through the temple' – to use the outer court as a short cut on their business errands? Many religious people might have agreed with him that the sacred area should not be turned into a bazaar, but a temple police force was stationed to protect its sanctity: who authorised Jesus to act as he did?

His cleansing of the temple was what would have been recognised in Old Testament times as a prophetic action – the kind of action by which a prophet would occasionally confirm his spoken message and bring it home to the people around him. Jesus protested that the temple was being prevented from fulfilling its purpose as 'a house of prayer for all the nations' (cf. Isa. 56:7). Gentiles were not allowed to enter the inner courts, but in the outer court they might draw near to the true and living God and worship him, like those 'Greeks' who, according to John 12:20, went up to worship at Passover. Because of this the outer court was sometimes called 'the court of the Gentiles'. But Gentiles were hindered in using it for its proper purpose if space within it was taken up by market stalls and the like. One of the latest Old Testament prophets had foretold how, when representatives of all the nations were to go up to Jerusalem to worship, 'there shall no longer be a trader in the house of the Lord of hosts on that day' (Zech. 14:21). Jesus's prophetic action was designed to enforce this lesson.

But by what authority did he perform such a prophetic action? By what authority did any of the ancient prophets perform prophetic actions? By the authority of God, in whose name they spoke to the people. So, when Jesus was asked, 'Who gave you this authority?' the true answer was 'God'. Why then did he not say so? Because his questioners would not have believed him. He tested them first with another question, to see if they were capable of recognising divine authority when they saw it. Reminding them of John the Baptist's ministry, he asked them whether John's authority was derived 'from heaven (that is, from God) or from men'. This put them on the spot: 'they argued with one another, "If we say, 'From heaven', he will say, 'Why then did you not believe him?' But shall we say, 'From men'?" – they were afraid of the people, for all held that John was a real prophet.' Could they recognise divine authority when it was expressed in the actions and teaching of John? If so, they might be expected to recognise it when it was manifested in the deeds and words of Jesus. But they professed themselves unable to say what the source of John's authority was. So Jesus said to them in effect, 'If you cannot recognise divine authority when you see it in action, no amount of argument will convince you of its presence. If you cannot tell me by what authority John baptised, I will not tell you by what authority I do these things.' There are some people who will demand authority for truth itself, forgetting that truth is the highest authority (see pp. 96–7).

Chapter 60

Render to Caesar

'Render to Caesar the things that are Caesar's, and to God the things that are God's' (Mark 12:17)

For many readers of the Gospels this does not seem to be a particularly hard saying. They pay their taxes to the state and give financial support to the Church and various forms of religious and charitable action, and consider that this is very much in line with the intention of Jesus's words. There are others, however, who find in these words material for debate, arguing that their meaning is not at all clear, or else, if it is clear, that it is quite different from what it is usually taken to be. Our first business must be to consider the setting in which the words were spoken. When we have done that, we may realise that some of those who heard them felt that here was a hard saying indeed.

Mark, followed by Matthew (22:15-22) and Luke (20:19-26), tells how a deputation of Pharisees and Herodians came to Jesus while he was teaching in the temple precincts during his last visit to Jerusalem and, expressing their confidence that he would give them a straight answer, without fear or favour, asked him if it was lawful to pay taxes to Caesar or not. By 'lawful' they meant 'in accordance with the law of God, the basis of Israel's corporate life'. Mark says that the questioners planned 'to entrap him in his talk' (Mark 12:13); Luke spells this out more explicitly: their purpose, he says, was to 'take hold of what he said, so as to deliver him up to the authority and jurisdiction of the governor' (Luke 20:20). The governor or prefect of Judaea was the representative of Caesar, and any discouragement of the payment of taxes to Caesar would incur sharp retribution from him.

It was, indeed, a very delicate question. After Herod the Great, king of the Jews, died in 4 B.C., the Romans divided his kingdom into three parts, giving each to one of his sons. Galilee, where Jesus lived for most of his life, was ruled by Herod Antipas until A.D. 39. Judaea, the southern part, with Jerusalem as its capital, was given to Archelaus (cf. Matt. 2:22). The sons of Herod received taxes from their subjects, as their father Herod had done. The Herods were not popular, but religiously they were Jews, so no religious difficulties stood in the way of paying taxes to them. But Archelaus's rule in Judaea proved to be so oppressive that, after nine years, the Roman emperor removed him to forestall a revolt, and reorganised Judaea as a Roman province, to be governed by a prefect appointed by himself. From now on the people of Judaea were required to pay their taxes to the Roman emperor, Caesar. A census was held in A.D. 6 to determine the amount of tribute which the new province was to yield.

The Jews had been subject to Gentile overlords for long periods in their history, but no prophet or religious teacher had ever taught in earlier days that there was anything wrong in paying tribute to those overlords. On the contrary, the prophets taught them that if they fell under Gentile domination, this was by God's permission, and they should acknowledge the divine will by paying tribute to their foreign rulers. But around the time of the census in A.D. 6 a new teaching was spread abroad, to the effect that God alone was Israel's king, and therefore it was high treason against him for his people to recognise any Gentile ruler by paying him tribute. The principal teacher of this new doctrine was Judas the Galilean, who led a revolt against the Romans (cf. Acts 5:37). The revolt was crushed, but its ideals lived on, and the propriety of paying taxes to Caesar continued to be a subject for theological debate. It would be generally agreed that Jews in the lands of the Dispersion, living on Gentile territory, should pay taxes in accordance with the laws of the areas where they lived. But the land of Israel was God's land; this was recognised by its inhabitants when they handed over one-tenth of its produce to the maintenance of his temple in Jerusalem. But the taxes which the Roman emperor demanded were also derived from the produce of God's land. Was it right for God's people, living on God's land, to give a proportion of its produce to a pagan ruler? When the question was framed in those terms, the obvious answer for many was 'No'.

What would Jesus say? While he stayed in Galilee the question did not arise: taxes in that region were paid to a Jewish tetrarch. But when he visited Judaea, he came to a place where it was a burning question. However he answered it, it would be almost impossible to avoid giving offence. If he said that it was unlawful to pay taxes to Caesar, the Roman governor would get to hear of it and he could be charged with sedition. If he said that it was lawful, he would offend those who maintained the ideals of Judas the Galilean and many would think him unpatriotic. This would lose him much of his following in Judaea.

'Bring me a denarius,' said Jesus; 'let me see it.' The denarius was a Roman silver coin; Roman taxes had to be paid in Roman coinage. When a denarius was forthcoming, Jesus asked, 'Whose face is this? Whose name is this?' The answer, of course, was 'Caesar's'. Well, said Jesus, the coin which bears Caesar's face and name is obviously Caesar's coin; let Caesar have it back. The verb translated 'render' has the sense of giving back to someone that which belongs to him.

Did he imply that the use of Caesar's coinage was a tacit acknowledgment of Caesar's sovereignty? Perhaps he did. There were some Jews whose orthodoxy was such that they would not look at, let alone handle, a coin which bore a human face. Why? Because it infringed the second commandment of the Decalogue, which forbade the making of 'any likeness of anything that is in heaven above, or that is in the earth beneath, or that is in the water under the earth' (Exod. 20:4). Jesus did not necessarily share this attitude – money of any kind was held in little enough regard by him – but there may have been an implication in his words which the Pharisees among his questioners might have appreciated: such coins were unfit for use by people who were so scrupulous about keeping the law of God, and should go back where they came from. Caesar's coins were best used for paying Caesar's tribute. If that was what Caesar wanted, let him have it; the claims of God were not transgressed by such use of Caesar's money. What was really important was to discover what God's claims were, and see to it that they were met. Once again, he laid primary emphasis on seeking God's kingdom and righteousness.

Some interpreters have discerned more subtle ambiguities in Jesus's answer, as though, for example, he included in 'the things that are God's' the produce of God's land and meant that none of it should go to Caesar, not even when it was converted into Roman coinage. But this kind of interpretation would render the whole business about producing a denarius pointless. Certainly his answer would not satisfy those who believed that for Judaeans to pay tribute to Caesar was wrong. If some of the bystanders had been led by the manner of his entry into Jerusalem a few days before to expect a declaration of independence from him, they must have been disappointed. And indeed, there seems to have been less enthusiasm for him in Jerusalem at the end of Holy Week than there had been at the beginning. On the other hand, if his questioners hoped that he would compromise himself by his reply, they too were disappointed. He not only avoided the dilemma on the horns of which they wished to to impale him, but turned it so as to insist afresh on the central theme of his ministry.

Chapter
61

Call No Man Your Father

*'And call no man your father on earth, for you have one
Father, who is in heaven'* (Matt. 23:9)

In his criticism of the scribes, contained in the discourse of
Matthew 23, Jesus speaks disapprovingly of their liking for
honorary titles: 'they love . . . salutations in the market places,
and to be called rabbi by men' (Matt. 23:7). Then he turns to his
disciples and tells them not to be like that: 'you are not to be
called rabbi, for you have one teacher, and you are all brethren'
(Matt. 23:8). 'Rabbi' was a term of respect given by a Jewish
disciple to his teacher, and a well-known teacher would be
known to the public as Rabbi So-and-so. Jesus was called
'rabbi' by his disciples and by others; it was given to him as a
mark of courtesy or respect. For Matthew, however, the word
'rabbi' has a dubious connotation: in his Gospel the only
disciple who calls Jesus 'rabbi' is Judas Iscariot, and he does so
twice: once at the supper table, when he responds to Jesus's
announcement of the presence of a traitor in the company with
'Is it I, rabbi?' (Matt. 26:25), and once in Gethsemane, where the
'Hail, rabbi!' which accompanies his kiss is the sign to the
temple police that Jesus is the person to arrest (Matt. 26:49).
This attitude to the term 'rabbi' may throw some light on the
setting in which Matthew worked and the polemics in which he
was engaged.

So, said Jesus to his disciples, refuse all courtesy titles: you
have one teacher, and you are all members of one family.
Members of a family do not address one another by formal

titles, even if some of them indicate high distinction. When John Smith is knighted, his brothers, who have hitherto called him 'John', do not begin to address him to his face as 'Sir John', although others may properly do so. To them he is still 'John'.

But what about calling no man father? Did Jesus mean that his followers ought not to address their fathers in a way that acknowledged their special relationship? It could be thought that he did mean just that, in view of the fact that he is never recorded as calling Mary 'Mother'. But this is unlikely: he is speaking of the use of honorific titles among his disciples. It is equally unlikely that he meant 'Call no man "Abba" but God alone.' For one thing, Matthew's Greek-speaking readers would not naturally take the saying to mean this; for another thing, the whole point of calling God 'Abba' was that this was the ordinary domestic word by which the father was called in the family, and to reserve 'Abba' as a designation for God alone would do away with its significance (see p. 137). But Jesus's meaning could very well have been: In the spiritual sense God alone is your Father; do not give to others the designation which, in that sense, belongs exclusively to him. Jesus was his disciples' teacher, and they called him 'Teacher', but they never called him 'Father'; that was his designation for God.

But did not Paul speak of himself as his converts' father, since, as he said, he had become their 'father in Christ Jesus through the gospel' (1 Cor. 4:15)? He did, but he was using a spiritual analogy, not claiming a title. Well, in insisting on his authority as an 'apostle of Christ Jesus' was he not infringing at least the spirit of Jesus's admonition? No, for again he was not claiming a title but stating a fact: he was indeed commissioned and sent by the risen Lord, and from that was derived the authority with which he spoke. Similarly, if someone is doing the work of a bishop (say) or pastor, then to call him 'Bishop So-and-so' or 'Pastor So-and-so' simply recognises the ministry which he is discharging.

Some Christians, as we know, have interpreted these words of Jesus so literally that they would refrain from the use even of the very democratic 'Mister', perhaps because of its derivation from 'Master', either using no handle at all or preferring something reciprocal like 'Friend' or 'Brother'. Others, considering (probably rightly) that it is the use of honorific titles in religious life that is deprecated by Jesus, would refuse the designation 'The Reverend' to a minister, replacing it by 'Mr.' (which is perfectly proper) or (in writing) putting it between brackets (which is foolish) or even between quotation marks (which is offensive). But, as with so many of Jesus's injunctions, this one can be carried out in a stilted or pettifogging way which destroys the spirit of his teaching. If the local Catholic priest is known throughout the community as Father Jones, I am simply being silly if I persist in calling him something else. If I stop to think what is meant by my calling him Father Jones, I shall probably conclude that he is not *my* father in any sense but that he is no doubt a real father in God to his own congregation. 'Father' in this sense is synonymous with 'Pastor'; the former views the congregation as a family, the latter as a flock of sheep.

When a new bishop arrived in a certain English diocese a few years ago, he quickly let it be known that he did not wish to be addressed as 'my lord'. That, it may be suggested, was a genuine compliance with the spirit of these words of Jesus.

Chapter
62

You Brood of Vipers

'You serpents, you brood of vipers, how are you to escape being sentenced to hell?' (Matt. 23:33)

The chapter in Matthew's Gospel from which this saying is quoted presents a series of woes pronounced against the scribes and Pharisees – or perhaps we should say laments uttered over them. The series may be regarded as an expansion of Mark 12:38–40, where the people who listened to Jesus as he taught in the temple precincts in Jerusalem during Holy Week were warned against 'the scribes, who like to go about in long robes, and to have salutations in the market places and the best seats in the synagogues and the places of honour at feasts, who devour widows' houses and for a pretence make long prayers. They will receive the greater condemnation.'

The scribes were the recognised exponents of the law. Most of them – certainly most of those who appear in the Gospels – belonged to the party of the Pharisees. The Pharisees traced their spiritual lineage back to the pious groups which, in the days of the Maccabees, resisted all temptations to assimilate their faith and practice to paganising ways, and suffered martyrdom rather than betray their religious heritage. In the first century A.D. they are reckoned to have numbered about 6,000. They banded themselves together in fellowships or brotherhoods, encouraging one another in the defence and practice of the law. The law included not only the written precepts of the Old Testament but the interpretation and application of those precepts – what Mark describes as 'the tradition of the elders' (Mark 7:3). They were greatly concerned about ceremonial purity. This concern forbade them to have social contact with Gentiles, or even with fellow-Jews who were not so particular about the laws of purity as they themselves were. They attached high importance to the tithing of crops (that is, paying ten per cent of the proceeds of harvest into the temple treasury) – not only of grain, wine and olive oil but of garden herbs. They would not willingly eat food, whether in their own houses or in other people's, unless they could be sure that the tithe had been paid on it.

From their viewpoint, they could not help looking on Jesus as dangerously lax, whether in the sovereign freedom with which he disposed of the sabbath law and the food laws or in his readiness to consort with the most questionable persons and actually sit down to a meal with them. It was inevitable that he and they should clash; their conflict, indeed, illustrates the saying about the second-best being the worst enemy of the best.

The Pharisaic way of life lent itself to imitation by people who had no worthier motive than the gaining of a popular reputation for piety. The rabbinical traditions illustrate this fact: seven types of Pharisee are enumerated, and only one of these, the Pharisee who is one for the love of God, receives unqualified commendation.[1] The New Testament picture of the Pharisees is generally an unfavourable one, but more so in the Gospels than in Acts. In Acts they are depicted as not unfriendly to the observant Jewish Christians of Jerusalem: the two groups had this in common (by contrast with the Sadducees), that they believed in the resurrection of the dead.

The gathering together of the woes or laments regarding the Pharisees in Matthew 23 probably reflects the situation in which this Gospel was written, later in the first century, when the Pharisees and the Jewish Christians were engaged in polemical controversy with one another. That provided an opportunity to collect from all quarters criticisms which Jesus had voiced against the Pharisees, and to weave them together into a continuous speech, with its refrain (as commonly translated) 'Woe to you, scribes and Pharisees, hypocrites!'

Pharisees as such were not hypocrites, and Jesus did not say that they were; he was not the one to bear false witness against his neighbour. 'Hypocrite' in New Testament usage means 'play-actor'; it denotes the sort of person who plays a part which is simply assumed for the occasion and does not express his real self. The 'hypocrites' in this repeated denunciation, then, are those who play at being scribes and Pharisees, who 'preach but do not practise' (Matt. 23:3), who assume the actions and words characteristic of scribes and Pharisees without being motivated by true love of God. The genuine Pharisee might disapprove of much that Jesus said and did, but if he was a genuine Pharisee, he was no play-actor. So we might render the recurring refrain of Matthew 23 as 'Alas for you, hypocritical scribes and Pharisees!' – alas for you, because you are incurring a fearful judgment on yourselves.

But what about the 'brood of vipers'? This expression was used by John the Baptist as he saw the crowds coming to listen to his proclamation of judgment and his call to repentance: 'You brood of vipers! Who warned you to flee from the wrath to come?' (Luke 3:7). He compared them to snakes making their way as quickly as possible out of range of an oncoming grass fire. In Matthew 3:7 John directs these words to Pharisees and Sadducees among his hearers. Jesus's use of the same figure may convey a warning that those who pay no heed to impending doom cannot escape it – cannot escape 'the judgment of Gehenna' (to render it literally). And if it is asked how they had incurred this judgment without being aware of it, the answer suggested by Matthew's context would be that by their unreality they were hindering, not helping, others in following the way of righteousness. (In Matthew 12:34 those who charged Jesus with casting out demons by the power of Beelzebul – see p. 89 – are similarly addressed as 'You brood of vipers!')

Finally, Matthew himself apparently indicates that this hard saying, with its context, should be understood as lamentation rather than unmitigated denunciation. For at the end of the discourse, after the statement that the martyr-blood of all generations would be required from that generation (see p. 227),

Matthew places the lament over Jerusalem ('O Jerusalem, Jerusalem . . .') which Luke introduces at an earlier point in Jesus's ministry. It is easy to see why Luke introduces it where he does: Jesus has been warned in Galilee that Herod Antipas wants to kill him, and he replies that that cannot be, since Jerusalem is the proper place for a prophet to be put to death (Luke 13:31–33). Then comes 'O Jerusalem, Jerusalem, killing the prophets . . .' (verses 34–35). Actually, the lament would be *chronologically* appropriate if it were uttered at the end of Jesus's last visit to Jerusalem before the final one, for it ends with the words: 'You will not see me until you say, "Blessed is he who comes in the name of the Lord"' (Luke 13:35; Matt. 23:39). This may simply mean, 'You will not see me until festival time'. (T. W. Manson compares two people parting today and saying, 'Next time we meet we shall be singing "O come, all ye faithful"', i.e. 'Next time we meet will be Christmas'[2].) But Luke and Matthew place the lament in contexts where it is *topically* appropriate; Matthew in particular, by placing it where he does (Matt. 23:37–39), communicates something of the sorrow with which Jesus found it necessary to speak as he did about those who should have been trustworthy guides but in fact were leading their followers to disaster.

Chapter
63

This Generation Will Not Pass Away

'Truly, I say to you, this generation will not pass away before all these things take place' (Mark 13:30)

This has been regarded as a hard saying by those who take it to refer to Christ's second advent, his coming in glory. If Jesus really affirmed that this event would take place within a generation from the time of speaking (which was only a few days before his arrest and execution), then, it is felt, he was mistaken, and this is for many an unacceptable conclusion.

Although this saying is not one of P. W. Schmiedel's pillar passages, many have defended its genuineness on the ground that no one would have invented an unfulfilled prophecy and put it on Jesus's lips. If an unfulfilled prophecy is ascribed to him in the gospel tradition, that can only be (they have argued) because he actually uttered it. In more recent times, however, the utterance has been widely ascribed not to the historical Jesus but to some prophet in the early Church speaking in Jesus's name. Rudolf Bultmann regarded the discourse of Mark 13:5–27 as 'a Jewish apocalypse with a Christian editing', and thought that this utterance would have made a suitable conclusion to such an apocalypse.[1]

Some students of the New Testament who do not concede that Jesus might have been mistaken are nevertheless convinced that the reference is indeed to his glorious advent. If 'all these things' must denote the events leading up to the advent and the advent itself, then some other interpretation, they say, will have to be placed on 'this generation'. Other meanings which the Greek noun *genea* (here translated 'generation') bears in certain contexts are canvassed. The word is sometimes used in the sense of 'race', so perhaps, it is suggested, the point is that the Jewish race, or even the human race, will not pass away before the second advent. Plainly the idea that the human race is meant cannot be entertained; every description of that event implies that human beings will be around to witness it, for otherwise it would have no context to give it any significance. Nor is there much more to be said for the idea that the Jewish race is meant: there is no hint anywhere in the New Testament that the Jewish race will cease to exist before the end of the world. In any case, what point would there be in such a vague prediction? It would be as much as to say, 'At some time in the indefinite future all these things will take place.'

'This generation' is a recurring phrase in the Bible, and each time it is used it bears the ordinary sense of the people belonging, as we say, to one fairly comprehensive age-group. One desperate attempt to combine the recognition of this fact with a reference to the second advent in the text we are considering, and yet exonerate Jesus from being mistaken in his forecast, is to take 'this generation' to mean not 'this generation now alive' but 'the generation which will be alive at the time about which I am speaking'. The meaning would then be: 'The generation on earth when these things begin to take place will still be on earth when they are all completed: all these things will take place within the span of one generation.'[2]

Is this at all probable? I think not. When we are faced with the problem of understanding a hard saying, it is always a safe procedure to ask, 'What would it have meant to the people who first heard it?' And there can be but one answer to this question in relation to the present hard saying. Jesus's hearers could have understood him to mean only that 'all these things' would take place within *their* generation. Not only does 'generation' in the phrase 'this generation' always mean the people alive at one particular time; the phrase itself always means 'the generation now living'. Jesus spoke of 'this generation' in this sense several times, and generally in no flattering terms. In fact, his use of the phrase echoes its use in the Old Testament records of the Israelites' wilderness wanderings. The generation of Israelites that left Egypt did not survive to enter Canaan; it died out in the wilderness – all the adults, that is to say (with two named exceptions). And why? Because it refused to accept the word of God communicated through Moses. Hence it is called 'this evil generation' (Deut. 1:35), 'a perverse and crooked generation' (Deut. 32:5).

Similarly the generation to which Jesus ministered is called 'an evil generation' (Luke 11:29), 'this adulterous and sinful generation' (Mark 8:38), because of its unbelief and unresponsiveness. 'The men of Nineveh', said Jesus, 'will arise at the judgment with this generation and condemn it; for they repented at the preaching of Jonah, and behold, something greater than Jonah is here' (Luke 11:32; see p. 97). In fact, 'this generation' has so capped the unhappy record of its predecessors that all their misdeeds will be visited on it: 'Yes, I tell you, it shall be required of this generation' (Luke 11:51). The phrase 'this generation' is found too often on Jesus's lips in this literal sense for us to suppose that it suddenly takes on a different meaning in the saying which we are now examining. Moreover, if the generation of the end-time had been intended, *'that* generation' would have been a more natural way of referring to it than 'this generation'.

But what are 'all these things' which are due to take place before 'this generation' passes away? Jesus was speaking in response to a question put to him by four of his disciples. They were visiting Jerusalem for the Passover, and the disciples were impressed by the architectural grandeur of the temple, so recently restored and enlarged by Herod. 'Look, Teacher,' said one of them, 'what wonderful stones and what wonderful buildings!' Jesus replied, 'Do you see these great buildings? There will not be left here one stone upon another, that will not be thrown down.' This aroused their curiosity and, seizing an opportunity when they were with him on the Mount of Olives, looking across to the temple area, four of them asked, 'Tell us, when will this be? And what will be the sign when all these things are to be accomplished?' (Mark 13:1–4).

In the disciples' question, 'all these things' are the destruction of the temple and attendant events. It seems reasonable to regard the hard saying as summing up the answer to their question. If so, then 'all these things' will have the same meaning in question and answer. The hard saying will then mean, 'this generation will not pass away before' the temple is totally destroyed. It is well known that the temple was actually destroyed by the Romans under the crown prince Titus in August of A.D. 70, not more than forty years after Jesus spoke. Forty years is not too long a period to be called a generation; in fact, forty years is the conventional length of a generation in the biblical vocabulary. It was certainly so with the 'evil generation' of the wilderness wanderings: 'Forty years long was I grieved with this generation', said God (Ps. 95:10, Prayer Book version).

But if that is what the saying means, why should it have been thought to predict the last advent within that generation? Because, in the discourse which intervenes between verse 4 and verse 30 of Mark 13, other subject-matter is interwoven with the forecast of the time of trouble leading up to the disaster of A.D. 70. In particular, there is the prediction of 'the Son of man coming in clouds with power and great glory' (see p. 246) and sending out his angels to 'gather his elect from the four winds, from the ends of the earth to the ends of heaven' (verses 26–27). Some interpreters have taken this to be a highly figurative description of the divine judgment which many Christians, and not only Christians, saw enacted in the Roman siege and destruction of Jerusalem; but it is difficult to agree with them.

Mark probably wrote his Gospel four or five years before A.D. 70. When he wrote, the fall of the temple and the coming of the Son of man lay alike in the future, and he had no means of knowing whether or not there would be a substantial lapse of time between these two events. Even so, he preserves in the same context another saying of Jesus relating to the time of a future event: 'But of that day or that hour no one knows, not even the angels in heaven, nor the Son, but only the Father' (Mark 13:32). This saying was listed by Schmiedel among his pillar texts, on the ground that a saying in which Jesus admits his ignorance (even if only in one respect) would not have been invented or ascribed to him by the early Church. But what is the day or hour to which it refers? Certainly not the day or hour of the destruction of the temple: what the whole context, and not only the hard saying of verse 30, emphasises about that event is its nearness and certainty. The event whose timing is known to none but the Father cannot be anything other than the coming of the Son of man, described in verse 26.

Luke, as he reproduces the substance of the discourse of Mark 13:5–30, lays more emphasis on the fate of Jerusalem, the city as well as the temple: 'Jerusalem will be trodden down by the Gentiles, until the times of the Gentiles are fulfilled' (Luke 21:24). When 'the times of the Gentiles' (the period of Gentile domination of the holy city) will be fulfilled is not indicated. But this saying, though peculiar to Luke in the gospel record, is not Luke's invention: it turns up again in the Apocalypse, and in a part of it which is probably earlier than that work as a whole and was subsequently incorporated into it. The outer court of the temple, John is told, 'is given over to the nations (Gentiles), and they will trample over the holy city for forty-two months' (Rev. 11:2). This is a prophetic utterance communicated to John by a voice from heaven, but it has the same origin as the words recorded in Luke 21:24.

Matthew, writing his Gospel probably a short time after the destruction of the temple, could see, as Mark naturally could not, the separation in time between that event and the coming of the Son of man. For Matthew, the one event had taken place, while the other was still future. He rewords the disciples' question to Jesus so that it refers to both events distinctly and explicitly. Jesus, as in Mark, foretells how not one stone of the temple will be left standing on another, and the disciples say, 'Tell us, (a) when will these things be, and (b) what will be the sign of your coming and of the close of the age?' (Matt. 24:3). Then, at the end of the following discourse, Jesus answers their twofold question by saying that (a) 'this generation will not pass away till all *these things* take place' (Matt. 24:34) while, (b) with regard to his coming and 'the close of the age', he tells them that 'of *that* day and hour no one knows, not even the angels of heaven, nor the Son, but the Father only' (Matt. 24:36). The distinction between the two predictions is clear in Matthew, for whom the earlier of the two predicted events now lay in the past; but it was already implicit, though not so clear, in Mark.

Chapter 64

There the Eagles Will Be Gathered Together

'Wherever the body is, there the eagles will be gathered together' (Matt. 24:28; Luke 17:37)

There is a slight difference between the two forms of this saying which does not appear in the English of the RSV (quoted above): in Matthew the Greek word translated 'body' means specifically a dead body, whereas Luke uses the more general word for 'body', alive or dead, although in the present context a dead body is implied.

The saying gives the impression of being a proverbial utterance, applied (as proverbial utterances regularly are) to some appropriate situation. But are the birds of prey mentioned in the saying really eagles? Might we not have expected a reference to vultures? Yes indeed; but there are two points to be made.

First, the Hebrew word normally translated 'eagle' in the Old Testament appears occasionally to denote the vulture. 'Make yourselves as bald as the eagle', the people of Judah are told in Mic. 1:16; but it is the vulture, not the eagle, that is bald. In those places where the Hebrew word for 'eagle' seems to have the meaning 'vulture', it is the Greek word for 'eagle' that is used in the Greek version of the Old Testament; so that for Matthew and Luke there was this precedent for the occasional use of the Greek word for 'eagle' in the sense of 'vulture'.

Next, even if (as is probable) the proverbial utterance referred originally to vultures, the change to 'eagles' may have been made deliberately, if not in the Aramaic that Jesus spoke, then in the Greek version of his words on which the Gospels of Matthew and Luke drew. 'Where there is a dead body the vultures will flock together' means in effect, 'Where there is a situation ripe for judgment, there the judgment will fall.' But the situation in view in the context is the city of Jerusalem, doomed to destruction because of its unwillingness to pay heed to the message of peace which Jesus brought. The executioners of this particular judgment were Roman legionary forces. The eagle was the standard of a Roman legion, and this may explain the choice of the word 'eagles' here.

T. W. Manson, who prefers the rendering 'vultures' here and sees no reference to the Roman military eagles, thinks the point of the saying is the swiftness with which vultures discover the presence of carrion and flock to feast on it.[1] So swiftly will the judgment fall 'on the day when the Son of man is revealed' (Luke 17:30).

In Luke's account, but not in Matthew's, the saying is Jesus's reply to a question asked by the disciples. He has just told them how, on that day, the judgment will seize on one person and pass over another, separating two people asleep in the same bed or two women grinding at one mill (one of them turning the upper stone and the other pouring in the grain). 'Where, Lord?' say the disciples – possibly meaning, 'Where will this judgment take place?' To this his answer is, 'Wherever there is a situation which calls for it.'

Among several instances of the kind of proverbial utterance illustrated by this saying special mention may be made of Job 39:27–30:

> Is it at your command that the eagle mounts up
>   and makes his nest on high?
> On the rock he dwells and makes his home
>   in the fastness of the rocky crag.
> Thence he spies out the prey;
>   his eyes behold it afar off.
> His young ones suck up blood;
>   and where the slain are, there is he.

Chapter
65

I Do Not Know You

'Afterward the other maidens came also, saying, "Lord, lord, open to us." But he replied, "Truly, I say to you, I do not know you"' (Matt. 25:11–12)

The picture of people arriving after the door has been shut and finding it impossible to gain entrance appears elsewhere in the teaching of Jesus. In Luke 13:25–28 Jesus speaks of such people who, seeing themselves shut out, protest to the master of the house, 'We ate and drank in your presence, and you taught in our streets.' But even so they are refused admittance; they are excluded from the kingdom of God. Matthew's version of the Sermon on the Mount contains a parallel to that passage in Luke; in Matthew's account those who are shut out produce what might be regarded as even stronger credentials entitling them to admittance: 'did we not prophesy in your name, and cast out demons in your name, and do many mighty works in your name?' (Matt. 7:22) – but all to no avail.

The most memorable setting of the picture, however, is in the parable of the ten virgins, as it is traditionally called. The haunting pathos of the late-comers finding the door closed in their faces was caught and expressed by Tennyson in the song, 'Late, late, so late! and dark the night and chill!' which was sung to Guinevere by the little maid in the nunnery where the queen had sought sanctuary. True, in the scene from real life depicted in the parable the maidens' disappointment was keen, but they suffered no irreparable loss: they had missed the wedding feast, indeed, but there would be other wedding feasts, and they would remember to take an adequate supply of oil another time. But in the application of the parable the loss is more serious.

The parable is one of three which Matthew appends to his version of Jesus's Olivet discourse – the discourse which has its climax in the glorious coming of the Son of man.

There was a wedding in the village. A wedding story with no mention of the bride seems very odd to us, but different times and different lands have different customs. Just possibly she does receive a mention, but if so, only in passing: some authorities for the text of Matthew 25:1 say that the ten maidens 'went to meet the bridegroom *and the bride*'. The ten maidens do not appear to have been bridesmaids, or even specially invited guests; they were girls of the village who had decided to form a torchlight procession and escort the bridegroom and his party to the house where the wedding feast was to be held. They knew that, if they did so, there would be a place at the feast for them, so that they could share in the good cheer. To this day there are parts of the world where a wedding feast is a public occasion for the neighbourhood, and all who come find a welcome and something to eat and drink.

No time was announced for the bridegroom to set out for the feast, and the day wore on. That was all right: a torchlight procession is more impressive in the dark. The 'torches' were long poles with oil-lamps tied to the top, and the more provident girls took a supply of olive oil with them in case the lamps went out. As the evening wore on and the bridegroom still did not come, one after another dropped off to sleep. However, their lamps were lit, ready for the warning shout. Suddenly the shout came: 'Here he is!' They set off to join his party, but as they trimmed the wicks of their lamps, five of them found that their lamps were going out, and they had n. extra oil. The others could not lend them any of theirs, for then there would not be enough to last the journey. So the improvident girls had to go and buy some, and that would not be too easy at midnight; yet by persistence they managed at last to get some. But by that time they were too late to join the procession, and when they reached the house, they could not get in. They hammered on the street-door and shouted to the door-keeper, 'O sir! O sir! please let us in.' But all the answer they received was 'No; I don't know you.' So they had to go back home in the dark, tired and disappointed, because they had not been ready.

The oil was good oil, while it lasted; but the oil that was used yesterday will not keep today's lamps alight. So perhaps we may learn not to depend exclusively on past experiences; they will not be sufficient for the needs of the present. Daily grace must be obtained for daily need. The explicit lesson attached to the parable is: 'Keep awake, for you know neither the day nor the hour' (Matt. 25:13). Later forms of the text (represented by the AV) add the words: 'when the Son of man comes'. Certainly in the context of the parable those words are implied, but the fact that the evangelist did not include them suggests that the parable has a more general application. Keep awake, because a time of testing may come without warning. Be ready to resist this temptation (whatever form it may take); be ready to meet this crisis; be ready to grasp this opportunity. Somebody needs help; be ready to give it, 'for you know neither the day nor the hour' when the call may come.

Chapter
66

This Is My Body ... This Is My Blood

And as they were eating, he took bread, and blessed, and broke it, and gave it to them, and said, 'Take; this is my body.' And he took a cup, and when he had given thanks he gave it to them, and they all drank of it. And he said to them, 'This is my blood of the covenant, which is poured out for many' (Mark 14:22–24)

The words of institution, spoken by Jesus at the Last Supper, were not intended by him to be hard sayings; but they may be included among his hard sayings if regard is had to the disputes and divisions to which their interpretation has given rise.

Mark's version of the words, quoted above, is not the earliest record of them in the New Testament. Paul reproduces them in 1 Corinthians 11:23–25, written in A.D. 55. He reminds his converts in Corinth that he 'delivered' this record to them by word of mouth (presumably when he came to their city to preach the gospel in A.D. 50), and says that he himself 'received' it 'from the Lord' even earlier (presumably soon after his conversion); he had received it, that is to say, through a (no doubt short) chain of transmission which went back to Jesus himself and derived its authority from him. There are differences in wording between Paul's version and Mark's, perhaps reflecting variations in usage among the churches of the first Christian generation, but we are not concerned here with those differences; it is more important to consider the meaning of what the two versions have in common.

The Last Supper was most probably a Passover meal. It may

be that Jesus and his disciples kept the Passover (on this occasion, if not on others) a day earlier than the official date of the feast fixed by the temple authorities in Jerusalem. At the Passover meal, which commemorated the deliverance of the Israelites from Egypt many centuries before, there was unleavened bread and red wine on the table, as well as food of other kinds. In the explanatory narrative which preceded the meal, the bread was said to be 'the bread of affliction which our fathers ate when they left Egypt' (cf. Deut. 16:3). A literal-minded person might say that the bread on the table was not the bread which the exodus generation ate: that bread was no longer available. But to the faith of the eaters it *was* the same bread: they were encouraged to identify themselves with the exodus generation, for 'in each generation', the prescription ran, 'it is a duty to regard oneself as though one had oneself been brought up out of Egypt'.

At the outset of the meal the head of the family, having broken bread, gave thanks for it in time-honoured language: 'Blessed art thou, O Lord our God, King of the universe, who bringest forth bread from the earth.' But at the Last Supper Jesus, as head of his 'family', having given thanks for the bread, added words which gave the bread a new significance: 'Take it,' he said to the disciples, 'this is my body.' The Pauline version continues, '... my body which is for you; do this as my memorial'. The Passover meal was a memorial of the great deliverance at the time of the exodus; now a new memorial was being instituted in view of a new and greater deliverance about to be accomplished. And if any literal-minded person were to say, 'But the bread which he took from the table could not be his body; the disciples could see his living body there before their eyes,' once again the answer would be that it is to the faith of the eaters that the bread is the Lord's body; it is by faith that, in the eating of the memorial bread, they participate in his life.

At the end of the meal, when the closing blessing or 'grace after meat' had been said, a cup of wine was shared by the family. This cup, called the 'cup of blessing', was the third of four cups which stood on the table. When Jesus had said the blessing and given this cup to his companions, without drinking from it himself, he said to them, 'This is my covenant blood, which is poured out for many.' (The Pauline version says, 'This is the new covenant in my blood, which is poured out for you; do this as my memorial, every time you drink it.')

When Moses, at the foot of Mount Sinai, read the law of God to the Israelites who had come out of Egypt and they had undertaken to keep it, the blood of sacrificed animals was sprinkled partly on the altar (representing the presence of God) and partly on the people, and Moses spoke of it as 'the blood of the covenant which the Lord has made with you in accordance with all these words' (Exod. 24:3–8). To the disciples, who had the passover and exodus narratives vividly in their minds at that time, Jesus's words must have meant that a new covenant was about to be instituted in place of that into which their ancestors were brought in Moses' day – to be instituted, moreover, by Jesus's death for his people. If, then, when they take the memorial bread they participate by faith in the life of him who died and rose again, so when they take the cup they declare and appropriate by faith their 'interest in the Saviour's blood'. In doing so, they enter by experience into the meaning of his words of institution and know that through him they are members of God's covenant community.

Matthew (26:26–29) reproduces Mark's version of the words, his main amplification of them being the explanatory phrase 'for the forgiveness of sins' after 'poured out for many'. In Luke 22:17–20 we find (according to the information in the margin or footnotes) both a longer and a shorter version; the longer version has close affinities with Paul's. On John 6:53–55 see pp. 21–5.

Luke's account is specially important because he is the only evangelist who reports Jesus as saying, 'Do this in remembrance of me' (Luke 22:19). In his account these words are added to those spoken over the bread (in Paul's account they are attached both to the bread and to the cup). From Mark's account (and Matthew's) it might not have been gathered that this was anything other than a once-for-all eating and drinking; Luke makes it plain that the eating and drinking were meant to be repeated.

According to all three synoptic evangelists Jesus said, while giving his disciples the cup, 'I shall not drink again of the fruit of the vine until that day when I drink it new in the kingdom of God' – or words to the same effect (Mark 14:25; cf. Matt. 26:29; Luke 22:18). He would fast until the kingdom of God was established; then the heavenly banquet would begin. But when he rose from the dead, he made himself known to his disciples 'in the breaking of the bread' (Luke 24:35); Peter in the house of Cornelius tells how he and his companions 'ate and drank with him after he rose from the dead' (Acts 10:41). This suggests that the kingdom of which he spoke at the Last Supper has now come in some sense (it has 'come with power', in the language of Mark 9:1): it has been inaugurated, even if its consummation lies in the future. Until that consummation his people continue to 'do this' – to take the bread and wine – as his memorial, and as they do so, they consciously realise his presence with them.

Chapter
67

Let Him Who Has No Sword Buy One

'But now, let him ... who has no sword sell his mantle and buy one' (Luke 22:36)

This is a hard saying in the sense that it is difficult to reconcile it with Jesus's general teaching on violence: violence was not the course for his followers to take. It is widely held that this saying was not meant to be taken literally, but if so, how was it meant to be taken?

It occurs in Luke's Gospel only. Luke reports it as part of a conversation between Jesus and his disciples at the Last Supper. Jesus reminds them of an earlier occasion when he sent them out on a missionary tour and told them to take neither purse (for money) nor bag (for provisions) nor sandals. Presumably, they could expect their needs to be supplied by well-disposed people along their route (Luke 10:4–7). But now things were going to be different: people would be reluctant to show them hospitality, for they might get into trouble for doing so. On that earlier occasion, as the disciples now agreed, they had lacked nothing. 'But now,' said Jesus, 'let him who has a purse take it, and likewise a bag' – they would have to fend for themselves. More than that: 'let him who has no sword sell his cloak and buy one'. If that is surprising, more surprising still is the reason he gives for this change of policy: 'For I tell you that this scripture must be fulfilled in me, "And he was reckoned with transgressors", for what is written about me has its fulfilment.'

It is doubtful if the disciples followed his reasoning here, but they thought they had got the point about the sword. No need to worry about that: 'Look, Lord,' they said, 'here are two swords.' To which he replied, 'It is enough' or, perhaps, 'Enough of this.'

Luke certainly does not intend his readers to understand the words literally. He goes on to tell how, a few hours later, when Jesus was arrested, one of the disciples let fly with a sword – probably one of the two which they had produced at the supper table – and cut off an ear of the high priest's slave. But Jesus said, 'No more of this!' and healed the man's ear with a touch (Luke 22:49–51).

So what did he mean by his reference to selling one's cloak to buy a sword? He himself was about to be condemned as a criminal, 'reckoned with transgressors', to use language applied to the Servant of the Lord in Isaiah 53:12. Those who until now had been his associates would find themselves treated as outlaws; they could no longer count on the charity of sympathetic fellow-Israelites. Purse and bag would now be necessary. Josephus tells us that when Essenes went on a journey they had no need to take supplies with them, for they knew that their needs would be met by fellow-members of their order; they did, however, carry arms to protect themselves against bandits.[1]

But Jesus does not envisage bandits as the kind of people against whom his disciples would require protection: they themselves would be lumped together with bandits by the authorities, and they might as well act the part properly and carry arms, as bandits did. Taking him literally, they revealed that they had anticipated his advice: they already had two swords. This incidentally shows how far they were from resembling a band of Zealot insurgents: such a band would have been much more adequately equipped. And the words with which Jesus concluded the conversation did not mean that two swords would be enough; they would have been ludicrously insufficient against the band that came to arrest him, armed with swords and clubs. He meant 'Enough of this!' – they had misunderstood his sad irony, and it was time to drop the subject. T. W. Manson rendered the words 'Well, well'. In contrast to the days when they had shared their Master's popularity, 'they are now surrounded by enemies so ruthless that the possession of two swords will not help the situation.'[2]

This text ... has nothing to say directly on the question whether armed resistance to injustice and evil is ever justifiable. It is simply a vivid pictorial way of describing the complete change which has come about in the temper and attitude of the Jewish people since the days of the disciples' mission. The disciples understood the saying literally and so missed the point; but that is no reason why we should follow their example.[3]

Chapter
68

Jesus said to him, 'Friend, why are you here?' (Matt.
26:50)

These are the words spoken by Jesus to Judas on receiving the
traitor's kiss from him in Gethsemane, as rendered in the RSV
text. Almost certainly they are a mistranslation. The
alternative rendering given in the margin or footnote is better:
'do that for which you have come'. Similarly the NEB text gives
the rendering: 'Friend, do what you are here to do'; the NIV
text says, 'Friend, do what you came for.'

The Greek word translated 'friend' is used by Matthew alone
of the New Testament writers; it might be translated
'companion', 'comrade' or 'mate'. Judas is the only person
whom Jesus addresses thus. The same vocative is used in two
parables: by the owner of the vineyard to the workman who
protested at the lavishness with which the last-hired men were
paid (Matt. 20:13; see p. 197) and by the king who gave a
marriage feast for his son to the man who came without a
wedding garment (Matt. 22:12; see p. 206). On Jesus's lips it
was particularly appropriate as a term of address to a man
who, an hour or two before, had sat at table with him and
'dipped his hand in the dish' with him (Matt. 26:23).

The rest of the sentence might be translated literally 'that for
which you are here'. It seems to be an adjectival clause; the
principal clause would then be an imper..ive like 'Do'. The
clause has turned up as an inscription on a few goblets of the
New Testament period, suitable for use at drinking parties,

where the principal verb supplied is 'Be of good cheer' or 'Enjoy yourself'.[1] The complete inscription means 'Enjoy yourself; that's what you're here for.' Matthew uses the clause in a much more solemn, and indeed tragic, setting; but his meaning is illuminated by the inscription. Jesus says in effect to Judas, 'You know what you are here for; get on with it!'

One further suggestion is that the clause might be an exclamation, as though Jesus said, 'Friend, what a thing you are here for!' But it is best to take it as an adjectival clause, and to render the words, 'Friend, do what you have come to do.'

Chapter
69

You Will See the Son of Man

Again the high priest asked him, 'Are you the Christ, the Son of the Blessed?' And Jesus said, 'I am; and you will see the Son of man sitting at the right hand of Power, and coming with the clouds of heaven' (Mark 14:61–62; cf. Matt. 26:63–64; Luke 22:67–70)

After his arrest in Gethsemane, Jesus was brought before a court of enquiry, presided over by the high priest. At first, according to Mark's narrative, an attempt was made to convict him of having spoken against the Jerusalem temple. Not only was violation of the sanctity of the temple, whether in deed or in word, a capital offence; it was the one type of offence for which the Roman government allowed the supreme Jewish court to pass and execute sentence at its own discretion. Two or three years later, when Stephen was successfully prosecuted before the supreme court on a similar charge, there was no need to refer the case to Pilate before execution could be carried out. On the present occasion, however, Jesus could not be convicted on this charge because the two witnesses for the prosecution gave conflicting evidence.

Then the high priest, apparently on his own initiative, asked Jesus to tell the court if he was the Messiah, the Son of God. (He used 'the Blessed' as a substitute for the divine name.) The Messiah was entitled to be described as the Son of God, if he was the person addressed by God in Psalm 2:7 with the words, 'You are my son', or the person who in Psalm 89:26 cries to God, 'Thou art my Father'. Jesus was not in the way of spontaneously referring to himself as the Messiah. But to the high priest's question he answered 'I am.' How Matthew and Luke understood this reply may be seen from their renderings of it: 'You have said so' (Matt. 26:64) or 'You say that I am' (Luke 22:70). That is to say, if Jesus must give an answer to the high priest's question, the answer cannot be other than 'Yes', but the choice of words is the high priest's, not his own. The words that followed, however, were his own choice. It is as though he said, 'If "Christ" (that is, "Messiah" or "Anointed One") is the term you insist on using, then I have no option but to say "Yes", but if I were to choose my own terms, I should say that you will see the Son of man sitting at the right hand of the Almighty and coming with the clouds of heaven.' (Here 'Power' on Jesus's lips, meaning much the same as we mean when we say 'the Almighty', is, like 'the Blessed' on the high priest's lips, a substitute for the divine name.)

What, then, does this saying mean, and why was it declared blasphemous by the high priest? It means, in brief, that while the Son of man, Jesus himself, stood now before his judges friendless and humiliated, they would one day see him vindicated by God. He says this in symbolic language, but the source of this symbolic language is biblical. Mention has been made already of the Son of man coming with the clouds of heaven (see p. 228); this language is drawn from Daniel 7:13–14, where 'one like a son of man' is seen in a vision coming 'with the clouds of heaven' to be presented before God ('the Ancient of Days') and to receive eternal world dominion from him. The 'one like a son of man' is a human figure, displacing the succession of beast-like figures who had been exercising world dominion previously. The one whose claims received such scant courtesy from his judges would yet be acknowledged as sovereign lord in the hearts of men and women throughout the world. His claims would, moreover, be acknowledged by God: the Son of man would be seen seated 'at the right hand of the Almighty'. This wording is taken from Psalm 110:1, which records a divine oracle addressed certainly to the ruler of David's line: 'Sit at my right hand, till I make your enemies your footstool.' The present prisoner at the bar would be seen to be, by divine appointment, lord of the universe – and that not in the distant future, but forthwith. '*From now on*', in Luke's version, 'the Son of man shall be seated at the right hand of the power of God' (Luke 22:69; see p. 154). (Luke omits the language about the clouds of heaven.) '*Henceforth*', in Matthew's version, 'you will see the Son of man seated at the right hand of Power, and coming on the clouds of heaven.' The right hand of God was the place of supreme exaltation; the clouds were the vehicle of the divine glory.

The Servant of the Lord in the Old Testament, once despised and rejected by men, was hailed by God as 'exalted, extolled and made very high' (Isa. 52:13–53:3); this role is filled in the New Testament by Jesus, obedient to the point of death, and death by crucifixion at that, being thereupon 'highly exalted' by God and endowed with 'the name which is above every name', in order to be confessed by every tongue as Lord (Phil. 2:6–11). It is the same reversal of roles that is announced in Jesus's reply to the high priest.

Why was his reply judged to be blasphemous? Not because he agreed that he was the Messiah: that might be politically dangerous and could be interpreted as seditious by the Roman administration (as indeed it was), but it did not encroach on the prerogatives of God; neither did the claim to be Son of God in *that* sense. But the language which he went on to use by his own choice did appear to be an invasion of the glory that belongs to God alone. It was there that blasphemy was believed to lie. The historical sequel may be allowed to rule on the question whether it was blasphemy or an expression of faith in God which was justified in the event.

Chapter
70

Why Hast Thou Forsaken Me?

And at the ninth hour Jesus cried with a loud voice,
'Eloi, Eloi, lama sabachthani?' which means, 'My God,
my God, why hast thou forsaken me?' (Mark 15:34; cf.
Matt. 27:46)

This is the hardest of all the hard sayings. It is the last articulate
utterance of the crucified Jesus reported by Mark and
Matthew; soon afterwards, they say, with a loud cry (the
content of which is not specified) he breathed his last.

P. W. Schmiedel adduced this utterance as one of the few
'absolutely credible' texts which might be used as 'foundation-
pillars for a truly scientific life of Jesus', on the ground that it
could not be a product of the worship of Jesus in the Church.
No one would have invented it; it was an uncompromising
datum of tradition which an evangelist had either to reproduce
as it stood or else pass over without mention.

It would be wise not to make the utterance a basis for
reconstructing the inner feelings which Jesus experienced on
the cross. The question 'Why?' was asked, but remained
unanswered. There are some theologians and psychologists,
nevertheless, who have undertaken to supply the answer which
the record does not give: their example is not to be followed.
This at least must be said: if it is a hard saying for the reader of
the Gospels, it was hardest of all for our Lord himself. The
assurances on which men and women of God in Old Testament
times rested in faith were not for him. 'Many are the afflictions
of the righteous, but the Lord delivers him out of them all', said

a psalmist (Ps. 34:19), but for Jesus no deliverance appeared.

It seems certain that the words are quoted from the beginning of Psalm 22. Arguments to the contrary are not convincing. The words are not quoted from the Hebrew text, but from an Aramaic paraphrase. (For the Aramaic form *Eloi*, 'my God', in Mark, the Hebrew form *Eli* appears in Matthew. Any attempt to determine the precise pronunciation would have to reckon with the fact that some bystanders thought that Jesus was calling for Elijah to come and help him.) Psalm 22, while it begins with a cry of utter desolation, is really an expression of faith and thanksgiving; the help from God, so long awaited and even despaired of, comes at last. So it has sometimes been thought that, while Jesus is recorded as uttering only the opening cry of desolation, in fact he recited the whole psalm (although inaudibly) as an expression of faith.

This cannot be proved, but there is one New Testament writer who seems to have thought so – the author of the letter to the Hebrews. This writer more than once quotes other passages from Psalm 22 apart from the opening cry and ascribes them to Jesus. In particular, he says that Jesus 'offered up prayers and supplications, with loud crying and tears, to him who was able to save him from death, and he was heard for his godly fear; Son though he was, he learned obedience through what he suffered, and being made perfect he became the source of eternal salvation to all who obey him' (Heb. 5:7–9).

In these words the writer to the Hebrews expounds, in terms of the sufferings which Jesus endured, the acknowledgment of Psalm 22:24: God 'has not despised or abhorred the affliction of the afflicted; and he has not hid his face from him, but has heard, when he cried to him'. But when he says that Jesus's prayer 'to him who was able to save him from death' was answered, he does not mean that Jesus was delivered from dying; he means that, having died, he was 'brought again from the dead' to live henceforth 'by the power of an indestructible life' (Heb. 13:20; 7:16).

The same writer presents Jesus in his death as being a willing and acceptable sacrifice to God. That martyrs in Israel should offer their lives to expiate the sins of others was not unprecedented. Instead of having his heart filled with bitter resentment against those who were treating him so abominably, Jesus in dying offered his life to God as an atonement for their sins, and for the sins of the world. Had he not said on one occasion that 'the Son of man came ... to give his life a ransom for many' (Mark 10:45)? But now he did so the more effectively by entering really into the desolation of that God-forsakenness which is the lot of sinners – by being 'made sin for us', as Paul puts it (2 Cor. 5:21). 'In His death everything was made His that sin had made ours – everything in sin except its sinfulness.'[1]

Jesus 'learned obedience through what he suffered', as the writer to the Hebrews says, in the sense that by his suffering he learned the cost of his wholehearted obedience to his Father. His acceptance of the cross crowned his obedience, and he was never more pleasing to the Father than in this act of total devotion; yet that does not diminish the reality of his experience of being God-forsaken. But this reality has made him the more effective as the deliverer and supporter of his people. He is no visitant from another world, avoiding too much involvement with this world of ours; he has totally involved himself in the human lot. There is no depth of dereliction known to human beings which he has not plumbed; by this means he has been 'made perfect' – that is to say, completely qualified to be his people's sympathising helper in their most extreme need. If they feel like crying to God, 'Why hast thou forsaken me?', they can reflect that that is what he cried. When they call out of the depths to God, he who called out of the depths on Good Friday knows what it feels like. But there is this difference: he is with them now to strengthen them – no one was there to strengthen him.

Notes to Text

Introduction

1. The material common to Matthew and Luke but not found in Mark is conventionally labelled Q. The teaching peculiar to Matthew is labelled M; that peculiar to Luke is labelled L.
2. T.W. Manson, *The Teaching of Jesus*, second edition (Cambridge, 1935).
3. T.W. Manson, *The Sayings of Jesus*, second edition (London, 1949).
4. *The Sayings*, p. 35.

Chapter 1

1. Augustine, *On Christian Doctrine* 3.16.
2. Augustine, *Homilies on John* 26.1.
3. Bernard, *The Love of God* 4.11.

Chapter 3

1. As is pointed out by T.W. Manson in *The Teaching*, p.308.

Chapter 4

1. *Mekhilta* (rabbinical commentary) on Exodus 31:14.

Chapter 8

1. R. Bultmann, *The History of the Synoptic Tradition* (Oxford, 1963), p.138.

2. E.g. by J.N. Farquhar, *The Crown of Hinduism* (Oxford, 1913); cf. E.J. Sharpe, *Not to Destroy but to Fulfil* (Lund, 1965).
3. *The Sayings*, p.135.

Chapter 10

1. E. Brunner, *The Divine Imperative* (London, 1937), p.350.

Chapter 11

1. H. Latimer, Sermon preached in St. Edward's Church, Cambridge, in 1529, quoted in J.P. Smyth, *How We Got Our Bible* (London, [1885] 1938), p.102.

Chapter 13

1. Eusebius, *Ecclesiastical History* 6.8.2.

Chapter 15

1. Théodore de Bèze (Beza) to King Charles IX of France at the Abbey of Poissy, near Paris, in 1561.

Chapter 16

1. A. Whyte, *Lord, Teach Us to Pray*, second edition (London, 1948), pp.33–35.

Chapter 18

1. *The Scofield Reference Bible*, second edition (Oxford,

1917), p.1,002. The sharpness of the antithesis is modified in *The New Scofield Reference Edition* (Oxford, 1967), p.1,000.

Chapter 20

1. *Didache* 9.5.

Chapter 21

1. E. Gosse, *Father and Son* (London, 1928), pp.265–267.
2. Plato, *Republic* 2. 382a–b.

Chapter 22

1. M. Arnold, *Literature and Dogma* (London, 1895), p.95.
2. D.S. Cairns, *The Faith that Rebels* (London, 1928), p.25.
3. *The Sayings*, pp. 89–90.

Chapter 23

1. Tennyson, *In Memoriam*, xxxvi
2. C.F.D. Moule, *The Birth of the New Testament*, third edition (London, 1981), p.117.
3. *The Teaching*, pp. 75–80.

Chapter 24

1. To this source (commonly labelled M) may also be assigned Matthew 18:17, with its direction that the insubordinate brother should be treated 'as a Gentile and a tax collector'.

Chapter 25

1. A. Schweitzer, *The Quest of the Historical Jesus* (London, 1910), p.357.
2. *The Quest*, p.369.
3. T.W. Manson, *Studies in the Gospels and Epistles* (Manchester, 1962), pp.9–10.

Chapter 26

1. S.G.F. Brandon, *Jesus and the Zealots* (Manchester, 1967), p.172.

Chapter 30

1. Justin, *Dialogue with Trypho* 88.3.
2. *Gospel of Thomas*, Saying 82; also in Origen, *Homilies on Jeremiah* 20.3.

Chapter 35

1. *Yalqut Shim'oni* (medieval compilation) 1.766.

Chapter 39

1. T.W. Manson, *The Sayings*, p.87.

Chapter 40

1. *The Sayings*, pp.72–73.
2. D. Hill, *The Gospel of Matthew* (London, 1972), p.162.

Chapter 41

1. *The Sayings*, p.73. Cf. M. Hengel, *The Charismatic Leader and his Followers* (Edinburgh, 1981), pp.1–20: in view of the urgent nearness of the kingdom of God there is no time to lose; all ordinary human considerations and ties must give way to this.
2. A. Gammie, *Rev. John McNeill: his Life and Work* (Glasgow, 1939), p.201.

Chapter 44

1. *Shir ha-Shirim Rabba* 5:2.

Chapter 46

1. Bunyan, *The Pilgrim's Progress,* Part 2.

Chapter 48

1. B.M. Metzger, *A Textual Commentary on the Greek New Testament* (London/New York, 1971), p.169.
2. H.B. Swete, *The Gospel according to St. Mark*, third edition (London, 1909), p.229.
3. Babylonian Talmud, tractate *Berakot* 55 b.

Chapter 51

1. C.S. Lewis, *The Problem of Pain* (London, 1940), p.115.
2. J. Denney, *The Way Everlasting* (London, 1911), p.171. It is noteworthy that, in the judgment of all the nations, it is similarly failure to care for those in need that incurs the sentence: 'Depart ... into the eternal fire prepared for the devil and his angels' (Matt. 25:41).

Chapter 52

1. *The Sayings*, p.308.

Chapter 53

1. Shakespeare, *The Merchant of Venice*, IV, i.
2. *The Sayings*, p.220.

Chapter 54

1. E. Schweizer, *The Good News According to Mark* (London, 1971), p.215.

Chapter 55

1. Plato, *Phaedo* 69 c.
2. Origen, *Against Celsus* 8.16.
3. *Westminster Shorter Catechism*, Answer to Question 31.
4. Burns, *Holy Willie's Prayer*, stanza 1.
5. J.E. Powell, 'Quicunque Vult', in *Sermons from Great St. Mary's*, ed. H.W. Montefiore (London, 1968), p.96.
6. J. Calvin, *Romans and Thessalonians*, English translation (Edinburgh, 1961), pp.114–115.

Chapter 57

1. Reprinted in W.M. Christie, *Palestine Calling* (London, 1939), pp.118–120.

Chapter 58

1. W. Manson, *Jesus the Messiah* (London, 1943), pp. 29f., 39f.

Chapter 62

1. Palestinian Talmud, tractate *Berakot*, 9.7.
2. T.W. Manson, 'The Cleansing of the Temple', *Bulletin of the John Rylands Library* 33 (1950–51), p.279, n. 1. (He, however, accepted the setting of Luke 13:35 as original and supposed that Jesus was bidding temporary farewell to the people of Galilee, saying that they would next see him in Jerusalem.)

Chapter 63

1. *Synoptic Tradition*, p.125.
2. Cf. G.H. Lang, *The Revelation of Jesus Christ* (London, 1945), pp.70, 387.

Chapter 64

1. *The Sayings*, p.147.

Chapter 67

1. Josephus, *Jewish War* 2.125.
2. T.W. Manson, *Ethics and the Gospel* (London, 1960), p.90.
3. *The Sayings*, p.341.

Chapter 68

1. Cf. A. Deissmann, *Light from the Ancient East,* second edition (London, 1927), pp. 125–131.

Chapter 70

1. J. Denney, *The Death of Christ*, sixth edition (London, 1907), p. 160.

Index of Biblical References

Index of Authors, etc.